THE RIDE TO REDEMPTION

RICK SWYDEN

Copyright © 2024 Rick Swyden
All cover art copyright © 2024 Rick Swyden
All Rights Reserved

This is a work of fiction. Names, places, characters and incidents are either the product of the author's imagination or are used fictitiously, and any resemblance to any actual persons, living or dead, businesses, organizations, events or locales is entirely coincidental.

No part of this book may be reproduced or transmitted in any form or by any means, electronic or mechanical, including photocopying, recording, or by any information storage and retrieval system, without permission in writing from the author.

Cover Concept – Rick Swyden
Cover Design – Jaycee DeLorenzo

Paperback-Press
an imprint of A & S Publishing
Paperback Press, LLC
Springfield, Missouri

Paperback ISBN – 13: 978-1-960499-81-3
Hardcover ISBN – 13: 978-1-963499-82-0

This book is dedicated to the memory of my mother

Myrtleona Swyden

who taught all five of her kids by pointing toward
the fence posts and power-lines dwindling
in the distance, or driving over bridges
and repeating her catchphrase

"Just Look At *All* That Perspective."

Because of this, I see and experience both
visual and human perspectives everywhere in life.

Thanks Mom For All *Your* Perspective.
Without it, this book would probably not exist.

Acknowledgments

Story Consultants

Michael Jezercak, PhD
Virginia Geddes, DNP-CNM

Book Editor

Cynthia Hilston

Additional Editing

Carolyn Woods, Alice A. Hearn, Melinda Moore,
Thomas A. Swyden, Elizabeth Hudson

Emotional Support Humans

Lon J. Darley III, John Pranter, Kim Burke, Dr. Charles Johnson,
Eric Dennis, Francine Ruokangas, Dale McKissik, Roy and Janis Roach,
Nicole Faulk, Marty Swyden

Thanks to my beautiful wife Susan, and wonderful children,
Christopher, Chase, Ryan, Alex, and Allison
for putting up with me for the seven years it took to write the book.

From the Author

To fully grasp the emotional ride you are about to embark upon, the journey requires the image of the 2012 Dedacciai Assoluto bicycle in Gleaming red. It is as crucial to the book as the characters themselves.

I pronounce the name (or possibly mispronounce it) as De-**Dah'**-Chi-Ay', according to a retired schoolteacher who helped spell that sound out for me. (Thanks, Alice)

So why is *this* Dedacciai bicycle so important? They are not sold anywhere in the U.S.A. (as of this writing), and it took me years to find one overseas. It is also the bike I rode the day this story fell into my mind. I knew something weird had just happened as suddenly there was not just an idea for a book but the entire movie version of the book playing in my head. It felt so powerful that I pulled over to take the picture above to immortalize this strange occurrence. The photo was taken at Lake Hefner in Oklahoma City in July 2016. OKC is where I was born and raised, and still reside in a suburb just north of the city.

Here's the thing, I wasn't a writer, or at least I hadn't written a book before. But the idea would not go away and gnawed at me day and night with the full-length movie version playing nonstop in my mind. The story was relentless and wanted to be fed, watered, and nurtured to life.

Three months later, with a little inspiration from *Tony Robbins* and his *Personal Power II* CD set, Robbins said the decisive words that encouraged me to script the story. I looked at the clock, which read 1:23 p.m., October 16th, 2016. My decision was absolute and grabbed parchment and pen and I began to write.

Four years later, to the exact date and time, 1:23 p.m., October 16th, 2020, my profound emotional journey hit my first tremendous writer's milestone. I completed my first draft.

I celebrated at The Cheesecake Factory with a piece of Oreo cheesecake. I was sitting by myself and crying from the completion of thousands of hours, countless all-nighters, and nearly a million words in writes and rewrites. All of it necessary to complete my EPIC first draft.

I was sixty years old, and I was joyous. However, the patrons at the Cheesecake Factory probably saw one of the saddest sights they had seen that day: a heavyset, sixty-year-old man sitting alone at the bar and crying on to his Oreo cheesecake.

The final product is *The Ride to Redemption*, with a name that will make perfect sense once you finish the book.

For seven years, every ounce of my blood, sweat, and fears were poured onto these pages. Each word intended to take you on a transformative and healing journey of redemption. I wrote the comedic attributes to help balance out the seriousness of the subject matter, hoping we can laugh at ourselves in a world where that seems lost. My hope is that I gave every ounce of what is important to me to you through wit and wisdom.

Additionally, I hope the life lessons on these pages are of significant emotional value and something you can take with you.

Thank you for giving my words a chance to earn a place in your heart, mind, and bookcase.
It is appreciated more than you could possibly imagine.

With sincere gratitude,
Rick Swyden

Contents

1. The Calm Before the Storm — 1
2. Carter Ducane — 33
3. The Awakening — 53
4. Cycledelic Bike Therapy — 73
5. Only in Dreams — 87
6. Kimmee James Attwood — 123
7. Godzilla — 137
8. Bellavia — 143
9. Papa's Letter — 165
10. "The Clicker" — 181
11. What Is Happening Here? — 195
12. The Theater of the Abyss — 211
13. Who Are We? — 217
14. Camp Carter — 245
15. The Burial — 267

16.	The Field Of Dreams and Despair	295
17.	Them Life Dominoes	327
18.	The Emotional Savant	343
19.	The Blessed Curse	353
20.	The Auras of Mankind	371
21.	Evan's Redemption	377
22.	The Friday Freeloaders	383
23.	The Clicker vs. The Macabre	405
24.	Master Yodacciai	415
25.	Follow The Yellow-Striped Road	431
26.	The Ride To Redemption	441
27.	A Mother Just Knows Things	465
28.	A Lot Can Happen In One Day …	477
29.	Even Bicycles Deserve A Second Chance	491

Three simple words the human ear
should never have to experience

— "Time of Death" —

— Rick Swyden

Chapter One

The Calm Before the Storm

Two firefighters sitting outside in their truck found it difficult to communicate with headquarters as the pounding rain echoed tenfold inside the encapsulated steel cabin. As they looked out their rain-soaked windshield, a small dog suddenly dashed into view and could be seen running in circles and sprinting excitedly about the front yard.

As they observed through the back and forth of the windshield wipers, the thought crossed their minds that perhaps the family pet shouldn't be running loose like that. But before they could act, a set of headlights swept the scene, and the little dog bolted, disappearing down Glenwood Trail and into the night.

Moments later, a dark gray minivan screeched alongside them and rolled down its window, prompting the driver's side fireman to do the same. Evan leaned across Amelia and shouted —

"Hey, excuse me, what's going on?"

"Just responding to some kind of accident."

"What sort of accident?" asked Amelia, alarmed.

"Sorry, I can't give out that—"

"It's okay, we're family!" interrupted Evan. "This is my parents' house!"

The fireman nodded. "All we have is the subject stopped breathing —"

"Jesus!" shouted Evan. He hit the gas, shooting forward and barely missing the ambulance ahead as he swerved around it. Thoughts barreled through his mind that something had happened to his Pops as he hastily pulled into the driveway. The two first responders watched objectively from their dry truck cabin as the man and woman jumped out of their van and sprinted through the pouring rain for the house.

—Earlier That Day—

Grandpa, as he was known to most, had several family distinctions. He was Honey to his wife, Pops to his three sons, and Daddy-O to his only daughter. But perhaps his favorite accolade of all was Papa to his granddaughter Addison.

That morning, he was preparing for a bicycle ride while seated at one of his favorite places on earth, his garage workbench. His garage was the ultimate man cave and where he surrounded himself with his prized art collection of over forty years. He presently owned nineteen stunning works of art, each more vibrant than the next. However, *normal* human specimens only saw nineteen beautiful bicycles, and each an artistic sculpture in its own right. But regardless of what *normals* saw, he saw magnificent works of art that he could ride.

In his collection was his masterpiece, the Dedacciai (De-**Dah**'-Chi-Ay'), a rare and exquisite Italian racing bicycle not sold in the United States. From the moment he first saw the gleaming red 2012 Dedacciai Assoluto online, it became his obsession to own one. Precisely nine hundred eighty-seven days later, his worldwide Google alert finally found the exact model Dedacciai living across the pond in West Yorkshire, United Kingdom.

After a rigorous price negotiation, *Grandpa made him an offer he couldn't refuse* in honor of the bike's classic Italian heritage. And now, this beautiful work of art was proudly displayed where he could gaze upon its beauty for hours on end, and he often did just that.

Grandpa went over his mental checklist for his morning ride. *Cell phone, wallet, bike shoes, check.* — *Helmet, water bottle, air pump, check.* — *Music, jersey, bike shorts* — *bike shorts?* He looked down. "Geez, not again!" and disappeared with grumblings of how it sucked getting old.

Upon his return, Grandpa reached into a bowl and drew from the eighteen individual names of all his bikes, except the Dedacciai, which he refused to ride because of its rarity.

Grandpa lived by his philosophy of 'bicycles are people too' as he ceremoniously announced the result of the drawing to his collection. "Okay, listen up everyone, today's winner is — drum roll, please. Congrats to our 1985 Bridgestone Grand-Vélo 2000."

He reminisced about the vintage pick as Grandpa considered it the first professional-level bike he had ever purchased. And almost forty years later, it still looked like it rolled off the showroom floor. He placed the Bridgestone in his SUV, returned to get his things, and again apologized to the Dedacciai. "Sorry, Pal, I hope you understand."

Grandpa loved driving to the lake to ride; actually, he loved driving anywhere, at anytime, because he had yet another philosophy that a car ride was a terrible thing to waste. He thought of learning on the road as Motor-Vational-University, where every traffic jam was an opportunity to learn, not a reason for concern.

Grandpa consistently listened to inspirational speakers while driving. And he always felt better at the end of his journey than before he began. Tony Robbins was his go-to speaker among the many speakers he enjoyed, and he currently owned sixteen different Robbins CD sets in his motivational arsenal. Grandpa's crown jewel was a poster of himself with Tony Robbins at an 'Unleash the Power Within' event three years earlier in Florida. Grandpa proudly displayed the poster in his garage, where he could routinely fist-bump Tony as he entered the house.

However, Grandpa's passion for seeking inspiration was not without its skeptics. Jesus understood this more than anyone when he prophesized, *'Only in his hometown and in his own house is a prophet without honor.'* Grandpa could sure relate because, in his own home, he couldn't ever listen to Robbins or any motivational speaker without someone giving him an eye roll.

Sadly, Grandpa also recognized that he had brought this upon himself. The motivational ban stemmed from a long history of getting excited and passionate about something and bringing everyone into his emotional orbit, only to lose enthusiasm and quit because life got in the way.

Grandpa had boxes of ideas mentally packed away in his mind, hoping to open again and continue someday. And he believed in them so strongly that he purchased a domain name for each idea in case one was successful. Unfortunately, he was currently paying for twenty-seven domain names that, in reality, he would never use.

He was now at the lake, riding with a brisk October wind at his back while he enjoyed the beautiful scenery and the familiar half-faces underneath their cycling helmets. It's a strange arrangement in the cycling world, as you often ride with people for years, yet only know each other from a smile or cyclist gesture as you ride past each other. But since you have never seen their entire face without glasses or a helmet, you may never know their name or recognize them publicly. All because they chose in life to ride counterclockwise to your clockwise.

Grandpa adhered to a strict cyclist's code of conduct while riding. Be considerate of another cyclist's time, and unless you know otherwise, assume they only have a certain amount of time to ride, especially early-morning riders who may need to get to work. And never impede on a cyclist's momentum as they may be training toward an important goal or event.

Grandpa was training for his annual 100-mile century ride and was behind on this year's preparation. He looked down at his GPS — 24.7 miles of an intended thirty-five-mile ride.

Suddenly, he flinched and felt a stabbing acidic pain in his heart. He grasped his chest and pounded his fist against his sternum. As he did, a strange vision of a man with a scraggly beard appeared in his mind. Grandpa swiftly pulled over and dismounted with as much composure as possible but wobbled as he slid his back down a nearby concrete barrier and sat overlooking the dam.

"Grandpa! – Are you alright?" shouted a fellow cyclist named Chris as his 28-mph sprint was cut short. "Grandpa, what's wrong? You don't look right?"

"Do I ever?" Grandpa sassed. "Your question pre-supposes I looked right in the first place."

"Yeah, that would be a tough sell," Chris jabbed. "But seriously, Grandpa, what happened?"

"I'm not entirely sure, but if I had to guess, the jalapeños on my pizza last night and stupidly again this morning weren't such a great idea."

"Well, maybe, but why don't we take you to the emergency room just to make sure?"

"No! I promise, it's just heartburn," he said adamantly.

"Here, take a drink and see if you feel better." Chris grabbed Grandpa's water bottle off his bike. "Lucky for you, I rode early because a rainstorm's coming later tonight. It's supposed to get nasty, lots of flash floods."

"Aww, yes — The proverbial calm before the storm," Grandpa acknowledged. "I hate that I don't get to ride with you anymore. We had some great bicycle therapy sessions out here."

"I know, I hate it too, but my business grew, and life got in the way. Hey, not to change the subject, but you look like you've lost a few—"

"Brain cells," Grandpa interjected.

"No, idiot — pounds!" Chris chuckled.

"Well, I am 287 days cupcake sober so far and have lost twenty-eight pounds."

"Cupcake sober, is that really a thing?" Chris uttered, shaking his head.

"It is to me!" he clapped back. "Recently, during my long-standing cupcake career, my addiction escalated to four cupcakes a day and six cupcakes on Nutella Frosting Day at my local cupcake shop, where I was named customer of the month. Truthfully, the only difference between me and an alcoholic is that I can't get an EUI for eating too many cupcakes."

Chris snickered in agreement. "That's a pretty good analogy, Grandpa."

"Thanks, at least it's working, as I'm down to 254 pounds. I'd lose a lot more if I applied the same concept to pizza. But since I'm defective, I only apply my sobriety rule of law to actual cupcakes. But at least I do that much because, trust me, as big as I am, things could be much worse—" Grandpa spouted with an inflection that was left unresolved and luring a response.

Chris had a *"should I?" or "shouldn't I?"* expression. "Okay, I'll bite; how much worse?"

"Well, I'm now the neighborhood Punxsutawney Phil, and every Groundhog Day, after my winter hibernation, my neighbors wait to see how wide my shadow will be for the coming year and if we'll have six more weeks of fat."

Chris rolled his eyes. "Geez, Grandpa, you're strange and profound all rolled into one. To think I would have missed out on all your oddness had we not ridden in the same circles. I truly regret that we don't ride together anymore. Can you believe we met out here ten years ago?"

Grandpa's demeanor changed as his smile left his face.

"I remember it well; that was such a dark period, but you helped me get through it. I'll never be able to thank you enough for introducing me to Al-Anon back then."

Chris patted his friend on the back. "It was my honor."

Grandpa lowered his head. "Damn addictions; my mentor still died, though."

"I know; I'm so sorry. Alcoholism is such a cunning and baffling disease. Are you still going to your Friday noon meeting each week?"

"Yep, hardly ever miss. We all miss seeing you in there, though."

"I know, but I also had to start attending later meetings because of work. But when I do make a Friday meeting, it seems I don't get to visit with anyone because I have to rush back to the office. I tell you what; I will make a concerted effort to come this Friday and see everyone. Maybe take a half day off work. Will you have time for lunch afterward?"

"Bet your ass I will! It will be great to have you since I'm chairperson this month. You know, Chris — thinking about my mentor makes me wonder about my own mortality. I've never been a sickly person, even with my weight. But this morning, I forgot to wear my riding shorts – again – before coming out here. But here's the kicker. I'm sixty-two, and my mom and grandmother both died at sixty-two of Alzheimer's."

Chris cringed at the coincidental numbers as Grandpa continued.

"Fortunately, my grandad lived to be a hundred and still arm-wrestled us whenever we saw him. So, hopefully, my genetic makeup leans in that direction. Maybe my heartburn is trying to tell me something else. Maybe the cosmos somehow changed the rules on me, like it did when I woke up one day, and my voice started changing. Perhaps this is my second resurgence of puberty fifty years later. Chris, what if I've entered into an undiscovered dimension of mortal puberty?"

"Grandpa, you haven't entered mortal puberty!" Chris retorted, trying not to laugh. "There is no such thing! Not one doctor has ever specialized in mortal puberty. Trust me; I help build medical buildings and lease them to doctors for a living. Have you ever thought that maybe the jalapeños are just doing what jalapeños do, and there is no cosmic message involved?"

"Nope, I think it's more plausible that I'm the cosmic guinea pig for what's to come. But regardless, those damn jalapeños aren't getting off the hook that easily. My mortality was mentally kidnapped today because of those little green bastards."

"Grandpa, you're a strange breed of man." Chris looked him over closely. "I still don't think you look right. I've decided that you're not riding anymore today. I'm going to finish my sprint and then come take you to your SUV — I'm not taking no for an answer."

"Whatever," Grandpa said, giving him a man-nod of approval and waving off his friend. Grandpa drove home, disappointed that his *mortal puberty*, as he put it, derailed his morning ride. But what if his mortal puberty was trying to tell him something? Besides the heartburn, he suddenly sensed another underlying explanation for this feeling of vulnerability.

He felt a mysterious notion that he had missed a significant anniversary of sorts, and somehow, it had something to do with his granddaughter Addison, who was coming up later that day for her weekly visit.

Puzzled, he looked at his phone — Tuesday, October 4th, 10:59 a.m. — but the date didn't ring a bell. Visions of the man with the scraggly beard appeared in his mind again. This time, the image was even more familiar and persistent— like it had a purpose. It almost felt like a premonition, urging him that he had indeed missed an important anniversary.

His thoughts assembled, and his eyes searched the upper quadrants of his mind, looking for the shadowy answer. As he sifted through his cluttered memories, he discovered one from three years ago that met the search criteria. He envisioned an encounter with a homeless man from that time, and Grandpa was mentally transported back to relive the event.

The encounter in his mind intensified as Grandpa heard the homeless man with the scraggly beard telling him about life lessons he wanted to teach his son. But sadly, he couldn't because the son tragically died at the age of three before the man could impart those lessons.

The man's tragedy prompted Grandpa to wonder: *What if that ever happened to me? What lessons would I have wanted Addison to learn?*

Grandpa decided the response in his mind needed to become a paper reality, and the urgency grew with each passing mile. By the time he pulled into his driveway, it was a full-on compulsion to write his life lessons down in a letter to Addison and to do it now!

As Grandpa opened the garage door, *his* Bellavia, as only he called her, stood in the garage to greet him with a smile that instantly transformed into a concerned look as her woman's intuition kicked in.

"What's wrong, honey?"

"It's nothing. I had some heartburn while riding at the lake and had to pull over. Thankfully, my friend Chris rode by and stopped to help me."

"Chris — you mean Al-Anon Chris? Are you ever going to tell me his last name?"

"My Bellavia, you know the rules of Al-Anon. Anonymity is the bedrock of our fellowship."

"Well, anonymity isn't good for us control freaks. I need to know what kind of people you hang around," she said, slightly tongue-in-cheek. "I think your heartburn was karma for stealing those jalapeños from my pizza in the first place. But I'm glad you're home. Now, why don't you sit here with your bike collection—"

"Excuse me— don't you mean *art* collection? How many times do I have to tell you — no one in their right mind would mistake these beautiful works of art for bicycles?"

"Honey, how many pieces of art do you have now anyway?"— She paused. "Never mind, I don't want to know and don't need to know."

"Ouchy wah-wah! That had to hurt your inner control freak. But it's sad that the one thing you don't care about anymore is my bikes. I miss you riding with me, but I know the deal. I ride, and you run. Got it."

"Hey, don't be sad. Your art collection is your deal. If you're happy, I'm happy."

Bellavia looked at him; she knew that look of introspection. "Honey, don't go there, there's no need to go dark on me — please be alright — are you alright?"

"I don't know; things feel off for some reason, probably because the jalapeños didn't let me finish my ride today. I just need to sit with my bicycles — because bicycles fix everything."

"Well, whatever you believe, I guess. But I know how to make you feel better instantly." Bellavia grabbed the garage TV remote, and soon, the movie Serendipity began to play.

"Honey, just relax and enjoy your favorite movie while I make you a tall glass of orange iced tea."

He lifted his head, looked into her eyes, and placed his hand lovingly on her cheek. "My Bellavia, you know me so well."

They hugged in a long embrace, and she felt his melancholy introspection melt away.

"Honey, how many times have you watched *Serendipity?*"

"My Bellavia, don't act like I'm crazy; this is only my two thousandth, one hundred and thirty-seventh time I've watched it — totally within the realm of normalcy."

"Yes, totally normal." Then, with a sultry voice, she added — "Honey, you know I won't be complete until I hear you whisper the line — you know you want to."

His eyes shimmered, and his voice lowered as he suavely conveyed his favorite *Serendipity* quote to her.

> *"You know the Greeks didn't write obituaries.*
> *They only asked one question after a man died. —*
> *Did he have Passion?"*

This quote was the essence of who he was as he gave *his* Bellavia that certain look and a devilish smile.

"Hey, don't you be filling your head with those thoughts," she said with a confusing blend of seductive mischief.

"What thoughts?" — he echoed slowly.

"You know — *tho*se thoughts."

"My Bellavia, *those* thoughts are simply here to answer the question, 'Do I have passion?' Which you should know better than anyone. Besides, my passion problem is all your fault."

"My fault — how's it my fault?"

"Isn't it obvious? It's how you walk around here looking like you do, blonde hair, blue eyes, and still able to fit into your cheerleading uniform. These items are of great interest and affect my hormone usage, perpetuating my passion problem with exceptional testosterone levels."

"Okay, calm down, tiger," she said, flattered. "Don't get yourself all riled up after your episode at the lake. Your granddaughter will be here before you know it, and I have a lot to accomplish before she gets here. I want you and your hormones to relax and enjoy your movie. Just be washed up before Addison arrives."

Bellavia reached for the remote, restarted the movie, and paused in thought. "You know, Honey, our trip to New York City to visit Serendipity was one of the best times of my life. I loved sitting with you at the same table where they filmed the movie while having our Frrrozen Hot Chocolate. Thank you for that." And with a loving kiss, she disappeared into the house.

Grandpa sat at his garage workbench, drinking the orange iced tea *his* Bellavia promised as he gazed at his prized art collection. He didn't care that others only saw nineteen beautiful bicycles; what mattered most was that he only saw magnificent works of art that he could ride. But there was a reason he viewed his bicycles as art. His mother was an artist, and bright colors were her passion. Although she passed, he felt connected with her through glorious greens, bold yellows, vivid reds, and prominent purples and blues, as seen throughout his collection.

He looked up toward the heavens, blew his mom a kiss, straightened out his riding gear, and wiped down his Bridgestone bicycle before placing it back on its designated rack.

Suddenly, he winced and swiftly grasped his chest while concern cloaked his expression. The pain vigorously returned, and he bent over and braced himself with one hand while pounding his chest with the other.

These darn jalapeños aren't giving up without a fight, are they? He closed his eyes and took a deep breath as an awkward solace entered his mind.

If these jalapeños take me out, at least my daughter pre-wrote my eulogy pleading the question, Did I have passion? And it was in a drawer he labeled Death-Drawer along with all the other disturbingly comforting documents his Bellavia would need when he passed.

Grandpa slapped himself — "You're not going to die, idiot!" — and took deep breaths while he drank his tea. The pain disappeared, but the intensity of writing his letter to Addison doubled.

It was 1:23 p.m. as he began to annotate his thoughts on paper. However, a curious thing happened during his creative thought process. The twelve hundred and forty-three words needed to compose the letter were already loaded in his memory as if his subconscious had previously written the letter. So, with pen in hand, the sentences already drafted in his mind effortlessly flowed onto the paper.

A Letter to My Granddaughter, Addison Hope

Dear Addison,

I have been a passionate man all my life; I have experienced love and joy to a degree that I thought could not be possible — then YOU arrived and proved me wrong.
Let me first say, "You're welcome," as I gave my heart and all its passions to your father and could not be prouder of the man he has become and the father he is to you.
Also, I knew from the moment I met your mother that she was special. However, I did not realize how special she was until YOU came into this world and changed mine! Now, let me put into words how I would change the world just for you if I could. — Here it goes.

Addison's Papa underwent an intense emotional metamorphosis for the next few hours as he cleansed his subconscious blackboard of the words written over the past three years. He took a momentous breath as he finished transcribing everything from his subconscious onto the paper. Then, he concentrated on finalizing the letter with a personalized touch.

In closing, Addison, as I write this letter to you, according to the Global Language Monitor, there are 1,057,379.6 words in the English language. The problem is, not one of these words is big enough to say just how much I love you — So, now, I need to invent new words just for you.
Addison Hope, I love you a Gazillion, Trentillion, Octillion, Quinnbillion, Threntillion, Artrillion, Fourlillion, Tridrillion, Gratillion, Catillion, Crazillion, Godzillion, and your daddy's favorite, BananaBillion X's Infinity Squared.
I know it's just a start, but with these new words, we have changed the world just a little.

Love, Papa

Handwriting the words Papa saw clearly in his mind astonished him, and he cried as an intense emotional fog lifted from his spirit. Grandpa now felt purged of the lessons he wanted Addison to have in case the unimaginable happened to him. Grandpa even appreciated today's darker emotions that renewed his appreciation for life and felt oddly free of further jalapeño attacks. He then went up to wash and rinse away all semblance of this morning's bleaker thoughts of mortality.

Soon, he was back in his garage, awaiting the three-year-old bundle of adorableness that would arrive at any time, and it was 5:03 p.m. when the doorbell rang. Papa acted like no one was coming and remained perched at his workbench, anticipating his opponent's entry into the art gallery.

Meanwhile, back in the living room, Bellavia, or Grammy Bell as Addison called her, was headed toward the front door to answer it. When she turned the doorknob — BOOM — in burst the three-year-old, thirty-six-inch, thirty-six-pound linebacker out of MU (Mommy University). Addison was wearing her Keep Austin Weird jersey and gave Grammy Bell a hug fake, then drove under her legs and was now at the five, the ten, scrambling past the couch. Oops! Make that over the couch, to the fifteen, twenty, weaving through the kitchen, past the dog, and breaking to the left. Down the hallway she went, taking a sharp right turn into the laundry room, slowing down as she approached the door into the garage.

Slowly and with stealthy precision, she opened the door and lowered herself so the one she called PAPA could not see her head. Gradually, she peeked around the corner and spied him at his workbench. Grandpa quietly paid no attention to the silliness that was about to ensue. A slight giggle squeaked out of the undersized linebacker that PAPA pretended not to hear. Then it started: two decibels: "PAPA." No reaction. Five decibels: "PAPA." No reaction. Ten decibels: "PAPA." No reaction. Then she launched straight to fifty decibels: "— **P-A-P-A!** —"

PAPA flailed his arms and legs as he turned swiftly to see little Addison. She had her left index finger placed under her left eyeball. Then she was tugging on the bottom eyelid ever so slightly, distorting the skin and making her eye look so silly that you couldn't help but laugh.

"Eye-Jobe, Papa!"

Now, Papa believed that every grandpa should invent some silly game to play with their grandchildren that is unique to them. And Eye-Jobes had been a forty-five-year tradition between Papa and his older brother, Marty. They invented the Eye-Jobe in their formidable high school years. To this day, the brothers still find unique and diverse ways to surprise each other. It's funny how small gestures can mean so much.

So, with the modern-day iPod, iPad, and iPhone, Papa brought back the **iJobe** full circle but still used the antiquated Eye-Jobe spelling. Papa was proud to pass it down to Addison as he reminded her, "Eye-Jobes won't Jobe themselves, you know, so that's why we do it for them."

But as silly as this little game was, Papa had a purpose in teaching it. He hung his hat on the premise that an unexpected gift at an unexpected time caused joy in life. Grandpa looked for opportunities every day through humor or with his unexpected gift philosophy to leave little joy crumbs wherever possible. He needed to teach Addison the same, which had taken root as she fired the first surprise Eye-Jobe of the evening.

Her papa responded and cried, "JOOOOOBE," as if mortally wounded and fell dramatically to the ground. The mini linebacker exploded with laughter and launched herself mid-air to land on her PAPA's tummy. The garage erupted into laughter as both players tried to out-tickle the other as if they were competing in a professional Tickle League.

Papa quickly rose from the floor, taking Addison under the arms, and lifted her to eye level.

"Control Tower to Addison, you are cleared for takeoff!"

"Roger that rabbit!" she replied, giggling as Papa counted down. "Three, two, *one!*"

And he tossed her gently two feet in the air, catching her seemingly at the last second. Addison squealed with delight. "Again, Papa! Do it again!" And she took flight a second time just as Grandpa's son, Evan, stepped into the garage.

"Pops!" he shouted while Addison laughed uncontrollably before Grandpa caught her. Evan walked over to Grandpa, grabbed him firmly by the shoulders, and looked him in the eyes. "Didn't I tell you just last week and the week before that to stop playing Papa Airways? I mean it, Pops. Don't throw Addison in the air! What if you drop her?"

Grandpa looked at his granddaughter as he started talking in a silly voice. "You know what I always say; it's only funny until someone gets hurt—*then* it's hysterical."

Addison giggled and repeated the words. "Then it's hysterical. You're silly, Papa."

The eccentric man looked back at his son. "Evan, you do realize you yourself have enough flight hours to go to Hawaii and back. You couldn't get enough flying time with me when you were her age."

"But Pops, you were younger and stronger back then, and Addison is getting heavier. I'm not asking; I'm telling you now I want this to stop — please."

"But Daddy, I don't want Papa to stop," Addison said with a sad face.

"Listen to your daughter. I'm a grandpa, and I've earned my Pilot's Wings for two-foot flight patterns. Do you really want to take that away from your daughter — and me?"

Evan had an anguished demeanor as he listened to his pops.

"I understand how overprotective you are of Addison, especially since she's your first child. But you must understand that you and your three siblings have flown around the world two feet at a time without one crash landing. And all of you have turned out to be some pretty amazing humans. Well – except for when you are making fun of my bicycles."

Evan reluctantly thought back and remembered his flights as well as making fun of his pops whenever a new bicycle brother entered the fray. He hesitantly smiled as he remembered joking with him all those years ago—*Pops, not another one. You do realize that you can only pedal one at a time?* When he saw the sweet grin on Addison's face from traveling on Papa Airways, he begrudgingly conceded to his eccentric pops— for now, and his demeanor returned to normal.

Evan hugged his pops before paying homage to his art collection so he could make fun of him. He lifted his pop's prized possession, the Dedacciai.

"Wow, that's light. Can I ask how much you paid for this? I've always been curious."

"Well, I bought it used and paid way more than I should have — but I had to have it," his pops responded. "I think I originally paid around $6000. But with the new wheels I put on, I would say it's now around $7500ish — give or take an ish."

"Wow, seventy-five hundred? — But it pedals just like the other eighteen — right?"

"Not to me," his pops replied defensively. "Hey, stop making fun of my bike collection and do your job and collect me some more grand-babies."

"But we couldn't make another one as great as Addison — so why try?" Evan joked.

Addison stood there with a massive grin as her Papa responded, "Well, leave that last part up to God. I read somewhere the technology for making babies in the heavenly baby factory has grown exponentially over the past three years. I'm sure this year's babies are much better than three years ago."

"P-A-P-A — I'm right here!" Addison giggled.

"Oops, sorry, Addison, I meant to say, 'earmuffs' first.'"

"Pops, you're just plain weird," Evan told the man wearing one of his many *Keep Austin Weird* T-shirts.

"Well, Evan, it's like I always say: 'When the going gets weird – the weird turn pro.'"

Evan shook his head as he scanned the collection of bikes that started years before he was ever a thought in his dad's head, then glanced at the workbench and saw the letter his pops had penned.

His pops leisurely covered the letter as he hadn't thought much about when or how he would present it to Addison, just that he needed to write it.

"Pops, are you working on another book idea? You do know they just invented these things called word processors. They're all the rage right now because you can type and make changes and corrections right on the word processor screen — it's a miracle, not to mention the *tens of dollars* you will save on whiteout!" Evan said, smirking.

"Oh, kids these days with your fancy gadgets. A penned letter is the heart and soul of what letters want to be when they grow up. They want to have curves and flaws and be individuals with a sense of purpose; no two alike. They want to be brought together by the oneness of the universe to form thoughts that bring a special tranquility and unique joy to the intended target. They want to be born into the world as ink, not a bunch of digital ones and zeros. So, respect the ink and know — That the pen is mightier than the computer. That's what I always say."

Evan tilted his head. "Pops, you never say that?"

"Well, I think it a lot; shouldn't that count?"

Evan rolled his eyes and looked at Addison. "Pops, you're like super-duper-luper weird."

Addison chimed in, "SUPER-DUPER-LUPER, that's like extra weird! — Right, Daddy?"

"Why, Addison, that's the nicest thing I've heard all day," her papa responded. "Now, repeat after me. 'When the going gets weird—'"

Addison laughs, "—the weird turn pro!"

Evan just shook his head. "The things you are teaching this girl...."

"Okay, how about we see what your Mommy and Grammy Bell are doing," Papa suggested as he lifted Addison to eye level with his Tony Robbins poster. "Okay, Addison, you know what to do." And they both fist-bumped Tony Robbins before entering the house.

"You know, Pops, if Tony Robbins knew just how weird you were, he probably wouldn't have let you into his seminar."

"Don't listen to him, Tony," his Pops replied. "The boy wasn't raised right." Evan shook his head and laughed as the men patted each other on the back and entered the house.

As they walked into the kitchen, his wonderful daughter-in-law, Amelia, was giving last-minute instructions for the care and feeding of little Addison. "Hi, Pops," Amelia said as she stood and hugged her favorite pops-in-law.

"I gave Papa an Eye-Jobe!" Addison exclaimed to her mother.

"Wow, good for you, Addison!"

"Then I flew in the air two whole times."

With no response, Amelia glanced at Evan, displeased, as she was *not* a fan of Papa Airways, and her look was a harsh reminder to him of their multiple discussions. Nevertheless, the glance ended, her smile returned, and she wouldn't let this ruin date night. As they headed out the front door, they seemed to be a little *extra giggly*, as Addison might say. Her parent's leaving was Papa's cue to distract Addison, as she would sometimes put on a sad face. But Papa had mastered the art of distraction with their enormous four-pound Pomeranian, Godzilla, or Zilla for short.

"Okay, Addison, let's go find Zilla so we can head to the park," Papa said.

Addison found Zilla under the living room ottoman chewing on her favorite doggy bone while Grammy grabbed the dog leash as part of their granddaughter's routine.

Papa and Grammy Bell lived near a park with slides, swings, and stones to skip over the duck pond. Addison loved the park and felt like a big girl as she walked all four pounds of Godzilla with her leash.

Addison felt special because of all the attention from other park dwellers. Everyone wanted to pet the four-pound fluffball, which made Addison "Princess of the Park," and she was all about the princess.

Grammy Bell leaned over to Papa and kissed him while Addison played.

"Hey, handsome, you know I love you, right?"

"OK, you know I don't like sentences that end with a double-dangling adumbden!"

"You are such an oddball. Do you even know what grammar is?" Grammy laughed.

"No, does anybody? But I'm pretty sure I resemble that oddball remark!"

"No wonder I married you; I would have hated to be with someone normal," she smirked but regained her composure quickly. "Listen, we need to talk about something serious. So, no more double-dangling adumbdums, or whatever you called them. And no more Eye-Jobes either!"

"Well, I can't promise on the Eye-Jobes, but you have my full 73% attention." (Which was probably accurate). "What did you want to talk about?"

"Did you notice anything peculiar about Evan and Amelia tonight?"

"They did seem excited about date night this week but also concerned about something."

"I'm glad you noticed. While you guys were in the garage, Amelia again mentioned her concerns about Papa Airways. She *truly* wishes you would—"

"—Stop handing out those awful peanuts," he injected rapidly. "I'll talk to the captain ASAP because I'm getting a lot of complaints about those darn peanuts lately. Maybe people wouldn't notice as much if I handed out liquor instead. What kind of liquor do you think Addison would like?"

Grammy Bell chuckled but quickly composed herself. "Honey — I love our banter, I truly do. It's what I love about you most. But right now, at this moment, please be serious and listen. Amelia wants you to stop with Papa Airways. She's afraid you might accidentally hurt Addison."

Papa lowered his head and softened his voice. "I know she does. Evan cornered me in the garage and scolded me as well. But Evan also saw how much fun Addison had and remembered all his flights from when he was her age. He finally conceded after I reminded him that Captain Papa has had thousands of flights over the years and not one crash landing."

Old habits were hard to break, and Papa didn't want to end Papa Airways. He saw it as the reason why Addison trusted him completely and how, someday, it would be easier for him to ask her to pedal for the first time with no training wheels. Addison riding a bike was a crucial event in how Grandpa saw the world. He had planned for it and even bargained with his son that he would ensure Addison had bikes for life if he could be the one to teach her how to ride without training wheels.

What they were asking Grandpa to give up was sacred, and his eccentric soul ached over this. Every time Addison launched in the air, he saw the faces of all his kids: Evan, August, Jack, and Jordyn, as well as a slew of neighborhood faces who were privy to fly.

Grammy Bell's voice pierced his thoughts. "Honey, it would be nice if you grounded Papa Airways. Your planes aren't as young as they once were, and you never know when an engine might fall off."

He jumped up. "My planes are in fine form and tip-top shape."

"Are they, though?" as she gently placed her hands on his stomach, "I think they might need some maintenance."

Grandpa looked down at his stomach. "I'll think about it. But for now, a reluctant maybe is the best I can offer on such short notice."

"Honey, you need to think a little harder. As much as you adore Addison, she's not your child. Maybe it's time to let Evan take over piloting duties."

Her words were like a dagger to the heart as he looked out at Princess Addison, who had a line of kids waiting to pet Godzilla. He closed his eyes in anguish. "We'll see — that's the best I can offer. I don't want to talk about this anymore. Tuesdays are my favorite night of the week, and I simply want to be happy with my granddaughter." He opened his eyes and looked at his wife. "I know it's important that I communicate with you. I want you to know that I heard what you said. But I also want you to know that this is a tough pill to swallow. Give me some time."

His Bellavia looked at him, smiled, and kissed him, allowing his jovial spirit to return. Then, the two embraced, which signaled a temporary acceptance of the 'terms of condition.'

Grammy Bell and Papa finished their park play with Addison by skipping stones and trying to break Papa's record of seven skips. But the pond would have none of it and put up a mean current from the winds that shifted as Papa shook his fist and talked like a pirate.

"Arrrrrrrr, I'll get you next time, Mr. Pond. I hope you and all your progeny get scurvy. You're lucky there's a gammy-bleedin'-gully-washer a comin', or I'd stay and topple ya'— Arrrrrrrr."

"Arrrr,"— Addison emulated. "What's a gully-washer, Papa?"

"Arrrrrrrr — shiver me timbers! My first matey doesn't know what a gully-washer is. Arrrrrrrr, there it is, in the distance, the dark clouds from the high seas, bustin' with rain. They're comin' to rain on us; a real gully-washer they are promisin' — Arrrrrrr."

"I like the rain, Papa, because when I get wet, I get slippery. And my daddy can't catch me when he chases me in the rain. It's funny!"

As they walked home, Addison practiced rolling her Rrrr's like a pirate as she and her papa got into an "Arrrrr"- off competition. It was just after 6:30 as they beat the storm home and prepared for the proper care and feeding of Addison.

While Grammy Bell prepared dinner, she yelled, "Grandpa, it's time for Puzzle Duty."

Papa and Addison looked at each other instantly, and their eyes got as big as quarters.

"Grammy said Duty!" Addison blurted out as she and Papa cracked up laughing. Without seeing Grammy Bell's face, they knew some severe eye roll was happening.

Papa got the puzzle boxes from the cabinet and turned around to head to the puzzle table. Addison had a perfectly formed Jobe as he looked down. "Eye-Jobe, Papa!"

There was a resounding "JOOOOBE" as Papa fell to the ground. And once again, like Pavlov's dog, Addison was right on cue as she flew mid-air to land on Papa's tummy. Papa loved how she learned the element of surprise from their silly game.

"I'm so proud of how you Eye-Jobed me this week that we're going to skip from the forty-eight-piece princess puzzle to the ninety-six-piece princess puzzle."

Addison's eyes got as big as saucers! "Addison, I'm not sure if you can handle this. We're getting into Big Girl territory here."

"But I am a Big Girl, Papa; I'm three whole years and ten whole months old now."

"Wow, that sounds extraordinarily grown-up. So how does a grown-up, such as yourself, put together a princess puzzle of this magnitude?"

"Like this, Papa," and Princess Addison began getting all the straight-edge pieces together, finding the four corner pieces, and setting them aside just like Papa had taught her.

"My goodness," he said. "Now what?"

Addison looked at the puzzle box picture and sorted the matching pieces into separate piles.

"Addison, remember your motto — *She started to sing as she tackled the thing that couldn't be done, and she did it.*" Before long, Princess Anna and Elsa were no longer individual pieces of funny-shaped cardboard but whole puzzles. Then Papa rewarded Addison, like always, by reading his favorite poem as she crawled onto his lap.

It Couldn't Be Done

By Edgar A. Guest

Somebody said that it couldn't be done,
but he with a chuckle replied.
That "maybe it couldn't," but he would be one
who wouldn't say so till he'd tried.
So he buckled right in with the trace of a grin on his face.
If he worried, he hid it.
He started to sing as he tackled the thing
that couldn't be done, and he did it!

Somebody scoffed: "Oh, you'll never do that;
at least no one ever has done it;"
But he took off his coat and he took off his hat,
and the first thing we knew he'd begun it.
With a lift of his chin and a bit of a grin,
without any doubting or quiddit.
He started to sing as he tackled the thing
that couldn't be done, and he did it!

There are thousands to tell you it cannot be done,
there are thousands to prophesy failure;
There are thousands to point out to you one by one,
the dangers that wait to assail you.
But just buckle in with a bit of a grin,
just take off your coat and go to it;
Just start to sing as you tackle the thing
that "cannot be done," and you'll do it!

Addison and Papa applauded for the poem, and Grammy Bell called out, "Dinner's ready!" The two raced to the table for Grammy's award-winning dinner, Addison, winning by inches.

Addison was a slow but cute eater who would succumb to the furry cuteness trolling below for table scraps. However, Zilla got sick last week and had an emergency overnight stay at the twenty-four-hour animal hospital. The nearly thirteen-hundred-dollar pancreatitis diagnosis was caused by eating too much 'people' food. So, Papa and Grammy Bell must keep an extra eye on Addison because Zilla's cuteness easily persuaded her to drop a scrap or two.

Dinner was over, and it was on to the next phase of the evening: bath time and then a movie starring a princess. Lately, *Frozen* and *Tangled* had been the front-runners, but *Beauty and the Beast* made a surprise showing last week.

Grammy Bell headed upstairs to start the bath ritual while Papa and Addison cleared the table. Papa did his usual accidental "Spraying of the Addison" with the dishwasher sink hose.

"Papa, you're missing the plates and squirting me!" she said as she went on a giggle burst.

"Oh, my, Addison, it's almost 7:30, and your mommy and daddy will be here soon. Time to head upstairs for a bath."

On the way, Addison stopped in her tracks. "Papa, aren't you forgetting something?" Her hands already stretched toward the sky.

The tradition was that Papa Airways flew Addison to her upstairs destination. But tonight, Grandpa hesitated and tried to calculate his guilt if he ignored everyone's plea to stop Papa Airways versus the joy Addison would experience if she flew. But her adorable smile and outstretched arms were like emotional kryptonite to Papa.

Oh, just one more round of flights; who will know? I'll ground Papa's airplanes next week. Addison soared up in the sky, giggled her way through imaginative clouds, and then landed back in his arms.

"Do it again, Papa!" And up she went. "Again, Papa!" And up she went. "Again, Papa!"

"Okay, Addison, once more, and then it's bath time." Up she went, but this time, as Addison landed in his arms, she was completely limp, like a rag doll. Papa looked down at Giggle Bum Addison and rolled his eyes.

"Okay, silly willy, quit playing possum." —But she didn't move.

"Oh, look at that, a princess riding a unicorn!" —No movement.

"Oh, my, the princess is eating your favorite ice cream, Neopolitan!" —Still nothing.

"Now they're flying over a rainbow. Look, Addison, before you miss it." —But no reaction.

"Okay, Addison, quit playing around. We need to stop this. You're scaring me!"

He held the limp body away from his, and her head fell loosely to her chest.

"Addison! — Addison!! — **Addison!!!**"

Panic struck; he instantly grew cold with sweat as he buried his ear against her chest but couldn't hear a heartbeat. He hyperventilated and sucked in a rebellious breath that wouldn't release. At the same time, a cold clamminess began gripping his heart, followed by a stab of pain — the same pain he had felt that morning while at the lake. *No, not now, you damn jalapeños,* but the blackness of nothingness began to swirl around him, dimming his world.

It's true, he thought as a barrage of life images flashed before his eyes for an eternal second. He suddenly woke to find himself on the ground, covered in sweat, with Addison lying lifeless on his chest. A thousand thoughts spun through his mind, rendering him speechless.

God, what have I done!? He screamed on the inside. *God, please trade me for her; please, God!"* His pleas to God morphed into berating himself repeatedly as he examined Addison. *Why couldn't you just listen, you idiot!? Why couldn't you just listen? Why!?*

She wasn't breathing, so he tried to resuscitate her. After a few tries, he wasn't confident in his ability and grabbed his phone to call for help.

"9-1-1, what's your emergency?"

"I need an ambulance at 700 Glenwood Trail — I was playing with my granddaughter, and she just stopped breathing."

"Okay, sir, the ambulance has been dispatched. Can you tell me—"

Grandpa snapped, "Just hurry!" and hung up. He tried to resuscitate Addison's motionless body once more. He shook as if an earthquake were tearing him apart from the inside out...

Grammy Bell had no idea what had happened downstairs with the water running upstairs, and because of Papa Airways, her husband was too terrified to yell for her. He continued the resuscitation process, praying for a miracle that Addison would merely start breathing on her own. Before long, she yelled downstairs, "Hey, where are you two? Hurry up; Evan and Amelia will be here soon."

Sirens in the distance grabbed her attention as they got closer. "Papa, do you hear those sirens? It sounds like they're in the neighborhood."

Without a response, she went to see what was taking Papa and Addison so long. As she got downstairs, she witnessed her husband leaning over Addison, performing what looked like CPR, and she screamed.

"Oh, my God, what happened to her!?"

His internal earthquake wouldn't allow him to respond, so she grasped for clues. *Why was he doing this?*

Her immediate thought was Papa Airways because of the guilt on his face. She knew he was hiding something involving him; otherwise, why didn't he yell for her when this happened? With the strength of an NFL lineman, she pushed her husband aside and took over resuscitation duties. Getting no response, she kept trying.

Stopping for a second, she yelled at him. "Look me straight in the eyes! What happened?" But he couldn't look because of his enormous guilt, and he continued to focus his watery eyes on Addison's body.

There was no doubt what happened here. And Grandpa not calling out for her was his most egregious and unforgivable sin. Because she believed, if given a chance, she could have saved Addison's life with proper CPR. In Grammy Bell's mind, the trial was over; the jury was back, and he was guilty on all counts. She was so full of rage at that moment that she slapped him as hard as she could. "You were throwing her in the air, weren't you!?"

His mind held his vocabulary hostage under a mental triage, and his wounded words could not answer her. If only Papa Airways had a black box that could tell her what happened instead.

She continued working on Addison but felt no pulse, no sign of life. Right outside, they could hear the deafening sound of multiple sirens pulling up, then abruptly fading, followed by the shrill screech of brakes and the hiss of released pneumatic pressure. Flashing lights strobed through the front windows as the promised rain began to streak against the glass.

"Go let them in!" Grammy demanded, but Grandpa was too emotionally paralyzed, fueling Grammy Bell's rage further. She harshly pushed on him to help her stand, digging her nails into him, then rose as quickly as her sixty-something-year-old legs could and rushed to the front door.

She quickly opened it and witnessed the promised gully-washer begin dumping sheets of rain over the city. Distant thunder rumbled ominously as two paramedics – one male, one female – clad in rain ponchos and carrying large cases of medical supplies navigated the driveway from the ambulance. "This way, hurry!" Grammy shouted, leading them into the house.

As the paramedics rushed inside, looking for who needed medical attention, no one noticed Zilla run out the front door behind them, as she did every chance she got. But there was no one to run after her this time, and Zilla would keep running. Her escape was not good for Grandpa. Because, as horrible as things were, they just got worse for him since the order of importance to Grammy Bell was Addison, Zilla, and then Papa.

Two firefighters, sitting outside in the truck cabin, were communicating with headquarters when a small dog suddenly dashed excitedly about the front yard, running in circles. As they looked out their rain-soaked windshield, the thought crossed their minds that perhaps the family pet shouldn't be running loose like that. But before they could act, a set of headlights swept the scene, and the little dog bolted, disappearing down Glenwood Trail and into the night.

Moments later, a dark gray minivan screeched alongside them and rolled down its window, prompting the driver's side fireman to do the same. Evan leaned across Amelia and shouted—

"Hey, excuse me, what's going on?"

"Just responding to some kind of accident."

"What sort of accident?" asked Amelia, alarmed.

"Sorry, I can't give out that—"

"It's okay, we're family!" interrupted Evan. "This is my parents' house!"

The fireman nodded. "All we have is the subject stopped breathing—"

"Jesus!" shouted Evan. He hit the gas, barely missing the ambulance ahead as he swerved around it. Thoughts barreled through his mind that something happened to his Pops as he hastily pulled into the driveway. The two first responders watched objectively from their dry truck cabin as the man and woman jumped out and sprinted through the pouring rain for the house.

Inside, the paramedics were doing everything they could to resuscitate little Addison. They powered on the defibrillator to try and restart her heart. As Evan and Amelia burst into the house, they both stopped in their tracks, their minds incapable at first of comprehending the near-motionless scene before them. Two paramedics were there, but they weren't administering aid to Grandpa. Seconds later, the word "Clear" rang out, followed by Addison's tiny, lifeless body convulsing from a defibrillator's violent charge.

Everyone awaited some hopeful movement from Addison. Evan and Amelia's minds raced with questions as everything seemed to move in slow motion. They anxiously awaited the results of the defibrillator's first attempt as silence filled the air except for the sounds of hands clasping together in prayer.

Again, the paramedic yelled, "Charge!" followed by its counterpart, "Clear," and the defibrillator's second chance to get it right.

The air was sucked out of the room by gasps of hope. Once again, the long silence drew out as everyone awaited Addison's response. Prayers thickened the air, but the body didn't respond; the chest did not breathe, and the body remained still.

The paramedic yelled, "Charge again — Clear!"

Once again, the air was removed from the room, only to witness the same result. The small crowd heard "clear" repeatedly — until they didn't. No one moved as the cold, metal stethoscope checked for a heartbeat. At the same time, the resuscitator airbag automatically filled and collapsed, taunting their emotions as it cruelly mimicked life.

The male paramedic gently removed the breathing mask from Addison's face, and there was a terrible eternity of silence before the female paramedic painfully checked her watch. Her voice quivered as she pronounced three simple words the human ear should never have to experience...

"Time of Death" — "7:48 p.m."

A massive lightning strike outside startled the roomful of mournful onlookers. It seemingly caused all light, all joy to vanish from their world. Moments later, a firefighter entered the house and walked as reverently as possible to the female paramedic. He whispered in her ear before respectfully leaving.

Evan's legs moved seemingly of their own volition, drawing him toward his daughter. The two paramedics calmly gathered their equipment, then rose solemnly and stepped back. Evan stood looking down at his little angel. "Oh, sweetheart... my sweet, sweet little girl," he sobbed. Then, a primal scream pierced the air, banishing the silence forever as Evan fell to his knees and folded over Addison's motionless body.

The loudest verified decibel level on record for a human scream was 129 dB, set by a woman named Jill Drake. Surely, this was louder.

All Grandpa could do was stare. He felt dead inside while still on his knees a few feet away. *This isn't right, God. You should have taken me...*

Evan looked at his pops, "What happened to Addison!?" he demanded.

But his pops had no words as his body visibly shook from his relentless internal earthquake. And now "Bella," as the name "Grammy Bell" followed Addison into Heaven, spoke up.

"Evan, your dad was—"

Before his mom even finished the sentence, he just knew. The voice in his head begged the question that he feared asking. *Please don't tell me she was flying! Please, please, please, NO!* Then, he had to ask the words aloud. "He was throwing her in the air, wasn't he?"

Bella tried to look into his eyes — but couldn't, confirming his belief.

—AND EVAN BROKE—

Evan's mind entered a realm of Hell that Hell didn't know existed. His primal scream must have created an alternate universe that took over everyone's lives at that moment. And violence Evan never thought possible had erupted from within himself. He grabbed the biological human that was no longer his father in this alternate dimension of Hell, and this gentle, kind-hearted, wonderful son and adoring young father of three short years broke.

"You killed her! *You killed my Addison!*" he shouted, face burning with anger. Evan clutched Grandpa by the collar and shoved him back against the wall, rattling the plaster, causing photographs to fall off shelves and large wall hangings to become unlevel.

"I asked you; I begged you, but you wouldn't listen! Is this hysterical to you, old man? So, is this hysterical, you fat turd!? Isn't that what you always say? 'It's only funny until someone gets hurt, then it's hysterical.' Well, tell me, is it? I don't see you laughing!"

Evan hauled back and punched the man who once was his father in his stomach – hard – as if to pound all his ridiculous fat away in a single stroke. The older man fell to the ground, consumed by guilt, not trying to defend himself. Addison's last breath took with it his will to live, and his life was not worth defending; he truly believed he deserved to die.

And Alt-Evan was only too happy to help him with his wish. He picked the biological human up from his knees and threw him over the couch with the strength of his newfound hate.

The paramedics, who had been on their way out when the yelling began, were sadly familiar with the escalation of domestic violence at a family tragedy. They didn't want this tragically altered family to experience another death, as this was shaping into a real pummeling.

The medics dropped their medical gear and ran out into the storm. They waved their arms toward the two firefighters, who were down the street working to remove a large tree that had been struck by lightning and fallen on a neighbor's car.

With the sound of an industrial-sized chainsaw and the pounding rain, the firefighters were unaware of the medics trying to get their attention.

The female medic ran down the street to inform the firefighters they were needed. But running proved easier said than done as the roads were beginning to flood. The second medic called for a police unit to investigate, as was protocol, whenever a child dies unexpectedly. He also called for the coroner's unit to pick up Addison's lifeless body, which her mother rocked softly.

Amelia was oblivious to what was happening around her as a deafening silence filled her world. She stared at Addison's face and tried to memorize every skin cell before mentally releasing Addison's life to her Heavenly Father and her physical body to the coroner.

But Evan was not finished with this horrible human. He jumped over the couch and managed to lift the old man to his feet, even though he outweighed Evan heavily, and pinned the man against the wall, hands to his throat while screaming at him.

"I hate you! I hate everything about you! I hate that you have always embarrassed me – not just me, but all your kids, by how fat and gross-looking you are! I never want to see you again. And don't even think about coming to Addison's funeral!" Evan's hands tightened around Grandpa's neck.

"You're dead to me, even more than Addison! You remember Addison, my daughter, who you killed because of how stupid and selfish you are?! At least Addison is still alive in my heart, but not you."

Bella sat watching, riddled with guilt because she knew a wife should defend the man she once called her husband. But mentally, she couldn't, as she felt the same way Evan did. Bella witnessed the possible end of her marriage as Evan grabbed the biological human again and threw him out of the room. This time, she and Evan watched him crawl away in disgrace and escape through the garage.

It felt as if all the years of wit, laughter, and joy this biological human gave them had been wiped out of their collective memories.

Bella wholeheartedly believed Addison would be alive if her husband had simply yelled for her, but his defiance in defending Papa Airways kept her from that, so he deserved what happened to him.

The two firefighters finally rushed into the house with the medics slightly behind them. As they arrived, they witnessed Evan practically choking on his putrid anger. One of the firefighters went to check on him, but Evan refused help and made his way toward Amelia and his mom.

The three of them huddled with Addison, and they could feel the warmth of her skin fade while awaiting the police and coroner's unit.

Meanwhile, it was all a cold, dark blur for this broken man who found himself stopped in the middle of the street a few blocks away. He stood frozen in the pouring rain, lost in more ways than one. His body clicked into survival mode as his head reminded his heart to beat again and again. But his soul needed to be on suicide watch. Both body and soul jockeyed for position to see which would win the battle. An odd image appeared in his head: a man with long hair, a piercing stare, and speaking faint words — *We'll see — Won't we?*

See what, Grandpa thought. He didn't even know where he was, where he was going, or what to do next. This was all a nightmare, and the rain was beginning to get to him. He folded his arms tightly against the chill and started hiking down the street. He had to concentrate and take in a few street signs to get his bearings.

He began to limp back toward Glenwood Trail and the structure that once occupied his hopes and dreams, both of which died with Addison. But it was now a forbidden place he couldn't foresee ever entering again.

As he rounded Glenwood Trail, he covertly snuck down his street. He ducked behind bushes or trees and stayed out of view of his neighbors, who watched the flashing lights and the comings and goings of the paramedics from their porches or discretely parted curtains.

A police car arrived, and two men in uniform emerged. The firefighters stepped out of their truck and briefly conversed with the officers before climbing back into their vehicle and pulling away. Grandpa observed the changing of the guard through a gap in a hedge before the police officers entered the house.

The rain was accompanied by heavy thunder and lightning strikes as it started to pour even harder, shooing the neighbors back into their homes. Grandpa walked out from behind the hedge and taunted the lightning as he stood with his eyes closed, arms open to the sky – *a lightning bolt right about now would sure solve a lot of problems, God.* But no such bolt was forthcoming. After a few seconds, he opened his eyes and looked at 700 Glenwood Trail — *Was God shedding tears because evil won the battle for this once-blessed residence?*

Through the downpour, the man saw another car slowly approach. He hid in tall bushes against one of the homes across the street. As the vehicle arrived, the already-flashing lights strobed the big block letters of CORONER glued to its side, which only thickened his pain.

Two men emerged from the vehicle and opened the back door. They pulled out a stretcher and one other item – an item that should never exist – a body bag the size of a small life. The agony drove Grandpa to his knees, yet somehow, his mind continued the vigil on his own life, reminding the heart to do its job — *Beat!*

Shortly after, the paramedics exited the house into the rain, again clad in water-proof ponchos. They loaded their equipment before driving away. No other activity followed. Grandpa finally gave in to his weakness and slowly lay down in the mud before he closed his eyes. He stayed dormant and hidden for what seemed an eternity.

Hours passed, and he eventually heard voices and looked up from his ground-level view. The two policemen had stepped out onto the porch, followed by Evan and his wife. They conversed in low, grave voices for a moment. Evan nodded. Then they stepped aside as the two men with CORONER on their jackets slowly and reverently carried out the stretcher with the small body bag resting on top. Even from across the street, Grandpa heard the rain pound against the thick plastic shroud from where he lay.

He felt every raindrop hit his soul as the men seemed to walk in slow motion. Their body language spoke volumes about what they saw. Their jobs were already one of the hardest to do nightly; surely, they must have mastered the art of indifference. But tonight, there was no indifference — there was only suck.

Grandpa's heartbeat rose slightly when he saw Bella come out to join Evan and Amelia. The three of them, together with the police officers, watched silently as the two men loaded Addison's corpse into the coroner's van. Then, they quickly got inside and drove off into the night. The police officers followed right behind, disappearing down the dark street.

Grandpa watched how Evan ran into the storm and started his van so he could pull it closer to the house. He got out with an umbrella to shield Amelia from the harsh elements as he walked her to the passenger side door. Then he hurried back to his mom and hugged her goodbye.

A strange thought permeated his mind as the older man watched from across the way, lying in thick mud — *I taught him that; he learned all of that from me.* Despite all that happened, the disconnected father couldn't help but feel immense pride for the son who verbally castrated him from his life a few short hours ago.

Watching them drive off, he assumed they were following the coroner's unit to the hospital to arrange for Addison's body. He watched closely as his wife walked back into the house. He remained in the mud, and his mind turned to survival mode, settling into a state of mental and physical numbness.

Time passed, and the garage door screeched open, startling Grandpa from his emotional abyss. He was puzzled as his wife's car backed out and wondered if she was going to meet Evan and Amelia at the hospital. With the numbness gone, the pain returned, knowing he should be with his wife at such a difficult time. He should be driving her and protecting her because she was a terrible driver at night and even worse in the rain.

He desperately wanted to rise from the mud, like a phoenix from the ashes, and fix everything for her. But who was he kidding? He was in no state of mind to do anything. And his trite, short-lived mystical whim produced only debilitating fear, which merely allowed him to watch her taillights disappear down the street.

He laid back down in the mud. Soon, a deafening silence penetrated the air, forcing the sound of the pounding rain to lessen into a disturbing silence. After a few minutes, a thought pierced his tortured solace: *NOW WHAT?*

He couldn't just lay there all night. He pushed himself up from the muddied ground and started toward the lifeless structure. He did not feel welcome. Halfway across the street, he stopped, raised his arms, and taunted the lightning once again to strike him. But just as before, the indifferent universe ignored his request. As he faced his old life, the rain washed the mud from every part of him, and his internal survival mechanism formulated a plan to answer the question of "NOW WHAT?"

He was a broken man with a fractured soul and shattered thoughts; however, the one constant that never left him was an overwhelming desire to die. He couldn't live with the guilt of knowing he had possibly killed Addison. However, it did present him with a conundrum.

On the one hand, he wanted to die. On the other, he didn't have the guts to kill himself because his faith kept him from that. He firmly believed that suicide would send his soul to Hell, and as bad as the current situation was, he still held on to a sliver of hope that he was once a good man and didn't deserve to spend eternity below. He would much rather God allow him to see his granddaughter in Heaven so he could ask her forgiveness. That ruled out suicide.

On the other hand, he also believed that the departure of his soul would be a gift to his family; otherwise, his living would always remind them of what he took from them and how he destroyed their lives. If only he could find a painless way to pass from this life, then maybe suicide was the easiest way out.

For the moment, he wouldn't make that life-or-death decision. So, as much as he wanted to die, he was condemned to live. The engine of survival was loud in his ear, and now he had to pay attention. It encouraged him to enter his garage for no other reason than to get out of the rain so he could think.

He entered his code, and the garage door rose with its typical annoying screech. Entering the main house was not an option, so he couldn't grab his keys, wallet, or cell phone and wouldn't do so if he could. He wanted to remain anonymous. He stood in the garage, shaking as his survival mechanism continued to work on the "Now what?"

Grandpa took a long look around the once cherished man cave. He fought off his vivid emotions by trying to delete the many hours of joy from his memory. There was an emergency stash of cash hidden in a garage storage box that he had accumulated since he was a teenager. All his life, he had emptied his nightly change into a piggy bank that he filled and cashed in for $100 bills. (Wash, rinse, repeat.) Over forty or more years, he had accumulated $5600. Ironically, it was all stuffed in an envelope that read, "Save For A Rainy Day."

He also had a money pouch his dad gave him long ago for a family trip to Italy. It kept his money safe from being pickpocketed because it was attached to his belt but hung hidden inside his shorts. It also came in handy for storing his valuables when he rode his bike in an unfamiliar city or dicey area of town.

He looked around and realized that although his bikes were vital to him, his wife lost interest around ten bikes ago. He owned bikes that no one knew he had, so no one would know if one was missing. The Dedacciai was the bike she knew about because of his excitement, but she also knew he would never, under any circumstances, ride it or any of his precious bikes in the rain, especially at night.

In his forty years of collecting, not one of his bicycles had felt a drop of rain or experienced the darkness of a night ride. And he had made it known to anyone who would listen that he hated reflectors on his bikes and de-reflectorized them the moment he acquired a new one. So, he was confident – even though the circumstances were far from normal – that neither Bella nor Evan would be looking at his bicycles as his transportation on this terrible night. He decided to ride one of his bicycles until he couldn't ride any longer. In his mind, since he had no reflectors or lights of any kind, it would be a risky game of riding roulette — *Are you paying attention, God?*

If he did perish in the night, weirdly – or perhaps not for him – he wanted to go out in style and therefore chose his cherished Dedacciai. He decided he would ride wherever the wind blew him. If God allowed him to survive the night, he would regroup tomorrow and buy the necessary bike clothes to continue his journey. Each tomorrow he survived after that would be up to God, and each trip would be determined by wherever the wind wanted to take him.

He was in jeans and wearing a button-down dress shirt left open over his Keep Austin Weird T-shirt. He dried himself off as much as possible with towels he used to wash Bella's car. He wore tennis shoes, which would work well on his bike, as he had SPD pedals with a flat side to use without the SPD cleat. He grabbed one of his six different-colored helmets and gloves for the journey, and his bike had the latest Garmin GPS.

He then transferred the Rainy-Day fund from the envelope to his money pouch. He secured it by running his belt through the double loops connected to his money pouch and tucked it safely inside his jeans.

Grandpa had no idea how long he would be gone or if he would survive this dangerous game. But he knew Bella needed a break from him, and he was painfully aware she might never forgive him.

He tried to stop the quaking that had never ceased from within as he straddled his shiny red bike. He was about to be alone for the first time in his life. The man wept as he put his life in God's hands. It was now His decision whether he lived or died or who would win the war between guilt and grace raging within his family.

He closed his eyes and took an exceptionally long breath before he slowly opened them — "What in the world!?" In the distance, a dog that looked a lot like a wet Zilla ran toward him in the dense rain. She barked in her high-pitched squeal as she saw her daddy. His heart seemed to take its first beat on its own when he saw her.

He dismounted to catch her as she slid into home base. He grabbed a towel to wrap her in and dry her off. He was confused on every level about why his dog was out here, lost in the rain. His wife must not have known that Zilla was gone because she loved this dog more than life itself – and probably more than him. But he was glad to be third in line after Addison and Zilla and accepted that role. Zilla had never been happier to see her daddy, and he cried as she frantically licked his face as if it were a competition.

Maybe it was a selfish desire on his part, but he was thrilled that Zilla was back home because he knew this dog would play a significant role in Bella's healing process and her ability to forgive him.

He finished drying Zilla, gave her the biggest hug, and then let her back into the house he believed he would never enter again. But that decision was no longer his; it was up to God.

He straddled his bike again and closed his eyes as he took another deep breath, only to hear Zilla's high-pitched squeals, asking, "Why are you leaving me, Daddy?" His body quaked from the inside out as the garage door screeched closed, returning him back to the reality of what happened a few short, eternal hours ago.

As his journey into the unknown began, his GPS read 11:08 p.m., and the wind determined he was headed north. It was the first part of October, and that year had been unseasonably warm in Austin, TX. Although he felt a little cold because of the rain, he knew it would not take long for him to warm up, causing the cooler weather to be welcome.

One last thought entered his mind: *Godspeed* and the realization no one was there to wish it to him. He was alone — excruciatingly alone — for the first time in his life. And with that, the first pedal strokes began.

Chapter Two

Carter Ducane

Carter Ducane walked in the back door at the six o'clock hour as his dad, Russell, slogged in through the front. There was no dinner on the table and, even worse, no beer to match. Russell Ducane blew a fuse, as he did most every night, and the evening's A++ level of verbal abuse was off.

"Where the freaking hell is my dinner?" he bellowed to his wife as he stomped into the kitchen to yell at her. But Rose was not there, only his son, hanging up his bicycle helmet on a hook near the pantry. The two Ducanes glared at one another for a moment as the sound of heavy thunder chimed in from the predicted storm headed their way. Even though Carter was a head taller than his father, Russell still had the advantage of weight, with a belly that could make a Sumo wrestler envious.

The staring contest continued a beat before Russell snorted, like a phlegmatic bull, and walked past Carter to the beat-up old yellow Frigidaire. Then he took out a beer, fuming because opening his first beer himself was a cardinal sin as far as he was concerned. He looked over at Carter. "Hey, son, lend me that fancy-schmancy nose ring of yours; I can't find the opener." He snorted again at the funny he made, twisted off the cap, and downed half the bottle in one long swig.

In a moment of monumentally lousy timing, the back door swung open, and in stumbled his missing spouse, Rose, awkwardly carrying two sacks of heavy groceries. She kicked the door shut with her heel and turned. When she saw the scowl on her husband's face, she automatically began apologizing profusely — which, as usual, had little effect. Russell Ducane had already opened his first beer of the evening, and for this, Rose must now pay the price. As she hobbled toward the kitchen counter, groceries in hand, he tripped her.

Carter stared in disbelief. His initial reaction was this had to be an accident. He gave his old man the benefit of the doubt since he had never seen this monster act this way and weirdly found it hard to believe. Russell had always been verbally abusive to them; Carter was used to that. However, physical abuse was never his MO toward Rose or Carter — *But tonight*?

What happened next created two opposite ends of a nuclear reaction that would have consequences for years as a birthday cake that read "Happy 25th Birthday Carter" slid out of one of the bags. Carter looked down at his mom, and a smile lit up his face for an entire two seconds before Russell's boot smashed through the middle of the cake.

"You mean you bought a birthday cake for this piece of shit, and that's why my dinner isn't on the table?"

Rose began to cry as she looked at the cake imprinted with a size 9½ Dickie's work boot. Carter exploded and raised his fists, ready to take on the piece of crap named Russell Ducane.

But Russell Ducane just smirked at him, unimpressed. "C'mon, boy, I've been waiting for this day for twenty-five years. I can still remember the day you were born as being the worst day of my life. And here you are twenty-five years later, a loser, still living at home, defacing your body with a Tooti-Frutti nose ring and ruining my life — *and* my dinner. I wish you'd just leave and get the hell out of here, you selfish bastard!"

Carter lurched toward him, fists still at the ready, but his mother staggered to her feet to block him. "No!" she yelled out through her sobbing tears. She looked at Carter, looked right in his eyes. "*No.*" Carter froze, transfixed by pity at this poor woman who was his mother. Then, obeyed and lowered his fists.

Rose turned toward Russell. "*I'm sorry!*" she blurted. "I should have had dinner on the table when you came home."

Russell stared at her momentarily, and then the scowl left his face. "Good," he said. "You hear that, boy? It's all her fault. But she knows her place. She's a good woman." Suddenly, he became downright friendly. "Here, let me pick this up for you." And unexpectedly, he stooped down and lifted the fallen grocery bags onto the counter, where he began putting the groceries away.

Carter gawked at him in utter disbelief. Rose saw the giant question mark on her son's face and hugged him.

"I'm sorry, Carter. It's not the evening I planned for you. I should've realized I couldn't order the cake in time, but I needed to try. Please don't hurt your father. In the end, it's my fault dinner wasn't ready."

Russell bellowed, "Yeah, boy, how many damn times does she have to say it's her fault before you shut your trap," then he thanked Rose again for knowing her place and continued putting away the groceries.

What the hell is happening here? Carter could not believe what he was hearing and how bass-ackwards it all was. But Carter's need to help his mother outweighed continuing what he started with his dad.

"Mom, you can't stay here with this Neanderthal," Carter said in a low voice. "Call Granddad to pick you up and move in with him."

But Russell heard him anyway, his inner Grinch returning. "Listen here, boy. That dream's not gonna happen. Your Momma doesn't talk much to her Daddy anymore. He hates me, and his new wife hates her, just like her Momma did, so mind your own damn bee's wax!"

He finished gulping the last of his beer so loudly you could hear it down the block. And just like Pavlov's dog, Rose was headed to the fridge to get the next beer open for him.

"What a good wife you are, Rose," he said in a gradually increasing slur. "Too bad Carter will never know what a good wife is. Hell, as far as I know, he's never even talked to a girl. Or if he has, I'm sure his wheels, all two of them, put a stop to that conversation."

Carter launched into a tirade of his own. "It's all because of you, you asshole! All this because you were never man enough to take care of your family and make sure we had even the basics, like transportation. Every other guy I know has a car by now, but I'm stuck riding a bicycle! You're supposed to be a role model, but the only example you've shown me is how to be a piece of shit!"

"Yep," Russell laughed, "Boy, you learned that lesson real good; got that one down, pat."

"You're the worst freaking human ever!"

"Really, I'm the worst freaking human ever. I thought I at least taught you how to curse better than that asshole." And he laughed, tilting back his second beer.

Carter was consumed by rage, confused on every level about what was happening. It was like they had entered an alternate universe because, as dysfunctional as they were, this night was *really* messed up! He couldn't believe how his mom took up for this turd she called a husband after he tripped her like that. But Carter realized all his mom knew how to do was diffuse conflict, and lucky for him, she did. Had she not, he might have been in handcuffs and headed to jail, or worse, prison, from the violence he had intended to inflict on that man.

But Russell was on a roll. "Hey, son, there's some cake that doesn't have my boot print on it. How about we put a candle in it so you can blow it out and make a wish? What do you say? How about one tug of your nose ring for yes and two for no?"

His taunts forced Carter's anger to boil again. But he thought of his mom and took a deep breath to honor her request. *Yeah, I'll make a wish*, he thought. *I wish I could start my life over and rewrite my whole freaking story – a story without you in it!*

They say that a person who decides to commit suicide suddenly becomes very calm and at peace, knowing their perceived misery is about to finally end. And so, it was with Carter. At that moment, he made a decision, and he knew it was the right one, the only one, the only way out of this horrible existence. He bent down and picked up the smashed disaster that was his birthday cake and set it on the counter. He looked at it, then over at his mom and dad. "I may not get my wish, but I'll grant you yours. I'm leaving — tonight. Congratulations, Dad. You win."

His mom rushed and grabbed Carter by the hand. "*No, son, you can't!* — you can't leave us — not like this. I promise to do everything I can to make things better — for all of us."

"Oh, don't beg, Rose, let him go. First smart thing he's ever done. He's worthless around here, and we both know it," Russell responded.

"Carter, don't listen to him! Please stay. You know how he is when dinner's not on the table. You know this will blow over. He's just —"

"He's just what? An asshole?!" Carter interjected. "It's my birthday; why can't he act normal and not be his charming asshole self for once? Why is it impossible for us to be a normal family for one night — just one freaking night?"

"Carter, he didn't know it was your birthday when he—"

"Mom, you're making my point," he interrupted. "What kind of father doesn't know his own son's birthday? And now you're taking up for him again!" Carter took her gently by the shoulders. "Mom, I have to leave. I need to start over without him and without you. I need to do this alone! So, please, please, please don't try to contact me because it will only make things harder for both of us. In fact, I'm going to shut off my phone, so you can't."

Carter didn't want the gravity of her voice pulling him back into her emotional orbit. But he had to give her something and looked firmly into his mother's tear-filled eyes. "I promise; I will call you in a couple of weeks to let you know how I'm doing."

Rose knew she hadn't been the greatest mother over the years and probably didn't keep an eye on her son's life as well as she should have. But the sudden impact of Carter leaving made her maternal instincts jump out of hiding after all these years. Hearing that her son didn't want her to contact him and realizing she would be left alone with Russell almost caused her heart to implode. As her son started to exit the kitchen, she said, "Please, wait —"

But Russell butted in. "Wait, hell! What about me? I'm still waiting for my dinner!"

Carter turned back to Rose. "It's okay, mom. Feed the Neanderthal his dinner before he throws another temper tantrum. I won't leave without saying goodbye." He spun away again and left, crossing quickly through the living room to the dark, picture-less hallway leading to the tiniest of the three bedrooms — his bedroom. He switched on the light, staring for a long moment at the depressing little room he had called home for way too much of his life. Suddenly, the reality of the decision he had just announced hit him like a ton of bricks.

What the hell have I done? He stood there another few seconds, buyer's remorse already knocking at his brain. But he refused to answer. *No turning back now*, he resolved.

He focused his attention on his room instead. It wasn't filled with much, certainly not anything he cared deeply about, which would make packing all that much easier. But where to begin? He grabbed his rather large backpack that had functioned like a car trunk all through high school as he rode his bike everywhere he needed to go.

So, now what? Clothes! Gotta have clothes! Carter went to his closet and scanned his meager wardrobe. *Let's see, I'm already wearing a decent pair of jeans and a shirt, and I'll save room by wearing a sweatshirt over this. Okay, I need my rainproof jacket since it's going to rain and some nice clothes for a job interview.* He was pretty sure he'd need to look decent for a job interview since he needed another job to afford his rash sink-or-swim decision. *Geez, what have I done?* He grabbed a nice pair of slacks and a dress shirt and tie to go with them. He grabbed one more pair of jeans, along with his bike shorts and jersey. *I'm gonna need underwear,* and he checked his dresser. *Three or four pairs should do, and socks! Don't forget socks!* He tossed it all onto his bed and folded everything neatly before stuffing it inside the pack. *Okay, we're down to essentials.*

He grabbed a few razors, a nearly empty tube of toothpaste, and deodorant, along with his charging cord for his cellphone, and put them in a Ziplock bag. Since he rode his bike everywhere, his backpack had several specialized lightweight bike tools for most roadside repairs and a mini first aid kit just in case. Carter prided himself as a self-taught shade-tree bike mechanic, born out of necessity since he couldn't afford to have his bicycle professionally repaired.

Carter sat at his wobbly little desk, which his father had found in a neighbor's yard on big trash pickup day, and yanked open the drawer. The rattle of old pain pills tumbling in a prescription bottle caught his attention. *"Why not? You never know,"* and he tossed them toward his backpack. He saw his checkbook and opened his bank app to see his current balance — about $950.

Damn, that was supposed to be for a car; now I'll never get one. Just get a hotel for tonight and start job hunting tomorrow — there, it's decided. He reached for his wallet to inventory how much he had. There was a lonely twenty-dollar bill, a debit card, and his state ID.

Carter eased back in his chair and sighed. He closed his eyes and tried to clear his head and not think about the self-inflicted dystopian adventure to come.

After a while, there was a knock at his door, and his mother poked her head in. "You all ready?"

"I'm all packed, if that's what you mean?"

"Come with me," she said. Carter rose, curious, and followed her down the picture-less hallway to the second back bedroom, which was used as a catch-all pseudo storage facility for the Ducane household.

She opened the closet door and rummaged around the stacked boxes of every size, shape, and color, looking for a particular one. It was found hiding in the farthest corner of the bottom of a stack. Carter had to help lift the other boxes while she wrestled the one box out of confinement.

She opened the old rectangular blue carton filled with letters, pictures, books, and other personal items she treasured. Sifting through the photos, she found the one she needed. Rose sat on the floor and patted the spot next to her for Carter to do the same, then handed him a picture of her father holding him as an infant. Her dad had a loving, adoring look as he gazed at his newborn grandson.

"My daddy loved you so much. You represented something he always wanted in his life – a son. He had two daughters whom he loved, but he would have treasured a son. He had every intention of being in your life and the best grandad ever. But too many battles between him and Russell prevented that. I'm so sorry."

Carter clinched his jaw hearing that but sat there and enjoyed the moment with his mom as she continued.

"Did you know your grandad was in the Marines when he was a young man? He would joke that being in the Marines was almost as hard as living with my mom. Sadly, I don't believe it was a joke. But after mom died, my dad gave me these."

And to his surprise, she showed him an old pair of brass knuckles.

"He bought these in Taiwan while stationed overseas. You can see the 'Made in Taiwan' emblem right here. He used to tell me he wasn't always in the safest of places overseas. So, he and his buddies bought brass knuckles from the actual souvenir factory because of all the barroom brawls they experienced."

"Is this why I got into so many brawls at school? Because I inherited Granddad's fighting spirit?!"

"That's probably partly true because your grandad was quite the stud in his day, and that's why you're so handsome today. But sadly, I wish you didn't live with so much anger. I only wish you were happier."

Carter leaned over and kissed his mom on the cheek as she wiped the tears from her eyes.

"Mom, I hate that I'm this angry, but none of it has to do with you. It's all him."

"I know, trust me — I know. Now, honey, my daddy gave these to me and told me that someday he wanted his grandson to have them and that I would know when the time was right. And I think this is clearly the right time," and she handed them to Carter.

"These brass knuckles are one of the most treasured things I have of my daddy. They meant so much to him from all his tales while overseas. He told me he honestly believed they saved his life several times during his scuffles. I don't want you ever to have to use these, but I know I haven't always been there to protect you as I should have. And now that you're going out into the world by yourself, I want you to have something to let you know I'm trying to protect you. — Happy birthday, Carter." She gave him a big hug. "I really did want you to have a birthday to remember."

"Well, mission accomplished, Mom," Carter said with a cockeyed smile. "I'm pretty sure I won't forget this one anytime soon."

Carter stood and helped his mother to her feet. He looked down at the gift, even slipped them on his fingers, and held them up, smiling and feeling slightly silly as he modeled them for her. She laughed and had to hug him again. He gave her one final gift in return: a moment of laughter with her son.

"Mom — thank you. Now I'll always know you're protecting me." Then he secured them safely into his left front pocket. Carter could not have chosen any better words. He could almost see the years of unforgiveness and guilt lift from his mother's face. Rose now knew she finally did what she should have done for all these years: try to protect her son.

They walked back through the picture-less hallway, stopping only at his room to pick up his backpack and slip on his jacket before journeying out into the war zone that was their living room.

"I love you, mom." Carter gave her one last peck on the cheek. Then he glared at his dad. "If I *ever* find out you hurt her in any way, I'll kill you!"

Russell, still sitting at the dining room table and finishing off the last of his fried chicken dinner, flipped him off. "Good riddance, asshole. Finally, after twenty-five years, the happiest night of my life."

Carter approached him, and as his father looked up from his meal, his son reached out for him somewhat threateningly... but at the last moment, his hand swerved down, grabbed the last chicken leg off the platter, and took a big bite. "Mine too, Asshole!" and performed a glorious Mic-Drop as it fell back on Russell's plate and splattered his mashed potatoes on him.

"Get the hell out of here, and don't ever come back!" Russell hollered.

Carter wanted to use his mom's gift on Russell's face but went into the kitchen and retrieved his bike helmet instead, shoving it onto his head.

"Get the hell out of here, and don't ever come back!" Carter said in a baby's tone, mocking his dad one last time.

"Screw you, Dad," then grabbed his bike and stepped out the back door, possibly triggering the rain to start. It was just par for the course for him, as he left one hell storm to ride to another.

The Hard Times Bar was an unassuming but friendly little pub despite being located in one of the seedier parts of town. When Carter turned twenty, he took the job and was promised full-time employment. But times turned hard, even for a bar named Hard Times, and work quickly fizzled to working from 8 p.m. to 2 a.m. three to four days a week — just enough to keep him a resident of the great State of Limbo, where there was no Zip Code.

His coworkers were older than him, but he got along with them okay, though they never hung out. And his boss, Arnold, was a burley ex-Navy man with Hula-girl tattoos on his biceps and a burr haircut. Although he looked rough, deep down, he was a good guy, and his customers liked him, as well as his employees.

As Carter peddled furiously through the powerful downpour along the three-mile route to the Hard Times Bar, he tried his best to keep the panic out of his thoughts but failed miserably. His mind spiraled with the constant realization that as bad as his life had been, he would be alone for the first time with no place to call home. Carter reanalyzed his plan of quitting his job, finding a hotel room for the night, and seeing where the day took him tomorrow. He needed time to think this through and wished there was a friend's place where he could crash. But he had no one, leaving him no choice but to follow his plan of finding a hotel room after his shift.

It's just one day at a time from now on, he realized.

It was almost dark when Carter pulled up at the Hard Times shortly after 7:45 p.m.

"You're early," remarked Arnold from behind the bar.

"Long story," replied Carter.

His boss signaled him to bring his bicycle inside and stash it in the storeroom, knowing how much Carter depended on it.

"Do you have a moment?" Carter asked.

Arnold nodded and led him into his small back office. Carter had hardly sat down before the terrible story of his confrontation with his father spewed out like an erupting volcano. Arnold sat patiently, not saying a word until Carter had finished.

Then he said, "Oh, man, that is messed up. I butted heads with my pop, but nothing like that."

Carter just stared down at the floor, too empty to reply.

"So, what's the plan?" his boss asked gently.

"Guess I need to find a hotel room for the night. After that...?" Carter shrugged.

"Well, if there's anything I can do—"

"Actually, that's what I wanted to talk to you about. This has to be my last night here. I'm... quitting."

Arnold just looked at him for a moment, not unsympathetically.

"You think that's wise?"

"*No*. But it's necessary. I need to find a job that pays more so I can afford to put as much distance between myself and that monster. I don't even want to be in the same town as that asshole, if possible. I need to figure out my life, and I can't do that knowing he's just a short bike ride away."

His boss lowered his head, nodding. "Yeah. Yeah, I get that. Kinda why I joined the Navy."

"Sorry to spring this on you—"

"No, no, you got bigger fish to fry. Can't say I won't be sorry to see you go, and I wish I had more hours for you. You're a good worker, so if you ever want to come back, you're always welcome here."

"Thanks, boss." He hesitated — "Just one more thing—"

"I know, your final paycheck. I'll have it for you at closing."

Carter left the office and entered the back room to put on his red Hard Times employee shirt to begin his shift. Luckily for him, it was a reasonably busy night, as the rain drove customers in and kept them there longer than usual, which didn't give him much opportunity to dwell on his situation.

Shortly after midnight, as the crowd started to thin, his fellow workers approached him with a box of cupcakes that someone had run out and bought at a 24-hour grocery store. It seemed his boss had spread the word that Carter was leaving, and they got together to wish him well on his last night. As they all toasted him with the sugary treats, some of his regular customers overheard and chipped in as well, leaving him some very generous tips.

As the night neared its end and the last few customers began to clear out, his emotional fear reasserted itself. Carter managed not to think about his plight much of the evening, but now his thoughts flooded back, and his self-doubt reached the point where he began to shake inside. Suddenly, his boss entered the barroom, jolting him out of his inner turmoil.

"Happy birthday, Carter." He handed him his final paycheck and put a cupcake with a single candle on the bar. "Just so you know, I had my wife bake this cupcake for you. I saw on my calendar it was going to be your birthday.

Carter was surprised and touched. "Thanks, boss, I appreciate that — How did you know?"

"It was on your application, and I noted it on my calendar. Can't make up for your mother's cake, but what can you do? Before I leave for the night, I wanted to wish you well, and I do hope you find what you're looking for out there." Then he fished a book of matches out of his pocket and set it next to the cupcake. "You can light it when you're ready to make your wish — Make it a good one."

Carter shook his boss's hand. "Thank you, sir."

Arnold started to leave but turned back. "Oh, and you can keep the shirt." And with that, his boss left the room.

Carter was finally alone to wipe off the final two tables of his bartending career. It was precisely 2 a.m. when the timed music from the overhead speakers shut off. Carter welcomed the silence in the only section of the bar with a view of the outside world. He grabbed his cupcake and sat at his favorite table by the window. He tried to look out, but the window had fogged over from the rain. He wiped the window clean with his towel and stared into the lifeless, terrifying night. A heavy sigh followed as he opened the book of matches and lit his single candle.

Carter was scared more than he ever thought possible. His self-doubt about his decision weighed like an albatross on his life. *What the hell have I done?* His boss had said to make a wish, and at that moment, he wished he knew how to pray. But he knew nothing of the religious ways of life – yet another thing Russell had never taught him. Instead, Carter closed his eyes, took a deep breath, and pleaded with the universe...

Whoever is up there, or out there, running this crazy world, this is my wish — I wish to find a way to rewrite my life story. For the better, if possible. Please, I could use all the help I can get.... Please, I beg you to give me a sign.

He reiterated his wish once more for a way to rewrite his life story, then blindly blew out his candle and slowly opened his eyes — "What in the hell—?"

Through the pouring rain, a blurry motion out the window caught his eye. Carter saw what looked like an oddly dressed, heavyset cyclist riding in the street. The cyclist rode what appeared to be an expensive road bike, judging by the 88-millimeter carbon-fiber rim on the back.

Why is this idiot riding in the rain at 2 a.m.? Does he have a death wish?

Out of nowhere, an older four-door sedan with its lights off rounded a corner and crept up behind the cyclist. Carter watched as the car seemed to purposefully run him off the road and onto the muddied grass. The car's front doors flew open with exact precision, and two hoodies with legs sprang out of the vehicle in perfect unison as if synchronized stealing were an Olympic sport.

Hoodie One ran over to the heavyset cyclist, yanked the bicycle out of the rider's clenched fists, and headed to stuff the stolen bike into their trunk. Hoodie Two then took over, rolling the older man onto his stomach, and straddled him as he rummaged through his victim's pockets, searching for coin.

Carter stood frozen, not sure what to do. His adrenaline levels surged as he watched the scene unfold, his heart racing as well as his mind. He needed to decide quickly if he wanted to try and rescue the cyclist and his bicycle.

Calling 9-1-1 would not have changed the outcome. The police would not get there fast enough, and the bicycle would be gone. *But why do anything at all?* Carter had no dog in this fight. For all he knew, the older man was a fleeing criminal and had stolen the bike in the first place. That would explain a thing or three, like his weight, odd dress code, and the late-night bicycle charter he was on at 2 a.m.

What if this was my bike, and someone else could have saved it but didn't? His mind continued to ping-pong: *And what if I get hurt trying to save a complete stranger's bike? Who would help me then?*

His adrenaline hit peak levels as he suddenly envisioned his mother falling in slow motion with his birthday cake sliding out of her bag. He saw the words "Happy 25th Birthday Carter," just before a Dickie work boot stomped his cake to smithereens.

His mom's dysfunctional compassion had kept twenty-five years' worth of Carter's pent-up resentment from being released on Russell Ducane. That resentment was now adrenaline, turned into rage. And it was cocked, loaded, and ready for action.

Carter took out his grandad's brass knuckles, weighing the cool, hard metal in his hand. He looked up and caught sight of his profile reflected in the bar's front window. There was a red, white, and blue neon Lone Star Beer sign above the window, buzzing softly like an electric beehive, and the muted rainbow of colors illuminated his image, causing it to almost glow. At that moment, he could almost have stepped right out of a poster for a Marvel superhero movie.

He had asked for a sign; if this wasn't a sign, then he didn't know what was. Carter grew a mental cape and a code of honor to protect his fellow cyclists. "What's that? It's a bird; it's a plane — No, it's Carter Ducane!" With superhero strength, Carter flew out of the bar, feeling his grandad's fighting spirit as he fitted his brass knuckles onto their rightful place. He was determined that no one would steal someone else's bicycle, not tonight, and especially not on Carter Ducane's watch.

He flew in behind Hoodie One, who had just loaded the ill-gotten bike into his trunk. Carter delivered a swift, rage-driven punch to the thug's lower back and another to his kidney. *Wow, what a difference brass knuckles made!* Hoodie One grunted in pain as he buckled to his knees, not knowing what hit him. Carter punched the top of his shoulders with both hands from behind, driving him face-first into the wet pavement, then stomped on his back, leaving him rolling in immense pain.

The mission continued as Carter rushed toward Hoodie Two, who had turned the cyclist on his back after searching his pockets. He then pummeled the man in his ribs for what Carter deemed no good reason. The cyclist shielded his face but did not attempt to defend other parts of himself while lying in the muddied grass.

Hoodie Two saw his assailant approaching from the corner of his eye. He kicked his boot into the right side of the older man's head before rising to meet his challenger. As Carter witnessed the boot strike, an angry red flash erupted in Carter's mind, and he relived the size 9½ Dickies work boot stomping its way into the middle of his cake.

Big mistake — It was like a red flag to a bull. There was now an extra level of hell waiting for Hoodie Two as Carter's physical, mental, and emotional momentum teamed up to lift the hoodie into the air like a cowcatcher on a freight train. It plunged him backward against a nearby tree, knocking both opponents to the ground from the impact, but not for long.

They instantly leaped to their feet, facing each other toe-to-toe and eye-to-eye. The hoodie saw, up close and personal, the beyond-crazed look on Carter's face, but not the quickness of his punch as Carter knocked him against the already familiar tree. Carter ripped a right-left combination punch into the matching left-right sides of the hoodie while the thug stood pasted against the familiar bark, knocking the wind out of him, and bending him over in pain.

The hoodie's upper torso angled down past the 2 p.m. position. Then, an adrenaline-filled, right-handed uppercut to the hoodie's lower abdomen hit so hard the hoodie rose slightly in the air á la Rocky Balboa in the 12th round. Hoodie Two landed face-first in the mud, gasping for breath. Carter had no mercy and stomped on his back and side to keep him down.

Both hoodies rolled around in pain and tried to gravitate toward one another as if there might be strength in numbers, just in case the crazed madman decided to attack again. Carter almost laughed at the thought. *Just let them try.*

The adrenaline in his veins was still pumping away like a fire hose as Carter turned his attention toward the *purple pimpmobile*. Its doors were still open from the synchronicity of the hoodie's earlier launch toward the cyclist. There was a glint in Carter's eye as he saw a baseball bat in the front seat and realized what must happen next.

He circled around to the still-open trunk, removed the old man's beautiful and pricey bicycle, and laid it safely on the grass. Then he returned to the passenger side door and took out the baseball bat that must have participated in several smash-and-grabs and seen its fair share of mailboxes. He hefted it in both hands, testing it, taking a few warm-up swings before stepping up to the plate, rainwater flying off its tip. And just as Ivan Drago warned — "I MUST BREAK YOU" — to Rocky Balboa before their heavyweight title fight, Carter Ducane applied the same attitude toward the purple pimpmobile.

The battered hoodies managed to reunite but were still on their hands and knees in the nearby muddy grass. They looked up toward a bizarre and unexpected voice cutting through the rain-infested air. The hoodies would soon discover they had ringside seats to witness what twenty-five years of pent-up rage and dysfunction, paired with a set of brass knuckles and a vintage maple-wood bat *circa* 1977, could do to a pimped-up Caprice.

What happened next should have required a ticket and a tuxedo to attend.

"*Ding-Ding-Ding! — Welcome to tonight's title fight — In the red corner, weighing in at two hundred and two pounds, the Don Juan of Dysfunction, the Rebel of Resentment, the Arbitrator of Anger. Let's hear it for a true American Hero — Captain Carter Duuuucaaaaane!*"

The hoodies' heads quickly turned toward their sedan in time to see Carter, bat in hand, pumping his arms in the air and prancing in circles like a prize fighter who had just entered the ring. As they watched, Carter continued in his announcer's voice, even adding applause and sound effects.

"*And in the blue corner, weighing in at 3,527 pounds — the Pied Piper of Pimpmobiles, the Monster of Metal, the Four Doors of Disaster. Give it up for the Hoodies' Hangout, The Most Purple 1984 Chevrolet Capriiiiice!*" Carter supplying the requisite boos.

"*Holy Crap,*" exclaimed Hoodie Number One, somewhat freaked. "This' dude's batshit *loco*!"

"*Tonight's "Might Meets Metal" mixed-species title fight is about to begin.*" And a new voice broadcast from Carter's vocal cords, emitting the familiar yet always electrifying signature mantra:

"*Ladies and gentlemen, boys and girls, now for the main event — rrrrrrRRR! LET'S GET READY TO RUUUMBUUUUUULE!*"

Carter began his boxer's dance around his opponent, cylindrical wooden glove in hand. He weaved and threw the first punch, a direct hit to the front passenger side headlight. *That one is dedicated to Russell Ducane's first D.U.I.*, as his mind attached a past event to each punch thrown.

The two thug's eyes went wide. "Holy Shit, you asshole — STOP!" yelled Hoodie Number Two as the pair of would-be bicycle thieves pushed to their feet and tried slip-sliding forward to protect their pimpmobile.

But Carter circled toward them and cut them off, waving the bat threateningly. "*You want a piece of this?!*" he screamed maniacally, "*Well, do ya, punks!*" he added, channeling his inner Clint Eastwood as he advanced on the twosome. He then pivoted back and delivered a high-flying blow to the pimpmobile's custom aftermarket hood ornament as it sailed toward an imaginary left field.

Evidently, the hoodies did not want a piece of this, as they tripped all over their own four feet while scurrying backward in the mud like a pair of rock crabs.

Carter pictured his dad backing away as well, as he closed in on that hated face. But he stopped and spun around suddenly, the bat emitting a loud whooshing sound in the rain, and – *WHAM!* – The passenger window was transformed into a picture puzzle of sparkling cracks.

He backed away as if his opponent were going to counterpunch. He bobbed and weaved his way over, staring down and focusing on the front driver's side headlight. Carter landed a second punch! Ooh! Another gut punch right to the heart of the driver's side headlight. *Carter dedicated that punch to Russell Ducane's SECOND D.U.I. and the reason mom had to walk to work every day.*

The flow of adrenaline through his veins was intoxicating. Carter felt invincible, like he could take on the world. BAM! Carter throws a third punch. *Ouch! Criminy!* A low blow to the passenger's side taillight. *That one I dedicate to Russell Ducane's third and final D.U.I. and my sophomore year in high school, where I lettered in being ridiculed for not having a car.*

Carter backed off, bobbing and weaving as if his opponent would try to counterpunch again. He even ducked, left then right, as if that imaginary opponent had, in fact, tried.

The heavyweight championship belt was in sight. Carter drove in and – POW! – A titanic jab to the center of the driver's side taillight sent red glass exploding all around. *And that punch is dedicated to... to...?* To what? He was all out of Russell Ducane D.U.I.s. — *This is for you, Granddad, for all the years of not being in my life because of Russell Ducane. Not that I blame you!*

Carter felt his grandad's military spirit come over him again and flung the bat far away. He rubbed the brass knuckles on his right hand with purpose. He wanted to re-live his granddad's barroom brawling days, using Russell's face as motivation. Once it started, the genie could not be put back in the bottle.

It was a furious round two knockout. Yet a possessed Captain Carter Ducane remembered little of the three minutes it took to decimate his opponent using only his brass-clad fist. He only remembered using his dad's face to produce the aftermath of broken side mirrors, dented fenders, smashed hubcaps, and mangled chrome pieces, some attached — some not. The front, back, and side windows looked like a plethora of spiders were in a drunken brawl and had cast their inebriated webs at each other like a game of darts.

When the frenzy was over, Carter stood exhilarated, like Rocky Balboa, after winning his first title fight — and it was time to claim his prize. The two befuddled hoodies watched in bewilderment as he lifted the stranger's bicycle high in the air as if holding the World Heavyweight Title Belt and yelled, "Yo, Adrian! — I did it!"

And just like that, like the air spluttering from a kid's balloon, he felt purged of the rage that filled his heart just minutes ago. As he stood in the rain holding his Championship Belt, the fog of his dad's face slowly faded from his mind as his senses clawed their way back to reality. As the Championship Belt transformed back into a bicycle, he lowered it to the ground. Carter spotted the hoodies, shaking in fear, staring at him, wondering if he was finished or just catching his breath for round three.

Carter calmly stepped back from what was left of the hoodies' car to give them safe passage to crawl back to their vehicle. He heard two car doors slam and a poorly tuned engine sputter to life. The purple Chevy sped off and disappeared into the rain with the trunk still open and bobbing with each bump on the road.

Carter stood in his lonely reality with his eyes closed, aware that his heightened state of being was slowing down and diminishing toward a deafening silence. One by one — the wind — the rain — the neon's buzz — and the locomotive in the distance — all dissipated, creating an airy canvas of silence with all sounds suspended in time.

With a deep breath, he accepted the silence. But through the soundless canvas, one rebel sound made its voice heard as it completed its journey to the crests of his ears. It was a sound that Carter had never heard before — and he turned toward its source: the older, heavyset cyclist.

Now Carter Ducane was no virgin to the many "ing" sounds a man makes — like smacking, yelling, cursing, chewing, spitting, sneezing, sniffing, sipping, slurping, gulping, laughing, and of course, belching, and farting. These two often performed simultaneously as Russell Ducane's superpower.

But what his virgin ears hadn't heard — was the sound of a grown man *crying*. However, it was much more than that. It was the sound of an emotionally tormented man, which Carter felt through the man's irrepressible sobs.

Carter stood, semi-paralyzed in the rain, not knowing what to do. He was nervous around strangers anyway, especially someone sobbing uncontrollably. Nevertheless, he walked over and tried to help him stand, but the man wouldn't cooperate. Carter leaned over and asked him his name, but there was no response. "It's going to be okay; I just want to help," said Carter. "The thugs are gone and won't be back—you're safe," trying to ease the man's fear of further violence, but the man only responded with silence and sobbing.

Then, after what seemed an eternity, the cyclist pushed out a single sentence through his aching, tortured cries, which would serve as his final decree: "Please — just let me die" —

Carter was taken aback and wanted to ask why but couldn't muster a response before the man lifted his hand off his blood-covered head. When he did, Carter saw a knot growing from the impact of the hoodie's kick, which was the size of a silver dollar and still growing.

Did he need a hospital? Carter wondered if he should call 9-1-1, but the thought re-emerged that this man might be a fleeing criminal.

Carter was reluctant. After all, he had just single-handedly destroyed an entire car's worth of personal property. What if the hoodies fled directly to the police and reported that some maniac beat them up and stole their bicycle from the criminal that stole it from them in the first place? Calling 9-1-1 meant they would have his phone number on record if the hoodies were innocent, and they decided to press charges.

A plethora of "what-if" scenarios played in his brain, convincing Carter to move the cyclist away from the "crime scene" — as *far* away as possible — with or without his cooperation. The twenty-five-year-old soon discovered it wasn't easy to haul two hundred fifty pounds, plus or minus, of a human being without his collaboration. Fortunately, the wet grass provided enough of a Slip-n'-Slide effect to move the man away from the street to a distant strand of three trees surrounded by bushes. The man cried out and grimaced the entire journey but, finally, was secreted away and propped up against a tree trunk out of the rain, safely hidden from view.

Carter returned to the street to retrieve the man's bike and hide it. As he rolled it back, the Garmin GPS detected movement and lit up, revealing the man had ridden 50.4 miles that night. *How could someone so big ride so far?* It was just one of the mysteries surrounding this odd cyclist who appeared out of nowhere and smelled of blood, sweat, and fear.

It was now 2:37 a.m., and with all the excitement, Carter forgot he had his bike and backpack waiting for him in the bar. He ran across the street to get them, hoping his former boss hadn't left yet and might have time to offer advice on how to help the older cyclist. Instead, he was just in time to catch Ed, the assistant manager, closing, and had his bike and backpack lying on the ground in the rain. Only two words are needed to describe all 5ft 5in of his former manager: "ASS" and "HOLE."

Ed saw Carter run up but asked nothing about the night he obviously had.

"I took the liberty of liberating the bar of anything resembling you. You don't work here, Ducane, and your crap isn't going to live here either."

"You mean you were going to leave my stuff out here to get stolen?"

"Get off your high horse, Carter; no one wants to steal your damn toy bicycle. You only worked here all these years because my uncle felt sorry for you, like a three-legged dog. If I had my way, you would've been gone long ago."

"That's just the thing. Your head is so far up your uncle's ass; you can't see your way."

Ed lined up square with Carter before laughing in his face.

"Ride your ass out of here on your banana-sized bicycle seat before I ride it out for you."

Carter sensed the brass knuckles vibrating in his pocket as if his granddad had communicated through a Ouija board. *Third times a charm.* He had already taken out a pair of hoodies and a car, but he might add Ed to tonight's resume in a few short minutes. He had the momentary thought of not getting dragged back to his high school days when being ridiculed was an almost everyday occurrence.

"Screw you, Ed! You're just jealous that you couldn't ride on my banana-sized bicycle seat unless I lowered it enough for you to reach the pedals."

Carter walked away with another reminder of why he wanted to rewrite his story. He grabbed his backpack and started rolling his bicycle back to where the man was, as his and Ed's middle fingers waved goodbye to each other.

When Carter returned, he leaned his bike next to the older man's bike and secured both to one of the three trees using his big-ass bike lock. They were all now – bicycles and humans – safely out of sight. He squatted down and tended to the cyclist's head trauma using a small washcloth from his backpack. Then, he examined his own right hand, bloodied and swollen from wailing on the hoodie's pimpmobile. Funny, he hadn't felt a thing.

Carter opened an anti-bacterial wipe from his mini first-aid kit. He then sat next to the stranger and tended to his own injured fist. As he cleansed his hand, the older cyclist was too exhausted to remain upright and fell over, wincing as his head found its way into Carter's lap. The man's body froze in a fetal position and cried its way to sleep.

Carter felt a weird, never-before-experienced panic rise in his chest. Cleaning the man's wounds while he leaned against a tree was one thing, but having his head in his lap was an entirely different issue. Even worse, he did not know what to do with his hands and felt uncomfortable placing them anywhere on the man as if to show affection. Carter was in deep, uncharted territory because caring for another human was not in his wheelhouse. Regardless, their two lives were now intertwined, and Carter tried to calm his panicked breath back to normal.

As he sat there motionless, waiting for his panic to subside, the surrounding silence grew louder, and the air turned cooler. And despite his jacket, Carter reached for a thin blanket in his backpack and covered them as best he could. Reality had officially reared its ugly head as Carter realized once again that he was painfully alone, even though a complete stranger's head lay heavy in his lap.

The outsiders remained under the tree, one crying on the outside and one on the inside. Yet, neither one knew what their futures held, and neither one knew the other's name. They knew *nothing* of each other, but for the moment, they didn't need to. The only thing the men truly needed was rest, and the sound of the pouring rain helped supply the backdrop that eventually lulled the two men to sleep.

Chapter Three

The Awakening

Time passed, and the pounding rain that melded the two strangers' lives succumbed to the stillness of the night. Against the backdrop of calm, only the neon crackling out the words "Hard Times" buzzed from across the street. But it was enough to wake the younger of the two men.

As Carter awakened, he noticed the bump on the older cyclist's head was even more prominent, and his head was still resting like a bowling ball in his lap. Carter's butt was numb, and he tried shifting to a more comfortable position without rousing the older cyclist. But the man was dead to the world and didn't budge. Carter sighed and closed his eyes, again wondering what to do about him. When he opened his eyes a few seconds later, his pupils immediately widened in alarm, and his heart rate spiked as a man stood roughly fifteen feet away, staring in their direction through the bushes.

In the available light, Carter saw a tall, thin man with long hair and a scraggly beard. He wore an old suit and a pair of sandals and wielded a wheelchair... *A wheelchair?* The man looked homeless, and Carter feared the homeless and even hated them as they reminded him of his dad, who was always drunk and obnoxious. Nevertheless, Carter was startled and scared of the man's intentions as his nervous system shot to DEFCOM-5 from the second unknown, oddly dressed character entering his world tonight.

Out in the distance sat a white, mid-sized cargo van with its moving ramp extended.

What in the—? His adrenaline pumped as he scooted out from under the cyclist. Carter was careful with his injured head, laying it down gently as he quickly stood up. He reached into his pocket and slipped the brass knuckles onto his hands in case it was time for Round Three.

"So, you awake?" asked the ghostly silhouette.

Carter's voice shook. "Who are you? What do you want?"

The man in sandals spoke in a gentle yet authoritative tone. "We need to get this man somewhere so he can rest and recover."

Carter stepped through the bushes into the open. "Do you know him? Do you know who he is?" he asked, puzzled.

The man saw the brass knuckles on Carter's hands. "Those won't be necessary. I'm only here to help this man get from point A to point B; then, you can take care of him from there."

The man's kind but somewhat matter-of-fact manner painted the intruder in a less threatening light. Carter slipped the brass knuckles back into his pocket. However, it did little to alleviate his anxiety from having to interact with yet another stranger on this increasingly bizarre night.

Carter was already beyond anxious from not knowing who this cyclist was that murmured to please let him die. And now, a homeless-looking character that 'poofed' out of nowhere informed Carter that he must start caring for the older cyclist after he drives them from point A to point B.

The man's voice interrupted his thoughts. "Carter, what time did you first see this gentleman?"

Carter did a double-take, surprised, alarm bells again ringing in his mind.

"How do you know my name?"

No response.

"I didn't tell you my name — How did you know it? Who are you?"

"Just answer the question. What time did you see this man?"

Carter thought about it and reluctantly answered, "I know exactly when I saw him – it was 2 a.m. on the dot. I saw him riding his bicycle in the rain right after—" Carter paused. "It was right after I blew out my birthday candle and made a wish to rewrite my miserable life story."

Carter had a lightbulb moment as his face pondered the unlikely possibility. *Does this man have something to do with rewriting my story? Is that why he's asking me? Is that why he knows my name?* Carter's anxiety levels retreated as his thoughts ping-ponged between "scared to help" or "needs to help" this man."

The man stared at the youth, allowing him time to process his thoughts.

"So, Carter, do you think we should help this man now?"

"I don't know; are you hinting that this man is somehow the one to help me? This is all very confusing. You won't tell me who you are, your name, or how you know my name! How did you even find us? We were hiding in the bushes, for God's sake?!"

"Oh, now you know something about God," the stranger stated calmly.

Carter looked up at the sky, frustrated. "No, I don't know anything about God — and I don't know anything about this man either! I don't know where he's from, his name, he just appeared out of nowhere, like you did. What I do know is that I saved him from getting robbed, probably even saved him from getting killed!"—

"But..."

"But?"

"There's always a 'but'," said the tall man.

"But... yeah, *but* – just before he passed out, he said something like, 'Please, let me die.' — It's been a really bizarre night, and now the one man who may be able to help me seems to have a death wish. It would be just my luck that he wants to die because he is probably a fleeing criminal that did something bad — really bad. And if he is a criminal, what if I beat up the wrong guys? — And now helping him out could open a whole Pandora's Box of trouble. Truthfully, I'm scared out of my wits, and I just plain don't know what to do here."

The man allowed Carter some space to reflect on his emotionally charged prophecy.

"Listen, Carter, instead of predicting your bleak future, let's get back to the realization that you don't know who this man is or know anything about him. — What scientists refer to as an anomaly. Do you know what scientists do when they discover an anomaly?"

"No, what?" Carter questioned, curious where the man's train of thought would lead.

"They give it a name. Usually something representative of the discovery."

"So, you're saying you want me to name him?"

"I'm just telling you what science does."

"Well, Mr. Scientist —you're an anomaly. Should I give you a name as well?"

"You didn't discover me; I discovered you. You have a name; he does not. Besides, you saved him, even though he asked you not to. So, now, you should care for him, even though he may not want you to. It's easier caring for someone who has a name. It will help transform your anomaly from some*thing* to some*one*. So, it's up to you. Do you want to name the man or not?"

As Carter pondered his dilemma, the man redirected the conversation.

"That sure is a nice bike he's riding, don't you think?"

Carter was momentarily thrown by the abrupt change of topic and looked back toward the bike. He let out a loud sigh and walked back through the bushes to look at the bicycle that he had risked life and limb saving. He unchained it and raised it up for inspection. Fortunately, besides being muddied and dirty, the bike seemed to have weathered the attack. He wiped some of the dirt from the frame. *What a freaking beautiful bike this is.* Then he looked closely at the name: 'Dedacciai.' Carter tried several times to sound it out — *Dedacciai* — but wasn't sure he was getting the pronunciation right.

"I give up," he said at last. "I have no idea how to say this name. But the bike is spectacular. I've never seen anything quite like it."

"He pronounces it – or rather mispronounces it as De-*Dah*'-Chi-Ay'," informed the scraggly-bearded oracle. "It's Italian. — So, Carter, you now know one thing about your anomaly. He rides a genuinely nice Italian bicycle."

"So how is it actually pronounced?" Carter asked curiously.

The tall silhouette shrugged. "Who knows?"

Carter almost laughed, still staring at the *Dedacciai* name as the mispronunciation unconsciously took root. He set the bike down and stood near the seemingly lifeless plus-sized form snoozing softly in the damp grass. He squatted next to the body, studying the bruised and battered face. "Well, if that's all I know about my anomaly… then until he speaks his name, I hereby dub him — *The Dedacciai*."

He said the name aloud a few times as if trying it on for size before buying it. "*Damn*…I like it! Sounds like a character from *The Godfather*, his best friend, and business associate, *The Dedacciai*." Carter fantasized: *Oh, hell yes! The Dedacciai could most definitely put a horse head or two in Russell Ducane's bed….* Carter then tried reasoning out the suggestion in his mind. *The Dedacciai — That should be a book or movie based on this very, very weird night.*

His fantasy was interrupted by the homeless-looking character's voice. "Carter, what were your plans for tonight before… before 'The Dedacciai' entered your life?"

Carter's mind bounced back to reality as he heard the neon sounds still crackling the words Hard Times from across the street.

"Well, my plans before the Dedacciai were to look for a hotel room because I need a place to stay. Last night, I packed my stuff and stormed out of my parent's house in a blaze of glory." For some reason, he felt comfortable sharing the intimate details of his apocalyptic evening with him.

"Last night was my birthday," Carter snorted, "and it was a marvelous event, complete with my asshole dad's boot stomped in the middle of my birthday cake because my mom didn't have his dinner ready at six freakin' o'clock. I hate that man so much, and I couldn't take another minute living with that drunken loser. I decided right then and there that I wanted a better life. My 'plan' was to put as much distance between him and me as possible. I even quit my job at that bar across the street so there would be nothing to keep me here. I need to find a new job tomorrow and prove to him and myself that I can be more than just some guy working at a bar."

He took a step closer to the man. "I made a birthday wish, you know. I blew out one lonely candle on a chocolate cupcake and wished I could start my life over – rewrite my entire life story without one page dedicated to that piece of crap father of mine – with one exception, his obituary!"

The tall specter looked at him for a few moments in silence. Then he asked, "And now?"

"What are my plans *now*?" Carter looked back through the bushes at the old cyclist. "I guess I need to help him first."

"Well, Carter, I can help you with that if you let me."

"I had a feeling you might."

The stranger pushed the wheelchair forward. "I feel for you, Carter, and I'm sorry about your night. Let's get the Dedacciai in the wheelchair so I can take you both to get some much-needed rest. I know where to go. It's a place where you can hopefully start the first page of your new story."

Carter thought about the sandaled man's offer and accepted his help. He needed to get a room anyway, so it worked out perfectly. They approached the cyclist to get him into the wheelchair. As they gently lifted him, he woke up and cried out in pain. Carter assured him they were not trying to hurt him as they placed him into the wheelchair.

The man struggled to open his eyes to inventory his surroundings and identify where he was and what was happening. But that simple act brought on a severe attack of vertigo, where it seemed like the world was spinning out of control. Feeling nauseous, he clamped them shut again. "Please, just leave me alone," he pleaded.

Carter was not sure the man understood what he was trying to tell him. He noticed the cyclist didn't have a water bottle and wondered if dehydration contributed to his sickness. The man in sandals rolled the cyclist toward the cargo van parked in the street, sloshing through the tall, wet grass. Carter grabbed both bikes and his backpack and was not far behind. The sloshing movement seemed to lull the cyclist into a semi-conscious state, and he quietly sobbed during the short trip to the van. As the sandaled man rolled the cyclist up the ramp, he leaned over and whispered in his ear: *"Just remember, the fiercest storms give birth to the biggest and brightest rainbows."*

When Carter reached the open back of the van, he noticed it was full of clothes and personal belongings as the homeless-looking character made room for the two bicycles.

"So — do you live nearby here or something?" Carter asked.

"I don't live anywhere," the man responded serenely. "At least, not permanently." He then looked at Carter. "I follow my heart. So, at this moment — I live here."

Carter was hit with the reality that the homeless-looking character was no longer a character but an actual homeless man who lived in his van. The two men exchanged non-judgmental glances before the younger one loaded the bikes and situated them so they wouldn't be scratched. Carter stayed with the cyclist, who fell unconscious as his sobbing diffused.

The bearded man started the engine and drove them to his chosen destination. Carter relaxed slightly in the quiet as no one spoke on the journey. What was happening was so surreal that he imagined he was in some kind of movie. And although Carter no longer felt he was in a horror film, his movie probably did involve a bed and a horse's head....

The thought reminded him of the night and his crippling fear of what would happen to him. But when he blew out his candle, wishing to rewrite his story, he never envisioned anything like this. *A night when an overweight cyclist with a death wish and a homeless character with no name yet knew Carter's name would mysteriously appear to drive him and the cyclist to an undisclosed location of the homeless guy's choosing.* Carter only hoped he would arrive alive in one piece and not in little pieces like the story unfolding in his mind.

The van took them from the seedier side of town before finally slowing and entering the front portico of The Lancaster Landing Hotel. It was grand in stature, old, but in pristine condition, with five stories and hundreds of rooms. Oversized red brick scaled the structure while white, ornate moldings adorned the outside walls, clinging to the brick and creating a beautiful contrast. It was the very essence of charming.

"OK, Carter, I'll wait here while you go in and take care of business."

Carter shimmied into his backpack, then exited out the side door of the van and looked up at the grand hotel. He turned back immediately with panic in his voice. "I can't afford this place. What the hell were you thinking? I need you to take me somewhere like a Super 8 or Motel 6."

"Carter, it won't end up being as expensive as you think — you just have to trust me," the homeless man said evenly, with a fervent look, which didn't leave him much choice. Carter turned and hesitantly began walking toward the hotel entrance.

"Carter," he yelled, stopping him in his tracks before making it to the entrance, "there is one other thing... The Dedacciai must stay in room 555, so make sure you ask for it — because it's important."

Carter had a strange look on his face with even stranger thoughts in his head as he turned toward the hotel again.

Why is he so specific about room 555? — Of course, it must be the room with the 13 ghosts or a horse's head already in place.

Everything about this felt wrong. The Lancaster Landing was much more luxurious than his budget allowed for his first night on his own...But even worse, he was anxious about leaving his bike – and the obviously expensive Dedacciai bike in the van with the homeless man. *You just have to trust me* didn't ring true in his mind. How could he trust him when he wouldn't even give him his name? *What if the van takes off while I'm inside, spinning my wheels, trying to get a room I can't afford? He could dump the Dedacciai anywhere and steal the bikes for himself.*

Carter made it within inches of the fancy frosted door that flanked the main revolving doors to the hotel before turning around yet again. He walked to the van's driver-side window, but the sandaled-wearing man wasn't there.

Carter froze as doomsday scenarios popped up in his mind like weeds in a garden. *Where the hell is he?*

Suddenly, he heard the van's rear doors swing open and the loading ramp being pushed out. He rushed back in time to see the sandaled man leading the two bikes down onto the pavement. "You don't need to explain — I understand," he said simply.

Carter almost fainted from relief. He took a calming breath and smiled sheepishly. "Thanks; I'm sorry I was worried."

"I said you didn't have to explain," as the homeless man handed the bicycles over to the younger man. "You've been through a lot with them. Take them inside where they're safe, and then come back for the Dedacciai."

Carter rolled the bikes just inside the lobby and leaned them against a wooden column where he could keep an eye on them. He turned to head back outside, but his eyes couldn't help but take a minute to look around the hotel.

It was astonishingly beautiful. A twenty-five-foot-tall ceiling arched overhead with one massive fifteen-foot-wide chandelier that defied description. Paintings scaled every inch of available wall space, starting six inches from the floor and topping out six inches from the ceiling. Each painting was a large, colorful story on canvas surrounded by a thick, ornate, antique-quality frame. No two frames were alike, but all were equally stunning. Carter knew nothing about art but sensed finding an art gallery as elegant as this would be difficult.

The hotel addressed each of the human senses with masterful delight. The aroma of the interior was as pleasing to the nose as the paintings were to the eyes. Two fragrances dominated its repertoire. Mahogany teakwood was their mainstay for most of the year. Yet, gold-leaf and hydrangea seemed the seasonal favorite during Christmastime. All Carter knew was that breathing took on a whole new dimension.

Carter stood there longer than he realized, taking in the sights and smells of the hotel. As he did, beautiful piano melodies proved just as soothing to his ears. Jim Brickman, America's Romantic Piano Sensation, seemed among the hotel favorites to be experienced by the listening audience. Just walking into the hotel could change anyone's state of mind as all three senses were massaged simultaneously, signaling the brain: *We are happy here; we want to stay longer; we will return frequently.*

Carter eventually tore himself away from the intoxicating sights, sounds, and smells and headed out the door to help the man get the older cyclist inside. Instead, he found the Dedacciai in his wheelchair, alone and unconscious. The sandaled man was gone, as was his van. It was as if he had never happened.

Carter's emotions were startled back into fear once again. The reality of his decision to leave home became highly questionable. He needed to calm himself and think logically. *Step one: Get the Dedacciai inside and check-in at the front desk.* But that plan only opened a whole new can of stomach-twisting worms.

Before encountering the cyclist, he planned to rent only one room tonight. Now, he was flooded with anxiety about having a roommate he knew nothing about and who could turn out to be a total lunatic or worse. Besides, it was never Carter's plan to spend what little money he had for two rooms — especially in such a fancy hotel – but interacting with a complete and possibly crazed stranger scared him even more. Renting one or two rooms could literally be a choice between life or death, depending on whether the older man was *just* a lunatic or *just* a mobster.

Two rooms, please! Flashed intensely in his brain as the only clear choice. Carter just hoped his internal warning system was wrong and the man was of sound mind and didn't actually want to die. Maybe he would get lucky, and the man would hopefully pay him back once he got some rest — but it was a lot to hope for.

Carter walked over to the cyclist to wheel him inside. But when he did, he found an envelope in the Dedacciai's lap with '*Carter*' hand-written on the outside and a matching letter inside.

Carter,

About your wish to rewrite your story— It is commendable of you to first recognize that your story needs to be rewritten. Like anything worth reading, the author you pick to help rewrite your story is most important. An author is the poet of your emotions, inspires what's already inside of you, and unveils the most buried parts of you. An author reveals the powerful capabilities that live within you and releases the unlimited possibilities of the human spirit. An author induces kindness and compassion by showing the same. You have a good heart; use it. Chapter One is sitting in this wheelchair. I hope your rewritten story turns out to be a beautiful and well-written novel.

~ Darius~

Carter shook his head and smiled, "Darius... Damn! He did have a name."

Carter closed his eyes, pondering the note. His spirit was suddenly uplifted, and his anxiety lessened. A new-found sense of optimism overcame him, and goosebumps overwhelmed his skin. His eyes almost started to water – *but they didn't* – and maybe they couldn't. They had never cried before; perhaps his tear ducts were the dodo birds of his own evolution.

He opened his eyes and breathed deeply as he looked down at the overweight Chapter One, sitting in the wheelchair. *How are you part of my story, and why do you want to die?*

Carter understood the pain of wanting to die, as he had experienced it many times while living with Russell Ducane. He cleared his mind for now and wheeled the Dedacciai inside.

When they entered the hotel, the calming, welcoming music continued to emanate from the speakers. As Carter stood alone in the lobby, he could hear other sounds in the nearby restaurant area, plates clattering as tables were set up for breakfast. But there was no one behind the check-in counter. Carter parked the wheelchair near the bicycles and walked to the counter. He took a few nervous breaths before he tapped the silver call bell three times.

It was like rubbing a magic lamp. A door opened, and almost as if a genie appeared out of a mystical cloud of smoke, a vision of ultimate beauty materialized before his eyes.

Carter was dumbstruck, literally paralyzed at the sight of her. The nametag on her neatly starched dress read CONNIE SUE LANCASTER, but its location only served to draw attention to her rather busty frame.

The forces of nature overwhelmed the red-blooded, affection-starved, All-American male named Carter Ducane. He was powerless to stop the telenovela fantasy that erupted like a geyser in his brain and read like a steamy narrative from some dime-store novel.

— She knew the power of being a Southern Belle as she stood there in an eye-catching, bright-red dress, like something seen on the red carpet. It had a long, thin, white stripe going all the way down the front with medium-sized, black buttons spaced equally along the contrasting line, all while the vibrant fabric hugged her body to perfection.

Connie Sue Lancaster looked to be the reincarnation of screen legend Raquel Welch. She was five feet six inches tall, with long, flowing reddish-brown hair that knew how to hold a curl. Her sultry features boasted big, mesmerizing dark-brown eyes, matching dark, full, expressive eyebrows, and long, thick natural eyelashes. She wore a powerful shade of scorching red lipstick across her perfectly formed lips, which were the ideal host to her faultless teeth and wide, sexy smile. And she was as ageless as she was faultless – she could be twenty, thirty, forty – not even the best guesser at a carnival could get it right.

She was every bit a Southern Belle and could teach a Masterclass in using the honey of her long, slow southern drawl to get anything she darn well pleased! And as an accent to her flawlessness, she had curves that rivaled the mountainous roads of the Italian Alps. Just one sexy curve after another, slowly winding their way down from top to toe.

And being the sensual being imagined by Carter, she understood the power of the senses. Sights, sounds, and smells were the tools she used to give tourists of the hotel not just a night's stay but an experience. An experience that prompted an immediate yearning for their return. Connie Sue was the reason the parking lot stayed filled, and the hotel had been in business for as long as it had. — And on this night, she stood, curling her long, reddish-brown hair through her fingertips, twirling her strands over and over with such precision that it could be an Olympic sport. Then it happened – her lips parted and created the most erotic words ever spoken —

"May I help you?"

Her voice was a pin, popping his fantasy bubble and returning him, startled and wide-eyed, back to polite society. Even worse, the subject of that fantasy was staring at him with a puzzled, even suspicious look. His face flushed with embarrassment. *Holy crap! How did that novella escape from its cage?*

He started to reply, but his mouth refused to function. In an instant, the few moments of confidence inspired by Darius's note had totally evaporated, returning Carter to his normal default position of being extremely anxious and terrified of beautiful females. He only knew one thing for sure in life, and that was from experience — Women Equaled Pain.

His high school days had taught him that as his mind filled with dreadful memories of being the outcast of his school and the emotional piñata of his class. The girls, especially the pretty ones, took turns swinging their emotionally charged bats at him while ruthlessly making fun of him because he didn't have a car and was forced to ride a bike. It forced him to live in a paradoxical world of hating bicycles and needing bicycles. — In this world, beautiful girls and bikes cannot coexist. Because of this, he was emotionally damaged goods when it came to beautiful women and relationships.

So, seeing the stunning woman behind the counter and knowing he needed to interact with her caused him paralyzing anxiety. He tried to speak again but stood there like a stone, humiliated by his thoughts and hoping she couldn't read minds.

Of course, Connie Sue Lancaster knew nothing of Carter's fantasy or background. When she emerged from her office at the sound of the bell, she was accosted by the image of a young man with a rather large nose ring who looked like he had just been through the wringer. He had bloodied knuckles, spaghettified hair and was in dire need of a shower. He was in rough shape, to say the least, and as he nervously stood there, she wondered if he knew how to put one foot in front of the other.

In the background, she saw two bicycles that weren't there before and an older gentleman in a wheelchair, muddied and passed out. *Well, this ought to be a whole-lot-of-interestin',* she decided, as one of her eyebrows rose to the occasion.

Carter finally managed to get his vocal cords to engage.

"I'd, uh, like a room, please, ma'am," he said in a low, quavering voice. "Er, I mean, two rooms." Then remembered to add, "Please, ma'am."

For a moment, he wasn't sure she was going to respond. Connie Sue glared disapprovingly at his rather prominent nose ring and overall demeanor. Usually, she was the essence of what Southern hospitality should be. But Carter's appearance didn't fit with her image of the clientele she preferred in her hotel, and she was not at her most charming with him.

"May I see an I.D. and credit card?" she said at last in a curt, business-like voice.

Carter jumped a bit at the sound but then searched his pocket for his wallet and handed over the requested items. Connie scrutinized his State ID photo, then studied his face carefully.

"How many nights were you plannin' on stayin'?" asked the sexy salesclerk.

Carter was unsure how to answer her, and he *really* wasn't sure what to do with his eyeballs.

He thought for a second. *It was already almost 5 a.m., and even with a late checkout of 1 or 2 p.m., it still may not be enough time for the Dedacciai to recover — which could take days. Carter wasn't sure if he could afford another night, let alone more.* His hands started shaking from the financial pressure and interacting with such a beautiful woman.

Crap, why did she have to be so freaking gorgeous!

"Uhm — can I just rent the two rooms for now? And then I'll let you know tomorrow if we need to stay another night. Would that be okay, — ma'am?"

Connie shrugged and turned to the keyboard. Carter used mental restraints by thinking of anything he could — puppies, kittens, nuclear holocaust — to keep his eyeballs from staring at the beautiful lady's chest as she checked the computer register for availability.

"Oh wait, I almost forgot!" Carter blurted suddenly, "I need to book this guy —" he looked back, indicating the cyclist passed out in the wheelchair "— into Room 555. Is that available?"

Connie looked at him like he had two heads. "Why Room 555?"

Carter bit his lip. "I don't know — But it's important."

The hotel clerk studied the man in the wheelchair, immensely curious. "So, what's his story? He doesn't look too good. Is he drunk?"

Carter gathered his thoughts, wondering if or how he should answer her.

"And why is he so muddy?" she continued.

"Well, he kind of got run off the road while riding his bike in the rain tonight."

"*Ouch!* No wonder — Is he okay?" she responded, a glimmer of concern coloring her voice.

"I hope so," said Carter worried. "A good night's sleep is all I can afford to do for him."

Her glance lingered on the cyclist. He seemed to be snoring. "That's good." She continued to stare. "Now, is it just me, or is he a smidge or two on the heavy side to be riding a bike in the rain?"

"It's not just you," Carter snickered.

"So, what exactly did you say happened to him again?" asked the salesclerk.

"Well, two thugs ran him off the road, and then one thug beat him up while the other tried stealing his bike."

"Ouch, that explains a thang or two," she said as her attitude toward the unkempt stranger was starting to thaw. "Now, which bike did those bad people try to steal?"

Carter glanced over his shoulder. "The one on the right."

Connie Sue surprised him by coming out from behind the counter and crossing to the bikes so she could get a closer look. "Now that's a pretty bicycle," she admired. "Looks like it has some sex appeal to it."

Couldn't agree more...Talk about the pot calling the kettle black, Carter's mind touted.

"Sure could use a bath, though." She suggested.

"Couldn't we all," murmured Carter.

"So, the blue bike is yours, I take it?"

"Yes, ma'am. My bike wants to be like that bike when it grows up someday."

She smiled at the reference. She was breathtaking before, but that smile solidified her in goddess territory.

"Okay, so I'm a bit confused. How did that man keep those bad people from stealing his bike?"

"Well – he didn't, exactly — I did," Carter said humbly.

"*You* did!?"

"Yes, ma'am. That's why we look like we do, all messed up," he explained. "I kind of had to slug it out in the mud and rain with them to steal it back for him."

She stared at him with new eyes. "Well, I reckon' that's what friends are for. How long have you two been besties? Is he your father or uncle or something?"

"Well...that's the thing. I have no idea who this man is."

That floored her. She just stared at him before replying, "So – you're telling me you stopped some thugs from stealing a total stranger's bike?"

"Well — I guess so," Carter shrugged.

"What do you mean, you guess? Mr. Carter, you're a *hero* the way I see it."

His mind flashed to that moment, standing in front of the window of the Hard Times with the red, white, and blue neon casting its superhero glow on his reflection. *It's a bird! It's a plane! It's Carter Ducane!*

"What time did you say this all happened?" Connie inquired, knocking him out of his superhero whim.

"I know exactly what time — it was 2 a.m. when this happened. It was also one of the weirdest nights of my life, and to top it off, it was my twenty-fifth birthday as well."

The hotel clerk looked over at the man in the wheelchair, then back at the bicycles. Then she looked past Carter's nose ring and saw him in an entirely different light.

"Well, I do declare! My, my, my, Mr. Carter. My daddy and I have owned this hotel for over seventeen years —" *Holy crap,* his mind blurted out, *you're the owner?! Connie Lancaster... the Lancaster Landing... Duh! —* "But I have never heard a story like yours or seen a bicycle quite like this one. You're a true hero in my book — and I've read a lot of books, Mr. Carter. Come on back to the desk, and let's see what I can do for you."

Carter sensed the change in her demeanor and attitude. The Flower of the South was now in full bloom as she returned to her terminal and searched for available rooms.

"You said you needed two rooms for the both of you?"

"Yes, ma'am."

"You are a polite one, aren't you?" she observed without looking up from the screen. "And you said you wanted Room Five-Fifty-Five for your new friend?"

"Yes, ma'am. Room 555. Can I ask you something? Is there anything particularly odd or special about Room 555?"

"Well, I can't think of anything. I usually try to put newlyweds or couples celebrating an anniversary in there. It's on our highest floor – a corner room at the end of the hallway. It's quiet and has what I think is the best view of the sunrise."

"Maybe that's why a man told me to ask for it," Carter said, low-key, puzzled.

"I reckon' he could have. Let me just check my little ol' computer here — hmmm, now this is odd. I show that someone had booked Room

Five-Fifty-Five for a late arrival but canceled about thirty minutes ago. It seems an emergency came up — Hope this Mr. Darius fella is okay - Bless his heart."

"Did you just say, Mr. Darius? And he just canceled about thirty minutes ago?" Carter was left wondering — *Could it be? No, it can't be — can it?*

Connie Sue's voice intruded, "Carter, are you okay? You look rather pale, like you've seen a ghost or somethin'. Well, I don't know about you, but it all just seems like kismet to me."

Carter stood there, dumbfounded, questioning what kind of kismet this was.

"Mr. Carter, few people surprise me in this world, and I have met thousands and thousands of different styles of people. But there's a little sayin' out there that teaches us: 'Don't judge a book by its cover.' I must apologize, Mr. Carter. I completely misread your book cover.

"So, I'll tell ya what I'm gonna do. Because I'm the owner of this fine establishment and because of what you did for that man, I'm going to give you a big ol' birthday present. Usually, it's three hundred and seventy-nine dollars per night, per room, before taxes and all. But since it's so late and there are just a few hours left in the morning, I'm gonna give you an extra night free for helping that total stranger. And the room charge for your friend over there – it's on me."

Carter stared with his mouth agape. He was at a total loss for words.

"I'm also gonna give you a big ol' discount on top of it all because the both of you are lookin' like you need a lucky break. So, I'm only gonna charge you an even two hundred dollars for the whole kit and caboodle. Also, I'm gonna set you up for a late checkout. Riskin' your life and all for a total stranger? That's the kindest thing I've heard of in a long time."

She finished processing his VISA and handed him the key cards. "Room 555 for your friend, and Room 556 for you right across the hall. Mr. Hero, have a charmed stay with us, and happy birthday."

Carter couldn't believe this was happening. He wished he could hug his mom or share the experience with someone who cared about him. But the realization that he was alone with an unconscious Dedacciai was his new reality.

"Wow, I... I don't know what to say," Carter stuttered, his face warm. "Just... thanks. Really. Thanks so much."

"My pleasure, hon."

He cleared his throat. "Um, ma'am, one more thing – would you mind keeping an eye on my friend while I take our bikes to the room?"

"Sugar, you can call me Connie Sue, and I'd be glad to."

"Okay, Connie Sue. Don't let anyone steal him — you promise?"

She crossed her heart with her long, beautifully manicured fingers and smiled pleasantly at Carter as he gathered his large backpack and walked the bicycles to the elevator. A quick ride later, the double doors opened to the fifth floor, and Carter navigated to Room 556 and slipped in his key card. He was immediately struck by how luxurious the place was and felt he had won some sort of lottery.

He settled the two bicycles against the wall, then crossed the hall to Room 555. But there he froze, hand inches away from unlocking the door. He looked up at the number plate 555. *I ain't afraid of no ghost* — But his nervous demeanor indicated that, yes, actually, you might be.

Exceedingly wary, Carter slowly entered the darkness to check for ghosts and/or a horse's head on the bed. He wanted a visual cue for why Darius insisted that the Dedacciai have this room specifically. Turning on some lights revealed an even nicer room than his... but no cobwebs or creepy sounds emanated from the woodwork, and no horse's head was lying on the luxurious king-sized bed. Even so, the stillness unnerved him somewhat, and there was no freakin' way he was going anywhere near that bathroom....

He hurried downstairs to fetch the Dedacciai... but when he got to the lobby, he stole another comforting glimpse of Connie Sue as he viewed her standing over the heavyset cyclist.

"Is everything okay?" he asked.

"Well, I was just hearing some strange noises coming from—" Suddenly, grumblings of hunger reverberated from the cyclist's belly. "There they are — that's the noises I was hearing!"

Carter responded with grumbles of his own as if they were competing for a spot in a Broadway musical.

"Hey, Carter, you got 'em, too!" she said, chuckling at the musical duo. "I've never heard such talented tummies before. I think people would pay good money to hear you two perform together. Tell ya what, I have a fresh box of donuts saved in the back for the breakfast crowd. I'm thinkin' you two could use them more about now."

She turned and walked toward the back room. Soon, she strolled back toward him with the promised box of goodies. Carter thanked her for the donuts and for watching the older man. The wheelchair's two-legged engine started, and shortly, the two men entered the possibly haunted, mysterious Room 555.

Once again, Carter stood there a moment in silence, listening for any signs of spectral activity or visions of the Macabre, before declaring to himself, "*I told you, dummy, you ain't afraid of no ghosts!*" He smirked at his foolishness, then rolled the cyclist over next to the luxurious king bed.

Before Carter knew Darius's name, he probably wouldn't have given much thought to the specific room request by the sandaled man. It would have just seemed another oddity on an already odd-filled night. But his views had changed since the disappearance of the scraggly-bearded enigma and the note he left behind. Carter felt that Darius knew something about the Dedacciai and why he was now in his life. He also sensed that his room-specific request seemed to have a reason and a purpose. Like it was somehow all connected and a part of Darius's diabolical master plan. But regardless of his conspiracy theories about what Darius knew and why, Carter needed to get the older man situated in his room for now.

The cyclist's clothes had muddy rainwater striped vertically on his back from the rooster-tail spray of his rear wheel. Carter decided to try and get his clothes off him so he could wash them in the shower and dry them by tomorrow.

Carter gently shook the older man. "Excuse me, sir — Sir? Are you awake?" But there was no response. He spoke a little louder. "Sir! Can you hear me?!" The man stirred a little into semi-consciousness. "Sir! I'm not trying to harm you, but I need to remove your clothes."

The cyclist opened his eyes to follow the voice, raising his head slightly. But as he did, his stomach convulsed from the debilitating vertigo that had plagued him all evening. He moaned and dropped his head again, closing his eyelids against the dizziness.

Carter sighed in surrender. *Okay, Dedacciai, we're gonna have to do this the hard way.* He removed the man's shoes and socks and unbuttoned his shirt. He leaned the man forward enough to slip one arm out of its sleeve and then the other, wrestling his shirt off and then his *Keep Austin Weird* T-shirt. His harsh whimpers of pain made complete sense as Carter witnessed the aftermath of the two hoodies' handiwork. As if the hardy goose egg on his head weren't enough, Carter became even more enraged as he saw the intense contusions left behind from the violent attack. He found his fists clenched and blew out an angry breath as his mind spun. *Freaking assholes, I'll kill those bastards if I ever see them again!*

He moved to the bed, tossed aside the throw pillows, and pulled back the silky-smooth bedspread and then the blanket, followed by the top sheet. He wasn't sure he had ever seen so many layers on a bed before.

"Okay, sir, don't open your eyes. I know this will hurt, but I need to raise you up to finish removing your clothes."

As Carter lifted the cyclist, his overweight body contorted as if it was tased. Carter managed to haul him halfway up, but the 250-plus pound load was too heavy for his grip; and gravity won the battle, sucking him back into the wheelchair. Breathing heavily, Carter reassessed the situation and approached it from another angle.

Maneuvering the wheelchair perpendicular to the side of the bed, he grabbed the man under the arms from behind and lifted him high enough to push him face forward onto the bed. The man grimaced and cried out as the upper part of his torso bounced a few times on the mattress.

In his delirious state, the cyclist tried to determine what had happened. He opened his eyes, but as before, vertigo caused his stomach to convulse, so he slammed them shut to avoid nausea. The man's combination of physical and emotional pain wouldn't allow for an assessment, and his body gave up trying. Within seconds, he was unconscious again, his face buried in a pillow.

Carter collapsed in the empty wheelchair, relieved but exhausted from his monumental efforts. – *Yep, Connie Sue was right; you really are a smidge or two on the heavy side.*

But the job was only half done. Carter got up from the wheelchair, regrouped, and finished lifting the man's legs on the bed and got him comfortably situated. He then turned the man on his side, unbuckled his plus-sized jeans, and laid him back on his stomach. With a gentle but steady tug, the man's pants slid off, carefully leaving behind his underwear and preserving his dignity. The plan was to wash and dry his clothes and return them to him with new underwear before he woke up tomorrow.

Carter headed to the bathroom for a towel to dry the man off — but hesitated outside the slightly cracked open door. One thing Carter did know is that horror movies almost always involve a bathroom mirror. With his breath held, he bravely reached into the darkened abyss and turned on the switch — then exhaled with the safety of the light. His horror mantra spouts off again: *I told you I ain't afraid of no ghosts.* Then, he returned unharmed with the towel and dried the remaining moisture off the man's chest and arms.

As he did, his head shook in disgust and anger as the man's bruises seemingly turned from yellow to purplish-blue before his eyes, and his goose egg was even more prominent than before. An ice pack was desperately needed. Snatching the ice bucket, he took it down the hall, filled it, and returned, placing it in the bathroom. He grabbed a hand towel and a few ice cubes from the bucket and tried his best to make a D-I-Y ice pack.

As he cinched the ice in the towel, his mind re-enacted the thuggery while his contorted lip and clenched fist conveyed the story to the mirror. Carter tried balancing the anger he was characteristically known for against an uncharacteristic caring that compelled him to sit on the bed and press the washcloth carefully against the protruding goose egg on the man's right temple.

Time passed, and the late hour took its toll. Carter needed to get settled in his own room. Before he left, he grabbed the ice bucket from the bathroom and set it next to the man's bed, along with a complimentary water bottle and drinking glass. Carter had eaten a few donuts while caring for the man, leaving the remainder for the Dedacciai. He silently said goodnight to the anomaly who had ridden into his life. With a few final careful pats with his homemade ice pack, Carter mentally pleaded with the man to *please, please, please* not be a lunatic.

He stood and grabbed the pile of wet clothes to take back to his room, leaving the light on in the bathroom as a night light. He began turning out lights and making his way out — but couldn't. He paused near the lonely lamp in the corner of the room that supplied enough light to observe the heavyset man sleep. After a minute or so, Carter took a deep breath to relieve the anger and anxiety. He found himself slumped against a wall, his emotions spent, and eventually, his exhaustion slid him onto the floor. While sitting against the wall, he decided to share a little about himself with the Dedacciai, even though he was sleeping.

"Hi, Mr. Dedacciai — my name is Carter Ducane. I know you can't hear me, but I needed to talk to someone, and it seems you are all I have. I don't know your story or why you want to die, but I can understand. My story, too, has been awful up until tonight — you could even say it sucks. And if you did, it wouldn't offend me; I say it all the time." Carter's thoughts slowed and deepened as he continued. "Do you want to hear something weird? I tried to pray earlier. But the bizarre part of that statement is that I don't know anything about the religious ways of life. So, I just pleaded my case to the universe for a way to somehow rewrite my life story. And you know what? As I made my plea and blew out my birthday candle, this heavyset, oddly dressed cyclist — which is you, by the way — appeared out of nowhere.

"And I keep wondering if you are somehow the answer to my would-be prayers – someone who can help rewrite my life story — that is, if you're not a criminal or something. Actually, even that's not a dealbreaker, depending on how bad of a criminal you are. Besides, you can't be any worse than my dad is. I know I'm rambling here, and I probably sound crazy, but does this all seem like a coincidence to you? Or is it all just wishful thinking on my part?

"I mean, what are the odds, you know? I mean, look at what's happened: I've had the most exciting night of my life. I fought off two thugs and beat their freakin' purple pimpmobile to a pulp with a baseball bat. I met this mysterious stranger in an old suit and sandals who wouldn't tell me his name, yet knew mine, and somehow prompted me to name you the Dedacciai after your bicycle — which is an awesome bike, by the way.

"However, I did finally find out his name was Darius, but only after he drove us in his old white cargo-van to this unbelievably fancy hotel, which I could never afford in a million years... but guess what? The most beautiful woman I have ever met calls me a hero and practically *gives* us two rooms for the night. I mean, can you freaking believe that?! Connie Sue Lancaster – *Geez*! I swear, this is all just a dream; It has to be. Nothing this exhilarating could ever happen to me. I know I'm going to wake up any minute with my asshole father standing over me, guzzling a beer." Carter caught his breath, his tone mellowing from the excitement as he continued his one-sided conversation. "Mr. Dedacciai, I would be very interested to hear your thoughts on all this."

Carter sat waiting in the amplified silence for the Dedacciai to somehow give him all the answers. But his only response was a deep, sudden snore.

"That's what I thought you'd say."

He sighed. "You know what hurts the most, Mr. Dedacciai? — Well, I'll tell you, since you seem so interested — It's the loneliness and desperation that hits you when you realize you have no one to share the most triumphant night of your life with — to the point of sharing with an unconscious stranger lying on a bed — just to try and feel something. When it comes down to it, I'm still just... painfully alone."

Carter closed his eyes, his skin flushed by a swarm of goosebumps, further reminding him how painfully alone he was, even though an unconscious anomaly he named the Dedacciai was a few silent feet away.

It had been a long, strange, and complicated night. He took one last deep breath and rose slowly from the wall to head to his room. Once again, he silently said goodnight to the strange being who rode into his life. And with that, he turned out the lights and shut the door as quietly as he could, carrying the pile of wet clothes with him.

Chapter Four

Cycledelic Bike Therapy

Your Totally Tubular Bike Shop

Carter entered his room carrying the Dedacciai's muddied clothes. Bone-weary and emotionally exhausted, he unpacked his backpack and gathered items needed for his shower. Before he took the much-needed shower, he quickly ran a shaver over his 5 p.m. shadow twice over, as it was past 5 a.m., and then separated the pile of damp clothes from the Dedacciai.

When Carter separated the jeans, he noticed something peculiar. A long, thin pouch with straps hooked onto the belt hung inside. He took a closer look, unzipped the pouch, and saw money inside — lots of it. Carter had never seen anything like this and grew pale as *Conspiracy Theories Part II* kicked his mind into high gear.

What in the hell is going on here? Who is this guy? Is this man a criminal? Is he dangerous? Was he in prison? Which prison? How did he escape? Why was he in prison? Oh, please be money laundering and not murder! Is he a mobster? Maybe he stole from the Mob? Did he steal money from the hoodies? Did he steal the bike from the hoodies? Did he steal the money and the bike from the hoodies? Oh, crap, what if the hoodies worked for the Mob, and they sent them to retrieve their money and/or bike? The only thing Carter knew for sure was somewhere, somehow, a horse's head would show up!

Carter breathed deep and shook his head, telling himself to calm down and stop thinking about all his conspiracy theories. *I mean, doesn't every older cyclist who is a smidge on the heavy side ride late at night in the pouring rain for a nice relaxing fifty-mile bike ride to enjoy nature? — With a butt load of cash well hidden in his pants! — Holy Crap!!! There's truly gonna be a horse's head!*

Carter breathed deeply, again trying to calm himself and reason things out. There had to be an explanation for all this mystery surrounding his anomaly.

He needed a mental diversion from his prisonous thoughts, so he grabbed the pile of clothes and stumbled into the shower. Using half a bottle of shampoo as his laundry detergent, he did a decent job cleaning the soiled and muddy garments – stomping them with his feet in the tub like a bunch of grapes for making wine.

Afterward, he felt revitalized as he dried himself off and tied the towel around his waist. He then tried ringing the clothes out as best he could before drying them with the hairdryer and folding them into a pile.

Slipping on a fresh pair of underwear, he collapsed into bed. But sleep was not immediately forthcoming. Being in a strange, unfamiliar place, coupled with a mind filled with new experiences and significant worries, he was now wide awake and needed to occupy his mind.

The Dedacciai bike leaned against the wall near him and looked every bit the part it played in tonight's adventure. Carter really wanted to see what the bike looked like underneath the caked-on mud and havoc it survived. Carter only had one skill in life – and that was working on bicycles. But it was his skill nonetheless, and what better way to help the Dedacciai with his Just-Let-Me-Die mindset than to see his beautiful bike looking all shiny and brand new? He grinned at the idea of reintroducing the pair — *Dedacciai, I want you to meet my good friend and bicycle, The Dedacciai!* Smiling, the mechanic squatted down and took a moment to run a critical eye over it.

Hmmm, grass in the sprockets; the mainframe covered in dried, dirty rainwater residue. Turning the bike upside down, Carter found the underbelly and foot pedals caked with mud, and the chain and gears clogged. While the mud was wet, the bike could still be rolled, but now that it had dried, the gears were nearly locked up. Turning it right-side up again, he noticed a tear in the handlebar tape from being run off the road, and it had begun to unravel.

Carrying the bike into the bathroom, he removed the GPS and cleaned the display with a damp wash rag. The readings were currently at 50.6 miles with fifty-five percent power. He realized it had the same connection as his cell phone, so he plugged it in to charge. Laying the bike on a towel, he grabbed a second towel, soaked it in water, and attempted to wipe off the mud. However, the effort proved futile – he only managed to rearrange the dirt.

Drastic times called for drastic measures. Carter was soon naked and back in the shower with his bicycle companion. The de-mudding began in earnest, and the bottom of the tub soon looked like the aftermath of the Muddy Day Massacre of 1912.

It took a while, but fortunately, the bathtub had a fancy, detachable showerhead on a metal-clad hose with several power-wash settings, and Carter got the bike as clean as showerly possible. He shook off most of the water droplets and carefully laid the now-gleaming Dedacciai on a new towel beside the tub. Removing the front and back wheels, he dried off every inch of the frame and even used ear swabs to get into the cracks and crevices, giving it the detailed cleaning of its life.

It was time to work on the costly and beautiful carbon wheels. With near-perfect hands, Carter wiped down every spoke, checking the tension to see if any needed to be trued, which some did, but he needed a spoke wrench, which he didn't have. Next, he wanted to remove the rear cluster of gears to clean and inspect them. Then, adjust the brakes, re-lube the chain, and perform a thorough tune-up. Unfortunately, his much-needed specialty tools and supplies were at home — the one place he couldn't go back to and wasn't sure he ever would. Carter wanted to see this project through and finish it with new handlebar tape and an excellent bicycle polish with protectant.

If he was going to do this thing, restore the Dedacciai – both the bike *and* the man – he would have to splurge on buying the supplies necessary for the task. Since he was gifted an extra night free by the wonderful Connie Sue, he was still on budget for his first two days in his new world. His usual bike-supply-buying options – Target or Walmart – were not an option because of the specialty tools needed for the job.

He decided if he was going to splurge, he might as well do it right. Of the two bike shops in town, his favorite was not too far away – Cycledelic Bike Therapy, Your Totally Tubular Bike Shop, as it touted on the sign. He called it his favorite because the name made him smile. But in reality, he had never purchased anything from there because the prices were beyond his usual budget of zero dollars.

However, tomorrow was a new day, and hopefully, the older cyclist would repay him since Carter knew he had the money. It was now almost 6:30 a.m., and although Carter was used to staying up all night after getting off work, he was ready to turn out the lights and get some sleep.

The ray of morning sunshine streamed past the slit of the poorly closed curtains, inching its way across the bedspread like the shadow of a sundial until it fell upon the 9:30 a.m. mark – which coincided with Carter Ducane's face. The sudden warmth and the red blast of brightness behind his closed eyelids were as effective as any alarm clock, and Carter came abruptly awake.

He quickly ran a shaver over his morning stubble, brushed his teeth, and dressed for the day in a fresh pair of jeans and a cotton shirt from his backpack. He wasn't riding that far, so he didn't need to wear bicycle shorts and a jersey. While his backpack was open, he noticed his pain pill prescription and thought of the Dedacciai as he grabbed them and headed over to see how he was doing.

Crossing to Room 555, the buzzing sounds of the old man's snoring permeated the hallway. Slipping in the key card, he poked his head in and saw the overweight cyclist precisely as he had left him, still out like a light. He approached and checked the makeshift ice pack on his temple; all the ice had melted, leaving a wet spot on the pillow. However, the goose egg was significantly better.

Carter took the makeshift ice pack and pain pills to the bathroom and put them on the counter beside an empty glass. Suddenly, Carter's stomach churned and gurgled, interrupting his web of thoughts. He was famished, so he returned to the Dedacciai, chose a donut from the box he left in the room earlier, and ate it to settle his stomach.

While eating, he watched the Dedacciai sleeping peacefully. As Carter studied his face, he noticed that the Dedacciai's REM was a step above what might be considered rapid eye movement — It almost seemed violent. The young man stared at it, his mind a strange blank, as he had never witnessed someone during REM sleep. It left him wondering what was happening inside the Dedacciai's dream world, about his anomaly, and about the conspiracies that accompanied him.

Carter took one last glance at the Dedacciai before returning to his room. Upon entering, he saw the complimentary coffee packets next to the expensive-looking coffee machine. Carter was not an avid coffee drinker, but the gourmet flavor of the Lancaster Landing donut needed something to help wash it down. The fancy packaging of the unheard-of expensive coffee brands intrigued his senses, and being the mechanic he was, the coffee machine was churning in no time.

Soon, an indescribably wonderful, aromatic brew a million lightyears beyond the cheap instant Sanka swill his father Russell Ducane insisted on was permeating the room. He poured the liquid black magic into an elegant coffee cup and tried to enjoy it along with a mental break.

But his mind turned back to his ward, the overweight cyclist. He remembered what Darius had said: *You saved him, even though he asked you not to. So, now, you should care for him, even though he may not want you to...*

Like it or not, he was responsible for him, and Carter sighed as a blip of negativity plopped in for a visit. *What do you know about caring for someone? You barely know how to take care of yourself.* He was still hoping against hope that the man's injuries were not as bad as they seemed, that a good night's rest and the ice pack would do the trick. And when he finally woke up, a hot meal would also help – *if* he woke up, that is. What if he had a concussion, broken ribs, internal bleeding, or something? Carter would have no choice but to take him to the emergency room. *What a mess that would be!* A thousand questions, the police would probably have to get involved, and they'd want to know the whole sordid story.... They'd find the mangled pimpmobile. *What if I was the one who ended up in jail after everything was said and done?*

He took a deep breath, trying to kick his negativity to the curb. *Okay, let's not get ahead of ourselves.* The Dedacciai was black and blue, that's true, but he looked much better and seemed to be in REM sleep, according to his face, so that was a good sign. Right? Carter continued to ponder his conundrum until the coffee cup was empty. *I need to hit the road if I'm going to finish the project, hopefully before the Dedacciai wakes.*

Walking his bicycle out through the lobby, he emerged into the bright sunlight of a beautiful late morning with a few traces of the pouring rain from the night before. Slipping on his helmet, he pedaled away and, 4.7 miles later, pulled up in front of the swirly, brightly colored 70's artwork of the Cycledelic Bike Therapy shop.

Carter entered the store as he usually did, somewhat sheepishly. He had dropped by occasionally from time to time to window shop and browse the aisles, looking at all the latest and greatest cool stuff he couldn't afford. Then, would slink out feeling guilty for not buying when the owner or bike mechanic wasn't looking. Trying his best to remain invisible, Carter picked out the specialty tools needed, along with lube, water displacing spray, bike polish with protectant, Armor All wheel cleaner and tire shine, and the best Deda-elementi handlebar tape he could find. Putting two and two together, he realized Deda-elementi bar tape was short for Dedacciai. *Hmmm, learn something new every day.* Then, screwing up his courage, headed to the checkout counter. He was met by the store's owner, Charley, according to his nametag. Carter already knew his last name was Mason because he heard him a few times joking with other customers with what was kind of his catchphrase – *It's Mason, not Manson!*

Charley was clean-cut, with thick, curly black hair, and was primarily business-like, with maybe a hint of an ex-hippie. But he certainly didn't match the appearance of the half dozen surfboards that decorated the walls. Carter imagined the owner would be an ex-surfer dude from California who had somehow found himself off-course in the Lone Star State.

"Good morning!" he said as if all mornings were good in his world. "How's my first customer of the day today?"

"So far, so good, I guess," Carter murmured demurely. He dumped his arm-load of items onto the counter. "Just these few things."

"I'm pretty sure I've seen you here before. What's your name so I can look up your therapy chart."

"I... I'm not sure I have a therapy chart."

"Well, everyone needs therapy, so it's my lucky day. Okay, kid, let's set you up so we can get you some help."

"Can't I just buy this stuff?"

Charley gave him the seasoned eye. "Can't give you drugs without a prescription. I need to know your problem to help give you the proper treatment. Name and address?"

Carter swallowed. "How about just a name? I'm kinda between addresses."

"Hmmm," the shopkeeper *hmmmed*. "Interesting-er and interesting-er. I'll settle for name and phone, then?"

"Carter Ducane."

Charley entered it with his phone number to set up his 'therapy chart.' "So, Carter — what kind of Cycledelic therapy session do you need help with today?" He glanced out the window at the blue *Specialized* bicycle parked in the bike rack. "Is that our patient?"

"Uh, no. I'm fixing up a bike for a friend. He kinda had a little accident last night. He has a Dedacciai?"

"A *De-What-Cha-Say*?" Charley questioned.

"It's called a Dedacciai — if I'm saying it right. The Jury's still out on my pronunciation. Have you never heard of a Dedacciai bicycle before?"

"Can't say that I have — but I'd love to see it when you're finished. I'm curious about any bicycle I haven't heard of before."

"I hadn't heard of one either, but yesterday, during the weirdest day of my life, I ran across someone who has one."

From the back bicycle repair room – a mechanic named Brandon– interested in "all things bicycle," sensed his ears pick up the scent of Carter's story. Almost immediately, a large, round head made even rounder by a retro 80's style head full of long, curly, sun-bleached hair popped through the repair window and thundered – "Dude! You had me at 'weirdest day'— what did you mean by that?"

Carter flinched, then inspected the Jack-in-the-Box head that popped through the window.

"Don't worry, folks, he doesn't bite," Charley interjected almost instinctively. "Carter, I want you to meet Brandon. He is not only a Master bicycle mechanic but the co-owner of this fine establishment and the heartbeat and personality behind the store. He is the real Kahuna in these parts, and his Cycledelic colors and surfboards grace the store's walls, inside and out.

Now this is what the owner should look like. Carter thought.

"Okay, Dude, the first rule of surfer-dom – don't leave another surfer dude out to dry. So, what did you mean by *you had the weirdest day*?"

Carter had to reorganize his thoughts before he could answer.

"Okay, well, yesterday was my 25th Birthday — let's just say that didn't go very well."

"Dude, I've had a few of those. Was alcohol involved?"

Carter envisioned his dad. "Well, yes. Sort of. Last night, my boss handed me a cupcake for my birthday and wished me well because it was also my last night working for him. Closing time was at 2 a.m., and I blew out the candle and made a wish. When I opened my eyes, I looked out the window, and out of nowhere, a heavy-set cyclist came riding into view on this beautiful bicycle in the pouring rain."

"That's messed up!" Brandon blurted.

"I know — right!? Then this old pimp-mobile with its lights turned off comes from behind and runs the guy off the road!"

"Dude, that's even more messed up!" Brandon's excitement added even more flavor to Carter's storytelling. "Dude — don't leave me hangin' — what happened next?"

"Then two thugs in hoodies simultaneously jumped out of their pimp-mobile and attacked the guy — and then tried stealing his bicycle!"

"Holy Shitballs, man! Pardon my Italian, but I can't stand that." Brandon was on the edge of his seat. "So, did they steal his bike or what?"

"Well — not exactly. I wasn't sure what to do at first, but when I saw the hoodies start to put the bike in their trunk, I decided to get it back. So, I ran out to confront them and ended up beating the crap out of both thugs before beating up their purple pimp-mobile just because it was there. Long story short — I got the freaking bike back!"

Brandon was over-the-moon excited and yelled, "DUDE!" then literally climbed through the window to give Carter a huge, man-sized Hi-Five. Charley made it a double as he chimed in. "Damn scumbags got what they deserved as far as I'm concerned."

"So, what happened to the heavy-set old guy?" asked Charley. "Is he okay?"

"Not really; he got beat up pretty bad."

The two owner dudes suddenly got very quiet, exchanging glances. "What do you think?" Charley asked. "Do you think the old guy might be — *The One*?"

The mechanic chewed his lip pensively. "Wow. I don't know. But how freakin' awesome would that be...?"

Carter was puzzled by this abrupt change in mood. "What are you guys talking about?"

"You've never heard the legend of *The One*?" asked Charley in a dark, conspiratorial voice.

Carter shook his head no as Charley stared him in the eye and typed something eerily into his computer. Charley then lowered his voice an octave as he began the mythical tale.

"For years, rumors swirled throughout our cycling community that a bike such as the one you're describing existed, or possibly it's the exact Dedacciai you're depicting. But legend has it, the bike was somewhere nearby in this vicinity. Precisely where no one could say. But people have claimed to have caught a glimpse of it—"

"Like a two-wheeled Big Foot," interrupted Brandon.

"*And it was always ridden by a heavy-set older man near a mass of water.*"

Charley let that marinate in Carter's cranium for a spell before he continued. "*And didn't you say your older dude appeared out of nowhere in the pouring rain when you first saw him?*"

Carter gulped, nodding yes. Then Charley abruptly whipped the computer monitor around for the young man to see a Meme of Big Foot riding a bicycle in the rain.

Brandon bellowed, "NICE!!!" and Hi-Fived Charley as their campfire horror story ended.

"Okay, Carter, fess up — who is this guy really... with the Dedacciai?" Charlie pressed.

"Seriously, I don't know his name. He didn't have any I.D. on him."

"Just like Big-Foot," Brandon interjected, "makes perfect sense him not having an I.D."

"And that's exactly why I named him 'The Dedacciai,' after his bicycle."

"Dude, that's awesome! I've renamed a few people myself over the years — most of which I can't repeat in polite society — *Yes,* alcohol was involved."

"But seriously, guys, the Dedacciai wasn't doing well last night. That's why I booked him into a hotel to let him recover, and he seemed to be sleeping okay when I left. The thing is, his Dedacciai bicycle is also in rough shape from riding in the rain and getting run off the road. So, I wanted to surprise him by cleaning it up and putting on new handlebar tape to make it look shiny and new before he wakes up. So, I need to be going. How much do I owe you for all this?"

Charley looked down at the pile of things on the counter: the tools, the lube, and the handlebar tape. "Nice tape. I never knew Deda-eleminti also made Dedacciai bikes. These two were made for each other. Using any other tape on this bike would have been sacrilege. They can throw you in Biker's Jail for that!"

"I know — Right? I just realized the same thing. So, how much do I owe for everything?"

Charley looked over at Brandon, and they gave each other the man-nod, which was the universal unspoken language for approval. "The handlebar tape is on us."

"Screw that!" Brandon added, pushing Charley aside and sliding the entire pile of items toward Carter as if they were poker chips. "You're on a valiant mission to rescue an international treasure. It's *all* on us!"

Carter was so overwhelmed with emotion he could barely speak. "Wow. *Dudes!*" he said. "I don't know what to say."

"Just promise us, when this old guy's up and riding again, you gotta bring him by to meet us," said Charley.

"And his bike!" piped in Brandon.

Carter shook his head as if to say okay, but his face didn't appear to agree.

"I know that look, Carter," Charley said, "what's wrong here? We can't make it any free-er than free, and paying our customers to take stuff goes against our economic policy of trying to stay in business."

"It's just that it doesn't feel right if I don't buy something," Carter said, "even if it's small, so I know I finally bought something here. I need to do this so I can feel good about myself."

"By all means, go wild," Charley said. "We understand the need for a man to feel good about himself."

"We got some damn good energy drinks and bars for the road," Brandon said as he popped open an energy drink.

"That's it, perfect. Give me twenty dollars worth of your best-selling energy bars."

Carter grabbed his debit card to pay. "Now, I'm complete." Then, he nodded and raised his fist, and a round of fist-bumps sealed the deal. Charley then packed his supplies in a plastic bag with a drawstring to hang from his handlebars. As Carter Ducane headed out the door, Brandon the Mechanic, unable to stop his inner ex-surfer-hippie demons from taking over his soul, bid him a final, "Okay, get your ass back in here soon so we can say, 'Welcome back, *Carter*'!"

Carter's puzzled look forced Charley to attempt a translation.

"You know, *Welcome Back, Kotter?* The TV show?" It didn't ring any bells. "Kotter? Carter? Potato? Patoto? Get it? Still nothing. Dude, Google '*Welcome Back, Kotter,*'" he said while smirking as Carter walked out the door.

That was the thing about Cycledelic Bike Therapy – it always made him smile.

On his trek back to the hotel, Carter stopped at a Dollar General to buy the Dedacciai some new size 2XL (he assumed) underwear using his tip money from his last night of work. As he walked toward their rooms on the fifth floor, he still heard the buzz-saw sounds of snoring echoing down the hallway.

Entering 556, he wasted no time getting to work on The Dedacciai Therapy Project. First, he focused on the carbon fiber wheels. Removing the rear cassette with his new tool, he cleaned each gear to perfection before thoroughly scouring the chain. Then, he reapplied the proper amount of lube to the rear gear cluster and chain and let the lube penetrate for a few minutes before he sprayed the water-displacing formula onto the entire drive train.

While he waited for the lube to penetrate, he checked the tension on the front and rear wheel spokes and found the ones that needed to be slightly adjusted with his new spoke wrench. To finish the carbon wheels, he cleaned them with Armor All wheel cleaner and finished with Armor All tire shine to blacken the tires and make them both – *POP.*

Next, he focused on the frame and generously applied polish and protectant before buffing it off, which caused the brilliant red color to widen the pupils like a morning sunrise. He was amazed at how beautiful this well-crafted Italian marvel was. It was time for the last piece of the puzzle as he tightened the wheels back into proper alignment and watched the bike jump to life before his eyes.

Carter ran through all twenty-two of its gears and determined the rear *derailleur* must have gotten slightly bent during last night's scuffle. He bent it back into position with impeccable precision, checked the front *derailleur* alignment on both chainrings and finished the needed rear *derailleur* adjustment.

Carter then opened the Deda-elementi bar wrap and applied it perfectly and evenly, even *artfully*, to both sides of the handlebars. As he finished, he heard an unfamiliar beep and realized the GPS had finished charging. He placed the device back into position, and with that, the icing was on the cake.

Carter stepped back to admire his accomplishment. It was stunning. There was simply no better way to describe it. He could hardly wait to return it to the Dedacciai with his newly cleaned clothes and safely secured money pouch.

But Carter's mind lingered on the money pouch a little too long before a vision began playing in his mind of all that cash alone in such a cold, dark pouch. Were they 20s, 50s, 100s... He tried to shake the image out of his brain. *You don't need to know what bills are there; it's none of your business...*

However, money – especially lots of money – can change people. Carter grabbed the pouch and continued to stare at it. He started to smell the genuine leather; the authentic aroma that made him even more obsessed. He felt his resolve begin to crumble.

Then it happened: A shift in his thoughts as his own DNA started a hostile takeover of his mind and body, then ideas of what Russell Ducane would do began messing with his head —

That's it, boy — you know you want that money, ain't nothin' like the smell of it. And if you listen to your old man for just a JIFFY, it'll be all yours, so pay close attention because class is in session. Let's just think about this logically. No one besides you knows about all this money. Here are the facts as I see' em'. You don't know the fat man's name, and he doesn't know yours. He's got no I.D. or phone – but was ridin' in the rain at 2 a.m. with a wad of cash and wanting to die. What does that signal ya, boy? It's simple; it says he's fleein' from somethin' he doesn't want to be found out about. This is basic 101 criminal handbook stuff.

He knows he was beaten up, and his money and bicycle were stolen. But here's the thing: he probably stole the money, bike, or both in the first place, just like ya suspected all along. But even if he didn't, he's obviously fleein' from somethin' nefarious and doesn't want no attention.

So, here's our plan: We have to fight nefarious with nefarious, so you'll have to grow some man-sized balls and develop a good poker face for the most critical part of the plan to work. Don't fret, boy; it's already in your DNA, so you're welcome for that. Now, here it goes...

When you check on the fat man, and he sees the freshly washed clothes, it'll let him know you were concerned about him. Then, when he sees how pretty you made his bike look, you explain how you beat up those thugs to rescue it for him and then wanted to fix it up before he saw it. Make sure your story sounds real good. He'll think you're a hero and won't believe you could have taken his money because no criminal in his right mind would have performed all this kindness for him. And that's why your plan is so instinctively brilliant. Because you got him and that pretty hotel lady both thinking you're practically a war hero for rescuing that darn bike.

And if he still asks about the money for some odd reason, you just tell him the hoodies must have taken it when they jumped him because you didn't see no darn money. Tell him the truth. You beat up the first hoodie to rescue the bike, then beat up the other hoodie who was already beating on him — but you didn't know to search the hoodie for any money. Then, a stranger with a van came along and helped you get him here. He won't remember anything, and he'll believe ya hook, line, and sinker.

Then, before you leave, wish him well and hand him a couple of 20s for food from your bar tips last night. Then ya play to his emotions and tell him you need to leave because your momma needs help moving something; everyone loves a boy wanting to help his momma. Oldest trick in the book to get someone to think good about ya.

Finish by telling him check-out is at noon and everything is handled; just leave the key card in the room when he leaves tomorrow. That's it, boy, you never exchanged names or phone numbers. You were just a good ole boy who came along at the right time and wanted to help. He'll be on his way, and you'll be on your way — and you'll be livin' on easy street for a good long while in a place of your own. It's a win-win for both of us. I don't have to see your ugly mug, and you don't have to see mine. And if your momma wants to see ya, she can take a bus or somethin'.

My spidey senses tell me that fat man's gonna walk right out of here askin' nobody nothin' and be happy as a clam havin' his clothes and bike back so he can continue fleein' from wherever he's fleein'. Besides, if he has that kinda money in cash, imagine how much he has in the bank. That's just a drop in the bucket for him... a damn annoyance at best.

Now, I know you have fancy thoughts about wantin' to see Connie Sue; nobody's gonna judge ya; just proves you got eyes. Then, come back tonight and tell her it was nice to meet her, and thanks for all her help and inspiration. Then inform her on how the fat fellas doing, that his head looks better, and that he's resting, and it's all because of her kindness. Then tell her all the fantastic things you did for him, how you washed his clothes and left him some money because he didn't seem to have any. Then you put on your poker face and act all concerned. I wonder if the thugs stole his wallet and phone when they beat him up because there was nothing in his clothes when I washed them.

Bam! She'll not only believe you but also think you're sweet and caring, adding to her hero scenario of you. Now that's an excellent start to becoming a con artist — congratulations.

Now for grins and giggles, let's play one last game of worst-case scenarios. Let's pretend the old fella wants a second opinion about ya and asks that pretty lady from the hotel about the money. You got your bases covered. You told Connie Sue the whole story about rescuing him. And what thief in his right mind would bring someone to a hotel like this if they were going to steal his money. They would have taken him to a seedier hotel that rents by the hour and left him for dead. Connie witnessed ya, scared about how much this was gonna cost ya. You never mentioned anything about no money except to give him some because he didn't seem to have any when you washed his clothes.

As far as she still reckons'– you're even more of a damn hero in her eyes. She saw how you cared for him; she ain't gonna suspect you of nothin' and has no reason to believe you stole no money. And if she does ask you, just stick to blamin' it on the hoodies.

Get my drift here, boy! This may be your only chance to get ahead in life. Besides, how do you know your first thoughts about this fat fella weren't correct? Maybe this is the rewritin' of your story, and you were always meant to find this money. Just accept it as a fact, boy, and take the win!

Carter was in a deep mental trance with the mindset of the DNA that created him. He looked more seriously at all that money and envisioned living in a place of his own. *He's right; this really could work. I could actually get away with it.* Then, this universal thought took over Carter's entire nervous system as he took a long, hard look at the Dedacciai bicycle.

I'm the one who rescued this bike. It would've been stolen if it weren't for me. I deserve this money as a reward. Just look how beautiful this bike is because of what I freaking did. This really could be how it's meant to be. I truly deserve this.

'Do it, boy; just do it! A few steps across the hallway, and you'll be on your way to rewritin' your story that you're always wishin' about. Just do it! A few steps further out the door and you'll be Scot-free —

Chapter Five

Only in Dreams

※━━━━━━━━━━━━━※

Quiet on the set!... Cue dreamer's fog.

THE TERRIFYING STORM

ACT I—DREAM ONE—TAKE ONE... And Action!

One of the most terrifying and lightning-enriched storms wreaked havoc on the city below. It was accompanied by a daunting soundtrack of dissonant lightning and boisterous thunder that could shatter glass and shake the rooftop.

A petrified three-year-old child trembled in fear while she cried a rainstorm of her own. She was spending the night with her Grammy and Papa and currently employed the death grip on her Papa as he carried her to the back porch. She clung to him vigorously as he opened the sliding glass door and stepped outside. Her death grip intensified, as did her crying, as he sat in his rocking chair.

"I'm scared, Papa. Please don't let anything bad happen to me."

"As long as I'm alive, I will always protect you and never, EVER, LET ANYONE or ANYTHING hurt you."

He looked at the storm and asked Addison to be courageous and look at it with him.

"Addison, there are going to be storms in life, horrible, terrible storms, and we have to face them, just as I am asking you to do now, with me. When you explore the heavens, try not to fear the lightning but see the beauty of it. What is the lightning brush trying to paint on the heavenly canvas? What if God is the artist creating a picture using beautiful streaks of lightning to paint the sky? Remember each lightning streak and envision what animal God might draw for you. Be brave, my little Addison, and remember this always — look for the beauty in situations and people who do not seem beautiful at first. I promise you it is always there. Will you try to do that, my little Addison?"

While her Grandpa sat on the back porch holding his granddaughter, the storm eventually calmed, as did the one called Addison. Sleep slowly overtook her as her clinging lessened and her tears turned silent. Smiling warmly, Papa gently whispered into her ear, "Just remember, Addison, the fiercest storms give birth to the biggest and brightest rainbows."

The next morning, 7:21 a.m. to be precise, Grandpa gently lifted Addison from her bed and carried her once more onto the back porch, where it was still dark outside. He sat in his rocking chair again as she wrestled the sleep out of her eyes with her fists. As she woke, a few rapid heartbeats ensued until she touched her Papa's burly arms and knew she was safe.

Without saying a word, he reached out and pointed toward the horizon as Addison's gaze followed. The first tentacles of light glowed, and her eyes widened as the crest of the morning sun made its presence known from the eastern hemisphere with spectacular pageantry.

Today, there was a special treat, as the sciences of the sky had an incredible show to display for the audience below. "Addison, do you want to see something extraordinary?" He pointed west, away from the sunrise, where the backdrop of clouds signaled that the curtain call was near. With perfect precision, millions of atmospheric actors put on their refractive costumes, and the magical cast of characters displayed their theatrical prisms of color and performed a breathtakingly beautiful rainbow for Addison.

It was one of God's finest early-morning displays as the arc stood proud from one end of the land to the other. Addison sat in awe of the pageantry until she saw it dissipate into the atmosphere.

"Wow, Papa! You were right! That was the biggest and bestest rainbow ever!"

"Well, it's Papa's job always to be right. It's also Papa's job to take you to IHOP for cupcake pancakes."

A loud squeal pierced the air as she ran into the house to get dressed for IHOP. It seemed only a few seconds later that Addison ran toward her

Papa and jumped into his arms. As he caught her, he threw her in the air. *Suddenly, without warning, the dream transitioned to a much darker and more intense dream state as the fog grew thicker and more turbulent.*

As she landed, her arms immediately reached for the sky. "Do it again, Papa, do it again!" And up she went as part of Grandpa's emotional reflex — But this time, his pounding heart remembered the outcome of her flight as his internal dialogue yelled in horror, "*Nooooo!*" He tried to suspend her in the air with his mind while repeating his failed promise: *"As long as I'm alive, I will always protect you and never ever let anyone or anything hurt you."* But it was to no avail. Her Papa was forced to relive her death as he caught her limp and lifeless body and screamed, "Addison — Addison — *Addison!*"

The scream thrust his body upright, and a punching-bag-type pain surged through him like electricity from his radical awakening. Cold sweat covered him as he gasped for breath. He was naked except for his underwear and sore from top to toe and inside to out. He briefly wondered if someone had tattooed "EVERLAST" across his body as he felt like a genuine punching bag. The suffering was too much, and he could not sustain his vertical position as gravity won out and pulled him back down. Everything spun out of control, and his mind was chaotic and confused.

Where am I? The last thing he remembered was actually a jumble of things — *death, pain, rain, God, boom, bike,* and the feeling of it ripped from his hands with a finale of *kicks and crying*. After that, everything became a blur.

The older man squinted in the darkness and noticed light slipping in from beneath the bathroom door, allowing his eyes to adjust. Judging by the furniture, layout, and smell, he was in a hotel room. *How did I get here? — Who brought me here?*

His battered skin was all he owned, and he wondered what had happened to his clothes. Then it hit him — his clothes were not the only thing he was missing. *Oh, God! My bike! My money!* He glanced furtively about the room; there was a wheelchair, which he vaguely remembered being pushed around in, but otherwise, his possessions were nowhere to be seen. Panic gripped him as he realized he needed to muster up the strength to get to the bathroom and verify if his clothes, bike, and money pouch were there.

With a series of gut-wrenching sit-ups, he managed to roll himself off the bed. Bracing himself, he used the strength of his legs to stand, causing his upper torso to throb. The cyclist headed to the bathroom to confirm whether his fears were justified; his strength imploded as he entered. *Nothing there.* All of it was gone — his money, bike, clothes — *all gone.*

He looked in the mirror and saw a monster – at least, that's what his mind interpreted. What other word described a man fleeing from the death of a little girl. He peered at his mostly naked body – and realized the extent of his beating. *You deserve this,* his mind chimed in convincingly.

He faltered back into the bedroom and opened the curtain to see if he could tell his location. He stood paralyzed, staring out the window into the night, then saw the first glow of the dreadful day to come, the first tentacles of light that sparked images to flash in his mind as he relived bits and pieces of his dream. He recalled his dream of holding his granddaughter through the storm and her joy as she witnessed the rainbow. Suddenly, a voice, as clear as could be, spoke in his mind — *Just remember, the fiercest storms give birth to the biggest and brightest rainbows* — But the voice wasn't his– and the words were spoken directly to him, not Addison. *I know that voice* and its familiarity ignited a momentary flash of him sitting in the wheelchair while sloshing through the sound of wet grass, mind-numbingly out of it.

He turned and stared at the wheelchair. He could feel the dark, cold night outside the hotel and focused on hearing the phrase repeatedly in his mind. He then closed his eyes and searched the quadrants of his mind for the distant but recognizable voice. After what seemed like forever, Grandpa questionably murmured — *Darius???*

As he came out of his fog, an actual rainbow now crossed the sky, one of God's finest displays. The man tried to process what all this meant and why his visions were so prevalent in his mind. In the past, a rainbow signaled an appreciation that he was alive. He would give thanks and praise for his family – his wife, kids, and even Zilla – but most of all, for Addison.

But today was a new day – a dreadful day. A day where none of those thoughts had a chance to survive in his mind as his state of being had changed. What happened last night roared to life and stampeded to the front of his prefrontal cortex. He envisioned Addison's final moments on earth as they ended in his arms. He would trade his life in a micro-heartbeat if it brought back hers in return.

Then, the courtroom of his subconscious took over:

"You are hereby sentenced to a life where Bella will not — and cannot — look at you. You will now and forever be a constant reminder of your failure to provide her the chance to perform proper CPR. It is her undeniable belief, and the opinion of this court, that if you had, little Addison would be alive today. But your pride kept Bella from having that chance, and for that, there will be no chance of forgiveness.

"You are further sentenced to a life where you will never be able to look into your son's eyes again, nor will the gentle creature once known as Evan ever want you to. You broke him when you took his daughter's life, and Evan will forever be filled with an immense rage toward the man he once knew as Pops. We find you guilty on all charges; do you accept your punishment?"

As he exited his mental courtroom, the former grandpa was not sure he could answer that question. Why would God start this new day with such a beautiful rainbow if there was no hope for salvation? Was this also part of his punishment? After all, God had to know the anguish it would cause him because He knew that the former grandpa did not appreciate being alive and wished he wasn't. The man clasped his hands in prayer.

"God, why are you doing this to me? I put my life in your hands; please show me a way out of this torment. Please, God."

He looked out the window in time to witness the rainbow's demise. *Was that His answer? Was his demise the solution for his family to heal?* His pain grew from the inside out, and he lay down in the silence to see if God would somehow provide a better answer to his plea. He was so overwhelmed with emotional and physical agony that survival mode took over and signaled: "*We need more rest.*" The pain got its wish, and he once again surrendered to the escape that was sleep — *Or so he thought....*

Quiet on the set!... Cue dreamer's fog.

THE DREAMATOLOGIST

ACT II—INTRODUCTION—TAKE ONE

Cue Tony Robbins.... And Action!

Spotlights sweep back and forth across a fog-shrouded theater stage, highlighting the majestic red velvet curtains. Suddenly, a booming announcement. "Ladies and gentlemen, we are proud to present a #1 New York Times best-selling author, philanthropist, and the nation's #1 life strategist. He has empowered more than 50 million people worldwide with his live seminars and many audio, video, and educational programs. So tonight, welcome to the stage, the one and only – Tony Robbins."

As he runs on stage, the auditorium roars with applause even though it is entirely empty except for the perplexed Grandpa. Suddenly, the spotlights sweep away from the elaborate curtains to pinpoint the singular audience member, where Robbins focuses his attention.

"Alright, Grandpa, welcome. I will be your acting Dreamatologist as I have been assigned to your mental court case. You did ask God to answer your plea — did you not?

"First, you must trust that I have a plan for what you will experience here. By listening to me, you know that I have developed what I refer to as the Dickens pattern to help people change. Think of this as your own emotional Christmas Carol, as I recreate the sights, sounds, and smells of certain events and immerse you into precisely what you felt while they happened. You and I don't have much time, so let's begin.

"'There are going to be storms in life, horrible, terrible storms, and we have to face them.' Do you recognize those words? You should. They are your words — good words — told to your granddaughter Addison. In the next segments, I will ask you to apply the lesson you were trying to teach Addison. You don't want to be a hypocrite, do you? You can't ask Addison to face the storms of life if you're not willing to do the same. Applying your own philosophy is what I am asking you to do here. So, let's get started — shall we?"

There was a sudden swooshing sound as the fog whisked Tony Robbins off the stage. Grandpa looked around the empty auditorium and wondered where Tony had gone. "I'm right here," Robbins said as he now sat beside Grandpa, where they shared a bird's-eye view of the dreamer's stage. He handed Grandpa a bag of movie popcorn. "This is going to be good," assured the Dreamatologist, smiling in anticipation.

The curtains opened, and Grandpa saw what, at first, he assumed was some kind of movie screen with an opening title of —

THE ENCOUNTER.

But it was like no movie he had ever seen. In this theater, he was simultaneously watching the movie and part of the movie, what the dream world's version of Virtual Reality would be. — Suddenly, it was three years ago...

Grandpa was in his Ford Expedition, headed down Statler Boulevard. He reached out and turned on the stereo, shoving an audio CD into the player. He had recently discovered motivational speakers and loved listening to them while driving. One of his favorite things about his discovery was learning to enjoy traffic lights, railroad crossings, and traffic jams, as they now provided an opportunity to absorb more inspiration. And that Sunday afternoon was turning into a good day as he was in a traffic snarl of glorious proportions.

Even better, he was on his way to IHOP to celebrate what he considered to be the little victories in life. The unsung moments that don't receive as much fanfare or recognition as they should. Moments like having a cake made that read *Happy Ten-Month Birthday Addison,* to surprise his granddaughter after lunch, or purchasing a ticket to his first Tony Robbins *Unleash the Power Within* event in Florida that December.

Tony Robbins nudged Grandpa, "This was when you had started listening to me before we met in Florida a few months later. It's why I'm part of your story and here with you now as your Dreamotologist." He then nodded to Grandpa and turned back toward the screen.

As Grandpa listened to the latest Robbins CD, he pondered what all the cars were blinking about while stuck in traffic. He checked his watch, then made light of the situation. *It's 1:23 p.m.; don't they know I will miss out on my favorite IHOP booth!?*

Finally, a large delivery truck, three blinkers ahead, angled over, revealing the culprit. A midsized white cargo van sat dead in the street. *What's wrong with everyone? Don't they even see the problem? There's a van stuck in the road, people — Hello!* He caught himself being frustrated and attempted to apply his new motivational principles and stop complaining.

Instead, he decided to become part of the solution. He pulled behind the cargo van, engaged his hazard signals, and walked toward the driver-side door. The man inside abruptly turned toward the window.

Holy crap! Grandpa's sudden rapid heartbeat forced him back a few feet as the mutual strangers looked at each other in awkward silence. Inside was a man whose face matched Grandpa's depiction of what Jesus with long hair would look like in modern times. But his facial expression and overall demeanor appeared to be cocked, loaded, and ready to yell at the next available human.

Grandpa was jarred by the unexpected scowl on the Jesus-looking man's face as he rolled down his window.

"Do you need some gas?" Grandpa said quickly, hoping his question offered a peace treaty to break their verbal void.

The Jesus-looking man's piercing blue eyes appraised the older gentleman outside his van before a curt nod of acceptance came from within the van.

"Okay, put it in neutral, and let me see what I can do." Grandpa walked to the back of the van and started to push, hoping it would signal other traffic-goers to help. Sure enough, within minutes, the cargo van was powered by an eight-legged engine that pushed it half a block to the nearest gas station. Grandpa thanked the legs that helped as they returned to their vehicles and swiped his credit card in the gas pump.

"Start filling your tank, and I mean, to the brim, and I'll be back in a few minutes," then trotted briskly to his SUV, which was now the traffic-stopping culprit.

When he returned, he pulled into a parking space near the store entrance and crossed the fueling island to the van. Glancing at the meter, he saw that the stranger had only put five dollars of gas in his tank. "I wasn't sure if you would come back," said the Jesus figure timidly and in a much calmer voice than expected. He squeezed the nozzle again to complete his fill-up. Grandpa closed his eyes with a glimpse of the man's experiences of broken promises.

"Hey, I said to the brim, and I meant it. You'll find I say what I mean, and I mean what I say, so, to the brim, good sir. I'm headed to grab a bite at the IHOP next door if you'd allow me to buy you lunch and fill up your other tank as well."

"Well, mister, I don't know. You've really done enough—"

"Nonsense. I've recently learned not to believe in coincidences; I think I was held up in the best traffic jam ever just so I could meet you." A kind smile was attached to his remarks as an attempt to remove the other man's scowl. "What do you say? Let me do this for you."

A few minutes later, they entered the cool air conditioning of the International House of Pancakes, where they were instantly greeted by the boisterous voice of the manager.

"There's my favorite grandpa! How are you doin' today?" announced Sid, a Mediterranean man familiar with Grandpa's quirks and preferences. "I've been holding your booth for you but wasn't sure if you were coming. Some people mentioned a traffic jam up the road, and I thought you might be delayed, so I saved it just in case. Looks like there'll be two of you today."

The rescued traffic culprit looked down awkwardly as the favored grandpa gave his guest a reassuring glance. Sid escorted them to the grandpa's favorite booth at the end of the row with a nice view out the window. "I'm a bit claustrophobic, so I like to keep my claustrophobia in check by sitting in a booth with my back to the wall," Grandpa confessed.

His guest pored over the menu like he had never seen one before. He was tall and thin, with a scraggly beard looming underneath all his long hair. He appeared to be in his late 40s or early 50s, wearing an old gray suit and sandals.

"Hi, I'm Joyce, and I'm new here, so take it easy on me," she preemptively warned them; "However, I've waitressed for a while, so give me your best shot. What can I get you gentlemen to drink?" The sandaled man asked for a simple coffee with cream, but before his benefactor could utter a word, the waitress cut him off. "I've already been warned about you," Grandpa noticed Sid smirking in the distance. "You want an unsweet tea with lots of ice — and an extra glass of ice for when the freshly brewed tea melts the original glass of iced tea. Then you need as many orange slices as possible, lots of Equal and/or Splenda, and most importantly, a teaspoon…Did I miss anything?"

"Yes — me falling in love with you," and they both laughed as she confirmed, "Comin' right up!" then winked for good measure as she scurried off.

The living Jesus icon stared at his overweight companion, who suddenly felt an explanation was in order.

"Sorry," he said, "I'm a smidge high maintenance regarding my iced tea regiment — a proud member of *The Tea-Drinkers Association* since '79. People here call me Grandpa, as I may have been here a time or two hundred, with and without my new granddaughter. She's ten months old today; the funny thing is I have a Happy Ten-Month birthday cake I'm taking to her when we finish lunch."

"Grandpa fits you. It fits your kind persona," the sandaled man remarked.

"Wow, thanks for that! I'm glad you decided to have lunch with me… er, I'm not sure what to call you."

"— *Sandals* — people usually just call me Sandals," he answered somberly.

Suddenly, his face had a confused look about it. He stopped sifting through the menu. His hands rapidly fidgeted while covering his face and holding down his hair.

"What's wrong? Are you okay?"

"Sir, I'm sorry, but I think I need to be alone today."

Grandpa became concerned. But before he could respond, the waitress returned with coffee and all the iced-tea requirements for Grandpa.

"What can I get for you two gentlemen?"

A silent pause permeated the air as Grandpa examined Sandals' facial expression.

"Joyce, I think we might need a moment or two longer," she took her cue.

"Sandals, I don't want you to feel like you have to be here, so if you need to leave, I'll understand. But I want to be honest with you. I know people have let you down, but I'm not one of those people."

The sandaled man let his hands fall from his face but continued to look down.

"Sandals, can I just ask you one thing?" There came a slight nod.

"You said you needed to be alone today — Is it that you 'need' or 'want' to be alone? Or is it specifically something about today, or today's date, that you need to be alone for?"

Grandpa studied Sandals' face, hoping to get an answer.

Sandals lifted his head and made eye contact. "It's the date."

"OK, Sandals, now we're making progress. How about you let me buy you some pancakes? After all, we are at the International House of Pancakes. I'm fairly sure I can hook you up!"

A slight smile emanated underneath the long hair as Joyce reappeared to take their order.

"My friend will take the specialty red velvet pancakes. Oh! And throw in the all-you-can-eat pancakes, just in case that isn't enough."

"The waitress eyed the skinnier of the two men. "Not sure where he's gonna put it, but I like a man with lofty goals!"

"And I'll take the country omelet, and I'd like to upgrade my three-dollar-size pancakes to red velvet pancakes because those small ones belong on the darn kids' menu — and I'm a man."

Joyce laughed. "Is this an eating competition between you two? Because I know where you will put yours" — eyeing the grandpa's plentiful-sized stomach — "but I don't know what Slim here will do with his. Competition seems unfair."

"Well, that's why I'm here, to plumpen up the competition," Grandpa retorted before the waitress smirked and walked away.

The high-maintenance grandpa organized and attacked his orange-sweetening iced tea ritual. First, he added extra ice to the glass to compensate for the melted ice. As stated in the Tea-Drinkers Association by-laws — *'It's called iced tea for a reason,'* and he preferred to keep it that way. Next, he squeezed the orange slices to get every drop of goodness before eating what was left off the rind. Lastly, he ripped open each packet of sweetener, stirring them in, one by one, and taste-testing between stirs until he achieved perfection.

"Er... Grandpa, that looks like a lot of hard work."

"Well, how else am I going to get such massive biceps?" Grandpa countered while performing a Hanz and Franz bodybuilding gesture.

His silliness caught Sandals off guard, and a small laugh escaped, but he immediately closed his eyes. He seemed guarded and shielding an emotional pain.

Hmmm, what's that about? He allowed the man to gather himself without asking, not wanting to push his luck. As he did so, the grandpa assessed his guest. Apart from his initial scowl, he appeared kind, with a hint of unpolished humor, maybe tarnished, like it hadn't appeared in a while.

Soon, the food arrived, and the two men took up their forks to dig in. The man with the sandals looked to have tears from seeing so much food. One bite of the red velvet pancakes set off a continuum of gratitude for such a flavorful explosion.

"I've never heard of red velvet pancakes before. But this has to be one of the best things I've ever tasted. And I once ate at the White House."

"The White House — really? How did that happen?" Grandpa asked. But before he could get a reply, they were interrupted by the waitress.

"Well, well, well. Slim here looks like he is putting you to shame. What do you have to say for yourself?" — glancing again at Grandpa's tummy, "I'm glad I'm not a bettin' kind of gal because I sure wouldn't be makin' a deposit today!" As she walked off, she glared sarcastically at Grandpa, and he sarcastically smiled back at her.

Sandals spoke up. "She's kind of a funny lady — Unfortunately, I lost my funny years ago."

The grandpa quickly replied, "What a coincidence, I just found a pile of funny the other day wandering the streets. How long ago did you lose your funny? Did it have any distinguishing scars or tattoos?"

Sandals nearly chuckled at the quick wit before he answered in a slow, more melancholy voice, "My funny would have been 25 years old — today."

Grandpa wasn't sure what he meant by that, but he knew it was significant to the Jesus-like man's story.

Sandals parted his long hair, his eyes probing before he started. "This will be hard to imagine, seeing me here, excited about red velvet pancakes and looking like I do. But I used to be a lawyer. A darned good one, I might add. That is how I once ate at the White House."

Grandpa was intrigued but not entirely convinced what he was hearing was true. He had heard illustrious tales from homeless people while volunteering with a church group before; nearly all of them ended in a request for money. But the sandaled man seemed different. He spoke with elegance and a vocabulary that could validate his lawyer background.

"I married the woman of my dreams when I was twenty-one but met her when I was sixteen. She was my everything. Neither of us came from money, but we were determined and hardworking, which was a great combination. I eventually got into law school, and she worked full-time to support us so I could concentrate on my studies. She believed in me, and she saw the big picture, and more importantly, she was right.

"In what seemed like a flash, I graduated law school, top of my class. I passed the Bar Exam on the first try and was recruited by one of the best law firms in the city. Didn't think life could get any better than that."

"I bet," Grandpa said, encouraging Sandals to continue.

"But a small pair of steel-blue eyes named Bronson was born and proved me wrong. Life did indeed get better! He was the most beautiful boy, and we were complete. I had a record-breaking year at the firm, and my work was exemplary. On the day of Bronson's one-year birthday, I made partner, the youngest to ever do so at the firm. That earned me my dinner at the White House because the partners knew people and pulled some strings. I even shook hands with the president."

"Wow," breathed Grandpa. "That's impressive."

"Oh, it was, it was." But then Sandals' eyes locked on his. "Now, what I'm going to tell you next might seem like it's from a book or movie — but I swear, it happened. I received a check with more zeros than I thought I would ever see in a lifetime. Nonetheless, there it was, a cool million. What a day! Partner and a bonus on the same day as Bronson's first year on the planet. Happy birthday, Bronson! I didn't think life could get any better, but there it was — better. I wanted to reward that beautiful woman for the years she worked to help put me through law school.

"By the way, Danielle was the name of that beautiful redhead. I wanted to build her the house of her dreams, so we designed one of the most beautiful houses you could imagine. She had never had a swimming pool and always wanted one, so we hand-picked our lot to accommodate a nice-sized one. To tell the truth, I think it was more for me because I was surely looking forward to seeing that redhead in her bikini on a regular basis. She was such a gorgeous woman."

The man's face lit up at the mention of Danielle while reliving his story. So far, Sandals' life seemed perfect — too perfect, and Grandpa wondered where this story was headed as he continued.

"It took us a year to finalize the floor plans. We celebrated Bronson's second birthday by giving him a plastic shovel so we could have the honor of breaking ground together. He was pure boy, through and through, and he loved playing in the dirt. We were all so happy and excited to see our new house begin construction.

"Every night when I got home, no matter how late, we would take Bronson to see the progress. It was amazing to watch every intricate design decision come to life. It took another year to finish, but the time flew by, and just like that, it was the morning of Bronson's third Birthday. On his first birthday, I made partner; on his second, we broke ground. It only made sense we would move in on his third."

"Makes perfect sense," Grandpa agreed, sipping his orange-infused iced tea.

"Yeah... perfect," Sandals repeated, his voice tinged with an odd bitterness. "I remember pulling up in the biggest moving truck I could rent, full of everything we had. A few of my friends were waiting to help me unload. I aimed to have all the furniture in place before Danielle and Bronson saw it for the first time. We also bought all new furniture, which three stores were scheduled to deliver that day. It was madness!

"My friends helped move until mid-afternoon that day, and Danielle and Bronson were scheduled to arrive at five. I was frantically arranging and rearranging furniture while directing the delivery of the movers. I even tried hanging some of our favorite art pieces so it would feel like home. But I didn't quite make it. At precisely 3:22 p.m., a small pair of arms grabbed my legs unexpectedly as I carried a chair into the living room. 'Daddy, Daddy, you're it!' the little voice cried out as I put down the chair and tackled him before he could escape."

"Nice," Grandpa said as he chuckled.

"We rolled on the plush new carpet as I tickled him into a giggling frenzy. Then, I caught sight of that stunning redhead laughing at me from the doorway. I leaped to my feet, swaggered to her, and planted the most passionate kiss I could muster, which must have lasted more than a minute. I finished in dramatic fashion by dipping her way down while continuing the kiss, reminiscent of Scarlett O'Hara and Rhett Butler in *Gone with the Wind*."

"Sounds very romantic, you sly devil, you," Grandpa teased.

With a sudden faraway look in his eye, Sandals continued as if he hadn't heard the other man.

"When we finally came up for air, we were laughing so hard, it hurt. We stood hugging each other tighter than ever and never wanted to let go. I'll tell you this: it was the pinnacle moment of our relationship — and we had never been happier than at that moment. I still remember staring at each other as we came down from our high and returned to reality.

"Turning our attention back to our son, he was gone. He must've left the room while we were at it. We thought nothing of it because Bronson was probably playing hide-and-seek as he always did while the house was under construction. So, we went to check the playroom, his usual hiding place. I tip-toed towards his room, ready to pounce and wrestle him to the ground. But there was no Bronson to be found.

"Grandpa, do you know the feeling when you just know something's wrong? Your brain takes over, and suddenly, you panic as your nervous system floods your belly with acid, forcing you to feel it churning inside you.

The grandpa stopped mid-chew as his stomach tightened, unable to speak as the other man continued.

"At that moment, I walked by a window and saw something that should have buckled me to my knees. Instead, I became a blur as my legs torpedoed me outside with my wife a fraction of a blur behind me.

"There it was, the most expensive swimming pool gate money could buy, with every safety feature imaginable — and it was propped wide open. I unlocked it earlier to make delivering our outdoor pool furniture easier and intended to close it before Bronson and my bride's arrival time. But they came early, and my excitement erased all thought of closing the gate. Hide-and-seek was over – we found him. The dichotomy of that moment split our psyches in two as we both saw Bronson's lifeless body at the bottom of the pool."

Grandpa sat in stunned silence, his back and bottom plastered to the sticky cushioned booth. Tears welled in his eyes.

"Just moments before, we were Rhett Butler and Scarlett O'Hara." His head dropped as his words turned silent, hair covering his face once again.

Grandpa reached out with a comforting grip. "You don't have to continue; I'm so sorry."

"Nope, you're wrong; I need to. We need to finish what we start; isn't that what we teach our kids? It's what I wanted to teach Bronson."

Grandpa was astonished at his resolve as he witnessed Sandals lift his head and part the curtains of his hair to continue.

"We fell to our knees in horror. I crawled toward the pool, falling over the edge and swimming as fast as my pain would allow. I swooped him in my arms and returned to the surface, then tried mouth-to-mouth and pumping his stomach — but to no avail.

"Whenever something horrible occurs, the mind seeks reasons for the event so it can accurately place blame. Bronson's lifeless body lying on the concrete was not even what Danielle's mind remembered or focused on. Instead, the open gate — the gate *I* left open seared its way into every level of her conscious and subconscious mind. My lawyer brain responded by coldly reasoning with the jury that if she had come to the house at the appointed time, the damn gate would have been closed — and our son's lifeless body wouldn't have been at the bottom of the pool.

"With those two contradictory sparks of thought simultaneously festering in our minds, it was the beginning of the end for us, the spiral down to nothingness. I lost everything important to my life that day. — But hey, silver lining — I'm here with you, partaking in the ingenious invention of red velvet pancakes."

Grandpa sat wordless, unable to produce a snappy comeback for the first time ever. He literally didn't know what to say in the face of such absolute misfortune. He sat sullenly, blinking randomly to dispel his tears, and focused his obscured vision toward the table.

After an eternal minute, Sandal's voice broke the horrid silence. "You were supposed to say — 'You bet your ass they are!'"

Grandpa looked up at him, startled. But after a moment, he realized that Sandals had just had a monumental breakthrough, and they laughed hard—the kind of laughter that garnered eyes from around the IHOP to gaze their way. Sandals, who never thought he would laugh again, laughed at the oddest moment he could imagine. In their ironic laughter, they found a common bond.

Coming down from their elation, Sandals felt compelled to continue the story. "The brain is a funny creature," Sandals said as he cut into his cakes. "Maybe it's just my own man-guilt, but I often think Bronson would still be here if it weren't for my selfishly wanting to see Danielle in a bikini so badly. And now, the punishment for my thought crime was diving into the pool that day to scrape our son from the bottom. It was the first and last time the pool was ever used. And believe it or not, trying to plan a funeral for a three-year-old isn't as fun as it sounds."

Sandals paused at the irony of his statement, realizing Grandpa had influenced his use of irony to lighten the heaviness of his story as he continued.

"My wife fought me on any idea or suggestion, not only for the funeral but everyday life. I couldn't concentrate at work because of my struggles at home, and bringing those struggles to work doesn't make for a good workplace.

"Next, I tried my hand at God and turned to the church to help me through this while Danielle turned to the bottle to help her. But neither the altar nor the alcohol brought Bronson back. Within a year, Danielle was a full-blown alcoholic, and I was full-blown unemployed.

"So, we sold the house and made an enormous profit, even though someone died there. Grandpa, did you know you have to disclose if someone died at a property you're trying to sell? I didn't know that either — just another tidbit you learn when you're part of the 'Dead Kid Club Society of America.' Regardless, we made a handsome profit, and I split it with her. I gave her every piece of furniture and everything inside the house because I had no use for it. We each left the marriage with over a million dollars."

Grandpa felt hesitant but emboldened to continue. "So, when you said you wanted to be alone today because of the date — is it...?"

The long-haired man paused momentarily before conceding, "Yes — Bronson's birthday. For the past twenty-two years, I have religiously returned on this day to drive by the house at exactly 3:28 p.m., the time of my son's death, then visit his grave and say goodbye until next year. I was driving aimlessly around town, killing time, when my van died, and now, here we are. Should've been paying more attention to the gas gauge." He shrugged, grimacing mildly. "Anyway — every October 4th, I follow my heart and come to pay my respects and reflect on the life that could have been." He looked at his watch. "Thanks to you, I won't miss out this year either."

Grandpa wanted to reach across the table and take the man's hand as a sign of friendship, but he kept it at his side, twitching. "That's... Wow, I'm so sorry."

"When I think about what Bronson's future would have been, my soul aches. Can you imagine going through life with the name Bronson? I loved that name. It was a powerful C.E.O. kind of name — and he would have grown up as a man's man, a friend to all, a gentle soul, yet strong.

"I was going to teach him things like how to treat women with respect and lead by example in the way I loved that redhead of mine. I also wanted to make him earn his way through this world; just because his dad had money didn't mean he had money. I worked for every penny, and he would do the same. I wanted to teach him so many things by example in an inspirational, caring, and loving way. He was genuinely going to be something.

"But now, here I am, twenty-two years later, just waiting to die so I can see the man he has become in Heaven."

Grandpa was in awe of Sandals' perspective of what and how he wanted to teach his son – which reflected much of his own intentions for his new granddaughter. But the long-haired stranger had said something else that caught his attention. Grandpa felt compelled to try and channel his inner Tony Robbins.

He wanted desperately to reach the sandaled man's eternal wound by repeating it to him from a different perspective. Besides, what good was it to listen to hours of motivational speakers if he never got to share it?

"Sandals, that was such a beautiful testament to Bronson — but you said something that caught my ear. Could I explore something here with you?"

Sandals became slightly nervous because Grandpa's tone had become more serious. He knew what was coming next and needed to nip it in the bud.

"Listen, Grandpa, people have tried to give me advice for years. No offense, but I really don't want to hear anymore."

"I know that's true; I can't imagine how true that is or how many times you've gone through this. But please, I'm too emotionally invested in you to not say something. I beg you to indulge me. Not to make this about me, but I've been really into listening to motivational speakers lately; in fact, I was listening to my favorite, Tony Robbins, when I saw you today.

"But I never get to apply anything I've learned with my family because they make fun of me for my rose-colored views these days. But this comes from a loving place, and I promise you can join everyone in making fun of me when I'm through — but my friend — I need to try."

The Jesus-looking man did not want to go through another version of this again. But even with all he'd been through, he felt sorry for Grandpa, like a three-legged dog, because no one in his family would even listen to him.

"Okay, Grandpa — Your gung-ho spirit gives me no choice but to give in. But no promises about any of this," and he gave the man-nod to the gentle grandpa to proceed.

"Thanks, my friend. I want to say you won't regret this, but we both know that may not be true," he said jokingly before he mustered the courage to begin. "First of all, can I ask your real name?"

"You would have to start with that...."

Sandals closed his eyes, placed his clasped fists against his forehead, and lowered his head to a thinking position. After a minute or so of deep contemplation, his head lifted, and his piercing stare grabbed Grandpa.

"My name died the day Bronson died," he stated frankly. "I lost everything, including my identity. Now, it's just easier to go by the name Sandals because they've provided me with the only identity I've needed. I don't think I've said my given name aloud in over twenty years."

A silence fell between the men. Grandpa patiently waited with a loving look for Sandals to decide. After a time, he gently prodded, "But you do remember it, don't you?"

The Jesus Impersonator smiled. "I can see why the manager called you his favorite grandpa. You have a way with people, and Grandpa really fits your identity, and I bet your granddaughter really loves you."

"Well, I really love *her*."

"You're also patient and kind and the only person to give me a hand today. Some people slowed down but then kept going, probably because of my long hair. I guess my appearance scared them away."

"Truthfully, I don't think it was the long hair as much as the scowl on your face that scared people away. I think you use it like a shield to keep people from entering your life, even if they want to help you. I was even afraid at first and had to back up a few feet before I asked if you needed gas."

Sandals looked at him. "*But you didn't back up and leave.*" Then, with a long pause and a deep breath, the improbable happened.

"Darius — My name is...Darius."

It was a significant moment for him. First, trusting someone with his story and now his name. Grandpa placed his hands over his heart, thankful for finally earning his confidence.

"Darius... Now that's a great name. Did you know the English translation means 'rich and kingly,' and another meaning is 'He holds firm to good'? I did a lot of research when picking names for my four kids, and Darius was a name I really loved. Thanks for trusting me with it, and I will never let you down now, or if our paths should ever cross again."

"So, what's your name, Grandpa?"

"You know, it's funny, but when I'm here, everyone calls me Grandpa, but I'm usually here by myself or with my granddaughter. I was just thinking how much I've enjoyed you calling me *Grandpa*. In fact, I want everyone to call me that from here on out." Then, with a dramatic pause, "So Let It Be Written, So Let It Be Done."

"Then, Sir Grandpa, it is," acknowledged Darius. — Well, I think Tony Robbins is working pretty well for you so far."

"Can I record you saying that so I can play it for my wife and kids?"

They chuckled, "It'd be a waste of time because my voice won't record anyway." Sandals replied with a straight face.

"Is that one of your superpowers," Grandpa clapped back.

"Yeah — something like that..." Darius said with a mysterious undertone.

Odd — Grandpa thought before becoming more serious as he began.

"I want to ask you something about a statement you made a few minutes ago?"

Once again, he gave the *Robbins* wannabe the silent man-nod of approval.

"You said you're waiting to die so you can see the man Bronson has become in Heaven, did you not?"

Darius nodded again while staring in quiet contemplation.

"So, when you see the man he's become in Heaven, won't he also see the man you became on Earth?"

A long pause followed.

"How do you think he's going to feel about what you did with your life? Will he be proud of you? Or will he have horrible guilt that you never again experienced happiness because of him?

"Darius, I know that if I died in some sort of accident, I would never want my kids to ruin their lives over it, even if it's their fault. I couldn't rest in Heaven knowing that they decided to destroy their lives in my honor. I would want the complete opposite, and I suspect you would too. So why shouldn't that philosophy apply on the flipside as well?

"I know without a shadow of a doubt that if something horrible happened to one of my kids and I was somehow involved, as hard as it would be, I would try to live the rest of my life by doing well and helping others in their name. And most importantly — I would strive every day to be happy because that's how you honor their lives, by living yours."

Darius stared at him skeptically, almost knowingly, "That's easy enough for *you* to say. It hasn't happened to you — *yet.*"

Yet??? And for a second time, Grandpa thought something odd about his guest. But it didn't deter him from his mission.

"Okay, Darius, let me try this from another angle. Since I'm always accused of being a kid by my wife and kids, I'm going to use a childlike analogy to make a grown-up point. Fair warning, I'm going rogue, so don't blame Tony Robbins for what you are about to hear," he cautioned before getting more serious.

What if it's our job as their loved ones on Earth to help the newbie angels —Bronson, for example —earn his wings? Picture in your mind a beautiful mountain where all the angels practice flying. Their goal in Heaven is to reach the top so they can go on to the next level of angeldom and eventually become guardian angels.

"But the only way they can reach the top is by their loved ones on Earth helping them by being happy and doing for others in their honor. And as we do on Earth in their name, their wings grow in Heaven, and they can fly a little higher with each bit of goodness we do.

"Do you think Bronson likes hovering at the bottom of the mountain for the past twenty-two years while all the other angels pass him by? That's right, Dar. You heard me. All the other angels are passing him by while Bronson is stymied, hovering at the bottom of the hill. And all because you're not living your life; I bet he's not pleased about that at all!"

As he continued, Darius stared, wondering how a man could be so passionate.

"Dar! Listen to me! It's not too late. You must start living your life for Bronson so he can soar up, up, up the mountain — and beyond! He wants to be your guardian angel and help you and his mother, the loves of his life, find your happiness.

"Help him — help you... Help him — help you – to find your 'funny' again, and take away his guilt and the shackles that keep his wings from growing! You can do this by closing the pool gate in your mind, which has caused you all this pain for so many years. Then the gates of Heaven can open and flood you with the ability to forgive yourself and free Bronson of the guilt you've placed on him. You do not deserve the life you have chosen. Darius, I believe in you!"

With that, Grandpa closed his eyes, took a deep breath, and stepped down from his imaginary pulpit. When he opened them again, he saw that Darius had lowered his head, hands clasped before him, contemplating Grandpa's third-grade assessment of how Heaven works and his sermon on Bronson's angel training. But before Darius could respond, his thoughts were interrupted by a familiar voice that thwarted the silence.

"Well, it looks like Slim here won your little eating contest," Joyce said cheerily. "Here's your loser's trophy," and playfully tossed the bill in front of the larger man. "And to think how much money I would have lost if I had bet on you," she snickered as he handed her a rectangular piece of plastic to complete the loser's trophy purchase. Then she winked and disappeared, smiling.

"Grandpa, I don't know what to say exactly, but I want you to know I heard every word. In all my travels, I've never met anyone quite like you. I appreciate what you've done for me, both physically and emotionally. In my world, this is considered a great day."

The waitress returned and handed Grandpa his credit card. "Well, this is the part where I usually say it's been a pleasure serving you — come back — blah, blah, blah. But in this case, it's truly been more interesting and fun than usual."

"Okay, young lady, I know where this is going. Grab your pen, and let's get this over with — write in the amount of tip you want." Grandpa ordered.

Joyce laughed, as no one had ever asked her to do that. "Hope you got you some deep pockets there, buddy," she joked, playing along. Then wrote in $15 on a near $40 tab with an asterisk denoting *$10 for tip and $5 for punitive damages for putting up with him.*

Grandpa looked over the bill, and his face lit up with laughter. "Nice! A 40% tip, which includes punitive damages. I think I will have to consult with my attorney on this. Darius, could you look this over for me? I'm feeling rather insulted here. I think I caused way more than $5 in punitive damages. I'm not sure this lovely lady will ever be the same. Could you instruct the court to have her write in another amount?"

The waitress quickly grabbed the receipt and wrote $10 for punitive damages.

Grandpa looked at the bill and acted disgusted, then yelled, "Preposterous," and shook his head as he returned it to his lawyer. "What do you think? Is that even close to enough for punitive damages?"

Darius glanced at the slip of paper and then back at Grandpa, a bewildered look on his long face. But then, the inner lost lawyer from twenty-five years ago rose to the occasion. The long-haired man's posture went from relaxed, almost slouched, to straightened back and squared shoulders. And then spoke with a more profound, authoritative voice.

"Grandpa, I think we should settle this out of court," he opined. He held out his hand to the waitress. "Pen, please." She quickly obliged, and he crossed out her tip suggestion and wrote in a counteroffer. He returned the document to his client and asked if he accepted the settlement. Grandpa laughed and gave him two thumbs up.

What started as a fun jest became a marvel to watch as the waitress held back tears from the man's generosity and the uniqueness of the tip presentation as Darius cleared his throat and read the final agreement.

"Joyce, my client has agreed to offer you $10 in tip and $90 in punitive damages for having to tell this story repeatedly for the rest of your life. Do you accept the above-aforementioned settlement in case #00001a, I.H.O.P court docket #RVPancakes02c3? If so, initial here and here, next to the amounts denoted."

Darius then slid the initialed receipt for $137.32 to his client and asked him to sign the document, hand it to the plaintiff, and keep a copy for his records. Joyce hugged the men and profusely thanked them for the joy they had given her and the over-abundant settlement tip. The two men said goodbye to the manager, Sid, and walked out to the fully-tanked white cargo van.

"Darius, it has been an honor to be a part in helping you laugh and hopefully continue to find your funny again. Would you mind if I... gave you my phone number? You know, just in case you needed something, wanted to talk, or possibly laugh some more?"

"Grandpa, I would, but I don't have a cell phone. I haven't needed one for years now. It's just a constant reminder that I have no one to talk to and no one who needs me. On the open road, I prefer doing things old-school; it's actually rather cathartic. Besides, you've done enough."

Grandpa reached for his shoulder with an understanding pat.

"Are you headed to the house and gravesite now?" Grandpa could tell the answer by the look in his eyes. Darius took out his keys.

"Wait! Before you leave, I just have to ask you something, which may seem crazy...."

"Crazier than paying almost $140 for breakfast?"

Grandpa laughed. "Not *that* crazy! But as my attorney, doesn't our afternoon fall under the privy of extenuating circumstances? Which is what I want to ask you about. Seeing you negotiate my tab in there was amazing. I'm not sure what it would take to re-establish your law license, but have you ever considered it? Maybe you could contact your old law firm to see if they would be willing to help. Perhaps they would finance you through school to help make you whole again — Bronson would want this for you. I think you know that now."

Darius slowly nodded in agreement. "You've given me a lot to think about, but I'm not sure about contacting my old law firm. It didn't end well when they fired me; I'm not sure they would ever consider helping me. You really can't comprehend what it's like being a member of the Dead Kids Club Society. The unwritten by-law states that when your parents die, you're an orphan; when your spouse dies, you're a widow or widower; but when your child dies, you are nothing — or at least that's how you feel. No one knows what to say; everyone thinks they have to walk on eggshells, and it's uncomfortable for everyone. I deserved to be let go."

It was Grandpa's turn to nod as he responded. "Dar, I understand what you're saying, and I realize I'm not a member of the Dead Kids Club Society, but what I do know, without a doubt, is that everyone loves a good comeback story. And everyone wants to be a part of one, especially one twenty-two years in the making. As humans, we all love to help someone who wants to redeem themselves. Life is all about redemption, which is why I think this has a compassionate chance to work for you if you try.

"Listen to me closely; the situation is different now. It's been twenty-two years since they let you go, and I bet many of those people have lived with terrible guilt over this. Trust me, it will be a healing force for them to see you back on your feet."

A long pause ensued as the two men looked at each other. Then, to complete the non-verbal conversation, both gave a respectful man-nod. With that, Darius got into his van and rolled down the window.

"Okay, Grandpa, to the mountaintop – and beyond!"

"To the mountaintop times two!" his counterpart echoed.

"Grandpa, I gotta admit, I think Mr. Robbins would be proud of you because this was not the worst advice I've ever heard."

"Would you *please* follow me home and tell my family what you said." Grandpa pleaded.

The two men chuckled, then fist-bumped and exploded hands.

"I hope this is a wonderful year for you, my friend; maybe I'll see you next year when you come back for Bronson's anniversary?"

Darius didn't respond. Instead, his whole demeanor seemed to shift. The man who smiled just a sentence ago was now intensely silent, looking straight ahead and contemplating everything. Moments later, he turned toward the grandpa with the same piercing look that started their relationship.

"Grandpa, do you really believe what you said? Do you truly think you could be happy in life if you played a part in killing one of your kids?"

With all the seriousness Grandpa could muster, he grabbed Darius by the wrists through the window and gazed intently into his eyes —

"Absolutely, unequivocally, I would. There is no other choice for me. No one likes a hypocrite. How can I say I would want my kids to be happy if something happened to me by accident if I couldn't return the favor?"

Darius looked straight into his eyes, quickly reversed hand positions, and grabbed his wrists. With a slow, eerie voice, he responded. "Okay, Grandpa.... We'll see — Won't WE?"

Grandpa didn't know what to make of his statement — *"We'll see, won't we?" — About what?* He was left unnerved but didn't want to derail what he had accomplished with Darius and brushed it off before his thoughts were interrupted.

"Grandpa, (this time using his normal voice — his kind voice) I want to thank you for everything you did for me today; like I said, this was a good day in my world."

"My friend, I'll be thinking about you as you visit your Bronson. Maybe our paths will cross again, but until then, I wish you all the best."

With that, the van drove away slowly.

Grandpa stood there, pondering the encounter, his emotions wide, confused. But in the end, he hoped he had done some good in this soul's tragic life. He looked down the street for one last glimpse of the van that started this adventure — but it was nowhere in sight.

The final image of the flashback unfolding on the dreamer's stage froze on the empty street as the majestic curtains swept closed. Tony Robbins turned toward Grandpa for his response.

"Darius... what a kind but sad man he was, and what a conversation we had. But now that we've relived it over again, I kind of see why maybe I've unconsciously tried to forget it. The way it ended kind of scared me. But now, I also realize its beauty and importance because it triggered something inside me to handwrite a letter to my granddaughter.

"I wasn't sure why until now, but what happened to his son and how he spoke about what he wanted to teach him made me want to do the same for Addison if something ever happened to me. I knew my intuition was telling me something!"

"Wow! There's a lot to unpack here," replied the Dreamatologist Tony Robbins as the majestic red velvet curtains swept open again, revealing an elegant but intimate interview setting.

Suddenly, fog *whooshed* them out of the auditorium seats and onto the stage, where spotlights highlighted each man sitting in lavish chairs opposite each other. In contrast, the rest of the stage remained dark as Tony seamlessly continued.

"You're right. Darius profoundly affected your life and inspired you to write your letter to Addison. But there's more to the encounter than just that. Do you know the real reason I brought you back to this encounter? It's because this is the day that changed your identity."

"Changed my identity?" questioned Grandpa. "How did it do that?"

"Well, let's think about it. We both experienced the same encounter as we watched it together. But the first thing that came to you was that this conversation gave you the inspiration, nestled within your intuition, to write a beautiful letter to your granddaughter Addison — But why is that? Why did you feel the need to write this letter? Haven't you experienced hundreds, even thousands, of conversations throughout your lifetime? Did you feel the need to write a letter after every conversation? Probably not. However, this encounter affected you differently because you were in a highly emotional state from experiencing Darius's story. Notice — I didn't say *listening* to Darius — I said *experiencing* Darius."

Grandpa stared, contemplating. "I never thought of it that way. But what's the difference?"

"The difference is that when you were in a highly emotional state, your whole physiology became involved. Darius's story became a part of you, thus creating an experience so powerful that when reliving it, even in a dream, the letter was the first thing that came to your mind.

"That letter hovered in your nervous system as a part of you for years. Then, one day, there was an emotional stirring so powerful that the words flowed from your heart flawlessly, creating a dynamic experience in itself. Writing it happened quickly because your subconscious had that letter cocked word for word, ready to shoot out onto the paper. So, how did all this happen? Let's analyze this, shall we?

"Recall when you and 'Sandals' first walked into the restaurant and how the manager greeted you with excitement. 'There's my favorite grandpa!' he said. So, when the manager associated the words 'favorite' with 'grandpa,' this created a positive anchor for you, and being recognized as the manager's 'favorite grandpa' in front of Sandals gave you a sense of personal pride."

"O-k-a-y..." the older man responded, anticipating where this was going.

"Once you and Sandals sat down and got acquainted, the conversation transformed from 'stuff' to 'story,' and so did the man as his scowl removed itself. The magical effects of red velvet pancakes also persuaded Sandals to open his heart, and you felt his pain.

"When Sandals talked about how he wanted to teach Bronson to become a man's man through example, you clung to his every word. That was when the letter began writing itself in your nervous system. Until that moment, you only saw yourself as a grandpa because, technically, that's what you became when your daughter-in-law gave birth to your first grandchild. But your new idea of self wasn't solidified until Sandals acknowledged you and said, 'I can see why the manager called you his favorite grandpa. You have a way with people, and *Grandpa really fits your identity, and I bet your granddaughter really loves you.'– That's* when things changed.

"A few short minutes later, he transformed from Sandals to Darius right before your eyes. It was his trust in your 'grandpa' identity that led him to share his real name. And in that instant, you likewise went from being a grandpa because your son had a baby to actually being 'Grandpa' as your main identity.

"Didn't you go home right after and tell your family and friends to start calling you Grandpa? Darius's story inspired you to write a letter to Addison from the perspective of your new 'Grandpa' identity, wanting to teach her life lessons you felt were important. Darius cemented your identity that day from being just a grandpa to being 'Grandpa.' You could say you re-created Darius, and in turn, Darius re-created *you*."

"Okay, now for the hard part, my friend. The nuts and bolts of the purpose for the encounter with Darius. I won't sugarcoat this, even if I am just your guest Dreamatologist here. My mission is to move you past the fragile mindset you are experiencing outside this dream world into a more powerful and productive state of mind. And I want to accomplish this now!"

Tony's secretary entered the scene and handed the two men transcripts of Grandpa and Darius's conversation. The "guest" glanced at the paper in his hands, and his heart filled with panic.

"Mr. Robbins—"

"*Tony*. Please, call me Tony."

"Tony... I'm not comfortable with this. It's not right that you keep referring to me as Grandpa. Addison is dead. Referring to me as such fills my soul with too much pain and guilt. Please, please, stop referring to me as Grandpa!"

"Listen here, my friend!" Tony said sharply, "You *are* a grandpa, and you will always *be* one. The death of a child doesn't make you cease being a grandparent. Think of Addison in Heaven. Is she now nothing? Suddenly, she doesn't have a grandpa because you decided this for her. You will always be connected to Addison; telling yourself otherwise will only increase your pain.

"Let me remind you what I quoted you when this dream sequence began: '*There are going to be storms in life, horrible, terrible storms, and we have to face them.*' Your words to Addison. In this next exercise, I'm going to ask you to apply the very lesson you were teaching Addison to yourself, to face the storms of life in order to get past them. You don't want to be a hypocrite, do you? You can't ask Addison to face these storms if you're unwilling to do the same. Now, turn to the first page of your transcript. I've bolded the important parts we need to focus on for your convenience. Please read the first few lines."

Grandpa shook as he began to silently read the words that felt like razor blades to his soul.

"*Out loud*, please, for our studio audience," insisted Tony Robbins.

The man looked into the auditorium but only saw rows of empty seats; however, he could hear the stirring of a silent audience in anticipation of him reading the transcript. So, he did as instructed, his voice quivering.

"Darius, you said you're waiting to die so you can see the man Bronson has become in Heaven, did you not?

"So, when you see the man he's become in Heaven, won't he also see the man you became on Earth? How do you think he's going to feel about what you did with your life? Will he be proud of you? Or will he have horrible guilt that you never again experienced happiness because of him?"

Grandpa's soul felt defeated by the first few statements as Tony spoke up.

"I know this is unbearable for you, but you must face this here and now. If you don't, you might find yourself twenty-two years later in your own van. You must take action now to avoid years of living life waiting to die. These are your words to Darius to get him to reclaim his life. So, pretend Darius is talking to *future you* twenty-two years from now. His first few questions will be: *What will you say to Addison someday? What kind of man is she going to meet in Heaven? Is she going to be riddled with guilt because you gave up living your life in her name? What will she think about what you've done with your life?* The answers depend on your choices when you wake from this dream cocoon you are experiencing.

"Let me tell you something — the outside *you* is not doing well. You would like to commit suicide but have been taught it is a sin. Nevertheless, you've been trying to get yourself killed by playing semantics, pretending you're taking the moral high ground by not officially taking your own life. But death is death, and you're putting yourself in harm's way, seeking out dangerous situations to try and get killed. This referendum on death is not an honorable act, my friend. You think Addison will be so welcoming, knowing you deprived your wife and family of their husband and dad?"

Guilt consumed Grandpa even more. He opened his mouth to speak but found no words. "Her dad, your son Evan, will need you, even though he doesn't realize it yet. Your actions now are going to determine his actions later. Do you think your death is going to better their world? No! Your death is going to cause your son so much guilt. In addition to working through the grief of losing his daughter, he must have the chance to forgive you in the future to rid himself of all his pent-up anger. But if he never has the chance to have closure with you because you 'semantically' took your own life, he'll find his own way to 'semantically' ruin his life in your name. Is that what you want?

"I believe people come into our lives for a reason. Let's discover the reason Darius appeared in yours. I believe he is here to give you a gift by showing you the consequences of the choice you are about to make. Let's analyze your conversation and the advice given to Darius...Shall we?"

"Please, I know what you're trying to do, Tony, but I can't read this anymore. It's too painful. I beg you to stop — please stop!"

The Dreamatologist was unwavering and determined to get through to Grandpa by pushing him to expand his emotional boundaries by facing his own words.

"You *must* read this. This moment is a matter of life and death. We're talking about *your* life and *your* death, even if it turns out not to be your physical death but the death of your emotions. Whether your soul thrives by having something to live for, or you choose a meaningless existence of meandering the rest of your days waiting to die, you'll ultimately face Addison.

"The destiny of our lives depends on our decisions, and this is the most crucial decision you will ever make. Your life and the lives of your wife and kids hang in the balance of what decision you'll make once you wake up. The man outside this dream is in no condition to make good decisions. That's why we're here now: to thwart that possibility by improving his odds.

"Read the words... NOW! The only way to get through Hell is to keep going through it. Besides, there are no devils in Hell. They're all here on Earth, recruiting souls by making them think they can play semantics with their lives and win. Now read it!"

Grandpa's hands trembled as he picked up the transcript, the psychic razor blades once again poised to shred his soul as he began:

"Darius, I know that if I died in some sort of accident, I would never want my kids to ruin their lives over it, even if it's their fault. I couldn't rest in Heaven knowing that they decided to destroy their lives in my honor. I would want the complete opposite, and I suspect you would too. So why shouldn't that philosophy apply on the flipside as well?

"I know without a shadow of a doubt that if something horrible happened to one of my kids and I was somehow involved, as hard as it would be, I would try to live the rest of my life by doing well and helping others in their name. And most importantly — I would

strive every day to be happy because that's how you honor their lives, by living yours."

Grandpa wept as he finished, and Tony spoke to him in a soothing voice.
"These certainly don't sound like the reassuring words of a man trying to kill himself. These are your words, spoken with absolute conviction about what you would do in his circumstance. I know you believed every word when you said them, so what has changed, besides everything, since you last told them?
"Addison wants these words for you. She wants to watch you be happy until the time comes when you will be together again. My friend, while you are in this intense emotional state with me here, you must confront these words and accept them. You must relive them, believe them, and make them resonate in your nervous system until they become part of your physiology. Isn't it through our actions that we prove commitment to our words? So, read these last few lines and believe them. Let them into your heart so they can take hold. Please, do it now."

"Grandpa, do you really believe what you said? Do you truly think you could be happy in life if you played a part in killing one of your kids?"

"Absolutely, unequivocally, I would. There is no other choice for me. No one likes a hypocrite. How can I say I would want my kids to be happy if something happened to me by accident if I couldn't return the favor?"

"Okay, Grandpa.... We'll see — Won't WE...?"

Tony Robbins began to clap as he witnessed Grandpa break through his barriers, and there seemed to be a round of applause from the invisible audience as well.
"Good job! You made it! And yes, You *Will* see — *Won't* you? From now on, you won't allow yourself to be a hypocrite, and you'll accept the challenge Darius presents. Now tell me, what choice will you make when you awake?"
This time, when he spoke, Grandpa shifted away from his scared state. He attacked the words with intensity and conviction: "I'm going to choose to live! It will be hard, but I will somehow work through my grief and try to

be happy. I will do this knowing I am making Addison happy and sending her to the mountaintop — and beyond!"

"You have come a long way, my friend. But now it's time for one final act. And as tough as that was, this will be tougher."

Grandpa's heart skipped a beat. "Wait! I thought we were finished! I learned my lesson!"

"People learn lessons all the time; they just never apply them. It's the application of a lesson that makes it useful; that's why we must test your conviction outside this dream world by having you relive your darkest journey, where every minute, every second, will be a battle for your soul," explained Tony Robbins calmly.

"This time, you will have a new perspective. You must apply what you have learned about yourself and your capabilities — but there is one caveat. No matter what happens, you must not wake up from your dream because, if that happens, depending on your emotional state, you may spiral back into a darker state of mind.

"That's why we need to analyze your emotional state before sending you back to the real world. If you happen to wake up while you are in this current emotional state, you will be fine. But if you wake up from your dream state in a darker state of mind before we can analyze what happened, you may go back to making a horrible decision, undermining everything we accomplished tonight.

Tony stood, and Grandpa did the same. He reached out to shake his hand.

"I believe in you, Grandpa, and I know Addison does as well, but for now, my time here as your Dreamatologist is complete. During your dreams, you have proven to yourself and to me that you have the tools and wisdom to make good decisions. But your inner self is in mortal conflict with your outer self, who sincerely wants to die. My friend, the following sequence is where the rubber meets the road, and in your case, literally.

Without warning, there was a *swooshing* sound as the fog whisked Tony Robbins away. Grandpa was now back in the theater seats, alone, with a bird's eye view of the dreamer's stage. Without Tony by his side, he found himself in a state of panic and yelled, "No, stop the curtains! I can't do this right now without Tony!" He yelled louder, "STOP THE CURTAINS!"

But his words had no effect as the majestic curtains swept open, revealing a title on the movie screen that read —

RIDING TOWARD THE DARKSIDE.

Suddenly, Grandpa was watching himself on the theater screen from his seat while simultaneously on his bicycle saddle as the Dedaccai racing bike's front wheel was determined to cut through the pouring rainwater. He felt every bump echo through his wrists as the cracked roughness of the concrete did not make the emotional journey any easier on the aging cyclist's battered body.

Pedal strokes per minute averaged 80 revolutions as the cyclist looked down at his GPS early in his solitary endeavor. This experience was new for him, as he had never ridden in the rain nor seen the darkness while seated on a bicycle. The loneliness of his venture allowed his mind to orchestrate a concerto of emotions composed from the constant barrage of sights and sounds compiled from the night.

By mile 7.8 on the GPS, there had not been one close call, as the pounding rain forced the few cars out that time of night to drive at a much slower pace. No one had even come close to completing his objective of being run off the road and ending his life.

The mental hell he experienced slowly matched his physical hell. The rough roads were a continuous reminder of the beating his son had initiated only hours earlier. With every pedal stroke, he relived each defibrillator charge, each word of his broken son's vocabulary, and each hate-filled punch to his physical body. He saw the look on his wife's face and felt the emotional trauma he caused her as he relived the slap in slow-motion that must have been the defining end to their love story. He saw Addison's beautiful face, silent and still, as death would no longer allow her beautiful smile to grace the planet.

As he passed the 22.3-mile marker on the GPS, a huge splash from the fastest mass of automotive metal so far nearly knocked him off his bike. The considerable spray served as his first drink of the evening. *I've tasted better,* his mind retorted, and he reached for a drink to wash the foul taste from his mouth, but the water bottle had been knocked loose from its cage. "Really? – no water!" In frustration, he began berating traffic. "What in the hell is wrong with you idiots!? Come on! Someone has to be texting and drinking."

He felt the continual dousing of rainwater from the rooster tail produced by his rear wheel as it lashed a north-south stripe on his back with each revolution. Keeping his gloves from slipping off the handlebar tape proved harder and harder, particularly when large cracks in the pavement jolted his grip without warning.

Mile after mile, he continued hoping someone would thrust him into the afterlife with their careless driving. *No lights– No reflectors– No problem,* was the mantra that swirled in his brain.

"What does a guy have to do to get hit around here?!" he yelled, annoyed that everyone drove white-knuckled in the rainstorm while paying attention to every inch of the road.

His legs continued to produce the constant squishing noises rubbing against the bike's seat as he passed the 25.4-mile marker per the GPS. He reached for his bottle out of habit but remembered it was gone, so he attempted to drink the rainwater falling from the sky instead.

A few miles later, the sudden rumbling in his stomach reminded him that his dinner from earlier was not sufficient for the mission he had chosen. His 15-mile-an-hour pace put him two hours into his fatigued mental journey. *Why the hell can't I die? People do it all the time! What is wrong with people? Is everyone suddenly a perfect driver now?*

He looked at the GPS, and it read precisely 30 miles. *What are the odds?* Experience had taught him that 30 miles was when he typically needed to refuel his rather large 'gas tank' with sustenance. He had ridden 50 miles before without eating but usually became very lightheaded and sick — which is why he never thought he would become a 50-mile Riding-Roulette survivor, especially in this weather.

He was already amazed and disappointed that at 30 miles, he had not experienced one close encounter with a metal fender. So far, the best anyone had offered him was a last-minute swerve, some elongated horn honks, and a few poetic anecdotes telling him precisely what they thought of his late-night voyage.

But then, as if these thoughts had tempted the Fates — *whoosh!* — a huge 4-wheel-drive truck came barreling from behind, and the sizeable wake sent the cyclist flying into the grass. He lay there on his back with the Dedacciai bike on top of him, his heartbeat significantly ramped up from the rush. For a brief second, his mind fogged and disoriented; he wondered if he had succeeded in his quest. But to no avail. He was pretty sure Heaven was more rainbows and unicorns than the wet, muddy grass where he found himself.

He pushed the bike away and started to rise but was so tired he laid back in the grass.

"Okay, five minutes," Grandpa decided. "*I can allow five minutes to gather myself.*"

But without having to concentrate on riding, his already horrible visions decided to amp themselves up to high definition in his mind. "Nope, *nope*," the old man said, changing his mind.

He forced himself to his feet and mounted the Dedacciai again, hoping the ride would lessen the visions back to their normal level of Hell. It worked for a while, but then it happened; at mile marker 35.8, a new image began to enter his thoughts — one unlike the constant barrage of hellish moments repeated continually up to this point.

At first, it was just a brief flash — *Addison smiling at him with outstretched arms* — but then the highlight reel from Hell returned. At mile 39.2, the image of Addison reaching for her papa reappeared; this time, it lingered in his mind a bit longer. He heard her giggle as he had on hundreds of occasions. With every pedal stroke, the letter to Addison rewrote itself in his mind as the original cruel montage played less and less until he finally visualized himself sitting with Addison, reading his finished letter to her....

This has to be a hallucination, Grandpa reasoned. *Or is God taunting my spirit with mercy before a steel bumper runs over me with thousands of pounds of heavy metal?*

The hallucination, or whatever it was, only grew stronger and more vivid, threatening to replace the reality of the rain-soaked night altogether. His pedal strokes, which now totaled 12,408, according to the GPS, increased in speed and wattage as if in hot pursuit. The cyclist tried attaching sensible thoughts to a nonsensical situation, attempting to decode the visions of Addison and her pure, gentle smile. Was he simply suffering from dehydration even though rivers and lakes were filling by the minute from the torrential rain?

But then he ceased, not wanting to reason this lovely vision away. He preferred it — it was what his soul longed for. And he raced even harder toward the phantom Addison, smiling at him with outstretched arms. The cyclist yelled, "I'm coming, Addison! I'll be with you soon!"

And then it happened — he went flying over the curb as a metal fender came out of nowhere and seemingly ran him off the road purposefully. The GPS read 50.4 miles as he screamed out one last time — "*Addison!*"

His body surged from 0 to 60 into an upright, sitting position as the hotel walls absorbed his screams of pain from the jolt. Grandpa fell back into his horizontal position, waiting for his throbbing heart to slow, and was covered in a cold sweat. He lay there, gasping for breath, totally confused about all that had happened to him.

He closed his eyes, yet underneath his eyelids were quickly fading dream fragments still swirling in his mind. He remembered a traffic jam and the taste of red velvet pancakes and questioned if he had shared them with Jesus. He saw Tony Robbins interviewing him and felt upset and scared by the conversation. He felt water splash against his body and saw Addison's face smiling before flying in the air, which brought him full circle as the dreadful events of last night bullied their way to the front of his mental food chain.

He instantly knew he was back to hard reality, where Addison was dead, and his money, clothes, and bicycle were stolen. He wanted to call the front desk and get answers to the madness within but didn't want to draw attention to himself. Surely, hotel security would ask questions about who he was and where he last saw his belongings. But even worse, they'd try to contact his wife and family, the last thing he needed.

The overwhelming experience of reliving Addison's death propelled his despair over the threshold to where he left off in his quest to get himself killed. But now, his thirst to die soared to its highest peak, and his internal pain made the dreaded decision to abandon his search for an accidental death and actually take his own life.

This–Was–Happening! Suddenly, the battered man stood and found himself staring again at the near-naked monster reflecting in the bathroom mirror. "How do I get rid of you?"

He closed his eyes to think for a second, and when he re-opened them, he noticed a prescription bottle on the counter beside an empty drinking glass. *Strange —those weren't there earlier,* and with a weird sense of gratitude, he wanted to know if they were from God or the Devil so he could thank them.

He filled the drinking glass with water, closed his eyes, and simply opened the orange container and swallowed what Heaven or Hell left for him. In the game of Prescription Roulette, the by-laws state that what kind of pills, how many, or what size milligrams are no longer your concern as they wash down your throat.

His emotions began bouncing around like a microwave popcorn bag ready to burst, causing his hand to shake wildly. Yet, he was unable to put down the glass. Suddenly, in an urgent sense of release, he smashed the glass on the countertop and stared intensely at the monster in the mirror before closing his eyes again.

He felt a sudden warmth on his wrist that jilted his eyes back open. Dark red reflected from the countertop and off the glass wreckage. He turned his wrist upright, saw a sizable gash, and grabbed a hand towel to curb the flow. But the emotions that caused the breakage furthered a message of curiosity as he sifted through the rubble for a potential weapon, found the largest and sharpest piece, and taunted himself to finish the job.

He filled the bathtub, turned off the light, and closed the door. In the shadows, the darkest cry of his life fell from the deepest part of him as he slowly lowered his nakedness into the warm water. Why he did this, he didn't know. Maybe it was an illogical response to a subconscious desire to recreate a movie scene worthy of his gasps of pain that echoed off the unseen walls.

Then, the fog of war in his addled mind initiated the final battle for his soul. It came down to a series of theological questions as he placed the sharpest point of glass at his wrist. Was there a heaven or a hell for him? — Or was he already in hell, and this final act the entrance fee into Heaven where he would reunite with Addison? — Or did the atheists win altogether, and there was only the darkness of nothingness? — Or worse, was it the entrance fee to something far more sinister?

As he pressured the glass weapon against his wrist, he asked himself one last time. Would he see Addison in Heaven or experience something far more sinister?

It was in the blackness of that moment that his faith, which had been the guardian of his soul, lost to the dark and was buried as strands of blood twisted in the water.

As blood accumulated on his wrist, he grew cold, although immersed in 112° molecular warmth. His mind numbed as it rebelled against the razor-sharp pain. He groped in the dark and wondered if his amateur attempt went deep enough or far enough or if he had simply created a glorified flesh wound worthy of a hefty bandage? If not, would the pills do their job?

He then experienced a sick sense of relief as he accepted the inevitable possibility that one way or the other, his inaugural attempt may have succeeded. Soon, his sense of self-awareness faded toward an empty void of blackness.

Chapter Six

Kimmee James Attwood

~~~

There she is, Kimmee James Attwood, experiencing first-hand what the streets of downtown Austin, Texas, felt like while on an invigorating early morning bicycle ride. With each crack and crevice, adrenaline surged through her wrists as she traversed the streets rich in history for the first time that brisk Wednesday morning in October.

Her accomplice in this endeavor was a brand-new $12,000 Project One Radioactive Pink Trek Madone bicycle she custom ordered from Mellow Johnny's bicycle shop, owned by one Lance Armstrong. Her inaugural ride was exhilarating, but even more exciting was knowing that today was the first day of the rest of her life as an exciting new career awaited her arrival.

And then it happened. On the horizon were the tentacles of light that would transform the darkness toward the lighter shades of the morning spectrum. Soon, the crest of the morning sun made its presence known with spectacular pageantry as the sciences of the sky had an incredible show to display for the female cyclist below. A few minutes later, the magical cast of characters revealed their theatrical prisms of color as a magnificent rainbow.

An astonishing arc stretched from one end of the land to the other. She felt blessed beyond belief because she knew it was a collaboration between her deceased father and the Creator of rainbows Himself.

Thanks, Daddy, for thinking of me today. Thank you for my new bike. Thank you for my life and for making it possible to start my new career in

Austin. Thank you! Thank you! Thank you! I love you so much, and thank you for letting me know you are with me today.

With the echo of gratefulness swirling in her mind, she continued to eye the rainbow from underneath her helmet as she watched the spectrum of colors eventually dissipate. It was time to head back to her new high-rise condominium in the 360 Tower, one of the finest residential buildings and the second tallest in Austin. It was located just across the street from Mellow Johnny's bicycle shop, where she rented a bicycle locker to store her new bike.

Mellow Johnny's had all the pleasantries that a five-star bicycle hotel could offer its guests, and she was sure her bicycle would make many new friends there. As her bicycle's guest, Kimmee would have access to the excellent Juan Pelota Café and Coffee Shop and clean showers. And not to mention another urbanite way to make life interesting for her as she began her new life of independence.

So why was living in Austin, Texas, so important? Kimberly James Attwood, her given name, was a twenty-four-year-old Dallas, Texas, transplant. Like her father, Kimmee had been riding bicycles most of her life. Her daddy's fanatical, fun nature and his love for cycling had been the most significant part of her life. From age two, she had watched every second of every minute of the Tour de France while sitting on her daddy's lap or by his side. Watching Lance Armstrong win all seven of his Tour de France titles from 1999 to 2005 was life-altering and some of her best years.

Her daddy even surprised her with a trip to Austin to ride in a LIVESTRONG event to raise money for cancer awareness. He also donated a significant amount, guaranteeing that Kimmee would meet her hero and icon, Lance Armstrong. Little did she know this meeting would affect her for the rest of her life.

The following Saturday, her daddy packed their bikes for an early morning ride around White Rock Lake in Dallas. Immediately, the crisp fresh air, the blueness of the water, the clean paved trails, and the lavish homes that kissed the water's edge became an integral part of Kimmee's soul. Experiencing the lake's beauty that morning changed her world and cemented her into becoming an avid cyclist. Their ride became an instant Saturday morning tradition and the most prized ritual of her life.

Kimmee was also incredibly loving and highly emotional. She had mesmerizing hazel-mint-green eyes, which she learned early on could get her out of almost any situation. Her parents knew it as well. Their little girl possessed spunk and vitality, mixed with a spoonful of villain, transforming her into one lovable rule-bender. To put it mildly, she was a loving handful to raise, and Mom and Dad kept an extra eye on her — always.

Kimmee's rule-bending skills became a force for good. As her emotions evolved, they transformed into the Robin Hood of her huge heart. But as she grew, her rule-bending skills developed one caveat — curiosity. She was curious about everything, and her parents swore she was Sherlock Holmes's cousin Shirley Holmes and would make detective by age ten.

Her eyes, coupled with her curiosity, allowed her to push the envelope further than most people. However, she knew when to stop; therefore, she didn't get into trouble at school or in life, and everyone loved her.

Although her daddy inspired her fun, playful, adventurous side with a passion for cycling and health consciousness, there was another side to Kimmee. This softer and more refined side also revolved around White Rock Lake. An outdoor amphitheater and the Dallas Arboretum and Botanical Garden, all located at the lake, served as her mom's special times with her.

Arts festivals of all varieties provided Kimmee with an eclectic cultural side, which added to why she loved the great outdoors. Free concerts of all makes and models gave her a love for all genres of music. Her mother also provided her with an ideal role model of a loving wife. What her parents taught her blessed her beyond measure. She had a perfect life.

It had been four years since Kimmee's daddy was diagnosed with cancer, and that dark day during her senior year was when she decided to do something in the medical field to honor him. Witnessing her daddy's refusal to become a victim as he faced cancer with such strength and humility inspired her.

She watched in amazement as he continued riding bikes with her every Saturday, way beyond the time most people in his condition could have. His healthy lifestyle allowed him that gift. Her father encouraged her until his last breath, and he passed with such grace, honor, and dignity that he almost made death beautiful.

Kimmee stood outside the hearse, holding the black umbrella used to repel the inaugural April shower that year. She also clutched onto her mother to keep her from collapsing from grief, which weighed heavy on them as they trenched their way across the uneven surface into the graveside tent.

The pastor spoke eloquently of remembrance and spiritual accolades depicting how her father lived to the many in attendance. Then, the beautiful brown veneer casket journeyed down the vertical, six-foot dirt hallway to the final abyss.

In her father's will, he ensured his timely investments as a financial advisor and real-estate investor would allow Kimmee to follow her dream of living in Austin. He gave her a generous life insurance payout with specific instructions that she live in Austin in the 360 Tower Condominiums directly across from Mellow Johnny's bicycle shop when ready.

In a separate envelope was a check for $12,000, with the date left blank, written directly to Mellow Johnny's bicycle shop. It gave her specific instructions to create her dream Trek Madone, Project One bicycle, from Lance Armstrong's bicycle shop. One final comment was on the back of the envelope in plain sight. *No monies shalt be left behind!*

It had been almost two months since her daddy entered Heaven. With his death, Kimmee carried twice the weight of the world on her shoulders, and Atlas could not shrug. She had to find the strength for two, as her mother needed to be cared for, and her studies needed to be kept current.

Professor Shroyer mentally documented Kimmee's ability to endure life's pressures at such a difficult time. He already knew Kimmee was bright but was more impressed by her fortitude under such emotional circumstances.

Soon, graduation day was here. *This is for you, Daddy,* as she looked to the sky, then walked across the stage after four years to receive her diploma from the UT Southwestern Medical Center in Dallas. Kimmee grasped the diploma that signaled her way into medical school and held it close to her heart. A bachelor's degree in biology was the first step toward doing something in the medical field to honor him, just as she promised herself. But even with her degree, she wasn't sure what path would make that difference.

Doing something toward cancer research in honor of her father was what she initially promised, but she loved kids, and specializing in pediatrics became a recurring thought. However, before her father was even diagnosed with cancer, Kimmee's initial dream was to be a psychologist, and she minored in psychology in case that door ever opened.

Whichever way, taking AP courses and dual enrollment during high school helped her attain her basic college credits and score a 34 on her ACT.

Her academic achievements assured her acceptance into medical school. However, she was still eight long years from reaching any of her career paths.

It didn't take long for the headhunters to emerge, as a job in the Travis County Medical Examiner's office in Austin came looking for much-needed pathologist technicians. A bachelor's degree in biology was the minimum requirement to become a pathologist technician. The ME's office was willing to train a worthy candidate and pay a generous starting salary. A particular professor from UT Southwestern Medical Center, who had mentally documented Kimmee's college career, highly recommended her for the position, unbeknownst to her.

The unexpected job offer was thrilling, and the thought of moving to Austin sooner rather than later overwhelmed her with joy. The idea that Professor Shroyer would even recommend her at all, let alone so highly, made her already feel accomplished.

But Kimmee had concerns about the position and had a series of long talks with her mother as she found herself missing her father deeply. Kimmee wanted to look into his eyes and know she wasn't letting him down if she accepted the position. She worried this would sidetrack her from her goal of making a difference in the medical field to honor him.

However, before any of this could happen, there was this tiny little elephant big-ticket item in the room that needed to be addressed — *death!* Kimmee's bachelor's degree didn't have concentrated electives in the forensic sciences. She had focused more of her electives on pediatrics. Although she had plenty of experience dissecting frogs and tissues from various species, she hadn't performed or assisted with a human autopsy. Sure, she studied human organs, but she didn't harvest them. They were just there, pickled and ready to be examined.

But her father taught her to take opportunities whenever they knocked, and he had a unique perspective that he always correlated with Kimmee.

"If opportunity takes the time to pack its bags, buy a ticket, and make a trip clear down to Dallas to land on my front doorstep and knock. The least I can do is invite it in, pour it a cup of coffee, and consider what it's trying to offer me?"

Was this her sign? This recommendation from her professor came strictly from his experience of what a great student she was, how brilliant she was, and her ability to learn quickly. And, since the Travis County Medical Examiner's office called for a recommendation for a much-needed pathologist technician. Was this opportunity the definitive sign that answered the question of which path to follow? Maybe she should consider the job because this was what fate planned for her — to become a pathologist and pursue cancer research over pediatrics.

"Kimmee, do you know why your father demanded you live in Austin and gave you that check for your bicycle? Sweetheart, your father had a new perspective, an awakening from going through what he did. As simple as it sounds, he realized and experienced the cliché that life is way too short. He would always tell me, 'Life is 'way-damn' too short,' with a smiling emphasis on the *way-damn*. I can hear him saying it, and it makes me smile how he said it.

"Kimmee, these are his exact words to me, 'I want to make Kimmee's life an adventure, and I simply want her to be happy doing anything she wants as long as it's in Austin, Damn, Texas.'" Kimmee's eyes watered as she heard her daddy's voice telling her those exact words; a smile accompanied her tears.

"Sweetheart, most people work all their lives just to make ends meet, and your daddy made sure you didn't have that struggle. He would not want you knocking yourself out for eight more years to fulfill a self-inflicted promise you made at a vulnerable age during a vulnerable time. Instead, he would want you to move to Austin, Damn, Texas, and be happy. Kimmee, as your mother, I only have three simple words of advice — Never postpone joy."

This past weekend, she moved from Dallas to the 360 Tower high-rise condominiums in Austin, TX, as instructed by the estate of Marcus Davenport Attwood. The 360-building shot 581 feet in the air to the tip of the spire and sits along Shoal Creek on the western end of downtown Austin. Her condo was on the 25th floor of the 44-floor high-rise and had a northern view from her window, allowing her to look down at Mellow Johnny's bicycle shop across the street.

Her custom-ordered bike arrived the following Tuesday, and she could hardly wait to see it. She conveniently walked over to Mellow Johnny's, and as she entered, a staff of three employees helped show her the bike. Tears of gratitude fell as she took in the radioactive pink color that had exceeded her expectations of how beautiful it would be.

Kimmee walked her new bicycle companion home and spent the evening personalizing it by adding front and rear lights, GPS, matching water bottles and holders, a nice-sized seat bag for extra inner tubes, CO2 cartridges, and repair tools. The radioactive pink was just that: radioactively bright, and she was overly excited about her inaugural early-morning ride tomorrow.

It was now 11:08 p.m., and she needed sleep. But, the anticipation of her day and the excitement of moving the past few days made it difficult to sleep. She looked out her 25th-floor view of the city, which was experiencing quite the rainstorm. The raindrops on her side bedroom window magnified the already beautiful downtown skyline.

She longed for her daddy. Often, when she couldn't sleep or if something was troubling her, he would surprise her with a late-night trip to Wendy's for a Frosty, just the two of them. The late-night backdrop deepened their conversations and led to some of their best talks ever. *He would want you to,* her brain negotiated as the SUV keys found themselves in her hand.

The familiar voice of Google Maps stated there was a Wendy's, 1.7 miles away and one 4.2 miles from her current location. On the way to the closer one, a medium-sized, white cargo van with its flashers had stalled out and blocked the road, and she turned on a different street to get around the van's misfortune.

As Google Maps was preparing to reroute her to where Kimmee needed to be, she had already missed the turn. It was easier to go ahead to the 4.2-mile location; besides, it would give her more quality time to reminisce about her dad as she imagined the wonderful conversation about everything happening in her life.

Kimmee reached her Wendy's destination and pulled into line. She was in 5th place overall for the Wendy's drive-thru Frosty trophy she promised herself.

The pouring rain caused havoc on her windshield wipers as she arrived at the window to pay for her yummy goodness. When she did, something illuminated in her headlights. "What the?"— She watched a rather large, oddly dressed figure on a bicycle make its way through the raindrop-infested headlight beams and then into the distance and out of view.

"Weird, right? — Nice bike, though." She wished her dad was there to see the late-night roadshow, as they would have summarized an opinion and taken turns creating a story to fit the stranger on a bike.

Her daddy sided on a made-up mystery while she trended toward something of the comical variety. She imagined him, in an ominous voice, would have storied that the man had just killed someone and was now frantically making his getaway on a bicycle he found near the crime scene with the money he stole hidden on his person in a secret pouch —

Then they would have looked at each other and laughed themselves into a comical frenzy. Kimmee also knew her daddy would have found the man to see if he needed help or wanted a lift. How he lived reminded her why she missed him and enjoyed a late-night Frosty in his honor.

※━━━━━━━━━※

Kimmee had the world by the tail as she pulled into the parking lot and parked her SUV. She turned to see her new bike sitting in the back. She smiled as she opened her door, her hand pinching her skin as she paused to read the sign: Medical Examiner's Building, Travis County, 1213 Sabine Street, Austin, Texas. She looked to the sky and relived the rainbow message — "Thanks, Daddy. Now, let's do this!"

Kimmee was met with first-day donuts, pleasantries, and a meet and greet with her fellow co-workers. She took in the sights, sounds, and smells of her new professional workplace as she looked around. The employees, especially the men, seemed to be on their best behavior for the newcomer. And there appeared to be an epidemic of advanced puberty that morning as stomachs sucked tight, chests puffed out, and voices lowered a third of an octave.

She was a *looker*, as they say in the business of looking. She was fit, strong, and could fill out a dress nicely. She had long, jet-black hair and, of course, her hazel-mint-green eyes, all of it packaged in a five-foot, three-inch-tall frame. She was radiant and could turn heads at the drop of a dime. But Kimmee chose not to. Her outfits were soft, buttoned up with no need for anything to fit snug — in a word, classy.

Kimmee learned from her mom, dad, and experience that she needed to be professional at all costs, and mixing business with pleasure was not a good idea. Besides, Kimmee James Attwood was able to take care of herself. Her daddy made sure of that. She didn't need anyone to be a financial crutch to her, nor would her pay predict her happiness. She was free of those burdens and would work where she wanted, and at a job she loved. She would also fall in love with a man of substance, with a personality that she desired to spend her life with, regardless of how much money lined his wallet.

Bottom line: finding someone at work to date would not be an aspiration of hers. Kimmee was smart and focused on one thing: to be the best pathologist technician who had ever graced the Travis County Medical Examiner's office.

Kimmee was shown to her office and quickly established her identity by placing the customary photo that told her most important story. That of her family before cancer took its toll.

They scheduled her to meet her main boss, the chief medical examiner, Dr. Charles A. Johnson, for orientation to discuss the rules and what he expected of her. Unfortunately, his administrative duties of dealing with the business of bodies at the state capital kept him busy trying to keep funding a priority for his office.

"So, you're the new pathologist technician." Dopamine flooded her brain, hearing her official title as she turned to read the name tag of Dr. Kevin Slavin. "It's time to get started on your first case," just like that, her first official call to duty began. She followed the senior pathologist to the room where she would spend hours learning how to solve the mysteries of the human cadavers placed before her.

He opened the door to a darkened room where two large surgical lights shone down on a medical examiner's table, blocked by four pathologists standing and staring silently. She cautiously approached the medical examiner's table to feed her curiosity about why these four grown men stood staring in such reverence. The examiners parted to make way for the newbie technician. There she was, lying on the table, the reason for the respectable silence: all 36 inches and 36 pounds of a small female Caucasian child brought in late last evening.

Kimmee was unprepared for the electrical impulses her eyes sent to her brain. Her emotional system immediately overloaded, propelling her into shock as she ran to the nearest trash can to take care of what her stomach thought of the matter.

Typically, the more experienced pathologists would poke fun at a newbie's first day. But today, there was an unwritten grace period. Today, no matter how long you'd been there or how many corpses you'd experienced, there were just some things a human being should never get used to seeing.

"It's alright, Kimmee. This job is exciting, but at times like this, it sucks. Thankfully, this is not the norm," the senior pathologist said.

However, Kimmee was embarrassed by her gut reaction and knew she was stronger than that. She owned up to it and was determined to tap into her father's strength and re-establish herself as the professional she knew she could be.

"Don't worry; you weren't the first and won't be the last. However, we have our traditions, and there's a reason that particular trash can is sterilized with no trash and so readily accessible. Now you must sign the back of it like all the newbies before you and ones yet to come."

Dr. Slavin was first in line for the small female Caucasian case since the medical examiner's office was backlogged and running thin on pathologists. Dr. Johnson would usually assist and pick up the slack, but since he was dealing with upper management problems at the capitol, Dr. Slavin would have to follow the upper chain of command. He feared he would have to somehow report to the top chief forensic electrophysiology pathologist — Professor Wolfrem Miguel Oswin Jezercak, the man everyone referred to as — "The Clicker."

As Kimmee recovered, she stared silently at the 3-foot cadaver of the little girl.

"By the way, I don't think I properly introduced myself; I'm Dr. Kevin Slavin."

Her focus shifted toward the voice that interrupted her thoughts.

"I'm the assistant senior pathologist to the chief medical examiner, Dr. Johnson. — Man! Try saying that ten times fast. Okay, Kimmee, are you ready to learn?"

She greeted the question with a reaffirming look. Her career officially began as she helped examine the tiny female corpse. As the two systematically searched the small corpse, a casual conversation took the mind off the tragedy they attempted to uncover. They looked for signs of trauma, track marks, scratch marks, needle sticks, shaking, bruising, and a long list of usual suspects before the official autopsy could begin.

"So, how did you get the name Kimmee? It's an unusual spelling if I saw it correctly on today's memo about our new star employee."

"I'm not sure about the star employee part, but my name resulted from a horrible dismantling of the word Kissimmee when I was a little girl at Disneyland in Florida. I couldn't pronounce my S's back then, and the Kimmee part was just left behind — and it just stuck, and I've been K-I-double M, double E ever since. My real name is Kimberly James Attwood."

"Well, then, K-I-double M-double E, let's get started!"

The two began, and Kimmee fought back her emotions as Dr. Slavin plotted the appropriate incisions on the small pale cadaver with markers.

Dr. Slavin's job was to teach Kimmee how to become a pathologist technician. He began by refreshing her memory on what they needed to accomplish on the autopsy list, then supervised her as she made the proper incisions along the dotted lines.

"Okay, Kimmee, we need to do this in six stages. The first stage is the Y-incision I have marked for you, and the second stage is the removal of organs. Our third stage examines the stomach contents, and the fourth stage is a sample collection. The fifth stage will be a head and brain examination, while the sixth stage will be to make a conclusion."

The look on her face signaled an apprehensive understanding, but it was difficult for them to begin cutting on the pale skin of the small female that lay soul-less on the table. But proceed they must, and as professional as Dr. Slavin's abilities allowed, they carefully did what their jobs asked of them.

As professionals, they were taught to set aside personal feelings of attachment at all costs so they would not develop an emotional connection to the cadavers before them. But what kind of monster could possibly do that with this caliber of a cadaver that was so small and innocent?

They had also been taught as professionals to avoid using names to help prevent attachment issues, but it was too late. Kimmee had been caught with her emotional hand in the cookie jar and was already attached. Now, her innate curiosity levels had to know everything she could about her first case. Not because it was her first case but because it was *this* first case. Had this been a 72-year-old man, she would have been as professional as possible. But the 3-foot cadaver and her love for children made it impossible not to make the rookie mistake of wanting the information that had congregated in her mind.

Dr. Slavin was deeply knowledgeable about the organs of the human anatomy. He asked Kimmee if she wanted to hear his thoughts based on his extensive experience with what seemed to be a "textbook" cause of sudden death. She gave him the female version of a male head nod, which was an approving look and was much more pleasant coming from the hazel-mint-green-eyed Kimmee James.

"Okay, are you sure you're ready for this? It's not too late to say no because once the geek comes out, it can't be put back in the tube."

She smiled but remained steadfast and curious about what kind of teacher she had before her. Slavin performed a ten-minute sudden-death word storm using an excessive amount of five-dollar words, phrases, and percentages. Slavin's highlight reel included coronary atherosclerosis, congenital and cardiovascular diseases, postmortem macroscopic and microscopic investigation, structural substrates, and forensic analysis techniques to identify subtle or functional disorders. And finally, electrical instability, arrhythmogenic, ventricular cardiomyopathy, mitral valve prolapse, myocarditis, conduction system, hypertrophic cardiomyopathy, and macroscopic, histologic examination.

"So, in conclusion, whether these are actually idiopathic or unresolved because we couldn't identify the subtle pathologic substrates remains to be elucidated. But, my theory was that the structural abnormality resided at a molecular level, which increased the need for a molecular biology investigation—"

He paused, embarrassed at how much geekiness he feared she might have attached to him because of this lecture.

"Wow, good job. I hope I can do that someday," Kimmee said.

"It's easy when you have zero social life. The heart muscle fascinates me, but believe it or not, I'm rather weak in that subject. I even read a lot of studies from different regions of the world. It's amazing how the different ratios of heart disease are affected by the cultures and lifestyles in other parts of the planet."

Kimmee was impressed and felt confident she could learn much from Dr. Slavin. His ability to perform his heart lecture off the top of his head gave her something to aspire toward learning.

Dr. Slavin looked at the clock, trying to conceal a stressful breath, and wished Chief Johnson was there to help with the case. The usual four-hour process was now north of the five-hour and thirty-minute mark. Between talking and teaching, emotions, uncertainty, and a newbie protégé, he was experiencing self-doubt as they compiled their findings.

The initial autopsy results showed no visual signs of abnormalities and nothing unusual that would point toward the cause of death. In other words, it was "inconclusive."

"I'll be consulting with Dr. Johnson first thing tomorrow morning to see if we can call in some forensic favors. If all else fails, we may have to summon — "The Clicker.""

Dr. Slavin instantly panicked as the two-word phrase escaped his lips. "Kimmee, forget you ever heard me say that. Please, it's for your own good — and possibly your own protection!"

Kimmee peered at Dr. Slavin. "Forget I heard you say what — the Clicker!?"

Gasps were heard outside the room as a large metal tray crashed to the floor, accompanied by the sound of medical utensils sprawling throughout the hallway.

As the gong sound equivalent resonated, voices referencing Dr. Slavin to losing his mind still echoed in the hallway. Within seconds, the door to the medical examiner's room opened briskly. Five faces transferred their fears toward Slavin without ever saying a word. Kimmee was left speechless and now felt like "The Clicker" could be released in a similar fashion to the mythical human equivalent of "The Kraken."

Kimmee's curiosity took hold. *Who in the hell is "the Clicker"?* She wasn't going to fail the first medical case of her life, and if she needed to risk life and limb to meet him, so be it. But until the time came before she had to prostrate herself before "the Clicker," she wanted to know everything about this case, starting with the little girl's name, where the incident happened, and the environment around her.

She wanted to look over the EMT's report. However, Dr. Slavin said they hadn't received it because all departments were shorthanded, which delayed everything in the pipeline.

Kimmee didn't know the rules. Was she allowed to get a first-hand perspective from the EMTs on their sense of congruency with their findings? Were they in tune with the stories they may have overheard from the police? Would she be allowed to accompany a forensic investigator to the scene to satisfy her intense curiosity and find the miraculous clue the police might have missed?

She decided not to push her luck on her first day and didn't think Dr. Slavin had the authority to make this decision. Nor did she want her first day on the job to be misconstrued as a slap in the face to Dr. Slavin's ego or abilities. When she met with Chief Johnson in the morning, she planned to steer the meeting toward what was swirling in her mind.

Her first day was now complete. The rollercoaster ride of emotions was palatable, and the ending bittersweet. The inconclusiveness of their results entirely overshadowed the thrill of her inaugural day.

She sat down for a moment to regroup from the emotional rollercoaster, but her feelings imploded unexpectedly. Her demeanor became bleak, and simply leaving the building became a physical challenge. *I don't get this; what is happening here?* Her mental struggle didn't make sense as she had been through much worse, and she knew she was much stronger. She looked up — "I need you, Daddy."

Chapter Seven

Godzilla

Kimmee left the facility feeling null and void and walked through the parking lot with her disappointment in tow. The sound of an engine sputtering but not starting grabbed her attention. A few spaces from her SUV heralded a van with its hood open. A man holding a small dog exited the driver's side and stuck his head under the hood. The dog was glued to his side with his right arm while his left arm poked around, pulling on any wire, harness, or hose to figure out why it wouldn't start.

The dog barked at Kimmee and wagged its tail voraciously until the man popped out from under the hood to see why the dog was excited.

The two of them glanced at each other while the dog became animated enough to wiggle out of his grasp. He bent down in time for the dog to leap a short distance to the ground and run to Kimmee.

"Oh, you're the cutest thing ever," she squealed, and her bleakness seemingly disappeared as she picked up the dog to take it back to the man.

"I guess it's true what they say; dogs know good people when they see them."

"Your dog is so cute; how long have you had him?" Kimmee looked at the belly to confirm, "Oops, I mean her. How long have you had her?"

"Funny, you should ask; she's not my dog. I found her on the way here, and I was going to try and return her, but now my van won't start. The problem is, neither will my cell phone, so I can't call the number nor get directions to the address on the tag.

"Plan B was to find a working payphone to call, but now I can't do that either. You know, it's just been one of those days," he said, calmer than his situation dictated.

Kimmee felt comfortable with the stranger's demeanor despite his scruffy appearance and engaged in conversation.

"Tell me about it — my day also ended on a sour note."

"Do you mind holding the dog a little longer while I poke around on my engine some more?"

"Not at all. Can I call someone to come help with your van?"

"That's kind of you to offer, but what would really help is if you could possibly help get that dog back to its owner. Can you imagine if that was your little puppy missing? The owner has to be heartbroken about now."

"You know what, I would love to help with that. I don't have anywhere to be, so it works out perfectly. And I'll get to know my new city this way."

"New city, huh? That sounds exciting. So what brings you to your new city?"

"Today was my first day working here at the ME's office. It was quite the rollercoaster ride — and still is. I even had difficulty walking out here, but this little puppy just made it better."

"Care to tell me about it while I unplug and plug everything back under the hood?"

"Well, today was my first day working as a pathologist technician. It was fascinating, and I assisted with my first autopsy. I have to tell you — it was every emotion at once and then some. But in the end, the result wasn't what I had hoped. I guess the disappointment just made me feel like a failure. But I'm not sure why it hit me so hard because I know I'm stronger than this."

"I'm sorry about that. I could tell you were disappointed. I could see it in your walk. But your day's not over; you never know how things might turn out."

"You sound like my daddy. He would have tried to find a silver lining as well."

"He – *would* have tried?" he asked gently with a look to match.

"He passed away six months ago of cancer — he was my hero."

"Well, I'm sorry to hear that, but at least you had a hero. Many girls don't get that in life, so I hope you consider yourself lucky. Besides, your daddy's heart will always be with you. I bet you felt him somehow on your first day of work."

"Wow, you're kind of like silver-lining the heck out of it out here. I know it sounds strange, but your kindness is just what I needed." Kimmee started to tear up. "And you're right; I've felt my daddy with me all day. You even remind me of him. He loved his sandals after he was in his suit all day. But you found a way to rock both at the same time," she reminisced while the dog licked at her tears.

"Yes, I know, I'm such a fashionista. I'm pretty sure *Scruffy* is the new black." Kimmee chuckled as he continued, "My sandals and suit have been through a lot over the years. People even call me Sandals; they say it's my identity."

"Well, it does fit your free spirit. I'm glad you were here for me today, Mr. Sandals."

"I'm glad too. You know, I believe that hearts can connect in ways we can't possibly imagine. Sometimes, a nudge is needed to guide one heart to another that needs healing or to find the heart they should be with in life. It's difficult to find a good heart; not everyone does. I know we just met, but I hope you find a good heart someday. I believe there's one out there waiting for you — you just never know."

"Wow, what a unique soul you have in those sandals of yours. You have such a poetic way of looking at the heart." Kimmee acknowledged.

"Well, that's because I follow my heart often, so I greatly believe in its power. Can you imagine a world without one?" Sandals got in the van to start the engine. "What do you know? It's my lucky day, after all. Meeting you probably had something to do with my luck changing."

"Mr. Sandals, you are just so positive and kind-hearted. Thanks for breaking down in my parking lot; you helped lift my spirit. — Did my daddy happen to send you?" she said, smiling.

"Would it be so wrong if he did? He answered in a way that was both comforting and confusing. Kimmee felt an emotional shift she couldn't describe as he continued.

"Thanks for helping to return that little puppy to her owner; I bet it's more important than we realize. You're an exceptional young lady, Miss Kimmee, and I think our hearts will meet again soon — you'll see," and he drove off as if he never were.

Kimmee walked toward her SUV and paused — *Wait a minute; I never told him my name.* — *Did I?* — She was perplexed as she entered her vehicle, but her furry passenger bid for her attention. The puppy forcefully rolled onto her back with her front paws held above her ears, and it looked like someone was robbing her at gunpoint. She sprawled with her tummy out as she pawed at Kimmee, demanding a tummy rub.

Kimmee obliged the puppy's demand as she read the dog tag and raised an eyebrow — *Godzilla* — *huh* — *really*? With a smirk on her face and biology in her thoughts, *Hmmm — I guess Godzilla would officially be an asexual species,* she concluded. "Okay, Girly Godzilla, let's get you back home."

Kimmee called the number on the tag first, but no one answered. Fortunately, there was also an address. Soon, Google Maps was up and reporting the 21.1-mile distance Godzilla had hitch-hiked that day. *That's a long way from home for such a little lady.*

"Welcome to Austin" played over and over in her mind as she admired the beautiful neighborhoods and Texas-sized shopping districts on the drive. She was happy to be *living the dream* of being there, as Austin was consistently rated a top-ten city in the United States in which to live.

Kimmee was low on fuel and stopped for gas. As she got out of her vehicle, Godzilla heard a dog barking in the distance. Not prepared for Godzilla's ability to escape, Kimmee saw her passenger off and running a split second later.

"Oh, God, please help me! — Godzilla, come back!" The puppy tore under her car, and Kimmee could not see where she ran to. *This darn dog should have been called Houdini!*

Moments later, horrific screeching pelted Kimmee's eardrums, and her nervous system braced for mental impact as tires painted the road with rubber. She ran toward the screeches, terrified of what she might find.

A large Texas-sized truck suddenly halted in front of her and blocked her view. She sprinted around the vehicle and saw five cars screeched to a halt, each with a varied slant. *— But where was the animal that caused the reaction?* The man in the truck rolled down his window while Kimmee was contemplating.

"Mam, I'm sorry I had to brake so fast. But there was a—" Before he finished, she saw the small, speeding fur-bullet known as Godzilla weaving her way through traffic and looking scared out of her mind. Kimmee suddenly became part of a volunteer dog-wrangling squad made up of the man in the truck and three other traffic goers, all after the same prize. The pup ran under one car and came running out from another to make another appearance.

The dog wranglers managed to redirect the dog out of the street. Godzilla was terrified as she ran toward the neighborhood next to where Kimmee had stopped for gas.

Kimmee thanked the truck occupant and waved at the other three dog-wrangling teammates. They hopped back into their cars and continued on their previously planned trajectories. *At least Godzilla was off the main road.*

Kimmee ran to her car, got in, and took a quick breather from the exhilaration. *What a day*! She started the SUV to search for Godzilla. Suddenly, the fur-bullet made a cameo and blazed in front of a car entering the neighborhood.

"Okay, Houdini, I'll find you if it's the last thing I do." Kimmee drove the neighborhood looking for the escape artist while simultaneously admiring the architecture of each home that seemed to put on a show.

Her gym bag lay on the front passenger floorboard, her running shoes poking out. She pulled over and put them on in case she needed some actual speed to catch the fur-bullet. Once again, out of nowhere, a blur caught the attention of her peripheral vision.

Within seconds, Kimmee found herself out of the SUV and sprinting around the corner to see if she could rescue the animal. Three blocks later, she found the critter doing what all dogs have done since the dawn of time — having a *smell-off* competition with another dog.

Kimmee approached Godzilla slowly as she was intensely smelling something the olfactory glands deemed significant to the tiny fur-ball. Kimmee's size-seven shoes inched their way toward the beast. But she sensed the nervousness in the pup's body language that looked like an Olympic runner ready to bolt, so she reconsidered her approach.

Kimmee had dogs growing up that would run away given the opportunity, so she did what she did back then to see if capture were imminent.

There was a small tree branch near the scene, and Kimmee sat alongside it, facing away from Godzilla but in plain view. She crept her hands out and reached for the branch, ensuring she didn't startle her. Then Kimmee slowly moved the branch in a windshield-wiper motion causing a sound that would surely grab any dog's attention.

In a matter of seconds, a playful growl was attached to the other end of the stick, using all its might to retain the item for itself. Then she drew the branch closer, making capture inevitable.

Well, I'll be, like riding a bicycle. And once again, Kimmee held the cutest Pomeranian pup she had ever seen. Only this time, much tighter as she returned to the gas station to refuel.

A few miles later, Google informed Kimmee to turn right in approximately 1000 ft. And once again, she drove through the neighborhood, admiring the architecture of each home.

"Okay, little Godzilla, we're almost there. We need to make a pact to never speak of this adventure. There's no need to mention our little mishap to your owner and worry them more than they already are." Kimmee then tried to teach Godzilla to lift her paw so they could pinky swear.

Chapter Eight

Bellavia

It was now the darker side of dusk as Kimmee found herself staring at a charming home that would make for a very romantic bed and breakfast. It was two-story and looked like a dollhouse covered with three-fourths siding and one-fourth red brick. It had a fresh, clean coat of white paint while trimmed in black. It was also color-coordinated with five sets of black shutters and two large black window boxes full of brightly colored flowers.

The roof was nearly black, completing the façade, which perfectly set off the home against the red brick. It had a large wrap-around porch, two oversized black rocking chairs, and a decorative black bench. The yard had three massive trees that reached far into the sky, each placed with ideal spacing on the front and side of the house. Beautifully landscaped shrubs lined up under the white railings, and four evenly spaced posts followed the wrap-around porch from start to finish.

Kimmee parked in the street and carried Godzilla toward the house. However, before they reached the porch, an emotionally distraught woman in a robe ran out after her pet. Godzilla cried out her high-pitched bark, and in an instant, the woman held her fur-child once again.

The lady rocked Godzilla side to side but could not produce the words of gratitude to let the kind stranger know how thankful she was. But watching the fur-child hold onto her mommy as if to say, "*I'll never let go again,*" was thanks enough.

Kimmee could only imagine the state of mind the woman was in, thinking she would never hold her puppy again. The emotions overwhelmed the war-torn-looking woman who could no longer sustain herself, and she sat down on her front porch steps, crying.

Kimmee was a bit confused, deducting that the woman's tears seemed to be from emotional pain rather than the joy of being reunited with her family pet. It was emotionally backward, as the woman was crying but wasn't smiling.

Kimmee placed her hand on the woman's shoulder to provide comfort. The lady gazed up at Kimmee as if trying to convey something other than the reactions from a missing dog.

Hearing the woman cry such harsh tears made Kimmee conjure up the emotions she experienced today and hosted a tear herself. However, she was still puzzled and sensed there was much more to this encounter.

Kimmee could tell a beautiful woman was hidden under her haggard appearance as she looked over the lady, who seemed to have way more to deal with than hygiene. In an unspoken agreement for Kimmee to become her caretaker, she sat beside the woman, gently placed her hand on her forearm, and squeezed slightly.

"Is there anything I can help you with inside? I'm sure you've had an emotional day with that little one missing. Would you like some company, even if just for a little while?"

The woman was hesitant to answer — but looked her in the eyes a few seconds later. "I would really like that; please, come in. I'm so sorry I'm a mess right now."

Kimmee stood and gently helped the woman to her feet. "There's no need for apologies; I'd be a mess, too, if my puppy were missing all day," she said with a smile.

Kimmee gasped as she entered the home. She was amazed by the continuation of the perfect bed-and-breakfast charm that matched the outside décor. The entranceway was spectacular. It hosted a staircase that went up to the second story via a landing halfway up and a stunning banister that followed.

Paintings large and small adorned every available inch of wall space and featured two primary artists. Four huge, contemporary, modern, colorful paintings by Lee Reynolds showed off the entranceway that followed the staircase walls up to the second floor — While an artist named J. Roybal had nine rather large paintings and a few medium-sized renditions sprinkled throughout the rest of the home.

Anyone who visited the home asked who the artist or artists were. And wherever you looked, you smiled at the colorfully dressed children with rounded faces either playing musical instruments, riding in a hot air balloon, or riding olden bicycles.

The exquisite, eclectic mix of modern and traditional furniture worked in harmony to make it an event just being in the home. However, the star of the show was a grand piano with a high gloss, dark-brown finish with two rows of wooden-carved antique applique moldings that accented and surrounded the piano. And three heavy-duty scrolled antique legs held it all together.

The home was too stunning to put into words, and Kimmee was amazed. She saw photos on almost every shelf or table of what looked like a common theme of a beautiful childhood. Love filled the home everywhere you looked as Kimmee followed the lady into the kitchen.

The woman wrestled around in her pantry and found an old-fashioned tea kettle while Kimmee sat and watched her organize the items necessary for a nice cup of hot tea.

"By the way, my name is Kimmee — Kimmee James Attwood, to be official. I tried calling the number on Godzilla's tag earlier, but no one answered."

"Oh, dear, I didn't even think of that. I've been on the phone all day dealing with some rather serious family issues on top of Godzilla running away. I guess it drained the life out of me and my battery."

"Well, in that case, is there anyone you need to call? Or rather, anyone I can call for you to tell them that Godzilla is back?"

"No, dear, I'm just grateful you found her and brought her back. I'm here alone and need this little girl more than ever to help me get through everything. I'm sorry, but I don't want to burden you. In fact, I need such an emotional break that having you here is the best thing right now. By the way, my name is Bellavia, but everyone calls me Bella," she said with the sweetest look in her eyes.

"Bellavia, what a beautiful name; I've never heard that before."

"It's actually my middle name, after my Italian great-grandmother."

"Well, it's wonderful to meet you, Bella. Have you eaten anything today?"

"No — I haven't eaten — or been able to do anything today."

The tea kettle started to sing as steam sent itself into an evaporating mist.

"It seems like fixing us tea is the first thing I've been able to accomplish all day," referencing her hair with a point of an index finger.

While Bella finished assembling the cups, saucers, spoons, and assorted sweeteners, Kimmee took a quick inventory around the kitchen. There was a bowl of fruit on the center island with an avocado and tomato, along with a toaster and Keurig on the kitchen counter.

"You know, Bella, whenever my mother was having an emotional day, I made her something to eat to help her relax. Would you allow me the use of your kitchen while you sit and relax? I make a mean avocado toast that is one of my mother's favorites. Could I make that for you?"

"Oh, that sounds wonderful! I haven't had avocado toast for quite a while."

"Well, you haven't had my avocado toast. I make a special version, just for moms, and made with extra love."

Bella placed the hot teas on their placemats, then gestured to Kimmee with a presentation á la the model from the *Price is Right*.

"Mi casa es su casa," Bella said most appreciatively as she sat down to relax.

"Is the bread in the pantry?" Kimmee asked.

With a look of affirmation from Bella, Kimmee turned the phrase "*mi casa es su casa*" into a verb, walked to the lady's pantry, and found some whole wheat bread, honey, and olive oil. She opened the fridge and found sliced cheese and some butter pats. She grabbed two slices of bread, placed them in the toaster, and found two matching plates in the cabinet. While in its toaster cocoon, the metamorphosis of bread into toast finalized and popped out light and crispy.

She placed the toast on the plates and spread pats of butter until they turned into liquid yum, with a splash of olive oil, followed by placing the cheese slices on top to begin melting. Kimmee then focused on the avocado and tomato sitting in the bowl. She sliced the avocado and used a fork to mash the avocado firmly on the buttered toast. Then she topped it with slices of tomato with a pinch of sea salt and pepper, then drizzled some honey on top to complete the project of avocado toast for the women to share.

"Are you an angel?" Bella asked with words and a look in her eyes.

Kimmee smiled and approached that question from Bella's point of view. First, she returned Godzilla to her, and second, she provided her solace and now was fixing her dinner.

"Yes, my Bellavia, I am an angel, and I have been ordered from above to have you relax and let me take care of you."

Bella looked at Kimmee with her sad but beautiful eyes and confirmed that Kimmee was indeed her angel. They had a wonderful dinner, and as they finished, Kimmee took away the dishes to leave the kitchen cleaner than she found it. As Kimmee washed the plates, there was a slight "yap" from below.

"Okay, Zilla, already back to your old bag of tricks, I see." Bella picked her up. "I'm so glad you're home, my little Zilla."

"Did I hear you call her Zilla?"

"Oh, yes, I shortened her name to Zilla to match her girly persona, and she's been my little Zilla girl ever since."

"So, how long was Zilla missing today?"

"I'm not sure when she escaped today. It might have been when I opened the door to get a package off the porch. It was the oddest thing, really. It seemed as if she was here one second and gone the next, but she darts out so quickly that sometimes I don't see her escape. Since the neighborhood knows her identity, Godzilla is typically returned to us rather quickly. But when we do see her escape, we chase after her for two or three blocks before we finally catch her."

Kimmee shook her head, relating to Zilla's escape artist tactics.

"I've had one of the worst days of my life. I'm dealing with family issues that no family should ever have to go through. I've been trying to get ready, off and on, all day, but I couldn't concentrate enough to make it happen. Trust me, you truly are an angel, and your presence here is such a gift."

Kimmee placed her hand on the woman's forearm and squeezed it.

"To answer your question, around three o'clock, I noticed Zilla wasn't harassing me like usual, and that's not like her. So, I checked under the bed and under the closet clothes rack, where she hides when she's not feeling well. I panicked when she wasn't there because I knew something was wrong. I drove everywhere looking for her while dealing with my kids. And I was crying the whole time about my family and hoping that someone didn't steal Zilla, or worse, run over her with a car."

Kimmee sensed Bella's body language reliving the trauma and jumped in.

"Well, luckily, Zilla hitch-hiked her way with another man to find me, and I'm so glad she did because she led me right here to you. Smart girl, Zilla," and Kimmee joined in petting Zilla.

"So, another man had Zilla when she found you?" Bella asked.

"Well, yes. Interestingly enough, I just moved here from Dallas this past weekend and started a new job today. After my first day of work, when I walked out to my SUV, a man in a van was holding Zilla while he looked under his hood — and that's when Zilla spotted me. The man was very kind-hearted and wanted to return Zilla to you, but since he was having car trouble, he asked if I would see to it that Zilla got home safe. And now, here we are."

"Wow, this little girl really did hitch-hike her way to you. You have a wonderful way of looking at life, don't you? How was your first day at your new job?"

Kimmee didn't want to mention where she worked and tried to keep the conversation light and playful to lift Bella's spirits. "I've had one of the best days of my life today because, in the end, I got to meet you. But it has also been a highly emotional day; let's just say it didn't produce the results I was hoping for — yet."

"Well, what a positive attitude. I'm sure you'll get the results you need soon. Tell me a little about yourself; you're such a beautiful girl, and your eyes are such a beautiful color. Are you dating anyone? I can't imagine there not being a line of men bidding for your attention."

"Aw, you're so sweet," Kimmee blushed — "but the answer is no; I don't have anyone. The love of my life was my daddy, who passed away a few months ago. He set the bar rather high as far as men go. I can't say this was his position all his life, but in the end, he just wanted me to be happy and meet a man of character and not worry about how much money he made.

"But he would have loved for me to have gotten married, not to have a son-in-law, but so he could have a grandbaby. My parents would have loved either, but they were dying for me to have a granddaughter just like me. My daddy would have been the best grandpa ever!"

Bella excused herself rather abruptly from the table. Kimmee sensed Bella's demeanor had changed as her face looked physically altered from the woman she was speaking with moments ago, for the lack of a better term — like she had seen a ghost.

"Kimmee, I'm sorry, but I need a moment — I'll be back in a bit; I need to do something about my hair — make yourself at home." She quickly headed toward the stairway with Zilla glued to her step-by-step up the stairs.

Kimmee knew she had said something to trigger such a harsh reaction, but she didn't know what. She reasoned that maybe talking about her daddy dying and having a family someday made Bella focus on what she was going through with her family. That, along with the stress of almost losing Zilla, may have overwhelmed her momentarily.

Kimmee moved to the living room and patiently waited for Bella there. She heard her footsteps upstairs as some squeaky boards gave away her location. Kimmee took in the beautiful artwork surrounding her and noted the artists for future reference, as her condominium would like to look like this home when it grew up.

She admired the beautiful carvings on the grand piano. She imagined a beautiful melody crying out from the eighty-eight black and white keys that sound like brilliant emotional colors when played correctly.

She turned her attention toward the heartbeat of the home, the photos, eclectically placed everywhere in the living room, no two frames close to resembling one another. She noticed what looked like four children at different stages of life and all happy.

She moved across the room to another section of photos. She saw one of Bella's sons holding an infant and another of a baby getting baptized.

A pink bow gave away that she must have a granddaughter. As she moved down the line, Kimmee witnessed the granddaughter getting older with each photo to a more concentrated gathering of framed moments. *Oh, how sweet, what a lucky girl.*

Without warning, Kimmee's face turned a shade of empty white as her blood cowardly rushed out and rendered her equilibrium challenged. Every skin cell tingled at once as her eyes fell on a small photo that gut-punched her entire nervous system. Her eyes amplified every pixel as her pupils widened to absorb the image — that of a small female Caucasian child already etched permanently into Kimmee's mind forever.

No — Oh, GOD — NO! — She gasped breathlessly. "*— No, NO, NO! This can't be right! — God, how is this even possible?* Kimmee grasped the photo as she recounted her last sentence to Bella and played it back in her mind.

"*My parents would have loved either, but they were **dying** for me to have a **granddaughter** just like me.*"

She felt sick to her stomach as she regurgitated her word choices. '***Dying,**' for me to have a **'granddaughter,'** Really? **'Dying,'** you just had to use the words **'dying'** and **'granddaughter'** in the same sentence?* Her knees grew weaker as all the puzzle pieces collided at once, and she could now see the bigger picture. And with a sudden intake of breath, she stumbled backward; with the couch catching her fall, the photo still clinched to her heart.

Kimmee took another look at the photo, hoping she was mistaken or hallucinating. She thought the picture would be different if she turned it upside down and back again, like the bottom of a Magic-8 Ball.

But the Magic-8 Ball trick didn't work, so she slid the picture frame behind the couch pillows as if the out-of-sight, out-of-mind trick might work. Neither did, and Kimmee gasped for air as a panic attack did precisely what the name implied it should do.

Her breathing escalated to high-pitched wheezing that captured Zilla's attention upstairs. Zilla scampered down to evaluate the situation and deemed it bark-worthy, sending Bella the message to come down and see why she was fussing.

Bella saw Kimmee struggling to breathe. In an instant, her mothering instincts bolted out from her prefrontal cortex to take hold of the situation.

"What is it, dear? What's wrong? Why are you having trouble breathing?" — Bella was panicking but calm, and for the life of her, she could not figure out what had happened.

"Let me get you a glass of water," and in a full parental second, she returned.

She had Kimmee take a drink to slow down her breathing pattern. It took a few moments, but the remedy took hold, and her breathing was regulated.

"Kimmee, are you okay? What happened?"

She squeezed Bella's hand to assure her she was okay. Bella leaned Kimmee's head back against her and began to rock her back and forth as she thanked God she was okay.

"Kimmee, you have to tell me what happened — you scared me!"

Kimmee nodded, saying she would tell her as she raised herself to face her.

"Okay, I'll tell you what happened, but I want to start over from the beginning."

Bella couldn't imagine what had happened here, but Kimmee had her full attention.

"I moved from Dallas this past weekend to start my new career here in Austin. I've wanted to live here ever since I was a little girl. Anyway, today was my first day at my new job." Kimmee looked at her nervously and couldn't follow through with the story, which became evident by a deep breath, long pause, and bowed head.

Bella placed her hands on Kimmee's forearms and looked at her kindly. "It's okay; you can tell me." —

Kimmee stole another deep, cleansing breath to begin.

"Today was my first day at the Travis County Medical Examiner's office."

Another long pause was required to summon the courage to finish.

"I'm a pathologist technician — and my first case — was a small Caucasian, beautiful little female angel that came in last evening."

Bella instantly gasped out, "— Addison —"

Kimmee softly repeated the word. "Yes — Addison."

She reached behind the couch pillow to retrieve the photo, and Bella realized how Kimmee made the correlation. Then, the two locked glances as tears streamed down both faces.

Bella trembled from the visions as she connected the dots between the Travis County Medical Examiner's office and what a pathologist technician must do. Kimmee held tightly onto Bella's wrists while she experienced so many emotions.

Suddenly, out of the fire of mixed emotions, one rose to the top — remembrance. Bella looked into Kimmee's eyes with such passion — and then with such envy.

"You held my angel's heart in your hands today — didn't you?" Somehow, Bella was strangely affected and unexpectedly comforted by the vision. She switched hand positions, so now — she — was holding Kimmee's hands.

"Yes — I held an angel's heart in my hands today."

Bella closed her eyes and drew Kimmee's hands up to her face, caressing them against each cheek and kissing them gracefully. She opened her eyes and stared at Kimmee for a few seconds.

"She used to call me Grammy Bell."

Love collapsed them into each other's arms, where so much emotional data was transferred and so much was said — yet only silence filled the room.

The two released from their embrace, forever connected by an angel, as two souls converged with a unique crossing-of-paths connection that was rare in life.

"They tell us not to get emotionally involved with our cases. But once I saw little Addison's face — I knew that would be a near-impossible task. I wanted to know everything about her: where she lived, what her parents were like, what happened exactly, how it happened, and where that little girl started her career as an angel.

"I wanted to look at the initial report, find the address, and just drive there to feel closer and more connected to her. But we didn't have the report, and if we did, I'm not sure if I would have acted upon my emotions. I do want to do things right, so I hope I wouldn't have acted on them because, in the end, I do want to be professional.

"Today, I was supposed to meet with my main boss for orientation but couldn't because he was dealing with upper-management issues. So, I don't know what the rules are or what they expect of me. But a senior pathologist came and got me, and that's how I came to know Addison.

"Tomorrow, hopefully, I'll meet my main boss and find out what I can and can't do. But today, I'm just lucky Zilla hitch-hiked and found me."

Kimmee smiled at Zilla, who seemed exhausted from her journey as she panted while resting comfortably in her favorite chair.

"Today, I woke with only one purpose in mind — to make my daddy proud on my first day of work. You see, the day he was diagnosed with cancer, I vowed to do something in the medical field to feel like I could make a difference and honor him. Honestly, Bella, I wrestle with this choice somewhat because I have eight years of schooling left.

"Then, out of the blue, the Medical Examiner's office offered me a job. At first, I felt guilty because it might derail me from getting my degree, and I thought I was letting my daddy down. But after a series of long talks with my mom, she told me daddy would want me to be happy here in Austin."

Bella grabbed her hand. "I'm so sorry about your dad, but trust me, dear, he is so proud of you right now, and you're already making a difference on your very first case. I don't know what I would be like right now had you not followed your heart. I'm not sure how it happened, but if you hadn't found Zilla, I don't think I would've made it through the night.

"God put you exactly where you needed to be — and where you need to be is right here with me. And you, Kimmee James Attwood, will be such a blessing to that office. I'm just the first day's example of what you're capable of."

Kimmee teared up. "Thank you so much for that. It means so much to me coming from you, and it sounds exactly like something my mother would say.

"Bella, you have shown such amazing strength tonight because you have spent the whole evening taking care of me, a total stranger, when the unimaginable has happened to you. You are so unbelievable and breathtakingly inspiring, and just for knowing you, I feel like a different person than the one that walked through your door earlier."

"Kimmee, if I inspire you, that thought is appreciated very much. But I'm struggling with horrible feelings of guilt and anger regarding my family. I'm not sure this is my finest hour—"

"—Which is my point," Kimmee interjected, "I can't imagine what you're going through, and yet, you cared for me and took me in — such strength!"

"Well, if that's the case, and I inspire you, you must listen to me — YOU are a remarkable young woman. And *you* are going to be an amazing mother someday. You saw my angel today, and your parental engine kicked in without realizing it. You wanted to learn everything about a little angel, who just started her career in Heaven, and help her family by discovering why."

"Thank you for that," and she drew Bella in for an emphatic hug before she continued.

"Kimmee, you told me about your father, but where is your mother?"

"Oh, my mom lives in Dallas and is wonderful, although we struggle with Dad's passing. I plan to drive back and see her on the weekends to make sure she is doing okay. Plus, we love to go to the White Rock Lake area in Dallas and take in the free concerts; it's our thing.

"But my daddy is the reason I'm here in Austin. When I was little, he surprised me with a daddy-daughter trip to Austin, and I knew this was where I wanted to be someday. He was the greatest man I have ever known, and he inspired me until he drew his final breath. In his passing, he made it financially possible for me to live here."

Bella leaned over and gave Kimmee another hug.

"Kimmee, you're not only going to be a great mother, but you are also such a wonderful daughter. You are completely beautiful, inside and out, and I love the person you are. I love you, Kimmee, and would be honored if you thought of me as your surrogate Austin, TX, mother."

"Well, you made me feel like I was talking with my mom all night, and I felt like I already was your daughter."

They teared up and grasped each other with a firm hug that notarized the binding signatures between their two hearts and that they were indeed mother and daughter.

"Okay, Mom, as your surrogate daughter, my job description is to take care of you, make you avocado toast any time you wish, and ask you about your day. And that means all of it: the good, the bad, the dark, and the ugly. I want to listen and learn about what you went through today and what you're still going through. But I'll completely understand if you're not ready or don't want to tell me."

Bella was apprehensive about the situation. But she mulled over her *daughter's* request as she took a cleansing breath and placed her head in her hands as her internal dialogue opened a mental court case in her mind.

I can't talk to her about this — or can I? Shouldn't I only talk about this with my family? But she feels every bit like my daughter. This wonderful stranger has given me so much solace and companionship, just as family should. Our bond is the most unique possible, given our angel connection. But for these same reasons, I'm afraid of what she might think if I tell her the truth about my struggles.

I can't scare her away — I need her. But sharing my life's darkest thoughts and feelings with her or anyone is a big ask. I want to tell her everything to help this stranger become my surrogate daughter. But talking to her about this will open the darkness, and I'll be right back reliving my most shameful parts — Do I really want to do this to myself?

Bella transformed out of thought and lifted her head from her hands. Kimmee could sense the war-torn woman's spirit return as the events from last evening recreated themselves in her mental palette.

"It's been horrible today; our lives — all of our lives — have been shattered by this. I had this wonderful family just yesterday, but today, we are a mere shadow of what we once were. We've fractured into pieces, and I don't think we will ever be the same again. Humpty Dumpty makes much more sense to me than ever before.

"My kids have been horrible to each other, and at a time when we need each other the most. But if I'm being truthful, I haven't helped matters, as it's just become an 'us versus them' stand-off because of what happened last night with their father."

"So, what did happen last night with their father? Kimmee asked, "I'm not sure about your situation. Are you two still married? — Is their father your husband? Or are you married to someone else? You told me when we first met you were here alone, and since no one's here, I didn't know what to think."

Bella's demeanor changed as the questioning led to mentioning her husband. Answers came but with a much sharper edge attached to each syllable.

"Kimmee, I'm sorry, but it's hard to talk about him, and yes, we're still married, but I'm so upset with him and don't want to see or talk to him right now... It's his fault — everything — the reason Addison is no longer with us. His fault! His damn stupid fault!"

Kimmee was taken aback by her anger and the woman's transformation from a few moments ago. Bella's emotional claws were out, and Kimmee was afraid to ask another question. But after a short pause, Kimmee gave the words in her brain marching orders and sent them into battle.

"Bella, where is your — where is *he* right now? Why isn't he with you today of all days?"

"I'm sorry. I don't know how to answer that question right now."

"Would you please tell me what happened last night so I can understand?"

Bella had a sharp look in her eyes, yet a tremble in her voice as she relived the painful story.

"Last night started as a typical Tuesday evening. Our son Evan and daughter-in-law Amelia try to have a date night every Tuesday, and we typically watch—" There was a pause while trying to verbalize Addison's name, her face squinched together, eyes closed, holding back the accompanying pain. Kimmee handed Bella a Kleenex from the nearby decorative box.

"It started as a wonderful night with my husband — everyone called him Grandpa." She mourned the word that no longer applied as she held the Kleenex to her eyes.

"Truth be told, he was on a roll last night. He has this ability to make me laugh with his wit and sense of humor — even when I'm angry with him. He was unique in that way. Fortunately, our life was more of the former than the latter.

"Where the night took a nosedive was when he played what he referred to as Papa Airways. He would always throw— Addison — in the air and catch her. My daughter-in-law Amelia, Evan, and I didn't like it when he did this. We've tried to get him to stop for over a year, but he's stubborn regarding his airways.

"Truthfully, Addison didn't help matters as she begged him to do it. We just couldn't get him to realize he's not the young man he thinks he is, and it's just a matter of time before someone gets—" her tears echoed the reality that hit hard in her mind.

Kimmee leaned forward and took Bella's hand, squeezing it.

"Last night, my son Evan confronted him about it *again*. Amelia asked me about it *again*, and I told him about it *again* on behalf of Amelia's pleas — but to no avail. He has this constant picture in his head from when our children were young and how he loved to do his airway thing with them. But that was then; this is now, and the results speak for themselves."

"So, when did the actual accident occur?" Kimmee asked as her inner Shirley Holmes became more investigative.

"Well, I guess it was after dinner because I went upstairs to run a bath for Addison while he cleaned off the table and rinsed dishes with her. Most of the time, Addison came up pre-soaked from being rinsed along with the dishes. Then I remembered hearing sirens in the distance and yelling down to hurry so we could get bath over with — but there was no response.

"I finally headed downstairs, and that's when I saw him leaning over Addison, trying to perform what looked like CPR."

Kimmee gasped, choking back tears. "Oh, no —"

"I screamed out — and screamed at him, trying to get answers on what happened. I was so furious with him for not yelling at me for help. If he had, you wouldn't be here asking me these questions. I could have — no, I *would have* saved Addison's life — had I been given a chance.

"I know how to perform CPR. I'm licensed to do it, but he is not! I remember how angry I was, and I slapped him as hard as I could before pushing him off her to perform CPR myself. Then the ambulance arrived. You're not going to believe this, but I had to stop giving CPR and open the door for the EMTs because my baby husband couldn't."

Kimmee allowed Bella a moment after reliving the scene.

"So, the truth is, you didn't officially see what happened? Is that correct?"

"... I suppose I didn't... You're right, dear. I was upstairs at the time."

"So why do you think he didn't call for you to come help?" Kimmee was now gaining more confidence as an investigative reporter.

"It's because he did something that caused her death. I think he finally dropped her playing Papa Airways. And he knew exactly how much trouble he was in, so much so that he would rather take a chance on performing CPR himself, over yelling for me so I could administer proper CPR and save her life. He gambled her life away, and for what? Because he was embarrassed and didn't want us to say, I told you so?

"I just can't let go of this anger because I know, given a chance, Addison would still be with us. Instead, I must live with the fact that I'll never know because he didn't give me that chance."

Bella captured Kimmee's gaze, narrowed her eyes on hers, and intensely asked, "Have you ever seen a glass break? And I mean, actually, watched it break? Or anything, for that matter, fall and shatter into tiny pieces and then stare at the fractured aftermath? Last night, when the EMT pronounced the time of death, I watched that happen to my son as if I were watching something shatter in slow-motion. My son Evan— broke—and I mean he broke.

"I honestly watched the human spirit of my son shatter. This man was the kindest and most non-violent of humans and had never once shown any sign of violence in his life. He lived for his wife and daughter. He loved everyone, especially his dad and me. He is incredibly fit and strong and works out every day before climbing the ladder of success at the oil company where he works. He's even a personal trainer on the weekends for extra money, just because he loves to help other people. That guy — BROKE!

"It's like he turned inside out and exploded at his father and blamed him for everything — just like me. But Evan was vicious. I remember seeing him throw my husband over the couch, then pick him up and shove him against the wall. He was hitting his dad, punching him repeatedly, especially in the stomach, so he could verbally abuse him about being so big. Then he threw him down the hallway and yelled to get out and not even think about coming to the funeral."

"Oh, Bella, I'm so sorry —"

"It was just horrible, and I did nothing to defend him. I felt so damn guilty about what was occurring, yet, I couldn't defend him. He was in the wrong. Evan is defiant in his conviction that his dad killed his daughter, even though the other kids try to convince him that he's wrong. He's more adamant than ever that he doesn't want his dad at the funeral, which makes the other kids try even harder to talk him into changing his mind — that he really doesn't mean it. But like I said, Evan is a broken, broken human right now.

"Kimmee, I don't know how I will survive this. I have so much anger and rage inside me. Not just because of what I told you. But ultimately, in an instant — in this moment of crisis — he robbed me of my future with him, or at least a happy future with him. And because I couldn't save Addison since I didn't have a chance, I'm forced to live with that fact.

"And it's because of this one moment that my perspective of him is gone. I'll always have blame and resentment in the back of my mind, a picture of Addison that will never go away whenever I look at him. It's just tragic because I loved that man so much; from the moment I met him, I knew — I just knew — we both knew.

"Kimmee, he was so funny, clever, and witty from the first second we met, and I wanted to laugh like this for the rest of my life — with this man. My life with him is built on his wit and passion for everything. And I mean e v e r y t h i n g — But also, I was drawn to his love and compassion, not just for his family and me but for anyone at any level of life." Bella began sobbing before her next thought could resume. "And in this one moment, all of that was gone — he has robbed me of my life — my future life with him, my future laughter from his wit and weirdness — and I can't believe I'm saying this, but from his silly Eye-Jobes!"

Kimmee had a strange look — *Eye-Jobes?* — but remembered several photographs where the husband and Addison placed their fingers under their eyes while laughing. *So that's an Eye-Jobe.*

"This is why I'm so bludgeoned with guilt because I know me — I know how I am, and I know he knows me," Bella said. "And that's why he's not here; he knows the deepest parts of me and knows that he must give me my space because of how I am. He also knows that Zilla must be here to help me if there's even a snowball's chance in hell for us.

"Kimmee, I hate this part of me, but I can be a little fireball when I get hurt, and what I'm feeling right now is way more than a fireball's worth of hurt. I'll never be able to look at him the same. This crisis will always live just below the surface with everything, and because of this, I won't ever give him a fair chance to make things better — not really."

"But you don't know that," Kimmee said gently.

Bella shook her head. "But I do. — His wit won't have the same impact; I'll be less patient than I already am, which is another boxcar to add to my guilt train. I'll always mourn the loss of our life together. Kimmee, I love and adore him, and yes, I will miss him, but not right now.

"And on top of all this, I miss Evan. It will be impossible for his life to be the same. I fear his rage will be right below the surface, just waiting to explode, and he won't want to be around his father ever again. And my husband won't feel like he can joke around with him or even look at him without overpowering guilt.

"It's an impossible situation and all of this because he wouldn't yell for help. Addison would have lived; I would have saved her. — Kimmee, I'm so sorry you had to endure all this, but this is also why I feel guilty about your admiration. I feel like a horrible person, and I'm petrified to live in my own future —"

Weeping didn't begin to describe the tears from Bella's collapsed soul. Without warning, a primordial scream erupted from the emotional volcano that had built up inside and reached its threshold.

Kimmee hugged her surrogate mother as the darkness Bella endured made Kimmee respect her even more. The daunting courage it must have taken to explore her darkest parts and realize her truth was remarkable. Knowing Bella's demons inspired Kimmee even more, and since she was Bella's angel, she was committed to finding a way to help her through this.

Bella's primal scream left her depleted.

"Kimmee, there's bottled water in the garage refrigerator if you want. It's down the hallway to the right and through the utility room; please make yourself at home. I'll be back in a few minutes," and Bella headed upstairs.

Kimmee accepted her offer and made her way down the hallway, once again enjoying the mixture of beautiful art and family memories. She opened the garage door and fumbled for the light switch. *Ah, there it is* — click.

Kimmee gasped — "Holy Moly!"

She recalled Bella saying her husband was passionate about everything, but this put a verb in her mind of how passionate the man was. *OMG, this guy's amazing!* — and she was in awe of what she saw. She made her way around the collection of beautiful bicycles, appreciating every detail, down to the color of each nut, bolt, and wire. Kimmee was so enamored with the Bikes that she didn't hear the door open as Bella interrupted her thoughts and chimed in.

"I know what you're thinking; this guy's crazy — right?"

"Well, actually — no — in fact, just the opposite. You're not going to believe this, but I wanted to move to Austin because when I was a little girl, my daddy and I watched every minute of the Tour de France, and every year, I became more and more of a Lance Armstrong fan. The daddy-daughter trip I told you about down to Austin. That trip was to ride in a LIVESTRONG event to raise money for cancer research and to meet Lance, who had won, I think, five of his seven titles at that time.

"Anyway, I've been riding bicycles ever since, and bicycles are the real reason I'm here in Austin. When my daddy passed away, he enabled me to live my dream of moving here. He even bought me a $12,000 bicycle that I custom ordered from Mellow Johnny's Bicycle Shop, which Lance owns, in case you didn't already know. Anyway, this morning was my first ride on my new bike.

"I can't believe what I'm seeing; this is amazing. There's something different about these bicycles; they look like every bolt and wire, seat and seat post, and every color on each bicycle is color-coordinated. These bicycles look more like beautiful art pieces—"

"I can't believe you said that." Bella interrupted, "he always referred to this as his art gallery and spent a lot of time sitting at his bench and staring at them for hours. I can already tell you he would love you — you're just like your surrogate father," she said with a smile. "You might end up with a whole surrogate family; riding bikes is a prerequisite to being in this family. Let me show you something, dear; wait here."

Bella headed upstairs and returned with a 5x7 photo. "Here you go, dear." Kimmee lit up as she scanned the picture of Bella and her husband riding bicycles with their hands raised high and smiling from ear to ear under their helmets.

"This picture is us crossing the finish line at the 'Hotter-than-Hell-Hundred' in Wichita Falls, TX. I was fifty-one years old at the time, and a few months later, I went on to run The Williams Route 66 Marathon in Tulsa, Okla. It was my third full marathon, and I ran with my daughter Jordyn in my first two marathons. You and Jordyn will love each other; riding bikes with her dad is one of her favorite things, just like you with your daddy.

"My daughter is quite the athlete; when we ran our first marathon, she was only fourteen, and we had to get special permission for her to run the full marathon. Jack Rector, the president of the running club we trained with, had to vouch for her because she was the youngest runner of the Inaugural Williams Route 66 Marathon that year.

"My husband became the running club's unofficial photographer. He went every Saturday at 6:30 a.m. for our training runs and rode alongside Jordyn and me for support.

"He began taking pictures of us to document our marathon journey, but then everyone got to know him, and he ended up taking hundreds of pictures of everyone. They eventually put the weekly photos on the running club website.

"He was quite good at taking photos while riding at the same time. He took some of the most amazing action shots without looking through a lens; he had a knack for pointing, shooting, and framing the pictures perfectly. Everyone wanted him to be at the marathon, so he found a way to weave and bob through the thousands of runners to take pictures of our running group members."

Wow! A cyclist who was a creative artist with an eye for photography, no wonder his bicycles all looked like art pieces!

"So, Mom — do you have a bicycle in the collection? I noticed a nice bright-red Specialized Allez that seems to be a smaller frame size than the rest."

Bella smiled as Kimmee continued.

"Maybe you, me, and Jordyn can ride together sometime! I would love to meet her; she sounds amazing. Maybe she could be my first official Austin, TX, friend," Kimmee said with a warm smile.

"Oh, that sounds wonderful! I can hardly wait for you to meet her, and I think you are about the same age. But as far as a bicycle ride, I'm not sure if I can even ride anymore or remember how to clip into my pedals, which was not my strong suit. This picture is probably the last time I rode my bike, and I did the Hotter-Than-Hell just to prove I could do it." Bella's face lit up as she reminisced.

"I remember having a lot of fun training for it with my husband, and it truly was an incredible experience. I've always been a runner, so I run while my husband rides when we exercise at the lake. Oh, my, I just remembered something." Her face looked like she was about to cry.

"I haven't thought about this for years. But it meant so much to my husband that I rode the Hotter-than-Hell with him, that he lost fifty-five pounds to have a full knee replacement just so he could start running with me." She reached for the picture of the two of them crossing the line and gazed at it with love and fondness.

Kimmee's eyes watered as she watched Bellavia stare at the photo as if she had just fallen in love for the first time. Feelings a few minutes ago she thought not possible.

"Oh, Bella — that's so cool that he did that. So how did the operation go?"

Bella smiled and was emphatic in her response. "It went TERRIBLE... He was in sooooo! — much! — pain!

"It was the most painful experience of his life. If you thought my primal scream was loud, double that, and that's what I heard every time his physical therapist came over to get his knee to bend to a specified degree. But week after week, he fought, and he screamed, and then he fought some more, and he screamed some more, and then he finally reached the degree of bendability he was supposed to achieve.

"Then I'll never forget this: on January 1st of that year, he jogged for the first time in thirty-eight years. He could only jog for about fifty feet, but he did it. Then, we would jog a little further every night when I came home – half a block the first day, two-thirds of a block the next, and so forth. Running was hard for him; he did not enjoy it and even hated it, but he was determined. Finally, three months later, he reached the three-mile marker. But he didn't want to run any farther because he wanted to officially run his first 5K race with me at an event.

"I researched a St. Patty's Day run called 'The Dash Down Greensville 5K' in Dallas. So, I surprised him with a trip to the Omni Hotel in Downtown Dallas, where we stayed when we married. Anyway, he did it — he finished the 5K with me and was so happy when we crossed the finish line.

"Although he hated running, he did that for me. But he hasn't run a single step since. After that, we both resigned to do what we loved; I ran while he rode, but we did it together and were both okay with that."

"Mom, that's so sweet. The two of you are so meant to be together. But that's not getting you out of cycling with me sometime. When these storms blow over, and they will, we're going on a bike ride."

"I don't know, Kimmee, it's been so long since I've ridden. That picture was taken over nine years ago — I really don't think I can."

"Oh, sure you can, Mom — it's just like riding a bike."

They laughed at the irony of the cliché.

A scratching at the door pulled Bella out of her inward gaze, and a bark let them know they had forgotten about someone.

"Kimmee, I better go back in and check on Zilla and see if she has food and water. Do you want to come with me?"

"Would you mind terribly if I looked around here for a while? I've just never seen anything like this."

"No problem, dear, take your time." Bella looked at Kimmee, who was becoming more like her daughter every minute.

"Kimmee, you're just like him, you know; it's bizarre how passionate you two are — and about bicycles, of all things." Bella felt a compulsion that she couldn't stop.

"Have you ever seen the movie *Serendipity*?"

"Are you kidding me? It's one of my absolute favorite movies! I can't even count how many times I've seen it. I've always wanted to go to New York City and go to Serendipity's to sit at the table where they filmed the movie and have a frrrozen hot chocolate. Then I'd like to go ice skating in Central Park just like they did in the movie. That's so on my bucket list of things I want to do. Why do you ask?"

Bella had a gentle look on her face. "Kimmee — that is a perfect answer; I truly hope you check that one off your bucket list."

Her response left Bella feeling reminiscent. The similarities Kimmee shared with her husband's attitudes and perspectives about life were genuinely bizarre. Bella began thinking that perhaps her self-imposed primal scream therapy helped lessen her emotional pain.

She hadn't spent any time around her husband's collection of bikes in nine years since they rode in the Hotter-than-Hell. But being around them now brought up some beautiful memories, and she heard his voice as some of his "bicyclisms" echoed in her head.

"*I have to go look at them; they're not going to look at themselves. — Hey, watch it; they can hear you. — Bicycles are people too, you know!*" And then she remembered one of his bicyclisms that had never meant anything to her. But tonight, it had a more powerful impact because she realized he only used it when he was feeling low or having a bad day. *"I need to go fix my bicycles — because bicycles fix everything."*

Watching Kimmee admire each bicycle as a work of art made Bella miss him. *Was he right? Do bicycles fix everything?* She wasn't nearly as focused on her emotional pain as before she entered the garage. *Maybe I should get to know my bike again?*

"Take your time, dear — spend all the time you need with his bikes; I think I get it now." Bella continued to watch Kimmee spend time with each bike as if she were making a new friend.

"Kimmee, I've thought about it — I'd love to ride bicycles with you."

A loud squeal exploded from Kimmee as Bella smiled before heading into the house to tend to Zilla.

Kimmee finished the tour de bicycles, then sat at his workbench, staring at the collection and wondering about the man who had his life ripped from under him. As she sat, she noticed a paper towel with some typing paper turned upside down on his workbench. Curious, she looked at it and saw the bottom page first. *Wow! What's this? — Handwritten! Who does a handwritten letter anymore?"* Then she saw the heading on the first page.

"A Letter to My Granddaughter, Addison Hope."

Goosebumps invaded her skin as her pupils widened, her hands trembled, and her soul opened to the emotional journey before her. What would she discover and hopefully understand about the essence of the man she yearned to find?

Chapter Nine

Papa's Letter

─────※─────

A Letter to My Granddaughter, Addison Hope

Dear Addison,

I have been a passionate man all my life; I have experienced love and joy to a degree that I thought could not be possible. — Then YOU arrived and proved me wrong. — Let me first say, "You're Welcome," as I gave my heart and all its passions to your father and could not be prouder of the man he has become and the father he is to you.

Also, I knew from the moment I met your mother that she was special. However, I did not realize how special she was until YOU came into this world and changed mine! Now, let me put into words how I would change the world just for you if I could. — Here it goes.

I want you to live in a world where children of all makes, models, and circumstances are kind to each other. A world where no one hurts any child, and a world where if a child is hurt, they can cry, and no one calls them a name — a world where the worst thing children have to worry about — is NOTHING.

I want you to live in a world where it is safe to ride a bicycle on any road and in any neighborhood. And I will be honored to witness the first pedal strokes that set you free of my hands as you learn how to ride a bicycle and begin balancing your way through life.

We will have so much fun navigating our way safely through neighborhoods, as well as around the lake. And as we do, you will learn the value of exercise while paying attention to the beauty of the world around you. We will stop and smell the flowers and gaze at the birds. And after our rides, we will have a picnic in the park and have lovely conversations about all the things we experienced. I will teach you to leave this place called "Earth" better than you found it, and we will do so by helping pick up trash.

We will talk about what you need to know in life and develop your mental toolbox with the right tool for every situation. You will learn to use these tools appropriately as you journey through life while becoming a young lady.

I will teach you about living what I refer to as an "Intention-Based Life." You see, Addison — people don't always say what they meant to say. Still, I believe you can develop skills to see past their poorly chosen words to determine what they truly intended.

These skills will help you understand and control your emotions as you get older. And this will help you with relationships and allow you to talk calmly and work through troubled times. Addison, there will always be some troubled times, but with the proper tools — not as many.

I make you a promise that "I" will not spoil you. (I cannot say the same for Grammy Bell) I want you to learn the importance of hard work. The satisfaction you get from accomplishing goals will give you great confidence and make you a great leader.

And when you reach an age of understanding, I want you to learn how important it is to experience giving to the less fortunate.

I will also teach you to look for opportunities to perform random acts of kindness. Oh, the fun we will have by doing just that! We will start with the drive-thru line at Sonic by paying for the car behind us without them knowing. And who knows, they might pay for the car behind them, and maybe we will start a movement! — Or, at the very least, we will put a smile on their face and brighten their day.

We will experience so much joy from giving because this is the most critical thing in life to learn. "An Unexpected Gift at an Unexpected Time" is what creates joy. And when we see a little girl or a little boy at a birthday party, I want you to shake their hand

and surprise them with a dollar bill of whatever amount we can afford at that moment. This act can cause great joy in a child's life.

Addison, you never know the impact of kindness on a person, but we know there <u>will</u> be an impact. However, my precious Addison, there are also these things called "Expectations." And when you are older, I will teach you how when expectations aren't met, "Expectations can become Resentments Waiting to Happen." When this happens, just as much happens negatively, which can cause resentment and hurt in a person's life.

My little Addison, this is what we do not want to happen in your life or to others around you as you journey to become a little lady. We will work on what I like to call your "Expectation Certification" as we journey through life together.

Oh, the times we will have, my precious Addison! I cry tears of joy as I look forward to when you and I watch the movie Serendipity together. This movie means so much to me because of one phrase. "You know the Greeks didn't write obituaries; they only asked one question after a man dies.

— Did he have Passion?"

This quote is how I live my life. I am passionate about all I do and all I love. And I dream of a day when you and I will travel to New York City to visit the famous Serendipity III restaurant and share a Frrrozen Hot Chocolate. And we will sit at the same table where they filmed the movie. I can't imagine a greater joy than doing that with you.

But for now, my little Addison, I must go, as you will be here soon, and I must get ready so I can see how much bigger you are this week than you were last, and in the blink of an eye, you are going to be all grown up. However, I already know what a beautiful, capable, and confident young lady you will be because I already know the tools you will have in life.

Addison Hope, as I finish writing this letter, I realize you will not understand any of this at such a young age. But when you are older, like me, I think this letter will become one of your most treasured possessions. We never know what life will bring or if life will give us another twenty-four hours. And that is why I choose to live the ones I have with passion.

So today, I want to have no regrets. I am an eccentric man, and these words filled my heart for whatever reason today, and a little voice in my head nudged me to get them on paper just for you.

In closing, Addison, as I write this letter to you, according to the Global Language Monitor, there are 1,057,379.6 words in the English language. The problem is, not one of these words is big enough to say just how much I love you — So, now, I need to invent new words just for you.

Addison Hope, I love you a Gazillion, Trentillion, Octillion, Quinnbillion, Threntillion, Artrillion, Fourlillion, Tridrillion, Gratillion, Catillion, Crazillion, Godzillion, and your daddy's favorite, BananaBillion X's Infinity Squared.

I know it's just a start, but we have changed the world just a little with these new words.

Love, Papa

It was one of the most poignant letters she had ever read. She almost fell out of her seat while reading the quote from *Serendipity* and how he wanted to take Addison there someday for a frrrozen hot chocolate.

It was now clear why Bella was curious if she had seen the movie. But something told her no one had seen the letter, and just in case they hadn't, she didn't want to spoil the grandpa's purpose for writing it, so she placed it back under the paper towel.

Kimmee thought the verbal painting of this letter was an absolute work of art. The lessons were perfectly chosen, as well as inked onto the paper. There were no mistakes or signs of whiteout used in writing the letter. But mostly, the words on the pages sounded like things her father would have written to her, word for word, and she became emotional thinking of him.

With her emotions came a vision of Addison lying on the medical examiner's table. But Kimmee saw her differently than before; this time, she knew all the tools this little girl would have been given in life. This time, she knew all the bicycle rides Addison missed out on with her grandpa, as well as the trip to Serendipity's to have a frrrozen hot chocolate.

Kimmee loved this man, this eccentric grandpa, as he referred to himself. His bicycle collection, his passions, *Serendipity*, his teachings to his granddaughter, everything. She had to meet the man who lost everything dear to him and was thrown out of his life during a moment of crisis.

This case could not get any more personal if she tried. And even though they didn't find anything yet from the initial autopsy today, Kimmee was determined they would. Somehow, someway, she was going to help exonerate Grandpa, and she was going to put Humpty Dumpty back together again.

Her gut feeling screamed there was no way this man could have harmed his granddaughter, as the family had blamed him. But regardless of gut feelings, the sciences must be there to back it up. She then asked herself what a forensic investigator would do. *Ask questions, gather evidence, and solve this puzzle so you can go on to the next.*

Kimmee looked around the garage, this time with new eyes pursuing evidence. She noticed a stack of towels with the top two folded differently from the four below. She checked the towels closer and could tell they were recently wet by how the fibers dried and had a slight crunch. She could also see a couple of hairs that looked to be the color of a little dog named Zilla.

The towels in the garage made sense, as there was a white Mercedes Benz that appeared to be quite pampered. But the top two towels had been used recently, last night most likely, to dry little Zilla.

Someone with the code to the garage door must have brought Zilla back last night and dried her off before putting her back in the house. I wonder if any neighbors have the code?

Kimmee found Bella back in the house, resting on a loveseat opposite the couch and staring at one spot on the floor.

"That's where it happened; that's where Addison started her career as an angel," she said as Kimmee sat beside her.

"Kimmee, how do I resolve this impossibleness? Between me, myself, and my demons? I'm trapped inside an emotional house of mirrors. Everywhere I turn, everywhere I feel, there's a different level of pain reflecting back at me. But in every mirror — I see and feel Addison and think she'll always be there because I know I could have saved her. These reflections will keep me from ever letting him be his true self around me again — all he had to do was call for me."

Kimmee handed her a tissue and hugged her while Bella dabbed her tears.

"I do have to admit something," Bella said. "Just being in the garage and watching how you interacted with his bicycles and called them art brought back a glimpse of my life with him. In fact, when we got together, our very first date was riding bikes together. He borrowed a bicycle for me so we could ride around the lake and then picnic.

"Bicycling fast became a significant part of our lives. We had great conversations while riding and loved being outdoors. But over the years, I lost interest in doing the one thing that brought us together. I guess I started to take things for granted.

"But hearing you talk about your dad and riding with him made me think about how Jordyn must feel when she rides with her dad. And reminiscing about the Hotter-than-Hell and his knee replacement reminded me of just how much pain he willfully endured to run a 5K race with me.

"Kimmee, you remind me so much of my husband that I had to ask you about watching the movie *Serendipity*. He has watched it over 2000 times, and all because of one line—"

Kimmee interjected, "You know the Greeks didn't write obituaries — they only asked one question after a man died — Did he have passion?"

"Oh, my God! You *are* him! After you told me about *Serendipity* being on your bucket list, I started hearing him say these bicyclisms of his. Things like, 'I have to go look at them; they're not going to look at themselves. — Hey, watch it, they can hear you — Bicycles are people too, you know!' But one of his bicyclisms I didn't get until tonight — because tonight I remembered him only saying this when he was a little down or having a bad day; 'I need to go fix my bicycles — Because bicycles fix everything.'"

Kimmee became emotional and reached for a tissue as well. For a man she'd never met, she felt everything about him.

"Bellavia, he's right, you know; maybe bicycles can fix everything. Perhaps his bicycles lessened his pain during the bad days and can help relieve your pain, too. Since bicycles are people too, let them remind you of what you once had so they can start you on your own bicycle path to forgiveness.

"I think you may be looking at your emotional house of mirrors all wrong; maybe the reflections of Addison aren't there to haunt you but to help you. Perhaps she's still in your thoughts because she needs you to forgive her papa so she can be at peace in Heaven.

"No angel should feel guilty knowing that an accident has ruined the lives of others back on Earth. Addison can't enjoy Heaven, knowing she was the one who begged her papa to throw her in the air. He couldn't resist that beautiful face with her arms reaching up high in the sky — Could you? 'Come on, Papa, just one more time, Papa?' Her papa made one mistake, and now his life is ruined.

"I get how you're angry because he didn't yell for you. But this split-second decision seems to be the defining moment you're willing to martyr your future for. So, if that's the reasoning, let's examine it."

Bella dried her eyes, staring at Kimmee in thought.

"No one can ever really know what they're going to do in an actual moment of crisis, at least not a crisis of this magnitude. Some people cannot think clearly, and some may be perfectly calm and think perfectly clear. Some people might faint, hyperventilate, or panic; some may not.

"The problem with a crisis is that you can't practice for one, even though you might think you can. But it's impossible to practice for one because you can't predict what your actual state of mind is going to be when that instance occurs. State of mind is everything in life. In some states of mind, you are a better version of yourself; that's why we have heroes. But in some states, you can't spell your own name, and that's why we have tragedies.

"Bella, you don't know this about me, but I was a very emotional little girl growing up and quite a handful — still am. Grandpa seems to be a very emotional and passionate man and probably a handful for you to raise as well."

Bella acknowledged, giving a small smile.

"If you say I remind you of him, then please listen to me. I believe with all my heart that if this had happened to me, I wouldn't have been able to think clearly. Maybe his only crime is that he may not have been in a state of mind conducive to thinking clearly. Maybe he didn't hide anything from you, but you assigned him a state of mind that you thought he should have been in and decided for both of you that you couldn't forgive him. But until you forgive Addison's papa, she won't be able to leave your emotional house of mirrors."

Bella's emotional demons poured out in a heavy rainfall of tears.

"Bella, I know your demons, but I'm your angel. And in order to get through this, you mustn't make this your crucifix that says you can't forgive your husband. Instead, when you think of or refer to him — refer to him as Addison's papa, not your husband. If you do this, it might be easier to forgive him that way. Listen to your heart. I think it's trying to beat your life back together by giving you emotional glimpses of what your life was — happy."

Bellavia gasped. "Kimmee, you're wise beyond your years, and everything you said is true. You must be an angel because how else would you know what to say?"

Kimmee responded, "I may have read an angelic piece of literature recently that inspired me. And maybe it gave me the state of mind to put you in the state of mind you needed. State of mind is everything; a mental state of forgiveness may help everything work out for you — I promise."

"Well, whatever you read, dear, sounds like something I need to read."

I hope so as well, Kimmee thought.

"Bella, can I ask you something about Addison's papa? Where do you think he is right now?"

"The detectives asked me that as well."

"I'm sure they did, but you were in a much different state last night than now. I want to find him; I want to meet the man you say I'm so much alike. Don't you want to find him as well?"

"Kimmee, I have to say, I am in a different place mentally than I was just a few short hours ago, thanks to you. You have blessed me so much by coming into my life. And yes, I am missing him — but I don't think I'm ready to see him just yet. I still need time to work through what you said, which was one of the most beautiful perspectives. It sounded like something he would've tried to say in his defense — but I wouldn't have listened to it coming from him. That's why God put you here, to say it for him so that I could give his words a chance."

Kimmee hugged her surrogate mom.

"Bella, let's think about this. After Evan threw him out, given his state of mind, where do you think he went? Everyone has a person they would go to if they needed serious help; who was that for him?"

"I'm not sure who that would be, but he just saw a man named Chris yesterday at the lake who goes to Al-Anon with him. Kimmee, are you familiar with Al-Anon?"

"Not really; I've heard the word before."

"Al-Anon is for people with a friend or relative with alcohol addiction. My husband had an employee who was very dear to him. He considered him not only a friend but a mentor — he was also an alcoholic. So, my husband joined to better understand the disease and help him. Sadly, his mentor died from the disease, but his brotherhood of men helped him through it.

"He loves attending meetings and has been a long-time member. Every Friday at noon, he goes to a men's meeting that is his favorite, and he hardly ever misses. He loves his 'peeps,' as he calls them, and I heard him mention Chris several times. The only problem is because of the anonymity of Al-Anon, I don't know his last name or any of his peeps' last names and only heard a few first names here and there.

"I told the detectives this and mentioned Chris as a possibility. They said they would go to the meeting on Friday and see if Chris was there or if anyone had seen him. Other than that, any of our mutual couples, friends, or church acquaintances would have contacted me to tell me where he was. They want to talk to him and get his side of the event. But I don't think they're treating this like a crime. I overheard the EMT telling them he witnessed my son throw him out, so the police knew he didn't run away from the scene. But they're looking for him just the same.

"Kimmee, I'm telling you — after my son threw him out, I don't believe he ever returned. He walks long distances routinely for exercise; a four-mile walk or more is no big deal. I think he walked to one of his Al-Anon friend's houses. The only other thought I have is this man knows me better than I know myself, and he knows I need some serious space. The man knows who I am and how I am; as I said, I can be a fireball, so he knows not to contact me because I won't answer.

"The only other idea I have is that he would try and go on a long bus ride. He loves resting and relaxing to the open road noise. He's always made these little jests over the years that if anything bad happened between us, he would go to Asheville, North Carolina. He has always wanted to see the haze of the Blue Ridge Mountains.

"I almost think he might go there as a poetic gesture. He prides himself on saying what he means and meaning what he says, so I think he would do it just to fulfill his poetic prophecy."

"Did the detectives ask you if you had any of his credit card information and cell phone number so they could track him?"

"That's the thing; he left his wallet, keys and cell phone on his desk and didn't come back for them. Last night, I gave all the information to the detectives to track him to see if he used any of his credit card numbers from memory. I also let the detectives take his phone to look at it in case it would help."

"Well, he would have needed cash to get to Asheville and stay in a hotel for a few days – a lot of cash. Did you guys have cash hidden anywhere that he could have grabbed?"

"Well — we don't have any cash that I know of — but if he really wanted to get there, he's resourceful; one of his buddies would have given him the money."

There was a pawing at Bella's ankles for her mommy to pick her up. Zilla was no longer tired from her sprint earlier but tired of not being the center of attention.

Kimmee couldn't help but get a little emotional from Zilla and her mommy's love for each other and the magnitude of the dog's cuteness. Kimmee helped pet Zilla, who obviously wasn't getting the attention she deserved.

"Today, when I first looked at her dog tag and saw the name Godzilla, I smirked because she was a girly Godzilla. — So, where did the name come from?"

Bella rolled her eyes as she answered. "We drove five hours to pick up this little girl — actually, we went to pick up her brother, but as we sat there holding him, Zilla crawled out from underneath the couch we were on. She was twice as small as her brother and the runt of the litter. It was love at first sight for me, but an extra $500 for my husband. But I didn't care. I had to have her. When we got in the SUV, my husband said, 'Okay, let's get you home, Godzilla.' I laughed at the sheer dichotomy of it, and from that moment on, she's been our little Godzilla.

"On the way home, my husband started thinking about the real Godzilla. According to him, Godzilla was asexual because, in one of the many Godzilla movies, Godzilla laid giant eggs that magically hatched at once and almost ate Matthew Broderick.

"Our first photo of Godzilla is her sitting in a small ice cream dish; it's the most adorable picture I have of her — she was so tiny. Like I told you earlier, I shortened her name to Zilla for more of a girly name. But as Zilla grew older, she started leaving little presents around the house, and my husband would yell, 'GOD – ZILLA! Use the pee-pee pad!' So, the whole he/she name worked out for all of us."

Kimmee watched Bella's face as she spoke about the love of her life, second only to Addison, and how her whole essence changed.

"Kimmee, I just remembered something odd about last night. After the coroner's unit left," — Bella paused as the thought robbed her of her breath, then started over — "After the coroner's unit left, Evan and Amelia followed to see where they were taking her."

"It was such a dark time, and I just stood there alone with my thoughts. But after about ten minutes, I noticed Zilla was not out wanting to be picked up and petted. I immediately panicked, and I looked everywhere for her. I was already an emotional wreck, but not finding Zilla? I had already lost Addison; now, the thought of losing two of the most important things in one night made me have a panic attack.

"I sat on the floor, hoping Zilla would magically appear out of hiding. I thought she probably ran out when I opened the front door for the EMTs to enter and set up their equipment."

"A lot was going on," Kimmee pointed out gently.

"But I wasn't paying attention or thinking about Zilla being gone. As you know, it was pouring rain last night, so I got in my car and drove around the neighborhood and surrounding neighborhoods looking for her. I searched for hours. I was crying so hard that I honestly don't know how I did it; adrenaline must have kept me going. I couldn't believe this was happening, and I blamed my husband the whole time.

"Anyway, when I finally got back and walked in from the garage, Zilla was here barking her head off. I picked her up and hugged her so hard that

I was afraid I might hurt her. I just cried and thanked God for this miracle of miracles.

"I'm telling you, Kimmee — if Zilla hadn't been here last night, I would have also been a part of your first day at work. I remember second-guessing myself. At first, I thought maybe Zilla was here the whole time, and I just panicked. But she was wet, or I guess more damp, so she must have run outside in the rain at some point but managed to sneak back in. Anyway, I'm not sure how she got wet; I was just glad she was home."

"It's interesting you said that because I wanted to ask you about something I found in the garage. Someone used a couple of towels to dry Zilla off because they looked like they had her hair on them. Do you think your husband could have possibly found Zilla after Evan threw him out of the house? Like you said, he knew you needed her to help you cope with everything. Maybe he found her and tried to come back and talk to you after all? — He may have been waiting for Evan and Amelia to leave before he did, but then you were gone, so he left her here and took off again."

"I guess that's possible — but if that's the case, why didn't he take his wallet, keys, and cell phone and drive off in his SUV, or wait around to talk to me, or at the very least call or text me to let me know he found Zilla?"

"Maybe he thought you might be with Evan and Amelia and didn't want to take the chance of calling or texting if they were around."

"No — I honestly think he didn't come back here last night; he knew better than to try and talk to me after what happened. He knew I needed my space, which is why his stuff is still here."

"In that case, who else had access to the house?"

"Well, a couple of neighbors have the code to the garage in case of an emergency."

"Do you think one of them found Zilla while you were looking for her and put her back in the house?"

"That's possible ... I suppose. Actually, that's more plausible to me...."

"I know it was raining last night, but would he have come back and grabbed a bicycle out of the garage without coming in to grab his things and then ride somewhere? Can you tell if any of them are missing?"

"Oh, no, no way! First, why would he take a bike instead of his SUV, especially since it was pouring rain last night? Kimmee, let me tell you something. He has never, ever — and I mean EVER ridden one of his bicycles in the rain. Nor has he ever ridden one of his bicycles at night. None of his bikes have reflectors on them anywhere. I've heard him say clear back when he was at, like, his seventh bicycle before I quit counting — that he couldn't stand reflectors on his bikes because they weighed too much and made the bike less aero-dynamic. The man is 260 pounds and very round — yet the reflectors weigh too much and cause the bike to be less aerodynamic?

"Anyway, after thirty-six years of marriage, I know for a fact that he would never ever take one of his babies and ride it in the rain or at night, no way. Like I said, even if he came back, why would he ride a bicycle in the rain instead of driving his SUV? And let's say you're right that he did come back specifically for a bike. Wouldn't he have come in and grabbed his wallet and phone? I know him better than anyone. Trust me, he did not take one of his bikes last night."

"Well, if he did, he wouldn't have been the only one riding in the rain last night. I saw another rather large cyclist riding a pretty nice bike while I was out getting a late-night Frosty treat — something my dad and I did when I couldn't sleep. Anyway, I thought it was weird to see someone that big out riding that late in the rain. — Bella, I have to ask again — Are you absolutely sure he wouldn't have taken one of his bicycles?"

"Kimmee — please don't waste another brain cell thinking about it. I'm absolutely sure it wasn't him. Austin is Lance Armstrong country, for goodness' sake. And one of the biggest bicycle towns in America. People of every shape and size ride bikes in all weather conditions, day and night. Lots of people here don't have cars and ride bikes instead, and almost all of them are pretty nice bikes, mainly because of your hero."

Kimmee began thinking about Bella's husband or anyone who had just been through a crisis of this magnitude. *Could they be prone to hurt themselves?* The detective in her had to know.

"Bella, after a traumatic event such as this one, I don't think people can often think logically or rationally. Given his circumstances, he would be at the height of emotion and maybe not thinking clearly. To me, leaving behind the things needed to survive is a sign of hopelessness — like he won't need them anymore. Bella, I have to ask. In his state of mind, do you believe your husband would be capable of hurting himself?"

Bellavia started to cry from the guilt. She knew she wasn't his biggest cheerleader right now, but she didn't want to be his funeral director either.

"Kimmee — what you're asking me is if he could kill himself? I've never known him to be even remotely suicidal. But perhaps that was yesterday; today, he is in unfamiliar emotional territory.

"The detectives weren't looking at it as if he was going to hurt himself because they knew Evan had thrown him out and that he didn't have the opportunity to gather his things first. They just wanted to talk to him and get his side of the story. But you're thinking this way because he may have returned last night and didn't take his stuff on purpose. Should I call the detective to tell him your theory that he came back but didn't take his stuff? I have his card right here."

"I don't think it would hurt to let them know it's a possibility."

"I'll call him and take care of that in the morning. Kimmee, I can't thank you enough for tonight. I know you are an angel because something spiritual happened here tonight; because how I felt when we first met to what I'm feeling now is nothing short of a miracle. It's the only explanation I can fathom because I hated my husband this morning, and then Zilla's escape piled on top of that feeling, and my kids fighting over the funeral piled on top of that.

"I was experiencing an emotional Jenga puzzle that I knew would crash and emotionally kill my soul. I felt like my life would be soulless for the rest of my days once it happened. But that was then, and this is now, and the thing that kept my emotional Jenga puzzle from collapsing was you."

Kimmee reached out with a gentle touch and tears in her eyes.

"I couldn't even say Addison's name when you first arrived or talk about my husband without the anger. But now I'm missing him, and being with his bicycles has affected me; watching you with his bicycles has saved me. Showing you the picture of us crossing the finish line reminded me of what I had. But most of all, your being his advocate and giving him a voice that I would actually listen to gives me hope that maybe I can heal from this.

"There's a picture upstairs in my husband's office that I suddenly have a deep yearning to see but, more importantly, feel. Would you mind coming with me to look at it?"

"Are you kidding me? My curiosity is running wild. I would love to go with you."

Once again, Kimmee is privy to even more beautiful art that adorned the walls on the way to the upstairs office.

Kimmee took a reset breath as she spied a blown-up photograph framed on the wall behind his desk. It looked like Bella and her husband when they were much younger, standing with a musician holding an instrument. Inside the framed glass were two concert tickets.

"What an interesting photo; who is that? I can hardly wait to hear the story behind it."

"So, my given name is Susan Bellavia Valliatti. Growing up, I went by the name Susan. But when I first met my husband, he was a musician who played in a 16-piece big band jazz orchestra in college and taught private bass trombone lessons for income.

"When he found out my middle name was Bellavia, he orchestrated this elaborate scheme that was months in the making that involved my mom and my boss — just not me.

"Imagine this: we lived in Oklahoma City at the time. One day, my boss asked me if I could work on a particular Saturday and said to put it on my calendar. He told me a big wig was coming in from corporate, and we needed to pick him up from the airport and take him to lunch and his hotel.

"So, on that Saturday, when we went to the airport to pick up the corporate big wig, my boss dropped me off at the entrance and said he would park the car and be back. — Instead, when I entered the airport, my boyfriend stood there with two packed suitcases holding two tickets for Austin, TX."

Kimmee clapped her hands together, applauding quietly, excited to hear the rest.

"When we arrived, he surprised me with two more tickets to the Austin City Limits Music Festival that night to see Chuck Mangione in concert. What I didn't know is that Chuck Mangione has this beautiful song called Bellavia, and when I heard Chuck Mangione play that song for the first time in that setting, my heart palpitated. I was breathless, and when the song was over, he was on one knee — and asked if I would be *his* Bellavia. And I have been *his* Bellavia ever since.

Kimmee clutched her hands over her heart as she took a savoring breath.

"So, to answer your question of who's in the photo with us, that's Chuck Mangione from the night we got engaged. If you look at the tickets closely, he signed them for us and wrote 'Good Fortune Bellavia.'

Kimmee's heart was now palpitating as she knocked on her chest.

"Oh, Bellavia, I have never heard of a more romantic marriage proposal. I hope I have an engagement story half as sweet as that someday."

Bella had an inward gaze as she looked outward at the picture. Kimmee could sense her inner conflict between the life she once knew — and the life she knows now.

Kimmee reached over and placed her hand on Bellavia's shoulder as she looked deep into her eyes, which swam with emotion. "Mom, can I pray for you?"

The surrogate mother accepted the invitation with a tear that ran down her cheek and onto Zilla's fur. Kimmee's words flowed from her heart and took refuge in her surrogate mother's soul. Bellavia grasped the hands that held an angel's heart and raised them to her face once again, kissing them softly while caressing them gently to her cheek.

"Bella, I'll call you tomorrow and check on you. — I love you, Mom."

"I love you too, my angel. Good night."

Kimmee was a jumbled mess of emotions from the day as she revisited each emotion. She started from the early-morning ride and rainbow to the first-day jitters and the subsequent holding of Addison's heart — to returning Zilla and gaining the love of a surrogate mother, and now a final prayer.

It seemed fitting that the D.J. on the radio told everyone to look up in the sky, as there was a rare *blood moon.* The crème de la crème of full moons that happens every three years in October.

Once again, she was sure her daddy had something to do with it. He always promised he would lasso the moon for her one day; it only made sense that he would choose tonight."

"Hey, Google, play 'Bellavia' by Chuck Mangione."

Kimmee sat in the driveway listening to 'Bellavia' and was swept away by the beautiful melody. She imagined the real Bellavia at the concert and the romantic proposal that started her life as '*his*' Bellavia.

Kimmee bowed her head and said a silent prayer for the man she knew so well but had never met. A man she knew her dad had possibly picked to take care of her along with her surrogate mother while in Austin.

"Please, Father and God in Heaven. Please be with a man whose life was torn out from under him. Protect his mind from his own self and perform a miracle to help him restore his family. Please be with this man, this grandpa, and teacher of life. Please do this in your name — Amen."

Kimmee drove away, guided by God, the moon, and 'Bellavia' on replay, as she drove home toward another tomorrow.

Chapter Ten

"The Clicker"

It was Christmas day in the German town of Fredericksburg, Texas. The family and friends gathered in the home that day were treated to an old, out-of-tune Bösendorfer upright piano that found a willing accomplice to tickle its ivories. As the melodic vibrations echoed throughout the living room walls, the musical atmosphere transformed the Christmas enthusiasts into joy-filled carolers.

Soon, the centuries-old German favorite "O Tannenbaum" began ringing out with joyful glee. Suddenly, a referee's whistle pierced the air as if to say, "Foul on the play," causing the many voices gathered to topple into submission to the whistle's mysterious meaning.

Now, because of certain lyrics written back in 1824 by the German organist, teacher, poet, and composer Ernst Anschütz, people think "O Tannenbaum" is the German equivalent of "Oh Christmas Tree." Fortunately for the crowd gathered that bitterly cold Christmas day. Wolfrem Miguel Oswin Jezercak, a six-year-old German prodigy with beady eyes, was there to save the day and guide them through German folklore Christmas history.

He quickly stood high atop a wooden chair next to a large, dark-stained, ornate fireplace hearth. Without a hint of doubt, the confident young word maestro addressed his audience of twenty-three family members and acquaintances from his makeshift stage.

"Okay, People, listen up! The German word for Christmas tree is Weihnachtsbaum, and *Ach Tannenbaum* started as a 16th-century Silesian folk song by Melchior Franck. This folk song later inspired Joachim August Zarnak in 1819 to write a tragic love song about a lover who had been unfaithful. The Tannenbaum is a fir tree with green leaves and needles all year round. And to composer Joachim August Zarnac, the fir tree symbolized everlasting faithfulness, which was the opposite of his unfaithful lover."

From this point on, the crowd became well-versed in the centuries-old "Ach Tannenbaum" writes, rewrites, and altered versions from different composers and in what years —

"So, in closing, 'Oh Tannenbaum' is a fir tree, and the lyrics do not refer to Christmas or describe a decorated Christmas tree at all. However, the takeaway here is proof that women causing pain has been well documented for centuries through song. But without this wonderful gift of painful inspiration, we would have approximately 32.7% fewer songs worldwide than we do now. That is, if my calculations are correct, which I'm sure they are."

He then nodded confidently, gesturing toward the two-foot cubically squared 39-pound *state-of-the-art* SCM Marchant Cogito 240 Electronic Business Calculator. Curiously, all heads turned to see.

With that, the Christmas lecture of 1966 circled in the air, hunting for the innocent eardrums of the audience members whose only crime was not having German ancestry in their blood. However, heads began to nod, and many eyeballs looked at each other, strangely bewildered and informed.

"Okay, everybody!" Wolfrem yelled — "Who's ready to open presents?" and then scurried under the Der Weihnachtsbaum, hoping the Jubilant Man in the Iconic Red Coat could decipher his Christmas list — a list that mirrored a requisition for a new forensics pathology laboratory.

"Here it is!" little Wolfrem yelled after sizing up every gift with his name by shape and weight to find the number one gift on his list. He then performed a reverse mud crawl maneuver to get out from under the tree with the 8½-pound present clenched tightly under his arm.

He sprang up from the floor and sat down to open it. Carefully, he began removing the wrapping paper with exact precision. With each new corner loosened, his beady eyes widened to reveal the scientific discovery he had dreamed about for oh-so-long.

What he saw through the clear plastic, misshaped cardboard opening on the front of the box was beautiful and almost brought a tear to his eye — almost.

"Holy momma cow, it's an AO Spencer stereo microscope with angled eyepieces, the greatest invention since sliced bread! Now I don't have to strain my neck looking straight down at slides for hours and hours! Isn't that amazing?"

The underwhelming enthusiasm from his guests did not deter him. He further informed everyone how it had a pair of 15X AO widefield oculars and how the three-lens turret with AO Spencer 1X, 3X, and 8X objectives accurately aligned for good focus with both eyes. He finished by informing them the internal prisms were rigidly attached, making the ocular screw adjustment smooth, thus allowing fine-tuning for focus. Just in case one eye had a different diopter from the other.

It was a fine instrument indeed, and it was his new best friend. As with all friendships, a name usually was associated; otherwise, how would you distinguish one friend from another? This friendship was no different as Mycroft the Microscope became as real of a friend as any. It was also a trait that would follow Wolfrem along life's path, as he would acquire many metallic friends requiring individual distinction.

Wolfrem was set to emulate his superhero, Englishman Robert Hooke, the 17th-century scientist who discovered *the cell*. Now, he, too, could experience magnificent pond scum in all its glory. Something he had only dreamed about or seen in pictures at the library.

That afternoon, he rode home on his OTASCO Flying 'O' bicycle with his first array of fresh virgin pond scum. He could feel the magnificent scum swishing around in a test tube vial named Gertrude and patiently waiting to become *living art*. Then he saw what the vial painted out before his very eyes. Thousands of organisms were swimming here, swimming there, swimming everywhere — and in an instant, biology became part of his human soul. It was like a dream had emerged from the deepest part of himself — and he found a new way to communicate with the universe at a deeper yet higher cerebral level.

But young Wolfrem was a realist at heart and understood that the same tantalizing piece of pond scum invoked different emotions in everyone. Just like *art*, pond scum was dependent upon the person, their mood, and their time of life. The word *art* itself had so many different accolades associated with it. For some, art is a painting; for others, art is sculpture, yet some may prefer the creative word or a piece of music as their artistic preference. We are all artists in our own various ways. On that day, Wolfrem Miguel Oswin Jezercak became a cellular artist — and the future of thousands of lives would be affected by the ocular path that had chosen him.

His love for microscopes grew year after year, and he already had two others named Boris and Yeltsin. A few years later, when other kids wanted to take field trips to the zoo, Wolfrem Miguel Oswin Jezercak, or Wolfrem Oswin Jezercak for short, pleaded that they have a fundraiser to visit the Golub collection of antique microscopes at U.C. Berkeley, CA. He knew the class would love learning about these historical optics if he could only get them there. Then they, too, would be hooked for life.

But his class only made fun of him and treated him harshly, calling him a weirdo and other similar verbiage. However, Wolfrem cared not and welcomed the silence of not dealing with the preteen ideocracy.

It was the perfect scenario for Wolfrem Oswin Jezercak, and school taught him a valuable lesson after all — that he needed no one's brain baggage to hold him back. In fact, he needed no one at all. He made it his life's mission to be independent of anybody and everybody, rendering the quote "No Man is an Island" laughable.

His fantasy class field trip never happened. However, his mother ensured that when Wolfrem Oswin Jezercak turned thirteen, he would indeed see, feel, smell, and touch Orville J. Golub's collection of antique microscopes.

Seeing the ancient microscopes, the earliest circa 1660, made Wolfrem wonder about his heritage, thus sending him on a lifelong quest seeking his ancestry. If he was going to be the most intelligent person in the room — any room — anywhere — he wanted to understand why and knew researching his unique genealogy would undoubtedly lead to the answer.

Then, one day, it happened. A call he made across the pond to his network of fellow genealogy enthusiasts helped him find the singular document discovery breakthrough that answered everything.

An archived page from his ancient past predicted his sterling future and revealed something that made perfect sense. Wolfrem Miguel Oswin Jezercak was a cellular descendant of his superhero, Englishman Robert Hooke. And, with that, his 17th-century long-lost relative was revealed to be his ancestral cellmate.

This cellular finding of his long-lost relative set the course of his life's sails — and cells. He was destined to be one of the top medical forensic pathologists ever. *How could he not?* Cellular royalty was in his DNA, and it was determined to crown him with his life's purpose.

Becoming an expert in genealogy made him want to get certified as a licensed genealogist. Not only that, but he would obtain certifications, licenses, and or degrees in any field that ended in *ologist* or *ology* — just because he could. As a bonus, he would continue stretching his brain, which was already a hobby but had now become a lifelong goal.

Because of his outstanding school aptitude tests, schoolteachers and principals alike tried using his brain to get national school recognition.

This recognition worked well for him because his goal of obtaining various *ology* degrees and certificates would become easier as colleges nationwide began recruiting young Wolfrem.

The intellectual floodgates opened as college representatives from the United States and other worldwide institutions began sending letters to his home requesting an audience.

Wolfrem took full advantage of every letter and phone call from every university worldwide. As part of the recruitment dance, he found which institutions would permit him to test out of entire courses to obtain various degrees in months instead of years.

At age sixteen, Wolfrem Miguel Oswin Jezercak proudly held his first licensed *ologist* certificate, that of a proud genealogist. And when he graduated high school, he had nine different *ologist* titles and entered college almost a senior.

After much consultation and thought, he decided to attend the prestigious Ludwig-Maximillian Universität München in Germany, recognized as one of the top institutes in the world in the field of biological sciences. As a bonus, he had relatives in Munich who would welcome him and make him feel at home.

But fate had something to say in the matter, as a paralyzing disease struck his mother just months before his departure. Wolfrem refused to leave his dad alone to battle the disease and care for his ailing wife.

Wolfrem had to chart a new course for his future and rotated his life's sails to head south 78.1 miles to the University of Texas in Austin, where he could be back home in an hour's time- if needed — any time of the day or night.

Wolfrem was now a senior in college as he stood there on that cold, cloudy Friday afternoon, representing the only biological offspring of Margaret Helena Strasbürg Jezercak. He stood tall next to his father, William "Bill" Jezercak. He needed to be there; it was crucial for his mentor and all-around rock.

During the private yet illustrious memorial service of her request, the taller of the two stood silent while the elder of the two wept deeply for the loss of his bride of forty-two years. A faithful marriage followed the casket that lowered along the dirt hallway and into the six-foot abyss.

Graduation day was quickly upon him as he walked across the stage to receive his coveted multiplex of degrees. His list of accolades caused an extended pause in the parade of graduates. It took so long to read that ironic laughter and sporadic cheering seemed the proper response for the graduating enigma — and Bill was in the audience that day to proudly cheer along with them.

Wolfrem loved the city of Austin and the convenience of seeing his dad consistently. He also loved riding his bicycle the 78.1-mile distance to Fredericksburg, which became a new rigid part of his existence.

Wolfrem was always rather pudgy growing up, but while obtaining degrees in Nutrition and Culinology, he discovered the culinary sciences intriguing and began cooking to the extremes of health.

It was more like a nightly chemistry experiment in his kitchen laboratory. He challenged himself to create 365 different recipes and never once ate the same dish twice in a year. It led to a critical lifelong decision that exercise would be a life staple, and cycling was the exercise weapon of choice against fat cells. "Die, Fat Cells, Die!" would become his mantra.

Years passed. — The beady-eyed German was now sixty years old and bald, not necessarily from genetics but attrition. His brain needed more space and pushed the hair follicles out of its way.

He was now fit; way fit — Mr. Clean fit. He mirrored his muscular counterpart and could be his German doppelgänger both in looks and cleanliness, and he could probably pin Mr. Clean in an arm-wrestling contest if such an occasion arose.

He would exercise 8 days a week, 25 hours a day, if he could, and made it a fundamental goal to do just that. He is still working out those pesky minuscule quantum mechanics and physics issues of quantizing space and time — but he's getting there.

His day started at 3:06 a.m., seven days a week, without fail, unless it was a matter of utter importance for him to miss. His wardrobe of exercise clothing was vast, and he had outfits for any predicted weather pattern. With an audiobook already cued up, he resumed where he left off the day before and performed his Ground Hog Day movie-like ritual.

For over thirty-five years, he had ridden at least thirty miles a day on his bicycle but would run six miles instead if it was raining outside. Either way, his routine was followed by a one-hour P90X exercise stint before showering.

He has accounted for every penny he has ever earned. He also performed a daily quantum mechanical forensic accounting assessment of all his investments and banking accounts worldwide. He has developed a theory that incorporated the superposition of states collapsing into the most significant financial gain once the commutator was known.

Wolfrem accomplished everything before showing up at work each day at precisely 6:30 a.m. — 90 minutes earlier than the 8:00 a.m. standard start time. He did all of it to avoid people and be safely tucked away in his office before everyone else arrived.

Transportation to work involved his commuter bicycle, with a vast array of panniers to carry everything he needed, or his 105th Anniversary Special-Edition Harley-Davidson Road Machine. He could be a certified Harley-Davidson-ologist if such a thing existed.

His office was at the Travis County Medical Examiner's Complex. It sat adjacent to one of the top Forensic Pathology Laboratories in the country and of his creation. Because, as they say— EVERYTHING IS BIGGER IN TEXAS — forensics was no exception.

His plush office space could teach the military a thing or two about organization and cleanliness. And no dust particle had ever survived the treachery of the cleaning compounds he had developed.

On his desk sat a custom, handmade, leather-bound journal full of his achievements. He currently had thirty-two college degrees, diplomas, licenses, and certificates; most were almost humanly unpronounceable. But of all his accomplishments, his Cosmetology and Genealogy degrees were the two hanging in his office since they significantly impacted his life the most.

A full-sized, neatly framed print of the human anatomy with see-through overlays was horizontally attached to the ceiling and perfectly placed so that he could lean back in his gray tufted leather office chair or lie on his matching couch and gaze at the organs while concentrating on the organ currently challenging his case. He had a bowl of rubber organs he used to squeeze to relax or throw at the organ-displayed poster. He would hit the suspect organ with near-pinpoint precision as if to say, "I'm going to figure you out — nobody beats me!"

Behind him sat six different potted flower plants on a large wooden credenza in six various degrees of death, which mimicked 'the evolution-of-man' poster seen behind the once-beautiful-custom-delivered-floriculture.

As a licensed Phenomenologist, Wolfrem Miguel had two current obsessions he was trying to conquer. The first was *spherical aberrations*, for which the only cure was a Magnetic Electron Microscope with Atomic resolution. The other was using scale-sensitive fractal analysis — to impress the ladies.

Yes, Wolfrem Miguel (*as he portrayed himself outside the workplace amongst his many suitors*) was quite the opposite of his inside professional persona of "The Clicker." His extracurricular activities were evident by the many flower arrangements delivered to his workplace on a regular basis.

Because of this floricultural parade, workplace snooping had become an art form and an obsession for his co-workers who were interested in all things *Clicker*. The curiosity seekers had kept a record for years of the names that appeared on the small envelopes that accompanied the weekly floricultural visits. So far, of the many suitors, "Bunny" seemed to be the name that accompanied the delivered custom floral arrangements with the most frequency.

He had earned the moniker of "THE CLICKER" after taking a month-long sabbatical to his homeland of Germany. Upon his return, anyone standing near or passing by could hear a clicking sound emanating from within him. There was a debate among the office dwellers about whether he ticked or clicked. After years of observance, the medical staff unanimously and scientifically concluded that depending upon their interpretation of the sound, this was a litmus test to determine whether an employee was left-brained or right-brained or had no brain at all. Because the simple fact was he CLICKED!

But regardless of what you thought you heard, there was a standing office pool with several conspiracy theories swirling about as to why he started clicking. Some said he was an underground science experiment gone awry; others predicted he was transitioning from no longer being human. Yet others predicted he would be Germany's first bionic soldier and part of the predawn rising of the upcoming 4th Reich.

Still, others conspired that he didn't use his original heart, at least not the emotional part, so he replaced it with a top-secret titanium one. But that wasn't all. He was also using top-notch organs retrieved from autopsies and secretly recycling the best organs from in and out of himself so that he could live forever.

Part of every new employee's orientation process was an in-depth, extensive warning not to go back to the forensic laboratory area. Paramount to the safety of all employees, there were two rules when it came to "the Clicker": 1) never bother "the Clicker" and 2) If an accidental clicker sighting should occur, whatever you do, never, ever make eye contact. If accidental eye contact were to occur, employees were informed that there would be consequences. All current employees had forcefully been made aware of this fact.

Just as a waiter does not want to piss off the cook, a pathologist doesn't want to piss off the top Forensic Pathologist; especially if they wanted their pathology lab results back quicker than the standard 10-day period or longer if the forensic pathologist was disturbed at any time.

To avoid clicker paranormal activity, a new mandatory "CLICKER WATCHERS" app for all employees was written secretly by the lead geek at the facility and discreetly distributed to all employees. It was simple and straightforward, with no sign-in or fingerprint recognition. Its design was for quickness of use only. When the app was launched, a big red clicking heart button appeared, and it automatically sent out a "CSS" (Clicker Sighting Signal). If the alert was heard, staff members were advised to assume the worst and head to the nearest office for safety.

On the app were also several amazing "CLICKERTOLOGIST" Trivial Pursuit-like games and "CLICK-CLOCK" games dealing with multiple-player organ removal races. Also featured were multiplayer suicide squad CLICKER ZOMBIE AND EXTINGUISHER games. These boasted some insightful ways to fantasize about how you would "Extinguish the Clicker" from this Earth while racking up as many ETC (Extinguish the Clicker) points as possible to win. The app could also add money to the office betting pool, which was handy whenever someone introduced a new clicker conspiracy theory.

It was a beautiful Thursday morning in October. The Clicker wanted to celebrate the rarity of the blood moon that bequeathed Austin last night. He often celebrated an astrological event by wearing a custom-made tartan kilt with a matching tartan sash in the German national clan colors of bright red and black. Every detail was authentic, down to the German buckle and black leather belt, sporran, kilt pin, knee-length hose, white Scottish Jacobite Ghillie kilt shirt with black leather cord, and shiny black Ghillie Brogue kilt shoes — just like they had done since the 1720's when the first kilt graced the hip of man.

Wolfrem Miguel, while sitting at his office that morning, was informed that another floricultural presentation was at the front desk waiting for him. He grabbed the least living of his current spectrum of living-to-semi-living potted plants and began the long, arduous walk to the front reception desk to pick up his prize.

The hallway encompassed the entire length of the large Medical Examiner's Office complex, making the path to his office lab sanctuary — as they say, less beaten.

The Clicker's weekly trip toward the front desk produced a variety of reactions. The CSS sounded off, as well as many old-school text warnings. People scuttled out of the hallways toward the nearest offices for shelter. Office doors that seemed to close just in time for his passing by were no longer a coincidence, and poor Johnny Montel of accounting thought maybe he could make his way to the — well, he couldn't.

He rounded the corner just 7.62 meters from the MEN'S metal plate on the door that could have saved him — but it was not to be for Johnny Montel that fateful day. His body stood frozen from eye contact with the Clicker, and his deer-in-the-headlights reaction debilitated any movement on his part. — However, Johnny Montel could not sustain his fear as a dribble sound hit his shoe just before a spot appeared below his belt line. Wolfrem stood silent, staring back through sunglasses he thought accessorized his outfit flawlessly. He was trying to ascertain whether he would give Johnny Montel a lengthy lecture on the history of centuries-old ancient Scottish clans' tartan kilts.

But the Clicker was kind that day; the rarity of the blood moon that happened every three years in October placed him in an unusual mood. It was his lucky day as the Kraken would not be released upon Johnny Montel, at least not then. Besides, the Clicker must complete his journey to the front desk to be surprised with this week's elaborate floriculture design and to see whose name graced the cardstock.

"Dr. Jezercak!" he heard called out to the hallway from an office as he made his way to the front desk. A reluctant figure appeared in Dr. Johnson's office doorway, wearing a Scottish kilt ensemble and holding a six-week-old death plant. No handshake or expression emanated from the demeanor of the kilted figure as Dr. Johnson stood up to greet him.

"Dr. Jezercak, I want you to meet Kimmee James Attwood, our newest technician. I was getting to know her and orienting her on how we do things around here."

Dr. Jezercak took over. "Alright, let me orient her on a few things around here. First, I'm not wasting brain cells calling you Kimmee James Attwood. It's a weird name, probably something to do with your childhood, so, barf, time to grow up. I'll call you K.J. — Maybe K.J. Attwood if I feel generous. And second, your green eyes, which I'm sure you have several other adjectives thrown in to describe them — don't get a hall pass with me."

He turned his attention back to Dr. Johnson. "So why am I meeting her exactly? I won't be associating with her. Come on, Doc, you know better than to waste my time."

Kimmee sat shocked, trying to process so many things wrong with this picture: a downright mean Mr. Clean wearing a kilt and holding a dead flower arrangement. And in this scenario, the dead flower arrangement made the most sense. With this one encounter, she understood the metal tray crashing to the floor and the terrified looks of the employees directed at Dr. Slavin yesterday. *Holy crap, maybe they weren't kidding— maybe he is the Kraken?*

"Dr. Jezercak, that's enough! I saw you walking and thought it would be nice to meet our newest employee. Come on, will you ever play nice?"

"As soon as you requisition my Magnetic Electron Microscope with Atomic Resolution that I've been bitching about for years. You know I need it to solve my eternal spherical aberration problems — then maybe I'll play fair. But never nice," The Clicker spouted.

"Come on, Dr. Jezercak; we've been through this a hundred times. The department isn't going to spend twenty million on a microscope. That's way overkill for what you need, and it isn't going to happen, so drop it!"

Damn! That didn't go well. Dr. Johnson tried to lighten the room with a calmer voice after his harsh reminder to Dr. Jezercak that he wouldn't get his astronomically expensive play toy.

"I'm sorry, Wolfrem; you know if it were up to me, I'd have your twenty-million-dollar monstrosity in a heartbeat."

Dr. Jezercak graced Johnson with a nonchalant expression before continuing to the front desk to exchange the future zombie floriculture for the elegant, floral living one.

"I'm sorry, Kimmee," Dr. Johnson sighed. "You didn't deserve that; nobody does. Please don't take it personally; he treats everyone the same — he's an equal-opportunity asshole. I wanted to warn you about him during your orientation, but then I saw him walking by and took a chance. I should've known better.

"Anyway, if you haven't heard, everyone refers to him as 'the Clicker' — but don't say it to his face. And one other thing. Management isn't supposed to know about the new employee-only mandatory app going around — but please use it to avoid him — things just go smoother around here."

"Dr. Johnson, can we get back to what we discussed earlier? I'm sure Dr. Slavin talked to you about the case we worked on yesterday?"

"Yes, he did; I tried to introduce you to Dr. Jezercak, hoping it would open a dialogue so that I could hedge Dr. Slavin's case for a forensic favor. But now that he's upset, I'm afraid it will have to wait until tomorrow." The phone rang. Dr. Johnson answered and found that he needed to leave to attend to some upper-management business.

"Kimmee, we will have to finish your orientation tomorrow, so come in first thing, and we'll start again. In the meantime, look through your employee manual and write down any questions. I'll text Dr. Slavin and let him know you can assist him in about an hour. I'll see you tomorrow."

Kimmee wanted to scream inside because of the freaking Clicker and the forensic leverage he held over everyone because of his oversized brain and asshole personality. She needed to find the right time to tell Dr. Johnson about how she met the grandmother of the case but was cautious about telling him, unsure of his reaction.

She had hoped Dr. Slavin's request for a forensic favor might come to fruition using the proper channels to expedite their lab results. But now that Dr. Johnson had pissed off the Clicker, she felt that would not likely happen anytime soon. She needed those results expedited, and she needed them now. Time was of the essence if she was going to help this family heal and, in her mind, save a man from possibly killing himself.

But the damn CLICKER stood in the way! And on top of everything, she was boiling inside, thinking about how rude he was to her. *Nobody — and I mean NOBODY's going to talk to me like that! And nobody's going to rename me either; DAMMIT!*

She walked back to her office in a headstrong state of mind. She did not realize that people were coming out of offices and turning around immediately. Since she didn't have the Clicker app downloaded, she walked the hallways naked of CLICKER paranormal activity. And not aware that the footsteps gaining on her were the sounds of Scottish Ghillie Brogue kilt shoes.

She turned to greet the fellow employee she heard behind her and came face to face with a beautiful flower arrangement before realizing who the man was transporting it.

"Dr. Jezercak," she said to the man, who didn't acknowledge her as he continued his path. — "Sir!" With a stronger infliction. She continued, "I would like to talk to you — please, sir?" But it was to no avail. She followed him and made her presence known; even if he didn't want to listen, she was going to be heard by him.

"First things first, my name is Kimmee James Attwood; you can call me Kimmee or Miss Attwood. You have the brain cells to do so, and in turn, I'll respond professionally. One K.J. directed my way, and I'll respond appropriately with 'The Clicker' or 'Dr. Clicker.' Do we understand each other? — Use your brain cells and decide!"

The kilted man turned abruptly yet spoke slowly, "Yes, K.J., come to the dark side; keep going, and let's see where you end up."

"Alright, Dr. Clicker, I don't care if you fire me or if you even can fire me. But what I do care about is an incredible family whose lives have been torn apart and need answers. Evidently, answers that only the almighty Clicker can give. There's a man that I believe might kill himself! Please! You can hate me; I don't care, but look at Dr. Slavin's case that came in two nights ago. A little girl, three years old. This man's future depends on you figuring out why she died."

The Clicker stood emotionless, unswayed.

"Sir, he has been thrown out of his family because they think he accidentally killed her — but I believe they're wrong. Regardless, I also believe he could kill himself over this. Last night, quite by accident, I made contact with the little girl's grandmother. The grandmother's name is Bella, and the little girl is Addison. I learned a lot about this family. The grandfather couldn't have hurt this little girl, but no one was around when she died, but the assumption is that he had something to do with her death."

"Listen, K.J., I don't care about your little problem. I have problems of my own, like getting this plant back to my office so I can water it."

Kimmee's daddy taught her that sometimes a little Texas Hellion is needed to achieve a goal. And when she summoned her inner Hellion to let loose, her heel could have pierced armor as it frightened the tile floor.

"That's your freaking problem! Listen here, Dr. Clicker. I stood in this man's garage, where he spent most of his time. He is passionate about cycling and has collected a lot of beautiful bicycles over the past forty years, and I—"

She was sharply interrupted by the Clicker, who lowered his sunglasses as his beady crab-blue eyes glared into the hazel-mint green eyes of his competitor.

"Why should I freaking care about some weirdo who collects bicycles? Why would you even tell me something like that!? Are you an idiot!?" Then demonstrated his profound ability not to blink as he stared her down.

Kimmee huffed and puffed but was too deranged with exasperation to answer. In a state of utter panic, she put her left finger under her eye and gave him an intensified Eye-Jobe, hoping to nullify his insurmountable non-blinking skills.

The Eye-Jobe immediately ended the Clicker's non-blinking reign of terror. Then he focused away from her, placed his left hand on his chin, and dabbled with his mustache while his eyes searched the upper quadrants of his mind.

"Now, why were you telling me about these bicycles, and why are they so important to you?"

"I told you that because — because — because that's how I connected with him. I love cycling, and his collection is like nothing I have ever seen. I wanted to get a sense of the man accused of something I know he didn't do. And I know you can help me find the answer to fix this. — Besides — Bicycles fix everything!" she said convincingly.

"What did you just say?" he responded. "Did you say, 'Bicycles fix everything?'"

"Yes — Bicycles fix everything, evidently a bicyclism, the man said, according to his wife."

"How old is he, this grandpa character?" the Clicker asked, even more perplexed.

"I think he's sixty if I heard his wife correctly."

The Clicker stood pondering the tenacity of Kimmee James Attwood.

"Okay, K — (he seemed to pause) — Miss Attwood. Ask Dr. Slavin for the file and bring it back to my office —"

Her knees shuttered and nearly buckled, "Thank you, Dr. Jezercak —thank you! I'll bring it back to you as soon as I can."

Kimmee wanted to run, but her legs needed to stabilize first as she realized she had just survived her solo Clicker encounter. Now, he wanted to look at the file. *Oh, my God, bicycles really do fix everything.*

Chapter Eleven

What Is Happening Here?

Dr. Slavin was in his office when a voracious knocking startled him from looking at his next case. "Come in."

A wide-eyed Kimmee Attwood opened the door, exhilarated.

"Kimmee, what's wrong?" Dr. Slavin had her sit down to gather herself.

"Dr. Slavin, you won't believe this, but I just pleaded our case to 'the Clicker,' and now he wants to see the file — It's a miracle! This morning, when I had orientation with Dr. Johnson, he tried to have Dr. Jezercak meet me, but he was awful. He even tried to rename me!"

Dr. Slavin laughed. "Let me guess, not enough brain cells? Kimmee, every employee here has an abbreviated name, and some are quite funny. By the way, did you not get the Clicker app yet?"

"That's the thing. I didn't have the app to warn me. I was so mad at him for renaming me that when I accidentally ran into him in the hallway, I said no one was going to rename me! I even called him Dr. Clicker!"

"Holy cow! And how are you alive exactly?"

"I started pleading our case and followed him down the hallway in his kilt ensemble, and then we kind of got into a fight."

"How in the heck are you still alive — seriously?" Dr. Slavin started to remember the last time the Clicker wore a kilt. "Kimmee, there had to be some rare astrological event like a comet or maybe the Southern or Northern Taurids meteorite showers— "

Kimmee raised her hand in excitement. "There was a rare October blood moon last night that I heard about on the radio."

"That must have been it. A rare blood moon would be kilt-worthy."

"Dr. Slavin, I know this is just my second day here, but can I take this file back to Dr. Jezercak, and, if he allows me an audience with him, follow through until he wants me to leave...please?" She widened her hazel-mints in persuasion that apparently damn well did get a hall pass as he responded.

"Sure, Kimmee, I was looking over the file for our next case, a sixty-two-year-old woman who wandered into the street, and a car tragically hit her. I'm thinking maybe an early Alzheimer's moment that sadly happened. I can handle it, though. If not, I'll get it covered. I've never known anyone to survive a Clicker encounter, so it must be those eyes of yours. Here's the file. Now go!"

Kimmee stood outside a door, staring at a metal engraved nameplate. *Dr. Wolfrem Jezercak - Forensic Pathologist.* She was nervous but composed herself as her hand raised to knock.

"Enter!" he commanded before she knocked, and she opened the door to CLICKERVILLE. The office was in meticulous order with a powerful and distinct smell of cleanliness, like nothing Kimmee had ever smelled. But if Pine-Sol and pineapple had a love child with cinnamon, this could be it.

Kimmee looked around and tried not to laugh when she noticed the Genealogy and Cosmetology degrees on the wall behind him. While below them, she witnessed a crime scene where six custom floriculture arrangements were slowly being murdered on the credenza.

One arm extended for the folder while the other turned a picture down suspiciously on his desk. Dr. Jezercak opened the file and propped his Scottish Ghillie Brogue kilt shoes on his desk. While he studied the file, his left-hand fingers and thumb worked seamlessly with contemplating strokes through his brownish-gray Van Dyke beard. As she patiently watched him review the file, she noticed that he no longer seemed to be looking at the file but more past it, his eyes no longer scanning the pages but fixed and slightly glazed.

Worlds ago, at the Tri-State Music Festival in Enid, Oklahoma, a husky boy carrying a rather large bass trombone case happened upon a pudgy, fifteen-year-old German boy sitting with his much smaller trumpet case on a lonely black rod-iron bench. He was staring at the two-story-high wooden stairway outside the back-alley entrance to Louise's Italian Peppermill Café.

"Mine's bigger!" said the huskier one to the slightly less husky of the two.

The beady-eyed German boy awakened from his trance of the back-alley stairway and turned to look at the source of the words. He was met with a vision he'd never forget.

"Eye-Jobe!" the husky boy said with a finger pulling down his left eye's periorbital skin, clearly aimed at him. The husky boy released the Eye-Jobe and again reiterated, "Mine's bigger," as he tapped his fingers convincingly on his bass trombone case. The bigger one then joined in on looking up at the stairway to a door that read: *Louise's Italian Peppermill Café: My English, not so good. Mia Spaghetti speak more better!*

It was dusk outside as the husky one thought out loud, "That spaghetti's definitely speaking more better to me. Let's go inside; the spaghetti won't eat itself, you know." He then introduced himself.

"People call me Groucho, but my friends call me Groucho Extendo. What's your name?"

"My name's Wolfrem."

"Sir Wolfrem, it is! So, do you want to be my friend, Sir Wolfrem? If so, let's do this; we can call it The First Annual Tri-State High-Flying Spaghetti Competition. What say you?"

The two boys were now sitting at a quaint round antique table draped with a red and white checkered tablecloth while eating complimentary bread. They looked around and tried to act well above their cultured fifteen-year-old ages as they took in the Italian art, themes, and decorations. Groucho began their high-societal conversation while holding a piece of bread with his pinky extended. In a sophisticated voice, he stated —

"I like farting for the band; it's my job, you know, as the bass trombonist. Besides, someone must do it; why not me? I'm exceptionally good at it. Some may venture to say — OUTSTANDING even. I'd like to do it professionally someday. Your thoughts, Wolfrem?"

Wolfrem extended his pinky on said bread and responded, "The valves on the bass trombone that make it easier for you to fart for the band were invented between 1813 and 1830. The newly developed valves inspired the instrument maker F.C. Sattler of Leipzig, Germany, to develop the tenor-bass trombone in 1839. He made it possible to integrate the additional piece of tubing, or crook, into the U-shaped slide in front of the bell without making any other alterations to the tenor trombone.

"The addition of this piece of tubing meant that bass parts could now be played using the slide of the tenor trombone. Players could now switch from tenor to bass pitch utilizing a valve. By the end of the 18th century, trombones came in three sizes: alto, tenor, and bass."

Groucho replied with his patented sarcastic smile. "Duh — everyone knows that, dwerb! — Now tell me something I didn't know."

"Did you know my dad just bought two brand-new balloon-tire Honda three-wheel ATVs exactly like the ones used in the new James Bond—"

Wolfrem was harshly interrupted.

"CHALLENGE ACCEPTED! I'll be there next Saturday to show you exactly how to ride them. My people will call your people to set up a time. Now, where do you live?" Groucho asked.

"I live in Fredericksburg, Texas. Where do you live?"

"Fredericksburg, Texas!!! HOLY FARTSVILLE, BATMAN — I live in Oklahoma City, America. CHALLENGE ACCEPTED AGAIN!"

Two rather large bowls of spaghetti arrived at the table, accompanied by a fresh basket of warm bread.

"America — is this a great country or what?" Groucho boasted.

The waitress smiled at his jubilance as she refilled their tea glasses.

"Can I help you two gentlemen with anything else?"

"Yes, ma'am," Groucho answered, "just one last thing — which one of us is *The Lady,* and which one of us is *The Tramp*?"

The following Saturday, a husky boy showed up in Fredericksburg, TX, ready to teach some ATVs a lesson on how to be ridden. It was the first of many trips the two boys would share during their long friendship.

Dr. Jezercak seemed to slip back into reality and repurposed his thoughts — "Let's Go!"

Kimmee was unsure what was happening here and what exactly "Let's go" meant.

"You're driving — now let's go!" he reiterated emphatically as he grabbed the picture off his desk and secured it in a locking desk drawer. He then took the least dead of his floriculture arrangements and began walking out the door.

Kimmee followed the fast-paced German clan colors of the kilted figure hurrying out of the building and had to jog to keep up.

"I have to grab my purse and keys; I'll meet you outside." She detoured to her office and then found herself outside with an impatient-looking Dr. Jezercak by her SUV. He was looking through the tinted rear window glass with his hands curved around both sides of his face while the flowers rested on top. A frightening thought entered her head: *how the hell did he know which car was mine?*

"It doesn't take a brain scientist to figure out that the vehicle I've never seen in the parking lot is yours, so quit wasting your brain cells."

Geez — he reads minds! She hurried to open the SUV doors. Once in, he looked back toward the storage area and studied Kimmee's bicycle.

"Project One — Radioactive pink, Top Dura-ace componentry — Nice choice — circa $12,000, I'd say?"

Kimmee thought that she just got hoodwinked like a circus guesser would do.

"How did you know that?" she asked.

"The Clicker knows everything," he said without missing a beat. "Now, drive to Bella's house."

Bella's house!? Kimmee was both excited and nervous. On the one hand, Dr. Jezercak took a vital interest in the case. On the other hand, the Clicker was taking a vital interest in the case and would come face-to-face with her surrogate mother. Let's face it — ordinary people shouldn't make contact with him, let alone someone in Bella's current state of mind. Kimmee was genuinely concerned and felt the need to protect her. Kimmee texted, letting her know she was coming with someone from her work who wanted to talk and look around.

It seemed like the longest drive of her life as a deafening silence played in the air. She initially dared not break the silence with a question because of how he might react but decided that his yelling was better than the awkward quiet.

"Dr. Jezercak, can I ask why you suddenly became interested in this case?"

"It's my job; I care deeply about people," he responded callously, cold, expressionless. "We can turn around if you prefer; I have other cases," he added.

"Oh, no-no-no! I'm so very thankful. It just seemed as if you had a moment — a realization of something while reading the file, and I just wondered."

"It's called a hunch, and I thought I'd see it through — We'll see."

He gave an approving glance unbeknownst to her, impressed by her intuition.

"Miss Attwood — tell me again. How did you come to know the grandmother on this case?"

Kimmee was reluctant that Dr. Jezercak would find some "Clicker" way to twist her story into something to use against her. But she decided the blatant truth would be best. After all, her mission was to have the Clicker look at the file to get a speedy diagnosis so she could vindicate Grandpa. Kimmee didn't want to lose her job over it but would survive any way this played out, assuming the Clicker remained interested in discovering why Addison passed.

Kimmee told him everything, from how she took Zilla to Bella's home and got to know her and relived the moment she saw Addison's picture and realized who she was. She also explained her happenstance of finding Grandpa's bicycle collection and her connection with him because of cycling.

"I see," he said evenly, "— I ride a Cervelo CSC Soloist bicycle."

"So, you ride bicycles, too? How awesome is that!" Kimmee's response was slightly more enthusiastic than she meant. She was embarrassed but safe from further scrutiny as she pulled into the driveway. She texted Bella to let her know they had arrived.

Kimmee trembled from what might transpire as she rang the doorbell and silently prayed Bella would be alright coming face to face with the kilted Clicker. The doorbell produced the yipping sounds of Zilla just before the door opened slowly. Bella looked at the Clicker holding the beautiful flower arrangement and burst out crying.

Yep — exactly what I thought would happen! Kimmee speculated. — Until what happened next stunned Kimmee as Bella reached for the Clicker with outstretched arms and cried out — "Professor Miguel!"

"My dearest Bellavia," he responded, gently lifting her hand to kiss it.

What in the freaking hell is happening here!? Kimmee's inner voice blurted.

Zilla took one look at the Clicker and growled vociferously, then scampered away in fear, not to be seen for the rest of the afternoon.

Bella's tears were quite confusing to Kimmee. They seemed to be a mixture of all the emotions she knew Bella was going through, but with one added emotion — joy.

"Professor Miguel," Bella reiterated as she kissed him on the cheek for the beautiful flower arrangement. Through her tears, her past personality sneaked through to make an appearance.

"Still rocking the kilt, I see. How is Verne doing?" Bella smiled.

Kimmee's mind ran wild with conspiracy. *Verne? Who the hell is Verne?*

"Why don't you see for yourself?" the Clicker responded.

Bella placed her head with her ear against his chest.

"Still clicking away, I hear. Groucho would be so happy to see you; it's been way too long." Professor Miguel was almost in tears.

"Bella, I'm so sorry for what you're going through. The moment I realized what had happened, I had to see you. I'm glad you met Miss Attwood; I want you to know that she truly went to bat for you and your family. I picked a good one in her, and I know she will be an excellent assistant to me. — Now, let's get to this. So, there's been no word from old Groucho Extendo?"

Kimmee was in shock as to what was transpiring between the two. There were so many different scenarios in her mind, with none of them leading to a gentle, heartfelt admiring Clicker, along with the words Grouch Extendo, Professor Miguel, and Verne? *Who the hell is that!?*

And why did he take credit for picking her as a good one? As if he had something to do with her getting the job in the first place. And then casually making her his assistant, unbeknownst to her and without her permission?

Her world of what she thought she lived in turned into an abstract construct after one day of work. But her curiosity about where this was headed and what else would be revealed had never stimulated her more.

They soon found themselves in the living room, each holding a hot cup of tea as the enlightened conversation followed many varied paths.

Bella felt comfortable telling Miguel everything. She revealed every struggle and every strand of guilt about her anger with her husband as she listed every detail of the night as it unfolded. After an hour of heaviness, the conversation lightened and turned toward a path of nostalgia.

Bella began to laugh-cry as she reminisced about their earlier days in life with all the adventures of Groucho, and Miguel. But as the kids came along, priorities changed, and as the kids grew, their adventures lessened. Eventually, the years took their toll on two lives that took different directions and innocently caused their relationship to distance itself into silence.

"Kimmee, did you know that Miguel was the best man at our wedding? He even played trumpet in the 16-piece big band my husband had for over ten years, way back when. Miguel would drive up from Texas every month to rehearse, and the two would always go on a nice long bicycle ride while he was here.

"In fact, Miguel was the one who pushed my husband to ride his first 100-mile ride. They rode from Oklahoma City to Enid and ate lunch at the Enid restaurant, where they first met in high school and became friends. Miguel is also why we ended up in Austin, so they could be close and ride bikes together."

Kimmee listened with wonderment. Miguel saw the picture of Bella and Groucho crossing the finish line at the Hotter-than-Hell 100. He stared intently at the picture and saw the old familiar bicycle he gave to his friend.

"Oh, Bellavia, can I see her?" he asked.

"Of course, I wouldn't let you leave without saying goodbye to her."

Bella led them to the garage, where Miguel spotted her still resting comfortably on the bike rack, where he last saw her over ten years ago. He walked straight to the purplish-blue Peugeot PX-10 with Columbus SLX tubing, the most expensive and lightweight Peugeot bicycle in the 1980s.

"How are you doin', girl?" He remembered the times they shared as he gently spun the back wheel to hear the ratcheting of the idled Campagnolo gear cluster that whispered so many memories back to him.

"Miguel — Kimmee has made me realize more than ever that "Bicycles are people, too.""

Without skipping a beat, Bella and Miguel said, "Because bicycles fix everything."

Then Miguel gave Bella an Eye-Jobe, and she gave him one right back as she walked over to Miguel and cried on his shoulder.

"I never thought I'd miss his silly Eye-Jobes. Oh, Miguel — if it were only true that bicycles fix everything — especially now."

Miguel, with much compassion, grabbed her and squared his shoulders with her.

"Oh, ye of little faith *(a phrase he heard his friend Groucho say quite often)* — "I'm here now, and my friend is out there somewhere. I will figure this out; all of it — Trust me on this!"

For the first time since the incident, Bella felt an ounce of hope in Miguel's words. He took a moment to look over the rest of the bicycle collection before becoming anxious, as he was determined to figure this out and needed to get back to his lab. They exchanged final hugs and goodbyes on the driveway.

"Bella, you notify me the moment you hear from him. You have my card, and if you can't get a hold of me, get a hold of Miss Attwood. I promise you — we will find my friend."

Kimmee's head swam with so many different takeaways from their afternoon as they headed back to the office. She wasn't sure where or how to begin questioning her new boss. Evidently, she was suddenly his new assistant. Which was both a terrifying and exhilarating proposition, depending on whether she worked for "the Clicker" or for the more compassionate "Professor Miguel."

"Okay, Miss Attwood, you have personal information about me that nobody else knows — What are you going to do about it?"

"I'll tell you exactly what I'm going to do — my job! As your new assistant, I will make sure I take care of the many day-to-day needs you have. And I will gain your trust by accomplishing everything without fail.

"The second thing is that I want you to have all available brain cells at your disposal working on this case and future cases. For you to do that, I don't want you to waste three whole syllables worth of brain cells calling me Miss Attwood. I'd like you to call me K.J. instead to save a syllable's worth of brain cells that you can apply to your work.

"You'll find I'm a quick learner, and I'll be a worthy investment of your time. Bringing in an assistant shouldn't mean you must change anything about how you work best. I'm here to enhance your workflow, and I'll guard the contents of the mystery photo and ensure it's locked away if you must leave. I won't let you down."

A few seconds later, she heard "— Nicely played —"

They entered the office complex at a fast pace. There was little warning, if any, for anyone to get the Clicker app started. Soon, desperate, panicking voices echoed in the hallways. And gasps of relief that Kimmee was still alive filled the complex.

She was the first known employee to leave the premises with the Clicker and return in one piece and still employed. The two made their way past the ebb and flow of frightened employees and back to the forensics pathology lab.

The Clicker was laser-focused on the prioritized task and already had the organ tissue samples tagged in his lab. They had an intense night of work ahead, and Kimmee soon found herself immersed in a world she thought was not possible.

"Alright, K.J., are you ready to meet my forensic family?" He placed one of his widened beady eyes against the military-grade retinal scanner to access the real CLICKERVILLE. As Kimmee entered the CLICKER universe, she marveled at the spectacle of high-tech forensics. He showed her around and introduced her as if they were at a black-tie affair. She noticed that each instrument had its own unique nameplate.

"Alright, people, listen up. This young lady is my new assistant, Miss K.J. Attwood." He leaned over and whispered in her ear, "They would clap if they had hands; I don't want you to think they're giving you the silent treatment.

"Okay, Miss Attwood, I want you to meet my forensic family, starting with Elfriede, my gas chromatograph-mass spectrometer, and Nadine, our high-pressure liquid chromatograph. Next is Francois, our Fourier transform infrared spectrophotometer. He thinks he's a real ladies' man, so watch out for him.

"This is Xavier, our X-ray diffraction spectrometer. Cyrano, the cyanoacrylate fuming chamber, is our class clown and everyone's favorite. Manfred is my atomic spectrometer. Ursula provides me with my arc spark spectrometry. And this is Petra, my precision ID NGS System for human DNA identification, who is best friends with Frieda, the fluorescence spectrometer.

"Bertha controls the gas chromatography analysis — and trust me on this; you do not want to get Big Bertha on your bad side. Continuing, we have Erma; she's in charge of my forensic DNA Analysis. Friedrich is used for forensic toxicology, and his friend Heinz is our histology tissue processor."

Kimmee gaped, trying to take this all in. "Wow, that's a lot of equipment."

He held up a hand. "Wait a minute; I'm not done yet. Here's Bridgit, the blood gas analyzer; she might have a wee bit of a drinking problem. Ernst, the electroencephalograph, keeps a close watch on her; I think he's her sponsor. Ingrid is our postmortem magnetic resonance imager. Helga and Olga are my twins; they're responsible for the macroscopic and microscopic investigations around here.

"Now, this little device, Miss Attwood, is Winchester. He is a 600 MHz Fourier transform nuclear magnetic resonance spectrometer. He is good friends with Bob, the only American in our group, who is also our transmission electron microscope. I have no idea how anyone can get by without one of these babies.

"However, my favorite instrument here, by far, is from my private collection — a circa 1960s Beckman DU spectrophotometer. Let me tell you about ol' Birkenstein here. This instrument was a significant advancement at the time. His construction is the unique and fun part. He has a bright light bulb that is shone through a slit to a grating, a shiny surface with tiny grooves. It acts as a prism, so depending on the light's angle, it reflects a given color. The light is passed through a sample and then to a photomultiplier tube. Basically, it's a vacuum tube like used in an old TV. It takes a weak light signal and multiplies it, with the results going to a strip chart paper recorder.

"I collect strip chart paper recorded charts of all kinds. I love practicing my craft of reading charts and figuring out someone's life simply by looking at their squiggles. The secret of why I'm probably the best at what I do, and I say, *probably* because I don't want to sound full of myself. But it's in the family histories and my ability to read their squiggles accurately that I determine why someone died when no one else can. It's my little secret of why I'm the almighty Clicker.

"Nowadays, it's all done using solid-state light-wave generators that do not need a grating, and electronic detectors now go straight to a computer interface. — How boring is that? I'll take a good read of an EKG strip chart any day.

"I know you smirked earlier when you came to my office and saw my genealogy degree, but the history of someone's genetics is what separates me from everyone I know in my field. Genealogy was the first 'ology' degree I ever earned and has, to this day, been my most surprising accomplishment. It has helped me as much or more than mastering any of these instruments I showed you.

"Anyway, I got this Beckman DU spectrophotometer back in the early '70s, and I still use it when I can. If you think all this is impressive, you should see my eclectic personal museum of microscopes, along with other early scientific instrument finds. It's quite something."

There were many other high-tech machines and forensic instruments he didn't introduce her to, as they would have been there all night. Still, Kimmee was intrigued by the ones she met and the Clicker's demeanor when he introduced them to her.

The seriousness the Clicker gave to each named instrument made weird sense. In his world, the phrase "Forensics fix everything" was a fact of life — or rather "death of life" in his case, and she could hardly wait to watch, learn, and study him in his element.

The Clicker gave a friendly pat to each instrument as he sat down to work every possible angle and was determined to do an extra methodical macroscopic and microscopic investigation. He also needed to address the spectrum of structural substrates of Cardiac Sudden Death and account for electrical instability by imploring molecular biology techniques to identify subtle or functional disorders.

Kimmee sat beside him and watched as he went from instrument to instrument. She studied his precision in cutting slices of the heart needed for the appropriate tests. Then a knock at the door disrupted his concentration.

"I'll handle it, sir," K.J. said.

"Sir? Did you call me, sir? I'd rather be called 'the Clicker'! How about 'Miguel' — all two of my other friends call me that. In fact, here is the name order when corresponding with people on the phone or by email.

"Wolfrem — to my colleagues.

"Wolfrem Miguel — to the ladies in my social circles.

"The Clicker — to the spineless office dwellers running about."

He then said with a Cecil B. DeMille epic pause, "This is the hierarchy of my name usage. SO LET IT BE WRITTEN — SO LET IT BE DONE."

They heard the knock at the door again.

"I'll get it, Miguel."

K.J. opened the door, and a nervous Dr. Johnson rushed in.

"Oh, thank God you're alive," as he hugged her, fearing what he might find.

"I'm keeping K.J. as my personal assistant. But don't worry; I'll let her help with an autopsy or two when we get in a bind."

Dr. Johnson looked at Kimmee to make sure she wanted to work for him, and she gave him a reassuring look that she did. "So, what case are you two working on?" he inquired cheerfully.

The Clicker's cold, hard look reminded him never to ask such questions. If he needed to know, the Clicker would tell him. Instead, Kimmee's eyes answered Dr. Johnson, and he understood, relieved at the outcome.

"Well, let me know if you need anything, and I'll make myself available."

As he started to leave, something caught his eye at the back of the room.

"Wolfrem! What are those boxes stacked in the back corner for?"

He walked back and moved a stack of decoy boxes blocking a stack of near military-caliber racing drones: ten boxes tall. A 3-D printing machine accompanied them with a realistically eerie composite of a face resembling "the Clicker" printed out before his eyes. He opened a large, tall, moving box filled with different-sized lampshades.

"Not again, Wolfrem! We almost had two heart attacks last year, and we don't need our own employees to become customers. You better tell me what the hell you're planning here—"

"I think you know by now," as a mischievous grin crossed the Clicker.

"God help us all."

Dr. Johnson left the office quite disturbed and shaking his head, while Kimmee was left wondering, *What the hell he meant by that?*

In years past, during October, Wolfrem Miguel had spontaneously let three of his many costumes come out to play at the workplace. His kilt ensemble had a double purpose: to honor last night's astrological blood moon event and start a new office pool.

Wagering what day he would wear his first costume in October made great fodder for the office betting pool, especially with the new app. Also, he would hate for no one to see his *Northern King* ensemble from *Game of Thrones*.

Yes, the blood moon from last night was the official start; Halloween was in the air, which was precisely when Wolfrem Miguel messed with his coworkers the most. Oh, the mayhem he had planned for the unsuspecting motley crew of the Travis County Medical Examiner's Office Complex. And be assured, of all the places where crazy Halloween happenings occur, the Travis County Medical Examiner's office had a bullseye on it from the great mystical beyond.

Wolfrem Miguel Oswin Jezercak had a fully funded account exclusively for his annual Hallowed-Eve trickery. Elaborate, you ask? Oh, hell yes! He pledged to take Halloween to another level this year as he became an officially certified and licensed pilot and drone-ologist. And his Embry-Riddle Bachelor of Science in Unmanned Aircraft Systems Science would be awfully handy.

What to expect, you might ask? Expect high-speed, high-tech maneuvering of flying lampshades — Good Golly, Miss Molly! — Very realistic "Flying Ghosts" — Bet your ass! And thanks to his MIT 3-D printing certificate in Additive Manufacturing for Innovative Design and Production — very real-looking 3-D printed faces would accompany such ghostly aberrations.

The one-two punch of the drone-3D printing combination was like the Batman and Robin of scaring the crap out of people. Let's just say Johnny Montel would not be alone in experiencing a personal Niagara Falls event. Turning the Travis County Medical Examiner's Office into the Niagara Falls of Texas was the greater goal.

PRICELESS...Oh, the stories yet to be told — Yes, indeed! Wolfrem Miguel Oswin Jezercak's favorite time of year! But for now, the eerie smile of Halloween future had to come off his face, for he had a case to solve.

"K.J., I need you to call Bella and tell her we need Amelia's maiden name and her family doctor. Then we need the phone number of Amelia's mother as well. You need to call her and find out all her kids' names, siblings' names, where they were born, and family doctors' names. We need as much information as possible about all of them.

"Find out if I could access an ancestry tree they might have. We might get lucky; someone might be into genealogy and have an ancestry.com account. Either way, whatever information you can get, I'll take it from there. K.J., this is far more important to solving this case than you know; take it seriously."

An hour later, K.J. had as much information as possible about the family's history. Miguel sent a quick text, and within five minutes, there was a knock at the door. K.J. answered, and standing in the doorway was an employee with an I.T. badge.

"Ray from I.T., this is K.J. You may know her as Kimmee, and you don't need to put the Clicker app on her phone. By the way, you did a great job on the app; it's working out just as I planned. But now, I have a different assignment. Take this list, K.J. prepared; I need every medical record on this family tree. Particularly, I need every EKG reading, every echocardiogram, death certificate, and what anyone from this family tree also died of — STAT! Retrieving this information will be a big job; tap into my worldwide network of hackers and send an S.O.S. to get this done. Don't dare leave this office tonight until you've finished. — Ray, I *need* this — Do we understand one another?"

"Y-Y-Yes, sir! I will not fail you." Ray responded with a nervous, stuttered response.

It was 1:47 a.m. when a knock from the door startled K.J. out of an intense trance from watching Miguel work. She felt like she had won the pathologist lottery sweepstakes to be Wolfrem Miguel Oswin Jezercak's first-ever personal assistant. She answered the door, and Ray from I.T. handed her a rather *War and Peace*-sized file.

"Let Dr. Jezercak know we hit the motherlode on this one," and then walked away. She gave the file to Miguel and relayed the message.

"He said motherlode, did he? Thanks, K.J."

Kimmee helped put the current organ samples back in their baggies as he was eager to look at the bulging motherlode file. He signaled K.J. to follow as he walked toward the connecting door from the forensic lab to his office.

He quickly resumed his default thinking position with shoes propped on the desk while running, contemplating strokes through his Van Dyke beard. The Clicker very much liked talking to himself while concentrating on the large file.

Kimmee found the tufted office couch to be quite comfortable, as a barrage of: "I'll be a monkey's uncle"s, — "You don't say"s — "No wonder"s — "How in the hell"s — "Come to Papa"s, and a slew of other gotcha type phrases hypnotized her to sleep.

Time passed. A voice accompanied her in a dreamlike state with no sense of time as Miguel talking on the phone played in her subconscious.

"Thanks so very much for your input on this one. I just wanted to confer with you on what your thoughts were as well. — Professor Shroyer, one last thing. Kimmee James Attwood — she's a winner. I owe you one. — A bottle of Scotch, you say. I'll send you my finest; she's worth it." Footsteps lessened out of the room.

Kimmee fought her eyes from opening from what she heard and continued to play possum on the couch. *This is officially the weirdest day ever! Professor Shroyer knows Dr. Jezercak. I guess I'm the monkey's uncle here because Miguel **is** the one who got me my job.*

This revelation stirred her subconscious mind as she tossed and turned. Soon, she opened her eyes long enough to notice a warm blanket covering her, and her head lay on a soft pillow. Kimmee smiled at the transformation of the human she hated a half-day earlier. She realized a great responsibility in knowing that she was now the gatekeeper to what lay underneath the man she was privileged to call Miguel. A calmness warmed her as fatigue overtook her.

The hour was late — far after the world had gone to sleep and long before it woke. In a lonely lab with spotlighting, the Clicker floated from instrument to instrument, gathering information much like a bee moving from flower-to-flower gathering nectar.

Then, there was a sudden halt in his movements. He rolled back in his chair amidst his legion of instruments and heaved a great sigh that produced a gentle smile. He whispered to himself as Kimmee slept comfortably on the office couch — "I got it."

Chapter Twelve
The Theater of the Abyss

(We pick back up on Wednesday morning with the Dedacciai's timeline)

As blood accumulated on Grandpa's wrist, he grew cold, although immersed in 112° molecular warmth. His mind numbed as it rebelled against the razor-sharp pain. He groped in the dark and wondered if his amateur attempt went deep enough or far enough or if he had simply created a glorified flesh wound worthy of a hefty bandage? If not, would the pills do their job?

He then experienced a sick sense of relief as he accepted the inevitable possibility that one way or the other, his inaugural attempt may have succeeded. Soon, his sense of self-awareness faded toward an empty void of blackness.

Wherever this was, there was no sense of time. Suddenly, blood-red colored spotlights shattered the darkened abyss and highlighted an unconscious man ebbing away in a tub. Tony Robbins and Grandpa flanked each side and watched while seated in red leather executive chairs.

As Grandpa watched himself fade away into a pool of blood, he didn't know whether to feel horrified or relieved. One might have expected him to feel some sort of doubt or regret for what he had done. Instead, he felt nothing, and that was worse.

"Let's try this again," Tony said. As if on cue, the house lights came up as his assistant, Carla, brought out another transcript of Grandpa and Darius.

"Grandpa, would you please look behind you?" asked Tony. When he did, eight giant 10x10 perfectly painted portraits of his family lit up one by one across the massive stage – *His* Bellavia, Addison, Evan, Amelia, August, Jack, Jordyn, and even Zilla.

"Would you please look at their faces and remind them how they are supposed to live when you die? Because, evidently, you might die here and now. When they find out how you killed yourself, they will experience unbearable regret for what happened. You sure had great advice for Darius. Would you give them the same advice?"

Grandpa lowered his head. He couldn't continue to look at the portraits or respond to Tony.

"Let me help get you started," Tony offered as he opened the transcript to the bolded advice.

"Darius, I know that if I died in some sort of accident, I would never want my kids to ruin their lives over it, even if it's their fault. I couldn't rest in Heaven knowing that they decided to destroy their lives in my honor. I would want the complete opposite, and I suspect you would too. So why shouldn't that philosophy be applied to me as well?

"That's why I know without a shadow of a doubt that if something horrible happened to one of my kids and I was somehow involved, as hard as it would be, I would try to live the rest of my life by doing well and helping others in their name. And most importantly — I would strive every day to be happy because that's how you honor their lives, by living yours."

The once powerful words given to Darius were now powerless to the soul that crossed the threshold as Grandpa folded his head into his hands.

"I warned you that you were in a fragile mindset, and if you woke up in the wrong state of mind, this could happen. But it was a tough ask for any man in your condition." Tony stood and kneeled in front of him and locked eyes.

"Read this to them; tell them how you'll live if you make it out of the abyss alive."

"Why bother? Look at me; you're right; I might be dead soon."

"But you might not." Tony pointed at the tub, "It's a shame; all those portraits won't have a husband, a father, or a grandfather because of your selfishness." Tony experienced a moment of realization. "It's not the first time you were accused of being selfish lately, has it? Maybe I'm going about this wrong; I'm having you read from the wrong transcript." Tony turned to his assistant. "Carla, could you please get us the transcript of Evan's last words to his pops?"

"You bastard, you're playing dirty," Grandpa grumbled at him.

"Good, now I've got your attention," Tony said as his demeanor took a stern attitude shift. "Maybe you won't do it for yourself, but you'll do it for Evan. You just need a clear sense of purpose of why you'll do it. I tried this the nice way last time and look at the results. No more, Mr. Nice Guy, as you may literally die in the middle of one of my sentences." Moments later, Carla returned and handed them each a transcript.

"You know what to do; read the highlighted parts. But this time, turn and talk to Evan's portrait. And don't give me any crap about how painful it is. We don't have time for that! Here, I'll get you started."

"'You killed her! *You killed my Addison!* I asked you; I begged you, but you wouldn't listen! Is this hysterical to you, old man? So, is this hysterical, you fat turd!? Isn't that what you always say? 'It's only funny until someone gets hurt, then it's hysterical.' Well, tell me, is it? I don't see you laughing!'"

"Ok, Grandpa, it's your turn. Read the next line — Now!"
Grandpa reached deep within his psyche and miraculously uttered the words.

"I hate you! I hate everything about you! I hate that you have always embarrassed me – not just me, but all your kids, by how fat and gross-looking you are! I never want to see you again. And don't even think about coming to Addison's funeral!

"You're dead to me, even more than Addison! You remember Addison, my daughter, who you killed because of how stupid and selfish you are?! At least Addison is still alive in my heart, but not you."

"So you're not invited to the funeral because of how fat and selfish you are. Since you won't hear the obituary, let's write one ourselves. You can put that quick wit of yours to use. What, writing an obituary for a three-year-old isn't as much fun as it sounds? Where have we heard that before? If only Darius had someone to warn him like I'm warning you."

"Tony, this only makes me want to die even more. Is that what you're going for?"

"No, what's going to happen to Evan because of your selfishness *is* what I'm going for. In fact, instead of writing Addison's obituary, let's write Evan's instead. Doesn't that sound fun? It can go something like this.

"Evan was born to a wonderful family, where love surrounded him, and he grew to become an amazing son, husband, and eventual father to a beautiful soul named Addison. Her parents, Evan and Amelia, cherished her every day, enveloping her with a kind of love they never knew existed until she came along.

"But all that changed one tragic night when Evan's three-year-old daughter died at the hands of his father, whose selfish refusal to listen to his family's concerns led to a tragic accident. Evan's pain was furthered as his dad's body was found overdosed and drowned in a hotel bathtub the next day.

"It was the beginning of the end for Evan and his wife, as their faith devolved and they blamed God. Eventually, they stopped going to church altogether. Eventually, Amelia left after their second child, who never knew the inside of a church, developed a devastating drug problem that their marriage couldn't survive.

"The stress of all of this contributed to Bellavia remarrying once Evan and Amelia's divorce was final, and her relationship with Evan and her grandchild collapsed. Like his father, Evan was found drowned in a hotel bathtub from an overdose. He was 47. Sadly, Bellavia died shortly after. Some say she died of a broken heart."

"At her service, the priest read a beautiful obituary that her new husband had written with you as a footnote as if you were nothing in their lives. A rather poetic ending, wouldn't you say, with his death mimicking yours. Like father, like son. Now that's a legacy worth leaving behind, don't you think?"

Grandpa had a complete emotional schism hearing Tony's epitaph of what could occur, as Tony relentlessly explained. "You are going to have to trust me on this. I've been at this for over 40 years. The consistency of a family's breakdown is staggering, especially in a case such as this, where you selfishly killed yourself after possibly killing Addison. And, as absolutely horrific as all that is, you are going to take it to another level."

"How could that possibly be possible?" Grandpa cried out.

"Because you're robbing your son of the opportunity to give true forgiveness. Because true forgiveness, and I must emphasize the word *true*, is one of *the* most consequential events in a person's life. Humans who have found the strength to forgive the unforgivable surpass normality and become extraordinary. They are people who feel compelled to meet with violent criminals who have murdered their children or family members for the sole purpose of reconciling their lives by offering true forgiveness to the perpetrator. But why do they do this?

"They do this to free the person they have become as a result of the hatred and vitriol that has infiltrated their soul. They have allowed their rage to determine their actions and influence their decisions. They have deteriorated physically and often experience severe medical issues. This cycle has created psychological problems that cannot be explained away to a therapist. For these people, there is only one way out — true and absolute forgiveness.

"And when this life-altering event happens, the giver and the receiver are graced with the chance for a new life. Your son Evan must be allowed this chance for metamorphosis, but that can only be possible if *you* survive. Your biggest misconception is that you think your death will better their world? But the truth is the complete opposite. Your death is going to cause your son tremendous guilt, as well as the rest of your family. If Evan never has the chance for closure with you, he'll find his own way to selfishly destroy his life in your name. Is that what you want?"

Grandpa, with no words, watched himself in the tub.

"Let's not be delusional here," Robbins continued. "It could take years for Evan to accept how desperately he needs to find a way through his pain to a place of intercession. And, if you are not around because you selfishly robbed him of the chance to confront you, you may add to his suffering. You may even make the situation worse. There is no guarantee that Evan will ever forgive you. But, as his father, aren't you willing to take that risk? Isn't that what it means to love unconditionally? Rather than preempting his decision by taking your own life, shouldn't you allow him to make up his own mind, even if it means risking his rejection?"

Grandpa looked up at the beautiful portraits of his family and saw their loving faces.

"You still have the power to do what's best — Redemption is now or never," Tony said as he handed him the original transcript of Grandpa talking with Darius.

"These may be the final words you ever hear. I want you to read these wonderful, heartfelt words you said to Darius and take them to heart. I believe you believed they could have healed Darius when you said them. And whether they're the last words that send you to Heaven, Hell, or back to Earth, I'm asking you to accept the possibility that they can heal you as well. And, if you do wake up in that bathtub, adopt them in your heart and live by them."

Grandpa grapples with opening the script but then closes it. "Tony, I know these words inside and out because they are already haunting me. Instead, I just want to talk to my dying soul still lying in that damned tub." he leaned toward his unconscious self in the tub and sighed deeply.

"You have made such a mess of things, but if, by some miracle, you survive this, your sole purpose will be to stay alive for Evan until his timetable for forgiveness happens, and you must maintain faith that it will. You must also strive to be happy, although you won't think you deserve it. The bottom line is this: you must live your life by doing well and helping others and strive every day to honor their lives by living yours to the fullest."

Suddenly, the scene returns to an empty void as an involuntary reaction to the pills causes Grandpa's stomach to convulse. What had seemed like hours were only minutes in the theater of the abyss. Grandpa started to hear sounds penetrating from the outside world. Suddenly, a knock on the door pierced the air before the room again went silent. After a momentary pause, a key card slid into the lock.

Chapter Thirteen

Who Are We?

Grandpa's eyes exploded open as he heard the door unlock and then open. A light turned on in the hallway and slightly illuminated the bathroom from underneath the door. He looked at his wrist — a silent gasp released from the deepest part of himself. But he was alive.

A state of bewilderment overpowered Grandpa as he relived the state of mind he was just in moments ago when he thought he would spend eternity in Hell. His fog-of-war mindset held him in profound conflict of how Heaven, Hell, or oblivion worked with the illogical way he saw things — and he wondered how his Creator now saw him in the emotional aftermath as well.

His life had become a living Bible verse, for he had betrayed his faith and had chosen death and eternal hell over life. He had crucified his faith and buried it — but after three minutes, his faith rose again from a knock on the door. Was this God's grace? Was he still worthy in His eyes?

Extreme guilt joined his mental plethora of emotions with the dichotomy of depression and relief living side by side within him. His now idled mind developed a vendetta against itself for what it tried to do to him, and it was torn into thirds as the three contenders of depression, relief, and profound guilt fought for emotional dominance.

Grandpa's thoughts returned from the blackness and focused on the knock at the door, which had temporarily saved his life. But who had saved him from Hell? Hotel security? The police? Either one would want to know why there was broken glass on the counter and a slit on his wrist.

"Dedacciai? — Are you here? — Where are you?"

The voice circling in his room triggered him. He knew it was the last voice he heard after being attacked and left on the side of the road with everything stolen. 'Dedacciai' also triggered an immense feeling buried deep inside him — hope. *But why is he calling out the name of my bicycle?*

As the room came into focus and his thoughts cleared, he felt the sharp glass almost used to kill himself. A dark shame accompanied the glimmer of hope of how deep and dark his life had turned. He attempted to rise from the tub to face the familiar voice but was unsuccessful. Instead, he grabbed a towel to cover himself before the bathroom door opened.

As the door handle rotated, a hand reached in and turned on the light. The transformation of darkness into light revealed the exact vision in the older cyclist's mind of a college-aged man sporting a large nose ring.

However, in this scenario, he was not attacking him and stealing his things. Instead, the young man was returning them as he held a stack of clean clothes, a package of new underwear, and the older cyclist's money pouch. The college-aged man saw the empty pill bottle and broken glass on the countertop and quickly noticed the blood strands painted in the water. He inventoried the cyclist and found the source of blood on his wrist.

Carter immediately put the puzzle together, as he had starred in this movie before in his life with Russell Ducane. Carter had a sense of calmness about him and didn't want to startle or give rise to the situation as he took command.

"Sir, you won't like this, but you have to throw up the pills. I'm not sure how many were in there, but we need to get them out immediately to be safe. I can help because this isn't the first time I've had to do this for someone."

The older cyclist looked at him silently, considering the directive, but also wondered about his statement. Then life took care of itself, as the man's stomach had its own remedy as it suddenly convulsed. He tried to lean over the tub to get to the toilet quickly but hurled half on the floor and half into the toilet.

"I got this, don't worry, I'll get it cleaned up." — Carter calmly knelt by the tub, handed him a washcloth to clean his face, and then removed the glass weapon from the older cyclist's hand with no resistance. Fortunately, the cut was more dramatic than it was deep, and Carter tended to the wound by temporarily wrapping a washcloth around the man's wrist.

"I know you had a rough night last night, but tell me what's going on — why are you doing this?"

The older man shook his head with no answers for the younger of the two. Overwhelming guilt prohibited a response as he stared at the glass weapon Carter took from him that almost changed everything. Fortunately, Carter's timely pattern interrupt rendered the sharp piece of glass no longer of interest.

"Everything is going to be okay. I'm here to help." Carter said. "I understand you don't know me and might not want to tell me anything. But is there someone we need to call that you could talk to?"

The older cyclist lowered his head with visions of the people he could call, but who would not want him to. He slowly and somberly shook his head no.

"Can you tell me your name?" asked Carter.

The man answered with silence and closed eyes, obviously avoiding the question. Carter stood and began wiping the shards of glass off the countertop and into the wastebasket.

"I've been there too — in the darkness — if you want to talk."

Carter felt a notion to share with the stranger as he had a vested interest in this man's story ending with something other than suicide. Not only did Carter want to help this stranger, but he also believed that if Darius was correct, this man was somehow the key to Chapter One of Carter's new life story.

"Yesterday was one of the worst days of my life. I wasn't at the point of darkness you are — mine was about anger and rage. But it was my 25th birthday, and my present to myself was almost killing my father — I'm just saying that I understand. So, if you want to talk, there will be no judgment from me."

Carter's sincerity painted the room with interest as the older cyclist lifted his head and opened his eyes. He was curious about the young man who shared such personal darkness. His eyes wandered toward the newly formed scabs on Carter's hands, evidence of his own bloody event. Then, a glimmer of Grandpa's former self made an appearance.

"I don't know who you are or how you are here — but I'm sorry about your birthday."

"Thanks for that; by the way, the name's Carter."

"Carter, is that how you cut your hands, fighting with your dad last night?"

"Actually, no," — Carter scoffed. "I cut my hands rescuing you!"

"Rescuing me? — Why would you do that?"

"Because you needed me to, and I did it despite what you said — 'to let you die!' What do you remember about last night?"

"I remember getting run off the road, getting beat up, and someone stealing my bike. The last thing I remember was getting kicked in the head, which was painful. After that happened, I either lost consciousness or was in a semi-conscious state. I remember snippets, but the world was spinning so fast that it made me sick when I opened my eyes, and my vision was blurry. Despite this, I recall hearing your voice and faintly remember seeing your face."

He closed his eyes, and the grumblings of hunger made themselves known by a rather loud voice coming from the belly of the cyclist.

"I'm not feeling well; my headache is coming back."

"Okay, I'll run down and get you some aspirin. I'm here to help you through this, and hopefully, you'll feel better once we get you cleaned up and fed. There's an IHOP just down the road. While I'm out, I'll get you a razor, shaving cream, toothbrush, toothpaste, and something to wrap around your wrist. Here, let me help you stand so you can shower."

Carter helped the man up as he winced in pain. The cyclist's bruises appeared to be turning more purplish-blue, and Carter concentrated a little too long on the bruising as his adrenaline from last night made a sharp appearance.

"Those thugs running you off the road and attacking you made me want to kill them, along with my dad." With a wry smile, he added, "At least I got to kill one thing — their car."

What does that mean? Did he kill their car? The man felt the intensity of Carter's rage and knew he had lived through quite a story last night.

"I'll be back; are you going to be okay? Do you think you can stand long enough to take a shower?"

The cyclist nodded that he would, and Carter unwrapped the soap bar and placed it in the shower with the shampoo and conditioner. He grabbed the wastebasket with the shards.

"I'm going to throw this away in my room. Weirdly, I think we have more in common than we know — I'll be back."

Twenty minutes passed, and Carter re-entered the man's room with the necessary hygiene items from the front hotel desk. The water shut off, and as the older cyclist opened the shower curtain, he saw a bottle of water alongside a purposeful plastic cup. Aspirin sat next to it, along with his necessary hygiene items. The hair dryer was unraveled and plugged in alongside a miniature hairbrush. There was a tube of ointment for the much-lessened goose egg on his head and bandages with some adhesive medical tape for the slit on his wrist. The man was fortunate he hadn't cut deeper than he did.

The bathroom door was 90% closed, as he commented to his caregiver.

"Why, thank you, Nurse Carter — truly."

"You're welcome," echoed back from the hotel living space.

The Nurse Carter statement hit Carter as he began contemplating what he was doing: caring for someone, especially a stranger. He felt something he couldn't assign a word to and didn't realize lived inside him — Selflessness. But even though he wouldn't know how to say the word out loud or think it, he was feeling it. More importantly, he was doing selflessness.

He remembered how scared he was for his future at the close of his last shift. But now, he hadn't thought about himself because he had become more worried for this stranger instead.

Was Darius right? — Is this man somehow the one to help me rewrite my story? His thoughts were interrupted as the hairdryer stopped.

"Carter—? Why did you yell the name of my bicycle when you entered the room earlier?" The question echoed as it drifted from the bathroom.

"I didn't know what else to call you. What is your name?" Carter replied.

The question once again met with silence.

"Exactly — that's why I had to name you last night," Carter added. The statement caught the older cyclist off guard.

"This sounds interesting. — Let's hear it; who am I?"

"You're 'the Dedacciai,'" Carter said. "That's why I was calling out 'Dedacciai'; I was looking for you. I'm fairly sure your bicycle wouldn't have answered."

"I'm sorry, Carter. I wasn't thinking clearly or expecting someone to yell the name of my bicycle. And why would you name me after my bike in the first place – I thought it was stolen?"

"It was stolen."— — —

There was a long pause as Carter almost heard the cyclist's disappointment emanate from the bathroom.

"That's why I stole it back. — My hands are scratched up because I beat up the thugs that ran you off the road and stole it back from them. And, as a bonus, beat up their pimp-mobile for good measure — just because it was there."

The cyclist opened the door rapidly to ask if he heard correctly. But the answer leaned against the wall in plain sight, and he had never seen his masterpiece look so beautiful.

He hadn't the words, but his silence spoke volumes as his knees buckled and fell to the ground. Carter attempted to catch him but couldn't get there in time. He knelt beside him to catch him as he tumbled sideways, forcing Carter to fall into a sitting position. The cyclist's head found itself once again resting in Carter's lap. The former grandpa's eyes were closed, and he shook from overwhelming relief.

"Yep, this was a perfect reenactment of how our relationship started."

Carter allowed the man a minute of solitude before the grumblings of hunger returned.

"Let's get you fed," Carter said.

The man winced in pain as Carter helped him out of his lap and eventually to his feet. The cyclist admired Carter's handy work while holding his bicycle again. Then he finished getting ready, and the two men exited the room.

"Dedacciai, I want to show you something before we go."

They walked across the hallway, and Carter opened his door. The Dedacciai saw the royal-blue Specialized Transition bicycle he knew all too well, as his collection had the same bike.

"See, I told you we have more in common than you know."

"Nice choice, Carter. Your bike is in great condition; do you have a particular mechanic that works on it for you?" he asked as he looked it over.

"Yes, sir — you're looking at him."

"You know your way around a bike. How is that? Cycling is almost a lost art form because of video games. And kids usually only care about whatever fancy car they expect their parents to buy for them."

Carter smirked at the irony.

"I don't have a fancy car or a car at all!"

The Dedacciai noticed the change in Carter's demeanor as he looked closely at his bicycle.

"I've had to ride a bike all my life if I wanted to go anywhere. My family has never been able to afford a car because of my stupid dad. I hate that man. It's all because of him that I have to ride my bike like a child when I should have a car! Anyway, I can't afford a car, and I can't afford a bicycle mechanic, so I've had to learn how to do everything myself."

The Dedacciai realized he had opened Pandora's Box to Carter's life as his emotions flared.

"From the moment I saw you riding your bicycle in the rain, I thought it was amazing, even from a distance. I had never seen anything like it. So, when I saw those thugs try to steal it, I felt the need to get it back for you. Like I said, last night was the worst night of my life. Lucky for you, I had a lot of pent-up anger. Let's just say it certainly helped in retrieving your bike.

"Anyway, after your rough night, I wanted to get it fixed and cleaned before letting you see it. I'm amazed how beautiful it is all cleaned up."

The Dedacciai stared at Carter and tried to thank him, but his facial expression said it all.

"So, what is your real name anyway?"

"Evidently— I'm 'the Dedacciai'—"

The two found themselves walking the elegant corridor toward the elevator. With each step, the Dedacciai seemed to feel stronger and knew he had previously walked these corridors of wallpaper. The elevator informed them they had arrived at the lobby level as they awaited the polished brass doors to part.

He wasn't sure which of his senses was titillated first — sight, sound, or smell. But a symphony of remembrance elegantly jogged his memories. And for a moment, every feeling of pain left his body to make room for the stimulations he received from the eclectic art that sprawled the grandeur of the twenty-five-foot walls. The familiar smell of mahogany teakwood lingering in the air was accompanied by the romantic piano melodies of Jim Brickman.

They all triggered the memory of a special Valentine's evening spent with his Bellavia. "The Lancaster" escaped his thoughts and became a verbal gasp.

"Oh, Lancaster," he said with closed eyes. How in the hell was he even here and in room 555? The mystery boggled his mind and brought him nearly to tears as his brain clamored with memory.

He envisioned his Bellavia wearing the little red cocktail dress he surprised her with as she spied it in the small boutique shop. He felt her rubbing his foot under the table as he held her hands and her gaze with his. The evening was accompanied by his devilish smile of excitement while she played with his heart using all the tools a woman has.

He awakened from his trance, and Carter wondered where his mind had gone. The Dedacciai wiped his eyes as the beautiful tears turned to dreaded ones, knowing his precious Bellavia would never see him that way again.

The momentary gratitude for the return of his possessions was quickly pushed aside when his emotional and physical pain escalated as he walked out of the grand entryway.

Upon his exit, he turned to look at the incredible architecture and recalled it instantly. The sight made him demonstratively silent as yesteryear swirled in his thoughts. The architecture was why his Bellavia wanted to stay there in the first place, as did he.

Carter felt Dedacciai's demeanor shift back to when he first met him. His mind relived the older cyclist begging, *Just let me die,* coupled with the bathtub scene from mere hours ago. The Dedacciai was noticeably silent, and Nurse Carter's confident state transitioned to his nervous self as the two men managed their way across the street.

Regardless of Dedacciai's state of mind, the primal need for food bullied its way past his thoughts of morbidity and was his primary need for survival at that moment.

The two-block walk was silent until a sight rolled past them that would solicit a comment from anyone. But, in this case, the reaction was far more personal as a tow truck transporting a 1984 purple Caprice passed from behind and drove into the distance.

The Dedacciai saw the car and the younger man's reaction next to him. The older of the two placed Carter's hands at the rolling crime scene and witnessed the severity of the crime that Carter had committed. The amount of duct tape bandaging the car was impressive and proved, once again, that duct tape had a wide array of uses.

Carter's legs quickened, taking him behind the nearest building with a "For Lease" sign as its only tenant. The Dedacciai followed at a much slower pace and saw Carter bent over and taking deep breaths.

"You really beat up a car — literally? I didn't realize the severity of your statement earlier — but I do now," the Dedacciai commented.

"Sorry, I panicked — I didn't want to be seen by anyone in case the two thugs might have been following in a different car." His breath surged, "Do you think the thugs turned me in to the police? If the police stopped them last night, what would stop them from lying and saying I'm the one that attacked them?"

The Dedacciai lifted his shirt — "We have proof otherwise," allowing Carter to catch his breath a little longer.

Carter walked around the building toward the street to see if any unusual cars were looking for him. The Dedacciai was compelled to comment on Carter's metal foe.

"That car had way more damage than I expected. How did you do that? The scratches on your hands don't equal the amount of duct tape used on the car."

"I had some help," and Carter reached into his pocket. "My mom gave me these before I left last night as a gift to protect myself. They belonged to my granddad, and she said they saved his life during some bar-room scuffles. Little did I know I would be using them a few hours later to save a bicycle — oh — and you," Carter said tongue in cheek.

"Now you're getting loopy. Let's eat something before you start thinking you're funny. I want to hear all about last night now that I have this visual stuck in my head. And by the way — thank you."

The hostess greeted the two as they entered IHOP. She had an aura about her that indicated she was relieved the lunch rush was over but glad to seat the two. She headed to where the remnants of a few guests were finishing their meals. However, no matter what the older cyclist's state of mind, he was always particular about where he was seated in a restaurant.

He instigated seating protocol One-Niner-Bravo, a rather lengthy substrate of criteria when looking for a table or booth that fit his needs. His mind and eyes decided, and he headed toward the other side of the restaurant where Carter and he would be seated. She had witnessed this protocol before, and the hostess followed and placed the menus on the table.

The Dedacciai was happy with his choice, which met his seating protocol. It was the perfect booth at the end of a row where he could sit with his back to the wall, and no one could sit behind him. It had a window view of the Lancaster Landing Hotel, and the sun had made its way past the point of needing the sunshade drawn. The Dedacciai, as a precaution, moved the nearest table an additional two feet away, just in case they tried to seat someone near them. No sooner did they get seated that Carter excused himself to use the restroom.

While seated alone and waiting for Carter's return, visions of the rolling crime scene faded as the Dedacciai contemplated his situation.

A portion of the Dedacciai's dream fragments from the previous night began playing in his mind. He heard Tony Robbins trying to break through to him and a vision of a tall, thin, Jesus-looking man sitting across from him in an IHOP booth. He saw sentence fragments as if he were reading a transcript.

"Darius, I know that if I died in some sort of accident, I would never want my kids to ruin their lives over it, even if it's their fault. I couldn't rest in Heaven knowing that they decided to destroy their lives in my honor.

"I know without a shadow of a doubt that if something horrible happened to one of my kids and I was somehow involved, as hard as it would be, I would try to live the rest of my life by doing well and helping others in their name. And most importantly — I would strive every day to be happy because that's how you honor their lives, by living yours."

He once again heard Robbin's voice as a vision of Addison played in his mind: **"I know you believed every word when you said them. Addison wants these words for you; she wants to watch you be happy and do good in her name."**

He knew his life forward would be a minute-by-minute rollercoaster ride of emotional darkness and light as he came out of his trance. Refocusing his thoughts, another familiar sight either following or haunting him appeared in the sky.

This time, there was a beautiful double rainbow displayed over the Lancaster Hotel. The vision made him question its meaning. Was the double rainbow a sign that Carter had been placed here for a reason and was to be his focus?

The Dedacciai's fragmented dream state dissolved when Carter sat down, causing the table to resonate through Dedacciai's body. Carter couldn't help but see the double rainbow, and the two familiar strangers watched as it soon dissipated.

His fragmented thoughts transformed into gratitude for Carter as the Dedacciai looked deeper at the man sporting the large nose ring.

The sound of singing preceded a sprite young forty-something waitress who came waltzing up with two glasses of water.

"Ya-mon, are you situated okay? Is this your final answer? I know your type. I'll not let people sit nearby unless they have their own seating ritual as well. Just an FYI —there are more of you than you know. I think you guys need your own twelve-seat program."

The Jamaican accent verbalizing her awareness of the Dedacciai's protocol caught him off guard. He smirked at the wisdom and cleverness of the statement. Carter didn't quite get the irony of the 12-step reference but was glad to see the Dedacciai smirk.

"What you havin' to drink?"

"I'll have a Coke," Carter replied.

"I'll take an unsweet tea with extra ice and a teaspoon. And could I have as many orange slices as possible with lots of Equal or Splenda?"

"Ya, a serious tea drinker, I see. I know your type; you are my brother from another mother. I'll bring you a bowl of orange slices and an extra glass of ice as well," and the waitress scuffled off to perform the task.

A few minutes later, she returned with the goods.

"Are you gentlemen ready to order?"

The Dedacciai knew what he wanted, but Carter had not decided on his order.

"I'll give you two a minute more." The waitress went over to check on the only other customer who had infiltrated their side of the restaurant.

Carter watched the Dedacciai organize and attack his orange iced tea sweetening process. He saw him squeezing the orange slices to get every drop of goodness, then ate what was left off the orange rind and rubbed what looked like a football mouthpiece against his teeth. He tore open each sweetener, one by one, and began stirring them in, taste testing between stirs till he got it right.

That sure looks like a lot of work for just one glass of iced tea, Carter thought as he sipped his prefabbed Coca-Cola.

The older cyclist spied a clock on the wall showing 3 p.m. His thoughts began to wander as he was flooded with memories of how IHOP had been his happy spot. Now, it was time to have a new experience, on a much different level, with Carter.

"Do we know what we are having yet?" the waitress interrupted.

"I'll have a turkey, bacon, avocado wrap, and a side salad with Ranch," Carter ordered.

"And you, my brother, what you havin' today?"

"I'll have the country omelet with the three dollar-size pancakes." Grumblings of hunger accompanied his order.

The waitress backed up, afraid something might bite her. "I read you loud and clear; I'll put a rush on it." With a smirk, she scuttled off.

The Dedacciai looked at the scratches on Carter's hands.

"Okay, Carter, tell me about yourself, starting with your childhood. I want to know about the man who saved my bike and everything that happened last night."

"Well, it's sort of a long story, and I don't want to bore you. I'm not sure where to start – are you sure you want to know?"

The Dedacciai looked at him intently and signaled with the universal man-nod to begin.

"Well, let's see — after a huge fight with my dad yesterday, I decided to move out of my parent's house and packed everything I owned in my backpack, except for these brass knuckles. Like I said, they belonged to my granddad. I never really knew the man because he didn't get along with my dad, which is a microcosm of my life — my dad ruining everything.

"I hate to even refer to him as a dad because a dad is someone you're supposed to love, not hate. And I hate Russell Ducane because he was a drunk and verbally abusive toward me and my mom. At one point, the abuse was so bad that my mom attempted an overdose. I was sixteen when I learned to stick my fingers down her mouth to make her throw up. And because of that, I have no good memories to talk about and hated my childhood. The silver lining is that I was prepared to save you, too. I'll have to thank my mom for you if I ever see her again."

The Dedacciai shivered at the darkness Carter's story reminded him of. "I'm so sorry that happened to you. No son should ever have to do that to his mother — or a total stranger. Would you mind continuing your story? I don't want to dwell on my darkest moment except to say thank you for being there for me earlier."

There was a non-judgemental moment of respect between the two before Carter continued.

"Things were only semi-tolerable because my mom would never stand up to him. And she knew he would be less verbally abusive as long as she had food waiting for him at six freaking o'clock every night, along with an opened can of beer. It's all I knew; it was our way of life — our normal."

The older man sighed, "It's amazing, in a sad way, what we get used to."

Carter snorted, "Isn't that the truth? But anyway, I knew it wasn't normal. The stupid bastard had three D.U.I.s, so we had no car. That's why I've always had to ride bikes to get to wherever I needed to. Which wasn't so bad when I was little, and true, it taught me to be a bicycle mechanic, but it sure doesn't impress the girls.

"Do you know how painful it is to have friends you rode bicycles with as kids turn against you when you turn sixteen just because you don't have a car? All the girls made fun of me, and everyone treated me like an outsider. Like I was *less than zero*. I hated bikes because of that. I've wanted to end my life so many times, so I understand getting to that point of no return." Carter took a deep breath and closed his eyes.

"Man, I'm sorry, Carter," Dedacciai responded.

"Yeah, me, too. Since I didn't have a car, fighting with kids who used to be my friends became another part of my new dysfunctional normal. High school was hell, simply hell. I'm not sure if graduating was the happiest night of my life, but it was the biggest relief of my life.

"Since I had to ride bikes after I graduated high school, I decided to at least buy my first real road bike. That's when I purchased my Specialized Transition; it was the first thing I ever saved and worked hard for that I've been proud of owning. It helped me not to hate bikes as much.

"Up until I bought my Specialized, I've had to fix my bikes because I had to — but now, I want to. I enjoy being a good mechanic and keeping my bike in great working condition. I like keeping up with the latest bicycle technology and frequent bicycle stores. However, I wasn't a customer until you came into my life."

"What do you mean by that?" the Dedacciai questioned.

"Buying some tools and handlebar tape to fix your bike was kind of my first purchase. All the tools I have are from my mom at Christmas."

"Carter, I will repay you for everything you've done for me. I want you to know that. So, how is it that I came into your life?"

"Like I was saying, I saved for my bicycle doing odd jobs and eventually worked at a bar called Hard Times. I've been there for five years now. I thought I could make enough money to move out, but they ended up not needing me full-time, so I made just enough to keep living in the great state of limbo — where there is no zip code, which is my life's motto at this point.

"I got this nose ring to help fit in at the bar, but more so because my dad would hate it. I wanted to show him exactly how much I hated him for being the worst dad ever. Truthfully, I never really wanted it; I just thought it might help with tips or something — but it didn't. — But it did piss off my dad, which was a win in my book.

"Anyway, life at home had been getting worse for years. But last night took a turn to the dark side when my mom walked in the door past six o'clock, and my dad's dinner and beer weren't on the table. My asshole dad got so mad; he tripped my mom while she carried in the groceries. When he did, the birthday cake my mom tried to surprise me with slid out of the bag and across the floor. He was so furious with her that my ass-wipe of a dad stomped on my cake. We got into the worst fight you can imagine. I hate that man so much. I still can't believe he stomped on my cake and tripped my mom. Like I said, if it weren't for her, I think my dad might be dead. Anyway, last night was the worst night of my life; you can't even imagine how horrible it was."

The older cyclist almost smirked at the irony; *you think you had the worst night of your life!* The eccentric part of the former grandpa wanted to compare notes but said nothing and let Carter continue.

"Anyway, after our fight and after I packed my backpack with everything I thought I needed, that's when my mom gave me the brass knuckles for protection. Lucky for both of us, she did. Then I rode my bike to work for what turned out to be my last night as I told my boss I had to quit. At least he was cool about it and understood.

"So, I planned to get a hotel room after my last shift, apply for a new job today, and start my life away from Russell Ducane — sink or swim.

"Dedacciai, I was so scared about my future and what would happen to me. I remember shaking and questioning everything. I even thought of going back home because I thought I was making the biggest mistake of my life.

"As I was closing, my boss gave me my final paycheck. He also handed me a cupcake with a candle and wished me a happy birthday. A few minutes later, the music shut off, and I knew it was exactly 2 a.m.

"I remember wiping off the window so I could see outside. I lit my candle, closed my eyes, and made a wish. Then I opened my eyes, blew out the candle, and looked outside. When I did, I saw this crazy-ass cyclist riding his bike in the rain. I remember laughing at first at what kind of idiot would be riding his bike in the rain at 2 a.m."

The Dedacciai pointed at himself, "This idiot."

Carter smiled slightly. "Then a car came from behind and ran you off the road. Two guys got out and attacked, and I honestly didn't know what to do. I thought about calling 911, but they wouldn't have arrived in time. Ultimately, I saw one of the guys take your bike and start to put it in his trunk. Suddenly, I had a cyclist code of honor to uphold and decided to rescue your bicycle from getting stolen.

"That's when I ran across the street with my brass knuckles. My adrenaline levels helped me beat up the two thugs, as well as their car, chrome, and windshields. Well, you saw the results."

"Carter —that's weirdly an amazing story." As Dedacciai reflected on the story, he looked out the window and focused on the Lancaster Hotel.

"Now, what made you bring me to this hotel? It seems odd; Millennials don't usually stay at a Lancaster-type hotel."

"Odd — you're telling me — odd. Everything about what I'm about to tell you wreaks of odd. Up until this point, our story has just been weird; now the odd part begins —"

"Do tell; I can't wait to hear it."

"Last night, after I saved you from the thugs, it was raining pretty hard, so I dragged you under a tree, where you fell asleep in my lap like our reenactment earlier. Eventually, we ended up falling asleep.

"After a few hours, the rain stopped, and I happened to wake up. When I did, this man was staring at us and had a wheelchair and a white cargo van parked in the street. He scared me at first. I had no idea who he was or how he saw us. He looked like he might be homeless, and I'm not a big fan of the homeless. They remind me of my dad. But this man calmed me down and said his only job was to help get you from point A to point B. He said he knew where to take you. We ended up here at the Lancaster, and he was adamant that you stay in room number 555. Do you know why he wanted you to stay in that particular room?"

Dedacciai went somber, mesmerized by the question. He closed his eyes gracefully — and for an eternal second, was transported back to a distant replay of a movie that lived in his mind.

COFFEE KNOWS BEST
SCENE ONE — TAKE ONE.... *And action!*

━━━━━✦━━━━━

It was five degrees outside as a freezing twenty-year-old college student hustled inside the "COFFEE KNOWS BEST" hot spot, "Where We Know A Bean Or Two About Coffee!" He loved going there just because of their infamous tagline.

As he reached the counter, an extremely attractive blonde was in the line next to him. As he ordered his grandioso-sized, white-hot chocolate, he noticed the digital clock behind the counter turn to 5:55 p.m.— At the same time, he heard the clerk tell the attractive blonde, "$5.55 is your change, and your ticket number is 555 as well."

"Wow— there are a lot of fives circling in the air around here! I mean, what are the odds that it would be five degrees on December 5^{th,} and I would meet the prettiest girl at 5:55 p.m., whose ticket number is 555, and who just got $5.55 back in change?"

Her eyes made their way over with a passive scan of the man next to her.

"I bet you use that line on all the pretty girls you meet at 5:55 p.m."

"Darnskis, you know me so well!"

"Sir, here you go. Your change is $5.55." They couldn't help but laugh as he counted it back. His eyes found their way back to hers, and he raised his hand, offering Hi-555s. The attractive blonde smiled and played along by slapping his hand back three times.

The two grabbed a table together, neither asking the other if it would be okay. It just seemed the natural evolution of their now five-minute relationship. And when they called ticket #555, he went to the counter to hunt and gather their heated goodness.

"So, the takeaway here is you think you are pretty?" he said excitedly.

"No — what I'm saying is that 'YOU' think I'm pretty." She responded. "I can see your eyes, you know, those nice round brown pupils all twitterpated."

"Well, lucky for me, you can't see what my heart is doing."

Causing one eyebrow to raise, she jabbed. "Well, what about your liver?"
"Being innervated by the autonomic nervous system," *he quickly taunted.*
"Well, how about your kidneys?"
"Filtering 200 quarts of very excited blood, my heart sent after seeing you."
Her facial expressions showed she was impressed by his answers and quick wit.
"Would you mind terribly much if I met you here tomorrow, let's say, 5:55 p.m.? Same bat-coffee, same bat-change?" *he asked.*
"I'm not so sure about that. — How do I know you're not part of some Russian mafia numbers gang where you pick up beautiful women using your mad math skills?"
"Oh no — you have me all wrong! I'm an alphabet man, through and through, a proud member of AAAAAAA."
Her coffee cup drew to her mouth while a puzzled expression furrowed her brow.
"Oh, I'm sorry. I just assumed you knew what that meant. It stands for the 'American-Allegiance-Against-Acronym-And-Alphabet-Abuse.'"
Not prepared, she snorted out loud, laughing while swallowing her coffee, causing much of it to come out her nose.
"Lady, you blew it! — I was supposed to say 'Abracadabra' first, and then the coffee bubble appears from your nose. We so need to rehearse," *and swiftly grabbed some napkins to minimize the embarrassment.* "If only I had a dime for every time that trick goes awry!"
She sat there, embarrassed yet smiling and comfortable with his company.
"So, what say you? I've already seen — well, you know — Your-Snot-Bubble-Made-of-Coffee. Which is more commonly known among my circle of alphabet friends as an **a**stounding **a**chievement **a**ccommodating **a**mple **a**mounts of **a**tmospherically **a**ttached **a**ir **a**wesomeness."
Gob-smacked by what her ears heard; her jaw unhinged as her face flushed.
"How about meeting me here tomorrow — 5:55 p.m.?"
She sat there, still gob-smacked — but thinking about it.
"Okay, it seems like I need another aberration. I bet anything your name has an 'A' in it?"
Her head tilted as she twirled her hair. "Actually, it does! That's either a lucky guess, or you're really good."
His raised eyebrow transmitted the answer — "I'm really that good."
She commented, "My middle name also has an 'A' in it. How about your name?"
"Actually, yes. Thanks for thinking about me. So, how about it, same bat-coffee, same bat-change? It will be fun, and we can talk all about our

A's together. Besides, I've already seen a snot bubble coming out of your nose. Aren't you the least bit curious about what else will go wrong?"

With a hearty smile, she stood and placed her hand out to shake on it. Then he played his part in this Tom Hanks, Meg Ryan movie scene by softly grabbing her hand and kissing it gently.

"By the way, in case you're wondering, my name is—" He quickly placed his finger perpendicular to her lips.

"Shussssh! Not now; I want to keep the mystery alive in our relationship. I really feel it has been kind of lackluster since the 7-minute and 38-second mark — don't you?"

"Well, for me, it was around the 6-minute and 53-second mark. But who's counting? — Well, okay, then, Mr. Alphabet man, the mystery waits until I see you tomorrow. — "

Faint words echoed in his ears and knocked the distant replay from Dedacciai's thoughts as he slipped back into the present.

"Hey, Dedacciai — Dedacciai — can you hear me? Are you okay?"

He fumbled his way back to reality, opened his eyes slowly, and lifted his head.

"Yes — and no. — I'm not sure. Sorry, Carter, what were you saying?"

"Dedacciai, what's going on? I've been asking you a question, but you haven't responded. Where did you go? You scared me."

"You asked if I knew why the man wanted me to stay in room 555. The answer is yes, I do. I stayed here years ago with my wife — room 555."

"But where did you go? You looked like you had a stroke or something. Like your life was passing before your eyes; it was weird."

"Part of it was — the best part, the beginning part. The part when I knew it changed the moment I met my future wife. Carter, it's incredible what can happen when you're in a peak emotional state. How you can become so passionate over the smallest detail — like the number 5, for instance. 5's became a staple of my life because a beautiful woman buying coffee simply received $5.55 back in change, and her ticket number was 555 while I was standing beside her in a highly emotional state.

"That moment led us to start dating, and the number 555 became our mantra. Back then, we had pagers and fax machines, so she would randomly page me with 5's, and I would fax back with 5's as well. It was our olden-day, modern way of saying, 'I love you.'

"We even got married on May 5th at 5:55 p.m. and stayed in room 1555 at the Dallas Omni Hotel located at 555 S. Lamar St. on our wedding night. And we have earned frequent flyer miles from always staying in room 1555 on our anniversary. The only reason we didn't stay in room 555 is that the 5th floor houses the swimming pool, exercise room, and day spa, so there aren't any guest rooms on that level. But we ask for room 555 every time we travel. Heck, our home telephone number even has three 5's in it!

"So, yes, I know why he wanted me to stay in room 555. But the odd thing is, how could this man possibly know that?"

"I told you this night was odd; I thought it would be the one room that was haunted or have a horse's head, but I like your reasons way better."

"Carter, I want you to continue telling me about last night; I don't want you to get sidetracked. So, you left off talking about the homeless man bringing you to the hotel."

"Hmmm, okay, what was I saying? Oh, I know. Anyway, you should've seen my face when we arrived at the hotel and I exited the van. I was scared to death. I knew it would be way too expensive, and I didn't have that much money budgeted for my first night. But somehow, he knew it was going to work out. I took the bikes into the hotel and returned to get you from the van. When I did, he was gone, and you were sitting in your wheelchair with this note on your lap. The man wouldn't tell me his name all night but then left this note for me and signed it —" Then he handed the note to the Dedacciai.

Carter,

About your wish to rewrite your story— It is commendable of you to first recognize that your story needs to be rewritten. Like anything worth reading, the author you pick to help rewrite your story is most important. An author is the poet of your emotions, inspires what's already inside of you, and unveils the most buried parts of you. An author reveals the powerful capabilities that live within you and releases the unlimited possibilities of the human spirit. An author induces kindness and compassion by showing the same. You have a good heart; use it. Chapter One is sitting in this wheelchair. I hope your rewritten story turns out to be a beautiful and well-written novel.

~ Darius~

The older cyclist was not prepared for such a beautiful yet heavy message from an alleged homeless man. But one sentence stood out: *Chapter One is sitting in this wheelchair.*

"Carter, what's this note about?" the Dedacciai asked.

"It's about everything that happened last night after I blew out my candle and made my wish right before I saw you in the rain riding your bike — and now here we are."

"So, according to this Darius man, I'm your Chapter One, and you think I'm the one who is to help you rewrite your story because you saw me right after you made your wish?"

As the former grandpa thought about his dream fragments, things began making more sense.

"Okay, here's another little oddity," the Dedacciai added. "Last night, I had this elaborate dream analyzing my life, and a man named Darius was a big part of that. I met him several years back when his white van had run out of gas and was holding up traffic. We eventually pushed it to the nearest gas station, and I bought him a tank of gas and lunch at an IHOP next door because I was curious.

"He told me he lived out of his van and traveled the country. He had a fascinating but sorrowful life, and I was trying to talk with him and help if I could. Part of that conversation is now trying to haunt me — or help me, and somehow, I'm going to have to choose which. But regardless, I'm having a hard time believing this could be the same Darius."

Carter chimed in, "Well, here's another tidbit of info — Darius is why I named you *the Dedacciai* in the first place. He suggested I name you after your bike when we tried to get you into his van. He said something about scientists naming the enigmas they discovered. It's like he already knew you wouldn't tell me your name. And I couldn't even pronounce the name of your bike at first — he had to do it for me."

"Truthfully, Carter, I'm not sure how to pronounce it either. I ran it through an Italian-to-English translator, and it pronounced it 'De-dah-chi-ay,' so that's what I've always called it. However, a friend ran it through a different translator, and it pronounced it differently. So, I'm not sure if anyone knows.

"Carter, it doesn't seem likely it could be the same Darius person to me — does it to you?"

"It wouldn't surprise me a bit because last night was the weirdest night of my life, and it all started right after I made my wish."

"Well, this clears up some things. It seems I showed up at the right time, so I now understand why you think this way, but I don't want you to get your hopes up because I believe it was just happenstance. Besides, I've let some people down lately; I'm not sure you would want me to help rewrite your story.

"Trust me on this. Grammatically speaking, I'm at a third-grade level, so if I did write your Chapter One —no one could even read it," — and the former grandpa made his first appearance, as Carter was caught off guard and laughed at the reference.

"Now that I know why you think I'm the one to rewrite your story, I could tell you a few things I've learned over my life's tenure. I wasn't always horrible at parenting, and after hearing your story, the bar is set so low that anything I say might help. My first baseline suggestion for you would be — *don't breed.*"

The former grandpa made a second appearance as Carter looked at the Dedacciai curiously and responded.

"Wasn't planning on it; trust me. After the way girls ridiculed me in high school, I'm scarred for life. In my world, *girls'* equal *pain,* and they scare me, so I don't think I'll ever breed."

"Okay, we're off to a great start," Dedacciai retorted.

"So, what's your actual name?" Carter asked. "I don't want my story rewritten by some ghostwriter!"

Dedacciai smirked at his cleverness but did not answer. He didn't want Carter googling or discovering anything about him or his family. For all he knew, Carter had a significant following on social media, and putting a picture of them on one of his sites could cause problems.

However, he was curious about one thing. Why Carter hadn't once taken out his phone to take a picture or text. This made him more curious about why he wasn't like every kid with a cell phone.

The older cyclist thought about Addison and the one conversation with Darius that kept making itself present. He knew why it was there and needed to decide if he would choose the side of a hypocrite or walk the walk of his own words.

Given what happened, was there an actual way to be happy on this earth in honor of Addison? Or was Darius a universal happenstance to make the former grandpa aware that it couldn't be done? — Either way, Carter was a welcome distraction to everything in his mind, and the older cyclist was willing to see what he could do to help him.

Once again, melodic singing preceded the sprite young waitress before making her grand entrance. With the grace of a ballet dancer, she spun around with everything balanced on her serving tray and placed it smoothly on the table.

"Do you boys need anything else?"

"No thanks, tiny dancer. You were great; your performance will be duly noted in your tip, my lady."

"I'll keep an eye on your tea levels and not fill up your tea glass too early and ruin your sweetness ratios. There will be no waiting on me; no, siree, I won't let you down." She left, smiling.

"Dedacciai, there's another part of the story I haven't told you about yet. Last night, when I rolled you into the lobby and checked into the hotel, this beautiful woman named Connie Sue Lancaster was behind the counter. I found out later that she and her dad owned the hotel.

"Anyway, when I tried to check in, I could tell she didn't care for me being a guest there. But then she saw you sitting in the distance and said you didn't look too good and asked about you — I began telling her how I saw you riding your bicycle and what happened. — And by the way — she said you were a smidge too big to be riding a bicycle."

"That only proves she has eyes," the Dedacciai smirked.

"Yeah, she does, and they're quite beautiful. Anyway, she wanted to hear more about what happened to you, and after I finished the story, she told me I was a hero in her book. So, when she went to check us into the hotel, I requested room 555, and she said the room became available because of the last-minute cancellation by a Mr. Darius. I thought it was the weirdest thing, but then she told me that because I helped a total stranger and she thought of me as a hero, she gave me both our rooms for $200 even, for two nights. She wanted to do that for me. Which reminds me — we need to be checked out of the hotel tomorrow by noon. But how did Darius possibly know that was going to happen?"

"I have no idea, but that is getting pretty weird. What did this Darius character look like?" the Dedacciai asked.

"He was tall and thin, had long hair, and a scruffy beard. He also wore an old suit and a pair of sandals."

"That is the same description of the man I had lunch with at IHOP that day. He called himself Sandals at first before finally telling me his name. It sure seems like the same Darius but seems awfully strange if it was."

"Dedacciai, like I said, it was the strangest night, so if something like this were to happen — last night would have been the night."

"Carter, maybe this is all your fault — maybe you put a little too much wish — on your wish and opened up an emotional black hole or something." The former grandpa made his third appearance.

"Dedacciai, if I did open a black hole, can I ask you a black hole-type question?" Carter asked hesitantly.

The Dedacciai nodded to allow it.

"Were you purposefully trying to get yourself killed last night? After what happened this morning, I thought about the first words out of your mouth when I found you. You told me to 'Please let you die.' I can't help but think I'm not a real hero; at least, it's hard to consider myself one, knowing you wanted to get yourself killed. You need to tell me why. I told you my side of our story from last night; what's yours? Please, I deserve to know."

"Carter, YOU are a hero regardless of what I'm going through. What you seem to be going through took a back seat when you saved me, a total stranger, last night and again today! You truly are a hero — or maybe the universe doesn't want me yet, which, in my case, kind of hurts my feelings.

"The thing is — you expected me to be something that I'm probably not. You made this wish, and poof, there I was. You put two and two together, and now you're convinced I'm your author. Darius left you a note that said I was your Chapter One, so it makes sense why you'd think that, but I'm not in the state of mind to rewrite anybody's life story. But like I said, I have tenure on this planet; I know a few things. Let's just see what happens."

"Okay," Carter mumbled. "We can do that — for now. But I'm not going to put up with you not trusting me forever. I think we should revisit this later. Not to play the 'I saved your life card,' but I did save you — twice now. I helped you when you couldn't help yourself. You may have wanted to die, but saving you is now part of my story — and helping you is now part of my story. When the time comes, I deserve to know your story, and I think I've earned the right to know your name."

"Carter — you're absolutely correct — you do deserve to know. But for now, I'm telling you not to push for that answer. I'll let you know if and when we'll revisit this. Learn this now, and moving forward, we will get along great. Listen to me very carefully — I say what I mean; I mean what I say, and I'm not mean when I say it. That is my normal. I understand I was far from normal this morning when you first saved me. Please, moving on, if you can accept and understand this, we will see where this goes, but I'm telling you — do not push —"

There was an intense pause in the conversation as Carter considered the Dedacciai's stout position, and the two men, young and old, sat in an extended, uncomfortable silence. Anger swirled through Carter's mind as he stared out the window, dismayed by Dedacciai's attitude.

Carter tried to calm himself by taking a deep breath and closing his eyes. When he opened them, he saw a homeless man coming from the back of the building, pushing a cart full of junk.

"I hate homeless people!" Carter blurted out.

The Dedacciai followed Carter's eyes and saw the junk-filled cart come to a stop, then watched the man's feeble legs help slide his torso down the cart so he could rest beside it. The Dedacciai signaled for the waitress to come over.

"Ya-mon, what do you need?" she asked.

"You see that nice man outside?" He watched as her eyes followed his question. "Could you please ask him if he would like to come in and eat? And if he does, give him anything he wants." Dedacciai reached into his pocket and handed her a $100 bill as a step toward doing good in Addison's name. "Keep the change for your trouble."

The tiny dancer hugged the Dedacciai and had a hard time letting go.

"I have always wanted to do this," she said. "I see these people, but I never have the money to help. I barely make enough to pay my own bills. Thank you, thank you, for the opportunity." Her tears dropped on his shoulder as she hugged him again.

The Dedacciai's kindness struck a dysfunctional chord in Carter. He clamped his hands together like a pressure cooker, then began a fidgeting regiment that crescendoed out of control. The thud turned heads as his hands slapped the laminate booth seat louder than intended.

"Why would you do that? You think it's going to undo your death wish, but it's not. Trusting someone who has helped you probably would. You're right about one thing: you're not the one to rewrite my story. I don't want someone so broken in life they can't even trust me with their name. I wanted you to be the one so desperately that I looked past the obvious first step — there is no real trust between us!"

Carter looked out the window with a hard silence on his face. He saw the waitress exit and make her way to the man with a drink and a handful of crackers. She then bent down and talked to him for a minute. The two men witnessed the man cry from a distance while grabbing her hands in thanks.

"I need to leave. — For the first time, I thought I had someone in my corner. You had me thinking and feeling differently about myself by helping you. You're supposed to be on my side, but I'm not good enough to trust, even though I saved your life!

"I'm supposed to be looking for a job today anyway. Thanks for lunch; it's the least you could do," and Carter stormed out with his anger in tow.

The Dedacciai questioned himself and hung his head while holding it in his hands with his eyes closed.

A few minutes passed before someone clearing their throat interrupted his internal pity party. The former grandpa lifted his head, and his eyes opened to the sight of the homeless man using his available teeth to smile.

"Sorry for bothering you, sir," the gravelly voice began, "but the nice lady over there told me how you bought my lunch today. She's making it to-go, so I can take it to my camp and share it with my other two campmates. I just wanted to thank you and let you know how thankful I was."

"You're not bothering me at all, and I don't want you to share your meal. Allow me the privilege of buying your campmates their own meals." He signaled the waitress over. "Whatever this gentleman ordered, please add two more for his friends."

The man pinched himself as if he had won the kindness lottery. "Please, have a seat while you wait," he pinched himself again for good measure.

"Sorry, I just had to make sure I wasn't dreaming. The name's Alabama; it's nice to meet you. Campsite's just a couple miles up the road, S.W. Seventh and Lee, third trailhead to the north. It's a fine site we got if you ever want to come by," he said with a grin, knowing the actuality was not a reality.

"It's good to meet you, Mr. Alabama. I'm the Dedacciai, and I'm glad to help."

"The Dedacciai, huh? Mighty fancy name you got there; I've never met anyone with such a big fancy name before. Are you like royalty or something around here? — It sure would be an honor to have someone with a fancy name like yours to come visit us. We probably won't eat until nine or better since you've blessed us with this big lunch. Maybe we can cook something for you to pay you back. I'll even try to get my campmates to behave if you were to come."

"I appreciate the offer, but I don't think I would be particularly good company right now. I have a lot on my mind and need to take time for myself tonight. I sincerely want to thank you for the invite, though." Three large to-go containers arrived as he finished.

"I better get going to get these back as hot as possible. — Mr. Dedacciai — I hope whatever you were thinking about earlier works out for you. Once again, pardon me for bothering you."

"I assure you, you were no bother. Enjoy the food and have a nice evening." The sentence was met again by his available teeth to smile with as he left.

A few minutes passed as the Dedacciai stared out the window and watched Alabama strap the three containers on his cart. The older man contemplated Carter's anger toward him and Alabama's kindness toward him as well. And the former grandpa's mind flooded with a vision of Addison looking at her papa with disappointment.

"It's not nice to turn down someone who invited you to eat with them, Papa. I think they will be sad. I don't want you not to go because you're sad. Do it for me, Papa; please, do it for me."

Alabama began pushing his cart when a familiar voice urged him to stop.

"I'll be there! — Mark my words, I'll be there. Tell your campmates they better behave. I'm also going to bring dinner. I'll see you sometime between 9 and 9:30. I promise!"

Alabama flashed his beautiful array of teeth as if royalty were genuinely coming to visit. He walked up to the Dedacciai with his blue eyes and paused. He then hugged him, hoping there would be no repercussions for not asking.

"In case I don't see you again, Mr. Dedacciai, or you change your mind, I want you to know I understand in advance. This lunch here is blessing enough."

Alabama's advanced forgiveness made him contemplate how many broken promises he had to experience in his lifetime to feel the need to say that. Dedacciai was determined not to let him down and, more importantly, not to let Addison down. And although buying them food was doing good in her name, Addison would expect more from him, just as her papa would of her. He made his way back inside.

"Well, where did your young friend go?" he heard as the waitress returned.

"I'm not sure where he went or if he is still my friend. I tried to be a substitute parent and set a boundary that he didn't like."

"We've all done that for certain; parenting is not an easy business. I'm sorry; I know it will work out. The boy certainly enjoyed your company; I could tell — he'll be back; you'll see. Is there anything else I can do for you?"

"Well, actually, I need thirty-five cents."

The change appeared instantly.

"You have been wonderful, Tiny Dancer." The Dedacciai shook her hand, leaving her another $100 bill and the waitress draped him in a hug for his generosity.

"Thank you so much for everything and for letting me help that man as you did. Thank you! Thank you! I'm working a double shift tonight; if you care to come back and see me — I'll be here till 7 a.m. tomorrow."

"I may do that — you never know. I've been known to visit an IHOP or two during the wee hours of the night."

It was 5:43 p.m. as the Dedacciai returned to the hotel lobby. Once again, he paused for his senses to enjoy Connie Sue Lancaster's handy work of sight, sound, and smell. He then walked to an old-fashioned phone booth he had spotted earlier with the change his waitress gave him.

He sat and waited until precisely 5:55 p.m. to insert the coins and listen to them pong their way to the belly of the old rotary phone. Then, he enjoyed hearing the old-fashioned rotary dial sing his home number back to him with each release of the finger. He knew his Bellavia would not answer because they never answered their phone. Their landline was one digit off the hospital's number, and they were riddled with twenty or more missed dialed calls daily.

But on his new journey, he wanted to at least dial it every day at 5:55 p.m. and let it ring five times anyway — rationalizing that his Bellavia would somehow know he was thinking of her.

Afterward, Dedacciai walked to the nearest grocery store and bought the items needed for tonight's campfire dining before returning to his room for a nap. The dichotomous emotional day had worn him ragged, as the roller coaster of emotional darkness and light was indeed a thing.

Meanwhile...

After a rather long and angry walk, the self-doubt and fear that returned and entered his body seemed to draw him back to his old familiar dysfunction. Was he the human equivalent of a moth to the flame? Because Carter somehow found himself outside his childhood home.

Thoughts of knocking on the door and apologizing flip-flopped in his mind as he stood in the street, secretly looking at it. But maybe this time, things would be different. Perhaps Carter and his old man were somehow more alike than he wanted to admit. Maybe Dedacciai was right; Carter just needed to believe in the fairy tale that someone would magically appear to rewrite his story. Perhaps this time, his failure could be the catalyst for Russell Ducane and him to build a relationship.

Maybe his dad wasn't as bad as he thought, and the only way to know for sure was to bow to his tyranny and learn from it. Besides, for a few days, he had heard his dad's tyrannical thought process swirling in his head in a come-and-go fashion as some sort of open house for the mind.

He started rationalizing that this two-day journey was a labyrinth to bring him back to where he was supposed to be all along. It was simply his destiny to be Russell Ducane's son, and he was somehow hoping his dad would show him a glimpse of mercy on his return.

However, trying to walk across the street was not a simple matter. Carter stood glued to the pavement, his mind wrestling with his feet for the direction of his next step. — Would it be left, right, forward, or back? — His destiny awaited his decision.

Chapter Fourteen

Camp Carter

Once again, the familiar plush office found the Dedacciai sitting across from his Dreamatologist, Tony Robbins. The two men bathed in their own global spotlight as Robbins read over a detailed transcript of what had happened since they last met.

"So, pattern interrupts; let's talk," Robbins began. "As you know from listening to me, pattern interrupts are one of the most valuable tools I use to get people to change. Evidently, they also save lives. I'm asking; would you have finished the job had Carter not interrupted?"

The Dedacciai hung his head in silence and shame before answering.

"In that moment? In that state?... Probably."

"How about now? Are thoughts lingering somewhere in the darkness, waiting to resurface?" Robbins asked.

"I don't think so. If I were to join Addison, it would still have to be at the accidental hand of someone else. — I'm pretty confident I'm no longer in the suicide business."

"That's good; glad to hear that. So, Carter Ducane, let's talk about him. — He's been a new addition to your life since our last conversation. I find him interesting. I like that he knows his life needs to be better and accepts that it has been dysfunctional up until now."

"Yes, Carter's pattern interrupt certainly gave me a smidge of hope. Because of him, I feel distracted from everything for the moment. Also, seeing the double rainbow made me realize I was to concentrate on Carter to take my mind off things."

Robbins responded, "I'm most interested in seeing how you will handle his dysfunctional anger. The young man has a lot of anger stemming from his father. You've already gotten a taste of it in two ways — his anger saved your life to start with, but that same anger is now showing itself in his desperation to have a father figure to guide him, to believe in him, or *be on his side*, as he thinks of it.

"Most of all, he wants to be treated as an adult. His identity is that of someone who has not grown up. He has felt stifled from having to ride a bike all his life, from not having a place of his own or a job that will support him in getting one. In his eyes, he threw a Hail Mary into the universe when he packed his backpack and quit his job. Now, he must succeed, or he might find himself back in the darkness — and he has all his marbles in one basket, YOU— the Dedacciai.

"His life has changed drastically from the moment he saw you. There is no mystery as to why he got so mad today. His dysfunction, which makes up a large part of his nervous system, will not allow him to get close to anyone who is a threat. He perceives you setting a boundary as a threat to the bond he desperately wants to create with you. He hasn't been able to get you to tell him much of your story or your name by simply asking, so he's reaching for the next and only tool he has in his toolbox — anger.

"You've got quite the dilemma because he needs you to set those boundaries, even though he doesn't know it. But if you cower now, you won't be able to rewrite his story later, which is your current purpose. Whether or not you want to accept this is up to you, but Darius *is* right."

"Tony, I question that. I know Carter wants me to be the author of his story, but I'm not sure I can handle that right now. Today, my former self appeared a few times when the opportunity to be clever presented itself, and it's like a knee-jerk reaction that I can't stop. I feel I'm betraying my family and Addison's death after it happens, and it feels like a needle is piercing my soul.

"Another struggle is that I can't stop my curiosity about Carter or anything. You would think that would change given my circumstances."

Tony stepped in.

"Let's analyze this, shall we? You're assuming that this tragic event automatically erased sixty years of who you are, which is rooted in your nervous system so deep, you can't even imagine. Yet, somehow, in an instant, your personality can be uprooted from itself, and your identity is gone, making you automatically different.

"You need to get this and get it now. Addison's death does not relieve you of being a grandpa. This former grandpa persona you're trying to adopt is not going to happen. If this were the case, Addison would no longer be your concern. But she's all you think about and why you want to die. Just know that every time this *former grandpa* crap appears in your mind, all 6'7" of Tony Robbins wants to jump out of your mind and kick your ass."

The former grandpa couldn't help but release a small, sad chuckle.

"Also, your cleverness and your curiosity are not going to disappear. Your cleverness has been the driving force behind who you are and the prime catalyst behind how you deal with life as a big person. For God's sake, it's how you got your wife. It wasn't because you were some kind of pretty boy. Let's not fool ourselves here; it's the prime instrument that has carried you through life. And now, you want to punish yourself by doing everything possible to suppress that attribute when, in actuality, it's needed now more than ever.

"Your struggle is that you're fighting with everything you have against your true self. And guilt is sending that needle-like feeling coursing through your nervous system. You're just interpreting it as a needle through your soul.

"Your biggest problem is that you know the right thing to do is to be exactly who you are. Why do you think that conversation with Darius keeps appearing? And I've got news for you; it isn't going away. That conversation with Darius is now a part of you, which is excellent because that conversation with him was spot on. That's why Darius wrote the note to Carter in the first place — because he knows you're the man for the job to rewrite his story."

The former grandpa gazed at Robbins skeptically, frowning. "I still don't know."

"What more do you need to know to believe Addison is begging from the great beyond for her papa to be happy? Addison sent the double rainbow to tell her papa that Carter can help you become whole again. And if you don't listen to what you know to be true, you will be the one traveling the countryside waiting for your own demise. Do I need to bring the transcripts out again with you and Darius?"

"No, Tony, please don't. That conversation is permanently etched in my brain. I'm trying to accept what you're saying, and I even get it, logically. But it just doesn't feel logical. And it doesn't seem right to do it or to be me — at least not yet."

"Now, I'm usually a gentle giant, but good God, man, when are you going to grow a pair? You can be yourself; I know you can, and I know you have all the tools necessary to help Carter and yourself.

"We need a new strategy. I suggest you simply allow your grandpa identity to shine the next time you have a sit-down conversation with Carter. Just go with it. Allow the cleverness. Envision Addison in Heaven, ascending to the top of the mountain with every stroke of laughter. The happier you are, the higher she'll go. There will be no more 'former grandpa' thinking unless you want all 6'7" of Tony to mentally kick your butt. And I will be back!"

"I don't doubt it." He held up his hands in surrender.

"Now, something tells me you will know the right time to begin the process of helping Carter rewrite his story. It will just happen, and it will start with one simple thought that changes the course of Carter's — and your destiny.

"Here's another idea. I think a bicycle trip to Dallas would be a great idea, and you can get a lot of rewriting done along the way on the open backroads of Texas. I've stayed at the Omni Hotel, next to the Dallas Convention Center, several times. Next time, I may request room 1555 as a poetic gesture to your life story. I, too, love the downtown view of Dallas. Maybe we will see each other sometime; weirder things have happened."

And with that, the former grandpa's 8:15 p.m. wake-up call left the dreamatologist session looming in thought. He again sensed conversing with Tony Robbins but cleared his mind and needed to go. He grabbed his grocery bags and left the hotel to begin his two-mile trek to the campsite for dinner, just as he promised Addison.

Meanwhile...

Across the hallway, another mental battle had been taking place as well. Carter had returned to his room after his cumulative nine-mile trek. He was staring at the Dedacciai's bicycle while on the edge of his bed. His dad's voice had convinced him to retrieve the bike from the older man's room before his walk to serve as a sort of punishment or leverage to be used against him later.

He was confused about everything, notably, the feelings of being drawn back to his former dysfunction and standing outside his home. But he could take solace that he returned to the hotel and did not pursue further dysfunction.

However, the Dedacciai's betrayal, as he saw it, was not eradicated from his mind. As Carter sat on the bed, he still felt angry, and the escalated anger somehow summoned Russell Ducane's voice to awaken.

"There's my boy; I knew you'd be back. You know, boy, it's not too late; you could still get his money. He might still kill himself; you never know. Walking out of the restaurant and ending your conversation could conjure up some of that dark stuff to return. You're all he's got. Whatever he's dealing with, killing himself could still be an option. You just never know — It might still be all yours, along with that pretty bike of his, in no time.

"By the way, good job taking his bike back to your room. I like it when you listen to your old man. You got some good leverage goin' on here; I couldn't have done it any better myself — That's probably a lie; I could have. But you and I are more alike than you know. You are a Ducane, through and through. This could still all work out for ya, after all, boy. That pretty bike would put you back on track and help pay the rent for a good long while. I think if you go over there and ruffle up them feathers of his, that might be all it takes for this all to be yours. C'mon, go back over there. If he hadn't done it already, ruffle him up till he does. It's one thing you're good at. See now, look at your old man being all positive about ya'. I know you will be just like me someday. You don't need to get a job when you can manipulate it out of this old man.

"By the way, I could feel you outside the house today. Next time, knock. There ain't nothing to be ashamed about. Failure is just how it is for a Ducane. I've had one menial labor job all these years, and you can, too. You can probably get your job back at the bar; be just like old times—or should I say, 'Hard Times'?"

Carter jumped off the bed and banged his head against the wall as if to kill Russell Ducane's voice, then held a pillow tight to his face and yelled at the top of his lungs, *"Get out of my head, asshole! I'm not you — I-AM-NOT-YOU! All you do is ruin my life!"*

Carter began thinking that if he didn't want to be like his dad, he needed to not act like him. He got angry at a man who tried killing himself instead of trying to give him a chance to speak, or the choice not to speak, without the immediate anger Carter showed him.

The only thing the older cyclist was guilty of was being the first person Carter saw after he blew out his candle. The instantaneous anger he had seen over and over growing up was a part of him. But if he was going to rewrite his story, maybe it needed to be up to him and not some mystical wish he had thrown into the cosmos.

"I am not you, asshole!" Carter grabbed the Dedacciai bike and rolled it over to reunite it with his owner. He knocked at the door and waited for the older cyclist to answer, but the door stood silent. *What if he actually killed himself, and it was my fault for pushing him back into the darkness?*

Carter panicked and slid the key card in, bracing himself for what he might find. He opened the door and sprinted the bicycle in quickly before running to the bathroom.

"Dedacciai, I'm sorry!" Carter flipped on the light, only to find him gone. His heart raced from the vision in his head, and he checked the rest of the room frantically, only to find nothing. Carter ran out of the room to head downstairs. The elevator took too long, so he sprinted down the stairwell two steps at a time and burst into the lobby. But the Dedacciai was nowhere in sight. In a panic, Carter dashed outside and looked around but saw nothing.

Carter tried to calm down and think clearly about what to do. He attempted to untether his emotions and drown out the city noise by closing his eyes. In the silence, he relived the conversation with the Dedacciai and enjoyed how he felt.

Once again, he also thought about the Dedacciai's fatal conversation killer and pondered the trust barrier between them. However, after standing outside his childhood home and his dad's voice now haunting him, Carter became more open to hearing what the Dedacciai had to say.

Carter needed to give the Dedacciai another chance, but this time, things would be different. This time, he would get a hold of his Ducane-bred anger. If he wanted a different story, he must do something different. He needed to find a way to listen to him without his anger interfering. He needed to not be a Ducane, at least not his dad's version of one.

He thought about approaching the Dedacciai to ask if he would continue their conversation because Carter was sure no one else could finish the Dedacciai's train of thought. And he didn't want to miss his opportunity to talk as they needed to check out tomorrow.

While contemplating his thoughts and looking for Dedacciai, a white van turned the corner in front of the hotel. As it sped by, Carter saw the profile of a scraggly bearded driver.

"Darius!—Stop!" but he kept going. Carter ran after the van but was no match for its speed. The van made a sharp left on the next block, creating an unobstructed view ahead and revealing a scenario that rendered Carter sad — yet relieved.

He spotted the Dedacciai more than a block away, carrying two large bags of groceries. *Now, where is he going?* Carter decided to follow him out of curiosity. He wanted to remain close enough behind as some sort of innate feeling that he was protecting the man. A quarter of a mile into the journey, he saw the Dedacciai stumble and abruptly put down the groceries.

Carter knew the charade was over, as this somehow didn't feel right. He ran up to him and found his head lowered onto his knees, trying to regain his strength to continue.

"Sir, would you like some help with those bags?"

The familiar voice caused the Dedacciai's head to rise, and the sight made him sad and relieved as he answered in a low tone, "I'm not sure I deserve to be helped."

Carter sat beside him on the curb. "I don't believe that you believe that. You see, I think you believe everyone deserves to be helped. I watched your kindness today as you fed a man I didn't think deserved your help. I even questioned and accused you of having something wrong with you. My dad has me so screwed up that an innocent man, who may be an alcoholic, doesn't deserve help. And why? Just because he reminds me of what my dad is. — I'm so sorry, Dedacciai — and I mean sorry-sorry. I need to grow up — I want to grow up. I need to stop reacting to everything just because my dad does. It's all I know — for now. But somehow, I could learn a different way, that is, if you would teach me. But before you answer, I have one condition, which is non-negotiable."

"Go on —I'm listening —"

"From here on out —you're 'the Dedacciai.' You're my enigma; I named you, and I don't need to know your given name. Besides, there's no way it could be as cool as the one I gave you, so I wouldn't let you tell me if you wanted to. Still, I was wrong for pushing. — It won't happen again."

The Dedacciai looked at Carter with pride and raised his curled pinky. Carter signed the contract as his pinky intertwined with Dedacciai's, and they swore on it.

"Well, that's good, Carter, because some amongst us think my name is big and fancy, that I'm royalty."

"I have no doubt," Carter laughed. "Now, where are you going anyway?"

"Well, Carter, you're going to have to trust me. Now help me up; we don't want to be late for our special dinner."

"We?" Carter inquired as he helped him up and grabbed the grocery bags.

"Yes, We! — and don't look in the bags."

Although curious, Carter obeyed as the two found themselves walking the streets and carrying groceries toward a destination that the Dedacciai kept private. With each block, Carter's anxiety grew a notch as the streetlamps seemed fewer and farther apart, and graffiti became more commonplace. The light became scarcer until they finally arrived at a dark open field, courtesy of the only broken streetlamp in sight. There was a tree-lined section in the immediate distance backlit by working streetlamps in the farther distance.

"Okay, Dedacciai, this isn't funny. Where are you taking us? This isn't my version of a special place for dinner!"

"Let me see your cell phone. Can you turn on your light for a second?"

Carter did as instructed as the Dedacciai read the instructions he wrote down.

"S.W. 7th and Lee, head north to the third trailhead. Carter, follow me."

Carter stopped. "No, Dedacciai! This is too scary. Are you trying to get us killed? Maybe you want to die, but I don't want to join you. I want to leave!"

"Okay, do what you must, but don't let your fear keep you from rewriting your story. Fear has dominated your life — so do you want to try and replace it or not? Trust me or don't; your choice."

The Dedacciai paced the grass field with Carter's phone, looking for the third trailhead. At the same time, Carter took out his brass knuckles and sprinted to catch up with him, and the two found themselves at the third trailhead. Carter gasped from fear as the Dedacciai grabbed him by the shoulders and tried to calm him.

"Trust me, Carter." The Dedacciai walked down the third trailhead toward a campfire beyond the thicket of brush and trees.

On the trail just before the entrance to the camp, three bicycles found themselves mangled together under a tree, all in desperate need of repair. Carter asked for his cell phone back and lit up the area. He took several pictures and instinctively observed what would be needed to repair them. Then, he quickly found himself on the heels of the Dedacciai once again as they passed under two tree limbs and entered the camp.

Three men were sitting around the campfire on makeshift seats, and two makeshift seats sat empty and available for guests. Surprisingly, the camp was organized, with a dedicated place for trash, hand soap, and a dozen or more one-gallon jugs of fresh water. Four tents were neatly displayed, three seemed to be living quarters, and one appeared to serve as the camp library. There were hundreds of books on shelves lining three sides of the tent and a dozen or more stacks of books on a wooden pallet to keep the books dry if rain flooded the tent. Carter recognized the shopping cart from outside the IHOP earlier and put one of the faces seated as its owner. The recognizable face stood up and rushed over to welcome his guests.

"You came! You really came! I told everyone to behave; we might have royalty coming to visit, so welcome to our humble abode. I can't thank you enough for our food today—"

Alabama was interrupted by a rather boisterous voice, the obvious alpha male of the three. He was tall, Black, and thin, with very distinctive features that would be hard to forget. He was layered with bling and wore dark sunglasses, day or night.

He had an oversized diamond earring in his right ear and a ring on every finger, big enough that his fingers had not touched each other since the early 80s. He wore a large assortment of gold and silver chains around his neck and a fake diamond-laced belt, all set against the backdrop of his pure-black wardrobe.

With all this, it wasn't even what stuck out about him the most. He had a head full of bright silver-gray spirals of hair tightly woven together and sprawling from his head in every direction. Each spiral was nearly two feet long but closer to four feet if he unfolded each by taking off the hundreds of rubber bands, keeping each sprawl together. He had a silver goatee and a friendly smile to complete the package as he hijacked the conversation.

"The problem is, we don't listen to Alabama, and behaving isn't really our thing. Miami Gambucci Hawthorne Rowland is at your service, but you can call me Miami. You already know Alabama, and that man there is M.C. Hammond, short for Military Chaplain. You can call him M.C. or Chaplain. He runs the community campfire library, which is well-known in these parts. He does his best to educate those he can during the day to help them get a job. Even has office hours for the library and uses his spiritual know-how's to counsel others.

"And if that's not enough, the man holds an open field Sunday church service for everyone." Miami huddled the Dedacciai and Carter close to him and lowered his voice so only they could hear. "M.C. has a bad case of them PTSD's, so don't make any sudden loud noises." Miami immediately yelled, "Boom!"

The Dedacciai and Carter were startled. They heard M.C. drop to the ground, then quickly get up and chase after Miami to punch him in the arm a few times. The three campmates began laughing; obviously, this was not the first time Miami had misbehaved. The men ended their charade with a group hug as they returned to their guests.

Alabama used his available teeth to smile once again. "I tried to tell them not to act up — I promise... Hashtag — epic homeless fail!"

Carter laughed at the reference and almost passed out from relief as he saw the men laughing and felt the excitement from the three to have guests. Carter slipped the brass knuckles back into his pocket and stood beside the Dedacciai while introducing them.

"Men — this is my friend Carter Ducane, and you can call me 'the Dedacciai.' We come in peace and with food. Now, who's hungry?"

The Dedacciai retrieved several packages of jumbo-sized hotdogs, buns, chips, condiments, cups, and a gallon of sweet tea. He also had large-sized marshmallows for roasting. The three campmates provided hangers and bent them into skewers. Carter watched with child-like eyes, as he had never done anything like this. He enjoyed sitting around the campfire and felt like he was fishing as the makeshift skewer roasting the hotdogs and marshmallows bobbed up and down over the open flame.

The Dedacciai stood and proposed a toast. "I would like to thank you for your hospitality and for allowing Carter and myself to break bread together. We sincerely appreciate it."

"Here, here!" as five plastic cups clacked into each other. M.C. rose to say a few words.

"Regardless of what you witnessed earlier, I'm actually a peace-loving man."

"Bullshit," disguised as a loud cough slipped from Miami's mouth as Alabama hit him to get him to shut up.

"Let's bow our heads and pray with our guests."

Carter experienced a prayer before a meal for the first time. However, it was more like a prayer performance. M.C. had a robust vocabulary and an incredible voice that delivered such an eloquent message. It was clear why he was a Military Chaplain.

The Dedacciai responded, "After what I just heard, M.C. doesn't do you justice; I'm going to call you Chaplain, and that was absolutely beautiful. But I'm not one for chit-chat. What's your story, Chaplain? Why are we privileged to be here with you?"

The medium build of what was once a ruggedly handsome man sat there. He had a full head of hair and a clean-shaven face. His external presence made you question why he was in the camp at all. He seemed to be in his fifties and took care of himself, given his circumstances, and with a deep, velvety voice, began his story.

"First, I don't want to start with a lie; I'm not an actual Military Chaplain. These two call me that because I was in the military and did some preaching as a hobby, but I have no formal training. The irony is that I wasn't religious at all growing up. But that was before two tours in Iraq changed how I look at life. When scud missiles are headed in your direction, there aren't many atheists sharing a foxhole with you.

"I saw things — things I can't un-see, and I held things that I can't un-hold. I never once imagined trying to decipher which body parts belonged to which soldier — dead or alive. I started listening to preachers on armed forces radio while in Iraq. I first started impersonating them because I had a voice that seemed to fit the mold. But soldiers seemed to react to my voice and my enthusiasm. The soldiers who heard me said I gave them hope. Then, one day, a colonel stopped by and heard me preach. He liked my voice and my preaching and took me under his wing. We became great friends.

"He loved books, as did I. He could speak six languages and had to be one of the most intelligent men I've ever known. He grew up Catholic and, for some reason, enjoyed hearing mass spoken in Latin. That started his wanting to learn different languages. He had a knack for learning, and it was no surprise he was a colonel. He also told me he was among the youngest to achieve that rank.

"Wow," Carter murmured, exchanging a look with the Dedacciai.

"He liked having me around," Chaplain grinned. "Especially when high-ranking officials visited the base and wanted me to say grace because it set a friendly tone for the evening. And, since I was well-read, he liked that I could have an intelligent conversation on almost any subject with any high-ranking officials visiting. He said I made him look good, and he appreciated me.

"I loved that man; he was a great mentor and influence on my life." Chaplain paused, struggling to go on. He breathed deeply and rebooted his emotional state before continuing. "Then, one day, I was in the colonel's transport when it got hit by an RPG-7. Somehow, I survived, and they kept telling me I was one of the lucky ones to be thrown from the blast — But I don't know how lucky it is to watch your mentor burn to death trapped inside a transport."

"Damn," Carter muttered, looking at the Dedacciai, who was shaking his head, eyes closed.

"They asked me to give his eulogy, probably one of the hardest things I have ever done. I didn't think I could do it, but I wanted to be as strong for him as he was for me.

"I didn't realize that just having him around helped me handle deciphering which body parts went to what soldier. When he wasn't there, I struggled. Hearing an explosion and knowing I would have to deal with the aftermath without him gave me severe PTSD. After that, I couldn't function in the military, and they gave me an honorable discharge. Bonus — I couldn't function normally in a polite society either.

"My family had a hard time being around me; I never wanted to get close to anyone again, as I associated closeness with pain. I seemed to sabotage any relationship and found that I was more accepted out here in the open-field community than in society.

"Preaching helps me escape my inner turmoil because I take on a different persona whenever I preach. I feel I'm helping people by using my voice to give them hope, so I hold a weekly open field service for everyone to hear me. I honestly feel that preaching helped save my life because I'm not sure I'd be here without it. I used to ride to other camp communities in other cities to preach, but my bike has been broken down for a while now."

Dedacciai observed Carter look toward the camp entrance as the other two men chimed in.

"We all used to ride our bikes together whenever M.C. was preaching. We miss helping all those souls in the surrounding fields."

Although Carter knew nothing of the religious ways, after hearing Chaplain's prayer performance, he was somehow aware that people in these other camp communities needed him.

Carter heard a voice speak behind him and turned and saw Miami.

"Young man, did you happen to see that blue bike as you entered the camp? That's mine. It's just like the one my son used to ride. My daughter had a sparkly red one, just like it. But that was before August 29, 2005, when Hurricane Katrina robbed me of my home, my wife, my kids, and my life. See this hair? I vowed never to cut it until their bodies were found. What do you think my hair follicles are telling you?"

"I — I don't think anything good," Carter said.

"Damn straight, nothin' good! — You can't imagine the stench from all those dead bodies lying around them streets. I must have put a hundred miles on my feet walking around and checkin' bodies that looked like my wife or kids. That shit messes you up — you gettin' me here, son?"

"I am; that's terrible, Miami."

"After Katrina and five years of livin' in a government trailer house, I had an opportunity to work in North Carolina, checking railroad lines. I loved the work and even found me a new girlfriend. Life seemed to be going alright. I even thought about cutting my hair and tryin' to move on from my past. But I felt too much of that hard guilt, so I couldn't do it.

"Then there was May 12th, 2012. Let me tell you something about tornadoes in North Carolina. They are different than the ones here in Texas. In Texas, radar and shit they have now would give us plenty of warnin' to find shelter. North Carolina tornadoes come up so fast; there is no warnin'. I come back from workin' on the railroad one day from the northern part of the state, and my house is gone, along with it, my common-law wife. The only difference this time is I saw the body.

"After that, I couldn't get up on time to get to work. I started drinkin' even more than I already was. I got fired, but as a goin' away gift, my boss talked them into lettin' me have a train ticket to anywhere in the country. I decided to come here to Texas and wound up in Austin. And that's why you have the privilege of listenin' to the one and only Miami Gambucci Hawthorne Rowland," and he slapped Carter on the back.

Carter sat there, not knowing what to say. He had never heard stories like this before.

Alabama stood and walked over to refill his glass with sweet tea.

"Looks like it's my turn, but my story is boring compared to these two losers," he said, flashing all seven leftover teeth.

"I'm a lawyer, believe it or not. Yes, indeed, the bottom of my class. I only took the bar exam six times before I finally passed. I had so much debt; you can't even imagine. But hey, I'm a lawyer, going to make them big bucks, everyone said. Guess what? I didn't make them big bucks; hell, I didn't make them little bucks, either. I hardly made anything. The pressure was just too much, and I couldn't pay the attorneys for the office space I had rented from them.

"My wife ended up falling in love with one of the attorneys who could pay the rent. I lost everything when that happened. Yeah, I'm not too proud to admit that I took up alcohol to numb the pain and possibly dabbled with some other things that helped me lose my radiant smile. That's how I ended up here, and I'm hoping we inherit a dentist with a tragic story one day so I can get my teeth looked after."

Carter and the Dedacciai exchanged an amused look.

"Yep, a regular off-off-Broadway version of an *Atlas Shrugged* community we got going on here. Or is it *Gilligan's Island*? I get the two confused."

His attempt at humor didn't resonate with Carter. A few moments later, M.C. tapped Carter on the shoulder and handed him a paperback version of *Atlas Shrugged* by Ayn Rand as Alabama continued.

"But truthfully, my friends here have helped me through it all. As you can see, we make fun of each other but do it out of love. I haven't touched as much alcohol as I used to for a good long while now, but hey, nobody's perfect. Still, Chaplain has been a big help in that regard and inspires me by how many people he counsels out here.

"So, I, too, decided to counsel several of our open-field community members with legal problems. Just because I graduated at the bottom of my class doesn't mean I don't know how the law works. I'm proud of what I've done for people here, especially dealing with social security and disability cases. — Well, that's my story, and I'm stickin' to it!"

Alabama hit Carter in the arm as he went to sit down and as Miami spoke up.

"So, what are we havin' for dessert? Surely you brought an apple pie or somethin' to go along with our all-American hotdog feast."

"Funny thing you should ask," the Dedacciai said. "My friend Carter is celebrating his 25th birthday tonight, and I thought you gentleman might help celebrate."

The announcement surprised Carter as the Dedacciai reached into the grocery bag and pulled out a red velvet cake with cream cheese frosting. The cake read, "Happy Birthday," with two candles placed side by side that read 25.

Miami, who seemed to be the spokesperson for the group, stood up.

"Carter, my man, we are honored to spend your birthday with you," and the other camp dwellers echoed the sentiment. "I just have one question before we light your candles. What's your story? — I'm curious, why ain't you celebratin' your birthday with your family?"

Carter wasn't over the unexpected announcement, let alone sharing his story about why he was there. He looked at the Dedacciai, who gave him a gentle nod of assurance. Carter stared at the cake that didn't have a boot stuck in it and let down his guard as he took a beat for himself.

"Dedacciai, this is strange and weird, but that seems to be our relationship from the moment I first saw you. — Guys, I met this man for the first-time last night. My birthday was actually yesterday, but that celebration ended with my dad's boot in my cake and my mom stopping me from killing him. — What kind of man would do that to his son's birthday cake? I hate him so much, and I wish he were dead. My problem is I wish it a lot, which is pretty much the story of my life."

"Last night, after almost killing my dad, I packed my backpack and moved out. Then, I quit my job at the bar I had worked for five years. Now, I have to take matters into my own hands and grow up, and today was supposed to be the first day of my new life. But I never imagined this on my first day. What's happening to me is all very strange. The feelings I've experienced since this man came into my life — to now being with you guys have been great. But I'm having trouble accepting your kindness because I don't deserve it —

"Alabama, I was in the restaurant today when the Dedacciai saw you outside and bought you food. I got so mad at him for doing that, and now that I've met you and know your story, I feel a lot of guilt — I mean, I really feel terrible. My dad's a horrible man and a drunk, and I automatically assumed you were like him and didn't think you deserved food today." Carter couldn't continue and looked at the ground.

In the silence, Alabama stood and then sat next to him. "But I am an alcoholic — It's not like you were wrong. I get it; you judged me. Guess what? You weren't the only one who saw me today and thought the same thing. Carter — It's okay — I forgive you." He reached over and hugged his newest campmate.

The Dedacciai studied Carter's body language as Alabama forgave him. He seemed humbled, giving a slow nod to acknowledge his kind understanding.

"I'm not sure how you guys do it. You have been through so much — yet here you are. My story is nothing in comparison, but it doesn't change the fact that I have so much anger living inside me, and I don't know how to deal with it or what to do with it."

"Sir Carter, I could help you with that," Chaplain said. "Anger makes us all fall short of who we're meant to be in this world. Your anger is deep-rooted, and anyone who looks at you can see it. We need to address this one step at a time. Forgiving your father is going to be quite an undertaking. But forgiving yourself is what sets the scene for your life to begin.

"It's hard to take that first step with so much hate weighing on your shoulders. You weren't born with your little metallic friend — hate drove you to undergo the painful mutilation of your nose so that you could, let me guess — 'piss off your dad.' I have one question for you: How attached are you to the hate?"

Carter sat stilted, wide-eyed, unable to answer.

"It's now clearly part of your identity. Without it, your dad feels he's won the battle between you two, but with it, you think that you have the leverage to keep the scale of hatred leaning in your favor. So again, I ask you — how attached are you to your hate?

"Carter, I'm going to ask you to come up here of your own free will — just know that you don't have to. I'm going to ask you to do something for me, yet I'm actually asking you to do something for you."

Carter sat there, nervous, put on the spot to perform. He didn't like anyone forcing him to do anything — as that was what his father did to him all his life. Much of him wanted to see this through, whatever Chaplain had planned for him. But the fear he entered the campsite with had him pinned to his seat.

"Carter — get your punk-ass up there! You know you want to!" Miami's alternative side said with authority, knowing Carter needed some Gambucci-style encouragement.

But Carter stayed put, unintimidated. He didn't know the religious side of life or what the Chaplain wanted of him.

"Chaplain, I need to ask you something first. I'm just wondering — why do you think you can help? No offense, but it's hard to take advice from someone who can't get himself to do the same. I mean, if you have all the answers, why are you still here?"

Miami got riled up by the question and sprang toward Carter, invading his personal space.

"You don't know what you're talking about, Carter. Just hear the man out. If you don't like what he's about, then you can go back to your wonderful life."

"Miami! Stand down — I'm perfectly capable of handling the situation. Carter has a right to his anger; it's who he is. Let him ask what he wants. You're right, Carter — I'm still here — haven't been able to get the visions out of my head. Loud sounds still cause me to see body parts all around me. — Miami can't seem to let go of his hair — Alabama doesn't want to work, and he's comfortable in what has become his normal.

"So, I understand you; I get where you're coming from on this, and I know how you see the obvious. But what you don't see here — is the hate. Go ahead, look at us. Do you see hate? Miami was showing you love just now. He's mad at you because he knows what it's like to give up the anger finally. He just can't quite give up the memories. One day, I think he will, but hate? You won't find it in any of us. So, when you ask — why do I think I can help you with your hate? — Because I have already done that — in all three of us and hundreds I have preached to and counseled. So this is your opportunity for a rather unique 25th birthday gift for yourself. You said you wanted to start your life over.

"The reality is all that emotional hate sits perched on your shoulder and weighs you down. But it doesn't have to. That is up to you — Keep it or don't — I'll sleep the same tonight. Will you? Ask yourself one simple question: What's the worst that could happen?"

Carter remained stilted, pondering the question, thinking about different scenarios. But every conclusion came back to the same dysfunctional outcome of thought —

If I give up my hate, my dad will win —

The Dedacciai felt Carter was backed into a corner mentally and wanted to interrupt his mindset as he spoke up.

"Hey, boys, these birthday candles aren't going to blow themselves out!"

The men turned to a cake with candles, ready for Carter to make his wish. The mood lightened as Miami yelled out.

"Carter, get your punk ass over there and take care of your birthday business!"

Carter walked over and studied the bootless cake. He smiled and laughed slightly at how much anger that image produced in his mind and embraced how he felt without it.

"Chaplain, before I blow out my candles. I want to tell you that I'll think about what you said. I'm not used to all this. Miami, I hope we're good; I don't want to let anyone down, but I'm not able to do what you ask for now. But I know where to find you when I am. Regardless of everything that's happened here, this night is weirdly the best birthday I've ever had." Carter made a wish and blew out the candles.

"Well, who's going to cut the cake? We all know by now it's not going to cut itself," the Dedacciai teased.

The men looked at Miami, who took over the cake-cutting duties and sliced everyone a man-sized piece that overflowed the paper plates.

The Dedacciai watched as Miami sat by Carter, took him under his wing, and apologized for his rough Gambucci-style motivation. Strangely, Carter seemed to enjoy Miami's Gambucci attitude and his coarse humor. Before long, the men all appeared to open up to Carter. He responded well as the newly bonded campmates compared dysfunctional tales.

Soon, volumes of laughter emanated from their adjunct dysfunctional tales competition. The laughter was loud enough to permeate the air and attract another group from a camp beside them. Two couples, Sara and Steve and Robyn and Mark, could almost smell the cake from next door.

"What's all the laughing about over here? Don't you losers know you're supposed to be depressed, homeless people!"

The statement caused the boisterous group to laugh even more.

"Depressed? How can anyone be depressed when we're celebrating this fine young man's 25th birthday?" Miami yelled.

The two couples made their way over to Carter to congratulate him, and Miami introduced Carter as his new friend. The Dedacciai was amazed as he watched Carter interact with the group and relived Carter's hatred for homeless people mere hours ago.

Chaplain walked over to the Dedacciai, "Good save; I'm glad you stopped Carter from spiraling. I'm sorry if I overstepped a boundary and pushed him, but I thought I could help with his hate."

"You did exactly what a man in your position should have. You planted a seed."

"Dedacciai, how about you? We never got your story. I'm guessing that's not by mistake. I know there's a story hidden behind your disappearing goose egg. But I'm more curious about the deeper story behind your overt kindness toward Carter. I know the two of you just met, but the important thing is *that* you met. I'm guessing the man upstairs has given you someone to focus on as a helpful distraction, which is perfect because Carter needs a father figure and role model. Just remember, if you need to talk, I might also be able to help you."

Dedacciai shook his hand and gave him an appreciative man-nod to confirm he understood.

It was close to 11:30 p.m., and the party had run its course. The Dedacciai and Carter said goodbyes and headed out under a full moon that brilliantly lit their pathway. As they returned to the open field, the Dedacciai stopped as they reached the entrance, fished into his pocket, and handed Carter $200.

"What's this for?" Carter asked with surprise. "Is this my birthday present?"

"No, Carter, that's not your birthday present. — Look closely at this field and tell me what you think about it."

Carter examined the open field.

"Well? It's kind of awesome. It's beautiful at night, especially with the full moon. The field seems to glisten, and you can see the tree line going into the distance against the streetlights in the background. The moonlight, I think, makes it even better than if the streetlight worked."

"Carter, you just described this field as beautiful, especially how the full moon makes it glisten. I didn't hear you describe it as fearful. What happened to the fear this field brought you just hours ago?"

The Dedacciai watched as Carter struggled for an answer.

"Carter, allow me to answer for you. You didn't even think about the fear, and here's why. Your fear no longer exists because you now have a positive neuro-association attached to this field. That's because it's now a part of your nervous system. When you visit this field or even just think about it, or this night, it will only produce happiness and warmth.

"Now think about what you would have missed if you had given in to your fear and run back to the hotel. This field is a lot like homeless people. You feared homeless people; actually, you told me you hated them. Is that how you feel about them now?"

"I don't even have that thought anymore!" Carter said with conviction.

"And that's my real gift to you — perspective."

Carter stared again at the empty field, glistening, and took in his gift as the Dedacciai started walking toward the hotel.

"Then what's the $200 for?" Carter said as he caught up with him.

"I think you know what to do with it. What you've wanted to do since we entered the campsite." Carter stopped in his tracks. The Dedacciai took two more steps and stopped to turn.

With a look of bewilderment, Carter asked, "How did you know that?"

"I knew the moment you saw that mangled mess of bicycles that you'd want to fix them, just like you did my Dedacciai. I also knew that, as badly as you wanted to help, you wouldn't ask for the money.

"Carter, growing up, my mother was an artist, and anytime there were trees, telephone poles, fences, or buildings going off into the distance and getting smaller, she would always say, *'Just look at all that perspective'* — and her art always reflected a visual element of perspective in it.

"When the field you described went from fearful to beautiful, that was internal perspective. Although the visual perspective she was talking about was different, it's the same in that both types of perspectives are all around us. But most of us don't see it or pay attention to it.

"My mother never — and I mean *never* — missed it, and she made sure all five of her kids never missed it either. But in reality, by doing this, we learned to pay attention to things in life that produced change, like the tree line changing in the distance and going from bigger to smaller. Situations in life do the same thing. They change with a new perspective. Big problems become small or even go away completely, with perspective. You simply need to pay attention."

Carter re-examined the open field once more with his new gift. "Thank you so much, Dedacciai. I think this is the best gift anyone has ever given me. I can't thank you enough. — And you're right, I really can't stand for those bicycles to be sitting there, mangled, especially after I heard Chaplain say that stuff before dinner—"

"It's called grace; Chaplain was saying grace," the Dedacciai said.

"Yes, that stuff he said, that grace stuff. I don't know much about it, but after hearing it, I know that people out here need it, and they need him to say it. I was formulating how much I thought it would take to fix those bikes for everybody."

"I knew you were, and that's why tomorrow, you're going to take this $200 and buy what you need to do just that. I'll accompany you to the bicycle store because I need a few things before continuing my journey to Dallas. I also need—"

"What's this about Dallas!?" Carter interjects.

"— As I was saying — I also need to rent a room to stay an extra night, but we'll have to share a room. Are you okay with that?"

Carter nodded, anxious for an answer.

"I think after another day of rest, I'll be able to continue riding. I need a new pair of riding shorts and new cycling shoes. I'm going to buy some cycling shoes that double as tennis shoes so I can walk even with the SPD cleat. Then I'm going to go back and rest while you come back out here to do what you do."

"Aren't you going to come back out here with me to help?" Carter asked with some trepidation.

"We'll see, but if I don't, you'll be fine out here by yourself. But something tells me you'll have plenty of help. I'd suggest buying more tubes and patches than you think. You can always take them back."

"Now, what's this about heading to Dallas? I've never been, but I've always wanted to go."

"Well, I was hoping you would say that. You're welcome to come."

"But I can't afford that; I need to stay here and find a job."

"Well, Carter, I have an idea. What if I lease space in your backpack? You ride with me and carry my street clothes, and every night after our ride, we can wash our cycling clothes for the next day. You'll also be responsible for all bicycle maintenance issues that may arise. In exchange, I'll give you an all-expense-paid pedaling trip to Dallas and back — Deal?"

Carter bypassed the handshake and went straight for the hug.

"My birthday wish was that you wouldn't leave so we could spend more time together. I honestly believe you can help me if I contain my anger long enough to listen. Thank you so much for letting me go to Dallas with you. But now, I'm curious. You didn't know I was coming tonight. Why did you buy that birthday cake and take it to the homeless camp?"

"I hoped I'd see you again eventually, even though you were angry. You have been an enormous blessing, and I wanted to give you the birthday you deserved. I needed to show you how much I appreciated you saving my life — not once, but twice. And not only for that but for caring for me when I didn't want you to.

"Funny how the universe works sometimes. I'm amazed how we can stand here in this empty field that had you quaking from fear a few short hours ago. And now we're standing in the same field, having a wonderful conversation without any fear. — Just look at all that perspective." The Dedacciai looked toward the sky, wishing his mother was with him.

"Carter, just so you know — I wasn't going to Dallas without you."

The two men were engrossed in conversation as they entered The Lancaster after their walk, which seemed to only take minutes. Outside their rooms, Carter hugged his friend once again.

"Thank you, Dedacciai; truly one of the best nights of my life. I don't think I have ever looked forward to something so much as riding to Dallas with you. I'll see you in the morning. How about we leave around 9:30 for the bicycle shop?"

With that, the two men gave their final man-nods of approval and entered their rooms.

Chapter Fifteen

The Burial

Once again, the familiar plush office found the Dedacciai sitting across from his Dreamatologist, Tony Robbins, as he analyzed what happened at the homeless camp with Carter.

"Okay, I see Carter accepted your terms of not pushing you for your name. I'm glad you held your ground because now, I genuinely believe you have set the table to induce real change in him. Also, celebrating his twenty-fifth birthday with the homeless was a fantastic idea, and the gift of perspective — genius! What an incredible gift your mom gave you and your siblings by teaching you about perspective so early in life. It's just another reason Darius was right about you being the one to rewrite Carter's story.

"The homeless camp could not have worked out any better for you. And kudos on supplying him with the money for bicycle parts and knowing how much he wanted to help them. But you should be there to witness what happens and not have him do it alone. I feel this will lead to a real breakthrough because Carter is primed and in a heightened emotional state. He's also very excited about his trip to Dallas. But what he's excited about most is that you're still in his life.

"Take advantage of the momentum you have going with this young man. He's here to help take your focus off Addison. Try something different that you haven't tried before. Let him get to know something about you. I understand you won't tell him about Addison, but maybe let him know something — but if you're not ready, at least confide something about your family situation to somebody. Bob Dylan said it best, 'Strange how people who suffer together have stronger connections than people who are most content.'

"Give him some insight into some of your life struggles. Maybe bond over these struggles the next time you two have a sit-down conversation. I think you'll succeed with this approach, as it will allow your grandpa identity to come out and play. And when it does, revel in it, allow the cleverness, and envision Addison in Heaven ascending to the top of the mountain with every stroke of laughter."

"But if you sabotage this by having a former-grandpa pity party, just remember, 6'7" of Tony is lurking in your mind to kick your butt mentally. I promise you — you'll know the right time to begin the process of helping Carter rewrite his story. It will just happen and start with one simple thought that changes the course of Carter's destiny. Allow this to occur, and I think you will get a lot of rewriting done on the open backroads of Texas. Until next time — Live with passion!"

The Dedacciai's body came alive, and his eyes widened to the darkness. His mind once again questioned the remnants of his dreamatologist session. *Tony Robbins, again? What is this?*

The numbers changed on the clock and grabbed his attention.

3:00 a.m.? — Tiny Dancer's still working. The gravitational invite of his waitress friend working a double shift lured him into needing a late-night IHOP session. He scrambled to get dressed and headed out the door.

Across the hallway, Carter was having a restless night as the excitement of his birthday celebration with his anticipation of Dallas left him energized and in bed awake.

In the quiet, he heard the Dedacciai's door open and close. *What is he up to this time? Maybe he's getting ice?* Carter waited for the Dedacciai to re-enter his room. Time passed, long enough for an ice run, yet no one re-entered. *I swear I'm gonna get a leash for that man; I know he's causing trouble somewhere!* Carter threw on his clothes and made himself as presentable as possible, then made the journey to find the Dedacciai.

The blue light emanating from the IHOP sign above the entrance cast a backward shadow behind the large-framed man who approached. A high squeal came from one very excited waitress.

"You came! You really came! I didn't expect this. I need to hug you for coming to see me again — Thank you, thank you, thank you!"

The exuberant Tiny Dancer hugged the Dedacciai before she resumed her waitressing. "Will it be only you tonight?"

"I hope not; I'm not sure how to run the place. I hoped you and at least one cook would also be here."

"You're a silly man; yes, indeed — you are a silly man!" She playfully hit him with a menu. "Now, go seat yourself. I know where you'll be."

Upon her return, she brought an unsweetened iced tea with extra ice, a teaspoon, lots of Equal, a bowl of orange slices, and an extra glass of ice. As an added first, she brought a few individually wrapped wet naps for his fingers after he finished squeezing the oranges.

"Wet naps…nice catch! You upped your game, I see. I have so won the waitress lottery!"

"No, siree! It's me who has won the customer lottery. I'm so glad you came back. I only wish your young friend were here with you. Have you talked to him since he left you last? I'm going to sit with you if that's okay," and she slid in on the other side of the booth.

"I know people. It seems you need to talk underneath your silliness. 3:00 a.m. is a magical time to get some of the best talkin' done. Besides, you're my only customer."

"Tiny Dancer, you're good. I did see Carter again. Do you remember that homeless man you served earlier? He invited me to his camp for dinner to meet his other campmates, and I accepted. I even brought groceries, including a cake, hoping to see my young friend again. It all worked out as he saw me carrying the groceries down the street and helped me. He had no idea where we were going and was extremely nervous and scared when we arrived. But as the homeless men shared their stories, it helped Carter see them differently."

"You gave him perspective; you did. Very nice, very nice."

"You're good, Tiny Dancer — perspective indeed. We even celebrated his 25th birthday, which positively affected him. And get this; all three homeless men have bicycles that need repair, and Carter is going back tomorrow morning to fix them."

"Very nice. I'm so proud of him; it will be good for the boy. You are good for the boy."

"I appreciate that Tiny Dancer, I do. Carter wishes to rewrite his story and thinks I'm the one to do it. But he has a lot of anger — Hell, let's call a spade a spade — he downright hates his dad. I'm not sure how to help him start over with a clean slate or if I can even help because Carter's slate has a lot of layers of dysfunction, anger, and hate. And I know he must get rid of the hate before rewriting his story. The thing is, up until a few days ago, I thought my wife, Bellavia, and I did a rather good job of raising our kids without any hate —"

The Dedacciai's voice quivered at the mention of his Bellavia as his eyes fought back the tears.

"I see you hit a live wire with that one. Tell me about your wife. What happened a few days ago?"

The voice across the table from her could not make its way out. She sat calmly and reached over to squeeze his hand, letting him know she would wait.

"Something terrible happened that has made my son and wife both hate me. Something unforgivable and something I can't talk about yet. My wife needs some space right now, but I think all the space in the world won't change how she sees me."

"My goodness – ya' mon, I knew something was underneath all the silliness, but I'd have never guessed something like this. Let me tell you; I know your heart, and you're a good man. I'm here to listen if you need."

The dreamatologist briefly appeared in his mind with a reminder. *"Strange how people who suffer together have stronger connections than people who are most content,"* prompting the former grandpa to refocus on Tiny Dancer's offer to listen.

"I'm haunted by a conversation I had a few years back. Somehow, I don't think this conversation is going away until I help Carter try to rewrite his story, and I'm having incredibly detailed and strange dreams about what to do. And they all lead to helping Carter.

"I think he's in my life to both save it and distract me from it by helping him with his request. At the heart of the matter is that I gave a man some advice that I was adamant would help him overcome the loss of his little boy who drowned in his pool twenty-two years ago. Let me ask you, Tiny Dancer. If something catastrophic happened to one of your children while under your watch, how would you live the rest of your days? Could you forgive yourself if you thought you had a hand in what happened?"

"My, oh my, my friend — I'm not going to pry, but my, oh my. That is far from the silliness of the man I know here. I've never had to think about such a thing. The fact you are here, still alive, tells me you are made of strength."

"That's the thing — I'm not. It's only because of Carter I'm even here. I'm overwhelmed fighting this wave of hypocrisy that's living in my subconscious and constantly reminding me of my words."

"My, oh my, my friend — I'm not going to pry, but I get the picture. Does your young friend know this?"

"No. — Carter only knows he saved me from my darkest moment. But because I came into his life when he wished to rewrite his story, he believes

I'm the chosen one to help him. My subconscious seems to think the same."

"So, you have talked with no one about this? — I feel special that you're here speaking with me. Would you consider sharing your advice so I have an even clearer picture? Maybe I can help you with a kind word or just being here for you with a polished ear."

"Tiny Dancer, I think you have been put here in my life as well, and at this very moment, so I have someone to talk with." There was a deep breath and a long pause before he began.

"Here it is, Tiny Dancer. I told that man who lost his son that if something horrible ever happened to one of my kids, and I was responsible, as hard as it would be, I'd live my life in honor of theirs. And I'd do it by being happy and doing good in their name instead of ruining my life in their name. And if the roles were reversed, I wouldn't want my children ruining their lives if something happened to me under their watch.

"But now, the cosmic afterworld isn't letting this conversation go. It's insisting that I be my *silliness* self, as you so wonderfully put it, and then deal with the consequences of guilt from being myself later."

"That's the best advice ever — I'd want to do as you say, or at least I'd want to aspire to do that. I must say, I'm most honored you're sharing these things with me. I wish I could be the voice in your corner the next time you talk with Carter. I'd be your biggest cheerleader and smile big as the sky watching you use your silliness to—"

The cheerleader's eyes grew as big as quarters as they drifted past the Dedacciai. She gasped loudly and became animated as an outside figure approached the entrance. She sprinted out of the booth, ran to the door, and practically tackled the figure who entered.

"Carter, I'm so happy it's you! Ya mon, I'm so glad to see you!"

She hugged him with a new understanding of the two lives about to mold each other's way forward.

"My two favorite people reunited together again. Seeing you makes me very happy! I believe you know that gentleman sitting in the corner."

Carter saw the Dedacciai over his hugger's shoulder.

"The celebration continues, I see. — What are you doing here?" the Dedacciai remarked.

"I couldn't sleep — because of you. Then I heard your door close and thought I better make sure you weren't getting into any more trouble."

Upon her return, Tiny Dancer brought Dedacciai an extra glass of ice, as his had melted during their intense conversation. She also had a Coke for

Carter. The Dedacciai looked at his fresh glass of ice and again marveled at how good she was.

"Carter, we've so won the waitress lottery!"

"Stop with the silliness. I'm just glad both of you are here together," she said while gazing in Carter's direction with a knowing look.

"Now, Tiny Dancer, you clearly understand the magical orange iced-tea phenomenon."

Carter looked at the Dedacciai with a funny expression as he witnessed the awakening of his personality.

"The orange iced-tea phenomenon?" Carter asked.

"It's a thing! Believe me — It is a thing!" the waitress confirmed, "and only a handful of serious tea-drinkers know about it."

Before she walked off, she squeezed the Dedacciai's hand and gave him a glance of assurance. After accepting her glance, the Dedacciai sensed a powerful shift in his mindset. He didn't know if it was because he shared an inkling of his story with her or the feeling of no longer hiding his secret that made him feel better — more normal. But an avalanche of his old self seemed ready to put on a show.

"Oh, young Carter, of course, you don't know anything about it; you're just a pup. I suppose you have the same tired Cola everywhere you go. Are you a tea drinker at all?"

"No, I'm not. Beers and pop were pretty much the only choices in my house growing up."

"Well, you know not what you're missing. Maybe it's time for a change, young Carter. There's nothing like a perfectly sweetened iced tea with the perfect balance of tea color, not too light and not too over-brewed, with the perfect proportions of orange-ness and ice. Or the taste of a perfectly blended Arnold Palmer iced tea, with the ratios of lemonade, tea leaves, and sweetness so beautifully blended that the taste must've been invented not by Arnold Palmer but by the angels themselves."

The waitress stood an earshot away and smiled just hearing her friend talk about orange tea and Arnold Palmers.

"You see, Carter, I've been a long-standing member of 'The Tea Drinkers Association' since high school. And I've learned that there are rules to iced tea.

"The first rule of iced tea: It's called *iced* tea. It must have the appropriate amount of iced cubage. It's in the name, for goodness' sake! Carter, that's why I knew our waitress was a winner because she volunteered to bring an extra glass of ice. You'd think every waitperson would know that, but they don't. Freshly brewed iced tea is hot, and it's going to melt the initial glass of ice. That's why it's imperative to have an extra glass of ice for anyone who truly knows iced tea.

"Second rule of iced tea: It must be stirred with a teaspoon. I'm amazed how many wait staff serve iced tea without a teaspoon. Come on, Carter, it's called a *teaspoon*. I mean, it literally has one purpose in life: to stir a sweetened substance of the drinker's choice into an iced tea glass. Yet so many wait staff never bring one. And if they do, they don't accompany it with the sugars and sweeteners needed to use the spoon. It's a phenomenon in itself of how many wait staff do not know this.

"Third rule of iced tea: Iced tea is to be served in a clear glass of appropriate size and weight. A 20 to 24-ounce glass is a perfect size, no more and no less.

"Last rule of iced tea: It must never be asked to endure its short life living in a clear plastic cup...EVER! It is not allowed and mentally diminishes the taste of what the heavens intended."

Carter was shaking his head and unsure what to think of his new friend. Thoughts of mental illness flashed through his mind as the man seemed too excited about his iced tea.

The point of view shifted as the older cyclist looked across the span of the table and saw Carter shaking his head. It reminded him of his son Evan shaking his head as he rattled off why handwritten letters want to be born of ink. He also remembered Evan shaking his fist at him before he was thrown over the couch and out of his son's life.

Carter witnessed the man's facial expressions telling a story he was not privy to and wondered what was happening inside him. But he was not about to ask. He was weirdly enjoying the awakening of the Dedacciai's personality, having just been schooled on the do's and don'ts of iced tea. Carter watched again as the Dedacciai organized and attacked his orange-sweetening iced tea process. This time, he had a better perspective and understanding of the Dedacciai's long history with iced tea.

He saw him squeezing the orange slices to get every drop of goodness, then eating what was left off the orange rind and rubbing the remainder against his teeth. Each rind looked like a football mouthpiece. Then he tore open and began stirring in each sweetener, one by one, taste-testing in between stirs till he got it exactly right. The entire process took seven minutes and three seconds. Carter watched him use his wet nap to clean his fingers before crossing the finish line. Carter thought he was watching a performance or maybe an audition for *America's Got Talent*.

"Dedacciai, my man — that looks like way too much work for just one glass of tea."

Then Carter mocked him and showed off by taking a sip of his prefabbed Cola.

The Dedacciai answered by placing a straw in Carter's ice water.

"Take a sip and swish it around to cleanse your palette."

Carter did as instructed.

"Now, close your eyes and open your right hand."

The Dedacciai placed his orange iced-tea glass in his opened hand, and Carter tasted its goodness. After the first few ounces passed his palette, his face looked like he had just seen Santa before his words immediately put him on the naughty list.

"Holy shit, that's amazing!" he exclaimed with his face still a glow.

The waitress returned to the table just as Carter finished his taste test.

"Ya mon, you look like you've gone to your happy place, young man," she observed.

"I think I have! Can I trade my Cola for an iced tea, ma'am?"

"Absolutely." She looked at the Dedacciai and winked, knowing another baptism conversion from pop to tea leaves had occurred.

It was now 3:47 a.m. as the Dedacciai spied a clock on the wall. He became entranced as he remembered the IHOP experience with his family. Carter could tell the Dedacciai had wandered off in his thoughts as he sat there with a smile mixed with a tear, trying to make an appearance. Carter interrupted the emotional concoction on his face.

"Dedacciai, what are you thinking about? — I'd really like to know."

The Dedacciai shook off the trance and felt the sincerity in Carter's tone. The older cyclist seemed to look through the college-aged, nose-ring-clad Carter as he gathered himself and his thoughts before he painted the silence with his words.

"It's Christmas break, and my four kids are home from school. One night during that Christmas break, I woke up at 3:00 a.m. and looked out the window. There was a beautiful snowfall that night and a full moon that glistened upon the white powder. It was an amazing sight, and I needed to share it with my family, so I woke everyone from a deep sleep and made them get dressed. My kids thought I was crazy.

"It was freezing outside, and there was snow and ice on the roads as I drove them to an IHOP, braving the weather to make the early-morning memory. The six of us had so much fun and laughter that night, and the kids still remember it to this day. I discovered 'the country omelet with three dollar-sized pancakes' on the IHOP menu that night and have never ordered anything else since."

Carter listened to how the Dedacciai retold his story and watched as he relived every word of his precious memory with such passion. *Orange iced tea, kids, and country omelets — Is he this passionate about everything in life, or is this just an excellent title for a country song?*

"Are you boys going to eat or only have a social tonight?"

Carter decided to pay homage to Dedacciai's story from long ago.

"I'm having a country omelet with the three dollar-sized pancakes."

"Alrighty, two country omelets with three dollar-sized pancakes because Carter is not eating alone. — No, siree, not going to happen on my watch. Two of them coming right up."

It wasn't long until melodic singing filled the dining room and preceded Tiny Dancer, making her grand entrance from the kitchen. Everything was balanced on her tray as she spun around, stopped, and unloaded everything flawlessly.

"Do you boys need anything else?"

"No, thanks, Tiny Dancer. You're perfect, as always."

"What did I tell you, Carter? The waitress lottery!"

The Dedacciai spent the next fifteen minutes between bites of their country omelets teaching Carter the textbook sequence of fixing a perfectly balanced glass of sweet orange iced tea. The two men shared the meal, and soon, the country omelets were no more.

"Dang, Dedacciai, that was a damn good omelet, and this iced tea is freaking amazing. Did you learn this as a part of the Tea Drinker's Association? Is this like a member's only thing?"

"No, Carter, that's years of me perfecting iced-tea R&B."

"Iced-tea R&B — Iced tea rhythm and blues? What the hell is that?" Carter asked.

"No, not rhythm and blues — ratios and balance, and the pursuit of perfecting ratios and achieving balance. The two work together all the time, and not just in iced tea, but in life. Life is all about ratios and balance."

"Really? Life's all about ratios and balance — why's that?"

"Because ratios make ordinary things extraordinary. Let's take our sweetened orange iced tea, for example. The different ratios of ice, orange, sweeteners, and brewing combine to produce a wonderful experience for the senses. It's in the minute details of ratios and the willingness to get them exactly right that transforms an ordinary glass of iced tea into an extraordinary glass of iced tea. Along with this transformation comes passion because the things in life you concentrate on while perfecting their ratios seem to be the things you are most passionate about."

"Hmmm, I can see that, I guess. So, what's balance? You said life was about ratios and balance."

"Balance is the key to life; surely you've seen *The Karate Kid*; you know — 'wax on, wax off?'"

Carter sat across, numb to the unheard term. Things quickly made sense to the Dedacciai as he unraveled the puzzle known as Carter Ducane.

"Carter! You can't tell me that the young pup of a man who sits before me here has never watched *The Karate Kid*?"

"No, sir, I haven't."

The Dedacciai gasped at young Carter for not seeing the movie that taught him the importance of balance in life.

"We didn't have cable because we couldn't afford it, so I didn't get to see a lot of movies unless they were violent enough to make Russell Ducane's approved watch list."

The Dedacciai gasped again, and Tiny Dancer appeared.

"Oh, no, we have a gasper, ya' mon! What are we gasping about?"

The Dedacciai pointed at his young protégé.

"Young Carter here has never seen *The Karate Kid*."

Not skipping a beat, the waitress gasped and played along.

"Wax on, wax off is the very reason your table was so clean this evening. Ya' mon, without that movie, who knows what horrible condition your table would have been in." She winked at the Dedacciai as she walked away, smiling.

The older cyclist thought for a second about how to teach the fundamentally most important life lesson in a way that young Carter could relate to and understand. — The lightbulb moment arrived, accompanied by a flash of Tony Robbins' voice in his mind: *"It will begin with one simple thought that changes the course of Carter's destiny."*

With that, the Dedacciai channeled his own inner Mr. Miyagi.

"Carter, did you know that the secret to life has been between your legs all this time?"

"Dedacciai, say what now? — Are you talking about — my junk?" Carter said awkwardly.

"No! Not your junk. I'm talking about your bicycles! You've had a bicycle between your legs all your life, have you not?"

Carter was somewhat relieved yet nodding and anticipating where this was going.

"Young Carter, think about your bicycle. The unifying principle for anyone who rides a bike is balance. Balance is the key. But what makes someone able to balance on their bike as they roll down the road?"

"— The wheels?" Carter answered, questioning.

"Okay, what keeps the wheels strong and stable in order to balance and roll down the road?"

"Hmmm — the spokes?"

"The spokes, good answer. Now, Carter, imagine there's a spoke for everything in life. There's a spoke for every emotion, every experience, and every part of your life, such as finances, health, relationships, career, race, religion, spiritualism, budgeting, fun, and recreation. Anything and everything, there's a spoke for that.

"Now, imagine that everyone has a metaphorical bicycle they use to ride through life, and everyone's bicycle wheels are custom-built from their own personal experiences and beliefs. Now, are you with me so far?"

Carter gave the nod.

"Okay. Now, for a wheel to roll smoothly down the road, doesn't each spoke need to have the proper tension for the wheel to be, in cyclists' terms — 'true'?"

Carter responded with another nod.

"What happens when a spoke loses its tension?"

"The wheel goes out of true."

"Okay, Carter, what happens when the wheel goes out of true?"

"The brakes start rubbing the wheel rim, sometimes leaving a mark and slowing it down."

"Can it be fixed?"

"Yes, you can usually tighten the spoke with a spoke wrench."

"Let's talk about the spoke wrench. What happens if you don't have a spoke wrench or have one but don't know how to use it?"

"The wheel will continue to go out of true until the spoke breaks."

"Carter, there's a saying; maybe you've heard it — knowledge is power. But the truth is knowledge isn't power; it's only potential power. The application of knowledge is power, just like knowing how to use a spoke wrench doesn't fix your wheel, but applying your spoke wrench to the spoke and tightening it will.

"What I want you to understand here is that just as you true a bicycle wheel by using a spoke wrench, you can true your metaphorical wheels by applying the spoke wrench equivalent, which is knowledge to your life spokes.

"And if that's the case, let's delve deeper into your life spokes. What if I told you that you not only have a spoke for every emotion and experience, but you have a spoke for every belief you have as well?"

Carter stared at the Dedacciai, nodding and following the metaphorical proposal.

"Now, here's a simple question. Why do you speak English?"

"I guess because that's what they taught us in school?" Carter answered, unsure.

"Carter, think about it a little harder. You could speak English before you started school. If not, how could you have communicated with other kids in your class or understood what the teacher said?

"You speak English because that's the language you were surrounded with when you were small. You picked it up through osmosis, hearing it spoken, presumably between your mom and dad or whoever you were surrounded by when you were little. There was even a point when you spoke your very first word. Every parent can usually remember the first word their child said. It's usually something like 'Mama' or 'Dada.'"

"I remember mine; it was 'Ass-Ho,'" his hate responded.

"You're probably right. But Carter, whether we learn things through osmosis or someone trying to teach us, our mind's job is to find a reference or an experience we've had to back up what we've learned.

"When our mind finds a reference in its memory banks, it will attach that reference or experience to that newly discovered piece of information, forming a belief and, eventually, our belief systems.

"The thing is, so much of what we believe was learned from osmosis — both big and small items. For example, how and why do you brush your teeth? Did you watch your dad brush his teeth and make the same motions with a toothbrush? Did you watch someone on TV brush their teeth, or did your mom or dad teach you how to brush them? Let's say the latter is true. What if your dad taught you how he brushed his teeth? But think about this: What if your dad was taught wrong? And the way he has done it all his life, your brain has now inherited?

"Now, let's look at the bigger picture where osmosis also applies to relationships. How did you learn about girls, and how did you learn how to treat them? How about your friends or family? Think about it. Initially, you learned these relationship guidelines by watching how your dad treated your mom and how your mom treated your dad. But you also learned when interacting with your family, relatives, or passerby's on the street. You watched how your mom and dad handled situations, how anyone you met treated you, or you watched total strangers react to a problem.

"Not knowing any better as a small child, you adapted these experiences in relationships as beliefs of how life and relationships are supposed to work. The problem is that we've created incorrect belief systems because so many of our references are wrong. The result is what everyone refers to as dysfunction because so many people end up with two types of B.S. — **B**elief **S**ystems and **B**ull **S**hit. And sadly, they're connected like the sea to the shore."

"Dedacciai, If what you're saying is true, I must be doomed. My dad was a horrible father. He never taught me anything. Everything I've learned has been by osmosis. It's why I have only one wish — to change everything about my life and rewrite my whole story somehow. Is that even possible, or am I just stuck with my childhood osmosis?"

"That question is why there's a whole industry called therapy. Therapists basically do one thing in a variety of different ways. They unravel the parts of life that have been learned incorrectly from childhood osmosis or any age of osmosis and have become a belief. Every decision, big or small, is based on our belief system. And because of this, we make bad decisions based on them, and our bad decisions then determine our future.

"But to answer your question, we're not stuck with our childhood osmosis. We store our beliefs in our resonant memory, and we can change one belief by replacing it with another — hopefully, one that is correct and more empowering. So, young Carter, you're a bicycle mechanic; how do you replace a spoke?"

Carter thought about it and wanted to get it right.

"First, you remove the old spoke, then insert the head of the new spoke into the empty hole in the hub. When the spoke is in place, you insert the nipple through the hole in the wheel rim and thread it carefully onto the end of the spoke. Then, you hand-tighten the nipple as much as possible before tightening or loosening the new spoke. Then, you align the spoke by plucking it and making sure its sound matches the other spokes. Once it does, it's in balance with the tension of the other spokes. Then, you make sure the wheel spins freely and evenly. And if it does, you're finished."

"Well, Carter, are you sure that's all to it? What about first getting the wheel off the bicycle to start the process? Don't you have to open the brake caliper, undo the quick-release skewer, and loosen it to get the tire off the bicycle before you can begin? And what about letting the air out of the tire before using the tire irons to remove the tire and tube from the wheel?

"There are usually more steps to dismantling almost anything than we realize. That exact process of dismantling your bike to replace the spoke happens when you want to replace a belief. You must first disassemble the old belief in your mind before replacing it with a new, more empowering one.

"So, young Carter, in the short time I have known you, I've learned that you hate your dad and blame him for everything wrong in your life. And you believe your life is so horrible that you want to rewrite your life story completely. So, what would be the first step if you wanted to rewrite your story?"

"Does it have to do with changing my beliefs?" Carter answered.

"Okay, you're on the right track, but in order to do that, you need first to identify which beliefs, or which spoke or spokes, are causing the most wheel rub and leaving marks on your rim, which, if left untrue, become emotional scars.

"So, let's go back to your spoke wrench for a second. Suppose your spoke wrench is knowledge, and you're trying to true a spoke with knowledge that is incorrect. Isn't it possible you may be doing more harm than good if you're applying incorrect knowledge for that particular spoke?"

"Dedacciai, this weirdly makes perfect sense. I like the analogy so far."

"Well, that's good, Carter. But now we must talk about something you won't like. Let's talk about your dad. Your *dad* spoke in particular. This spoke seems to be so out of true that your wheel can hardly turn. It has kept you working at a dead-end job for five years, and until now, no matter what, it feels like there has been no hope because this one spoke exists. This singular spoke has caused your life wheel to be so untrue-able, if that is such a thing, that you believe you are damaged goods sitting here now. All because of the reckless actions of one Russell Ducane — Is this correct?"

Carter nodded in agreement.

"Well, Carter, if you genuinely wish to rewrite your story, there will be parts you won't want to face. Maybe we need to take a break and talk about this later. — Because unless you're ready to face what I have to say next with courage and an open mind, I'm afraid we won't be able to continue.

"Listen to me. Do you remember what happened this afternoon? I'm not going through that again, so you'll need to let me know if you think you can handle what I say like a man."

Carter's face turned pale with worry. He had already learned his lesson that the Dedacciai said what he meant and meant what he said, and Carter didn't want to blow his chance of learning more from him.

"Dedacciai, you're making me nervous."

"Don't be nervous; be a man. Your destiny — and the rewriting of your story, all hinges on how you react to my next statement."

Even more worried after that statement, Carter sat contemplating what the Dedacciai had to say as the waitress came by to check on them.

"Are you boys thinking of dessert? If you are, the cook made a special tray of homemade cinnamon rolls that are out of this world. They aren't on the menu, but I think I can pull some strings to bring you boys a couple."

"I'd love that!" Carter responded quickly, and the Dedacciai nodded in agreement as the waitress headed off.

"Dedacciai, you have me so nervous; I just want to eat my feelings!"

"Welcome to my world. I've been eating my feelings since birth. Let's put this topic down for now and enjoy our cinnamon rolls. — Carter, are you following me so far?"

"I am Dedacciai. I've never really thought about anything you've said tonight — like, at all. Ratios, balance, a spoke for everything, spoke wrenches, knowledge, living life in true. It's fascinating, but you have me worried about what's next — that I won't like."

An aroma preceded the tiny dancing waitress as she approached them with the cook's homemade cinnamon rolls.

"Oh, my, that smells amazing!" Dedacciai said as he reached into his pocket and grabbed a $20 bill. "Tiny Dancer, please hand this to the cook for allowing us to have one of his creations."

"I don't think anyone has ever tipped our cook before. You're about to make someone's night!" She headed off to deliver the good news.

Carter thought about himself at that moment. Although nervous, he had never had anyone try to help him understand anything in life — certainly not Russell Ducane. Carter craved the words the Dedacciai spoke, and his thoughts convinced him that Darius really knew this man was the one to help him rewrite his story.

Carter knew it to be true because, in the few hours he had spent with this man, he already felt differently about things, himself, and his future. And he knew he wanted to hear more of what the Dedacciai had to say.

The two men enjoyed their amazing cinnamon rolls before Carter served notice that he was ready to continue their conversation.

"Carter, I want to start by asking you two simple questions. What color are your dad's eyes, and what's his favorite color?"

Carter seemed surprised at the simplicity of the questions and confident he could answer as his eyes looked to the upper right, scouring the universe for the answers. Seconds later, his head lowered with a side-to-side admittance that he didn't know.

"I know you believe Russell Ducane is a horrible man, but what if he wasn't? Let's go back to our bicycle analogy with our custom wheels made from all the different spokes that get us down the road of life.

"When they are out of true, the spokes cause the wheel to rub against the brakes, causing our life to slow down. Sometimes, our wheels are so out of true it causes the brake pads to mar our rims. If left untrue, the brake pads can permanently scratch the rims. These varying degrees of wheel rub create our emotional scars. Unfortunately, these emotional scars become part of our belief system, which we rely on to make every braking decision, good or bad.

"Bad braking decisions can cause some horrible wrecks. Sometimes, we might fall over unscathed, and sometimes we might fall and scratch our frame. Prolonged bad braking decisions can lead to addictions that dent our life's frame. And serious addictions can crack our frame. Some addictions are so deep that when we crash, we break our frame. What we call hitting rock bottom, which can often lead to death."

"That's rather intriguing," Carter said, "I've never thought about a frame like that."

"I think our frame can represent two things in life. First, I believe it represents our spirit. And in many ways, our emotional scars and addictions can break our spirit, causing us to hit rock bottom mentally. But there is also the physical body that it can represent. If we make bad breaking decisions, we can scratch our skin or break a bone, and horrible breaking decisions can leave us paralyzed or even kill us.

"But there is also the possibility that someone with perfectly trued wheels can hit one of life's unexpected potholes, which causes them to wreck. But even worse, something can come out of nowhere and crash into us and crack or break our frame, which can also lead to death.

"We know your dad has a big dent, or possibly even a crack in his frame — but what put it there? Did he grow up in a dysfunctional environment, or did something happen that sent him toward a dysfunctional path? What if Russell Ducane was once a good man?"

Carter snorted, "Yeah, right."

"Keep listening, Carter, because you're not going to like what I have to say next. This is where the rubber meets the road and the reason you've been nervous. This is what determines whether we can continue and possibly rewrite your story. Let me remind you one more time. If you get up and leave, we're done. It would be best if you let me explain my reasoning behind the question. Are we clear on this?"

Carter was not expecting that the rewriting of his story would begin with this level of intensity as Carter looked at him intensely, knowing a lot was at stake. The waitress anxiously hovered in the background, awaiting the outcome.

"Okay, Dedacciai, I'm ready. I'll try not to let you down."

"Wait a minute here; let's be very clear. You won't be letting me down; this is for you. This is for all the wishes you've made that are on your front doorstep right this second. Do you understand?"

He braced himself. "Yes, I understand."

"Okay, what if I told you that *you* are the problem and always have been? Would you believe me?"

"WHAT! — Hell no, I wouldn't believe you! Dedacciai, are you crazy? No way! How could you even think that?"

"Listen, Carter, do you want to stop? If this is going to work, you must control your emotions and keep an open mind. We can't make progress if you close your mind after one question you don't like. So, are you in or out?" the Dedacciai asked firmly.

Carter sat quietly for a few seconds, took a deep breath, and quickly gained control of his emotions.

"Dedacciai — It's just that for the first time, I thought I had someone in my corner. But your question makes it seem like you are on my dad's side. You're supposed to be on my side, not his. You don't know the man; you haven't experienced him."

"That's a good point. I haven't experienced him — but I have experienced you. Carter, I want to tell you first how much you've done for me. You saved me from myself when I had a terrifyingly tough moment; your timing couldn't have been better. You've helped me in ways you don't even know. From cleaning my clothes to what you did for my bike, it's appreciated beyond words. But above all, your innate sense of decency and honesty is admirable.

"I know you looked in the pouch, which, by the way, is not stolen money, and I have no ties with the mob or anything else you have concocted in your mind. But you returned it all the same. I just want you to know one thing. I'm so very proud of you for that, son."

In twenty-five years, Carter had not heard the word *son* used that often in his life, at least not by a male role model, and especially not in reference to something he did that pleased someone. Carter had heard it used in sentences that started with "son" and ended with "of a bitch," — "I'm going to kick your ass," and the number-one answer for $200 — ding, "you're worthless."

"I'm sorry, Dedacciai. I've never met anyone like you. I can't ever remember being around someone this long who hasn't somehow criticized me or put me down. But it felt like you were putting me down when you told me my relationship with my dad was my fault. I felt like I was nothing again after you made me think I was truly worth something. I'm not sure where this is going, but I promise to listen to anything you say. If I'm the problem, as you say, then I want to know why."

"Well, just look at all that perspective," the Dedacciai said while looking across at his nose-ring-clad apprentice.

"Carter, let's begin again. Chapter One: The Russell Ducane Spoke. What if it was your job as his son to find out what happened to his frame? What if you weren't so hell-bent on doing things that pointed out your dad's failures? If you had done either of those things, do you think that maybe he would have treated you differently? And if he treated you differently, is it possible he would have shared his life with you, and you would know why his frame had a massive dent? Perhaps if you knew what color his eyes were or expressed any interest in his life, it would have been the equivalent of the two of you finding a carbon-fiber repair shop to repair his frame. Sure, they're hard to fix — but it can be done. And, even if you were to fail in your endeavor, do you think some benefit could come as a result of the attempt?

"However, in the few short conscious hours I've known you, I've only heard you refer to Russell Ducane with great disrespect. You tell me how much you hate him with every verbal jab you've thrown at him. You've lived such a life of hate for this man; it's become your identity. He lives in your head, rent-free, 24/7. And worse, he also lives in your nose.

"You hate this man so much that you were willing to go through the pain it took to place a rather large piece of metal there that you knew he would hate for the very specific reason of escalating hate. Did I understand you correctly? Didn't you say you hated your nose ring but kept it because he hated it more? Carter, who do you think is more complicit here, you or your dad?

"Besides hating him, what do you know about him? Have you ever once asked him anything? Who was his best friend in high school or college? Did he have any hobbies growing up? Carter, you have blamed your dad for ruining your life from all of the *whats* he has done in life — you missed the more important fundamental question of *why* he was doing everything in life."

Carter stared, dumbfounded.

"Is it possible you could be wrong about the Russell Ducane spoke? Were you just the most incredible son in the world? Have you ever tried easing your dad's burden of providing for his family? Or were you so hell-bent against him for not providing you with a car, like you thought he should, that you decided to put an alien piece of metal through your nose? Yet everything is your dad's fault, and you're completely innocent in all of this. I ask you again, what's your dad's favorite color? Mark my words, Carter, all the horrid things your belief system tells you are wrong about Russell Ducane have a *why* to them.

"I'm not trying to blame you for what's gone on between the two of you. But I'm not accusing him either. Each of us has our own cross to carry, and it seems that too often, we humans forget that. Carter, think about this. Russell Ducane, too, has a wheel with spokes trying to stay balanced so he can roll down the road of life smoothly. And he has a Carter Ducane spoke. How incredible do you think it is having a son like you? It's probably not fun for your dad to have an ungrateful turd for a son. It's true; you didn't have a car, but you had a roof over your head.

"Somehow, Russell Ducane provided the fundamental needs of food, shelter, water, and clothing. He kept you from being homeless, people you seem to hate through the osmosis of having an addiction like your father.

"Carter, there's zero difference between your dad and me. I have just as serious an addiction as he has. Have you noticed that I'm a smidge overweight? Listen, having an addiction is downright evil, cunning, and baffling. My weight loss career has spanned over sixty-two years, and the last decade was mostly fueled by a severe cupcake addiction. Did you know that I'm currently 289 days cupcake sober as of today?"

"Cupcake sober — are you messing with me?" Carter asked.

"Nope. The only difference between my cupcake addiction and his alcohol addiction is that I can't get an E.U.I. for devouring too many cupcakes while driving. And another difference is that I would have never stomped on your cake. — But that's only because I would have eaten it after everyone went to bed."

Carter opened his mouth to protest, but The Dedacciai held up a hand.

"Not now, hear me out. It's utterly baffling to me why some lives are controlled by alcohol instead of dessert. I have leftover beers in my garage refrigerator from a hotdog cookout I hosted over eleven years ago, and these beers residing in my refrigerator are now married with a grown family of their own.

"They read the story of *Goldilocks and the Three Little Beers* to their children each night as they slumber comfortably in my fridge. I'm pretty sure I have a few grandbeers and possibly great-grandbeers by now. But a brand-new bag of Oreo cookies hasn't a snowball's chance in hell of making it through the night in my pantry.

"The addiction is the same for both your dad and me. The part of our brain that craves sugar obtains it either through the liquid form of alcohol or the solid form of food. Both addictions wreak havoc and cause great pain destroying our relationships with ourselves and those around us while physically destroying our bodies from the inside out. Now, do you understand what I'm saying here? I'm not that much different from your dad."

Carter crossed his arms over his chest and shook his head from what he had heard.

"I get where you're going, but I gotta be honest, you and my dad are nothing alike."

"That's only partly true. What we need to ask is why does your dad have an addiction? Why is a spoke on his wheel so out of true that his frame developed a considerable dent? Or worse, what happened to him that cracked his frame? That's the pivotal question that needs to be answered. And I realize I don't know your dad, but my guess is you don't either.

"Have you ever considered that your dad might be a good man hidden underneath life's trials? We need to remove the filters from your eyes of how you see him. What if you were the son to him that you've been to me? What do you think Russell Ducane would think about the way you treat me? What would he think of the kindness you've shown me by putting your life on the line for a total stranger? You've shown yourself to be selfless with me, but have you ever once been selfless with him? Would he even recognize the person you are with me?

"Carter, consider there might be other possibilities for how your life could be more balanced — because balance is the key to life. But for now, all I'm concerned about is you. And what I absolutely know to be true is there's no possibility of you rewriting your story while living with so much hate.

"So, let's first concentrate on taking steps toward getting rid of the hate. It's obvious that emotional hatred runs your life from what you display to the world and, up until this point, has served you well in pushing people away, but let's take a different approach — what about the effect of your anger on your physical body? Hate is horribly unhealthy for your well-being. The amount of acid that hate produces can lead to creating cancerous tumors. You could literally die from the amount of toxic hatred eating you up inside.

"I want to try something here. I want you to close your eyes and keep them closed. Think about how much you hate your dad. Think about that feeling from your birthday cake or any incident when your dad was abusive toward you. Now, focus on your body. Just feel the amount of acid that hatred floods your body with inside. Feel the acid churning in your stomach as well as the feeling in your chest around your heart. Isn't that an awful sensation?"

Carter nodded.

"Okay, now clear your mind and try to relax. Think back to a few hours ago when you were standing in that open, moonlit field as you unwrapped the gift of perspective with your eyes. How did your body feel then? Was it quite the contrast to what happened when you focused on your dad? Keep your eyes closed and concentrate on that for a few minutes."

While Carter had his eyes closed, The Dedacciai signaled the waitress over, indicating to come quietly with his finger to his lips. He whispered instructions in her ear that turned her face curious, but she did what he asked and went to perform the task.

"Now, Carter, breathe deep and focus on the different sensations as you switch between the two different states of mind."

While Carter continued thinking with his eyes closed, the waitress returned with a large Styrofoam to-go container and a piece of Texas toast. The Dedacciai placed it on the table in front of Carter as silently as possible.

"Okay, Carter, you can open your eyes."

He did so and furrowed his brow at the Styrofoam container and Texas toast.

"What's this for?"

"It's for you, another birthday present. Go ahead, open it."

Carter opened it and found it filled with used coffee grounds.

"What the heck is this?"

"Isn't it obvious—?"

"Not really."

"It's a burial ground," the Dedacciai explained.

"Is anything buried in it?"

"Not yet, but I'm hoping there will be soon—"

"What are you hoping to bury?"

"Your hate."

"You're gonna need a bigger container!"

"True, but we have to start somewhere. You see, for another birthday gift, I wanted to allow you to bury your hate so we can truly start rewriting your story."

"Dedacciai, I'm telling you — We're gonna need a bigger boat!"

The Dedacciai smirked at the *JAWS* reference, surprised Carter had seen it.

"I think it's time we bury Naustris."

"Who in the hell is that?"

"Naustris Damien Ducane — your nose ring."

"What in the...? Did you smoke some of these used coffee grounds or something? What blend of CBD coffee do they use around here anyway?" He looked at the Dedacciai and realized he was serious.

"Carter, it's time for the proper burial of Naustris Damien Ducane. It's my opinion that he's no longer needed in your life. I even have a few words that I'd like to share."

A rather large man with a pancake batter-stained white apron exited the kitchen and looked for the man who gave him a twenty-dollar tip. Tiny Dancer stopped him in his tracks so he wouldn't disturb what was happening in booth twenty-one.

The Dedacciai noticed the two and signaled them to join as he began. The innocent chef who just wanted to thank him for the tip was now shushed and elbowed in the ribcage as she forced him to join her for the ceremony. The waitress and cook grabbed chairs from the nearest table and sat perpendicular to the spectacle.

Carter was astonished at what was happening and hadn't the words to stop the Dedacciai. — This WAS happening!

"Would everyone please bow their heads as I give the eulogy?"

With all the reverence of an actual funeral, IHOP had changed to the perfect sanctuary for Naustris Damien Ducane's final resting spot as the ceremony began.

"Carter, I'd like to start by asking you if you would volunteer to give up your symbol of hatred by removing it and placing it in the palm of my hand."

Carter was hesitant of the Dedacciai's request as he made accidental eye contact with the two additional funeral attendees. The waitress had soft eyes and the beginning of a tear. He noticed an emotional acceptance and pride in her eyes that said he should do as the Dedacciai asked. His eyes wandered to his second, much larger funeral attendee. His eyes said something much different: *Dude, you better do this, or I'm gonna kill you for wasting my time.*

Both pairs of eyes had a compelling argument for what action he should take, and he gently removed the metal hatred and surrendered it to the Dedacciai. He wiped it clean, using a napkin, and raised it high into the air for everyone to see.

"Although it's not something that we normally do in our American culture, that is, give a name to an inanimate object. In this case, since this particular inanimate object is filled with hate, I feel we would be doing a grave disservice if we didn't. Hate is something not found in other metallic vestibules, so it goes without saying that this object, which has the human emotion of hate living inside it, should also take on a human name — AMEN!"

The amen echoed back as an elbow to the cook's side signaled his participation.

Two other cooks exited the kitchen, looking for the head chef, followed by another waitress who had caught sight of the makeshift ceremony. They, too, were drawn in by the unusual man holding a nose ring high above his head.

"With this understanding, we are gathered here tonight to pay our last respects to Naustris Damien Ducane. He was conceived as a weapon and born from hate the moment he joined Carter's life. For five long years, he lived a miserable existence on this earth, which must have seemed like an eternity. Naustris has now passed, as he is no longer needed to cause pain and push away love in the life of his master.

"I'd like to break bread on this special night and with these special people, just as Jesus did with his twelve disciples. As we get ready to partake in the two-thousand-year-old tradition of breaking bread. I ask that we all consider what we can do to move on from our hate, addictions, or any other personal demons holding us back from what our lives should be."

The Dedacciai handed the Texas toast to the head chef.

"I'm assuming your hands are clean," the Dedacciai said with a wry grin and wink. "Would you please distribute the bread?"

The head chef broke the bread and gave the now-seven-member congregation each a piece.

"We've learned some things about Naustris. We know he has caused a thousand times his weight in emotional baggage for one so small, and he was never used as part of a way to express oneself as a unique person or connect with other unique-minded people. Oh, no! His entire purpose was to hurt people and push away love.

"When an artistic object is brought into this world, it's the job of the human who has conceptualized it to take responsibility for its purpose. Humans must ask themselves a series of questions before considering the possibility of giving birth to a nose ring, piercing, or tattoo.

"Do you love yourself? You must love yourself first before giving birth to an artistic object. If the responsibility is placed on the artistic object to help you love yourself, you have set yourself up for an epic fail.

"Do you know who you are as a person? You must know who you are and the precise reason for giving birth to any form of artistic uniqueness that will become a part of your identity. If the sole purpose is to impress another person by mutilating your body or permanently altering your skin out of fear that they will not love or accept you — then this is a terrible choice. If you're birthing an artistic object in order to intimidate other people, you should reconsider.

"Bringing an artistic object into this world is only an act of goodness if you're doing it for yourself as an expression of love and connection with others or as a positive symbol of hope and remembrance. When people die, they want to know that their lives meant something, that during their life, they did something to contribute to making someone else's life better. Instead, Naustris died a self-expressionless piece of art never appreciated by anyone — not even his master.

"Before we conclude our service, ask yourself one last question: What's the greatest need of a human? — to be loved? — Actually, the answer is no. The greatest need for a human *is* to love. We begin our lives with a clean slate and a pure heart. As we go through life, our experiences create references, which turn into beliefs. Our beliefs create our values, which lead to our identity. We assume that our beliefs are correct, but, in actuality, we often go through life believing things about ourselves that simply aren't true.

"When our identity is built on partially correct or false references, it can lead to destructive values and beliefs. We end up living a life upside down from those around us and find ourselves not fitting in and asking ourselves why. So, we sabotage relationships and drive others away by hurting those we should love. And then, one day, in a desperate attempt, we decide to create an identity that works against our primary need, which is to love.

"Carter, by keeping you emotionally stunted for five years, Naustris kept you from your one primary human need— to love."

The Dedacciai pauses reverently, "I now commit Naustris Damien Ducane to these hallowed coffee grounds for his final resting place. May his definitive act upon this earth be to relieve Carter of his hate and allow him the freedom to move on with his life, to experience love, peace, joy, and happiness. Naustris, with this as your last act, your life will finally have meaning — Amen."

The seven unsuspecting funeral crashers sat silently, thinking about the eulogy's lessons as the lid to the burial ground was respectfully closed. At the same time, Tiny Dancer moved to Carter's side of the table and hugged him.

"Very handsome young man, you are. You did very well. Your parents would be very proud of you," she added, then moved to the Dedacciai's side of the table and hugged him.

"You're doing very well, my friend; your advice is very becoming of you. Thank you for your beautiful words."

The relatively large funeral attendee looked at Carter.

"I didn't know what the hell I was getting myself into here. Evidently, you're kinda messed up — but I'm weirdly glad I was part of it."

The man then turned to the Dedacciai. "I originally came out here to thank you for the tip, but I think you stopped me from making a big mistake. I honestly was going to get a tattoo next week, but I might need to answer some of those questions before I do. My mother told me to save money and buy a bumper sticker instead."

The man reached into his pocket and pulled out some sketches of the tattoos he wanted. "Is there any room in there for these?"

The Dedacciai opened the burial ground and watched as the large cook named Owen buried his drawings alongside Naustris, then shook his head — "You two are some weird-ass dudes."

"Owen, when the going gets weird — the weird turn pro!" the Dedacciai responded.

He shook his head even more and punched the two in the arm as he rose and disappeared behind the metal swinging kitchen door that rocked itself to sleep after four quick swings.

The congregation had all dispersed, and Carter sat there mesmerized. He was happy, joyous — yet troubled, sad, and confused. *How is it that this man who knew so much about life was seconds away from taking his?*

And thus, it happened. At 4:39 a.m., IHOP store 687, booth 21, a twenty-five-year-old man named Carter Ducane entered a new chapter of his life as he cried his first tears that washed away his hate and transformed him from an ungrateful child into a father's son.

"Just look at all that perspective," Dedacciai admired. "Amazing what happens when we dismantle the things in our mind and replace one belief with another."

"You two are exceptional people," Tiny Dancer said as she slid into the booth next to Carter. "I'll never forget this day! Your money is no good here tonight — I'm buying your dinner with the cash you blessed me with earlier. There will be no discussion. I have always said I'd pay it forward if I were ever blessed. Today is that day. I want to pay it forward.

"It is my gift to you both for blessing me with your presence. That was a truly special service. And I'm keeping this container; I'll give it a proper burial. It doesn't seem fitting to simply throw it away."

"You think of everything, Tiny Dancer! That is exceedingly kind. Thank you so much for dinner; you are just as special to us. Your presence made this experience even better because you are you."

She saw a patron enter. "I better take care of this customer. I pray our paths to cross again," and Tiny Dancer hugged the two before leaving.

"Okay, Carter, let's head back to the hotel so I can pay for the room."

"Crap!" Carter said as he bolted toward the bathroom. A few minutes later, he came out with dampened hair combed back with his shirt tucked in and straightened.

"Is there a spoke for this 'Crap' situation'? What's going on here? Why did we feel the need to get spruced up? By the way, you do look much better without your hate showing."

"Connie Sue is the owner of the hotel I told you about, who is so freaking beautiful. I just wanted to look nice for—"

Wham! — Out of nowhere, Carter's face jilted forward from Dedacciai's slap to the backside of the head, followed by his playful yet stern voice. "Don't even think about pretty girls. We have a lot of work to do before you can even fantasize about a relationship. — So, until then, there will be no breeding for you!"

The two shared an odd moment as the Dedacciai was both serious and playful but mostly serious as Carter rubbed the back of his head.

"I will let you talk to this Connie Sue person and observe how you handle the situation, then decide how to proceed with your training. — Now, let's head back."

The two stopped to take in Connie Sue Lancaster's handiwork upon entering the hotel lobby before walking toward the check-in counter. There was no one at the counter, so they rang the bell. Out walked Connie Sue in another form-fitting, award-winning blue dress with two black stripes down each side, highlighting her perfect curvature.

"Why, hello there, Mr. Carter! How are you doing this evening?" she inquired as she looked him over.

"Why I do declare, Mr. Carter, you seem taller than I remember. Something's different about you tonight," as she continued to analyze him.

"Oh, my, I got it! Just let me say, you look mighty handsome without your little round friend. Now, is this just for tonight, or did you get rid of the little rascal for good?"

"For good, ma'am. In fact, we just got back from burying the little rascal in a styrofoam container full of used coffee grounds while our waitress and cooks attended the funeral. My friend here said the eulogy."

"Mr. Carter, are you storying here? You had a funeral service for your little round friend? Whose big idea was that?"

"Glad you asked. Do you recognize this gentleman?"

"Not without his wheelchair and mud all over him. You clean up well, Mr....um?"

"Dedacciai. It's nice to meet you, Connie Sue Lancaster. Thank you for what you did for young Carter last night. That was exceptionally kind."

"Well, it isn't every day you meet a real-life hero; I was mighty proud of him for what he did for you. So, is Carter storying to me, or did you actually have a burial service for his little friend?"

"Yes, ma'am, we did. After meeting this young man and getting to know him, I thought he was wearing his little friend for all the wrong reasons. It was my birthday present to him to bury it so he could move on with his life.

"Earlier, we went to a homeless camp for a hotdog cookout, and Carter met three men who all had bicycles needing repair. In the morning, he's going to buy the parts needed and head over to surprise them by fixing their bicycles."

"Why, I do declare, Mr. Carter, you are full of surprises. I have never heard tales like the two of you have. By the way, Mr. Dedacciai, your head looks much better than last night. Your little goosey egg didn't stick around much, did it? You two handsome men are really something. Now, how can I help you this evening?"

"I'd like to go ahead and pay for an extra night for tomorrow night, but just for room 555. And could you have a rollaway bed added to the room tomorrow?"

"Anything for my two favorite storytellers. Now, Mr. Dedacciai, I'm going to ask one more time. Did this incident really happen? Did you really have a memorial service for his little round friend? Do you pinky swear on your children's lives and the lives of their children that you're telling me the truth?"

"More than you could possibly imagine," he murmured.

Connie Sue Lancaster watched as the Dedacciai's face quivered slightly. "Are you okay, Mr. Dedacciai? You look kinda pale. I tell you what. Since Carter looks so handsome without that pesky rascal blocking his face, I'd like to show you my appreciation for helping my young friend." Connie Sue printed out a receipt for the room marked "paid in full."

"What can I say? The two of you fascinate me. What good is it to own this big old hotel if I can't see fit to do something nice for two of my most interesting guests? You two should write a book someday. Good luck with whatever comes your way, and do me a favor. Keep me apprised of what's happening with you two, and come back and see me anytime — Deal?"

"Yes, ma'am, absolutely," Carter said.

The two men headed to their rooms. Carter was bouncing off the walls from talking to Connie Sue and experiencing the best day of his life.

"Well, how did I do, Dedacciai? You know, with handling myself around Connie Sue."

"Let's just say I'm going to give you a hall pass on this one — she's quite the challenge for any man not to make an idiot of himself. I'll see you at 9:30 to head to the bicycle shop. It was a good day, Carter. It's good to see you like this."

Carter walked across the hallway and gave his friend another hug.

"Thank you so much — for everything!"

The hug ended, and the two entered their keycards into their locks. The Dedacciai looked back at his friend. He thought about how Carter's thirst for what he had to say made him feel useful and lessened his physical and emotional pain.

He knew God had put Carter in his path to help him feel what it felt like with his children growing up. He saw the excitement Carter had when hearing his life wisdom for the first time. Watching him absorb knowledge was like seeing Addison learn things for the first time. He felt a kinship, even a sonship, with Carter — if that was a thing.

Was Carter my second chance? — "Just look at all that perspective!"

Chapter Sixteen

The Field Of Dreams and Despair

"Welcome back, Carter!" Brandon shouted as he saw Carter looking for bicycle parts.

"Dude! Didn't expect you back so soon. But seriously, welcome back," Brandon reiterated while bent down on his current repair before doing a double-take and popping back up.

"Wait a minute — Hold the phone — Something's amiss — Something's awry — Dude! What's different about you?" Brandon's boisterous investigation of Carter's appearance caused Charley to come over and join in on the mystery.

"I can't smell you from back here — Did you shower? No, sorry, that's not it...." Brandon joked as Charley took his turn.

"You look taller; have you grown since we last saw you? No, that's not it either, although you do seem taller somehow."

A few seconds later, an animated Brandon concluded, "You're missing your facial component — Dude! I must say — you look rather dapper. Is it just home taking a nap or something more serious?"

"Well, if you call a man I saved a few days ago saying a eulogy, then burying it in a Styrofoam container filled with used coffee grounds while complete strangers attended the funeral service at 4 a.m. in an IHOP serious, then yes, it's something more serious."

"BEST FUNERAL EVER!" Brandon yelled as he fell to his knees and cued Charley to join in. "We're not worthy! We're not worthy!"

The Dedacciai, recognizing the Wayne and Garth "We're not worthy" reenactment, rounded the corner with his bike. Brandon recognized the name on the bike as the one he and Charley had been googling ever since Carter left the store. Without missing a beat, they both scooched on their knees toward the Dedacciai bicycle and continued worshiping the bike with their "We're not worthy" mantra.

"HOLY S-H-I-I-T-E-! — You weren't blowing smoke up our asses, were you, Carter?" Brandon used the opportunity to speak the bicycle's native tongue as best he could while petting it as if it were a childhood pet.

"You are *Stupefacente*! I mean *Sei la bicicletta piu incredibile e bell ache abbia mai visto! Dedacciai, come ti stai godendo il tuo soggiorno in America?*"

Charley leaned over, "Maybe the bike doesn't speak Italian?"

"Nonsense! Borderline blasphemous!" Brandon argued as the comedy duo lifted themselves off the floor.

"It would be impossible for a bicycle like this not to speak its heritage."

"Bicycles are people, too, is what I've always thought," said the more human of the two Dedacciai's.

"Exactly, dude! — Sorry, I meant *Esattamente Amico*! I don't want the bicycle to feel left out of the conversation."

"Brandon, I'm the Dedacciai. I'm also the Dedacciai's owner."

"No way — Double Dedacciai! — Sounds like the best board game ever! That's awesome! It's great meeting you, sir. I just wanted her to feel at home here in America. Did you, like, totally say a eulogy for Carter's metal dude?"

"Yes, and I think he looks rather dapper as well."

Charley, the owner, drooled over the Dedacciai bicycle as he walked over to the register and opened it. He counted how much was there before going to the backroom to look in his safe. A loud voice yelled from the back —

"I'll give you five-thousand three-hundred forty-three dollars and thirty-four cents for your beautiful steed! I'd offer you more if I had it," then exited the back room with his own personal bicycle.

"Or I'll trade you for this Trek Madone 9 team-issue bicycle. It's the same one they rode in the Tour de France. It's three years old but cost $13,000 when I bought it new."

"Charley, is it? Nice to meet you as well. Thanks for the offer, but my beautiful steed is not available at any price. Nice try, though. I would have done the same."

Carter was mesmerized by the Dedacciai bicycle's effect on anyone who saw it. So far, he had witnessed two thugs try to steal it. He, himself, risk life and limb to save it and then restore it — Connie Sue Lancaster's great admiration for it, even at its lowest moment. And now, Brandon speaking to it in Italian while Charley was trying to leverage anything and everything to own it — and that was after they weren't worthy of its presence. The Dedacciai bicycle was its own spectacle.

"Well, since you broke my will to live, what can I charge you twice the amount for today?" Charley asked.

"I need to look at some clothes, a water bottle, and new SPD bicycle shoes. My friend Carter is the one who really needs your attention."

While Carter was turned away, the Dedacciai leaned over and whispered in the owner's ear, "Ask him what project he's working on."

Charley walked over to Carter. "It seems you had quite the night last night; what project are you working on today?"

Carter pulled up the list on his phone and showed it to him.

"That's an interesting array of items you need. What's this for?"

Carter showed the picture of the three bikes.

"Well, last night, my friend took me to a homeless camp for dinner."

Once again, Brandon's ears never missed a beat as he walked over to hear Carter's story.

"I was scared at first, but it ended up being — well, kinda a game changer! The Dedacciai even brought a cake, and we celebrated my 25th birthday with them. Anyway, I noticed the three bikes in the picture, and after hearing their stories, I wanted to help them by fixing their bikes. Kind of my gift to them for helping me overcome my fear of the homeless and stop hating them."

"Carter, dude! Why do you hate on the homeless in the first place? What did they ever do to you?"

"That's the thing; it's not really what they did to me. It's more about who they remind me of — my dad, who was always drunk. But, Brandon, I want to be absolutely clear on this. I don't hate them anymore. I now have a new perspective from getting to know these guys and hearing their stories. It gave me perspective, which Dedacciai said was my birthday present from him.

"That hate I had living inside me for them, and my dad, was buried with the nose ring. I'm trying to redeem myself, and that's why I'm here. I want to help them by fixing their bicycles."

"Carter, I used to be homeless," Brandon said nonchalantly.

Charley, with a double-take, stared down his friend.

"Dude! Really? All these years in business together and nothing! Nada! Not once has this come up."

"Dude, not my finest moment, and in my defense, you never asked. But with the help of a mentor who was there for me during my homeless phase, I learned to live life by my own surfer's code: 'You cannot stop the waves, but you can learn to surf.' So, that's what I do — surf through life and try not to get knocked down by the waves behind me. Besides, this was fourteen years ago."

Carter spoke up, "Brandon, I want to hear your story; I think it will help with rewriting my story."

"Yes, do tell!" Charley added. "Start at the beginning. I want to know how you became the awesome dude you are today."

"Well, if you insist. Here it goes. I grew up surfing around the delta in Louisiana. I also rode bikes all my life and found I was excellent at fixing bikes, just like you, Carter. In the delta area, all my friends were in the same boat, financially speaking. It was an extremely poor area, so we all rode bicycles, and none of us had a car. But we had fun every day because that was our competition creed— the best surfer out there was the one having the most fun.

"My dad worked construction and traveled around the country, moving from disaster to disaster for months on end. That was until my dad returned from a construction stint in the California wildfires to a 'Dear John' letter from my mom. She had met someone while cleaning houses, which she did along with substitute teaching. I was sixteen when my mom left us after twenty-two years of marriage. She even took our dog! That hurt almost as much as her leaving!

"So, it was just us. To make things worse, my dad found out he had an advanced stage of liver cancer, had no insurance, and couldn't work construction anymore. He drank heavily, not just then but during the marriage, too. But he was never abusive toward us when he did.

"My dad was awesome. He began teaching me how to speak Italian to fill the void of quietness. My dad encouraged me to party and live life to the fullest while I still could. So, I did just that. I loved to surf and party down in the delta and had many surfer-dude friends I hung out with daily. But within six months, we lost the house. When that happened, I had to decide to either party till I died young or grow up. But I hadn't yet decided."

"Dude," Charley breathed while Carter and Dedacciai were dumbfounded.

"Yeah, exactly," Brandon said. "Anyway, we drove from Louisiana, headed to Arizona, where my dad had an uncle we thought might help us. But the old Pontiac didn't make it, and my uncle didn't have money to help us complete the journey.

"Two days later, when my dad called him, he said his wife blew a gasket and that he couldn't help us at all. He told us not to come, even if we got the car fixed. My dad was devastated. We panhandled and saved enough money to get the Pontiac moved near a homeless shelter in Austin.

"We stayed in the mission some, but the old Pontiac more. My dad was getting sicker and sicker and drank more and more. The missions have a zero policy on liquor, and if you're not inside the mission by 7 p.m. and sober, it was just tough luck — no matter the weather. We lived in that old Pontiac for six months until—"

Brandon lifted his shirt and showed a cross tattoo with his dad's name close to his heart.

"I've never touched a drop of liquor since the day I found my dad dead. You'd think I'd be sad, but he was free from the pain. That day changed my life. It was also the day I met a homeless man named Chaplain."

Carter and Dedacciai glanced at each other immediately. The Dedacciai put his hand out silently toward Carter, urging him not to say anything as Brandon continued.

"Chaplain was just a stranger on a bike. I saw him in the distance when we both heard a gunshot. I could see his reaction from behind when he heard the shot. I saw the man flail his arms and yell. It looked like he dove off his bike for cover. Later, I learned he did.

"But at that moment, I didn't know the gunshot belonged to my dad's brain. If that weren't such a tragedy, it would have been one of the funniest things I had ever seen. I mean, the man looked more like a Charlie Chaplain movie as he flailed his arms like a wild man before taking a dive. Isn't it strange some of the stuff your brain remembers so vividly?"

"Dude," Charley murmured again.

"Anyway, he got up quickly and ran to the car to help. Later, I learned he did that instinctively during the war, to run toward his fellow soldiers to help, But, in his case, he did it mostly to pray with them, often just before they died, which he was doing with my dad when I rode up and saw him."

The three had an unscripted moment of silence before he resumed.

"I had just panhandled enough money to buy my dad some more vodka to numb his pain. Chaplain stayed there with me while someone called the police. Here's a new life tidbit I never knew — you can donate whole dead bodies to science. I donated his body to a forensic body farm since I didn't have money to bury him. He never had a funeral except the one Chaplain had enough foresight to have with me as he said a quick eulogy for the man and son he just met."

The Dedacciai could tell Carter wanted to interrupt the story but gestured not to disrupt him as Brandon continued.

"Dad was gone, but this man thought I shouldn't be alone, so he made me ride to his camp and stay with him. He counseled a small group of people on grief, and I became part of that group. He did the same for a lot of people in the field, under bridges, anywhere there was a need. And he always rode a bicycle everywhere to help them.

"He would stay up late at night to help me get my life together and always made me read and keep my mind busy. Best of all, he continued my Italian education by making me converse with him in Italian.

"I stayed with him for about four months. He made me take aptitude tests at the library and then encouraged me to fix things because I was mechanically inclined. He told me to visit every bicycle shop in a 100-mile radius and show them how good of a mechanic I was by working on a trial basis.

"Guys, that's how I met Charley. He was thinking of opening his bike shop when he met me while working for another bike shop in Austin. Charley approached and asked me to go into a partnership with him. He handles the office and business side of things, and I run the bicycle repair part. We've done well together. But Chaplain was the one who saved my life back then.

"I never knew what happened to him because his number went dead. He must have lost his phone or something because, after a while, someone else answered his old number. I have always wondered if he is okay and where he is. Because I wanted him to know how much he changed my life."

Carter and the Dedacciai looked at each other, wondering who would ask or say what first. But Charley chimed in before they decided.

"Brandon, I'm confused about something. I hear you talking to your mom all the time. What happened with that, and how did she get back in your life? I mean, didn't you hate her for leaving you?"

"Damn straight, I did! Growing up, I was always closer to my dad because we both thought life was a party. But I had good times with my mom as well. She was just quieter. But witnessing the pain she caused my dad by leaving and what he went through toward the end forced me to hate her. But that was before Chaplain got a hold of me. During our grief counseling and just in talking, he told me I could never move forward with the weight of hate holding me back."

Carter physically reacted to the vital truth of that statement.

"Chaplain made me recognize that my mom was simply a flawed person, like all of us. He taught me about the yin and the yang of relationships. He taught me that my mom had emotional needs that were hard to get when her husband was gone for months and that she simply didn't have the emotional know-how to tell me she was leaving.

"Believe me; Chaplain had a lot of experience counseling on that subject. He said mail call was the most exciting and dreaded part of the military. Dear John, letters were quite common, and so was dealing with the painful aftermath.

"Anyway, before he allowed me to graduate from his homeless camp, I had no choice but to forgive my mom. And since I was no longer drinking, Chaplain encouraged me to use my panhandling money to buy extra minutes for my phone to reconnect with her.

"He also called her on his cell phone and counseled her for hours and hours into forgiving herself. And we had three-way counseling sessions all together while on speakerphone.

"It was odd at first, but it worked. I love my mom now, and we're closer than ever. One of the last things I remember him saying to me was, 'You cannot stop the waves, but you can learn to surf.'" Brandon sat quietly after reliving his emotional journey, while Charley sat amazed that he never knew any of this.

"I'm so proud to call you my friend," Charley said as he hugged his friend, then yelled— "DUDE!"

In an instant, Brandon reemerged from his tales of yesteryear.

"DUDE!" he yelled back — and bicycle operations resumed.

"Brandon, here's Carter's list of parts he needs. Take a closer look at that picture and make sure he didn't miss anything."

Brandon took a closer look to ensure they had everything they might need. He then went to the supply room and whistled for Charley to join him.

The Dedacciai huddled with Carter. "Don't you say a thing! Let's just see what happens on its own. Got it?"

Carter nodded as he listened to the two men's muffled voices in the backroom while the Dedacciai finished shopping for what he needed.

"Okay, Carter," he heard as the two emerged from the backroom. "Here's a buttload of extra patches, as well as new and used tires and tubes of all different sizes that we have accumulated over the years. There's also extra cabling, miscellaneous pedals, bar tape, and a few extra tools we no longer need."

"But I only need the stuff on my list for those three bicycles! What in the heck is all this other stuff for?"

"It's for me to help you kick some bicycle ass because I'm going with you. I need to do this," Brandon said. "Charley, can I call Ken to work for me today?"

"No problem, in fact, let me take care of that," Charley said.

"Carter, you're gonna have to trust me here. When I was living on the street, anytime someone pulled up at the mission with food or clothing, they were bombarded. It can also be dangerous, as people would fight over a pair of socks or if someone got an extra Twinkie.

"That field is not only a field of dreams for their lives to somehow get better, but a field of desperation. I promise you, not if, but when one other person sees you fixing bikes, the floodgates will open. These aren't your grandparents' homeless; today's homeless have cell phones and group texts ready to send. That's why I need to meet you there as soon as possible — just in case."

"Okay, Ken just texted and can come in at one o'clock," Charley informed everyone.

"I'm going to stay till he gets here and then come out," Brandon confirmed. "Now, where's the field again?"

"It's at S.W. 7th and Lee, but the homeless camp where the bikes are is the third trailhead north of that. That's where I'll probably be," Carter answered.

"Okay, Carter, your portion of the bill comes to $100," Charley interrupted.

"Wait a minute! I know you guys are trying to help with all that other stuff, but I know my part is more than $100."

"Nope, you're wrong. The register says $100. And it's not wise to upset the register by questioning its mathematical skills."

The Dedacciai was in the background, watching and listening to everything.

"Carter, just say thank you," he advised as he came out from his obscure vantage point with his shoes, jersey, water bottle, and riding shorts.

Charley rang up the Dedacciai, using Carter's account and applying a heavily reduced-price tag to his purchase as well. Carter handed the $100 bill he didn't use to the Dedacciai.

"Here's your money back," Carter offered.

"Why don't you keep it? I have a feeling you'll find a need for it."

With that, the four men had to engineer a way for Carter to carry his winnings to the homeless camp. Hidden in the back of the shop was an old bicycle buggy they found to haul everything to its planned destination.

"Okay, I'll see you soon," Brandon said as he returned to the shop.

"Dedacciai, why didn't you let me tell him about Chaplain?"

"I just didn't want Brandon to have unrealistic expectations of how Chaplain might look or how he would be. Carter, it's like when someone sees a movie and tells you it was one of the best movies they have ever seen. And they enthusiastically say that you must see it because you won't believe how great it is. But then you see it, and it just doesn't seem like it was that great.

"That's because you have these expectations that this movie will somehow change your life, but it ends up being a letdown. Yet ten years later, that same movie comes on when you're not expecting it, and you remember how it wasn't that good. But watching it now, the movie ends up being great, just like the person said it was initially — So that's why!"

"Damn, Dedacciai, can't you just once not make sense," Carter smirked.

"Not to change the subject of how much sense I make, but Brandon is freaking amazing with what he has overcome."

The Dedacciai paused as he heard his voice say "overcome" and reflected on his own mental state. The constant flow of horror that played in the backdrop of his mind had become his norm. But he had, in his own evaluation, overcome at least the ability to keep his personal horror playing only in the background and not focusing on it.

Carter's story was his focus, as well as doing good in Addison's name. The combination served him well toward his hopeful triumph to honestly be happy and not have this hypocritical feeling of happiness that he deserved an Academy Award for playing. Still, he was headed toward overcoming what Darius never could, which gave him a reason to keep moving forward. Soon, he returned from the mental evaluation of himself to continue the conversation.

"What Chaplain did for Brandon is miraculous, and I bet he has done that hundreds of times with people out here. Just think of all the people he can reach because of what you're doing for him. You should feel very proud of yourself. I told you yesterday I might not go today to rest, but that was before I knew Brandon's story. I wouldn't miss this for the world. Now, let's go get you some more perspective."

The shaking man who entered the darkened grassland last evening was no more. Today, he held his head up high without the weight of his metallic friend pulling it down. The two soon found themselves riding their bikes across the open field that had a familiarity about it and a positive neuro-association in Carter's nervous system.

As Carter made his way across the field, he acknowledged total strangers. He even acquired a new friend as a medium-sized golden retriever with matted fur took to his rear wheel.

"Hey, Dedacciai, look at me! I got myself a riding partner! Hey, boy!"

"Doesn't surprise me a bit. Dogs know good people when they smell them!"

As they entered the third trailhead north of SW 7th and Lee, no one was there. The two dismounted as the furry newcomer with big dim-brown eyes and a visible rib cage watched them with high hopes for food or attention, but hopefully both.

"Well, Carter, you seem to be making new friends everywhere you go. See if there's a collar with a name tag hidden underneath his fur."

Carter tussled through the matted fur and found nothing.

"I've never had a dog or any pet because Russell Ducane would never allow it. *'Cost too much damn money for what you get in return,'* he said half-jokingly. Regardless, nothing with fur or feathers ever lived in our house. Anyway, look how his ribcage is showing; we need to feed him."

"He definitely needs food. I'm sad that you never had a dog and sad for him that he doesn't have a family. I bet he did at one time; golden retrievers are one of the best breeds for families. But when you're poor and desperate, something must give. I bet someone dropped him out here, hoping he'd find a home. It appears you might have a doggy for a day. Maybe you should name him?" the Dedacciai suggested.

"It wouldn't be the first time this week I had to name something," Carter smirked. "And maybe this time it will turn out much better for me," he added, laughing.

"Haven't a clue what you're talking about," Dedacciai smirked back. "Well, my friend, if you feed him, he's going to be your friend for life, so he needs a good bicycle name, don't you think?"

Carter felt his hands vibrate over the ribcage of his malnourished friend as he looked at him. "Well, it's obvious what your name should be here in Armstrong country. Come on, Lance; let's start fixing some bicycles."

"Lance, now that's the perfect name; when our campmates get back, I bet they'll know if anyone has some dog food out here."

Carter removed his backpack and started finding makeshift ways to organize his tools as his new friend sniffed each one as part of a dog's protocol. The Dedacciai also explored the buggy of bicycle parts and worked to separate all the tires, tubes, tools, and accessories.

Carter's pop-up mobile bicycle repair was now in business. His first clients were three metal bicycles that he meticulously untangled from each other.

He decided to first work on Miami's blue Schwinn sting-ray bicycle, with a sparkly blue banana seat that Schwinn bicycles were so famous for back in the day.

With help from WD-40, the skilled mechanic removed the wheels from the frame, and in fifteen minutes, the old, rotted-out steel-belted tires were removed and replaced. He went the extra step of applying Armor All tire shine and made the wheels look wet-black and shiny, then cleaned and lubed the chain before truing the wheels. While truing the wheels, he couldn't help but remember the Dedacciai's late-night IHOP lessons. *There is a spoke for everything and to live a life of true.*

Carter smiled and enjoyed the process of returning the bike to its former glory as he wiped it down with metal cleaner to remove the rust. The Schwinn now had life breathed back into it, and it looked good — actually, it looked great. Better than Carter thought as he did one last wipe of the seat that returned it to its shiny, sparkling reality.

Carter found that Lance made it fun and was good company. They discovered their unique rhythm of working together as *pet, work, sniff, work, bark, work, and repeat* became the order of their working relationship.

He performed the same routine on Alabama and Chaplain's bicycles. But this time, he was in the middle of the repair as Lance barked and rushed to sniff the three campmates who returned from helping a distant camp dweller with his depression.

The sight of Carter working on their bikes produced exceptional levels of gratitude for the unexpected mechanic. As Miami looked closer at his blue bicycle glistening in the sunlight, his knees weakened. He quickly found himself on the ground, eye-level with his old metal friend, as he laid his head against the top crossbeam.

His eyes were closed, but underneath his eyelids, the real story of his kids before Katrina shone brightly. It was a magical time when a herd of Schwinn stingray bicycles made their way through the neighborhood streets of New Orleans as a family. His eyes leaked heavy tears as he watched the show play on the silver screen of his mind.

His two campmates were unsure what to do, as they had never seen Miami in this state, and Alabama wanted to hug his friend to make sure he was okay. But Chaplain stopped him quietly, not wanting the picture show of his mind to be interrupted. He wanted Miami to relive the good memories, not the ones that ended with the levee's failure.

Miami opened his eyes after a few minutes, pushed back up, and squared shoulder-to-shoulder with the mechanic. The others watched, waiting to see Miami's reaction. Miami was speechless — almost.

"What the hell happened to your face?"

"There he is!" Alabama said as *The Gambucci* made his triumphant return.

"Why, holy shit, Carter! Your punk ass went and did it! — Or is your hate sittin' in a drawer somewhere?"

Lance barked at Miami for using such a tone with his new human.

"Well, who's this tryin' to take up for you?"

"This is Lance, my new friend that followed us here. Guys, do you have any food we can feed him? Or know anyone who does?"

Chaplain spoke up. "Here, boy, follow me, Lance; I can find you something. Let's get you a water bowl started."

Carter saw Chaplain with new eyes and took in his compassion not only for others but for Lance. He looked forward to seeing his reunion with Brandon as he finished working on their bicycles.

Chaplain began walking with Lance but paused to turn around.

"Carter, I think your lack of hate is a good fit. After I get Lance settled, I'd like to hear more about how you did that."

Carter nodded.

"I want to help with the pooch," Alabama said as he followed the two into the camp.

"Damn you, Carter!" The Gambucci scorned, "We need to get somethin' straight. I don't need nobody seein' me get all up in my emotions. Them ass-holes might exploit my reputation as a hard ass. 'The Gambucci is The Gambucci.' Got it? Now, what can I do to help you finish?"

"Well, you could—"

"Holy crap!" was yelled from a distance as Alabama stumbled on a site worthy of his decibel usage. Miami, Carter, and the Dedacciai hustled into the camp to see what the fuss was about. There, the three campmates stood stunned as the Dedacciai bicycle stood proudly next to Carter's.

"That's some kind of beautiful shit!" Miami exclaimed, staring at the pair. "But you better lock that shit up before one of these crazies out here steals 'em. Surprised you even made it in here without your asses getting mugged."

Miami put thoughts into Carter's head about Brandon's 'field of desperation' statement and locked the bikes, then took a moment to search his backpack for his grandpa's brass knuckles — just in case.

"See, I knew you were royalty," Alabama declared. "Isn't that your name there on that frame? Is that what they do in your country, name a bicycle after you? What should we actually be calling you? Your Royal Dedacciai? — Your Dedacciousness? — Sir Baron von Dedacciai? — The Flying Dedacciai?"

"— '**Thee**' Dedacciai will suffice. '**Thee**' has a certain oomph to it, don't you think?"

Carter watched in wonderment and added their responses to the growing list of Dedacciai bicycle reactions in his mind.

"Okay, Carter, Lance is cared for and has food and drink. I'd like to hear more about what happened to your hate," Chaplain curiously inquired as Carter acknowledged the camp groupies that gathered.

"Well, guys — last night, the Dedacciai and I ended up at IHOP around 3 a.m. He started teaching me things and related life in a way I could understand by using a bicycle analogy to help explain everything." Carter related the story of his nose ring's memorial service and eulogy to his captive audience, then brought it to a close.

"All I can say is — it was super weird, yet amazing. It was the perfect ending to Naustris and a great start to rewriting my story. It's also why I'm here. This is my way of thanking you guys for last night. After hearing Chaplain say grace and learning that you could no longer ride to other campsites to preach, I wanted to do something to help. Those people need to hear your words. So, here I am."

Chaplain spoke, "Nice job, Dedacciai. A eulogy for a nose ring and referencing the amount of acid you produce while in a state of hate — now that's interesting. Do you mind if I borrow those little teaching nuggets to help others with hate? Approaching it from that perspective could be a game-changer. It sure worked for Carter."

"Absitively, you can! I would be honored."

As the men looked at the bicycles, a homeless lady appeared at the trailhead with her bike in tow that needed repair. She was thin, medium in stature, and wore a red sweater that had seen better days. A green, red, and blue plaid scarf adorned her neck, while a new pair of black sweats and blue tennis shoes finalized her ensemble.

"Excuse me, sir. I'm Julie. I saw you crossing the field earlier and followed you here. I saw you fixing these bikes — I thought I'd take a chance to see if you could fix mine. I'll understand if you can't or don't want to."

Miami immediately took over —

"Jules, absolutely, you can. In fact, text anyone in our community and tell them to get their bicycle asses over here pronto!"

Carter's adrenal glands surged from the thought of helping Julie and maybe others, so he finished the final repairs on Alabama and Chaplain's bicycles and moved on to Julie's bike. Carter had Julie help him move his tools and her bike out to the front of the trailhead so he could see when anyone else entered the field.

As he removed the wheels, he witnessed the field of dreams come to life as bicycle despair rolled in from every direction. While working, he noticed bikes were mainly ridden, some rolled, and others delivered out of truck beds and car trunks.

As Carter replaced Julie's brake cable, she stood silent with kind eyes and medium-length auburn hair that showed signs of frizz against a pale complexion. Her demeanor was meek, her confidence null, but her freckles plentiful — what little Orphan Annie would look like all grown up. While petting Lance, Julie's and Carter's eyes met.

"God bless you—?" her meek-sounding voice said loud enough with an inflection that signaled him to fill in the blank with his name.

"It's Carter."

"Carter, that's a nice name. God bless you, Carter, for doing this for me."

"I heard Miami call you Jules. Is that what you go by?"

"Miami calls everybody something out here. It's Julie, but Jules is fine. He's pretty gruff and all, but he does as much as anybody to protect us. If you're unfortunate enough to be out here, you definitely want him on your side.

"As crazy as that hair looks, he has that crazy inside of him, especially when justice doesn't go like he thinks it should. Trust me; his Gambucci persona is not something you want to mess with."

Jules looked down the trailhead back at Miami's bike.

"Just God bless you for fixing his bike; it looks great. That bike is all he has to remember his kids by; what a tragic story. He used to give me rides to the grocery store on that long banana seat before his bike broke. It was a challenge with all that crazy hair flying back in my face, but it also made it fun.

"Whenever I needed groceries for my five-year-old daughter and me, he was always willing to take me—"

Jules sat down as tears rolled down her pale skin at the mention of her daughter. Carter stopped the repair and watched her sadness take over.

"We had to run away in the middle of the night from a very abusive relationship with a man I took up with. He started out nice enough, but it went south quickly. I took my daughter, and we first went to the mission in Austin, but he found me and threatened us. They had to call the police and everything, so I couldn't stay there. Then, I heard about this little camp community outside of Austin with a good reputation. It got a 4.5-star rating on Yelp."

Carter looked at her funny. "Is that a thing?"

"No, it's not a thing. I was trying to make a silly. At least, that's what my daughter used to call it. *Sillies* help take away the real pain, if even for a moment. What I'd give to hear my daughter say that again." Her tears were thick with emotion.

"They took her from me! Child Protective Services took her because I couldn't provide for her, and now she's in the foster care system. If only I could get my life together. This bike is my only transportation for now. If I could keep it running, maybe I could hold a job, any job, and possibly dream of a future.

"I don't seem to have enough in me to do it for now, but who knows, maybe this is the day. The day when all my *One Day* I'll do this, and *One Day* I'll do that propositions finally turn into my *Day One,* I did this, and *Day Two,* I did that. That is my elusive dream out here in this field." She continued crying while keeping her eyes closed or looking down.

"Wow, Jules — thanks for sharing that. I'm so sorry about everything you're going through. Have you talked with Chaplain about this? I learned today that he helped a friend of mine while living on the streets, so maybe he could also help you?"

"I've talked to him a little bit. He's kind of part of my *One Day* narrative that I'll get my life together by talking to him more often. And maybe I can now since my bicycle is being fixed. He helped me a little by giving me some books on writing poems. He thought I could write about my daughter, and it would help. Truthfully, it did. But then I stopped because I simply lost hope."

"Jules, earlier today, I told someone I was coming out here to fix some bicycles. He mentioned that this was not only a field of despair but a field of dreams for a better life. What if you're right? What if today is a *Field of Dreams* day for you? A *Day One,* as you put it. I know you don't know me; I'm just a guy out in this field fixing your bike, but I'm out here because I want to rewrite my life story as well."

Carter paused while his eyes presented a more meaningful look. "You know what, Jules? If I think about it — I'm homeless myself. Do you see that man over there?" pointing toward the Dedacciai. "I met him two days ago after I had a huge fight with my dad and moved out. Truthfully, I was scared to death after that happened, but that man rode into my life, literally. Ever since then, I haven't had the chance to think about myself because I was too busy worrying about him. The thing is, that complete stranger somehow gave me hope when I thought I only had despair. What I'm trying to say is that I want to be that complete stranger who gives you hope.

"Jules, I'm discovering something out here in this field of dreams and despair; I'm discovering that bicycle repair is something valuable I have to offer this world. The weird thing is, I've always hated my life because of my bicycle. — But now, what I thought was the most broken part of my life is actually the best part of my life. I just needed the gift of perspective to realize it. Jules, look at me." Carter extended his hand to help her stand. "Try your brakes now."

When she did, her face lit up.

"Your bike is all better, just like you will be someday. Because from this day on, you don't have to worry about your bike. I promise you; I will work this out so you can get your bike fixed whenever there is a problem — I know a guy." Carter smirked.

"I've always wanted to say that, but I've never had a reason until now — until you. But really, I do know a guy. He's even going to come out and help me in a little while. I'm going to talk to him about your situation. So, the next time you have a problem, come see Miami; we'll have a plan in place to get you fixed up."

Jules extended her arms, "Is it too much to ask for a hug?" she voiced in her meek way.

"Not at all. I've only learned in the last two days about the power and the importance of a hug."

"Good, because I need to hug you. It would mean the world to me."

She fulfilled her statement as she held on much tighter than he thought — all the while crying and repeating her mantra. "God bless you for this; God bless you, Carter."

While hugging him, Jules told Carter that inquiring for her bike to be fixed earlier was a rather bold ask for her, spawned from her desperate state. She was usually timid, insecure, and unsure of anything.

Jules finally mustered the strength to let go of him. Carter saw the slightest glimmer of hope that wasn't there in her eyes before. She then walked her bicycle through the field, glancing back periodically, then into the distance, to hopefully find her elusive Day One.

The theory of Dedacciai's "Bicycles are people too" took on a new meaning for Carter. Bicycles were more important to the homeless than he ever knew. They were almost family in an askew version of how the homeless experienced life. He was learning that a bicycle wasn't just a bicycle. It was transportation; it was a chance at a job; it was a chance for Julie to someday reunite with her daughter. It was hope for a better tomorrow.

As this realization took hold, Carter looked at the growing field of Dreams and Despair. The text messages produced approximately twenty bikes in the approximate thirty minutes it took to fix Jules' bicycle. The number grew close to forty bikes strong waiting in the Field of Dreams and Despair within the hour.

Carter's ability stood ready to do battle with all the repairs. Carter smiled inside, knowing Brandon did indeed know what would happen here. Without panicking, Carter recruited the Dedacciai and his three campmates to go out and get people's wheel sizes and to assess whether the wheels just needed air or needed to be repaired. If they needed repair, they would grab the correct size tires and tubes and place them with the bicycles.

Carter knew something was happening within him. He felt a new spoke on his life wheel. A spoke he never had before — Inspiration. And from this Field of Desperation came Carter's Field of Inspiration from what Jules said, when "One Day" transforms into "Day One."

He now knew that somehow, someway, today was a "Day One" in this field — his field. And it was not a place where dreams came to die. Not today anyway, and not on his watch, as Carter took command of his field.

"Okay, people. Listen up!" Carter yelled with strength and authority. "My name is Carter; I'm here to help everyone as much as I can with your bicycles. It will probably be a long day out here, so everyone needs to be patient. Now, how many people out here could fix their own bicycles if they had the parts? Raise your hands." He looked out and counted twelve. "Okay, would you twelve please line up over here by Miami."

Miami instinctively raised his hand.

"We're going to concentrate on getting your bikes fixed first, but only if you agree to then help everyone else in the field with your mechanical skills. Do you agree?" Carter waited for confirmation. "Good; this way, we can get everyone's bike fixed quicker if we do this as a team. Does everyone understand? Thank you. Now, let's do this!"

As the sea of bicycles parted, Carter noticed Brandon sitting on his bike in the back after witnessing his battlefield deployment command strategy. Carter quickly called to the Dedacciai to inform him of Brandon's arrival.

The two greeted him as he rode up on an expensive Specialized cross bike that had seen its fair share of competition trophies.

"Dudes, nice turnout! What did I tell you? Not your grandparents' homeless. Carter, did you even know that guy I just heard taking charge out here before today? I didn't realize how much of you was hidden behind your little metal friend, but I like what I see. Now, enough of that before your head explodes. Let me get my stuff set up so we can get busy. I'll help get the self-mechanics started over here."

From behind Brandon, a distant past reemerged as a soothing voice with a recognizable timbre spoke. *"Vedo ancora andare in bici. Ciao mio Vecchio amico stai bene. E Bello vederti."*

"Che, CAZZO! Oh, scusa, Chaplain. Tipo!" Brandon dismounted his bicycle with authority, and the momentum was too great to stop his hug from plunging the two to the ground. Screams of joy thrust out of Brandon's soul as the two returned vertically.

"YOU! YOU! YOU! YOU! Changer of lives - You! Chaplain, I can't believe this! You look awesome! You hardly changed a bit. I can't believe the awesomeness of seeing my mentor dude again. How are you?"

"I can't complain, and I've learned not to. I'm still in the business of helping others like your former self out here. You know better than anyone; it's what keeps me alive. And keeps me from the bombs."

"Chaplain, don't take this the wrong way because I'm not glad you're still out here, but I am happy you're still helping people. I've tried reaching you many times, but your phone number stopped working and eventually went to somebody else.

"I got so much stuff to tell you that I don't know where to begin. Let me start by telling you how freaking happy I am and how alive I feel because of you. And I'm so grateful for what you did for my dad when everything went down. As the years passed, I realized how significant it was that you prayed for my dad and gave him a funeral. And just how fortunate I was that you took me under your wing and taught me how to handle my mind afterward. Dude, those brain exercises honestly helped me reboot my brain. One of the biggest lessons for me was training me to empty my mind and how that enabled my brain to reach full processing speed by deleting unnecessary memories."

"Yes, if people understood that although we call it mindfulness, it's actually mind-emptiness or mind-calmness. That's when you get to be in control and reach your full juggernaut potential. You seem to have done just that. I'm incredibly proud of you, Brandon."

"Chaplain, if it weren't for you, there would have been no relief, no emotional morphine for me. You were both my hero and my heroin, especially at a time when I needed both to survive." Brandon said sincerely, powerfully, and with no surfer slang as Chaplain responded.

"It's hard for me to accept hero status. I'm no hero, not yet, and not until I've deleted the bombs from my mind and the ones out of my nervous system. But helping others is still the main substance that keeps me going around here."

"Chaplain, if helping others gives you substance, you should have plenty of it because those brain exercises, as well as those aptitude tests, did help me to succeed. And I worked at a bicycle shop like you said I should. While there, this dude, Charley, approached me and asked me to be his business partner. So here we are in Georgetown, with one of the biggest bike shops and doing an awesome business.

"Then today, this Carter dude said he was coming out here to fix three bicycles, and I know how it works out here. I knew he would be overloaded if anyone saw him. So, my biz partner and I gave him extra bicycle stuff — just in case. I can't believe yours is one of the bicycles he came out here to fix."

"That's how the man works — Mysterious ways and all. Brandon, it's wonderful you came out here to help Carter. Proves you have good in you, which I never once doubted," Chaplain touted.

"Well, he seems to be 'crushing' it out here! I didn't realize he had this much Kahuna Juice inside him until I saw it with my own eyes. The dude has totally taken control out here, I mean, like totally!"

Chaplain interjected, "I think everyone is getting restless. How about we get you set up fixing bikes, and then we can continue our visit?"

Carter looked at the Dedacciai. "Wow, they picked up right where they left off. Now, I understand why you didn't want me to say anything. Once again, you weirdly make sense. Yeah, yeah, yeah — look at all that perspective, I know."

"Carter, your 'perspective' spoke has served you well. By the way, what made you step up and take control like that? Because whatever it was, you were impressive. And that's coming from me, the Dedacciai," he winked.

"It was Jules. She told me her story while I fixed her bike. She told me her own little analogy of life. Which is how to transform our 'One Day I'll do this' mantra into 'Day One I did that,' which hopefully leads to a 'Day Two.' It made me think about how true that is."

"Ah, yes, I see it now. You were inspired. The 'perspective' spoke along with the 'inspiration' spoke. Now, that's a bicycle wheel any man would want to have. Now, we better get back to it. I will resume my duties, Commander." The Dedacciai headed back out among the field of bicycles.

Carter remembered seeing the first bicycle to ride up while working on Julie's bike, so he signaled the rather large-in-stature man to roll his bike up to him.

A deep, gravelly voice rolled out of the intense 6'4" man. "God doesn't hate me; He just hates my sins. At least that's what I learned from Kairos."

Lance made his presence known as he rejoined Carter with a bark and immediately gave the man a good sniff over.

"His name is Lance; he seems to be my helper today. So, who's Kairos? Is Kairos someone like Chaplain? Because that sounds like something Chaplain would say."

"No, but that's a rather good guess. I take it you haven't been around a field of people like this before, have you?"

"No, sir, not really. I came out here to help with three bikes, which grew to this. How did you hear about getting your bike fixed?"

"My friend forwarded me a text from a lady who texted him about it. He knew my bike needed help."

"Well, what's your name?"

"Robert Greene. You think you can get this metal turd to roll down the road again?"

"Not sure; let's turn her upside down and look. — Hmmm, your inner chainring is cracked, your crank arm is bent, and your front derailleur isn't shifting to the big chainring."

"Can it be fixed, Doc?"

"Fixed is a stretch, but I think some aggressive hammer therapy might convince this bike to roll down the street from point A to point A½."

"Sounds good, Doc, that's all I need. To get from A to A½."

"So, Mr. Greene, you never finished telling me who Kairos was — the guy who said that Chaplain-like God stuff."

"Doc, Kairos isn't a person. It's the prison ministry that helped me when I was doing time." He watched as Carter tightened up and got quiet.

"Doc — don't do that. I can see your Adam's apple doing a hard swallow. Anytime someone hears you did time, they assume you killed someone — which I did," and a few long seconds drew out. "Just messing with you. I meant to say, which I 'almost' did." He used exaggerated air quotes to make his point.

Carter's face was ghost-white.

"I'm messing with you, Doc. You're safe, man. It's just a little street humor to man-you-up a little, especially if you're coming out here to do God's work. I'm just going to come out with it. It was for burglary and armed robbery. But I didn't kill nobody. I did twenty-five years in the slammer for it. I was a young and stupid punk kid and a bad-ass dude.

"Just didn't have that proverbial Father figure I needed. At least, that's what my Kairos ministry volunteer told me. This man, John, came out every month to see me. Gave up time with his wife and family to see an unworthy nobody like me. That changed my life in prison. Gave me somethin' to hope for one day. And this is it, the dream.

"I might sound like I'm making light of this. But being out here with this metal turd is a fantasy compared to prison. So, yeah, God doesn't hate me; He just hates my sins. And church-goin' people like yourself who come here and help people like us are extra special. Doc, it helps way, way, more than you could ever know. Yep, indeed. — Livin' the dream out here."

Carter thought it was strange to be considered a church-goin' person but didn't want to tell Robert how he had never been in a church, weirdly afraid Robert would judge him. Besides, Carter's Adam's apple had enough of a workout trying to show Robert how he wasn't nervous. So, as calmly as he could, he explained what he had done.

"Okay, I removed your inner chainring and fixed the front derailleur so that it will stay on the big chainring for now. If you ever want to buy an inner chainring, any bicycle shop could get an inexpensive one and install it easily. I also knocked some sense into your crank arm and got it back where it belongs. Your turd can now make it to point A½."

"You did wonders, Doc. God bless you, my man, and Merry Chris-tober. Never too early to start Christmas, you know."

As Robert rode off, Carter shook his hands toward the ground, walked around the corner, and sagged against a tree. He closed his eyes and tried to get a hold of himself. But it didn't help rid the guilt. He knew he was judging Robert for being in prison. His intensely overwhelming and intimidating size perhaps amplified his guilt for fearing the stranger.

But the actuality was the man was nothing but kind and truthful, and he had a sense of humor. Carter continued to breathe deeply and shake his hands to release the tension. A loud slurp began as Lance licked his hand to comfort his human.

Carter bent down and looked into the big brown eyes of his friend, "You're a good boy, Lance." And he licked his master's face to let him know he, too, was a good boy.

"Hey, Lance, let's check on Brandon and Chaplain."

They found the pair who had done a great job getting all the parts for the abled mechanics. Even more surprising was that most were already out in the field helping others with their bicycles.

"Carter, Dude! Your Kahuna Juice levels are off the chart with your mad organization and leadership skills. And I'm stoked about what an incredible triage bike mechanic you are. We could use a good mechanic dude at the shop to help lighten the load if you're interested?"

"Brandon, are you serious? That sounds great! But I want to take this bicycle trip to Dallas with the Dedacciai. Can I give you my answer when I get back?"

"Sure, Dude. And to sweeten the pot, Lance would make a great mascot to have around the shop. Besides, golden retrievers are great with kids, and I'd like to help get some meat on his bones."

The Dedacciai stood within earshot and heard Brandon's offer. He was proud of how far Carter had come in a few short days. He headed over to the three campmates.

"Gentlemen, I'd like to propose something. I'd like for Carter to be able to come back to Lance when we get back from our trip. I know it's a big ask, and I'm not sure Carter might want this, but I'd like him to decide for himself. Could I give you some money for dog food and to keep him at your camp? Lance would be good for Carter when I'm gone because his life works best when he has someone or something to care for that occupies his time. He has a need that he never knew he needed until now. Is this something you can do for him?"

"Hell yeah, it is!" said The Gambucci. "I owe that dude for fixing my bike."

"Dedacciai, I couldn't agree more," Chaplain added. "I was going to suggest the same to everybody. Lance is exactly what Carter needs when you're gone. Which will be sad for all of us."

"Well, I don't know what I'm returning to in my life or if I even have a life. But I want this for Carter, and I want to thank the three of you, in advance, for taking Carter under your wing when I'm gone."

"I'm already sad just thinking about having no more royalty around here," Alabama interjected. "I just want you to know that accepting my invitation at IHOP that day did wonders for me and for all of us."

"Well, Alabama, the thing is, your invitation was a great blessing for both Carter and me. Just look at him over there in this field of bicycles. Does he resemble anything like the scared young man you met?

"You never know how the simplest thing can turn into a life-changing event. I love you guys for everything you've done for us." The Dedacciai handed Chaplain a $100 bill. "Here's some money for room and board and to buy dog food for Lance while we're gone."

"You know this is way too much, right?"

"Not to me. Treat yourselves to a nice dinner with anything leftover or whatever you want to do with it. Now, let's get back to helping everyone out here."

After his rounds, Carter returned to his workstation, where he found a young couple anxiously awaiting his arrival.

"Sir, thank you for being out here. This is my wife, Cathy, and I'm Tim. Timothy Morton. These bicycles were given to us by a friend who said to get our butts out here because a bicycle mechanic was here fixing bikes.

"We don't know anything about them except they don't work. Is there any hope of getting them fixed? My wife and I are having a hard time right now, and we need transportation. Our credit union informed us that they're repossessing our car this week, and we're desperate. We have a place we can barely afford, and on top of everything, we just found out we're pregnant. We can't lose our jobs, so this will be our only way to get to work." The man paused to breathe. "Sorry, I'm very anxious and scared of losing everything."

"Honey, breathe; this poor guy doesn't want to hear about all our problems."

"Cathy, is it? I'm Carter. It's okay to tell me your story. I'd like to hear."

"Oh, sir, God bless you for that." She responded, "And God bless the way you are with everybody. We watched you while we waited, and your attitude toward people out here is wonderful. You are such a huge blessing to everyone, and getting these bikes working would be a huge help to us. We really need a break. We need a win at something and are hoping you'll be the one to give it to us."

"Cathy, Tim, let's see what I can do to give you that win." Carter took a closer look at the bikes. "Wow, by the way, I love these bicycles."

"Thanks, I looked them up online," Tim responded. "One's a vintage 1974 Kool Lemon yellow Schwinn Continental, and the other is a Sunset-Orange Schwinn Varsity."

"Well, all I know is that they are way cool and might be in great condition underneath all this dust. Do you mind if I show my friends? I'll be right back."

Carter ran over to the Dedacciai, who happened to be in the same vicinity as Brandon.

"Hey, guys, I want you to see a couple of vintage bicycles I think you'd enjoy. I think they may be kind of rare. Collectors' bikes even, come see."

As the three approached, the Dedacciai knew precisely what he was about to see, but Brandon was the first to comment.

"Dudes, these are some awesome bikes. And they look like they could be in great shape once Carter gets them going. By the way, my name is Brandon. I'm one of the owners of the Cycledelic Bike Therapy shop here in town. If you want to sell these someday, I'll give you a fair payday, so try to keep them in good shape if you can."

The Dedacciai reminisced, "You're not going to believe this, but I owned this exact bicycle when I was young. It was the first 10-speed bicycle I ever bought."

The group saw the Dedacciai fade back into his childhood memory.

"This gentleman is a 1974 Schwinn Varsity Sport bicycle in Sunset Orange. I knew from the moment I saw one in my local bicycle shop that it would be mine. I even memorized the pamphlet, and I quote: —

"'Schwinn's most popular 10-speed lightweight bicycle with so many features usually found on bikes costing much more! Diamond-style carbon-steel frame with Twin-Stik gear shift controls and a 10-speed derailleur that handles the 38 to 100 gear ratios, 27"x 1 ¼" gum wall tires, drop handlebars, and dual position brake levers in beautiful sunset orange.'"

The owners of the two bicycles somehow felt better about what they thought was a desperate situation. They felt a sense of pride and hope and looked forward to seeing the bikes cleaned up and working.

"Well, Carter, what are you waiting for? These bikes won't fix themselves," said Tim.

The Dedacciai watched as the man's wife smiled and laughed at her husband. He also remembered when he said similar quips to make his Bellavia laugh.

He watched as Lance stood by Carter's side and had a sense of belonging in his dim brown eyes. He thought of Zilla and hoped she was earning the $1,500 purchase price to comfort his Bellavia.

Please, God, be with that woman. Please allow her to look past my stupid act of pride and forgive the unforgivable. Please give me a home to return to and a family that can heal. And please take care of your newest angel. Please, God, please.

As the Dedacciai emerged from his silence, a hand rested on his shoulder, followed by a soothing voice.

"I know where you went, and He is listening. Keep the faith, my brother."

The Dedacciai turned to see Chaplain, who understood the inner turmoil of having wisdom and nonsense living side by side within the psyche. The two gave the proverbial man-nod and then continued their roles in the field.

"Dedacciai, before you go, I want to meet my customers here. Tim and Cathy, this is my friend, the Dedacciai. He's like royalty out here." Carter touted.

"Please, don't listen to him. I put my pants on like everybody else out here — backward."

Cathy and Tim laughed.

"I forgot to mention he's a professional weirdo — Dedacciai, by the way; Cathy and Tim are having a baby."

"You are? That's wonderful; congratulations. Do you have a name picked out?" the Dedacciai queried.

"I do," Cathy replied. "I grew up in the foster care system. My mom and dad died in a car wreck when I was five. I had no siblings or family members I know of left. My mother's name was Addison Monroe, and at one time, I had a foster mother I was close with named Addison. She helped me a lot when I entered the system, but she died when I was fourteen. Anyway, I think Addison must be my little angel's name if we have a girl and Andrew if it's a boy." Cathy saw Dedacciai's reaction, as he seemed very emotional and lowered himself to the ground.

"Sir, I'm so sorry; are you okay? Did I upset you?"

Brandon and Carter attended to the Dedacciai to make sure he was alright. The Chaplain, Miami, and Alabama showed up as well as Gambucci started in—

"Carter, what the hell did you say to him this time?"

"There he is!" Alabama once again alerting Gambucci's mental arrival.

"Dedacciai, sir, I'm so sorry to upset you," Cathy interrupted Miami's take. "I was the one who upset the man, not Carter."

The Dedacciai gathered himself and looked up at Cathy with the remnants of tears in his eyes.

"Cathy, please, believe me, you did not upset me in any way. You reminded me of a blessing in a very profound way. Believe me when I say this. You could not have picked a more angelic name for your daughter or son. I hope the good Lord blesses you both." The Dedacciai stood and gathered himself. "Now, Carter, get busy doing what you do so Cathy and Tim can show me their bikes before they go."

Cathy couldn't help herself as she hugged the Dedacciai and whispered in his ear, "Sir, I don't know what you're going through, but there is always a rainbow after the worst of storms."

Of all the phrases she could have said, the Dedacciai thought.

"Cathy, your little angel already has a most beautiful voice." He whispered back. "Your angel will be such a blessing, and you will be one terrific mother."

The two let go after sharing their momentary whispers.

"Okay, Carter, you heard the man; these bicycles aren't going to fix themselves. Let's get to it and get these things rolling," Gambucci commanded.

An hour and a half later, two vintage Schwinn bicycles, accompanied by their proud owners, came to show Brandon and the Dedacciai Carter's handy work.

"AWESOME!" Brandon exclaimed as he saw the bicycles in their full glory. "Holy freaking moly, Carter! This is impressive, dude! You have to come work for us!"

"Tim and Cathy, I know I said I would give you a good payday if you ever wanted to sell these. But I have an offer you can't refuse. I'm prepared to trade you two brand-new city bikes I think will be much more useful for your commute to work. And you'll be able to carry things to work much easier with these bicycles, and they'll have a warranty.

"Trust me; these bicycles are what you truly need and will not require near the maintenance of these bikes. Also, when you are further along with your pregnancy, you will be thanking me. I'll make sure and get you the most comfortable seat possible. I'll also give you $750 on top of that for these bicycles. Guys, I have to have these bicycles, and you can visit them any time you wish."

Tim interjected, "Make it a thousand, and you got yourself a deal. That will totally help us buy a crib and baby stuff."

"Totally, dude! You got yourself a deal."

The two high-fived each other as they worked out the details of their transaction.

Cathy came over to the Dedacciai for one more whisper.

"I felt almost hopeless when this day started, and somehow, we're ending up with a crib. What an unexpected blessing this day has brought. I'll be praying for you, Mr. Dedacciai, and I'll think of you often when my angel arrives. Whatever I reminded you of, I hope you get what you need to comfort yourself."

The Dedacciai had no words big enough to thank Cathy and broke the unwritten rule of manhood by giving her a man-nod for her kindness as they walked away.

After witnessing the event, Brandon became silently animated as he waited for Cathy and Tim to get out of earshot before confronting the Dedacciai.

"Dude! What the freakin' hell did you just do? I just saw you give that woman a man-nod. Don't you know that will unravel the fabric of life and tear the spacetime continuum apart? Dude, don't ever, and I mean EVER, out the man-nod like that again. It's man's finest invention yet. It's the one thing we hold dear that is ours and ours alone. It's the one thing we have to show another man immense love, affection, appreciation, and emotion — yet it displays none of what it conveys.

"Besides, women have 'The Look' that they use on everybody, including animals! It's not gender or even species-specific like the man-nod. Think about it; how many times has your wife or girlfriend said, 'I'm fine' with their lips, yet a few inches above, her eyes have said — 'How stupid can you possibly be? I'm the furthest thing from fine!' — or 'You ain't ever getting that again' — or 'I'm not your mother!' and finally — 'You're MOTHER said WHAT about me?'

"And, gentlemen, how often has a woman said to another woman, 'Oh, I love your haircut,' or 'I love those shoes,' or 'That dress looks so cute on you.' Then turn around and give you a look that says, 'That haircut, those shoes, or that dress looks hideous?

"There isn't a man alive who hasn't experienced 'The Look' in some way, shape, form, or fashion. It's impossible not to because they have a look for *everything*. —But the nod…That's ours! And no woman is ever supposed to see that and know that we are emotional creatures.

"What the freaking hell is wrong with you? This could put man back centuries! I'm telling ya, dude; it could return us to the tree where Adam and Eve started this mess. Which I'm pretty damn sure started with Eve giving Adam *the first look* that lingered just a little too long, making him bite the apple in the first place.

"Let's face it, dudes; ever since the apple debacle, women have had a hard time choosing what to eat or picking a restaurant because the first time they did, they doomed humanity! Only this time, we're the ones who will have to carry the emotional burden for the great civilizations to come — and all because you gave a woman the man-nod which has been solely ours — until today!"

Carter was stunted in thought, not realizing Brandon was just as weird as the Dedacciai, who made a feeble attempt at defending his actions.

"Gentleman, I understand the man-nod is one of the greatest forces on the planet, but you must understand, there's an angel involved. For that very reason, Cathy deserved to be shown the *nod*. However, it is possible my emotions clouded my decision-making ability.

"I have a friend from yesteryear; his name is Professor Miguel. He is a quantum mechanics savant. I assure you that he will fix the spacetime continuum and restore us, men, back to a noble normal. If I make it through this journey to Dallas, I promise I will reunite with him and figure out the quantum physics and mechanics of my mistake. If not, I will go before the Universal Man Council to shamesplain everything. If I must endure an epic punishment, then so be it. But until then, I think it best if we all go to the grave with this incident and never speak of it again."

The three shared a three-way man-nod event to close the matter.

"What did I tell you, Carter? When the going gets weird — the weird turn pro! Brandon, speaking of which, I'd be honored if you joined my Pro Weirdo League. We meet on Tuesdays at 7 p.m."

Carter couldn't contain himself. "I'm extremely worried about you two. You truly are so unbelievably freaking weird. Besides, aren't I supposed to be the dysfunctional one here? Why are you guys stealing my thunder?"

The three couldn't keep up the façade and burst out laughing as another round of man-nods was earned before they all returned to what they were doing.

"Dedacciai, is there a spoke for that? And is the weirdo spoke all crazy and spirally looking? How your wheels roll down the road is such a mystery." Carter chuckled before resuming his rounds.

As he went around the field with Lance as his shadow, Carter was amazed at how fast the bicycle field mechanics could fix their bicycles and help others do the same.

He was on top of the world with the feeling of accomplishment. His organizational skills did indeed come to life. He was somehow a born leader; he just didn't realize it until this moment. He was passionate about helping these people fix their bikes and began thinking he didn't want this to be a one-time thing.

"Hey, Miami," Carter summoned, "we need to talk."

"Hey, nobody talks to Miami without going through The Gambucci — especially when he hears the words 'We need to talk…'"

Lance barked at Gambucci, instinctually knowing he was a smart-ass.

"Miami, Gambucci, or whoever I'm dealing with, you're becoming as weird as the Dedacciai."

"Why, thank you. We all need to strive to reach new levels of weirdness. Now, me and all the voices in my head will listen."

"Oh, in that case. — Attention, all people living in Gambucci's head, I have an idea. I want everyone who came here today to be able to get their bicycles repaired, even when I'm not here to help. And I want you all to be a part of it and help me. What do you think?"

"Carter, you got my attention. I'm listening. Now, what do you have in mind?"

"Well, for starters, I want you to get everyone's number out here who is a mechanic. I'd like you to be the go-between for when people need help and me. The first step will be to have one of our twelve field mechanics look at the bike and determine if they can fix it and what parts they need. Then you can let me know, and I'll try to get the parts. If I can, I want you to pick them up from Brandon at the shop and take them to the mechanic assigned to the job.

"I'll try to come out on a more consistent basis and maybe have a first Saturday of the month type of thing where all the mechanics come together…You and I could do this together. Miami Gambucci Rowland Hawthorne — what do you think?"

"What do I think? I thinks I want what you have. I didn't get to tell you earlier, but what you did to my bike and how you came out here and surprised us all, I don't think I've ever felt more grateful for anything in my life. I'm shocked by your punk-ass mechanical know-hows. You did me a solid today, so hell yeah, consider me in!"

Gambucci once again gave his signature gesture punch to Carter's arm.

This time, Lance took up for his human and playfully chewed on Gambucci's punching arm.

"This is an awesome dog you got here – too bad you can't keep him."

"I know. Lance has made being out here a lot of fun. I've never had a pet before. I didn't realize how fast you can get attached." Carter got on the ground and let Lance lick his face, all the while telling him what a good boy he was.

The three returned to the bicycle field triage unit. They continued fixing the bicycles that needed more time to repair than those that only required minor adjustments.

Time passed, and they had completed the last repair of what must have been forty or more bicycle patients.

"Dudes, this has been super awesome!" Brandon boasted. "Chaplain, seeing you again and helping all these people while they told me their stories has been an incredibly emotional ride. Lots of twists and turns, just like my cyclocross courses."

Brandon hugged Chaplain and had a hard time letting go.

"You, my friend, are a huge part of my success journey. You have my number; don't you dare lose it. Let me know if you need anything, and I mean anything!"

A round of man-nods ensued, and Brandon rode off.

"Okay, Miami, I'm entrusting the remaining bicycle parts over to your care," Carter said as he bent down for one last emotional goodbye to Lance.

"I wish I could take you with me, boy. You've been awesome. I'm sure going to miss you," and Lance tried to lick his master's face.

"Guys, I don't know what to do. I need you to hold him until we get away."

"We got you covered," Miami said. "Don't worry; we'll find him a place while you're gone," and he gave a private nod toward the Dedacciai, confirming his plan.

There was a special bond among them, for this day would be etched permanently into the history of their minds. Because of them, the Field of Dreams became a reality — even if only for a day.

It was a little after five as Carter and the Dedacciai began walking their bicycles out of the camp. Lance did a sudden launch and escaped from Miami to catch Carter at the end of the trailhead, where he had learned about perspective.

Carter got on the ground one last time with his canine friend. "I don't know where you came from, boy, but I think you blessed me today."

He recounted the number of times he'd heard people wanting him blessed for helping them. "I think you helped me understand something important today, the meaning of the word 'blessing.' I love you, boy."

Lance got in his final licks of Carter's face as Miami walked up the trailhead to retrieve him. Miami paused for them to finish their goodbyes without any smart-ass remarks to ruin the moment.

Alabama nudged Chaplain. "Why, I'll be a monkey's uncle!" as they witnessed Miami, not Gambucci-up the moment.

"Is Miami dying? That is the only explanation that makes sense. Maybe he thinks this is his way of getting into Heaven."

They smiled and watched the tender goodbye from a distance.

Carter finished and made sure Miami had a firm hold on Lance so that he couldn't escape.

"Which hotel are you staying at again?" Miami asked before leaving.

"The Lancaster Landing, room #555. Why?"

"No reason, just couldn't remember."

"Miami, I'll contact you when I return from Dallas. I'm looking forward to working on this project together."

"Me, too. Now get your honky ass out of here."

"There he is," Alabama hollered in the distance as he and the Dedacciai rolled their bikes away and left the Field of Dreams and Despair.

Chapter Seventeen

Them Life Dominoes

The men arrived back at their hotel. As they accompanied their bicycles into the room, the Dedacciai noticed the clock's display at 5:43 p.m. No sooner than he walked in the door, the Dedacciai needed to exit.

"Carter, I need to get something from downstairs; I'll be back."

"Do you want me to go with you?"

"No, I'm fine; I got this. I'll be back."

"Well, the last two times you exited this place without me, I somehow got involved in some sort of life-altering adventure. Are you sure I can't go?"

"Not really, but if you're going to tag along, make yourself useful and get us some more toothpaste, mouthwash, and shampoo."

It was 5:56 p.m. as the Dedacciai exited the antique telephone booth and saw Carter standing in the lobby with the hygiene items needed for their last night.

"What were you doing in there?" Carter asked.

"Oh, I just needed to emerge from a telephone booth to see if my Superman outfit still works. — Apparently, it's broken."

"YOU! - ARE! - SO! - WEIRD!" Carter said emphatically, prompting a jeopardy-style round of questioning.

"Dedacciai, at what age did you realize you weren't like other humans?"

"What is three years of age for 600?"

"Are there others like you who aren't like other humans?"

"What is Wolfrem Miguel, a.k.a. Professor Miguel for 1000?"

"Quantum Physics, Professor Miguel? Is he a real person? I thought you were making him up during your 'pro-weirdo time' with Brandon."

"Oh, no, unfortunately, he's real, alright." The Dedacciai wandered off mentally to recall his first encounter with his longtime friend.

"We met back in high school in Enid, Oklahoma, at the Tri-State Music Festival and became fast friends. I guess we have been a couple of strange ones from the moment we first met. I introduced myself as Groucho Extendo. Groucho was my nickname back then."

"You — Groucho...?"

"I know, right? Anyway, it came up in our very first conversation that his dad had bought a pair of Honda ATV three-wheelers with the old-style balloon tires. I said, 'Challenge accepted' and invited myself to come and show him how to ride them. Of course, that was before I knew he lived in Fredericksburg, TX, and I lived in Oklahoma City at the time.

"But I was a kid of my word and worked it out to take a Greyhound bus to visit him. We had more fun riding those darn things, and what made it even better was that it had rained the day before, so when we finished, we were covered in mud."

"That sounds like a blast." Carter injected.

"It was, it really was. Anyway, in college, we started riding bikes together. Miguel was the one who convinced me to ride my first 100-mile bike ride from Oklahoma City to Enid, and we ate at the same restaurant where we first met. He became a professor at The University of Texas, and that's when I started calling him Professor Miguel. He truly was a quantum physics and quantum mechanics savant.

"Miguel was an extraordinarily private and strange person, and he was extremely German. He used to wear kilts for some reason, something about his genetics or German clan's colors; I'm not sure why. But he would go out in public like it was no big deal to celebrate events that were above my pay grade to try and explain.

"It's sad, but we lost touch years ago. Life just gets in the way sometimes. I have no idea what he's doing these days; heck, I didn't know what he was doing back then. He never talked about his work; besides, it was so far above my brain capacity; he learned the juice just wasn't worth the squeeze to explain. He changed jobs at some point, and I don't know where he went. But I'm sure it was quantum physically, mechanically, or medically related."

"Dedacciai, it makes perfect sense that you, a.k.a. Groucho Extendo, would indeed have a weird kilt-wearing friend. I can certainly empathize with him. Sometimes I wonder if the juice is worth the squeeze trying to teach you things about life." Carter smirked.

"Son! Standing in the sun all day and not eating has caused some sort of dysfunctional chemicals in your brain to mutate. You're starting to think you're funny. — Not to change the subject, but I will anyway.

"Now that we have the bicycle buggy, we should get a small ice chest with Gatorade and snacks for the road before we leave in the morning. I'd offer to help haul the buggy to Dallas, but I came to my senses and invoked the older cyclist's rule where 'you pull while I drool.' Besides, you're the young buck here and are already used to carrying such a heavy burden from lugging Naustris around all these years. — Metaphorically speaking, the bicycle buggy is much lighter."

Carter shook his head at the plight of his Naustris heritage as heard through the Dedacciai's viewpoint. He raised his hand as if to be called on.

"Yes, I have time for one last question. You! With the red face, what's your stupid question?"

"Yes, Mr. Dedacciai. Are you going to be this weird the whole way to Dallas? I'm asking for a friend who is reconsidering riding with a lunatic."

"Your friend sounds rather smart. And yes, our trip to Dallas is where the weird meets the road."

"So that's a hard NO! He shouldn't ride with a lunatic?"

"Probably not, but then again, it *is* a free trip to Dallas."

"Is it, though? My friend feels more like a Sherpa."

"I wish your friend was a Sherpa — because Sherpas usually don't bitch about carrying the load and going the distance!" Carter shook his head while they laughed it off.

"Okay, Carter, tonight we carbo-load before tomorrow's adventure. Let's have dinner in the Lancaster Lounge to celebrate our last evening in this fine hotel."

The two men walked the corridor back to their room to get cleaned up for their final dinner at the hotel.

As they entered the Lancaster Lounge, the aroma created a delectable excitement for anyone who dined there. The food was a fourth dimension in the arsenal of Connie Sue Lancaster's already three-dimensional assault on the senses.

"Will there just be two of you this evening?" the hostess asked as she seated the two men while placing menus in their hands. Moments later, "HARPER," as her name tag read, put two elegantly shaped glasses of water, a plate of warm cheese rolls, and homemade honey butter pats on the table.

"Tonight's specials are a vegetable lasagna, topped with grilled pineapple rings, and a side salad with an orange-pineapple vinaigrette dressing…or the chef's special of handmade spaghetti with ham balls, topped with a sweet pineapple marinara sauce. They are both amazing if I say so myself," Harper added.

"We will have one of each," the Dedacciai responded. "And could we please have that split for each of us?"

"Of course, my pleasure. Would you like anything to drink?"

Carter interjected, "Absolutely, two unsweetened iced teas, with extra glasses of ice, lots of Equal and or Splenda, and as many orange slices as you can possibly spare. But, most importantly, two iced teaspoons."

Harper laughed at Carter's authoritative iced tea order as her eyes made contact with his and lingered a tad longer than expected before walking off.

The thud to the back of his head was heard, but more importantly felt, as Carter quietly yelled, "Why the hell did you do that for?"

"Don't you remember today's lesson from Brandon? That's how it all begins, with the widening of the pupils and the lingering. Harper's look lingered a bit longer than necessary. You, my friend, are nowhere near the point of having a relationship. We'll talk about the 'relationship' spoke on the way to Dallas and work on getting you ready to pass the breeder's license exam."

Carter shook his head, then took on a more serious demeanor. "Dedacciai, is that how it happened with you? Did you get the look?"

The Dedacciai sat quietly as he drifted back to that cold December day at the coffee shop — "Yes, I did," and continued his silent journey before drifting back into reality, "I knew the second I laid eyes on her that she was my one. What I'd give to—" His words fell silent before a vision appeared.

It's okay, Papa; finish the sentence. Please, Papa, don't make me sad. Please don't be sad; I'm so happy here in Heaven watching you be silly. Be happy, and say something funny — before you forget how. Do it for me, Papa.

Carter realized that he had pushed an emotional button but considered it a win that he spoke at all, even if he couldn't finish. He changed the conversation to interrupt the possibility of the Dedacciai going dark.

"Can you believe that Brandon offered me a job today? And to think, if I hadn't followed you to the homeless camp, none of this would be happening. Today was absolutely one of the best days of my life. It was a day without hate, anger, and fear.

"I felt alive — I felt in charge. Hearing people's stories made me feel energized, like I was truly making a difference. While fixing their bicycles, I kept thinking of what you said at the bike store that was funny but interesting: 'Bicycles are people, too.'

"That's funny, but it also made me think of how these bicycles are more than just pieces of welded steel. They are transportation, freedom from boredom, even job security. When making the rounds, I heard at least eight people tell me that they lost jobs because they couldn't get to work when their bicycles had a flat and couldn't afford a patch kit.

"It put things in perspective of how important a bicycle can be in their lives. So much so that everyone said 'God bless you' for doing this, and they were so sincere about how they said it. It's like they really chose the phrase, 'God bless you' instead of 'Thank you.' And it seemed especially important to everyone that 'He' blesses me.

"I'm not sure if I'm qualified to say this or even think it. But I felt like maybe God was genuinely blessing me for this. Which is confusing because I thought God's only job was to *damn* everything, according to Russell Ducane.

"But today, I learned that's not His job at all. And I think Lance helped me realize that. He made me feel what I think everyone felt out there today — he made me feel blessed.

"Am I crazy to fall in love with a dog so quickly? With Lance by my side, I felt there was more to his presence than I knew, like something was guiding me. A presence I've never felt before — like I was experiencing the God that everyone wanted to bless me. I felt surrounded by love. Am I weird for having these thoughts? All this is strange and new for me — Dedacciai, am I crazy?"

It was interesting for the Dedacciai to listen to a spiritual virgin talk of their first God encounter. And hear him relive his experience in such a profound and wonderful way, then ask if he was crazy.

"No, Carter, you're not crazy. It's always been my assessment that God is love. Full disclosure: I've been struggling with that notion the past few days, but then again, maybe I'm not. Somehow, I feel challenged to believe in his love again, especially when I see the evidence, like what I witnessed in the field today.

"I watched you grow as a man out in that field. I watched you take charge and become a confident leader. I watched you have compassion for the very same people you hated just days ago. I watched you fall in love with a dog that opened a new part of you. Lance made you feel something new, powerful, and greater than yourself. I witnessed you give up Naustris and saw hate toward your dad dissipate.

"While witnessing all this evidence and experiencing you rewrite your story, it's hard for me not to believe that God was with you today. When Lance showed up, you felt God was present. Think about it, DOG spelled backward is GOD, and I don't believe that is a coincidence. Dogs are pure love, and to me, a dog's love is how I have always envisioned God's love — unconditional. And trust me, I hope I'm right about this because the key to my life rests in the heart of a four-pound dog named Godzilla."

The kitchen door swung open as a prelude to the culinary masterpieces Harper placed before them. MacKenzie-Childs courtly check-patterned dishes hosted the chef's creations so the eyes could also partake in the feast.

"Gentlemen, how does everything look?" Harper asked.

"Stunning," the Dedacciai responded.

Once again, her glance lingered toward Carter's as she walked out of view.

Carter quickly raised his arm in defense. "Don't even think about it!" he said quickly before the Dedacciai could thump him. "Besides, I'm not responsible for my confidence — You are!"

After a few seconds of contemplation, the Dedacciai replied... "You're right — I suppose I am responsible." He then looked at the chef's pasta creations. "Young Carter, dig in. Tonight, we carbo-load for our epic trek tomorrow."

His half-joking words transported him back to the first marathon his Bellavia and fourteen-year-old daughter, Jordyn, ran together. He relived the night before the inaugural Route 66 Marathon as they ate at Andolini's Pizzeria in the historic Cherry Street District in Tulsa, Oklahoma.

He remembered the ambiance of the old, converted grocery store that now sat with a substantial antique bar that hosted ninety-five different beers on tap. A full-view pizza kitchen spotlighted national pizza champions performing mild renditions of their freestyle acrobatic pizza dough-throwing competition routines.

To cook the award-winning dough was the best of the best, a Rotoflex four-tier stone rotating-slab pizza oven capable of cooking twenty-seven large pizzas at a time. The owner had an Italian lineage that he proudly boasted about as he made the rounds. He made sure his patrons realized that what they experienced was the best that could be — anywhere in the world.

His words felt true as the patrons smelled the authentic flavors and Italian seasonings that lingered about and were in no rush to leave. But most of all, The Dedacciai heard the laughter from his two favorite women, making light of their attempt to perfectly carbo-load from the spaghetti and meatballs that sat before them.

Whether or not they were doing it perfectly correctly didn't matter. What mattered was that it was partially true and did indeed help them cross the finish line together. It also mattered that he was there to capture their historic moment at the finish line.

He earned that moment by riding his bike the length of the marathon course. He earned it by weaving his way through runners and streets to capture their historical journey and using the photos to create a poster-sized collage that hung proudly in their exercise room to spotlight the momentous event forever.

— "Carbo-loading for our epic trek — really?" Carter asked sarcastically.

The question relieved the Dedacciai of the memory and brought him out of his fog.

"I'm sorry; what did you ask?"

"Dedacciai, where did you go? I can always tell when you've gone somewhere else."

He took a few beats of silence. "A better place and time, I suppose. One I'll probably never have the chance to experience again."

Carter again sensed the Dedacciai going dark and changed the subject.

"So, carbo-loading for our epic trek tomorrow. How many miles is equivalent to Epic?"

"Well, it sounded good when I said it, but that was minutes ago. I'm not sure how far Epic is or how far I'll be able to make it each day. I'll just see how the roughness of the road affects my bruised ribcage. Hopefully, I can do around thirty to fifty epic miles a day. Carter, you may not know this, but every year, I always do at least one century ride."

"Do you really? You told me you rode your first one with Professor Miguel, but I didn't know you rode one every year. I've never done a century ride. I'm impressed!"

"Maybe we can get one in on the way back if I feel strong enough. I'd love to do that with you. It's a huge accomplishment, and the timing is perfect with everything you've experienced."

"Dedacciai, speaking of experiencing things, can I ask you something about what you said earlier, about what happened in the field today?"

The Dedacciai returned to a seriousness that he felt Carter's question might need.

"I know you thought I had experienced God today, but what I'd like to know is when have *you* experienced God?"

The Dedacciai looked at Carter to answer. He thought about how easy it would have been to answer that a week prior and how hard it was now. Every thought about experiencing God was neutralized by a tipping scale of pain. The day Addison was born versus the day she was lifeless. The love in *his* Bellavia's touch versus the pain from her slap. The love of his kids versus the brokenness of Evan.

Just a few days prior, he would have said he experienced God the first time he met *his* Bellavia and then again when she said, "I do." How he experienced God the first time he heard the words, "I'm pregnant," and with each delivered life that followed.

He experienced God when he heard Mama or Dada for the first time and with every birthday candle celebrated. And he experienced God when they learned they would be grandparents and when they held Addison Hope in their arms for the first time.

He also experienced God's strength when they heard "malignant" and experienced an even higher level of God when *his* Bellavia was pronounced cancer-free. After that day, when he opened his eyes each morning and drew a conscious breath, it was better.

God was there when he seized the goodness of his days by riding his bike and taking in the beauty God had created. He experienced God when he shared that experience with his family and friends. — His mind paused — He wanted to experience God as Addison rode around the lake for the first time with him by her side. With that, his thoughts died.

"Dedacciai, are you okay?" Carter asked softly.

He looked at Carter, who deserved some sort of answer from him about God since he was helping to rewrite Carter's first chapter. Because of him, Carter's story of transformation was happening before his very eyes —

"You know, Carter, I believe we are experiencing God at this very moment. I'm realizing that God has been watching over us for the past few days. I think He feels our pain exactly how it is, and then He works through every good heart and mind around us to help alleviate our suffering. I believe you were put in my path, and I in yours. We both needed each other to deflect our pain and keep our minds busy.

"Think of the people He has used to help rewrite your story: Darius, Connie Sue, Tiny Dancer, Naustris. Miami and his alter-ego Gambucci, Alabama, Chaplain, Brandon, Charley, and every homeless person in that field today. I believe God put each heart and mind there to help alleviate your pain. I think it was His calling card for you to experience Him and help guide you in a different direction by letting you realize your potential.

"Think about it; ever since you threw that universal Hail Mary into the cosmos, life's been quite different for you — has it not? You believed so strongly at that moment that you thought I was the one sent to rewrite your story when I appeared.

"On the flip side, I believe God also put you in my path. I have some serious issues with how he put me on your path. But, in the end, I thank God you saved me because I'm not sure which side of the sky I would have ended up, given my darkest moment. The cast of good hearts and minds that have surrounded us has helped us both. So, yes, I believe we are experiencing God."

Carter pondered his words. "But Dedacciai, don't I need to believe in God to experience Him? Or should I start attending church first to believe in Him? I don't know what the rules are to all this."

"Carter, I don't necessarily think you don't believe in God; you just don't know where you stand yet. You hadn't experienced Him until you asked Him to help rewrite your story and believed. Let me ask you something. When did you last think about your dad?"

Carter tilted his head. "Wow, I haven't thought about my hate for him since the funeral."

"Interesting. I asked about the last time you thought about your dad, but you responded, 'I haven't thought about my *hate* for him since the funeral.' If that's not God, then I don't know what is. You must start realizing and enjoying His blessings that every customer wanted you to experience."

"I don't know. For some reason, I've always thought only church people got to experience God."

"Let me tell you something. I've been in church all my life, and I love my church and the people in it. But if you were to ask me when I experienced God's presence the most or felt the closest to Him, I'd say it was not in a church but in the four walls of a room called Al-Anon."

"Al-Anon, what the heck is Al-Anon?" Carter asked.

"Well, Al-Anon is for people whose lives have been affected by someone else's drinking, just like yours with your dad. It helps people have a much better relationship with someone who suffers from alcohol addiction and offers tools and wisdom to deal with the situation."

"Wow, I wish I knew about this sooner. So how did you get involved with it?"

"I discovered Al-Anon when my mentor, who also worked for me, struggled with addiction, just like your dad. I wanted to help him, but I didn't know how. One day, I was riding my Dedacciai around the lake and praying for my friend when a man named Chris rode by and asked about my bike. Our conversation led him to tell me about Al-Anon, and he invited me to attend a men's Al-Anon meeting with him. When I did, I loved it, and I found my new spiritual home.

"Al-Anon makes it very clear they are a spiritual fellowship, not a religious one. We avoided discussions of any specific religious doctrine, and members of all faiths, or no faith, were welcome. Al-Anon helped me deal with my friend, but sadly, he died from his addiction a few years later. But those four walls helped me through that, allowing me to experience God in a way I had never felt before.

"I chose to attend men's-only meetings and heard stories very similar to yours, Mr. Carter. Would it surprise you that you're not alone? The great thing about Al-Anon is it's an anonymous fellowship. We introduced ourselves using first names only, and we were not to publicly acknowledge each other.

"But that room and those four walls brought me closer to those men than anything I had experienced. And I had no idea whether they believed in God, what religion they subscribed to, if any, or even their last names. But I didn't need to know because I knew something far more important — their hearts. Because in Al-Anon, you didn't just see their life through their eyes. You heard about their life through their hearts.

"The anonymity of it allowed for the truth of these men's situations to pour out unscathed and not be sugarcoated from fear. Men could talk freely without fearing retribution from their wives or girlfriends. — But most of all, from judgment."

"Wow," Carter breathed. "That sounds pretty amazing."

The Dedacciai nodded. "You bet it is. The friendships you make are on such a different emotional and spiritual level. The man Chris, who introduced me to it, is still my friend; in fact, I just saw him Tuesday while riding at the lake.

"A men's Al-Anon meeting is the most honest place I've ever experienced. Women think men never cry, but men are amazingly emotional creatures when judgment and façade are removed from the equation. Men weep, yet they only do so when the threat of someone using it against them as a weapon later is removed.

"And along with that comes a level of God I've never experienced. I gained so much wisdom during my tenure there, and it made me a better person. It also became my new spiritual home and lifted me to a level of knowing God I hadn't reached before.

"Honestly, between the wisdom of Al-Anon and all my years in church, I use the best of both worlds. I strive to live a life where people and animals — well, maybe not spiders — know I'm a Christian by how I act and treat people of all different sizes, shapes, makes, and models."

"Spiders," Carter smirked. "Dedacciai, that's some interesting stuff. I sure wish I knew about it earlier and that my mom would've known about it, too."

"Carter, it's never too late; Al-Anon would be a good fit for you, and it would help you with your dad. Chaplain would also be someone you might want to talk to about God. I certainly don't want to keep you from pursuing any spiritual path or church because the two can coexist nicely."

"When we return from Dallas, would you consider going with me to an Al-Anon meeting and maybe a church service?" Carter asked.

"I'd be honored, my friend. I highly recommend visiting different churches and seeing if one calls your name. And speaking of something calling your name, how about this meal? It's a God experience in itself — Am I right?"

Carter nodded in agreement as the two enjoyed their meal.

"Would you gentlemen like to see our dessert menu? The chef's special is an Oreo cheesecake that's superb. He personally comes out with a culinary torch to caramelize the sugar on top that takes his special recipe cheesecake to a new level."

"You had me at 'dessert menu.' How could we possibly say no? Carter, do you want to split one?"

"Split? Are you crazy? I'm pretty sure this is God trying to bless me still."

"Say no more; he's right. What was I possibly thinking? Bring us each one, please?"

The two men could barely walk as they left the Lancaster Lounge.

"Dedacciai, I have never eaten anything as good as that in my life. That was spectacular — the food, the surroundings — everything. Definitely a dining experience I'll never forget. Thanks for that."

"You've had a special day, my friend. You deserved it."

Carter looked at the Dedacciai and gave him an exaggerated man-nod. With an exaggerated breath, the Dedacciai return-volleyed the nod.

It was 10:17 p.m. as the two men finalized getting packed and organized for their trip when the hotel room phone rang.

"Must be for you, Carter. I'm certainly not expecting a call."

"Hello?" Carter answered.

"Yes, sir, this is Carl, one of the concierges at the hotel. Is this a Mr. Carter?"

"Uhm — yes?"

"There are some gentlemen in the lobby for you, sir; they would like to speak to you. Shall I tell them you are on your way, sir?"

Carter felt paranoid and wondered if his pimpmobile brutality had come back to haunt him.

"Are these police officers?"

Carter heard a scoff from the man's voice as if to say "hardly" before he answered.

"No, sir, certainly not. One of the men wanted me to relay a message to you, sir, and I quote, 'Get your punk ass down here!' What should I tell him?"

Carter looked at the Dedacciai. "Miami's down in the lobby and wants to see me. You're coming with me!"

"Okay, Carl — tell him I'll be down in a minute."

As the elevator doors opened to the lobby, Carter and the Dedacciai saw Alabama and Chaplain standing in the distance and approached them.

"Where's the third Musketeer?" Dedacciai asked.

"He started flirting with one of the waitresses leaving from work; he'll be back," Alabama noted.

'What are you guys doing here this late anyway?" Carter asked.

"You'll see — trust me," Alabama answered. "Someone needed to see you before you left on your fancy-ass trip tomorrow. He said he called your cell, but you didn't answer."

"I don't turn my phone on unless I'm going to use it," Carter replied.

Just then, the revolving doors motioned that someone was entering the hotel as the unique sounds of rubber seals swished against the doorframe. A distinguished-looking, tall, thin, bald Black gentleman they didn't recognize walked in.

"I thought Miami was coming in. Should we go outside and find him?" Carter asked.

A familiar voice exited the unrecognizable Black man.

"Why do that when Miami's right here in the flesh, baby?"

A stunning doubletake-of-the-man revealed a pair of smiling, beady dark brown eyes, usually hidden behind dark sunglasses, day or night. He wore nice gray dress khakis with a pressed, navy-blue, button-down shirt, minus his assortment of Mr. T.-style gold chains.

"What? You two act like you've never seen a black man before."

"What the conspiracy theory happened to you?... You look..."

"Come on, spit it out. I look what?"

"Amazing! You look — amazing! What happened?" Carter said, exhilarated.

"You happened — that's what happened! You started them life dominoes falling. It started with you fixing my bike, and then your punk-ass went and got rid of your hate. It made me jealous. You turned it into a competition, like, how can this kid be better than me? Then you fixed Jules' bike and helped to inspire her —"

Miami motioned toward the revolving door as the seals slapped together again.

"Jules!" Carter yelled as he ran and hugged her, "What are you doing here?"

"I needed to see you; I have something for you." Jules pulled two envelopes from her purse and handed one to Carter while holding on to the other. "Here, open this one first," she said with a smile. He opened the large blue envelope and removed a beautiful thank-you card.

As he looked inside, there was a sea of Thank You's, God bless You's, kind sentiments, and signatures covering the inside and backside of the card.

"Everyone wanted to thank you for what you did today. People texted me and asked if we could get a card for you, and Miami and I rode around on our newly fixed bicycles to get their signatures. Honestly, I think he just wanted to show off his bike to everyone."

"That sounds about right," Carter said as he fought back his emotions.

Then Jules handed him the other card. "But this one's from me."

Carter was quietly emotional as he opened the envelope. He pulled out a beautiful handmade card with a big title on the cover that read, "ONE DAY" by Jules Benton. Carter opened the card and saw a beautiful handwritten poem.

"I'd like to read it for you if that's okay?" Jules asked.

Carter was unsure how to act from such a personal and emotional gift as he handed her the card. Soon, her meek voice began the words.

ONE DAY

by Jules Benton

One day, we'll do it — that thing that needs to be done,
that thing that might get us to surpass Day One.

When the sun comes up from yesterday's night,
we have another chance to get it just right.

In the early dawn's light, the decision is then,
to capture the promise or lose it again.
If the covers come off, the decision is made,
our future's unshackled, no longer delayed.

If we string hours together until they become days,
these sequenced steps will become our pathways.
Then hope is formed, and our battle is won,
when we can see what we have become.

Then, a year from now, we'll hold it up high,
or be viewed in the mirror while passing by.
It will live in the pages we wrote or the art that we drew,
all because we followed Day One with Day Two.

Now, the lesson in life is to remember this,
the next time our life hands us a twist.
It only takes that thing that needs to be done,
to transform our life from One Day to Day One.

Jules paused. "This poem came to me today after we talked. I wrote it down so I could share it with you. I also wrote two personalized stanzas for you that aren't part of the original poem."

One Day in a Field of Dreams and Despair
came a man re-written to do bicycle repair.
Two paths crossed from human desperation,
and a bike once broken became my inspiration.

In that instant, the poetry of my life had begun
as my life transformed from One Day to Day One.
A year from now, I will hold my daughter so tight,
with a kiss in the morning and with every goodnight.

Dedicated to a guy in a field who fixes more than bicycles.... With much love, Jules.

She cried as she finished, while Carter stood highly emotional.

"See what I'm talking about? Miami chimed in, "Them life dominoes. After you fixed her bike, Jules texted and wanted to show me what she wrote. It was so beautiful, so simple, and beyond poetic. One Day to Day One. Her words are perfect, and she wanted to give them to you.

"Then she needed me to take her around to get signatures because all these people wanted to thank you and bless you. Man, it straight up pushed that last life domino that made me realize it's time, and today is my Day One as well. Jules and I are going to celebrate our Day One anniversary from now on. I guess your punk-ass Day One anniversary is today as well.

"Carter, let me tell you somethin' about Jules. With this new Day One attitude, she *will* get her daughter back. And she *will* get a job with her bike fixed, and she *will* put in the work. You'll see. But besides all of this, you think I'm gonna let some punk-ass kid get rid of his hate and think he's better than me?"

"There he is," Alabama said as Miami continued.

"Drastic times call for drastic measures. Jules knew a hair parlor that would cut my hair and donate it to somethin' called Locks of Love. Then she took me to a thrift store and picked my new threads. — Now, to be clear, since it's a competition and all, I donated my hair, which makes me the obvious winner over your honky ass... Day One, baby, that's how it works!"

"Miami, you win hands down. I'm–I'm–thrilled for you. You look awesome — seriously!"

It was hard for Carter and the Dedacciai not to stare at Miami's stunning transformation.

"Carter, I know it's late, but I tried callin', and you didn't answer. I hope we didn't stop you from getting your beauty rest." Miami touted.

A large, beautiful grandfather clock chimed in and sang 11 p.m., and then Chaplain spoke.

"It's been a long and wonderful day, one of the best I've ever witnessed. But these boys need to get rested for their trip. I'd like to pray if I could before we leave."

The six joined in a circle, with Jules emotional as she linked arms with Carter on one side and Miami on the other.

"Dear Lord, what You have shown us today in so many of what our brother Miami calls *them life dominoes* is a rarity. These life dominoes have toppled so much hate and pain and cleared a new path for so much inspiration.

"It's Day One for Brother Carter without hate and Day One for Brother Miami without hair. And we know Your strength will be with our sister, Jules, as she begins the path of getting back what was always hers. And we all know You will be there every step of the way.

"Please be with our brothers as they make their way to Dallas. Keep them safe from traffic and texting and be there in every way they need. I pray that You bless Carter for what he did today for so many of your hurting people and show him what *You* are about in the coming days. With Your goodness and grace, be with us all — Amen."

"Carter, don't get your honky ass killed riding to Dallas! Dedacciai, take care of my boy here and get him back in one, maybe two, pieces at the most." Miami hit his friend in the arm before he hugged him.

Jules hugged Carter and once again had a hard time letting go. "God bless you for everything today, and please be safe."

The four visitors exited the hotel, leaving Carter and the Dedacciai reflecting on what just happened. Carter read more closely what people signed on his card as the Dedacciai walked out the front door. Soon, Carter finished reading and caught up with him.

He saw the Dedacciai watching as the four visitors grew smaller in the distance.

"Just look at all that perspective," Carter said, getting the jump on the Dedacciai, who would have said it in a few seconds anyway.

"Yep, that is certainly a big bowl of perspective for one day — pardon me, for Day One," the Dedacciai said with a smile.

Carter put his arm around the Dedacciai as they stood silent, watching their visitors disappear under the distant streetlights.

"Your mom was onto something with the whole perspective thing. I can't help it. Now I see it everywhere! Whatever tomorrow brings. I wanted to say thank you in advance for everything."

They gave a mutual man-nod and headed inside to get some sleep. Carter was joyful as he bounced off the walls with the thrill and wonderment of what his first Day One brought him and what his future Day Two trip would bring.

Chapter Eighteen

The Emotional Savant

Carter was restless as he saw 2:00 a.m. appear on the blue-lit clock next to the snoring Dedacciai. He quietly lifted himself from the trundle bed and got dressed, hoping to catch a final glimpse of Connie Sue Lancaster and talk with her. As he entered the lobby, he saw her looking perfect as usual in a stunning black dress with oversized white lapels and a large, colorful southern belle booch.

"Why, Mr. Carter, I was hopin' I'd get to see you before you leave tomorrow. Now, what are you doin' up so late?"

"I couldn't sleep; too excited, I guess. And if I was being truthful, I wanted to show you something — if I could, ma'am."

"Ma'am! — Now, Mr. Carter, we're way past the ma'am stage. Will this take very long?"

"Well — I'm not sure – It just depends, I guess. But if you don't have time, I'll understand."

"Don't be silly, Mr. Carter. Let's sit a spell so you can show me." Connie Sue led him to a quiet nook of the hotel lobby with an elegant table and two matching chairs where they would not be disturbed.

"Is this table okay? It's where I get some of my best creatin' done late at night."

Carter answered by nodding but mentally shook his head in disbelief as he was unprepared for this fantasy scenario. The confidence he thought he had when he came down seemed to disappear. Suddenly, he was in high school again, scared he would say something stupid.

"Well, Mr. Carter, what is so important that you came all the way down here to show little ol' me?"

"It's — Well — I wanted to — Uhm —" He breathed deep and tried to gain his composure. At least enough to answer in a complete sentence.

"Now, Carter, we're not gonna get a whole lot of conversatin' done if you continue to stop mid-sentence. Don't be shy; just spit it out."

"Okay, I'm sorry. I just — It's just that — Well, I wanted to tell you what happened earlier tonight and show you something to prove that I wasn't storying to you about today."

Carter began the self-doubt cycle in his mind. *Now she thinks I'm stupid and weird, a loser, like all the other girls. Why did I think I could come down here and talk to her?*

Connie Sue could tell he struggled with his words and reverted to the shy man she had met a few nights ago.

"Carter, try and relax. Consider me your friend; how would you tell your friend what happened?"

"That's the thing. I don't have any friends. And I have never had a friend like you. I mean, one that was a girl. And it's not that I'm shy around girls; it's that I'm scared of them.

"Do you remember the first night I checked in and I showed you my blue bicycle? Well, a bicycle has been my only form of transportation in life. We didn't have a family car because my dad had too many D.U.I.s and couldn't drive. And when I turned sixteen, we didn't have enough money to buy me a car, so it's always been just me and my bicycle."

Carter stopped and realized the lack of acid coursing through his chest.

"What is it, Carter? What are you thinkin' about?"

"I don't think I've ever talked about my dad without saying how much I hated him in the same sentence. I'm beginning to understand how important it was to literally bury Naustris."

Carter placed his head in his hands, shielding his emotional scars. But this southern belle was masterful at reading people. As an emotional savant, her job was to know what people needed, wanted, and liked. She knew Carter needed to realize it was alright to be vulnerable at that moment as he felt a gentle hug come from his side and a voice that soothed him.

"Carter, it's okay — you can talk to me. It's safe."

He raised his head, slightly watery-eyed, and looked at his friend.

"Connie Sue, how can you be so beautiful and so kind? Every girl I've ever known has been cruel because I didn't have a car. They put me in the loser category, and even kids that were sort of my friends were pressured to be mean, or they'd be in the loser category as well."

"But, Carter, you're not a loser."

"Well, it sure felt that way. High school was absolute hell. It was like I was at war every day. First at school, then at night when my dad came home from work. It all gave me a P.T.S.D. mentality about girls and life. I never felt worth anything, so I worked this dead-end, part-time job at a bar for years. I got the nose ring, thinking I was doing it to fit in at the bar, but I realized after the eulogy that it was a weapon to use against my dad. I didn't know any of this until the Dedacciai came along. Saving him saved me, and caring for him has changed me.

"Connie Sue, today was one of the best days of my life, but I didn't have anyone to share it with — well, that's not entirely true. I had the Dedacciai and the men at the camp. I guess what I really mean is — that I couldn't share it with a girlfriend-type person.

"And then I was given two cards tonight from a lady I helped in the field today, and they're amazing! They're something that gives me proof that my life matters. Something that maybe a girlfriend would be proud of me for doing. It's just that you're the first girl I've gotten to know who is nice to me, so I wanted you to see them."

Connie Sue inhaled and placed her hand over her heart as he continued.

"I know you weren't thrilled about the Carter that entered your establishment a few nights ago. But still, you could look past that after you heard my story."

Carter caught himself and checked his emotions. "Wow — sorry to unload my woes, not sure how I got so off course. It seems like I was just supposed to tell you about today's adventure fixing bikes."

He took a beat from his emotions and found Connie Sue stroking his arm gently.

"Carter, let me say something first. I'm sorry about how those girls treated you. The young man I've watched change before my eyes is a handsome man with a good heart. Girls want a man with a good heart. But they also want someone with confidence. I think it was sweet and brave to come down here to share your day with me. If talking to me can help you gain confidence — I'm on board. I'll be your friend, and you can talk to me anytime. I'll help you in that department because I've enjoyed watching the scared young man who could hardly look at me change in a matter of days. Now, let me see these cards so I can see what all the fuss is about."

She opened the thank-you card first and took the time to read every word. Her lips tugged with each other, the upper and lower working together to whisper the words silently.

"Mr. Carter, that is quite a card you got yourself there. You truly do matter to everyone out there. But just so you know, you matter with or without that card."

Connie Sue then opened the card from Jules and read the poem. Her silent-whisper demeanor changed with each passing word. At the end, a gasp, followed by silence. She clasped the card to her chest and closed her glistening eyes.

"How did this poem come to be? Tell me, what happened in that field today that inspired Jules to write this poem? It's special — and I mean incredibly special."

"Wow, I thought the same thing, but hearing you say it makes it even more real. Okay, as I was fixing one of the bikes, Jules saw me and asked if I would fix her bike. One thing led to another, and she texted everyone she knew, letting them know I was out in the field fixing bikes.

"Evidently, they forwarded the text to others, and eight hours later, we fixed close to fifty bicycles. It was awesome! — Anyway, a man everyone called Chaplain, one of the three men I met at the camp, seems to help a lot of people out in the field with their problems. He had talked with Jules about writing poetry to help her deal with her circumstances. She mentioned that she wants to get her five-year-old daughter back one day. Child Protective Services took her from her because she couldn't afford to take care of her, and now she's in the foster care system."

"Oh, that's terrible," Connie Sue said, clearly affected.

"Jules said having her bike fixed gave her hope that one day she can get a job and someday get her daughter back. We talked about somehow turning our 'One Day I'll do this' into 'Day One I did that.' Jules went home and said she was inspired to write that poem.

"She said people texted her and wanted to get me a thank-you card and sign it. So, she and Miami, one of my other friends from the camp, rode around on their bikes that I had just fixed and collected signatures. Jules and the three men we met at the camp showed up at the hotel tonight and gave me the cards. And if that's not enough, Jules' poem inspired Miami, who hasn't cut his hair for over fourteen years, to finally cut his hair, all because of this poem."

"My, my, my, Mr. Carter, I'd like to meet with this Jules person. When I read her poem, I knew it was exceptional and very inspirational. And I thought that poem would be perfect for hanging in our exercise room.

"I'm also well connected with many hotels and hotel chains across the country that I bet would think the same way. I attend several of the largest hospitality conferences in the country and happen to be a keynote speaker this January at one of the largest ones. It may surprise you, but I'm rather popular at these conventions."

Nope, no surprise here! Carter thought.

"I can envision that poem in every gym nationwide, and I'd like to help get it there. I'm pretty darn good at this little ol' thing called business. If Jules wants to start writing poems and gets enough together, maybe we could get her published.

"Carter, I mentor young girls to help them with relationships and business ventures. My daddy and I don't publicize this little tidbit much, but we have a foundation specifically to help women get into business. I will personally see to it that Jules has her daughter back in no time."

"Connie Sue, that would be amazing; you're brilliantly amazing! Everything you touch seems to turn to gold, doesn't it?"

"I've had my share of successes. I don't get turned down much. Trust me; I'll get that poem everywhere it needs to be."

"I have no doubt," Carter said. "I have another success story I haven't told you about that happened. Brandon offered me a job at his bicycle store when I return from my trip. He was impressed with my mechanic skills while fixing everyone's bike today."

"My, my, this has certainly been your day today, hasn't it? — Pardon me, it's actually been your 'Day One.' — You know, I like that a lot. You just gave me a new perspective, Mr. Carter."

"There's been a lot of that going around lately. I also got a little of that perspective with dogs today. Connie Sue, do you have a dog?"

"Why, of course, I have a dog, a little sable-colored Pomeranian named Bob. Why do you ask?"

"Today, a stray golden retriever followed me out in the field. I named him Lance — he was so awesome. I've never had a pet. I didn't realize how fast you could fall in love with a dog."

"Oh, yes, it happens instantly, but that's so sad you never had a puppy growing up. There's nothing like the love of a dog."

"The Dedacciai said the same thing. He said that DOG spelled backward was GOD and that a dog's love was unconditional and the closest thing to God's love."

"The Dedacciai's exactly right; a dog's love is unconditional. It would be nice for you to experience that kind of love daily. Carter, I want you to promise me something. One day, when you get settled and have your own place, I want you to consider getting a dog. It will help your already good heart grow even more."

"I will, Connie Sue; I promise. It was hard leaving him today, but my friends at the camp said they would try and find him a good home. Brandon said he thought Lance might make a great mascot at the bike shop if I took the job. I hope the new owners might let me have Lance back once I get a place of my own. But then again, he is so awesome that I'm sure they won't — I wouldn't.

"Connie Sue, can I ask you something else? And I promise you don't have to answer if you don't want to. But — Do you believe in God? I'm asking because today, I felt He was blessing me for the first time in my life."

"Why, Mr. Carter, I'm a southern belle; we have to believe in God. Besides, how can we give a backhanded compliment if we can't nullify it with a 'Bless your heart'? That's just a little Southern humor for you. I will tell you this: I very much believe in God, but God and religion, that's a tricky subject."

Carter leaned in, wanting to know more.

"My daddy is a wealthy and powerful man, but before we opened this hotel together, he had political aspirations to become governor of this great state. I observed, even when I was little, how he tried to convince people to change to his political and or ideological viewpoints. But no one really did.

"He lost many friends during that time, and it aged and emotionally scarred him. I learned a valuable lesson watching him all those years. You can't talk about religion, politics, or the latest newcomer, tattoos, without someone getting upset and resenting the other person.

"When my daddy first approached me about going into business together, we made it the main staple of our agreement that we wouldn't talk about such matters to each other or our customers. And all these years later, I haven't spoken with customers about tricky subjects because I want customers to return again and again. So, it makes perfect economic sense not to initiate a conversation that may result in them not coming back.

"But I will tell you this: Because you're my friend, I'd love to see you follow your heart in this matter because I believe it's taking you in the right direction. Carter, I want to give you somethin' – I'll be right back." On her return, she handed him a Bible.

"Here you go, Mr. Carter. I've had this treasured Bible for a while, but I want you to have it. I think it will help you get started with following your heart and knowing God and such."

"Thank you, Connie Sue; this will definitely help get me started. I want you to know that giving me this Bible and asking me to sit with you tonight has made today even better. I can't believe how amazing it feels to have someone like you in my life."

"Mr. Carter, I think someday, some young lady will be mighty fortunate to have you. But you may need a smidge more of them ol' life lessons first. I can tell you're emotionally scarred and not quite ready for a relationship."

"The Dedacciai says the same thing, just not as nice. When I even look at a girl, he hits me upside the head and harshly informs me, 'No breeding for you!' And then mentions something about getting my breeder's license."

"Well, he's right, for now." Connie laughed, "But maybe one day soon, you'll be able to get your breeder's license."

Carter laughed and felt on top of the world from hearing her encouraging words. But hearing Connie Sue say "breeder's license" was priceless. "Connie Sue, I don't know if this is weird to ask, but do you have any relationship advice about women you can teach me?"

"Carter, I counsel young ladies with their relationships, and I can tell you a few things. First, I want you to promise that you will be respectful toward any woman you pursue. Women need respect, and men need appreciation. When you go on a date, listen to her, and I mean intently listen to her — it's a form of respect. Also, put your cell phone on silent, and don't be checking text messages or fiddling with somethin'.

"And don't interrupt and 'one-up' her by telling her what happened to you while she's talking. You will get your time to shine at some point. And another thing, don't jump in and try to fix everything either. Sure, she will be telling you about her problems, but listen, really listen, without trying to fix them. Trust me; more brownie points will come your way from listening than anything else you can do.

"Carter, that's a few basic things to get started, and I promise we can delve into this more seriously when you get back. Truthfully, before worrying about relationships, continue with what God began today. That's a better place to start, and relationships will follow — you'll see."

"Connie Sue, I appreciate you getting me started with some womanly advice. Do you have any advice for me with the Dedacciai? He has been so wonderful, but underneath every sentence, every tidbit of wisdom and wit, I can tell he's crying — tortured, even."

Carter paused; his face mimicked his confused thoughts.

"What is it? I can see you want to tell me something," the emotional savant asked.

"I don't know if I should tell you this. Can it be our secret?"

She grabbed his forearm and squeezed it, and he heard the answer in her touch.

"Connie Sue... The first night we came here, the first thing he said to me right after I rescued him was, 'Please — just let me die.' And the following morning, when I went in his room, he had a piece of glass in his hand and an empty pill bottle on the counter and was trying to kill himself."

"Oh, my God, Carter, I had no idea. I can't believe that; he seems so jovial — and normal."

"Okay, trust me; he's the furthest thing from normal," Carter joked a bit before turning serious. "I know he's hurting; I just wish I knew why. He always seems to disappear mentally, and when he returns, he usually says something rather cryptic.

"But I promised him I wouldn't pry into his life. I still have no idea his real name; I thought maybe he'd see that it's safe to tell me by now. But he isn't giving up the ghost, and I've learned one thing about the man. He says what he means, and he means what he says. I had to learn that the hard way. But I want to keep my promise because the man has been the answer to the universal Hail Mary I threw into the cosmos, as he puts it."

"Wow, Carter, he's come a long way himself since you came into his life. He needs you, and you need him. The two of you are certainly the most fascinating people I've met. As simple as this sounds, especially with you trying to learn about God and all, maybe pray for him. Your first Hail Mary into the cosmos worked pretty well."

"Thanks, Connie Sue. I will." Carter had a reminiscing look about him.

"Well, I guess this is it for a little while. I can't thank you enough for everything you've done for me. You've made my night tonight — Truthfully, you've made my life tonight. It was special — like very, very extra special, talking with you."

With that, Connie Sue Lancaster gave her friend a lovely kiss on the cheek. It was a confidence-building event that was more than a peck, close to the lips without touching and with enough pressure to leave a lipstick mark. Carter would never want to wash his face in that spot again. — Yes, Connie Sue Lancaster was a master at what humans needed — wanted —and really, really liked.

Meanwhile, in an office approximately fifty miles away sat a sizeable wooden credenza with six different flower arrangements in various degrees of death. Two people had been working all day and night putting together their findings for an 11 a.m. meeting with a young married couple who had lost their three-year-old daughter three days prior.

The one who clicked had implemented one of the most crucial quantum forensic genealogical medical investigations of his career. He had called in favors and enlisted a team of hackers worldwide to help him prove a theory. At the same time, the other one with hazel-mint-green eyes organized the hundreds of printed research pages, including medical charts and graphs hacked by his team that he most needed to prove his case. The two would not sleep this night until the wee hours of the darkened abyss.

Chapter Nineteen

The Blessed Curse

"Mom, Amelia, and I would really like you to go with us to the medical examiner's," Evan said over the phone. "They want us there at eleven. I think it would be good for Amelia — actually, for both of us if you were there. It doesn't seem possible that I'm asking another human when I can get my dead daughter's body back—"

The call went silent underneath his anguish, and her heart ached from hearing his distraught silence scream out from the other side.

"I know, Son, I know. You'll make it through this; you'll see. Evan, you're stronger than you know."

Bella heard his silent struggle to push his words out beyond his tears.

"Mom, I don't know that, and that's why I need you there."

"Evan, we all need each other right now."

"We'll be by at 10:30 to pick you up. Thanks for going, Mom." The call ended.

A Gray Honda minivan with three inhabitants pulled into the visitor parking lot and studied the building marked Travis County Medical Examiner, 1213 Sabine Street, Austin, Texas. A handful of sad-looking cars were parked within their allotted stripes and blotted the parking lot in the name of official death business. Evan parked near the entrance next to a medium-sized white cargo van so his mother wouldn't have to walk far.

As they exited their minivan, they saw the length of a black hearse sitting around the corner, forcing the mind to wonder if the body was coming or going.

Upon entering the building, they made themselves known by their signatures, and they were treated with meticulous respect as the trio was asked to sit among the other visitors with whom they shared a horrible commonality.

Seating in the waiting area was limited, but fortunately, they found three available seats. Bella sat next to a man and found herself staring down at his sandals to avoid eye contact with other visitors. She soon heard a soothing voice.

"Yeah, I have no idea why people keep calling me Sandals, either. I just don't get it."

Bella looked up at the man with a soothing voice, long hair, and a scruffy beard and smiled.

"I was wondering how many miles your sandals have walked and about all the stories they could tell," she said.

"Well, as long as they don't tell them to the authorities," the man responded.

Bella was caught off guard and smiled.

"Truthfully, I was keeping my mind occupied," she added.

"I think we're all trying to keep our minds busy from the real reason we're here," Sandals responded.

"Death is complicated. I believe everyone in our little community hopes to hear something in that room that will put their Humpty Dumpty lives back together again. Or maybe it clears up a misunderstanding that allows them to forgive someone, maybe even themselves. I have a friend who could sure use some forgiveness right now. I'm here with his family, but he's not here because his family doesn't want him around. It's very sad."

Bella looked at him, bewildered, hearing a storyline that hit too close to home. But before she could respond, the receptionist summoned her family to the front.

"I must go now, but it was nice meeting you, Mr. Sandals."

"Please, my dad goes by Mr. Sandals. I'm just plain old Sandals," he replied.

Bella needed to leave, but her feet disobeyed as her curiosity about his cryptic subject matter begged her mind to know more.

"Sandals, do you know why this man's family doesn't want him around?"

"As you can imagine, there's a lot of emotional family drama and blame; like I said, deaths are complicated. The sad thing is, it's probably a huge medical misunderstanding. I know you need to go, but can I ask you something? I realize you don't know me, but you seem like a very loving and sweet lady. My friend is pretty lost right now. I was wondering if maybe you could say a little prayer for him. It would help him more than you could ever imagine. You see, he lost his granddaughter three days ago, and right now, he has no one who cares about him—"

Bella clasped her heart from the proximity of his story to hers and didn't know how to respond.

"Mom, we need to go! They've called our name twice now," Evan pleaded.

"Sorry, I have to go." She gathered her things quickly and began to walk off. As she did, she heard his voice.

"Take care, Bellavia. I hope you hear what you need to forgive him. I'm sure your granddaughter would want it that way."

Bella froze as the blood rushed from her face, leaving her pale. An indescribable feeling about the man wearing sandals left her uneasy. She stood there quietly, reviewing their conversation. *Did I tell him my name? — How did he know I was here for my granddaughter or that I needed to forgive my husband?* — She turned to inquire, but he was gone.

"Are you okay, Mom?" Evan asked as she came out of her internal dialogue.

"Son, everything's fine. I got caught up in thought. Evan, have you ever seen that man who was talking to me?"

He looked at her — "What man?"

She glanced around as if looking for answers. She considered that maybe her guilt conjured him up in her imagination. Or maybe her subconscious wanted him to be real to obtain what it needed and wanted from this meeting.

They were escorted back to the first available sterile office where the phrase 'I'd like to be a fly on the wall' would not pertain. These four walls had but one job: to hold the telling of autopsy reasoning and hold the sadness of the families changed by such findings.

A light knock at the door preluded two familiar faces who greeted Bella with hugs. Then, a familiar face greeted Evan. He had met him a handful of times growing up and knew he was a friend of the biological human who killed his daughter. Amelia knew neither.

Dr. Wolfrem Miguel Jezercak matched the black embroidered name stitched onto the white lab overcoat he had chosen to wear in reverence of his friend's granddaughter. Kimmee James Attwood accompanied him and already had tears after her prolonged hug with her surrogate mother, Bella. She wiped any evidence of tears from her eyes as she turned to her professional side to greet the grieving parents of the angel who had brought them all together.

"Evan, Amelia, my name is Kimmee Attwood. On behalf of Dr. Jezercak and myself, we'd like to express our sincere condolences. We've prepared many documents which Dr. Jezercak will go over with you. Bella, I'm sorry, but I didn't have one printed for you; I didn't realize you'd be here." She handed each of the grieving parents a three-ring binder that rivaled *War and Peace*. Dr. Jezercak took over the consultation.

"Okay, are we ready to proceed?" he asked before delving right in. "I want to start with the elephant-in-the-room question that needs to be answered — Addison did not suffer; she was gone in an instant —"

The pause was thick with emotion — their breaths eerily grateful.

"Addison had an exceedingly rare congenital heart defect referred to as Ebstein's anomaly. What happens is the septal and posterior leaflets of the tricuspid valve are displaced toward the apex of the right ventricle of the heart. It only happens in one per 200,000 live births and is classified as a critical congenital heart defect. In Addison's case, I believe she had another heart defect, sometimes associated with Ebstein's anomaly. It is called Wolff-Parkinson-White syndrome, often referred to as WPW.

"What happens is an extra electrical pathway between the heart's upper and lower chambers causes a rapid heartbeat. The additional pathway is present at birth and is extremely rare. An abnormal gene is the usual cause in a small percentage of people with WPW. The Wolff-Parkinson-White pattern is usually discovered only by chance during a heart exam.

"People of all ages, including infants, can experience the symptoms related to Wolff-Parkinson-White syndrome. An episode of a speedy heartbeat can begin suddenly and last for a few seconds. Episodes can occur during exercise or while at rest. Herein lies the rub. The problem with Wolff-Parkinson-White syndrome is it cannot be detected postmortem.

"So how do I prove my theory, you ask? I'll get to that. But in the meantime, open your binders to page twenty-three. I have provided everything you need to know about Ebstein's anomaly and Wolff-Parkinson-White syndrome. And I would be glad to go over in-depth with you if you prefer."

Dr. Jezercak looked at his notes and organized his papers for stage II of his presentation. He did not realize his target audience had a deer-in-the-headlights look about them as they tried to assimilate his findings. Since they didn't respond, Dr. Jezercak delved back into his theory.

"What I want to get across to you in this binder is why I—" Dr. Jezercak felt a hand on his shoulder, grasping his attention. Kimmee made him look up to see why she interrupted him. Wolfrem Miguel saw the audience frozen in thought as Kimmee took over the meeting.

"I want to apologize. I realize all this may have been too much to absorb so quickly. As I helped assemble this information, I learned a lot about this syndrome. We've all experienced that moment where our heart skips a beat or beats twice as fast for a moment. Often, we joke about it, even calling it love, but the heart is not designed to skip a beat or have an extra-fast beat.

"However, those who might experience the heart skipping a beat, or rather throwing in an extra beat, think of it as normal since these heart palpitations happen so quickly. In retrospect, I wonder if Addison ever alluded to having a heart palpitation that maybe was passed off as 'that's what happens when you love someone so much' or something along those lines. Anyway, I want you to be open to a memory of something she said or did about something she felt. So, please take a moment while you gather your thoughts and ask Dr. Jezercak anything else you'd like clarified before we proceed."

As Evan thought more about what Dr. Jezercak said, he realized the doctor may have proven his case against the biological human who killed his daughter. He verbalized his feelings with a zero-to-sixty intensity.

"Well, if that's the case, and my daughter did have this — Wolf-Parking Lot-Whatever-syndrome. My dad probably caused her heart to misfire when he threw her in the air after we repeatedly warned him not to!"

His every word of righteous anger fueled his complex hatred toward his dad as Dr. Jezercak felt his Clicker persona eager to come out and play.

"Now, listen, Evan. I understand you need to blame something or someone for this tragic event; it's what our human nervous system needs, but that's not how it works. Your dad didn't kill your daughter. Using your thought process, why didn't this happen every time she landed in the sand after going down a steep slide or jumped down from one of the other playground toys? Plenty of jolting goes on there that could've caused this.

"If you want the hard truth, your wife's family genetics killed her. Are you going to hate her as well?"

Amelia's head drew back immediately as a cold heaviness expanded in her core as the Clicker's tirade continued.

"And while you're at it, how about blaming your God!? Or better yet, why not turn to your God! — Evan, I've known your dad for years. I know he was a believing man, so I'm sure you are, too."

Evan fired back, "You're just trying to protect that piece of crap friend of yours by finding something, anything, to use against me. Now you're trying to twist science against my wife to blame her. What kind of turd does that?"

"This is why I'm an antitheist! Because of people like you! Instead of using your faith to turn to your Jesus, or your God in Heaven, for strength and forgiveness, you turned immediately to your hate and the need to blame. I'm pretty sure your supposed devil is rejoicing with this one. He instantly demolished an entire family, using you as his guinea pig. So how does that feel?"

Kimmee instantly jumped in. "Wolfrem Miguel Oswin Jezercak, you're out of line! Both of you are! Everyone needs to take a beat here! I didn't stay up all night to help prove a theory that's not going to be presented. We need to settle down so we can present our facts."

The room quieted, and the aftermath found Bella and Amelia embracing one another. Evan saw the pain he caused his wife and mother, and his spirit collapsed. He sat there in reticence, his hands clasped over his head as it hung close to his chest. Kimmee signaled the Clicker to pause with his findings. The room took a break while the internal dialogues all played out.

Evan pleaded his case to the courtroom of the mind.

Your Honor, if he's right about all this, and she can be here one second and gone the next, then I've been the worst son ever. What if I had killed him? I hit him hard enough! I wanted him to be dead with a vengeance. I'm her protector, and I'm the judge, jury, and executioner when it comes to my daughter. I tried him with a fill-in-the-blank justice system. He was there, and we warned him not to throw her into the air — done. He's guilty; case closed. — But, Your Honor, now I'm told with a novel full of evidence that the science is against me. How do I accept and make sense of this? I need help. I need you to overturn the verdict from my mental courtroom where the previous trial took place. How do I convince myself and accept I'm wrong? Because once I acknowledge this new verdict, I'll be accused of an unforgivable act — for which I can never be forgiven.

Evan took a deep breath through his pain and unclasped his hands.

"Dr. Jezercak, are you absolutely sure you are right about this?"

"Yes, Evan, without a doubt. Addison's congenital heart defect killed her, not your father."

Evan succumbed to the sciences, and his righteous belief that his dad had killed Addison began to diminish along with his pain. But it was not easy, as this pain had comforted and served him well as a buffer from the truth. Without it, he was wrong about everything and the worst son ever. Through his thoughts, he turned to Dr. Jezercak.

"I'm sorry about my outburst. I have no idea how to forgive myself for accusing my dad, who is innocent, from what you say. I must trust you on the science and admit you're right about the devil winning this one. But how can I ever forgive myself?"

Evan put his head down and cried as he grew mentally dark. His body shook while he experienced an exorcism of sorts as the truth propelled his painful belief about Addison's death out of his consciousness.

As they witnessed Evan's pain, Bella and Amelia began to cry as they prayed for Evan's painful journey to forgive the unforgivable part of himself.

Bella wanted to rid herself of her overwhelming guilt toward her husband and forgive him. She prayed intensely for him and the man Sandals described as lost as well.

The Clicker spoke through the chorus of sobs that bounced from wall to wall and the thick emotions that filled the room.

"Colossians 3:13: 'Bear with each other and forgive one another if any of you has a grievance against someone. Forgive as the Lord forgave you.'

"Ephesians 4:31-32: 'Get rid of all bitterness, rage, and anger, brawling and slander, along with every form of malice. Be kind and compassionate to one another, forgiving each other, just as in Christ God forgave you.'

"1 John 1:9: 'If we confess our sins, He is faithful and just and will forgive us our sins and purify us from all unrighteousness.'

"Mark 11:25: 'And when you stand praying, if you hold anything against anyone, forgive them, so that your Father in heaven may forgive you your sins.'

"Matthew 6:9-15: 'This, then, is how you should pray: Our Father in heaven, hallowed be your name, your kingdom come, your will be done, on earth as it is in heaven. Give us today our daily bread. And forgive us our debts, as we also have forgiven our debtors. And lead us not into temptation but deliver us from the evil one. For if you forgive other people when they sin against you, your heavenly Father will also forgive you. But if you do not forgive others their sins, your Father will not forgive your sins.' —

"Shall I go on? — Maybe this will encourage you to forgive your father, yourself, and hopefully both of you."

The others in the room sat stunned by this astonishing act performed by the Clicker.

"Evan, Amelia — I know this may be hard to grasp right now, but this man accused of killing his granddaughter gave you one of the biggest blessings ever. Suppose Addison died on your watch while you were holding her. Would you live the rest of your days with an underlying mentality that maybe you did something to cause her death? Maybe you could forgive yourself — but then again, maybe not. Fortunately, you're not left with that burden, are you? But your dad is. Just think about that for a second."

Once again, Evan was left contemplating the ugly truth of Dr. Jezercak's statement.

"Evan, you know your dad would never hurt his granddaughter. I know that logically, you know this to be true, but you must accept it in your heart and mind. I also want everyone to think about this statement, which I can tell you with 100% certainty —

"Addison's last sounds that trumpeted her entrance into Heaven were made up of laughter and giggles. And the last emotions she felt were love and joy — something every human would choose if given the choice of how they would want to exit this life."

With that, Kimmee signaled her boss to pause so the family could emotionally absorb such beautifully horrible thoughts.

After some time passed and the sobs quieted, she signaled Dr. Jezercak to proceed.

"Now, before we continue, I need everyone here to know this. If I thought in any way that your father did something to hurt Addison accidentally, and if the science led me there, I'd tell you. But that is not where the science led us. There was no post-mortem bruising, no indication or infraction whatsoever that he dropped Addison. So, let's get back to the actual cause of Addison's death. This binder shows evidence of why I believe Addison died from Wolff-Parkinson-White syndrome.

"Kimmee and I performed the most extensive forensic genealogical timeline of a family's history that I have ever done before," and then added with a wry smile. "And maybe accidentally used the Department of Defense's experimental quantum computer to do so — a statement I can neither confirm nor deny. But I needed a complete account of both your families' genealogical trees to help prove that Addison also had another heart defect that caused her death.

"Evan, I found very quickly that a genetic propensity for Alzheimer's dominated your side of the spectrum. Obviously, Addison did not have Alzheimer's since the youngest diagnosed case of Alzheimer's was at twenty-seven, a young man named Jayde Greene; obviously, Addison was much younger than that.

"So, we concentrated on your wife's family tree. Please look at the synopsis I prepared for you beginning on page 243. It shows you every relative who suddenly died of natural causes without an explanation. As you can see, the list is plentiful. Ages range from six years of age up. And the ages are widely dispersed throughout your family's genealogical timeline.

"In other words, these ages are well below the average lifespan expectancy. The takeaway is that I sincerely believe that Addison's symptoms would have been apparent once she began participating in intense sports, especially in her teenage years. And, had we known, the fix would have been a simple routine in which a catheter-based procedure known as ablation could have permanently corrected her heart rhythm problems. But since no one had put two-and-two together before, there wasn't a natural continuity to reference that would explain these other premature deaths until now.

"Addison's death will not be for naught. In fact, I can predict with a 73.26% probability that Amelia may also have this syndrome. Here's what you need to know. Many people go undiagnosed with Wolff-Parkinson-White syndrome and live a perfectly normal life. But with your family's genetic makeup, you have a much higher risk that it will raise its ugly head."

Amelia grasped Evan's hand with a force that matched the strength of her concern.

"Your brothers and sisters will need to be checked out as well. Usually, but not always, Wolff-Parkinson-White syndrome can be diagnosed by doing a routine ECG, showing some slurring between the P wave and the QRS waves and—"

Kimmee touched Dr. Jezercak's shoulder and took over the consultation.

"Amelia, given your family history, we shouldn't waste time using a heart monitor or do any of the multitudes of tests we could run first. We'd want to skip to the front of the line and do the one test that shows if you have Wolff-Parkinson-White syndrome.

"Dr. Jezercak explained it to me earlier. He would infuse a chemical called adenosine and send it through an IV while repeating an electrocardiogram or ECG. He said this will definitively show whether Wolff-Parkinson-White syndrome is present."

Kimmee continued, "Amelia, Evan, although I could never feel the pain you're going through, there's something here: given time, you may find solace. From this point on, Addison's death will save other lives, and not just any lives, but the lives dearest to you on your genetic family tree. Your brothers and sisters must listen to you and get checked out, as Dr. Jezercak recommends; this will change your family timeline forever. And when you're ready to get tested or plan to have more children—"

Kimmee stopped as she noticed Evan and Amelia quickly cling to one another. Bellavia gasped as she instantly knew she was going to be a grandmother and began to cry.

Amelia reached out to her. "We wanted to tell you the other night, but..."

Bellavia's tears shared the burden of so many emotions. She wished they were all tears of joy, and part of them may have been. But it seemed so sad, wrong, and empty that her husband wasn't there to hear the news and share it with her. Her pain grew stronger as she thought of her last moments with him. She felt herself slap him again as if it were happening for real. She collapsed to the floor, repeating, "I'm sorry. I'm so sorry."

Kimmee jolted to the floor to lighten the fall, then took her surrogate mother in her arms and rocked her. Evan also tried to catch his mother but arrived a few seconds later. He watched as Kimmee held his mother while stroking her hair. She showed why his mother spoke so highly of her.

"Mom, I'm so sorry you had to find out like this; after everything that's happened, there just wasn't the right moment to tell you."

His mother reached out and clasped his arm. And with a loving squeeze, she let him know she understood as he helped her up on her seat.

The Clicker, who was believed not to have a human heart, felt a phantom pain for his friend in his absence as he watched Kimmee hold Bellavia. He had difficulty speaking through the hurt he witnessed but knew there was more to discuss.

"Evan and Amelia, with your new baby, we will monitor him or her closely. I can personally guarantee this will never happen on my watch. That binder has all the proof you need to show your family and relatives across the country and worldwide what they're up against. Addison's life will save many. Amelia, I have people standing by who owe me favors and are ready to help do this procedure immediately. When you're able, we need to get that done.

"Lastly, I know you came here for Addison. Now that we're through with everything, you need to decide which funeral home you want to use, and we will release the body to them." He paused, obviously deep in thought.

"Personally speaking, I would not relinquish her to you at this time. At least not, if you still plan on having her funeral without my friend in attendance. I know you're broken, but you no longer have time to be. Let me keep her here a while longer while you use your Jesus, your God, or whatever means necessary to be the man you were just days ago.

"I would much rather you spend time looking for your dad than planning a funeral. I'm sending the ME report to the investigator on the case to let him know there was no foul play. Actually, I'll call him because I have a hunch about something and might need to call in a favor. In the meantime, if there is anything you need from me in any way. Let me give you my card."

Evan stood with authority to face the Clicker after his stout but necessary words. He felt ready to face the challenges ahead as the Clicker handed him the card.

"Keep me apprised of what's going on with the investigation. Now, get your ass out of here and go find your dad!"

"I can see why my dad always loved you. But I've got to ask. If you're such an atheist, or whatever you called yourself, how did you know all those scriptures?"

The Clicker smiled. "That's simple. It's because your dad was a great adversary. He always challenged me as we went back and forth, talking about God. I decided that I needed to know the Bible better than anyone else so I could take on the enemy. Let's put it this way: I'm permanently on the do-not-disturb list for missionaries worldwide coming to my house. I'm the Clicker; nobody stands a chance against me."

Although Evan wanted to debate him as his father did, he wasn't about to challenge him. Instead, he felt grateful that his dad had him as his friend — a friend who stood up for him even under dire circumstances.

With that, the two men hugged, and Evan smiled for the first time in days. Bella experienced an emotional lift she thought she would never feel again. She walked up to the Clicker, and first, with her hug and then with her eyes, she said everything she needed to say. Then, she hugged Kimmee to complete her emotional journey as she left.

The Clicker and Kimmee were left in silence as they gathered their documents and case files. They headed down the long corridor to his office, all the while hearing Clicker alerts, followed by scampering shoe sounds and doors closing.

The Clicker turned to his protégé. "Nice, isn't it, having the hallways to ourselves?"

"You're right. It's actually pretty bad-ass."

They entered his office and straightened up the mess after pulling their all-nighter. The Clicker turned to Kimmee.

"You were outstanding today; I couldn't have asked you to handle the situation any better. It's hard to say this, but thanks for reigning me in when I was out of line. I also want to acknowledge your professionalism, organizational skills, and determination to get the job done, no matter how long it took us. That truly says something about your character and how great your ability is. — Now, let me say this, and then I'll get back to being an asshole. Your dad would be proud of you and the path you chose."

Kimmee looked at him with gratitude and sincerity and replied with a bit of a wry smile, "Just don't let that emotional crap happen again... EVER! I didn't work my way up the corporate chain of command to work for some emotional manbaby who can't contain himself — Capisce?"

The Clicker looked at her with much pride, "Capisco — and if we're going to speak our minds, I want you to get the hell out of here. Now go! Leave early! Drive home and surprise your mom, surrogate mother, or both!"

Kimmee looked at him with pause and respect.

"I can't thank you enough for taking on this case and doing what the Clicker does. You were great. Now I'm leaving before that bald head of yours explodes. See you Monday, Boss Man."

And with that, she gave him an Eye-Jobe as a symbol of poetic justice for the grandpa, then did what she was told and left.

The Clicker had absolute pride for his protégé and reminisced about his old friend, hoping he was safe. *We're going to find you, old friend; you'll see.*

Word traveled fast via the Clicker app in the medical examiner's office. Fellow workers congratulated Kimmee on a job well done as office doors opened along her trek toward the parking lot.

Dr. Johnson and Dr. Slavin stood together at the end of the hallway and greeted her.

"We were just talking about you," Dr. Johnson said. "I reviewed the medical report Dr. Jezercak sent and signed off on the case. His work, and yours, was spectacular. Congratulations, you did us proud. We were just about to head to The Hula Hut for lunch. Care to join us? My treat for having to put up with the Clicker. You deserve a medal, but food will have to do."

"Sure, why not?" Kimmee answered. "What exactly am I getting myself into here? What kind of food is at a Hula Hut?"

Dr. Slavin jumped in. "Kimmee, trust me, you're in for a treat. The Hula Hut sits on a pier overlooking Lake Austin; it's beautiful. They serve Mexonesian, which is Mexican and Polynesian infused. We usually order Hawaiian fajitas, with a combination of beef and chicken, glazed with Polynesian plum sauce, red bell peppers, green onions, and Hawaiian pineapple. It's incredible; everything on the menu is.

"It's one of our favorite restaurants in Austin, along with The Oasis that overlooks Lake Travis. Interesting side note: The Oasis is the largest outdoor restaurant in Texas and seats 2,500 people. It is built into the side of a cliff and has over forty decks, all interconnected with stairs. It's called 'The Sunset Capital of Texas,' as it has the best view of a sunset you'll ever see. Every night, they ring a bell to toast the sun as it disappears on the horizon. It's way cool. We'll take you there the next time we go."

Dr. Johnson received a text. "Excuse me, guys. I need to take care of something quickly before we go," and abruptly returned to his office.

Dr. Slavin turned to Kimmee. "Dr. Johnson told me about Dr. Jezercak's findings: Ebstein's anomaly and Wolff-Parkinson-White syndrome. Only the Clicker could find a way to prove a theory like that. I'm so amazed at how that played out, and all thanks to you."

"Why, thank you, Dr. Slavin. I want to thank you for the time I spent with you. You were patient and kind, and your work and knowledge were inspirational."

"Thanks, Kimmee, but as I told you, I have much to learn about the heart organ — and I will. But the Clicker defies logic on every level."

"You can say that again. Can you believe that I'm working for him now? It's the weirdest thing ever — right?"

"It's why he's the Clicker. He immediately knows when something or someone is great and surrounds himself with who and what he needs to be the best. He recognized that in you instantly, but just so you know — I recognized it first."

"Thank you, Dr. Slavin, you're the best. I'm grateful to have met you."

Dr. Johnson reappeared, and the three headed outside. As she walked out of the building, a mid-sized white cargo van caught her eye. *Hmmm — I wonder what Sandals is doing here?*

As she walked up to Dr. Johnson's Jaguar SUV, she turned toward the building. As she waited for the doors to unlock, she remembered seeing the sign on the ME's building as she parked in the lot for the first time and thanked her daddy. She took in how much had happened in three days.

And now, she had been asked by the chief medical examiner to lunch. She sensed this was probably not the norm for a newbie and looked to the sky.

"Thank you, Daddy, for being with me and for everything. I couldn't have done it without you. I love you. I'll give Mom an extra big hug for you when I get home."

❋━━•••━━❋

Meanwhile, at the end of the corridor, Dr. Wolfrem Miguel Oswin Jezercak sat alone among the five stages of floriculture death, his collection of microscopes, and a very thick binder full of diplomas and certifications.

However, none of them seemed particularly relevant to him. Instead, he found himself staring at the one item that meant the most: his picture of Bunny.

As he stared at the picture, his phantom pain still permeated his thoughts; this case got to him. Bellavia, Kimmee, Evan, Amelia, Addison, and his missing friend all got to him. And he wanted to be with the one thing he loved more than anything.

So, he did something he had never done in his career. He got up, gathered his things, left his office in disarray, locked the door behind him, and left early. Today, he had a new perspective on what was important, so he headed home to be with someone he loved — his pet rabbit, Bunny.

As he walked down the long corridor to the parking lot, the hallway cleared via the Clicker app. Ahead, he saw the door to the morgue open and a man exit and head toward the front of the building. Wolfrem saw from behind that the stranger had long hair and wore an old suit and sandals. He was sure the man shouldn't be wandering out of the morgue unaccompanied by a staff member. The Clicker hurried his pace to catch him in the parking lot.

As Dr. Jezercak exited the building, the man hurried into an old white cargo van. The Clicker caught up to him and knocked on the passenger side window as the van started. He signaled for him to open it, and the man leaned over to use the crank to lower the window.

Dr. Jezercak observed that the long-haired, scruffy-looking stranger resembled what so many would assume to be Jesus.

"What are you doing here? And why were you exiting from the morgue area without accompaniment?"

"I was paying respect to a friend of mine's granddaughter for him because he couldn't be here today."

"Who were you visiting?" he asked, not believing him.

"It's good to see you're leaving early to be with someone you love. Following your heart is a good thing. I do it every year at this time. I know Bunny will appreciate it."

Okay, here we go; this just got personal. Wolfrem didn't react so that he wouldn't give the man mental leverage.

"Do you believe that things are meant to be, Dr. Jezercak? That a hunch can bring such marvelous realizations, such as Wolff-Parkinson-White syndrome, for example?"

"Who in the hell are you, and how did you know that? Tell me now before I call security!"

"I'm a friend, and I'm here to tell you that your friend would be so thankful for everything you've done for Addison. And for helping his family begin putting Humpty Dumpty back together again."

"I'm only going to ask this one more time — Who are you!? — Dr. Jezercak allotted him a three-second window to comply before calling for security.

"Don't bother calling security; I'll be long gone before they get here. Don't waste your time. Go home to Bunny and celebrate the God-given gifts that allow you to do what you do. And on a personal note, thanks for what you did for me all those years ago."

"What the hell are you talking about? — What did I do for you!?"

Dr. Jezercak looked closely at his face, noticing a distant familiarity about it.

"Since you know so much, where is my friend? I promise I'm not calling security; talk to me. Tell me where he is!"

"I've told you enough. You'll be able to take it from here, Wolfrem, or do you prefer 'the Clicker'?" With that, the Jesus-looking character looked at him and gave him an eye-jobe before leaving.

How in the—? Wolfrem grabbed his phone and took pictures of the man, the van, and the license tag as he drove from the parking lot. Wolfrem ran and jumped on his motorcycle to follow him wherever mystery men went after leaving parking lots. Wolfrem was determined to find precisely where his hidden lair was as he sped off in hot pursuit. But the van was gone, missing, with no sign of it in either direction.

How in the f — There's no way he could have gotten away that fast!

The Clicker pulled back into the parking lot to make a call. He dialed his top investigative hacker for this one as he looked at the pictures of the van's tag number.

A thick Russian accent accompanied the voice that answered the phone.

"My Clicking American friend, what the balls are you calling about this time?"

"Ivan, my friend, I have a case. I need it done now; yesterday was too late on this one. You will be rewarded handsomely for your effort. I'm texting you some pictures of a man, his van, and his license tag."

Wolfrem waited for his contact to receive the photos before hanging up.

"The pictures are blank; send me the correct pictures, you American Clicking Dummy."

"Ivan, are you messing with me?"

"No, I promise. Ivan not making mess with you, my Clicking friend."

"Ivan, I know we have a history of bantering with each other and pulling pranks, but this is not the time."

"No, no, promise! Ivan not pranksting with you or making turds up your ass. The pictures are blank, my friend. Send them again; maybe cosmic sunspots are making astrological mess with airwaves. Please, send again."

Wolfrem waited and once again got the same result.

"Ivan, I don't know what the hell is going on with your damn Russian Wi-Fi, but it's the worst! Here's the damn number, Texas plates, FWY-332."

"Such old license, my friend. Texas plates now seven digits after 2009. What's expiration sticker number?"

"Ivan, how in the hell do you know that kind of crap off the top of your head?"

"KGB trivia — not normal trivia, my friend, not normal. People get bullet in brain not knowing these kinds of things. So, what is expiration year on your Texas motor plate?"

The phone went silent as Wolfrem zoomed in on the expiration date. The Clicker found himself having a deer-in-the-headlights moment.

A few too many seconds passed before Ivan began... "Hello, Hello? Testing, 1,2,3 — Is this thing working? — Test, Test, Syllabus, Syllabus — Gorbachev, Brezhnev, Bolshevik — Test, Test,1,2,3 — Is this thing on? Where are you, my Clicking friend? Do I need to hack into parking lot cameras to see if you are lively still?"

"Ivan, I'm here. The expiration year on his sticker is from twenty years ago."

"My friend, cannabis not good for your country. American cannabis making you crazy. Maybe I mail you good stuff to try. I send in discreet package for you."

"Ivan, I'm not crazy! That's the expiration year, twenty years ago. It's an old white cargo van. Find it!"

"Okay, okay, don't get panties in wad. I work on it. Say goodnight to Bunny for me, good, good, rabbit. — Make nice stew someday. I have recipe I send to you. No charge. Goodbye, my Clicking friend."

Wolfrem Miguel smiled as he put his helmet back on. He could hardly wait to get home, share a carrot with Bunny, and tell her about his day. He felt a new level of excitement from meeting this mysterious adversary, a Phantom Moriarty, if you will. Wolfrem Holmes accepted the challenge. Wolfrem Holmes had the resources, and Wolfrem Holmes had come out to play. *Game on, Mystery Man — Game on!*

Chapter Twenty

The Auras of Mankind

It was 9:32 a.m. as Carter and the Dedacciai were in the hotel getting ready to head to the store before they left for Dallas.

"Man, I'm going to miss this hotel!" Carter announced in a giddy voice.

"Carter, your voice is two octaves higher than usual, and you're acting peculiar, and — **what** is that? — Is that lipstick on your cheek? Did you purposefully not wash your cheek? Okay, — spill. What's this whole demeanor thing you got going on this morning?" the Dedacciai inquired.

Carter walked to the bathroom in his robe to look in the mirror and see if Connie Sue's lipstick was still in plain view. The smile in the mirror reflected the answer as he put on his riding shorts and walked back into the room to grab his shirt.

When he did, something struck the Dedacciai, something he had not noticed before on Carter. He saw a faint but rather long scar on Carter's chest that lurked under his chest hair.

"Carter, fess up; what is going on with you? I thought I heard you come in extremely late last night — So, where were you? Because if you went to IHOP, I'm going to be pissed."

"No, I didn't go to IHOP; I'd never go without you. Do you think I'd use my own money to buy food? That's just plain crazy talk! Maybe you're not so well after all." Carter chuckled. "But I did do something even better."

"BETTER! Better than IHOP!? You blasphemous bastard! What could be better than IHOP at 3 a.m.? Do you have a secret flask around here because you're acting like you're tipsy or something?"

"Nope, not tipsy, but a fair analogy. I just feel — alive! Last night, I couldn't sleep. I couldn't stop thinking about everything in that field yesterday that led to Miami cutting his hair and Jules writing that poem. It was the best day of my life, and I just wanted to share it with someone — Someone other than my hairy-legged man friends. Okay — I'll just say it — I wanted to share it with a girlfriend-type person. So, I went downstairs and showed my cards to Connie Sue, and she was awesome! She took the time to sit with me and seemed genuinely interested in what I had to say. She even talked to me about girls and wanted to help me with relationships and my fear of them.

"She was amazing. I mean, she was truly a great friend. I even asked her about God, and she gave me one of her Bibles to learn more. In the end, she kissed me on the cheek. So, yeah — maybe I didn't want to wash it off. Sue me for wanting to remember the best night of my life as long as possible."

The Dedacciai looked at his protégé with pride. "No judgment here, my friend, and you should relish the day you had with someone who doesn't have hairy legs. Connie Sue was the perfect one to share that with, and I'm sure she can help you with your breeder's license. Spending time with her was a confidence builder for sure, and the Bible — now that's a wonderful gift. I'm proud of you, Carter. Now, can I ask you something?"

"I guess. What is it?"

"What is that scar on your chest? Care to tell me about it?"

"Well, truthfully, not much to tell. I was young when it happened, and I really don't even remember it. But evidently, I had a bum heart and had to have major surgery of some kind." Carter kind of chuckled as he got lost back in time. "A few days ago, this is where I would have accused Russell Ducane of a genetic crime against me. But now, it's a different world — because of you," and he sat beside the Dedacciai.

"I'll never be able to tell you how much I appreciate you in my life. Everything, and I mean EVERYTHING, is different. I have wanted to forget everything about my life and childhood because of my dad. But now, I can sit here without Naustris — and talk about him, unaffected, with forgiveness in my heart."

The two paused to absorb Carter's new perspective before he continued.

"Anyway, it seems like I had to go to the doctor for regular checkups for a few years after this heart thing happened. What I do remember is how Mom and Dad never really talked about it — ever! Looking back with my new gift of perspective — I think maybe they were trying to protect me." Carter had a puzzled look on his face as he continued. "I'm trying to imagine Russell Ducane protecting me, but it hurts my brain," Carter smirked.

"The more likely answer is that it was simply part of our family dysfunction to not talk about monumental stuff and scream at the mundane. But either way, it just wasn't a big deal to me. Because if it was painful, I don't remember because I created my own dysfunctional pattern of blocking out everything to numb the dysfunction that was my childhood." Then he stood, and in a deep professional radio voice, announced, "This has been another episode of *Carter's Life: A Retrospective in Perspective.*"

"You are a strange, strange man," the Dedacciai joked.

The two cyclists found themselves outside the grocery store. Carter practiced locking up the bikes with his big-ass lock as he would have to replicate this routine often on their trip. The two men entered the store to hunt-and-gather all the necessities for their journey and headed to the cashier lines.

"Dedacciai, this checkout line is way too long; I'm going to cash my paycheck while you wait." Carter walked off.

It didn't take a clairvoyant to sense the auras of disdain emanating from the line of cart holders. On a day when multiple cashiers were needed, the line for the singular cashier lengthened to approximately fifteen carts long. And then came the straw that morphed the auras into an angry frenzy; a family made up of a mom, dad, and four small, adorable children on normal days, but devil children on this one.

The family did not understand why their EBT card didn't work; to make matters worse, they didn't speak English. The amount on the L.E.D. display topped out at $179.32. as the eyes rolled back in the head of the poor cashier, whose job would be to restock all the items since they were shorthanded.

The Dedacciai waited patiently for the outcome and observed the frustration brewing in the line. Cart holder #7 placed his items harshly on the gum rack and stormed out of the store, making sure everyone was acutely aware of his grand exodus.

"Speak English or go back to where you came from!" cart holder #6 yelled. A man no one chose to confront, as the ugly truth was others felt the same vile words.

Papa, those people look scared; you need to help them. The Dedacciai heard Addison's voice and went to pay the bill, but something caught the Dedacciai off guard. Carter Ducane had walked over from the customer service center and handed the cashier $200 to pay the unresolved grocery bill.

The mom screamed and threw her hands in the air, clasping them together and thanking her evident God for their miracle. Then she wrapped her arms around Carter as if he were the Jesus incarnate of her mind. The father had a quivering lip and took his rightful turn, hugging Carter. The cashier tried to hand Carter back his change, but he gently grabbed the woman's hand and extended it to where the cashier could place it.

The mood of the line instantly lifted as the auras transformed from disdain to a host of emotions that garnered Carter's attention. As he walked past the fourteen faces, he sensed their admiration for what he did and their disappointment for what they didn't. Each facial expression seemed an eclectic concoction of gratitude, disappointment, shame, or guilt.

At the end of his journey, under the Physical Reactions Category, the humanity scorecard read: Cart-holders 1,5 and 14 shook his hand. Cart-holders 2,8 and 12 gave him a pat on the back. Cart-holder 3 gave him a fist bump, while cart-holders 4, 6, 9, 10, and 13 looked down, avoiding eye contact. Finally, cart holders 11 and 15 gave a man-nod.

Under the Verbal Attribute Category: One cart-holder said God bless you, sir, while three cart-holders said God bless you. He also received a Bless you, young man, along with a Good job, kid. There were also five instances of Null verbiage from the five cart-holders that looked down. In addition, the two cart-holders that gave man-nods need not give verbiage as a man-nod conveys everything that needs to be said.

Of special note, cart-holder #8, Beatrice, the elder of the line, had tears in her eyes as she hugged Carter and told him she wished he were her grandson.

Carter's story was being rewritten in real-time as the young man who walked up to pay the grocery bill was not the same man as the one who stepped back from paying the grocery bill.

"Just look at all that perspective," the Dedacciai said. "I knew you would know when to use the leftover money."

"Well, that's the thing — I didn't. That was the money from my final paycheck. This one's on me. I wanted to show the universe my appreciation for the experiences it's given me since I asked it to rewrite my story."

The Dedacciai took a beat, fighting back a public display of tears.

"I'm so proud of you, son; you just can't imagine."

"Actually, Dedacciai, I can," and he hugged his author.

"You're a great writer! — I knew — I just knew you were the one to help me rewrite my story. I can feel my heart changing."

Carter looked toward the line and noticed Beatrice checking out.

"Dedacciai, I'll be back. I need to be someone's grandson for a moment. I'll meet you by the bikes." And with that, Carter hurried back to the front of the line to help Beatrice carry out her groceries.

The Dedacciai couldn't help but think his sons would have done the same. He looked toward the sky — *Addison, that's what your dad and uncles would have done, wouldn't they?*

He smiled, hearing Addison's sweet voice: *I know, Papa, just like you.*

It was now 11:08 that Friday morning. The Styrofoam chest was full of ice and starting the molecular slowdown of kinetic energy to cool the electrolyte-replenishing drinks for their ride. The Dedacciai witnessed the utter joy emanating from Carter's aura as the two men began their journey north toward the emerald city of Dallas.

Chapter Twenty-One

Evan's Redemption

A saying is sometimes heard within the four walls of an Al-Anon meeting: "Eating crow is a dish best served warm." It is often referred to while sharing on steps 8, 9, and 10 of the 12-step program regarding making amends. At this particular Friday Al-Anon meeting, thirty-nine of the usual forty participants found themselves in place. When the noon meeting should have begun, a bevy of confused faces was apparent as the scheduled chairperson had not shown, but a police detective accompanied by a police officer had arrived instead.

The emotional concern was palpable in the room for the missing chairperson as the detective explained that Grandpa was missing. One member, Chris, was hit with the news especially hard as he had seen Grandpa at the lake that Tuesday morning and was scheduled to have lunch with him after the meeting.

Initially, the detective was only there as a courtesy to the family to talk to Chris, get his full name, and discuss what he and Grandpa had last talked about at the lake. But an emergency phone call from Dr. Jezercak calling in a favor because of his growing concern for Grandpa's state of mind prompted an impromptu mini sting operation to interview each participant, then monitor Grandpa's cell phone to see which members contacted him and gain information on his location.

Each group member was more than willing to answer questions regarding Grandpa, and they seemed legitimately worried about his whereabouts.

They knew something was terribly wrong because Grandpa would never miss a meeting without someone knowing why.

It didn't take long after the meeting for Grandpa's cell phone to light up with a flurry of calls, voicemails, and texts.

Meanwhile, it was 1:38 p.m. as Evan, Amelia, and Bella walked in their front door carrying the aftermath of their emotions lingering from the autopsy report. Evan had a better-than-expected ride home from the medical examiner's office with his wife and mother. The burden of hate that had accompanied his heart to the meeting did not join him on the journey home.

But now, it was time for Evan's redemption. He asked his mom to find the police investigator's number so he could call for an update.

"Honey, the detective told me they were going to his weekly Al-Anon meeting today at noon to see if he was there or to talk with a man named Chris if he isn't to see if he or anyone else knew his whereabouts. They said they would call me if they found anything. They were also checking on train and bus tickets to Asheville, North Carolina, to see if he tried to go there."

"Asheville? Why the heck are they looking there!?" Evan questioned.

"Your dad always joked that if something happened between us, he would end up there. The police think he may have been telling the truth under his façade."

Evan shook his head in dismay but needed to release some emotional energy. His need for redemption took center stage in his emotional tundra. Finding his dad was paramount to thawing his scattered emotions and melding them together to find his new normal without Addison. He felt an urgent need to find his father and beg forgiveness before he could even think of arrangements for Addison's funeral.

"Mom, I'm going to the garage to look around for a little bit — I just need to."

"I get it, son. I've found myself standing out there as well. I'll make lunch and visit with Amelia since we need to catch up on the new grandbaby, so take your time."

"Bella, you have to know, it was just too hard to share the news with you. We wanted to make a big production of it the other night when we came to pick up..."

"Amelia, say no more; I completely understand. I'm sorry you had to hold all this in; that must have been hard."

As the women found comfort talking in the kitchen, Evan went to the garage. As he opened the door, he surveyed the room full of bicycles and the garage walls that unleashed the memories it had saved for his return. Evan remembered how he made fun of his pops every time a new bicycle brother entered the fray. He vividly relived the conversation with him the last time they spoke.

"Pops—not another one. You do realize you can only pedal one at a time?"

"Hey! Stop making fun of my bike collection and do your job and collect me some more grandbabies."

"We couldn't ever make another one as great as Addison, so why try?"

Evan envisioned Addison standing there with her huge smile as her Papa responded.

"Well, just leave that last part up to God. I read somewhere the technology for making babies in the heavenly baby factories has grown exponentially over the past three years. I'm sure this year's babies are much better than the ones made three years ago."

"P-A-P-A — I'm right here!" Addison giggled.

"OOPS, sorry, Addison, I meant to yell 'earmuffs' first."

"Pops, you're just so weird!"

Evan could picture his dad wearing his "Keep Austin Weird" T-shirt as he responded.

"Well, Evan, you know what I always say: 'When the going gets weird— the weird turn pro.'"

Evan sat down at his dad's workbench and looked out among the bicycles from his pop's perspective. As he gazed at the collection, he remembered his pops working on a handwritten letter and relived their conversation.

"Are you working on another book idea? — Pops, you do know they just invented these things called word processors that allow you to type and make changes and corrections right on the screen. — Not to mention the tens of dollars you will save on whiteout!"

Evan found himself smiling from his cleverness.

"Oh, you kids these days with your fancy gadgets. A penned letter is the soul of what letters want to be when they grow up. They want to have curves and flaws and be individuals with a sense of purpose; no two alike. They want to be brought together by the oneness of the universe to form thoughts that bring a special tranquility and unique joy to the intended target. They want to be

born into the world as ink — not a bunch of digital ones and zeros. So, respect the ink and know that the Pen is mightier than the computer. That's what I always say."

"*Pops, you never say that?"*

"*Well, I think it a lot; shouldn't that count?"*

"*Pops, you're like super-duper-luper weird."*

Evan could hear Addison respond, "*SUPER-DUPER-LUPER, that's like extra weird! — Right, Daddy?"*

"*Why, Addison, that's the nicest thing I've heard all day; now, repeat after me. 'When the going gets weird—'"*

"*—the weird turn pro!"* He could see Addison laugh as she finished the mantra.

"*The things you are teaching this girl...."*

Evan came out of the fog and remembered his pops tucking the letter away when he commented on it. He looked underneath a paper towel on top of some paper. There it was, the handwritten letter with the headline: *A Letter to my Granddaughter, Addison Hope.*

He began to read the letter but stopped after a few lines as an onslaught of emotions hit him, and his horrible guilt increased with each tender word written. He relived the dreaded eve of punching his pops, calling him fat, blaming him, and throwing him out of his own home. He heard himself tell his pops he could not come to Addison's funeral.

With the help of the Clicker, Evan had begun the process of forgiving his pops. But the scene that currently lived in his thoughts seemed unforgivable. He felt the notion of letting out a primal scream but somehow reigned it back as he heard the Clicker's Bible verses.

He was determined to be a better and stronger man this time around. He had to be! His new baby would need him to be. And they would not need a father who was weak with emotion. He must talk with them about their older sister's life without making them feel guilty that they were alive when Addison was not. They must not live a life of competing with Addison as an unattainable standard. That would not be part of their story.

He looked up at the sky. "Welcome back, God." He continued reading the letter with new strength — the strength of forgiveness.

The letter provoked a trove of tears formed from many different emotions as he looked up again. "Okay, God, where is he? Would you please show me the inevitable clue needed to find him? Please, God, show me where my dad is." With that, he smiled as he grabbed the letter to show his mom and Amelia. But before he did, Evan felt he must pay homage to his pop's bicycle collection so that he could make fun of him in his mind.

But something was different than the last time he was in the garage. His pop's prized possession, the Dedacciai, was missing. Evan had been so angry with his dad since the incident that he wanted nothing to do with finding the man. But now — it was a must. As he looked around, he wondered why his mom hadn't thought his dad might have been on one of his bikes, especially his prized possession.

He rushed in to show them the letter and interrupted their conversation by gently placing it on the table. He wanted them to experience the words without interruptions. Evan provided them with Kleenex as the two began reading. They instantly clung to one another, and their arms held tight throughout each emotional word.

Bellavia was especially struck as every drop of doubt that she was no longer in love with this man evaporated. She was all in and knew that all could be forgiven. As she finished the letter, she reacted as if it was a love letter written directly to her heart, although its intended target was Addison.

"That is from the heart of the man I married. And who I would marry again and again. We have to find him. Let me call the investigator and see what they found out."

"Mom, before you do, I know how Dad left. He took one of his bicycles — the Dedacciai. It's not in the garage, but it was here that night because I picked it up and talked to him about it. Why didn't anyone think of this?"

"Evan, if his bike is missing, he must have snuck over and gotten it out of the garage. Several times, Zilla has barked for no reason, so maybe he did open the garage. But I don't believe he took off on the bike that night — especially **that** bike in **that** rain. Listen, you know the man; how often has he mentioned something about de-reflectorizing his bikes because they made them less aerodynamic? Has he ever ridden any of his bikes at night? And have you ever seen him ride in the rain — ever?

"These are two things he has said and proved to me over the years that he would never do. So, if that bike is missing, he must have returned for it at some point," his mom said adamantly.

"Well, tell the investigators about it when you call him, and let me know what they say. — Mom, where would he have ridden to?"

"Evan, I honestly don't know. He'd probably ride to one of his Al-Anon buddies and stay with them to give me some space. But if that is not the case, I think he'd ride somewhere with the most scenery; that's why he always takes you guys to the lake.

"He used to love to escape to Dallas and ride around White Rock Lake, then stay the night at the downtown Omni Hotel. We did that a lot back in the day when we used to ride together, which I'm going to do again when we find him — because bicycles fix everything!" she said with a hopeful smile and a reminiscent spirit.

Her cell phone rang, and she recognized the investigator's number.

"Hello, this is Bella — Do you have any updates on my husband's whereabouts?"

She left the room and returned with an update a few minutes later.

The detective said they originally went to ask Chris his name, what they last talked about, and if he or anyone else had heard from him. Then he mentioned getting a last-minute call for a favor from Dr. Jezercak to do a full-scale separate interview of everyone there.

"The investigator said he and another officer went and interviewed everyone, one by one, but no one had a clue what happened. The last member to see him was Chris, who said he had seen him at the lake Tuesday morning. The detective said the men were all sincerely concerned for their friend. Evidently, he was supposed to be the chairperson, and the group was confused about why he hadn't shown up, which is a sign no one had talked with him since they didn't have a substitute.

"Afterwards, they monitored his phone to see if anyone would leave a voicemail or send a text that would give them a clue, but no luck. He said everyone was trying to reach him out of concern. The investigator made it a point to tell me he had an honorable group of men as his friends. He also said they had no leads about him taking a bus, train, or plane to Asheville.

"I mentioned your theory that maybe he's riding one of his bicycles. I told him I'd send him a picture of him with the bike, but I don't think I have one because that was after I stopped riding. However, the investigator said they would look on his phone to see if he had a picture before returning it."

Bella sat and breathed a heavy sigh from the tremendously emotional day. She looked up and then reached out for Evan and Amelia's hands.

"I think we should pray for his safety." And they did just that.

Chapter Twenty-Two

The Friday Freeloaders

Carter and the Dedacciai were now four hours into their journey when they ran across a fleet of cyclists, approximately 75 to 100 strong, calling themselves The Friday Freeloaders. They were highly organized and well-funded, evidenced by the most expensive bicycles in the expansive pack of the relatively loose peloton. They met on Fridays, as indicated by the Bat-signal sent out on their Facebook Friday Freeloaders group page.

The Friday Freeloaders' ride schedule for this Friday was a social fun ride, not a racing one — and would 100% end in beer. The 100-mile voyage had a large U-Haul at the end of the destination with 200 large pads to safely bring back the bikes that rode the entire distance. And they had a large, privately owned ex-Greyhound bus to get all the riders back to their point of origin. The bus had a million-dollar renovation with all the amenities. The members were mostly made up of wealthy retirees and many professionals who could take off on any chosen Friday that the Bat-signal dictated.

The Dedacciai was feeling great on this day. He felt strong, and the Everlast title fight that plagued his body was now three days removed and null and void so far into the journey. Carter's joy was infectious, and he was having the absolute best time on his voyage. The Dedacciai felt that a century ride was inevitable today and was privileged to accompany Carter on his first-ever 100-mile ride.

It was a great afternoon to ride as the unseasonably warm weather continued, with a solid southern breeze pushing them northerly. The Freeloaders' Bat-signal was based on the wind's direction, and they had a route for every direction the wind might choose. Today's destination would take them to Slovacek's West, a travel center in the town of West, Texas. It was known for its bakery and BBQ at the Kissing Pig Café and was renowned as a people-watcher paradise.

Slovacek's had a tremendous gift shop to appease travelers with many eclectic items for sale. The Sczechskadoodle (chopped brisket and sausage in a tortilla wrap) was a favorite menu item among the Freeloaders, as was the Klobasnek, a unique sausage kolache found in the bakery. But their crown jewel was a fantastic dog park. It was perfect for travelers who made Slovacek's a planned destination so their dogs could stretch, sniff, run, and play while their owners ate or relaxed. Yes, indeed, all the hallmarks of a people-watcher's paradise.

Carter had never ridden in a large pack of bicycles before and conversed with any cyclist who rode near him. Suddenly, the Dedacciai overzealously congratulated Carter as he hit the metric century mark of 62.13 miles, as shown on the GPS. The news of Carter's accomplishment sailed up and down the peloton, and bikes from every which way made it a point to pat Carter on the back or give a fist bump to the metric newbie.

And then it happened — the event known as Frank Andrewchow Beansley. Colorful, boisterous, a stand-up comedian in a past life. He was medium to short with a thick build; you may not call him fat, but he wasn't too far off. He was balding with plenty of hair on the sides that was rarely seen because of his expansive collection of ball caps. Additionally, his gray-streaked beard added a dash of handsomeness and was the perfect accessory for his cosmic smile of perfectly white veneer teeth. He was proud of his multicultural Italian and Hawaiian heritage and knew he rocked his Polynesian skin tone.

But the real fun began when his Polynesian, Italian, Texas-infused hick accent came out to play. There was no one word to describe the complexity of Frank Andrewchow Beansley, but a couple of multisyllabic words came to mind — Sesquipedalian loquaciousness.

"Ciao, amigo! Congrats on your first metric. The names Frank Andrew 'Ciao Baby' Beansley. But mi amigos call me 'Frank and Beans' for short, but even shorter — just plain 'Beans' to my dedicated followers of 'Bean-heads' that made up my now deceased fan club. May it rest in peace." (as he made the sign of the cross). "So, what's your name, Metric Man?"

"Carter's the name, and this is my friend 'the Dedacciai,'"

A round of fist bumps ensued.

"Beans? That's a great stand-up name. Were you really a comedian? The Dedacciai asked. "Or are you just being funny for our comedic pleasure?"

"Pleasure!? If my comedy was pleasurable, I might still be one," he joked. "I did the comedy circuit for twelve years back in the day. My 15 minutes and 37 seconds of fame was opening for Jay Leno once. Tough life on the road, tough, tough life, and I have five wives to prove it. But that was so five wives ago. Divorce was the new black back then and allowed me to become a professional ex-husband and an EX-PERT in womenology. So, if you need to know something — anything about women, I'm the guy — the mystical male unicorn to have this secret wealth of female knowledge."

Dedacciai shook his head seconds into the routine, and Carter was at full attention.

"People travel from all over the world to tell me I'm full of crap, and I get emails from the lazier haters who also need to remind me I'm full of it. Fortunately, I don't have kids to remind me as my 'Frank and Beans' were neutered early during wife numero-uno's reign over my soul. Hence, there are no little Beansleys to take my place. Trust me, Earth caught a break or dodged a bullet — you pick. Metaphors are all the same difference to me.

"Before I go on, Mr. 'the' Dedacciai, it's awfully rude to have to stop my routine to tell you what a hell of a bike you got there. I thought I had seen every bike ever created riding with these rich, freeloading clowns. Hey, is that your own brand of bike? I'm confused, which is not meant as an oxymoron, as I'm always confused about something."

Carter chimed in, "Beans; it's much easier to call him 'the Dedacciai' and not waste any brain cells thinking about it."

"Done!" Beans stepped back into his routine without missing a beat.

"My Act II in life is owning 'FRANK'S GLUTEN-FREE HANDY-MAN SERVICE.' Specializing in DIY rescue, where I put the 'Y' in 'DIY in the hell did I start this project? For when a man's eyes are bigger than his toolbelt."

Dedacciai laughed and had to give Beans a fist bump in honor of men everywhere.

"I offer a discreet handyman-client privilege protection service where I cover up my signage to stay incognito because I believe no wife needs to know of a man's epic DIY fail. My policy has saved more relationships than you could imagine. There's a saying in our secret handyman lair where we all meet — 'Behind every good DIY project, there's a local handyman.' Here's my card for your next DIY project that turns to crap," as he slipped it into the back of Carter's jersey.

"I also specialize in hanging Christmas lights for the lazy masses or the scaredy-cats that don't like climbing on roofs. But truthfully, I've found that people just don't want to deal with female light strands."

"Female light strands?" Carter questioned. "Is this a routine?"

"I wish this were a routine. Female light strands have haunted men at Christmas ever since Tesla, Westinghouse, and Edison invented the darn electrical stuff. Trust me, there are definitely male and female light strands, and I never know which I'll be dealing with when I get to a job.

"People usually have boxes of lights handed down from generation to generation of garage sales and Craigslist ads. I have only one prerequisite when doing a Christmas job. The customer must untangle all their light strands before I get there, or I make like snow and blow away."

During Frank's word storm, Dedacciai's head was in a perpetual loop of head shaking.

"Anyway, once I plug them in, I separate them into male and female strands. The male strands are the ones that come on no matter what; even if one bulb is out, the whole strand still works — logical, right? Find the bulb and replace it. Boom, done! But the females are the ones you plug in that won't come on until you check every single bulb to find the one damn bulb that doesn't work and replace it.

"Just like real life. Every single emotional thing that has ever happened to a female is interconnected into one long historical, emotional strand of metaphorical lights. When the man screws up, the whole emotional strand shuts down until the man relives every emotional failure he has provided the female until he finally reaches light bulb #37 (counting backward from 100, of course), which is the ultimate culprit.

"Ah, lightbulb #37, yes, indeed, she remembers that fateful day twenty-three years ago like it was yesterday. It was March 3rd at 10:03 a.m. on a Wednesday, with partly cloudy skies and a 64% chance of precipitation moving in by 11 a.m. from the southwest. She was wearing a pink poodle sweater and having a bad hair day when you told her that her sister was prettier than her, which you never actually said. But when she asked you about her sister — YOU HESITATED! And for that, you must suffer, as have all men who have collectively suffered together because female light strands kept exposing men's 'Male Hesitation Syndrome.'"

Carter's face was lit up like Christmas time; his cheeks were aglow from laughter. At the same time, the Dedacciai was mesmerized by Bean's ability not to take a breath, even while pedaling at 19.2 m.p.h. — He wondered if his genetic makeup was an air-breathing fish and looked closely to see if he had gills as he seamlessly continued.

"Now, here's something that never made the history books. During the great 'Men's Suffrage Movement.' A movement brought about by female light strands exposing men's faults from 'Male Hesitation Syndrome.' Men pleaded for a Male Hesitation Reform Act from Congress to help men's plight, but it fell on deaf ears. Ultimately, female Christmas lights led to why we now have two different emotional banking systems for males and females."

Both Carter and the Dedacciai looked at him like some sort of alien. But Beans was no stranger to such looks as he continued his comedic yet *isn't this obvious* way of thinking.

"So, Metric Man, before I go on, you got you a woman?"

"Well — no. According to the Dedacciai, I'm not allowed to enter a relationship until he deems it so. He claims I need a breeder's license before I'm fit to date."

"Damn! A breeder's license. I could've run with that one in the day. Each license could have checkmarks next to what a man was good and bad at. When you meet a woman, you simply hand them your license so they can examine it and see what they are willing to put up with and what they think they can change. There would be no need to ask anyone out ever again."

The trio chuckled.

"I hate to break it to you, kid, but if you want to succeed with women, you'll have to learn their secret decoder ring credit score rating system. First, you must understand that women use an entirely different emotional banking system than men. So, as long as you remember this emotional financial institution lesson I'm about to teach, you will be a step closer to getting your license. Otherwise, I'm your Christmas Future."

"Okay, Frank, I gotta know — how do these different banking systems work?"

"Well, Mr. Carter, I'm glad you asked. Okay, the female bank is the First National Bank of Bed Cred, established well before money was even a thing. In fact, it started with Adam and Eve. Think about it. Here's Adam, thinking he had it all. I mean, he had the first woman ever created and was destined to live for eternity with his lovely wife in the nude until he ate that damn apple. Next thing he knows, Eve is asking, 'Adam, does this fig leaf make my tushy look big?' And when he hesitated, right then and there, the First National Bank of Bed Cred was established."

The Dedacciai shook his head even more as he anticipated Carter's lesson.

"Here's how it works," Frank began. "A man walks into the First National Bank of Bed Cred and up to the first available teller.

"'Good morning, I would like to see the balance in my Bed Cred account?'

"'Certainly, sir, let me look at that for you. What would you like to know?'

"'I'd like to know if there's enough in my Bed Cred account for me to *(wink, wink)* "exchange tools" with my wife tonight.'

"'Yes, sir, of course you would; let me see here — it certainly appears you do.'

"'Oh, that's great, I'd really love to *(wink, wink)* "exchange tools" with her tonight because there are some things that need fixing around the house — if you know what I mean?'

"'Sir, of course I know what you mean. I work at the First National Bank of Bed Cred.'

"'While you have my account open, can you tell me how close I am to getting a *(wink, wink)* bell and whistle?'

"'Just a second, let me switch screens here to take a closer look at your bell and whistle statement. I see here on the 24th, you told her how pretty she was at 8:03 a.m. And at 10:36 a.m., you invited her to lunch and took her to her favorite restaurant. I see you didn't use a coupon, which works well in your favor, and it seemed as if you had a lovely time, and she made a nice deposit in your account.'

"'Let's take another look here. On the 26th, you filled her gas tank in 32°-below-zero weather while she sat in the warm car. Keeping women out of the cold is an excellent move for men, and she made a nice deposit in your account for that one as well.'

"With that deposit, you had enough to *(wink, wink)* 'exchange tools' in the next few days. It shows here that you probably need to buy her some flowers and or handwash her Mercedes. And don't forget to put tire black on her tires so they will shine, and vacuum out the inside as well. With that, you would probably have enough Bed Cred for a *(wink, wink)* bell and whistle.'

"A week later, the man skipped his way to the First National Bank of Bed Cred to check on his account.

"'Good morning, young lady; I would like to check on the balance in my Bed Cred account to see if I have enough for a (wink, wink) bell and whistle, please?'

"'Certainly, sir, you seem very chipper this morning; I'll be happy to look for you — Hmmm? I'm sorry, sir, but I show here there are no funds in your account at the moment.'

"'What? A few days ago, I almost had enough for a *(wink, wink)* bell and whistle! I worked extremely hard for this bell and whistle; I don't understand what happened. I mean, the other morning, I got up early and made her breakfast and brewed her favorite coffee. Then I went out in the snow in below-zero weather to bring in the paper for her and surprised her with warm towels fresh from the dryer when she got out of the shower. I also slipped a romantic card inside her purse so she would be surprised the next time she opened it. We texted all day and had a nice texting conversation, and then that night, I took her out for a nice dinner. Are you sure there's not enough in my account for a *(wink, wink)* bell and whistle?'

"'Let's look at each line item for you, sir. Okay, on the 30th, I can see that you did all those things, and you had plenty of deposits in your account for your *(wink, wink)* bell and whistle. Wow! You even had enough for her to wear lingerie as well. Well done, sir... Oh, here's the problem.'

"'What is it? What happened to my bell and whistle?'

"'At 10:03 p.m., it shows here that you hesitated when she asked you a question, and she emptied your Bed Cred account.'

"'What the hell? I thought we had the perfect evening together!'

"'Yes, sir, it did appear that way. I do see here there's a note on the account. It looks like you hesitated when she asked if she had cellulite on her ass.'

"'What! She never asked me that! She asked if her jeans made her butt look big."

"'Sir, women consider that question to be one and the same. — So, did her butt look big in her jeans?'

"'—— Uhmmm, I don't know, maybe a little. But she looked great; her ass looked wonderful; she looked wonderful! I worked ridiculously hard for this!' I love my wife so much; why would she withdraw the funds needed for my bell and whistle?

"'Well, sir, in all fairness, you hesitated when I asked you what you said to her, so I'm guessing you hesitated when she asked about her cellulite.'

"'What the freaking hell? That question isn't fair! Besides, I don't care if she has cellulite.'

"'But she cares, and you hesitating just confirms that not only does she have cellulite, but it's now the size of craters from meteorites that have hit the earth.'

"'But I didn't say anything like that. How in the hell could she come in here and withdraw my funds like that?'

"'Well, sir, is she beautiful and a woman?'

"'Of course, she's beautiful! I love her so much.'

"'Well, that's why she could come in and make a withdrawal like this. Sir, I might suggest you check your Bed Cred account frequently during the day; accounts like these can be full one minute and empty the next — and this can often happen several times a day. You see, sir, we have learned over the years from thousands and thousands of customers that the golden rule of banking here is 'There is no golden rule of banking.' You know, like *Fight Club*.'

"'This just doesn't make sense!'

All the tellers in the Bed Cred bank burst out laughing.

"'Sir, we don't mean to laugh so hard, but did you just say, 'This just doesn't make sense?' We think you have the First National Bank of Bed Cred confused with the First Federal Reserve of Logic.'

"The man, distraught with emotion from his loss, slowly walked out of the building."

Carter's eyes reeled in every word while simultaneously feeling educated as Frank and Beans flawlessly continued.

"Meanwhile, down the street at the First Federal Reserve of Logic, the wife of the distraught husband walked in to check on her account. She went up to the teller, and with sadness in her voice, asked to check on her First Federal Reserve of Logic account.

"'Ma'am, is everything alright? You seem sad.'

"'I am sad. Last night, I got upset with my husband, who has been so wonderful and had a lot of money in his Bed Cred account. He worked and saved enough for a really great bell and whistle. I even bought new lingerie and everything, but then, as I was getting ready—'

"The teller stopped her mid-sentence, 'Let me guess. He — hesitated.'

"'Why, yes! How did you know?'

"'And did he tell you that you were the fattest woman on the planet? And first thing this morning, did you go down to The First National Bank of Bed Cred and wait in a long line of women in the freezing cold for the doors to open so that you could clear out his Bell and Whistle account?'

"The music in the lobby abruptly stopped. The tellers all bowed their heads in a moment of silence for another wasted bell and whistle's life that ended prematurely — and not in a good way. And they gave reverence for the husband's emotional pain from such a loss.

"'Wow, a moment of silence — really! Is a bell and whistle really that important to a man?'

"The tellers gasped in horror and disbelief.

"'I didn't realize how much I've been hurting my husband. I've been punishing him for years whenever he does something to upset me.'

"The teller then asked her, 'Are you here to check on your account and see if your husband withdrew all the nice things he planned to do for you? Did you want to know if he retaliated and withdrew all your funds?'"

"'Why, yes, that's exactly why I'm here.'"

"'Ma'am, can I ask you — did he actually say you looked fat in your jeans? Or did he simply hesitate when you asked him the question?'"

"Well, uh, ..."

"Ma'am, we tellers have learned a thing or two in the emotional banking business. The way we see it, the failure of most "banking transactions" comes down to men hesitating when a woman asks — "Do these jeans make my butt look big?'"

Frank continued without allowing a word in edgewise.

"'This one question has destroyed civilization as we know it because there is no correct answer. If a man confidently says, 'Yes honey, those jeans make your butt look big,' his bed cred goes to zero and stays there for a VERY long time. If a man rightfully says, 'No, honey, you look great,' his bed cred can still go to zero if his wife suspects him of lying.

"'However, lying at least has a remote possibility that he may eek by and get lucky. Sadly, men have been conditioned to believe that they must lie to be able to "exchange tools" with women by surviving these impossible tests.'

"Even mankind's hero, Capt. James T. Kirk of the *Starship U.S. S. Enterprise*, who is the only starship fleet captain ever to beat the Kobayashi Maru training exercise and who could pick up alien women from any galaxy or constellation in the known universe, could not have answered that question correctly.

"But this phenomenon goes deeper than deep space even; it's biblical, which brings us full circle to where it all began, with the story of Adam and Eve. This finally explains how Male Hesitation Syndrome has plagued the male species ever since Eve asked Adam, 'Does this fig leaf make my tushy look too big?'

"It makes perfect sense that the first male and female conversation on the planet would start with a Question and Hesitation session. And although there is no actual evidence, this happened. A certain snake who started the whole thing witnessed the conversation and thought, *Hmmm, I'm pretty sure I can use this against humanity somehow.*'

"And for the ultimate proof that it's biblical, at the wedding of Cana, when *Mary* Magdalene, Martha, and *Mary* of Bethany asked Jesus, "How do we look? Do these burkas make our backsides look big?"

"'Jesus responded, "It's gonna take a miracle to answer that question, and I need a drink!"'

"BOOM! Men and women explained! — That's all, folks; you've been a great audience. Frank and Beans is going, going, GONE!"

Carter laughed hard as the Dedacciai looked to the sky to see if lightning would strike, hoping the heavens had a sense of humor.

"Carter, the moral of the story is — Don't Hesitate! Which will definitely be a key item on your breeder's license exam. In fact, all men need to start bitch slapping each other whenever a man hesitates to keep us in check with our women — and scene."

Frank and Beans then took a bow while riding and transformed from his metaphorical comedic stage to his version of normality.

"So, where are you two cats headed?"

And with that question, the three were inseparable and bonded on a comical and emotional level for the remaining two-hour ride. The Dedacciai relaxed and listened as Carter came alive, telling Beans his life story from his new perspective. The positive attributes of what happened to him the past few days far overshadowed his dysfunctional past. And Beans? He simply "spilled the Beans" of his life back to the two men.

As the Friday Freeloaders arrived at Slovacek's, two bicycle valets handed out ticket numbers and safely loaded the bikes that were returning to their starting point into the largest U-Haul made. They had a 100% record of not scratching or damaging any bikes to date.

The Slovacek's takeover from the Friday Freeloaders was a rabble-rousing event of teenagers trapped in retirees' bodies. The 100% beer policy for the overaged teenagers was joyful to witness and a big help in contributing to why Slovacek's was a people watchers' paradise.

The now solidified "Three Amigos" pulled into the Slovacek's parking lot. Beans and Dedacciai found themselves on each side of Carter. They yelled congratulations as they raised his arms triumphantly for his first century ride. Cyclist after cyclist picked a form of congratulatory pageantry for Carter as they passed him.

The three men, energized from their accomplishment, needed Slovacek's Barbeque to recover. As they headed to the café, Carter reflected on the day and saw the Slovacek's dog park.

"Hey, guys, can we go to the dog park for a bit before we eat?"

The Dedacciai knew Carter was reminiscing about Lance, and The Three Amigos changed course and waddled their way toward the dog park after their long ride. The Dedacciai noticed the time and excused himself to make his 5:55 p.m. five-ring phone call to his Bellavia to signify his love for her. His heart raced as the thrill that she might answer rivaled the terror that she would answer. Once again — no answer. It was 6 p.m. as he re-entered the park and joined Carter and Beans as they watched the cross-country traveling mixture of dogs running, sniffing, and playing with each other.

As they found a seat, a man named Rusty greeted them.

"Are you here for Skyler's going away party?"

And before anyone could answer, a beautiful Alaskan husky came waltzing clumsily by, bumping into Dedacciai's leg and tried smelling his inseam up and down.

"Well, who's this beautiful creature?" as the Dedacciai dropped eye level to look into the mesmerizing bright-blue eyes of his canine companion.

"This is Skyler," his human said, walking up.

"So this is Skyler," the Dedacciai said while rubbing him. "Rusty just asked us if we were here for his going away party. But we're here to relax before eating at the Kissing Pig Café."

"I can certainly understand that. I'm Drew, — Drew Simmons. I'm Skyler's dad. My wife Kelly and I love this place. Skyler, too. He loves coming here to play while we eat and has pretty much tried everything on the menu. I asked the owner if we could book the dog park for his going away party, and he graciously accommodated us."

Beans interjected, "I thought I noticed some 'fuzzy,' or rather 'furry,' math. The people-to-dog ratio seems way off tonight."

Drew smirked, "Yes, nice observation. That's because there are a lot of Skyler's friends here to say goodbye."

"I'm sorry, is this a private party? Do we need to leave?" the Dedacciai offered.

"Listen, you're welcome to stay. Besides, Skyler's already sniffed your inseam; you're practically family."

The Dedacciai smiled and nodded to confirm he accepted the invitation for the three of them. "So, where is Skyler going, if I might ask?" The Dedacciai was still mesmerized by Skyler's beauty.

Drew looked down upon his furry companion of fifteen short years as tears welled up in his eyes. "He's going to Heaven — He'll be there tonight at 10:30."

The three realized this beautiful spirit would be gone in a matter of hours, and their emotional avalanches hit each of them. Images of Addison playing with Zilla in the park flooded Dedacciai. He latched onto Skyler's neck and hugged him, and he had a hard time letting go as he heard Addison's voice play in his mind: *Don't cry, Papa. It's okay. I'll take care of Skyler. We will walk to the park every day and play a game of fetch together.*

With the freshness of his first pet experience with Lance, Carter could already feel the pain of what this loss must be like for his owners. Frank Beansley relived all the dogs that emotionally saved him through the dark and lonely times between wives as his comedic alter ego Beans left his mental stage.

Drew felt his mysterious guests' bond with Skyler after a few short sniffs of each of their inseams while Drew's eyes continued what they had started.

"I'm sorry. I thought I'd be stronger than this. Skyler is eaten up with cancer and can hardly walk in a straight line anymore. The vet says he's in a lot of pain. He's coming to the house tonight at 10:30 to set him free. But we wanted to give him a real party and have everyone who loved him say goodbye. It's obvious you guys love him, so I'm glad you're here."

Skyler's mom, Kelly, appeared as her husband's body language signaled that he might need her.

"Are you alright, honey?"

"I'm fine — just having a moment watching Skyler make some new friends here. Skyler wants them to stay for the party. I hope that's okay?"

"I'm not sure — did they pass the smell test?"

"Yes, Skyler knows every inch of their inseams."

Carter helped the Dedacciai stand, as he could tell his emotions drained him of that ability for the moment.

"Hi, Kelly, I'm the Dedacciai, and these are my friends, Frank and Carter. We didn't mean to intrude on your party but are truly honored by your husband's invitation."

"Hey, the party is for all those who love Skyler. It seems you qualify. But we are all here to celebrate fifteen years of love Skyler has given us. So, please don't make me ban you two crybabies from the party. No raining on his parade! We're going to laugh and enjoy what time we have left with him tonight.

"For his last supper, the owner is fixing him a special meat platter with every meat on the menu and an assortment of menu items and sandwiches for the rest of us. There will be plenty, so please stay and eat with us."

"Kelly, we'd be honored to celebrate his life with everyone."

She stood on a bench and addressed the crowd of approximately forty partygoers.

"Thank you, everyone, for sharing your time and love for Skyler with us. Just a reminder: This is a celebration of Skyler's life, so no crying. I've already had to warn my husband and his new friend, the Dedacciai, not to be crybabies. I don't want to ban them, but I will if I have to, and that goes for everybody here. So, let the celebration begin." With that, Kelly signaled the owner to bring out the food.

Carter watched the Dedacciai's reaction to the news of Skyler's impending doom, which concerned him. He didn't want him to relapse into the darkness of whatever he was going through.

"Hey, guys, since I've never had a pet, is a going-away party like this something everyone does?" Carter asked.

Before the Dedacciai could answer, a field of strangers approached the newcomers to introduce themselves. Beans quickly reappeared as laughter emanated from whichever section of the dog park he was at. Carter found himself once again shaking hands with strangers and enjoying it. The Carter of four days ago wouldn't recognize the Carter of today. But he maintained a vigilant watch over Dedacciai for any signs of sadness or darkness after the stern warning that this was a no-cry zone.

"Okay, everyone." — The baton motions from Drew's extended arms signaled everyone to chime in at once.

"For he's a jolly good fellow — For he's a jolly good fellow — For he's a jolly good fell-ell-looowww— which nobody can deny!"

Hoots and hollers of all different sizes and shapes rang out, and laughter and joy emanated from the partygoers. Beer bottles and cups filled with many different substances clanked against each other in celebration as the barbeque hodge-podge was served.

Kelly's request for partygoers not to cry was an epic fail as they watched Skyler struggle to eat his final meal. After everyone had consumed the barbeque feast, Kelly resumed her rightful place on top of the bench.

"Okay, everyone, I'd like to open the evening up to anyone who would like to say a few words for Skyler."

She started by giving her heartfelt tribute to what Skyler meant to her life as Drew stood on the bench next to her and seamlessly continued what she had started. There was a flood of emotions among the crowd and a slight pause for who might be the first to pay tribute when they finished. It only took a few seconds before the lid of stage fright lifted, and once the first commoner spoke, it was hard to stop. While everyone gave a tribute, Addison's voice chimed in her papa's head.

Papa, you need to say something. Tell them about the doggy poem you wrote. I love that poem. Papa, please! Do it for me. I want to hear your voice again. Please! I think everyone would love to listen to it, Papa.

The inner-defuncted grandpa struggled with Addison's request. But if he was to hold true and honor her life, it must happen now, as it was getting toward the end of the tributes. There was a pause at the tribute pitching mound, and the Dedacciai stepped up to the plate.

"Hi, everyone; for those that don't know me, I'm the Dedacciai. My friends and I happened upon this extraordinary celebration, and Drew graciously invited us to stay. Drew and Kelly's kindness toward complete strangers is remarkable.

I know everyone here has a dog that has made an enormous impact of love on their life. I wrote something long ago about our furry companions that I read to my kids (*and granddaughter,* he thought). And if I can remember it, I'd like to recite it for you. It's called 'These Things That Go Bark.'

"These things that go bark are lots of fun
and love to run, walk, and play.
And they love to do it with the ones they love,
every single day.

There's not a day that goes by that they hold a grudge,
and never do they judge.
But more than that, these things that go bark,
they never hold back love.

These things that go bark wake each day from the dark,
and each time with a great attitude.
Because they love what they have
and don't need what they don't,
because they live in what's called gratitude.

They don't ask for a toy, and they don't postpone joy,
and never, ever do they live in the past.
They only live in the present moment they know
and not in a future forecast.

These things that go bark aren't about the color of skin,
or whatever size seems to be you.

And they don't care about the color or length of your hair
or if you don't have hair or you do.

And they don't care about the clothes that you wear,
so wear your worst dress or holey best sweats.
And it doesn't matter how much makeup you smear,
because however you look, they like best.

And they will watch whatever channel you want,
and never will they want the remote.
And they don't care about what's in the bank,
or how expensive your house, car, or boat.

But when you are feeling blue, then they will too,
until they lick all your troubles away.
And if you are hurt, they will lie next to you,
until everything is okay.

There's a reason they call them man's best friend,
because they implore only one strategy.
They give love away, with one guarantee:
That their love will forever be free.

"Here's to you, Skyler; we wish we could simply lick all your troubles away. We will miss your love."

Silence overcame the dog park as everyone held their dogs or knelt beside them as they listened. Just then, Skyler made his way to the Dedacciai and began licking his hand. The roar of sniffles echoed in the park as the Dedacciai kneeled to the ground and hugged Skyler. He imagined he had read the poem to his young kids and the impossible dream of Addison's ears swallowing his words again.

Drew and Kelly knelt beside him and hugged their mystery guest and Skyler simultaneously. Skyler had a lick fest that started with the three humans but grew into a mound of humans bidding for a healing lick from Skyler himself.

As the pile let up, Carter was there to ensure the Dedacciai was okay and looked for signs of darkness. He stood back with Frank and waited patiently for the crowd to disperse from thanking him for his poem.

Kelly and Drew stood up on the bench one last time.

"I can't thank everyone enough for your kind words today. Thank you, Dedacciai, for those perfect words to end our celebration of life. Thanks for coming, everyone; you are officially dismissed."

The Three Amigos watched as Drew and Kelly loaded Skyler into their SUV.

"Carter, you asked if everyone has a going-away party for their pet. Truthfully, I've never heard of anyone doing this before. But now that we're in attendance, I'm surprised people don't do it more often. I know the thought of it is rather sad, but the reality of it is really loving."

"Dedacciai, you need to become a professional funeral crasher and start giving random eulogies for people, pets, or objects," Carter said. "Beans, you should've heard the eulogy he gave for my former nose ring in IHOP at 3 a.m. as he buried it in a container of coffee grounds."

"Damn! This is not a good time to be out of the comedy loop; you two are ripe with material. I can get them laughing one minute, and then BAM! Hit them with something serious. I could be a Thinking Man's Comic, something I've never been accused of before — thinking. Guys, I don't live that far from here; you two should stay at my house tonight instead of finding a hotel. If you want, I could have someone pick us up in a few minutes?"

Carter spoke up. "I'm in; that's a great idea! How about you, Dedacciai? You in?"

"As long as Mr. Beans doesn't keep us up all night with his comic routines," Dedacciai said sarcastically.

"No way, dude! I'm counting on it!" Carter said.

"Guys, there's plenty of room for you to spread out so you can hear or not hear my performances. Bonus: you can fart in peace. You can also wash your clothes and be ready for Dallas first thing. I haven't had company in a while; this sounds fun. Let me call someone — I know a guy."

Within forty-three minutes, an unmarked black Mercedes cargo van pulled up to a massive set of iron gates protecting a rather large mansion in the Texas countryside.

"Damn, is this your — house?" Carter's voice quivered.

"You mean my quaint cottage in the woods? Yes, this is it."

"How many times did you open for Leno again?" Dedacciai asked.

"Just the once, but I did help the man write jokes for years, along with a team of writers."

"Okay, that explains things. So why do you do handyman repair if you have all this?" the Dedacciai queried.

"Well, all this has taxes and upkeep, and I find it's best to keep my mind and body occupied. I tell ya, it's a dark place, running around in your own mind. Not a safe neighborhood at all, not one bit! Besides, I enjoy helping people repair their DIY failures and making them laugh at themselves. It gives me a sense of giving back," Beans said proudly.

"Mr. Frank A. Beansley, the saying 'never judge a book by its cover' sounds rather appropriate here. You're a good guy underneath all that comedy stuff. Aren't ya? Aren't ya? Aren't Ya?" the Dedacciai escalated jokingly.

"Hush, I don't want my neighbors to hear. I have a reputation to uphold!" Beans defended.

The midnight hour came and went amongst the verbal jousting, comradery, and private Beans Comedy Show Performances. The Dedacciai eventually wore down and excused himself for the night.

"Carter, let's head out tomorrow around ten. We only have approximately seventy miles or so to reach Dallas, so we should make it tomorrow unless we want to rest and get there Sunday instead. — Frank, thank you so much for your hospitality; you made this day fun. Thank you for the laughter — Goodnight."

"No problem, and by the way, I'm one hell of a cook. I'll make you guys breakfast for a proper send-off. Belgian waffles with cream cheese icing are my specialty if you care to try them. It may sound weird, but you'll never be the same after you try one. Plus, I can also do boring traditional bacon and egg stuff."

"You had me at 'I'm one hell of a cook.' I'll see you guys in the morning." And with that, a round of man-nods ensued as part of the Dedacciai's send-off.

"Carter, what's this thing you got going on with Dedacciai about earning your breeder's license? How did this even come about? I mean, you're a handsome devil. I find it hard to believe that at twenty-five, you haven't practiced breeding before."

"It's because they scare me — women scare me," Carter answered.

"Well, not to scare the world, but with a name like Frank and Beans, I have been breeding since I was sixteen. But only practice breeding, not breed breeding. Once I bought my first car, nothing was the same. My backseat and I became best friends.

"I named the backseat of my bright red '75 Mercury Cougar Backseat Sally, and she was the guardian of my escapades. She was also the longest female relationship I've ever had. Even longer than my mom, as she died when I was nine. It just might be why I was married five times. I didn't have her love and guidance when it counted. But I still have her in my garage."

"Wait a minute; you still have your mom in your garage?" Carter asked, confused.

"Hell no, I don't keep my mother in the garage! What kind of barbarian do you think I am? She hated the Texas heat. Besides, she's in the urn on that bookshelf near the air vent to keep her comfortable and where she has a great view."

"So, who's in the garage, then?"

"I keep Backseat Sally in the garage," he shrugged as if to say, *Who doesn't do this?*

Carter's face countered with a *Who in the hell does do this?* as he awaited an explanation.

"After I totaled my beautiful bright red '75 Mercury Cougar with a gorgeous bright-white vinyl top in wreck number three. I couldn't part with the bright-red Corinthian leather of Backseat Sally, so I kept her. Backseat Sally is where I write much of my material to this day — like I said, B.F.F.s forever. So, Carter, let's get back to why you're so screwed up and need a breeder's license."

"Well, I'm screwed up for the opposite reasons you are. When I turned sixteen, we couldn't afford to buy me a car; we didn't even have a household car I could borrow. My dad had multiple D.U.I.s, three I know of for sure. When you're sixteen and don't have a car in high school, you get left behind and alienated, which is bad enough. But I rode my bike to school, which gave people an extra level to make fun of me — and most of the girls were vicious.

"I didn't have a father figure who taught me anything about relationships except how to have a bad one. So, I had kind of a P.T.S.D. reaction around girls until I met the Dedacciai and Connie Sue Lancaster.

"Anyway, between these two, they're determined to help me get over my fear of women. Connie Sue is the most beautiful woman you'll ever see, and she's my friend because of the Dedacciai. She talked to me last night about some relationship stuff and said she'd help me when I got back. She even gave me a Bible to help me with some God stuff, which I will use to read up on that Bible routine you did."

"You know, Carter, I've learned a few things from my failed marriages. Most importantly — in a relationship, love that keeps score is not love." Frank paused. "Sorry, dude, maybe you don't want to hear relationship advice from a guy who's been married five times. But if you want my two cents worth, I'd gladly share. And I promise I'm not setting you up for a routine."

"Dude! I most definitely want to hear it, like, *definitely-definitely*. I'm talking double, definitely!"

"See that — I knew you were a smart kid. I don't want you to make the same mistakes I did. I also don't want to say anything about relationships if you don't want to hear it. Trust me, unsolicited advice is exactly that — unsolicited! It is usually considered criticism in disguise and never given any emotional gravity by the ears that don't want to hear it." But Frank was excited that Carter really did double definitely want to hear what he had to offer.

"Frank, your routines are fascinating, so your relationship advice should be quite interesting, to say the least. Besides, I'm not sure about this — but I think the Dedacciai has only been married once, so what can he possibly know about relationships? He's still a rookie and not a pro like you." Frank smiled at Carter's teasing, then they found themselves gut-laughing from the irony.

As the laughter subsided, Frank became more serious and spoke in a calm, slow relationship counselor-type voice.

"Okay, Carter, here it goes, but stop me if you have a question or lose interest. As I started to say, in a relationship, love that keeps score is not love. However, many people unknowingly think it is. For instance, people like me had to learn this the hard way, so let me explain.

"At the beginning of any relationship, when everything is shiny and new, one person will usually do something sweet and romantic, and often as a surprise, which creates joy in the recipient. And when two people are courting, the other participant usually does something back to create joy in return. This leads to two people unconsciously establishing an attitude of 'Okay, I did this for you; now it's your turn.' Then, they wait for the other person to respond before doing something else. This one premise led to my marital demise five times in a row. It is Trouble with a capital 'T,' and here's why.

"At the beginning of my relationships, when everything was new and exciting, the person I was dating would want to reciprocate with a loving gesture, which is okay — great even. But love in and of itself isn't reciprocal. The problem with reciprocal love is the expectation that it creates, that someone *has* to reciprocate for it to be love.

"Herein lies the rub. When my relationships lost their 'new car smell,' which almost every relationship does, the person I was dating didn't want to respond as much. Once one of the members of any relationship skips their turn, the other participant may not put in as much thought or effort on their next romantic gesture. Then, the other participant will notice that the valiant effort once given by their partner has become noticeably lackluster, and not what they're accustomed to, and not what they expected.

"Remember this always, Carter. Expectations, more than anything, create resentment. This resentment leads to anger, then to hate. And ultimately, what causes two people in love to fall out of love, which is what happened to me."

Carter stared, mesmerized, and absorbed every syllable.

"Do you know how long men and women have courted each other? We've been playing this game since the first caveman dragged home a woolly mammoth with a *Montsechia vidalii* plant hidden behind his back as a grand gesture of love. Let's analyze this mysterious little thing called courting. Let's start with the word 'court.'

"A court is something used to play a game. Thus, we have the tennis court, basketball court, volleyball court, and now, the relationship court. Let's take tennis as an example. When someone stops volleying the tennis ball back, the game ceases to be fun. Suppose one of the players continues to serve without the other attempting to volley it back. In that case, the server with no response is likely to find someone else who is willing to volley the ball back to them. And this is not a good thing for any relationship. Carter, when love becomes a game between two people, it's fun while you're playing, but just like in any game, someone must lose.

"To avoid falling into this relationship trap, you must consciously adopt a different love strategy. The best love strategy on the market today has been employed by dogs for over 15,000 years to stay at the top of the man's best friend list. And after what we witnessed tonight with Skyler, this is the perfect time for you to understand this.

"Carter, it's this simple — Love isn't love until you give it away, which is a textbook definition of a dog's love. I have never heard of someone falling out of love with their dog, let alone their pet bunny rabbit. And you never see headlines about celebrities breaking up with their dogs. The dog is man's best friend for a reason; it's simply the result of the love strategy a dog uses to be loved forever, just like the Dedacciai said in his poem.

"With this love strategy, imagine what your relationship could've been with your dad. And what your future relationships will be once you obtain your breeder's license and are cleared for take-off — which still cracks me up.

"If I practiced what I preached, I might still be with wife number one myself. But I didn't, so it took five failed marriages and three rounds of marriage counseling to finally understand what I was doing wrong.

"I just want to reiterate this one last time — Never hesitate! Male Hesitation Syndrome is a real thing! When a female asks if these jeans make her butt look big — there's no time to explain the emotional chess match in your mind to answer each scenario before giving her a logical answer.

"Logic doesn't work in this line of emotional questioning, so practice, practice saying NO — immediately! And then backtrack with an 'Oh, I'm sorry; I misunderstood you.' If you stop the female from filling in the blank with her own answer to what she thought you should say, you might have a chance! I can't emphasize this enough, but not hesitating is monumental in a relationship; it is vital to everything, along with a dog's love strategy.

"Dedacciai's poem tonight was an amazing portrayal of what a dog's love means. If you truly base your relationship on how a dog loves, I think it will be the greatest gift you can have to succeed in a relationship and pass the breeder's exam with flying colors. Okay, with my advice, you should be able to become the King of Kings, the Dude of Dudes." Frank bowed and curtsied. "That's all I got — What-cha think? — make sense?"

"It makes perfect sense. On the road tomorrow, I'm going to explain to Dedacciai what I've learned from you and Connie Sue about relationships before Dedacciai can even bring it up. What you said truly makes perfect sense, and I believe the Dedacciai would probably say his version of what you said anyway. I might blow his mind; at least, that will be my goal. I might just earn my breeder's license and be closing in on a chance for a relationship after all."

Beans agreed as he mimicked a mind-blown emoji, complete with sound effects, before firing off a man-nod in Carter's direction.

"Well, Carter, look at that; it's almost 3 a.m., and you need to get your beauty rest. Thanks for listening tonight. I usually don't get many captive audiences to hear the more serious side of Frank A. Beansley. It was nice to feel heard, which I frequently heard as a complaint from my wives, but it applies to everybody. People simply want to feel heard."

"Dude, Connie Sue told me something like that as well. She said to be present during your relationship, turn off your cell phone, and listen without trying to fix everything. I've had some great advice, haven't I? Thanks, Beans, I guess I need to get some sleep — I might have another long day in the saddle."

"Until tomorrow — Ciao, amigo!" Frank Andrewchow Beansley gave his signature greet and retreat phrase and the last words of the night.

Chapter Twenty-Three

The Clicker vs. The Macabre

The wolves were howling, beckoned by a full blue moon out of some horror movie opener. The cobblestone streets, which begged for a horse's clip-clopping hooves to echo throughout their corridors and alleyways, lay quiet. Even the animals dared not venture into the dark early morning London hour, where the lampposts flickered eerily, stubbornly, as they shined defiantly into the charcoal night while sharing their amber glow with the pavement and giving the shadows rest as they intersected each other's way of life — Back and forth, yin and yang, darkness and light. What their relationship dance expected of each other — regardless of whether anyone admired it.

In the heavy soot that descended from burning coal and amplified the choking London fog, Sherlock "the Clicker" Holmes searched for clues left behind by his nemesis, the Phantom Professor Moriarty. The hairs on the back of his neck stood on end, particularly where the streetlamp's flickers were distanced from each other.

Oh, the privilege to have the skill of a great detective. To have the mind and eye for clues, the legendary power of deduction, of which his prowess had no equal. Sherlock, "the Clicker" Holmes, was the brightest of the famous unravellers of mystery. On this eldritch night, he was armed only with his signature silver and chrome magnifying glass, long-stemmed cherrywood pipe, custom-made deerstalker hat, and a bespoke Kilt patterned in German clan colors.

In this lonely hour, was he the only beating heart, the only being of warm blood and flesh that dared the cobblestone streets that night? Or was his Nemesis, the Phantom Professor Moriarty, lurking in the fog before or behind him?

Then something appeared, a vague outline in the fog ahead. He hastened his pace to catch the mysterious suspect. In four lampposts' distance, he found himself ten paces away from confronting his Machiavellian criminal mastermind, the Phantom Professor Moriarty. Then suddenly, his nemesis stopped post haste, spun around, and espied the eye of his mental foe.

Sherlock was met by a gruesome encounter of the Macabre, an image, scraggly in nature, with chest wide open and absent of heart.

The Macabre scene receded instantaneously as the Clicker bolted upright due to a rapid infusion of adrenaline, which interrupted the thrilling arena where dreams exist. The vision that awakened him left him exhilarated and smiling from the Phantom Moriarty confrontation — but what did this mean?

One definition of the macabre is "an entity representing or personifying death." The Clicker's new real-life Phantom Moriarty was clearly the personification of the macabre in his mind. Their parking lot clash had awoken the Clicker's alter ego. 'Wolfrem Holmes' was now part of his reality, both real and in dream, and who had kept his subconscious sleep-wake cycle entertained for most of the Clicker's mandatory 8.162 hours of sleep that night.

The Clicker wrestled with this whole macabre line of thinking, as his anti-theist belief system did not allow for such nonsense to exist outside the human body. But now, he had to put himself in a spiritual realm and start thinking like the macabre, as if they exist, to find clues to what they thought happened after death.

Wolfrem Holmes continued thinking of the macabre imagery from his dream and the verbal parking lot confrontation. He dissected every syllable and action and compiled a verbal saga and action imagery roadmap of clues from his deductive construct.

The Clicker didn't go looking for the macabre, although surrounded by its potential daily. But today, the macabre came into his house looking for him.

After the photos didn't seem to appear on Ivan's internet, Wolfrem Holmes began to suspect this visitor to be the personification of the macabre. What he knew was that if the macabre was here, then its every action was a clue, and every word should be taken literally. The macabre are not stupid, and this Phantom Moriarty obviously had an intellectual prowess that beckoned the Clicker to analyze their clash in extreme detail.

1st Clue — The macabre exiting from the morgue — *What an oxymoron, such a desperate play to grab my attention.*
2nd Clue — He obviously knew of the meeting and heard the results. *He must have overheard Addison's family say Wolff-Parkinson-White syndrome. And he possibly made contact with Addison's family to know I was helping put Humpty Dumpty back together again.*
3rd Clue — The Macabre said, "I was paying respect to my friend's granddaughter for him because he couldn't be here today. I left earlier than the others in the room; that's why I was alone." — *If true? The macabre is genuinely aware of his friend and where he might be.*
4th Clue — Acknowledging he knew I was leaving early to visit Bunny and people lovingly referred to me as "the Clicker." — *Typical macabre, trying to use personal knowledge of routine, nickname, or loved one to scare me in order to gain leverage — so typical.*
5th Clue — "Following your heart is a good thing. I do it every year at this time." — *A bleeding-heart macabre with feelings — geez, maybe they are stupid.*
6th Clue — He said he gave me enough clues to take it from here — *Meaning? If I follow this scavenger hunt of sorts, it will lead me to my friend. Not sure why the ghost and pony show.*
7th Clue — He said, "And on a personal note, thanks for what you did for me all those years ago." — *Obviously, I have crossed paths with him in my career. But when, why, and what did I do for him?*
8th Clue — He gave me an Eye-Jobe — *Once again, using very select personal data to let me know there is no doubt he knows my friend.*

3:06 a.m. — The phone rang as the Clicker answered to a screaming thick Russian accent.

"WERE YOUR BALLS BURNING!? You know, human people talking behind your balls. Not sure which metaphor — English, — hard language, very hard. — Russian metaphor — much easier. Ivan now begin. — YOU CLICKING AMERICAN — Now you've pooch screwed us! — Busted Universe Ecosystem. Halloween portal now open. — Ivan scared, very scared. Your fault Ivan work from underground bunker last night — yes, your fault! I know Ivan help with elaborate Halloween pranks, but are you doing pre-Halloween farking with me. — You must be pre-Halloween farking with me — Ghost not real — Serious — I not make turds up your ass!"

"Ivan, get a hold of yourself; what the hell are you screaming about this time? I pay you to find out stuff, not yell broken Russian English at me. What the hell did you find you babbling cosmonaut?"

"Ivan find out October 4th — bad day, very bad day. — Too many people die this day. Oh, before Ivan forgets. I love watching Bunny. You and Bunny look so cute sleeping together. Bunny make good reality TV. Ivan might need upgrade bedroom camera. American bunnies just so cute. — Russian bunnies — not so cute. — Chernobyl not good for bunny population. Extra bunny parts, not cute — well, sometimes cute, depending on extra appendage."

"Dammit, Ivan! Would you stay on point and stop going down the literal rabbit hole with your bunny obsession? I hired you to make it impossible to hack into my system. —You know I know assassins as well! Don't you...!?"

"Oh, my clicking American friend — no need for an assman, no need. — I promise — your place impenetrable, very impenetrable — Everybody but me — impenetrable."

"I don't have time for this, Ivan; what did you find?"

"Ivan find October 4th not good day — Too many people want to die this day. — No more October 4th for me — must mark off all Ivan's calendars. —joining 13th Floor and dodo birds."

"What are you talking about? Who all died?"

"Addison die, Bronson Montgomery die, Darius Montgomery — all die this day. — Darius man now ghosting people — and not the cell phone way. — Real ghost way. — Driving 20-year-old van way. — You somehow open Halloween Hellhole with Clicker antics you do. — Ivan had to go down bunker and dig out American microfiche to find original news clippings."

"Ivan, would you please calm down, take a deep breath, stop babbling, and focus? Take some of your Russian cannabis and chill so you can try putting some sensical words together."

"Good idea, Ivan be back — few minutes."

"Ivan, I don't have a few minutes! —" The Clicker's words were useless and heard by no one as the yearlong minutes passed before Ivan returned.

"Okay, my clicking friend — Russian cannabis in system, — Ivan try again. Man kill himself 20 years ago on 5th anniversary of son's death — Bronson, — which also son's birthday — which also three days ago — same day Addison die. — Darius Edward Montgomery, his name was.

Newspaper article reports man slit wrist outside Austin hospital — include handwritten letter to hospital to use his organs for current hospital patients and not nationwide donor list. — Specific request to help local patients only. — He kills himself in mid-sized white cargo van — same license plate you give me. That's why Ivan know macabre after you! — When macabre find you — so sad see you go, so quick — so sad. — I find Bunny a nice home, maybe buy friend for Bunny to make screw with. Ivan read somewhere bunny rabbits like screw-time."

"Dammit, Ivan, there are no ghosts, and I'm not going anywhere! Now, back up for a second. You said he had a letter telling them to use his organs. What happened with his organs?"

"Yes — that's why Ivan know you open Halloween hellhole. — Ivan e-mail you document from microfiche — Clicker at hospital October 4th hellhole night. See for selfie how Clicker signature on documents. Clicker work hard to save organs and find human homes for them."

The other end of the phone went silent as the Clicker's hair lifted off the back of his neck as he recalled that night. And then the resurgence of the Phantom Moriarty statement in the parking lot merged with the macabre imagery from his dream. Everything became evident in his mind.

"Ivan, this Darius man said to me that following my heart was a good thing; he does it every year at this time. Then he said, 'On a personal note, thanks for what you did for me all those years ago.' So that's what I did for him — give away his organs, and that is where we crossed paths. Ivan, he must be leaving us a clue. He's talking figuratively *and* literally. He comes to visit his heart every October 4th, but I don't think he's just talking about the anniversary of his son's death. Who did his heart go to? Do you know?"

"It's in microfiche articles I send you — Ivan check." — There was a long pause while Ivan researched articles.

"Dr. Gary Stidham — name sound familiar? That is doctor name on document that performed transplant. Shows you consulting doctor that help place heart organ in patient by name of — let's see here, young boy — Carter William Ducane —"

"That's it, I remember now! A young boy in the hospital had just turned six or seven that day and needed a new heart. Their blood type was a perfect match, and I had to determine if the young boy's chest cavity would hold the deceased man's heart.

"I remember that the heart from this Darius man was uniquely small, and the chest cavity on the boy was rather large."

The Macabre imagery of a scruffy man with an open chest flashed like a road hazard signal in his mind as his dream now made perfect sense.

"Ivan, for all the crap I put up with, you're once again worth it. Send me everything you have so far; I'll take it from here. Check your Swiss bank account soon. You will be extremely pleased on this one. One last thing — if you need to upgrade cameras to watch Bunny, I'll allow it. Thanks, my crazy-ass Russian friend."

"Oh, my clicking American friend, you make Ivan so happy, so, so, very happy. — Good luck with ghost people. Ivan promise to buy Bunny friend for screw time if ghost people eat you — Ivan do that for you — Russian scouts honor."

It was 4:38 a.m. as Dr. Wolfrem Jezercak called his old colleague, Dr. Stidham, to discuss the now twenty-year-old case.

"Wolfrem, what are you doing calling this early? Is everything alright? Are you okay?"

"I'm okay, Gary. I've had a rather bizarre thing happen that has to do with a heart transplant case you and I worked on twenty years ago. I wanted to see what you remembered."

"Okay, Wolfrem, I'll try. My thinker isn't as good as it once was, but I'll give it a shot. What do you have for me?"

"Back when I was working with you at the hospital, do you remember when a man killed himself outside the hospital in his van one night and requested his organs go to patients in the hospital? According to what I have here, we consulted on a young boy named Carter William Ducane. What do you remember about that case?"

"Wow, that's a doozy question for 4:45 in the morning. Let's see here. I do remember that night, us working on that case. I remember they were a perfect blood type match, and everything worked out as far as fit because the donor's heart was on the small side, and the boy's chest cavity would support it.

"There were absolutely no complications with the surgery. It went beyond perfect, but I do remember this: the parents did not have insurance, and it was a tremendous financial burden for them because they were supposed to make frequent follow-up appointments, but after a couple of years, they quit coming altogether. I remember thinking his dad was a piece of work. Over the two years that I did see Carter, it seemed like the family took a nosedive, for lack of a better phrase."

"Gary, could you send me your files on Carter and any contact information you have? I'd greatly appreciate it. I don't want to be a pain, but this is extremely urgent. Are you still a scotch man? I will send you a bottle of my best for your expediency."

"If I remember, your scotch is top shelf! It will be there within the hour. Is that email still valid from when we worked together?"

"Yes, sir, thanks, Gary. Come by the examiner's office when you can, and we'll catch up."

"Wolfrem, it's odd that this case has resurfaced. I've always wondered what happened to Carter because he seemed to be a miracle case. He was such a perfect genetic match for his heart that his anti-rejection drugs didn't seem necessary for him to live. The problem was his dad used that as an excuse to stop coming. As I'm sure you know, heart transplants rarely last this long. If Carter is still alive, it would be a miracle — and if he is still alive, you need to take a serious look at how he's doing.

"What concerns me most is that Carter might need a new ticker, and soon! I would be glad to be in your camp and help however I can, just like in the old days. Remember, I have some pull because Carter probably needs to get on a transplant list, and I know people."

The hunt for the Red October heart had begun. The Clicker took over hacking duties and worked alongside his stateside hacker, Ray from I.T., to learn all they could about Darius Montgomery and his son Bronson. — But mainly focusing on the living of the three, Carter Ducane, his family, and his current occupation and location.

The Clicker read everything Ivan sent and saw that Darius Edward Montgomery had no surviving family members when he died. His ex-wife had passed from liver disease due to alcoholism earlier that year. Texas state law found the nearest distant relatives and distributed the deceased's assets.

Darius Montgomery's van was eventually taken to a plot of land owned by one of the receiving relatives and never heard from again. The Clicker was pleased with Ivan's extensive hacking job, as he had already listed the address of where the white metal clue might be hiding.

Further reading provided the cemetery map of where Bronson Edward Montgomery's headstone lay as well. The Clicker was sure the cemetery was part of the whole 'I follow my heart' theme of his October visits.

The Clicker and Ray from I.T. now concentrated on finding as much information as possible on Carter Ducane. They looked for his residence, cell phone, and banking records.

The first piece of information that intrigued the Clicker was that Carter William Ducane had no driver's license registered with the Texas Department of Public Safety. But his Texas state ID was scheduled to be renewed this year by the end of December, so his DPS photo on file was now six years old. A lot of physical changes happen between nineteen and twenty-five. Furthermore, he had zero social media presence. Cell phone records indicated no texts or phone calls since Tuesday, October 4th, which would have been his 25th birthday on the now-evident macabre Holiday of Death.

The Clicker had the fleeting notion that maybe there was a fourth victim on this death holiday somewhere in the form of Carter William Ducane. Further hacking discoveries showed a 5 a.m. debit card transaction at the Lancaster Landing Hotel for $200 that early October 5th morning and another for $20 at 10:30 a.m. at Cycledelic Bike Therapy. As far as they could tell, no other debit card transactions had happened since that date.

The $200 amount prompted skepticism and a visit to the website where $200-a-night rooms existed only in one's dreams and not at the Lancaster Hotel. It was an odd amount for a hotel where $200 wouldn't buy a night in the janitor's closet.

The Clicker deemed this needed serious contemplation and leaned back into his familiar position. His left-hand fingers and thumb unconsciously worked with seamless strokes through his brownish-gray Van Dyke beard while his shoes laid propped on his desk.

His first counter-conclusion to the notion that Carter was a fourth victim was that Carter's ID, debit card, and cell phone were stolen. The perpetrator spent a luxury night at the hotel, then used it again at the bicycle shop to possibly buy parts to flee on a bicycle. That would make sense, as perhaps a poor or homeless bicycle thief would have wanted to sleep in a comfortable bed before traveling the next day. And now the thief has dispensed with his debit card.

The Clicker instructed Ray to hack into the security cameras at both places, starting at the hotel to look at the night in question. Once Ray hacked his way in, he found only static-filled footage from the outside camera. But before the inertia of static overloaded the image, it seemed like a white cargo van approached the entrance. Ray then found the lobby camera footage from a few minutes later. The image of a white male who might fit the description of Carter Ducane was walking into the building, rolling what looked like two bicycles before the static monster swallowed the footage.

"What the hell is happening here, Ray? Can't you do something to remove the static with some super-secret software spy program that only you dark-webbing hacker guys have?"

"Someone has been watching way too much *NCIS*. But I'll admit, this is the strangest thing I've seen. The timing is highly suspect. Here's a thought. Maybe this Carter guy is already part of the macabre and can't be seen because he has his heart or something."

"Okay, Ray, now you're just talking crazy talk. Keep digging into everything on our list. But the bicycles probably mean I was right. Someone stole or found his ID, and he and a bicycling buddy used it for a good night's rest. So, what about the bicycle shop cameras? Anything there?"

"I couldn't find any at the bicycle shop. They may have an older private system not hooked to the internet."

"Okay, I'm going to visit the hotel first and then the bicycle shop. Let me know if Carter's cell phone pings or other debit card transactions occur."

A few minutes later, at 1:07 p.m., the Clicker's 105th-anniversary special-edition Harley-Davidson Road Machine started to rumble before the Doppler effect echoed into oblivion.

Meanwhile, Evan was home trying to accept his new normal without Addison and contemplating where his father could be. He was obsessed with figuring this out and felt he was one thought away from *'the something'* that would change the tide. His need to find his dad burned in his soul as Evan longed to be forgiven by him. He appreciated the forgiveness he had for his pops and the burden of hate that he no longer carried. The tide of hate pulled into the ocean, and the forgiveness washing up in its place was life-changing, although difficult to delight in still.

He sat in his office, staring at a clock that read 2:37 p.m. He yearned to reconnect with his pops as he grabbed his latest edition of *Bicycling* magazine, a subscription purchased by his pops as a gift. He thumbed through the magazine, looking for anything that could lead to a piece of the puzzle. As he did, he turned on the TV to watch something golf-related, as he was an avid golfer. He found it relaxed him and quieted his mind.

As he flipped through the magazine while listening to the golf game, a commercial came on for the newest Garmin Golf watch. His magazine page displayed a full-page ad for the same product. A small smile released from the coincidence and then hit him like a rock as he heard the commercial boast that the golf watch could be used for all outside activities, including biking. The same words jumped off the page as well.

"Holy Moly! How did I not think of that?"

Evan couldn't boot up his computer fast enough. Although a painful sight, his current screensaver was a picture of Addison, adored by her grandparents, while just about to blow out her 3rd birthday candle.

His hands couldn't type 'garmin.com' fast enough, and after a few clicks, he found himself at the www.connectgarmin.com website to track his pops' whereabouts. Evan assumed he had been using his Garmin GPS and hadn't let the battery run out. Even if it had, he might be able to see the vicinity and direction of where his pops had been.

Finding the correct username and password to sign into his pops account proved more problematic than he thought. Evan picked up the phone to call his mom to see if she might know.

"Hi, Evan. Is everything okay?"

"Yes, it might be great, but I need your help. I think Dad might have his GPS on his bike, and we can track him, but I don't know his username or password, and I'm afraid I'll get locked out if I try too many times. Can you see if you can log onto his computer? Maybe his user ID and password are automatically saved."

"Evan, his editing computer that he worries about is password protected to the gill. The problem is we had an electrical power outage at some point, and it isn't on. Even if I boot it up, I don't know his password to get past his home screen. Evan, honey, try this; try 'happy grandpa' spelled backward, followed by his birth year and three asterisks. I think I heard him mention that as one of his usernames for some reason. I think it might work. But I don't know his password; he changes those quite often."

"Mom, that helps me a lot!"

She sniffled, and he could speculate her tears.

"Mom, are you okay? Do I need to come over there?"

"Evan, I'm better than okay. I never thought I'd see the day that you could forgive him."

"Truthfully, I didn't either, but I have to find him to truly forgive myself. — But what if he doesn't forgive me?"

"Honey, that's an impossibility. That man has more love for his kids than you could ever imagine. Just find him; you'll see."

"Okay, thanks, mom. We'll talk soon; I love you."

Evan ended the call and typed in the suggested username.

"Holy crap — it worked!" He shook with excitement as he continued his password guess. — *Now, what could It be? Don't overthink it* — he searched the upper right quadrants of his mind, then the left, and then it hit him —

"But it can't be... Can it?"

Chapter Twenty-Four

Master Yodacciai

It was 1:38 p.m., as the two cyclists had forty-five miles of the Texas landscape under their belts. Carter enjoyed the rugged backroads of Texas and riding across aged iron-covered bridges once meant for the old iron horses of yesteryear. Although the train rails had been replaced with wooden planks, you could almost hear the locomotive's steam engine chugging, bellowing out its smokestack songs, while the steam whistle communicated a warning of a cowcatcher headed their way.

Maybe it was the sound of the bicycle wheels hitting each plank from one end of the bridge to the other, much like a giant piano glissando. Or maybe it was the view of the rapidly flowing river or small lake below that added the emotional element to the ride. But Carter was fascinated and enthralled by all of it. Even better, he didn't have to perform as a Dallas Sherpa as Frank offered to keep the bicycle buggy.

The two cyclists decided to have lunch as they passed a diner that begged their taste buds to stop. It looked as if a construction crew of grandma engineers designed and built it from scratch, which best described the aromas that filled the air. It had to be as good as it smelled, given the parking lot was filled with cars from several counties that deemed the drive worthy.

Carter and Dedacciai considered the 'granny fortress' appearance safe and didn't bother with Carter's big-ass bike lock as their hunger trumped safety, and they hurried inside. The wait was considerable, but the Dedacciai insisted that this was a 'stop and smell the flour' moment, and they had plenty of time.

While they waited, Carter divulged all he learned from Connie Sue Lancaster and the less edgy "late-night" version of Frank and Beans. Carter bombarded the Dedacciai with a flurry of womanisms that impressed him.

Carter learned much from Beans and his relationship lessons based on his five wives' failed recommendations of what Frank should have done during each marriage. But Frank honestly listened and learned from each wife. His caveat was he couldn't apply the lessons to his situation and lived the cliché "those who can't — teach," even if their own self-enlightenment was unattainable.

The Dedacciai sat, impressed, proud of Carter's absorption of knowledge. His evident co-authors were helping young Carter rewrite his story with their chapters inching him closer to obtaining his breeder's license. He felt Connie Sue was a perfect fit for Carter with her promise of continued relationship advice. Just having her in his corner would bid well for his confidence. Beans seemed to have some unique insight into differences between men and women that would additionally help if applied.

There were roughly two hours left before reaching Dallas. The Dedacciai needed to wrap up his portion of Carter's education and tie a bow around it before releasing him into the world of relationships.

"Relationships — learned well, you have, young Jedi. To complete your training, enter the Dagobah Cave; you must. A final quest for your mission, this is."

Strangely, Carter was well-versed in all things *Star Wars*.

"Master Yodacciai — What is in the cave?"

"Only what you take with you," Master Yodacciai responded. With that, the scene was complete, and the two laughed as Master Yodacciai patted his protégé on the back.

"Good to know you're a fellow *Star Wars* aficionado."

"Kind of had to. It was on Russell Ducane's approved TV-watching list, as he loved rooting for the Dark Side. My life was pretty much the central storyline between 'The Force' and 'The Dark Side' and the complex galactic relationship between father and son."

"Yes, makes sense, that does. But if I may impart one last lesson of relevance to your training. The Dagobah Cave metaphor is the final chapter of sorts to rewriting your story. And although there will be a plethora of new lessons that you will learn throughout your life, the rewriting of who you are with my help is complete with what happens next."

"Master Yodacciai — exactly what does happen next?"

"You must face Russell Ducane, just as Luke Skywalker faced Darth Vader in the real Dagobah Cave — your house. And when you enter your old house and face your father for the first time, it will be the real version of the metaphorical symbolism of the Dagobah Cave. 'What is in the cave?' will be imperative to finalize your training. The answer, 'Only what you take with you,' will be determined by what you've learned during your time with me.

"Take this seriously; you will, young Carter. Because what you take with you truly determines your future, and you must choose wisely." Master Yodacciai paused and reached out to his pupil.

Carter looked up from the ground he was concentrating on while his head bobbed as he listened. The Yodacciai demanded his full and clear attention before he continued.

"If you enter the house with hate, anger, and revenge hiding in your depths, your outcome will not be good. You must only take love, forgiveness, and God. And although God is a rather new tool for you, take Him with you. I saw you reading your Bible at Frank's, and I'm happy about that. But now you must apply what you read as faith and believe God is with you. If I might ask, what part of the Bible did you read?"

"Well, the first thing I read was John 3:16 because I saw it on a billboard and a couple of church signs while we rode yesterday, so I was curious why that was so important to churches."

"You picked a good one; you did. John 3:16 is considered the most famous verse in the bible. That's why you saw it. Do you remember it?"

"Maybe — it says that God loved the world, He gave His only Son, and we need to believe in Him to have eternal life, or something like that. I'm sure I butchered it, but it's something like that."

"You did good for a rookie; you'll get your Bible verses down in time. But the important thing is that you are a rookie, and everyone who believes starts somewhere. Connie Sue believes in you, as do I.

"Now, like I was saying, take God in with you, and you can do that by saying a prayer or memorizing John 3:16 and repeating it over and over as you enter your old house. Remember — the last time you threw a prayer into the cosmos — you did pretty well.

"But you need to be prepared because Russell Ducane is going to push your emotional buttons with weapons of hate, manipulation, and guilt. It is who he is and what he does — for now. But you will not, at any cost, reach for the same weapons. Understand me – you will?" he emphasized in his trill Yoda voice.

Carter looked at his mentor, Master Yodacciai, with gratitude.

"I understand, Master. Now answer question, you must — Important this is. I realize I must forgive my dad, but what does it have to do with getting my breeder's license?"

"Young Carter Ducane..." once again with Yoda-ism inflection.

"Yes, Master Yodacciai?" Carter strikes back.

"Wonderful human, you are — Wonderful woman, there will be. And this woman that will be is going to happen upon you when you least expect it. You will be twitterpated from the moment you see her, and this woman does not deserve the emotional baggage of your not getting along with your family. It's not something that will impress her, but a loving family will. And this woman will pay particular interest to how a son treats his mother because it reflects the treatment she can expect."

Carter felt the overwhelming task ahead as the Dedacciai continued.

"But the most important thing is that you will break the cycle of hatred that has plagued your life. When you carry 'the Dark Side' on your shoulders as you go through life, it interferes with all aspects of everything. And it's hard even to imagine this — but someday you will breed, and having family around as a community of love for your child is so important.

"However, too many people use a child as a weapon to get leverage against their family by threatening never to let the grandparents see their grandchild. If I *ever* hear of this from you, I will personally kick your ass.

"Your wife and kids deserve peace — peace inside the home, peace within their minds. No child should ever have the thought of not wanting to spend time with their grandparents, and no wife should dread seeing her in-laws. So, the peace you must strive to provide for your relationship is essential to foster an atmosphere of normalcy. It keeps love alive and helps relationships thrive. That's why this is imperative for your breeder's license.

"Carter — I know you feel you have completely forgiven your father as you sit with me now. But when you sit eye to eye with the man who has caused you so much pain and hear him say something you don't like, your knee-jerk reaction will be the ultimate test. You will know in that instance whether you've truly forgiven him."

Carter felt the realization that this was not going to be as easy as he thought.

"But here's the deal, Young Carter. Everyone in life deserves the chance for redemption because redemption is everything. Russell Ducane also deserves the chance for redemption. Redemption with himself, his son, and his wife — so he can make his family whole. When this redemption between father and son happens, you have rewritten your life story and finished your book. But your next book will be an adventure of love and relationships experienced by the person you are now, and it will be magnificent. With love, forgiveness, and God, miracles can and will happen—"

"Carter, party of two," the featured grandma hostess declared, and she escorted them toward their booth.

As they were walking, a grandma-sized piece of cake that could plumpen up an NFL linebacker made its way past them and onto a table where an eight-year-old girl was having her birthday. The Dedacciai stopped in his tracks and handed Carter a $20 bill.

"Wow, cool, handing out money again, I see! But what's this for?"

"Carter, fold the $20 bill up in your hand and tell that girl happy birthday, congratulate her by shaking hands, and surprise her with it. Just trust me on this."

Carter found himself hugged by an overly excited eight-year-old as she jumped up and down while clinging to him. The squeal was proof enough that Carter did what Dedacciai asked and that the "unexpected gift" routine did indeed work. He was thanked by her parents as well for his kindness.

He had a grin from 'here to there' as he found his way back to the booth where Dedacciai sat. "That was awesome! Thanks for letting me do that, but what's the story behind it? I know you got some elaborate backstory."

"Well, Mr. Carter, the same thing happened to me almost fifty years ago on my birthday. But it was a $5 bill back then that a stranger left in my hand, and it was at a time when five dollars meant something. Anyway, it hugely impacted my life, and I have been doing it ever since whenever I see someone having a birthday. You just never know what this unexpected gift will do for the future version of that little girl."

"Damn you, Dedacciai!" Carter said with a joking seriousness. "This is gonna cost me a lot of future money, isn't it?"

"Yes, Young Carter. — Use the Force, you must — Give birthday money, you will." Master Yodacciai gave off a prideful smirk and a man-nod to confirm young Carter would enforce his new code of birthday conduct.

"Hi, I'm Gretchen," as two glasses of water smoothly land on the table. "I'll be serving you two gentlemen today. You have that tea-drinkers look about you; am I right?"

"Gretchen, you couldn't be righter," the Dedacciai answered. "And could you bring us extra ice and lots of Splenda or Equal, and do you happen to have orange slices?"

"And he means a lot of them!" Carter chimed in.

"Darlin', of course we have oranges! It'd be hard to have fresh-squeezed orange juice without 'em — We have a sayin' in these parts... 'When life hands you lemons — trade 'em for oranges.'"

"Gretchen, I love that!" Dedacciai said exuberantly.

"Dedacciai, how have you never said that before in the world of all your weirdness and Dedacciai-isms?"

"Truthfully, I have no idea how I missed that orange-ism. As the lady said, the saying is from these parts, and I just haven't been to these parts before — I guess? But now that I have, I officially deem this Orange County, Texas! So let it be written — So let it be done."

As the two men sat relishing in the new verbal orange-ism, the Dedacciai saw a police officer standing in the rather long line, waiting to be seated. Addison's voice appeared.

Papa, remember the nice policeman who brought Zilla back after running away? You should ask the nice policeman to sit with you.

The Dedacciai found himself in a rather odd mental quandary. How does he explain to the Addison of his mind that the 'nice policeman' might be looking for her papa as a suspect in *her* death?

Papa, ask the nice policeman to sit with you.

"Carter, I can't explain this logically, but I need to ask that police officer in line to have lunch with us."

Carter looked terrified as he flashed back to the homicide of a purple 1984 Chevrolet Caprice by a baseball bat and brass knuckles.

"Dedacciai, are you in your right mind right now!? I mean, I killed a car, and you have a lot of hidden money on you, which you've never really explained why. Is that something the police might want to know? Just remember, I beat up that car to save you! — Not a good idea!"

Papa, what's wrong? Why aren't you asking him to sit with you?

"Carter, you don't understand. I have to, even though it's risky. It's hard to explain."

"What!? You're making like ZERO sense right now."

"Carter, we are in a small town 150 miles from where that happened; surely, they aren't looking for us this far away."

"US!? You said 'US'!? So, they are looking for you? Then are you part of the mob, or did you escape prison just like I thought — which one?"

"Carter, get a hold of yourself; it's neither of those!" *But he might want to question me in the death of a small child,* his mind continued.

While Carter and the Dedacciai bickered, a voice that sounded the furthest thing from a Gretchen interrupted them. It belonged to a Black police officer named Brandon Scott. He had a well-groomed beard and bold brown eyes, and to say he was burly was putting it mildly. His forearm alone was big enough for his tattoo of the old Texas territorial flag with large capital letters underneath that touted COME AND TAKE IT. If you were a criminal, this would not be advised. The man could be a badass, if necessary, but otherwise, a gentle giant with a kind voice.

"Excuse me, gentlemen. I couldn't help noticing you were wearing cyclists' jerseys. I'm assuming those are your bicycles parked outside?" said Officer Scott, who arrived unnoticed during their verbal scuffle.

Carter and Dedacciai sat, mimicking deer in the headlights as they stared at the officer's burly size. *The jig is up*, they internalized as their faces turned pale with worry. They had visions of what prison was like as they prepared to hear *You are under arrest for the murder of a child and a car*, but instead —

"I have to tell you, those are some sweet-ass bicycles, but the Italian-sounding one — it's incredible! I'm an avid rider myself and have never heard that name. So, whose bike is it?"

"It's his!" Carter said quickly while pointing viciously at the Dedacciai. "He bought it!"

"Whoa, slow down, tiger," the officer said. "May I join you for lunch and talk bikes? Lunch is on me," he added as the Dedacciai gained his mental composure and hoped Carter would do the same.

"Officer Scott," (according to the badge), "we'd be honored to have you join us, but your money is no good here at booth seventeen — it's policy," as the ceremonial man-nod occurred to accept the terms and conditions and grant access to the booth.

"Well, Officer Scott, joining our new guests, I see," Gretchen confirmed. "I brought your usual coffee, or did you want to change it up today?" And she placed the coffee, two iced teas, oranges, Equal, extra ice glasses, and two teaspoons without being asked.

"The waitress lottery," Carter mumbled to the Dedacciai as Gretchen started her spiel.

"The special today is a BBQ-glazed meatloaf with caramelized onions and peppers, with a helping of sautéed vegetables, and a side salad with our secret granny recipe vinaigrette. Gentlemen, it's out of this world if I don't say so myself."

"I can attest to that," the officer touted. "Gretchen, a round for everybody. I'm not letting our guests leave this county without trying the special."

She smiled and walked off to place the order.

"I heard you say waitress lottery. Let me guess; it's either the extra glasses of ice or the teaspoons? Yes, indeed, if you're talking about Gretchen, she's a lottery waitress and one of the many reasons people drive from multiple counties to come here."

"Well, for us, the incredible aromas bursting from here made us stop and smell the flour," the Dedacciai added.

Officer Scott chuckled. "Amen, brother, you're preaching to the choir. Best darn food in Texas, as far as I'm concerned. But the desserts are from another level of granny-dom. It's like they all combined their grandma superpowers to create a hostile takeover of our senses and waistlines. So, prepare; there will be dessert."

"Officer, you can see my stomach — right? It has a superpower of never having said no to a dessert — apart from a recent, self-imposed ban on cupcakes and being 289 days cupcake sober as of today. — But that's a whole other thing."

"A whole other thing, huh?" The officer laughed. "By the way, I never caught your names."

"I'm Carter, and we call him the Dedacciai — after his bike," Carter answered purposefully so the Dedacciai didn't have to grovel with his mysterious real name.

"Dedacciai — so that's how you say it. Yes, tell me about it. Where did you get that?"

"Well, I saw a picture of one years ago and made it my life's mission to get one. I had several alerts on my computer searching worldwide when one appeared in Yorkshire, England. It was quite an ordeal to get it here, but here it is. I added the wheels and some other custom pieces to get it to look how I wanted, but I haven't seen one like it for sale since, as I still have my alerts set up."

"Well, it's awesome! — I suppose it's not for sale?"

Officer Scott could tell by the look on his face that it wasn't. Carter smiled as he added the officer's request to the long list of how that bike affected people as the officer continued.

"I ride with a group called the Friday Freeloaders when my schedule allows."

"You've got to be kidding! We rode with them yesterday quite by accident as we were heading to Dallas. Talk about a small world — even if we are in Texas," the Dedacciai responded.

"The Freeloaders have every bike imaginable, but I've never seen a bike like yours. I really wanted to go yesterday because Slovacek's is one of my favorite routes."

"That was my first century ride!" Carter touted as Officer Scott gave him a fist bump.

"Do you know Frank and Beans by any chance?" Carter asked.

"Know him? I've arrested him; I don't know how many times," he joked. "No, really, it was just the once — How can you not know Beans? He's the funniest human ever — assuming he's even human."

"Very true. We stayed at his house last night," Carter said, animated.

"Real dump, isn't it? He invited some fellow freeloaders over for poker night, which is code for cheese, nacho, and beer fest. He took us to the cleaners at the poker table. But, at the end of the night, he donated his winnings, plus some, to the Dallas Assist the Officer Foundation. Most people have no idea how charitable he is behind the scenes. He's a great guy underneath all that 'Beans' stuff. What a crazy small world and crazier with Beans in it!"

"Alright, gentlemen, here's your feast," as Gretchen lifted each dish fluently off the platter and placed it on the table.

"Okay, I've been instructed that there are three pieces of our grandma's recipe, homemade, red velvet cake with buttercream cheese frosting, waiting when you finish. And it's on the house because any friend of Officer Scott's is a friend of ours," and she patted the officer on the back and walked away.

"Wow, how awesome is that! I bet that happens often, doesn't it?" the Dedacciai remarked.

"It does; most citizens appreciate law enforcement, but believe me, it's not all free meals and late-night donuts."

"Really? In a small town like this? What do you mean?" the Dedacciai asked.

"Let me paint you a picture of my life. Every day, I exit my home, knowing this may be my last journey on Earth; not only this, but my family knows it as well. And although I have a gun, I must also wear my mental armor to face the world's results from poverty, greed, poor parenting, addictions, and dysfunctional lives that threaten our peaceful communities. Inattention in the family unit and a lack of fathership drive young boys' mental neurons to clatter for the streets to get validation.

"Even in small counties, we have gangs, or groups of thugs, that provide the attention they yearn to have. Many are young and provide easy targets for older criminals who are happy to groom them. Unfortunately, this is where our paths cross, as these young recruits usually perform an illegal act to gain membership and thug approval.

"And so, I go into the world's garden that should be beautiful and is, for the most part, but it is also full of weeds. And according to the Constitution, they have as much right to be there as the grass and flowers. Yet I am not allowed to pull the weeds; instead, I must protect them and their right to freedom so they can get high, use drugs, and often try to kill me."

"Damn," Carter muttered, exchanging a glance with the Dedacciai as Officer Scott continued.

"I don't wake up relishing the thought of seeing my weapon in my hand, other than placing it in my holster at the start of the day. I do not enjoy or look forward to arresting kids I see as lost and victims of their dysfunctional surroundings, especially the boys from fatherless homes. Their fathers' mentorship is vital to their success in becoming responsible, law-abiding young men.

"I see my children's faces as I place handcuffs on these young people who make me question what has happened to them to make them rebel against society. I don't want to arrest anyone and would be happy rescuing cats out of trees all day."

Carter snorted at that last part, but Dedacciai's firm gaze silenced him.

"No joke," the officer said, shaking his head. "I'd rather be a role model, not an obstacle. I'm here to protect people from themselves and their dysfunction. Under my mental armor, I have feelings, compassion, and a love for humanity.

"I hate when people see me as the enemy, a robot with no heart, when I'm a person who sometimes fears them as much as they fear me. But I can look past their dysfunction; I just wish they could look past the badge and understand the job I must do to keep themselves, their neighborhoods, and the city safe.

"I want to get home to my family so I can give them the love and attention they deserve and that so many of my opponents on the streets have craved from their parents. I understand how that wasn't fair for them, but when that inattention forces our paths to cross, I want them to be able to ask me for help rather than ask me not to shoot. I don't want to die, and I don't want them to die, either.

"I'd gladly make a pact that I will make sure they get home at night if they'd do the same for me. I want to draw up a treaty where we no longer use weapons against each other. But instead, use tools called education, respect, appreciation, hard work, and achievement so that together, we can build up our communities, not destroy them. But that is far from the reality I face. So, when the opportunity presents itself to talk shop about bicycles, I take it. Because you just never—"

Like a lightning bolt, Officer Scott leaped to his feet and yelled for everyone to get out of his way. He ran toward the front door but changed directions like a jackrabbit and headed out the side emergency door as the Dedacciai and Carter watched a teenage thug trying to get his footing on the pedals of the Dedacciai bicycle.

As he pedaled the bike down a grassy knoll, Officer Scott pushed him off the bike before making it to the street, where a truck waited for his fellow thug to deposit his find. Fortunately, the Dedacciai bicycle landed in the padded grass. Officer Scott held the assailant to the ground while calling in the tag of the late-'90s green truck that tore off down the road.

The restaurant was a gasp with excitement, watching the officer. Once he obviously had control of the situation, many restaurant inhabitants stepped outside to applaud the man who protected their freedoms.

The Dedacciai and Carter hurried over and grabbed the bicycle as Officer Scott wrestled the cuffs onto the delinquent.

"Dedacciai, how much would you say is the value of that bicycle?" the officer asked loudly so the perpetrator could hear.

"Around six to seven —" the Dedacciai answered.

"Hundred?" the officer asked.

"No — thousand!" the Dedacciai replied.

"Randall — it looks like you picked the wrong bicycle to steal today. That makes it a felony charge. Maybe this time, you'll finally learn. I'm gonna call your mama, and she's not gonna like this one little bit."

Officer Scott read the would-be thief his rights as he marched him toward the police car and placed him in the back of the unit. He headed back into the restaurant to grab his hat and received a hero's welcome as a wall of grannies took turns hugging him.

As he exited, Carter and the Dedacciai waited for him.

"Duty calls, gentlemen. Maybe this time, Randall will learn a lesson. The bikes and stuff he usually steals only add up to a misdemeanor. Perhaps a felony charge will finally straighten his ass out.

"It was nice talking shop with you men. But maybe next time, actually use the bike lock. They call it that FOR A REASON!" he emphasized, with a jokingly serious attitude.

"Dedacciai, I'm beginning to think we're not that smart. Why did we decide not to lock up the bikes again?" Carter queried.

"I guess we got caught up in the aromas and thought no one would be looking for trouble outside a granny fortress with so many people around.

But I guess the parking lot had cleared out quite a bit when the thievery occurred. So, what are you waiting for? Lock the bikes up — Cake awaits! All this excitement needs to be quashed by sugar."

As they walked back in and made their way to their table, all eyes encircled the two men in cycling clothes who caused the excitement. They wished them well and were glad the thievery was unsuccessful.

"Carter, it's been an interesting ride so far, hasn't it?"

"Yes, it has. And the box score is now two to two."

"Oh, boy, what box score are you talking about now?"

"Well, two people have tried to steal the Dedacciai, and two have tried to buy it. However, the important part is that no one stole my bike, and I could have continued without you. And that's *The Ugly Truth* presented by the *Carter Ducane Dallas Road Show*."

"The *Carter Ducane Road Show*, huh? Your head's not right. You spent way too much time with Beans yesterday. And by the way, technically — three people have tried to steal it so far. Now, let's eat cake and get on the road."

As the two men finished eating their pieces of granny-infused-superpower red velvet cake. They found themselves on high alert with an extra pair of eyeballs taking note of everything happening outside the windows. Carter noticed a minivan had pulled up earlier toward the back of the parking lot, and the driver never emerged.

When leaving the diner, Carter's curiosity got the best of him, and he asked the Dedacciai to help check it out. The two kept their distance and noticed a woman hunched forward over her steering wheel. But it was more than that; this woman was crying so loudly, they could hear her from where they stood, but she was not alone — the cries of a small child accompanied hers.

"Duty calls; let's go," Carter said, and the two approached carefully, trying not to startle the woman, who had her eyes closed.

They tried getting her attention, but she couldn't hear them while she and her child were crying, so they knocked on the window loud enough to overpower the cries. The woman jolted back, startled, with her eyes nervous and wide as she analyzed the men's intentions.

"Ma'am, are you alright? Is there anything we can do for you?" the Dedacciai began.

Knowing they wanted to help, she rolled down her window.

"I'm sorry, but I'm having the worst day. My baby has been fussing all day, and I'm trying to get to the emergency room to see if she's sick. I thought a car ride might calm her, but she's been screaming the entire time.

In my rush out of the house, I forgot my phone and wallet and found out only after trying to get gas. So now I don't know if I have enough gas to get to the hospital or back home."

"Ma'am, I'd be glad to buy you a tank of gas," the Dedacciai offered.

"Thank you for that, but now I've got even bigger problems; my van won't start — like I needed that, too! It's just freakin' me by myself, and I can't afford to go and see what's wrong with it, much less get it fixed!

"I pulled in here because my baby was screaming, and I needed to try and calm her down. As you can hear, an epic fail. I can't catch a break!" She screamed to relieve her frustration and saw the two men exchange suspicious looks.

"Oh, God, I'm sorry! I'm acting like a crazy person, which I'm not — even though I am, for the moment," she said while struggling to quiet her baby.

"It's okay, calm down, breathe deeply; no one thinks you're crazy. Who wouldn't be frustrated by what's happening to you?" the Dedacciai said.

"I don't know what to do."

"Ma'am, you don't need to. Let me call a tow truck for you," Carter offered.

"You can't call a tow truck; I don't have my wallet! And even if I did, I can't afford it!"

"Let me call a tow truck for you; let us talk to them and see what we can do. Listen, I don't want you to worry; we'll pay for the towing. Do you have a particular auto mechanic? Maybe they have their own tow truck," Carter said.

"Yes, there's a Jerry's Automotive not too far from here," she said slowly.

"While we get the tow truck handled, why don't you go inside to see if you can calm your daughter in the air conditioning while we wait?" Carter offered.

"There are several grannies inside that would enjoy fussing over you and your baby. If you need anything to eat, it's on us," the Dedacciai added.

She got out of the car and hugged Carter while crying on his shoulder.

"I'm Emily; what's your name?"

"I'm Carter, and my friend here is the Dedacciai."

She hugged the Dedacciai as well.

"The world needs more people like you, and I hope someday my daughter meets a young man with your character, Mr. Carter."

"What? You don't want her to meet someone with my character?" the Dedacciai joked as she was caught off guard and laughed.

"Not really," she kicked back. "I'm on Team Carter for my daughter." She laughed harder than she might have expected.

"I can't believe I'm laughing like this. You two are just — special. But I still choose Team Carter," she jabbed as the two men witnessed her fun-natured personality emerge. She went to the other side of the van to get her diaper bag.

Dedacciai's instincts kicked in, and he knew, as sincere as this seemed, that sometimes people try and scam you. He would at least try to start the van and check the gas gauge to see if she was being truthful. Even if she wasn't, she had to be desperate to go to this length, and he would want to get to the root of why – but still want to help.

"Emily, would you mind if I tried to start the car and take a look?"

"Sure, anything you want." She attempted to get her daughter settled.

The Dedacciai tried to start the van and could tell by the sound what the problem likely was, and he was thankful it wasn't a scam.

"I'm pretty sure it's the starter; let me talk to Jerry's to see what I can work out with them to get this paid for."

"Who are you people?" she exclaimed.

"Well, just so you know, I taught Carter everything he knows, so technically, you're Team Dedacciai."

"I can live with that," she said as the three of them hugged before she headed into the granny fortress.

Carter turned on his phone and called Jerry's Automotive to take care of business.

"Dedacciai, we're in luck! They have a tow truck available and said $100 will cover it since they're only three miles away."

Time passed, and Jerry's tow truck had the van on the back of the rescue vehicle. They paid Big Bob (as he introduced himself) a total of $600. Carter gave his $100 left over from the bicycle repairs for towing, while the Dedacciai gave $500 toward a starter and gas. The receipt clearly stated any balance to be given to Emily if there was any.

Several grannies were standing about, still fussing over little Audrey. She was giggling profusely while Big Bob cleared space in the cab to fit the baby carriage so he could take them home.

"Well, once I calmed down and everyone fussed over her, she seemed back to her perfect self."

"That's great! It all worked out, and we have you completely paid for." Dedacciai informed her.

"I can't believe this is happening. I have no idea how to thank you for this. Can I get your number so I can pay you back when I can?"

The two hugged her, acknowledging the answer was a hard no. A few minutes later, she waved goodbye as Big Bob left the parking lot. The two cyclists walked over and unlocked the bicycles.

"What a day, young Carter! You have done much; you have."

Carter laughed as Master Yodacciai turned on the GPS and waited for it to get its bearings. "Dallas awaits, young Carter. Use the Force; we must."

"How's this for using the Force?" Carter rose off his seat and let one rip, laughing as he tried to speed off.

"You're more like your father than you think!"

Chapter Twenty-Five

Follow The Yellow-Striped Road

The two were laughing as the cycling journey resumed. Neither was aware that Carter's tow truck call had garnered the attention of Ray from I.T. — while the Dedacciai's GPS signal had now given Evan a fix on his location.

"Ray, what do you have for me?" the Clicker queried, leaving The Lancaster Landing.

"Dr. Jezercak, I received a ping from a cell tower in a small town a few hours south of Dallas. There's not much there except a small diner that's extremely popular, according to Yelp. I texted you with the location. Did you find out anything at the hotel?"

"Well, they wouldn't give any private customer information and didn't want to confirm whether Carter stayed there. But I did manage to get security to admit they had some electrical problems for a few days with their security system from all the rain. I think that could explain the footage going to static," as the Clicker was willing to accept any theory where static did not mean ghost.

"Ray, good work; I have someone trying to reach me. Text me with anything else that pops up. I'm on my way."

"This is Dr. Jezercak."

"Hi — Dr. Jezercak, this is Evan — you know, Addison's dad."

"Yes, Evan, good to hear from you. I know it's been a rough twenty-four hours. How are you doing?"

"You know, I'm doing better; a lot of it has to do with you. I want to thank you for that. You answered some tough questions that explained away my reckless blame. I'm in a much better place now and determined to find my pops, which keeps me focused on something other than — well, you know. Anyway, I'm calling because I think I've located my dad."

"What!? That's great; where is he?"

"Well, if my theory is correct, one of his bikes is missing, and my mom thinks he came back sometime during all the chaos and got it. I remembered he had a GPS and figured out his password to his Garmin account to see where it was. A few minutes ago, the GPS started and was headed north on an old back highway. It looks like he's headed to Dallas. I'm gathering my stuff now and headed that way. As I said, this is just my theory because Dad's resourceful. If he didn't want us to find him, he would give his GPS to one of his long-distance cycling buddies to throw us off track. Or maybe someone stole it off his bike and is using it. Regardless, I need to find it to see if it's him. I just wanted you to know."

"Evan, I'm busy working on a rather interesting scavenger hunt myself, or I would help. Would you text me the last known address so I can have it? I hope it's him. Keep me posted, and thanks for the call."

Meanwhile, the two cyclists were groaning from being stuffed and blaming the grannies for the excess sugar, causing them to feel parched. They stopped at a quick mart to replenish their water bottles with a thirst-quenching sports drink.

While in line, the Dedacciai saw the winning lottery numbers for the 555 million-dollar Powerball ticket, which were 05-15-25-50-55 with Powerplay number 05. *What are the odds of that many 5s in a 555 million Powerball number?* he thought while reminiscing about his Bellavia.

"Five hundred fifty-five million, that's a lot of green," Carter stated as they walked out and filled their water bottles. "What would the all-powerful, all-knowing Dedacciai do with that kind of dough?"

"Off the top of my head — hmmm, I'd bring back 'The Ball.'"

"Come again — say what now?" Carter countered.

"You heard me. I'd bring back 'The Ball.'"

"The Ball? What exact ball are we talking about here?"

"The winningest ball of all time, personal property of one Lance Armstrong."

"You talkin' about — his testicle?" Carter questioned in a high-pitched voice while scratching his head.

"Testicle, tosticle, whatever! Carter, it's all about redemption. Like I've been saying all day, I believe all men should be able to redeem themselves, including my personal hero, Lance Armstrong. Now, before you get your panties in a wad, let me preface this with a little story."

"Please do; I gotta hear this," as their riding resumed.

"Years ago, whenever my wife and I pulled into our housing addition, there was a home where the owners had started replacing their wooden fence. Initially, we were excited because the old fence was an eyesore. So, about half the fence was torn down and piled to the side of the yard, which we saw while driving home each night. After the initial burst of the project, it seemed there was no progress whatsoever. For months, it was a terrible eyesore.

"We couldn't stand it because every time we drove into our neighborhood, it put us in a bad mood, and this went on for a good six months — maybe even a year. Obviously, the owner wasn't going to finish the project. I got so mad that I decided to confront the horrible troglodyte who was determined to bring down the neighborhood. With my mental marching orders, I marched myself right over there one fateful Saturday morning to take care of this situation once and for all and demand justice."

"Oh boy, this sounds like an episode of 'The People's Court' waiting to happen."

"Yes, as I rang the doorbell, I thought the same thing. I was both nervous and determined to face the troglodyte responsible for the mental hell it caused us. But no one came to the door in the allotted time, which I thought reasonable. I wish I could call it a knock, but I banged on the door rather voraciously, demanding the troglodyte show itself.

"Finally, the door creaked open, and my heartbeat escalated, wondering if I bit off more than I could chew. At last, I'd have my answer as the troglodyte's face did, indeed, show itself.

"I'll never forget the disgust I felt — not for the troglodyte, but for myself, as an older woman named Margaret answered the door.

"'Hello, may I help you?' she said with her tiny voice and beautiful but sad and lonely eyes.

"She explained how her husband had started the project but died soon after. She didn't have enough money for the funeral and had to use the money they set aside for the fence to pay for her husband to be cremated. They were blessed with two children but had outlived them and didn't have grandchildren. She became a recluse and could barely pay her bills with the social security she received."

"Geez, Dedacciai, that's harsh!"

"It was harsh, and even worse, I saw the real troglodyte reflecting from her front glass door as I stood on her porch. I'll never forget how bad I felt about my self-righteous need to confront the perpetrator of what caused me so much pain. — Damn perspective."

"Hey, don't be bad-mouthing perspective. That was your own damn fault."

"True, but as I walked home, my perspective gave me an idea. I decided to talk with neighbors and tell them the story, and then I asked if they would sponsor a fence panel or volunteer to help put them up. One teenage boy overheard me talking with his dad, grabbed their lawnmower and weed eater, then marched over to the house and began mowing her yard because he wanted to help."

"Wow, now that's an impressive kid."

"He was for sure, and the following Saturday, we showed up as a volunteer workforce to fix her fence. My wife was with me as we knocked on the door to inform Margaret we were there to fix the fence and then added we would have to charge her. She said she couldn't afford anything, but we had everything she needed to bake chocolate chip cookies for the crew, which would be her payment.

"My wife asked Margaret if she could help her make the cookies. The best part was she said no. The lady rekindled her inner determination and wanted to repay the men for putting up her fence by making the cookies herself. She wanted to feel that accomplishment on her own. So, instead, my wife started to help clean the house and vacuum. She made a list of what other items she needed to clean. As word spread among the wives, they pitched in, bought the cleaning supplies, and went into the home and gave it the spring cleaning of a lifetime.

"Word spread within the neighborhood as people stopped and asked what was happening. When people saw, they were also inspired to help. Soon, men were checking her furnace and air conditioner, adding freon, replacing filters, fixing the toilets, and replacing ceiling fans. It was a thing of beauty watching her inner spirit come alive."

"Damn, Dedacciai, just look at all that perspective."

"I still feel bad that I complained for a year about that fence. But I learned a valuable lesson — to stop complaining and become part of the solution instead. To this day, Margaret's cookies were some of the most meaningful chocolate chip cookies ever baked. And from that day on, a community of people made sure they took care of Margaret.

"The thing is, Carter, I always believed that what happened in my neighborhood could happen in our nation. So, with my 555 million, I'd bring back 'The Ball' to lead us in a way where we stop waiting for the government to rescue us and provide a way to save ourselves.

"And I have a way for the greatest cyclist of all time to help our country, and in a far greater way than anyone could imagine — except for me, of course, because I have a pretty big-ass colorful imagination!"

"Most people would probably call it psychosis," Carter interjected, laughing.

"Psychosis, Schmychosis! Take heed, young Carter, in what your elder has to say because you never know what you could learn from one's mental excursion of thoughts — May I continue?"

Carter rolled his eyes while laughing and gave permission. "Bring it!"

"Oh, it's brought! And it all starts with the redemption of Lance Armstrong — for 'Give Lance a Second Chance!' we will chant across this nation because it doesn't matter if he only has one ball — We need that Ball! We need the Man! The Bike! The Ball!"

"Oh Boy, here we go," Carter said in anticipation.

"I honestly believe Lance should not only be able to rewrite his story; he should be able to re-ride his story. And when Lance redeems himself and the history books are finalized, they will not focus on the seven Tour de France titles nor the infractions of his demons — they will focus on his redemption.

"I will ask Lance to be chairman of the BE THE ONE FOUNDATION that I will fund with my winnings. We will sustain it by taking a page out of the Lance Armstrong playbook and why his vast experience in fundraising will make him the man for the plan.

"Now, mind you, this is a two-pronged approach, with both needing the Man! The Bike! The Ball! — Prong numero uno: THE BE THE ONE FOUNDATION.

"I would start a foundation patterned after the microcosm of what happened in my neighborhood. I want to provide a way for all people to take kindness to a new level, regardless of their differences. And I would do this by giving them the resources to help one another."

Carter was now more interested in where this was going.

"It would start with one simple slogan: BE THE ONE TO HELP SOMEONE. It will be launched by selling a multicolored wristband of pink, purple, red, yellow, orange, and blue, with all six words landing on a different color. And I will accomplish this for less than fifteen cents a word, and here's how I'd do it.

"We have the most hands-on DIY volunteer handyman force in the country: retirees with the time and skills to help someone but not the resources. We also have people with the resources to help, but they don't want to help if they can't deduct it from their taxes — but what if they could?

"And here is why our great nation needs 'The Red, White, and Blue Ball of Lance Armstrong.' He will go before Congress to petition the government for new legislation based on the current 501c3 charity, calling it a 501-IDC, which stands for Individual Documented Charity.

"The technology we have sitting in our pockets can change our country if the government would allow D-I-Y volunteers to document a project from start to finish with before, during, and after pictures. These pictures, along with images of store receipts for materials purchased, should be a tax write-off for the D-I-Y volunteers — but not their labor. No one gets paid for this; it's a nationwide volunteer force to improve our impoverished communities.

"I believe this new tax law would cut through the red tape of bureaucracy and inspire people to help each other in the most creative ways. And I firmly believe we would help disintegrate racism in the process. And when we unleash the creativity of giving and helping one another, the good Samaritans of our country will come out in droves, and we will flourish as a nation.

"And when social media shows people of all colors, pink, purple, green, orange, red, yellow, and blue, helping each other transform impoverished neighborhoods. Then, DIY volunteers from across this land will help rebuild communities, which will help unite our country.

"People want to help when they see an opportunity, exactly like what happened in my neighborhood. And when this happens, the racial divide will lessen, and goodwill will reign the auras of humanity.

"'BE THE ONE TO HELP SOMEONE' will heal our nation. It will be the will of the people to help one another, not another branch of a government welfare policy that enslaves an individual's destiny.

"The money raised selling millions and millions of multicolored wristbands will aid the volunteer workforce. It will help those DIY volunteers with the time and skill to help people buy the materials needed to do the job. The impoverished property owners can also supply their labor to help fix their properties. It's essential for them to be able to take pride and share in the feelings of accomplishment with their DIY counterpart to build a bond and pay this feeling of accomplishment forward.

"I'd also try to inspire a volunteer workforce of teenage kids to mow lawns in their neighborhoods and communities, not for money, but for a feeling of accomplishment that comes from individual giving. If we can get these kids, who yearn for acknowledgment, to get that from hard work instead of gangs, it will forever change their destiny.

"They will recognize what individual accomplishment feels like to take on an entire street in their neighborhood. And by helping each homeowner upkeep their lawns, they'll feel proud, as they can physically see their accomplishment daily.

"If we get enough of these kids to discuss their accomplishments with their friends, other kids may want to do the same. And if they can't afford a lawnmower, kids can raise money by selling BE THE ONE wristbands to buy the necessary equipment. And we can help by matching what they sell to help them get the lawn equipment or tools for whatever endeavor comes their way. And opportunities will come their way when business owners who need hard-working employees can be shown pictures of the streets they call their own.

"These individuals will protect these neighborhoods and not pilfer them had they turned to the gang's way of life. Hard work and personal accomplishments are what move our nation forward.

"Just imagine the kindest nation on earth raising its standard a notch more by adopting the nationwide motto 'BE THE ONE TO HELP SOMEONE.'

"And to further the redemption of Lance Armstrong, there will be another prong. One that will show how One Man, One Bike, and One Ball re-rode the history books. Because bicycles are people too, and too many bikes die a horrible death to rusticytis — when they could have been restored and cured of their disease."

Carter chuckled. "Wow, Dedacciai, that's some dream you've got."

The Dedacciai leveled him with a serious gaze. "Don't interrupt, Carter. I'm just getting to the good part because 'The Ball' will change the landscape for the American bicycle. Once again, a separate fundraising project in the form of a multi-colored wristband will forever cement Lance Armstrong's redemption. 'RIDESTRONG AND REDEEM YOURSELF AND or REDEEM YOURSELF AND RIDESTRONG AND' — This time for twenty cents a word, these five words read in an endless circle will present a positive message no matter which word you begin reading.

"We will attempt to revitalize and redeem our neighborhoods with the multicolored pink, purple, green, orange, and blue wristband. And we will do so by ensuring every kid in America has access to a bicycle. Either new or one that has been restored and cured of its rustic past.

"We need 'The Ball' to organize rides and raise millions through the RIDESTRONG AND REDEEM YOURSELF wrist bracelet. Bring back 'The Ball,' I say unto you and organized rides of millions of bicycles will restore our health and fight childhood obesity. The redemption of Lance Armstrong will lead to the redemption of so many bicycles that will help fight the war on fat cells everywhere."

The Dedacciai was now full steam ahead for the Red, White, and Blue as he rode upright with one hand over heart and one in the air like the Statue of Liberty screaming out his patriotic tone.

"Bring back 'The Ball,' I say unto you, and as a great nation, we will give testimony to the testicle because The Red, White, and Blue Ball of one Lance Armstrong will become our new Liberty Ball. And it will let freedom ring, like One Nation, under One Ball, indivisible, with liberty and justice for all balls.

"A nation where pink, purple, green, orange, and blue Balls will be rolling together with the Liberty Ball. And our Liberty Ball will give us hope and prosperity as we become a Brotherhood of Balls. Because whether you are odd or even or have no balls at all, ALL BALLS MATTER!

"And from sea to shining sea, balls will be rolling under spacious skies, and through amber waves of grain, over purple mountains' majesty, and above the fruited plains. I'm talkin' about America! Where black and blue balls will roll together to protect each other while rolling through neighborhoods of brotherhood because this is the freaking United States of America. Where every ball has an inevitable right to redeem itself — Carter, It's not just Spectacular — It's Testaclular!"

Carter was laughing his ass off as he yelled, "Now that's what I call America!" and then had a lightbulb moment of conviction as his body surged with excitement.

"I GOT IT! I know what I want to do with my life!" His adrenaline pumped as he sped over a rustic bridge before dismounting his bicycle and soaring down the slanted hillside to the river's edge.

"What's all the excitement about?" the Dedacciai yelled, not far behind.

"Dedacciai, your craziness has inspired me. Because of all your blathering about redemption and how bicycles are people, too, I absolutely know what I want to do with my life. And it's all your fault because you finally said something useful!" Carter exclaimed with a wink and mile-sized grin.

"Sure, blame the messenger. It wouldn't be the first time. But of all the blathering of things that I said — what did I say?"

"You said that in the realm of redemption, everyone deserves a second chance, even bicycles. You made me wish I could make a living fixing bikes because I really enjoy helping people. But then it hit me. Maybe I can? What if I opened my own bicycle shop and called it —?

— Redemption Bicycle Consignment —
'Where Even Bicycles Deserve a Second Chance.'

"I could be the one to sell and launch a 'RIDESTRONG AND REDEEM YOURSELF' wristband campaign. I would somehow make the community aware that they could donate their bicycles to be fixed so they would be free to kids who couldn't afford them. But I would want the kids to do something, like work around the shop and be taught how to fix bikes as part of working toward a bike. This way, they could feel like they're earning their bike and take pride in it rather than seeing it as a handout. And the money raised from the wristbands would fund the parts needed to restore the donated bikes.

"We could also service homeless people's bicycles in the community and make sure they have transportation to get to work and sustain a job. And that would be a community outreach program to have people donate to and sell wristbands to fund that endeavor as well.

"Of course, we'd also have our nicer inventory of bikes we take on consignment to sell to people who want a used, more expensive bike.

"Dedacciai, I was built for this! You have made me realize my calling in life. I could start by working at Cycledelic Bikes with Brandon and learn the business, and maybe they'd help with taking trade-ins on new bikes and let me sell the trade-ins on consignment. Maybe they'd be open to something like that? I could make this work, and my skills as a bicycle mechanic will be used for something important. I'm so freaking excited about this!"

The Dedacciai felt the enthusiasm emanating from Carter.

"It doesn't get any more American than that, Carter. It's a perfect idea, one of the best I've ever heard. And you're so right. You were built for this. Now, throw one of those cosmic prayers into the cosmos, and let's see what happens. You just never know."

Chapter Twenty-Six

The Ride To Redemption

It was nearly 5:45 p.m. as the two cyclists weaved through traffic and neighborhoods, making their way toward White Rock Lake. The Dedacciai watched for a pay phone to make his routine 5:55 p.m., 5-ring phone call to his Bellavia. Carter was on an all-time high from seeing Dallas for the first time. He felt like a changed man, but now, with an element of confidence and certainty, knowing his life now had a purpose — to somehow open the Redemption Bicycle Consignment Shop, where even bicycles deserve a second chance. How that purpose would come to fruition had yet to be determined. But Carter Ducane tossed his plea into the cosmos, this time with an actual Biblical backing, courtesy of Connie Sue Lancaster.

The Dedacciai spied an old payphone and pulled into the Quick Mart parking lot that housed the relic. It was a dead-end, as the phone was broken and caused him a slight panic. He needed to implore his superstitious belief that this daily attempt to call his Bellavia was his miracle thread of hope.

"I need to borrow your phone, Carter," he said with a subtle panic inflected in his voice. "Will you buy us some more energy drinks while I make a call?"

Carter knew the importance of his silent endeavor and reminded himself not to ask the Dedacciai about his personal life.

As Carter exited the Quick Mart, he saw his friend with his back to him while holding the phone to his ear in silence. As he hung up, he seemed to hang his head in a sheltered, silent pain that only the Dedacciai knew while he kept up his façade.

"Okay, young Carter, we're less than a mile from one of my favorite places on earth. Are you ready?"

"I was born ready!" Carter said with a bantering intensity.

"Were you, though?" Dedacciai asked with a tilted head and a questioning expression.

Within minutes, their destination came into view as they approached the south side of the lake, where an entire community of cyclists of all sizes, shapes, and speeds enjoyed the area. The Dedacciai was excited for Carter to experience the lake trail as he reflected on his first time there.

Carter was overwhelmed with emotion and pulled over to the water's edge, where beautiful benches accompanied the waterfront for such an occasion. He took it all in while he enjoyed the accomplishment of his journey.

The two men sat silent, appreciating the serenity of White Rock Lake. Carter gave his mentor, his author, a watery-eyed man-nod, conveying everything he needed to say.

The Dedacciai put his arm around his friend. "It's been an honor, but the journey's not over. We still need to get around the lake so we can properly celebrate with a thick, juicy steak at Bob's Chop House inside the hotel."

A few miles passed, and Carter was astonished as they reached the west side of the lake, where multi-million-dollar homes lined the streets to his left and the beautiful lakeshore to his right. He had never seen anything like this and had difficulty grasping such abundance.

With each mile around the lake, it was hard to keep his emotional fortitude together. His mind traveled back to the moment he decided to rescue the Dedacciai. He played an emotional game of '*What if* he decided not to save the Dedacciai's bicycle that fateful night?'

His body shuddered at the thought of being that nose-ring-clad, self-hating victim of his father's tyranny over his soul. For a moment, he relived the constant bombardment of acid coursing through his body and felt his heart beat putrid hate for his father.

He thought of all the people he would not have met along the way and the experiences he would have missed had he not helped the Dedacciai. He thought about the lessons he had learned and the perspectives he'd gained. He was incredibly grateful for the emotional spokes he had removed from his bicycle wheel of life and the new spokes that now took their place.

Carter saw a row of trees lined in the distance. "Just look at all that perspective!" he shouted out from a place of utter joy. "Is there a spoke for this? I can't believe this is my life! You truly rewrote my story!" he yelled to the Dedacciai.

"It's just the beginning. Now, Carter, I don't want this to go to your head, but I have decided to bestow unto you — your breeder's license dating permit. But mind you, this is only a permit, which will allow you to enter into a relationship — but not to go any further. You must still face your father to earn your permanent breeder's license. Be patient, my friend, because in life, you never know what's around the corner."

And just as the Dedacciai spoke, there was music in the distant air.

"Carter, do you hear that?"

"I do. — It sounds like a concert, but where's it coming from?"

"I think it's coming from the Dallas Arboretum and Botanical Gardens, not too far away. It looks like we're going to a concert! Let's hurry."

"Don't worry, Dedacciai; I'll use *the Force* to get us there!"

"Nooooo!" the Dedacciai yelled, but it was too late as Carter rose once again.

Carter locked up the bikes outside the arboretum where the concert was as the Dedacciai spied ahead to see who was playing.

"It's the Dallas Jazz Orchestra. Hurry up! The concert's over at seven — only twenty minutes left."

Big band jazz wasn't something Carter had ever experienced, but that night, it became another memory he would never forget. Although he couldn't appreciate what he was hearing, the lead trumpet hitting double C's and emulating one of the greatest trumpet players of all time, the late Maynard Ferguson, was exciting to him.

After the concert, Carter got separated from the Dedacciai by the sizable crowd. He went toward the bicycles to wait, as he presumed The Dedacciai had gone to the men's room.

Carter found it hard to navigate the crowd, so he stepped outside the throng and waited for the line to slow before resuming his way to the bicycles. While he waited, a smile bigger than the moon lurked a nose length below his closed eyelids as he caught up with his emotions. Suddenly, he felt the moist tongue of a dog lick his hand and was brought back to reality.

"Hey, boy, who are you?" And he bent down eye level with his assailant, a golden retriever, and thought of Lance.

The retriever's owner was a nice-looking, older woman with her even nicer-looking daughter, who looked to be his age.

"What's your dog's name?" he asked.

"We haven't decided. We're still trying a few names on for size," the woman said.

"I had a golden retriever — actually, I still might. But that's a long story. I named him Lance."

"Lance?" The daughter's eyebrow lifted. "As in Lance Armstrong, I assume —?"

"Pffff," he sounded off jokingly. — "Is there any other? Duh!"

Immediately, her eyes perked up for the young man in cycling clothes.

"So, where did you ride from? Do you live around here?"

"Oh, no, that's a longer and even more bizarre story. I rode here from Georgetown over the past two days with my friend — a very strange man, I might add, who insisted we ride here since I've never been to Dallas. It's been quite a journey."

"My daughter's a cyclist," the woman interjected approvingly.

"Really, you're a cyclist? What kind of bike do you have?"

"Well, I have a new project one—"

"Nice!" he interrupted. "I'm sorry to cut you off, but I already know it's amazing. I'm assuming it's a Trek Madone. What components and color scheme did you go with?"

"Wow, you do know your stuff, don't you? I went with a radioactive-pink Madone with Shimano Dura-Ace Di2."

"Nice, dude! Right to the top of the bicycle food chain!" He instinctively gave her a high five as she enjoyed playing along.

"So, how do you know so much about bikes?" the daughter asked.

"Well, it's because I'm a bicycle mechanic. Actually, I want to open up my own bicycle consignment shop with a mission and purpose. I want to help poor people get bikes and help the homeless maintain their bikes so they can get and keep a job. I have this whole idea of how I want to do this. But, for now, I have a bicycle mechanic job waiting for me back in Georgetown until I figure out how to make it a reality. Wow, sorry. That's a lot to unload on someone I just met."

"Not at all. I'm glad you shared that," as the daughter cyclist caught a glimpse of the mechanic's heart.

"Where's your bike now? Can I see it?" she asked.

"Sure, it's on the other side of the crowd."

The three pierced their way through to get to the bicycles.

"My friend, the Dedacciai, should hopefully be there by now. I'd like you to meet him. He's very — odd. He says weird things like, 'You know, bicycles are people, too.'"

The daughter stopped in her tracks as she saw the Dedacciai bicycle while hearing the mantra.

"Did you just say the owner of this bicycle says, 'Bicycles are people, too'?"

Carter nodded. "Uh, yeah —"

"Where's your friend? I need to talk to him — NOW!" She became animated from pure adrenaline that amplified a vision of a rainy-late night bicycle that crossed her path.

"Kimmee, what is it? Are you okay?" the mother asked, as both she and her daughter had a look of concern.

"I don't know; please find your friend for me; it's vital that I find him!"

"He should be here any minute," Carter reiterated.

"Why do you call this man the Dedacciai?"

"Well, I call him that because—"

Suddenly, the thunderous throttling sound of a 105th-anniversary special-edition Harley-Davidson Road Machine interrupted as it parted the crowd like the Red Sea.

"What in the world?" the mom asked, covering her ears.

Kimmee yelled, "Mom, that's my boss — Dr. Jezercak." Then she shouted in her ear, "You know, the Clicker!"

Her mother's initial reaction was to hide. But their new dog was a step ahead and found his way nestled between Carter's legs while snarling at the Clicker and whimpering for shelter.

Kimmee ran over to her boss.

"Dr. Jezercak — what are you doing here!?"

"Oh, it's you! Well, it's too bizarre to explain — and that's coming from me. But a lot of unexplainable weird crap has happened since you left work yesterday. Bottom line, I'm looking for someone, and he's in this vicinity because I've been tracking his phone to this location. It's possibly a life-or-death situation," as the Clicker scanned the crowd.

"K.J. — what are you doing here anyway?" he added.

"My mom and I came to a concert tonight. It's our weekend thing we do. — So, tell me, who are you looking for and why?"

"I'm looking for someone by the name of Carter Ducane."

Carter was bent down comforting their unnamed dog when he heard the man say he was looking for him, and it was possibly a life-or-death situation. Carter's first thought was this had something to do with him beating up the hoodies that night, that maybe something had happened to one of them. But he also wondered if something happened to his mom

— or Russell, and strangely, he felt concerned for his dad. He stood up and walked over to Kimmee and the man.

"Did you say you were looking for someone named Carter Ducane?"

"Yes, do you know him or know where he is?" the Clicker asked harshly.

"Is he in trouble for some reason?" Carter questioned.

"Okay, kid, who are you, and what do you know? He's not in trouble with the law if that's what you're getting at. But he may be in danger with his health. It's imperative I find him. Now, do you know where he is or not? Because I'm tired of you wasting my time!"

"I'm him — I'm Carter Ducane. Why are you looking for me?"

Kimmee looked at Carter, surprised — and realized they had never introduced each other during their conversation. Not missing a beat, the Clicker grabbed a stethoscope from his storage compartment and walked straight over to Carter.

"Take off your backpack and raise your shirt."

"Wait, why!?"

"Do it, kid! Now!" He placed the stethoscope on Carter's chest.

"Whoa, dude, what are you doing here? Why in the heck are you listening to my heart?"

"Well, technically, it's not *your* heart."

"Okay, what are you talking about? — What does that even mean?"

"Do you know a Darius Montgomery by any chance?"

Carter was taken aback by the oddity of the question from this bizarre stranger.

"Darius Montgomery?" Carter searched his mind. "I met someone named Darius a few nights ago. What does he have to do with you listening to my heart?"

"You mean the night of October 4th, your 25th birthday? Is that when you met?"

"What's going on here? How do you know any of this?"

"Because I met the former owner of your heart, Darius Montgomery — That's why!"

"The former owner? Dude, you're bizarre! The Darius I'm talking about is alive; this doesn't make sense."

"Are you sure about that? Just shut up and let me listen!" the Clicker demanded.

"Carter — what's going on here?" the Dedacciai queried as he walked up from behind to what looked like a very odd crime scene, with a biker-looking, bald man listening to Carter's heart with a stethoscope. He approached, not realizing that it was his friend, Professor Miguel, and Professor Miguel didn't hear his friend approaching from behind.

Suddenly, a voice yelled from a distance, "Pops!" A voice the Dedacciai's nervous system knew very well, and he recoiled from the mere timbre. His nervous system took over immediately and replayed the entirety of Addison's death. He relived every punch, every slap, every emotion — and the response was a primal scream that rang out and rivaled shots fired, which both scared and captivated the crowd leaving. But most, if not all, stopped and peered toward the drama unfolding as the grandpa was now coiled on the ground near a tree. His hands shielded his face, and he was flinching at the imagined punches as he yelled out while crying from the phantom pain.

"Nooooo, I'm sorry. I'm so sorry. I didn't mean to."

Kimmee saw Evan, Amelia, Bellavia, and the rest of the grandpa's family run toward the man coiled on the ground, which confirmed the man she saw in the late-night rain at Wendy's was, indeed, the grandpa.

"I'm sorry! I'm so sorry. I didn't mean to." he screamed again as the crowd shushed all those wanting to witness the drama unfold.

Carter tore away from the Clicker to protect his friend. Kimmee questioned if Carter knew what the grandpa had gone through as she equaled his pace and confronted him.

"Carter — it's okay; this needs to happen. You need to stand down."

The Clicker, too, was shocked that finding Carter had somehow found his friend. He let the family know of his presence, gave Bellavia a hug and Evan a man-nod of confidence, and then backed away from the drama.

"Pops, — Dad! It's okay; your family is here for you!"

"Nooooo, Addison's gone! I killed her; I broke everything; I broke my family. Nothing will ever be the same."

Carter leaned over to Kimmee. "He killed Addison — Who's Addison?"

His question confirmed her suspicion that Carter never knew what happened. However, he held all the secrets of what had happened to the grandpa, which made her mind run wild with curiosity, and she was now determined to find out.

The crowd had managed to quell their way into silence as the pageantry of forgiveness began.

"I'm sorry; I'm sorry; it's unforgivable," the man pleaded his mantra once again.

"Pops, you're wrong; you've got it backward! I'm the unforgivable one — the worst son in the world. I threw you out of our lives without a fair trial. I blamed you for Addison's death, but it's not true. Addison died of a congenital birth defect in her heart that we didn't know she had. If you don't believe me, ask your friend Dr. Jezercak. He's here; ask him — Ask Miguel."

The grandpa lifted an elbow, allowing his eyes to contact his longtime friend. Miguel approached and lifted his friend up to his feet to look into his eyes.

"It's true, every word. Addison had what's called Wolff-Parkinson-White syndrome. No one could have ever known — well, except for me, of course."

The grandpa felt a micro-moment of relief from the unexpected blatant truth that only Wolfrem Miguel Oswin Jezercak could present before returning to his emotional default position of pain. Miguel extended his arms and placed his hands firmly on his friend's shoulders.

"It's going to be okay, my friend. It will take some work, but we'll go through this together, and I'll be there every step of the way. Now, I believe Evan needs to purge himself of his feelings. Accept his words as the truth," and gave his friend a man-nod to confirm.

Evan stepped in and placed his hands on his dad's shoulders.

"Pops, please look at me," pleaded Evan.

His dad tried, but the invisible weight of Addison's death still weighed heavy.

"It's okay, Pops; just listen then. I was filled with rage that night. A rage for a man who gave me life — and a wonderful childhood. And his only real crime was that he was determined to give my daughter the same wonderful experiences I was privileged to have. The same experiences that made me into the person I am today."

The grandpa's head hung heavy.

"After the anger and after Dr. Jezercak made me realize I was wrong about what happened, I was left searching for the greatest man I've known. I couldn't live with myself, knowing you wouldn't be at Addison's funeral because of what I did. But what I didn't tell you that night — is that you're going to be a grandfather once again."

Addison's voice appeared — *Papa, I'm going to have a baby brother or sister.* Her papa found the strength to lift his head and look Evan in the eyes.

"Pops — the most important thing you need to know at this moment — is that if God needed an angel in Heaven — and if Addison needed to give up her earthly body, there's no place I'd rather she enter into the Kingdom of Heaven — than through your arms."

A universal chorus of emotional sniffling emanated from the crowd.

"Dr. Jezercak made me realize that Addison's last sounds on Earth were giggles and laughter. And the last emotions she felt were love and joy — something we all would choose if given a choice how to exit this life."

Utter gasps went up from those in attendance as Evan continued.

"And because Addison died in your arms instead of mine, you saved me from being unable to forgive myself. I would've lived the rest of my days with an underlying mentality that maybe I did something to cause her death. Maybe I could've forgiven myself — but then again, maybe not. But I'm not left with that burden because you saved me from that. And just like our Heavenly Father absorbs so much of our pain, my earthly father did the same for me."

Evan shook with emotion as his harsh, watery eyes made it difficult to power through and finish.

"Pops, I can't live with myself, knowing the horrible pain I caused you. And I'm not sure how to ask this because I don't know if I'm worthy — but could you ever forgive me? — Please?"

Pops lifted his hands and placed them on Evan's shoulders.

"Forgive you? There's nothing to forgive — I love you, Evan."

This act of forgiveness shattered their emotional walls as father and son embraced, and the pageantry of forgiveness took hold. They cried, they laughed, they forgave, and then cried some more. The onlookers responded with an emotional encore of sniffling and tears as a forgiving spirit haunted the group. Many in the crowd embraced and confessed how much they loved the person they were with, while others found themselves asking for forgiveness.

His Bellavia took her turn as she stepped into view. Their eyes connected as their foreheads engaged one another softly, quietly, saying nothing yet everything. But some words needed to be said.

"I want you to know that I called you. — I called every day at 5:55 and let the phone ring five times to let you know I loved you."

She separated her forehead from his and placed her hand on his cheek as she looked into his eyes to lovingly confirm.

"Somehow, I knew that." She leaned in and gently kissed the cheek she had slapped, then laid her head sideways over his heart.

"Jacob Jobe Garrard, you are the love of my life. I'm so sorry I slapped you. Can you ever truly forgive me — for how I reacted?"

"Only if I can ask for forgiveness for not calling for you when—"

"Don't say it. Kimmee helped me understand why you didn't call out for me. I know why you didn't come back; I know you were giving me my space. I know that you know everything about me, and had you not stayed away, I wouldn't have had the space to realize how much I loved you and will always love you."

They reveled silently in their truth while nestled in each other's arms. After some time, they released their silence as his Bellavia spoke first.

"But truthfully, honey, it was your new surrogate daughter who you truly need to thank."

"Wait, I have a new surrogate daughter? — What happened to my old one?"

His Bellavia laughed out loud, proving once again that only he could make her laugh at the darndest of times. And with her laughter, she was now complete.

The Dedacciai family overtook their mom and dad with a joyous family group hug that solidified their love before hugging their father individually. The crowd clapped and cheered for the successful pageantry of forgiveness before they dissipated.

"Okay, I'm curious — How did you know I was here?"

"Your GPS," Evan answered, "and a logical but lucky guess of your Garmin password. Really, Pops, Addison's name, birthday, and exclamation point?"

The two men looked at each other with a slight smile and a man-nod. "You know, Dad, I had a hard time saying her name before, but it's easier now that you're here."

"I know, me too, Son. We have to live our lives in honor of hers, always. All of us will."

The family wept and grew together as Kimmee stood back, watching and relishing the reunion.

"Honey, come here; I want you to meet your new surrogate daughter, Kimmee. She's the one who truly went to bat for you in so many ways. Kimmee James Attwood, I want you to meet my husband, Jacob Jobe Garrard."

"Please, call me Jake, but soon — I understand I will be going by Grandpa again."

Kimmee threw her arms around her surrogate father. The man she predicted might have killed himself, the man who became her obsession to redeem, and now the man she had difficulty releasing. But as she did, she couldn't help herself as she placed her finger under her teary eye and gave her new surrogate father, an Eye-Jobe.

"I love her. I love her so much already!" He laughed as he return-volleyed an Eye-Jobe back. "Kimmee, we need to get to know one another, and soon. You must come over for dinner so I can learn all about my surrogate daughter."

"Jake— sorry — Dad," she said jokingly, although accepted by her surrogate father as okay. "I'd rather get to know you on a nice long bike ride instead. And not just one; we'll need many miles together."

"I love you already— truly. I mean, I got an Eye-Jobe already, and now I get to go on a nice long bike ride. Since you're a cyclist, have you met my new cycling friend, Carter?"

"Yes, I have. We met while looking at your Dedacciai bicycle, which you will ride when we ride together."

"No problem, as long as Carter can keep it running for me. He's a great mechanic if you need one." He scanned the crowd for Carter, who was talking to Dr. Jezercak, and excused himself to approach them.

"I was just discussing a plan for a full medical workup with Dr. Jezercak," Carter said, strangely excited, knowing Kimmee would be helping to poke and prod him.

"Apparently, not only do I get a new story for myself, but I'm doing it with someone else's heart —"

"What in the world are you talking about?!"

They were interrupted as Dr. Jezercak walked up to his friend.

"Miguel, it's been way too long." Dedacciai said, "We need to talk about everything: Carter's heart and how all this came about. I can't tell you what it means that you were there for my family. It's amazing to see you, my friend. The Dos Amigos will reunite soon to cuss and discuss all this."

The old friends hugged each other, and Dedacciai suddenly yelled, "Wolfrem Miguel Oswin Jezercak — you're still clicking!"

Kimmee almost fell to the ground laughing when her surrogate father yelled that to her boss. The two men instinctively gave each other an Eye-Jobe as they laughed, and Miguel walked to his Harley Davidson to leave.

Kimmee introduced her mother to her new surrogate family, with Carter meeting them also.

Dr. Jezercak watched as the family reunited. He smiled, knowing he had put the proverbial Humpty Dumpty back together again. As he placed his stethoscope in the storage compartment to leave, he heard a familiar voice.

"Now, that's what I call the art of forgiveness. If I had a heart, I would've cried."

The Clicker looked up to see his nemesis, his Phantom Moriarty.

"FYI, your heart sounded really good, perfect even. Carter wears it well."

"Hmmm, interesting, you should say that. Have you ever wondered why Carter has survived all these years without anti-rejection drugs? It seems odd, doesn't it? Unless it's a near-perfect genetic match, that is. I thought you were good, Dr. Jezercak; maybe I was wrong about you."

"Darius Montgomery, you are not getting to me again. See how calm and cool I am? I know you're just a figment of my imagination."

"Am I, though? Are you sure about that?"

"You're right, I probably have a brain tumor causing these crazy hallucinations. Regardless, I know you're just screwing with me, that no one can see you standing there, that you're going to try and haunt me in my dreams — yada-yada-yada. If you don't mind, I'll do my own poking and prodding of your heart. I'll figure it out on my own."

"Yeah, maybe. But maybe you should talk to Dr. Stidham some more, or better yet, Ivan could use his American microfiche to help."

The Clicker closed his eyes, breathed deep, and opened them.

"I'm still here. The old closing and opening eyes routine is an old myth of how you get rid of — whatever I am. You know, it's amazing how you have four names. Six if you include 'The Clicker.' There's a lot to a name. It's interesting how we all get our names in life, don't you think, Wolfrem Miguel Oswin Jezercak?"

The Clicker tightened his jaw; his head trembled slightly with an inauspicious look. *That asshole just dropped another freaking clue, didn't he?*

"Do me a favor; take care of Carter. He has a great life waiting for him. I'll be here if you need me."

Dr. Jezercak looked over at Carter, then turned to respond to the macabre.

"I'm not going to need you!"— But the phantom was gone. "Damn macabre!"

A call was warranted.

"My clicking American friend — Ivan going to call you! Ivan got new cameras installed while you go gallivanting after American organs. 4K Images of Bunny so beautiful — make Ivan cry, but afraid 4K not a good look for Clicker — Ivan leave discreet package full of Neutrogena skincare and much theatre makeup. Now, what the balls do you need help with?"

"Dammit, Ivan! One of these days, I'm going to fly over to Russia and kick your—"

"Ivan suggest not do that — Bunker hard to find. Much barb-wire."

"Listen, Ivan, I thought you were good! But evidently, you're not?"

"Why is Clicker man Clacking that Ivan not good? Ivan better than good; ask many Russian comrades. Why you do big doubter balls on Ivan?

Ivan think Clicker need anger derangement course. Maybe learn to stop and smell the balls in life? Ivan think be good for Clicking man to stop and smell more balls. If Clicker smell more balls, Ivan think Clicker man be in more happy place."

"Ivan, it's supposed to be 'stop and smell the flowers' — you idiot."

"No, Ivan plant balls firmly in ground holes for balls to start life. Now, who's idiot?"

"It's Bulbs; you plant bulbs, not balls. Flowers start as bulbs — Geez!"

"Now Clicker ruin Ivan 4K Bunny vibe. How do Ivan make you have un-doubter balls?"

"Here's how! I found Carter William Ducane. He is still alive and doing great. And that's the problem — Why!? We need to figure it out because Darius Montgomery just revisited me."

"Again! — Ivan head to bunker — Don't want to be ghosted, Ivan much scared of Ghost Man."

"While you're down there, use your American microfiche and figure this out. He gave me another clue, which has to do with how we get our names in life. He may be screwing with my head and sending me down a rabbit hole, but I need to find out! — Damn macabre!"

"Okay, Ivan beat the midnight balls till find American answer."

"Ivan, the phrase is 'Burn the midnight oil'!"

"Beat balls, Burn oil. Is really that different? Ivan think not. Ivan like beat balls better."

"Of course you do, never mind. Ivan, figure this out because we might be missing something — And Ivan, one more thing — I'll say hi to Bunny for you."

"You make Ivan happy. We end conversation on high balls. Ivan decide not to beat midnight balls, but beat balls now and find answer — Ivan be right back."

The Clicker sat on his motorcycle and watched the families mesh while waiting for Ivan to get back with him.

"Ok, Ivan back. Ivan figure Ghost man must be relative of heart boy. Took Ivan thirty extra seconds to hack into sealed adoption site. Good news, Clicker man now have two choices, Darius Montgomery or Ghost Man original name — Darius Ducane."

"Darius Ducane? — Damn, he's a Ducane. So, Carter's heart is a Ducane. This makes sense, but how?"

"Ivan find old private social media blog from Darius Montgomery ex-wife. She explain to a friend that Darius found out he had an older brother and tried to find him for years. She say after Bronson died, while Ghost man was still lawyer, he finally found his brothers address.

She also explain they found that Russell and Darius Ducane were left at a firehouse when Darius was born. They didn't know what happened to his older brother Russell, but Darius was placed with a foster family that later adopted him and changed name to Darius Montgomery.

"She said they drove to Russell's house once after Bronson die to try and have some type of family connection. They thought it might help her and Darius heal. But night they went, Russell sounded drunk, and they could hear him yelling at his family outside the door. It was painful to hear, and she felt terrible for them. Blog say her and Darius were on brink of divorce, who were they to interfere with Russell's broken family when her family was broken even worse. She say they weren't mentally strong enough at time and didn't think it would help if they intervened."

The phone went silent on both ends as the men reflected on the sad situation.

"Ivan sad for Ghost man, if only Clicking man could have heart feelings."

"Darius asked me to do him a favor and take care of Carter because he has a great life waiting for him."

The Clicker looked out at Carter, realizing what he was witnessing.

"The only thing I can do now is make sure that his heart is as healthy as it can be. Ivan, you did good. But I'm now curious how Darius knew Carter needed a new heart and how he was outside the hospital that exact night. If the ex-wife and Darius only went by the house once, and chose not to interfere that night, they would not have known about Carter's heart. Are there any more blog posts that mention anything that can connect the dots?"

"Ivan beat more balls and try connect ball-dots for Clicking man — Ivan be back."

The Clicker again watched Carter's life meld with the two families while he waited for Ivan.

"Clicking man — Ivan sad to say Ivan can't find anything to connect ball-dots. But Ivan find last post of ex-wife. It say this is her final blogpost. Tomorrow, my divorce is final."

Again, it was quiet on both ends of the phone as the sorrowful words that entered Clicker's ears did not match the jubilance of what his eyes were witnessing — a family's redemption.

"Ivan, thanks for trying. You've been a tremendous help. Enjoy watching Bunny in 4K."

"Ivan go watch Bunny in 4K to help Ivan get out of sad heart feelings for Ghost-man family. Goodnight my Clicking American friend."

Soon, the doppler effect of the Clicker's 105th Anniversary Special-Edition Harley-Davidson speeding off could be heard in the distance.

Meanwhile, the families went to their respective cars and Carter and the Dedacciai found themselves alone to talk after all the revelations.

"Jacob Jobe Garrard — huh?"

"Well, I go by Jake, but if you ever call me that, I will punch you. It's Dedacciai to you!"

"I accept — Dedacciai." Carter's voice struggled with emotion. "I'm not sure what to say."

"My friend, you don't need to say anything."

"I always knew something tormented you, but I had no idea it was something like this. I'm so sorry. I had to ask Kimmee who Addison was once you said her name. I hope you don't mind, but since Kimmee seems to know a lot about what's going on, I thought about talking to her about this so you don't have to relive it with me."

"I very much approve. Besides, I just discovered she is my new surrogate daughter and wants to go on a long bike ride and get to know each other."

"Wow, that's awesome. She's really awesome."

"Carter, follow me to the bicycles for a minute."

Soon, the cyclists stared at the Dedacciai bicycle that started their relationship.

"Carter, it's strange to think, but your dysfunction is what got me through Addison's death," his voice quivered slightly. "Your wish to rewrite your story, your hatred for your dad, your nose ring, all of it kept me distracted from everything and saved my life. But now, since you're all fixed, this can't ever happen again because if it does, I'm screwed!"

The two laughed at the insanity of the statement, although it was a painful truth.

"Dedacciai, you're the weirdest person I've ever known!" Before the Dedacciai could start his mantra, Carter interjected, "When the going gets weird — the weird turn pro. You're just too slow these days," he touts.

"Listen, Carter, about your Redemption Bicycle idea — I absolutely love it and believe in it 100% because I believe in you. I'm proud of the man you've become. And because I'm so proud of you, I need to tell you something. And what I'm about to say, I won't take 'no' for an answer. Do you understand me? Do we have a deal?"

"Dedacciai, you always make me nervous when you do stuff like this — But yes, we have a deal."

There is a heartfelt pause before the Dedacciai starts — "I want you to have the Dedacciai; it's yours. I'm giving it to you, and I want you to sell it and use the proceeds toward opening your shop. Take it to Brandon and Charley and see if they will help you sell it for top dollar — Because bicycles are people, too — they deserve a second chance. And they need a place like Redemption Bicycle Consignment more than I need the Dedacciai."

Carter was emotional on so many levels. But the first thought was one of utter sadness. The idea of detaching his mentor, his author, from the Dedacciai bicycle itself was a harsh reality to accept.

"Dedacciai, I can't... I just can't — I won't."

"Carter — you can, and you will! 'The needs of the many outweigh the needs of the few — or the one.' I think Spock said that, and it's not wise to mess with Spock logic. Young Carter, will you do what I ask of you?"

Separating the Dedacciai from its master caused Carter great emotional pain. And on top of that, he was torn from the possibility of never seeing the Dedacciai bicycle again. It was too painful, and he wanted it to be a deal-breaker. But if there was one lesson Carter learned from the Dedacciai early on — it's that he says what he means and means what he says, and it was futile to resist.

"Yes, sir — I'll do it."

"SO LET IT BE WRITTEN...SO LET IT BE DONE!" the Dedacciai commanded.

The cyclists shook hands before Carter threw his arms around the man who changed his life.

The Dedacciai's family, along with Kimmee and her mom, made it over to Carter and their dad.

"Honey, I want to get you home; we all do. But we don't have enough room for Carter and the bicycles."

The Dedacciai thought for a second. "Carter, why don't you get an Uber big enough for both bikes and go to the Omni Hotel? I promised you a night there when we got to Dallas. You can call Frank and arrange for him to pick you up tomorrow," and he began handing Carter some money.

"Nonsense, Carter and the bicycles are coming with us," said Kimmee's mom, surprising everyone. "We have plenty of room in my SUV and plenty of room at the house. Carter can stay with us tonight, and Kimmee can take him back to Georgetown tomorrow on her way back to Austin. It's settled!" Mrs. Attwood said with authority.

Kimmee was secretly excited and intrigued with Carter because her insatiable curiosity would be satisfied learning how Carter and the Dedacciai's lives intersected.

Final goodbyes took place, and everyone made their way toward their vehicles. But the Dedacciai and Carter stood hugging from the journey that brought them to this moment.

His Bellavia stood there in pure joy, watching her husband say his last goodbyes to Carter. Suddenly, the hair on the back of her neck tingled as she heard a familiar voice.

"Hi, Bellavia."

"Sandals," she said, startled, before a calm came over her. "What are you doing here?"

"Oh, you know, my sandals and I are always traveling somewhere. We had to see a friend of mine here in Dallas. Remember my friend I was telling you about that I asked you to pray for in Austin? It turns out his family forgave him after all; just a big ol' medical misunderstanding. Anyway, I saw his family tonight, and I think they are going to be alright. How about your family? Did you find what you needed to put Humpty Dumpty back together?"

"Humpty Dumpty is being put together as we speak. That's my husband, standing there with a young man who seemed to help him while he was gone."

"Oh, yes, Carter. Nice young man, has a really good heart."

"You know him, too? What a crazy small world."

"Truthfully, it's more like a small universe, and Carter and I go way back. I know him very, very well. What a beautiful sight, those two!"

"Sandals, thank you for letting me know about your friend. I'm truly happy for him."

"Why, thank you; I knew you would be. Before I go, it was great seeing you again — and one last thing. Your granddaughter is going to be absolutely beautiful, just like her grandmother. — Goodnight, Bellavia."

Mystified by Sandals' prediction, he was gone before she could respond. Yet, somehow, she was at peace this time with the disappearing stranger as she refocused her attention on her husband and Carter.

"Okay, Carter, here's your phone back. I forgot to give it to you earlier. That darn phone is probably how Dr. Jezercak found you since I never turned it off. Plus, I answered it in the restroom to stop it from ringing and annoying everyone. By the way, I think you're qualified for an extended warranty for your vehicle — she sounded very sincere."

"Well, did you ask her if the warranty covered bicycles?" Carter said with a straight face before they exploded with laughter.

"Oh my God, that's too funny; anyway, here's my cell number. Let me know about your appointment with Dr. Jezercak."

"Your doctor friend is half crazy, you know. And why does he click?"

"Carter, no one knows why he 'clicks,' but everyone knows he's crazy. Tell me something I don't know!"

"Okay, he told me he knows who the former owner of my heart is — It's Darius!"

"Darius — our Darius? — The Darius that's alive?"

"Yep, one in the same. He said he would try to explain later."

"Okay, that's bizarre. I'll wait to hear from you about what Miguel says — Darius, that's just a big ball of weird."

The two men looked at each other, and with one final man-nod, they parted ways.

Carter headed over to unlock the bicycles and found Kimmee waiting with her dog.

"My mom went to get the SUV."

"Oh, that's nice of her. Your mom is amazing! I can't believe she's giving me a place to stay tonight." He unlocked the bicycles and took off the front wheels to make it easier to place them in the back of the SUV.

The new golden retriever was also involved in helping and was in and out of Carter's legs with the nonstop licking of his hands when available.

"You know, if my mom approves, I think I'm going to name him Armstrong. I think My dad would like that as well."

"Oh, yeah, that's a great name. Sorry about taking Lance already because there can only be one dog named Lance — and well, because there's only one actual Lance in this world! Duh," he said, tongue in cheek.

"Yes, you name-stealer. I see how you are!"

"Hey, I resemble that remark." Carter stole from Dedacciai's vast repertoire of Dedacciai-isms, which worked as Kimmee laughed at the banter.

"I meant to tell you earlier that your bike is awesome, but I was more focused and taken aback by the Dedacciai bike."

"Speaking of that, evidently, it's my bike now, so officially, you were taken aback by *my* bike."

"What do you mean by that?" as his claim enthralled Kimmee.

"The Dedacciai just now gave it to me. He wants me to sell it and use the money to open the REDEMPTION BICYCLE CONSIGNMENT shop — where even bicycles deserve a second chance. Actually, it makes perfect sense since he is always saying—"

"'Bicycles are people, too.'" as Kimmee hijacked the bicycle-ism.

"Yes, how did you know that earlier?" Carter asked.

"His wife told me when I found myself over there one evening by a serendipitous fate."

"Wow, not sure what that big-name means, but—"

"What! Do you mean you haven't seen the movie *Serendipity*? — I'm not sure we can be friends."

Carter stood there with pause — and wonderment.

"Hmmm, is that a possibility? — Us — being friends? Because I have a solution. We could just watch it together — like, maybe tonight?"

Kimmee looked at Carter. In the dark, he couldn't notice, but the pupils that belonged to her hazel, mint-green eyes had widened.

"It's possible, I suppose. I'd like to hear more about your bicycle shop with a mission and *a purpose,* as you put it. — So, the Dedacciai actually gave you his bike to sell and open your shop with?"

"Yes, he said he wouldn't take no for an answer."

"He believes in you that much, huh?"

"Duh! It's me, so yeah," Carter asserted a comical confidence.

"Well, maybe you can make a pitch to me. Are you taking on any other investors?"

"I don't know," Carter said, mystified. "This all literally happened a few hours ago."

"My dad used to invest in a lot of properties and businesses — he died recently of cancer."

"I'm so sorry; is it okay to ask how long ago?" Carter reached out with a kind and gentle touch. When Kimmee felt his hand on her shoulder, she was shocked at the warmth and sincerity as she looked back at him with a mixture of excitement and sadness.

"I guess it's been around six months now. We rode around this lake every Saturday morning until he didn't have the strength. I think he'd love your idea."

"Maybe I can follow in his footsteps with an investment of my own. We should go for an early-morning bike ride around the lake tomorrow before my mom and I go to church. We can talk about it some more. 'Redemption Bicycle Consignment: Where even bicycles deserve a second chance.' I love that! It's brilliant if you ask me."

"I have a Bible in my backpack. Would it be possible for me to go to church with you? It's kind of a new part of my life, and I'd like to hear your thoughts on what you believe."

Carter had no idea, but Kimmee's pupils widened even further.

"Hey, you never finished telling me why you call Mr. Garrard 'the Ded acciai.'"

"Jacob Jobe Garrard," Carter smirked. "He said he would punch me if I ever called him that. In fact, we had a huge fight because he wouldn't tell me his name. Now, I can't imagine him as anything but the Dedacciai."

The headlights of her mom's SUV approached, and she pulled past the bicycles before releasing the rear door.

"Finish telling me in the car."

"I'm sorry I took so long; I had to make a phone call and got caught up in the drama." Truth be told, Mrs. Attwood had been praying to her husband about a handsome young man who was a cyclist and taking her time to let the two talk.

Carter placed his blue Specialized bike in first, careful not to hurt the interior of the SUV. He then removed his blanket from his backpack to protect the Dedacciai bike as well. As he picked up the Dedacciai to place it in the SUV, he heard a familiar voice from behind.

"Excuse me, sir, that's one hell of a bike you got there. Is it for sale by any chance?"

Carter turned and saw the Dedacciai standing there.

"Hmmm, I'm not sure. It would have to be someone pretty special that I would want to own it."

"Will $5,000 make me special enough to own it?"

"Five thousand dollars, huh? I don't think that's going to cut the mustard."

"Oh, really, $5,000 won't cut the mustard? What kind of mustard do you have?"

"It's an incredibly unique and strange mustard blend, just like the man who owned this bike. You see, the unique and strange man who owned this bike taught me that 'bicycles are people, too,' and that everything I need to know can be learned from a bicycle. He taught me about balance and how balance is the key to life. He taught me there's a spoke for everything and to live your life in 'true.'

"He taught me about belief systems and why I believe the things I do. He taught me to have compassion for the homeless, and he taught me how to give. He also taught me about forgiveness. But most of all, he changed my life because he taught me how to live."

"Really? He taught you all that. Sounds kind of strange if you ask me. But okay, whatever. How about we settle on $6,000?"

"Six thousand dollars, huh? I'm not sure about that because the man who owned this bike changed how I look at the world around me as I ride.

He changed the way I see the road, the telephone poles, and the fences in the distance. He even changed how I see an open field.

"You see, the man who owned this bike gave me the gift of perspective while celebrating my birthday on a day other than my actual birthday. A celebration with people who became my adoptive family who live in a homeless camp. A camp where good people struggle to survive, and a community of good men take care of their own. A camp where you can learn more about yourself than you ever thought possible and learn not to be afraid of the darker places in life. And now, I can just look at all that perspective that surrounds us, just like his mom taught him."

"Well, how's this for perspective? I'll give you $7,000."

"Seven thousand dollars, huh? I'm not sure about that because the man who owned this bike made me realize that I had a lot of misplaced anger for my dad and helped me remove the hate and acid coursing through my veins. He made me realize that I had not been the greatest son and that things could've been better between us.

"He made me realize the physical pain I was willing to undertake to keep a wedge of hate between us. The man who owned this bike performed a memorial service and gave a eulogy for Naustris, my former nose ring, which represented the hate I had living inside me. And he buried Naustris and my hate in a Styrofoam container full of coffee grounds."

"Geez, kid! Your friend sounds like a real weirdo."

"He is a weirdo. In fact, he's a professional. He even has his own weirdo league; they meet on Tuesday nights — if you're interested."

"I'll consider it, but in the meantime, that doesn't change the fact that I want that bicycle. I'll give you $8,000."

"Eight thousand dollars, huh? I'm not so sure about that because the man who owned this bike taught me that 'when life hands you lemons — you trade 'em for oranges.' And then you take those oranges and partake in the orange iced-tea phenomenon. He taught me that there are rules to iced-tea and that life is all about ratios and balance. It's about how the different ratios of ice, orange, sweeteners, and brewing combine to produce a wonderful experience for the senses.

"He taught me that it's in the minute details and the willingness to get the ratios just right that transforms an ordinary glass of iced tea into an extraordinary glass of iced tea. He taught me that the things in life you choose to concentrate your efforts on seem to be the things you're most passionate about."

"Come on, kid, really? All that from a glass of orange iced-tea. Are you sure the owner didn't have one too many Long Island iced teas when he taught you that? Regardless, I'll give you $9,000 for the bike!"

"Nine thousand dollars, huh? I'm not sure about that because the man who owned this bike took on the very challenging task of rewriting my life story. A hopeless story full of pain, dysfunction, and hate." Carter paused, fighting to continue. "But more than anything, while he rewrote my life story, his own story was crumbling underneath him. — While he was living an untold tragedy that almost took his life — it didn't stop him from helping me change my life.

"And I can't ever tell him how grateful I am that in rescuing him, I rescued myself. Because I don't believe the words exist that encompass the pain he was going through, with the pain he removed from me. He is the greatest man I have ever known. He is my Hero — He is my Author — He is my Dedacciai."

The two men paused before the Dedacciai broke the silent appreciation for what Carter had just amplified between them.

"Yeah, that's probably true, but he's probably a first-time author. If you ask me, he's probably not even good enough to be an author. Maybe he's just an aautgir. You know the old saying, 'I'll be an aautgir for now and then an author somehow.' But regardless, did he accomplish his goal? Did he rewrite your life story into a great novel?"

"It's the greatest story ever written — Just look at me!"

The Dedacciai looked him up and down.

"You — could use a shower."

Carter laughed while having tears of gratitude as the two cyclists, one older and one younger, approached each other.

"Just my luck, I'd get an aautgir like you to rewrite my life story."

"Okay, kid, final offer. I'll give you $10,000 for the bicycle and the rights to your story."

The two men shook hands and agreed on the terms and conditions with the unbreakable bond of a man-nod.

"You take care of my bicycle now; it better be in perfect running condition when I get it back."

"Well, it's not officially yours until I see the green stuff. Besides, I might need it for a few days. Kimmee asked me to go on a bike ride around the lake before going to church tomorrow. She wants to talk about investing in Redemption."

"So, what you're saying is you want to ride my bike to get her to—"

"Excuse me, my bike—" Carter reiterated while rubbing his fingers and thumb together, reminding the Dedacciai 'not until the green stuff.'

"Okay, you think riding the Dedacciai will somehow help seal the deal of her investing in your Redemption?"

"Duh — yeah!"

"I can see that. Remember, you only have your breeder's permit, not your actual breeder's license. Do yourself a favor. If God blesses you with a relationship with my surrogate daughter, read your Bible, attend whatever church she attends, and grow spiritually with her. You're already a virgin; it won't hurt to stay that way a little longer, until marriage, if possible. Have your friendship and love for God take center stage. The rest will follow beautifully. And one more thing — Love you, I do, young Carter," Master Yodacciai said one last time.

"I know," Carter struck back once again.

"You're not Han Solo." The Yodacciai responded.

There was no better possible outcome for Carter as he threw his arms around his author, his mentor, his Dedacciai. His entire nervous system was exuberantly relieved that his future endeavor would not separate Dedacciai, the man, from Dedacciai, the bicycle. And he had a hard time releasing his mentor back to his reality.

He watched as the minivan's side door opened, and all passengers emptied to hug the man they desperately needed back in their lives. Bellavia was the last to hug him after his children had finally let go.

Carter heard the utter sounds of joy emanating from 'His Bellavia,' as the Dedacciai referred to her. She was the love of his life, something Carter could only hope to experience. — But then again, every love story begins somewhere.

Chapter Twenty-Seven

A Mother Just Knows Things

Kimmee and her mother couldn't help but hear most of the exchange between Carter and the Dedacciai. They had tears in their eyes from the unique banter and emotional sentiments exchanged while the men negotiated the price. Kimmee was entranced as her curiosity was on fire, and she was determined to learn everything about their time together. As Carter approached, she got out of the passenger front seat and opened the rear door for Carter.

"And they say chivalry is dead," Carter smarted off as he got in.

"Well, scoot over, dummy, or you're going to be dead!"

Carter gladly slid over to make room for Kimmee to share the back seat. They left the parking lot, and a short while later, Kimmee's mom pulled into a drive-in.

"I hope you kids don't mind. I know Carter has to be starving after his long ride, and we haven't had dinner yet, so I'm going to order some food while we talk."

"That would be great, Mrs. Attwood."

"Please, call me Diane." And she placed their order.

"Can you believe he bought his bicycle back for $10,000 after giving it to me in the first place — just to help me open my bicycle shop?"

"That's pretty amazing, alright!" Kimmee agreed.

"I sure would like to know what happened to Addison so I can have some perspective on what the Dedacciai was going through. I mean, I know Dr. Jezercak is your boss and figured out how she died and that you met Bellavia through a serendipitous fate. And although I haven't seen the movie yet, can you tell me how all this is 'serendipitously' connected? And, by the way, how does your boss know about my heart? He thinks he knows who it belongs to, but the man he says is alive. Forgive me for saying this, but he's rather mean — and he clicks! Has anyone ever told him that?"

Kimmee once again laughed at the Clicker reference.

"He's so mean that they developed an app specifically to warn everyone when he's walking down the hallway. So, you're not that special; he's an equal-opportunity asshole to everyone. I hated him when I first met him, and I just started working at my new job on Wednesday. And by Thursday, I was working for him — once again, by a serendipitous fate."

"But Dr. Jezercak said that something bizarre happened yesterday after I left work, and then he showed up here out of the blue looking for you. So, I have no idea what happened to make him do that."

The carhop delivered the food, and they divided up the goodies and got situated.

"Kimmee, tell me about Addison. How did you find out about her?"

"This probably isn't the best dinner conversation, but I had just started my new job at the Travis County Medical Examiner's office as a pathologist technician, which basically assists pathologists with autopsies. And by fate, my very first case was a three-year-old little girl."

"Addison? She was your first case! So, you what? — performed an autopsy on her on your very first day?"

"Well, I assisted another pathologist, but he was teaching me, and I did a lot of the autopsy."

"So, do you know what happened and why they blamed Dedacciai for killing her?"

"Bella told me he was throwing her in the air after being warned several times to stop."

"Oh, man, did he drop her?" Carter asked.

"Well, that's the problem; no one knows precisely what happened. But from what Bella said, he was throwing her in the air, and then she somehow ended up dead. I think he panicked and hoped she would start breathing while he was trying to resuscitate her.

"But he made a terrible decision by not yelling for his wife because she thought that if he had, she could've saved Addison. And in the end, Evan and Bella blamed him for her death. As I understand it, Evan even beat up his dad and threw him out of the house. He was brutal and told him he couldn't come to the funeral. When Evan threw him out, the Dedacciai thought he killed her, too."

"Wow, I'm telling you, I think you're right. That explains a lot because when I first rescued both him and his bike, the first words out of his mouth were, 'Please, let me die.'"

"Wait a minute, back up, Mister. What do you mean 'when you rescued him? Back up to the beginning, and don't hold back. Tell me everything," Kimmee insisted.

"Well, okay — last Tuesday was my 25th birthday. It also ended up being my last day at the bar where I worked. A few minutes before we closed at 2 a.m., my boss handed me my final paycheck and a cupcake with a candle. He wished me well and told me to make a wish.

"My wish was to rewrite my life story because of my dad, which I don't want to bore you with. So, at 2 a.m., I lit the candle, closed my eyes, and made my wish. When I opened them, I saw this rather large cyclist riding in the rain—"

Kimmee interrupted.

"I saw him riding in the rain at a Wendy's that same night! That's why I got so animated when I saw his bike. I thought he might try to kill himself, especially after knowing what happened to him!"

"He did try to kill himself!"

"What? When?" Kimmee exclaimed.

"Wednesday morning. But I entered his hotel room just after he tried to overdose with pills and slit his wrist. Luckily, I stopped him."

"Oh, my God, I was right! — I knew it! When he was thrown out, he didn't take his wallet, keys, or phone, which I knew was a sign that he didn't need them because he might try and kill himself. Now, Carter, go back to where you said you rescued him," Kimmee insisted.

"You kinda like being right, don't you?" Carter jabbed.

"Bet your ass I do!" Kimmee counter-jabbed.

"Kimmee, that's not very ladylike!" her mom corrected her.

"That's okay, Diane; I already know that about her."

Kimmee punched Carter while laughing.

"Now, finish your story so I can see what else I'm right about."

"Okay, okay! After I made my wish and saw him, my initial thought was, 'Why is this idiot riding in the rain at 2 a.m.?' But after I took a closer look, I saw he was riding one heck of a nice bike but dressed rather oddly. I mean, no one rides a bike like the Dedacciai with a pair of jeans and a button-down shirt! I thought, 'Something's not right here.'

"Then suddenly, an old pimped-up car with its lights turned off came up from behind and ran him off the road. Two guys with hoodies flew out of the car and began attacking him. I thought, 'Hey, I'm a cyclist; it's my duty to uphold the bicycle code of honor and help the man' — am I right?"

"Darn right, you are! You go, Carter," Kimmee egged him on while Diane sat, compelled to hear more.

"So, I bolted from the bar and flew across the street to take out hoodie number one, who was stealing his bike and trying to stuff it in the trunk. I had to rescue it first from being stolen before taking out hoodie number two, who was beating him up and trying to rob him. Then I kinda-sorta-maybe-possibly beat up their car — but I don't want to brag."

"Oh, no, you didn't!" Kimmee sparked and hit him in the arm.

"Oh yes, I did! Nobody messes with the Dedacciai! I don't care whether you're human, fish, fowl, or car. And believe me, that car knows never to mess with Carter Ducane again, and he can tell all his friends."

"So, your kind of a badass with a big heart, aren't you?"

"I'm like the Robin Hood of beating the crap out of cars," Carter said comically, proud.

Diane found herself laughing as well.

"Okay, so after I let the hoodies drive off in what was left of their car, I went over to the older cyclist, and that's when he asked me to please let him die. At the time, I thought he was in horrible pain from the hoodie's attack — but now I know Evan beat him up before that. Ouch! And that's not counting the emotional trauma from Addison. — No wonder he wanted to die," uttered Carter, who realized a few things before continuing.

"But that's when things took a turn for the weird," Carter added.

"You mean, things weren't weird enough?" Kimmee bantered.

"Evidently not. I thought maybe he was dehydrated from riding fifty miles with no water bottle since he had horrible vertigo. He was so far out of it that he couldn't open his eyes without getting sick. So, I dragged him under a tree to get him out of the rain. He somehow fell over in my lap and went to sleep — we both did. Then, a few hours later, I guess the rain stopped, and somehow, the quietness woke me up. But when I did, this homeless man was standing about fifteen feet away, and he scared the heck out of me! I mean, who wouldn't be — am I right?"

"No kidding, absolutely, you're right," Kimmee concurred.

"Once I started talking with him, this homeless guy seemed to know things about me he shouldn't know. And he hinted for me to name the Dedacciai after his bike like he knew the man wouldn't tell me his real name. Come to think of it, the homeless man wouldn't tell me his name either. It wasn't until we got to the hotel that I discovered his name was Darius. He said the older cyclist was an anomaly and that a scientist who discovers an anomaly gets to name it. So, I named my discovery after his bike, and that's why I call him the Dedacciai."

"Wow, Carter, what a story!" Diane exclaimed. "You're a real hero!"

"Hey, wouldn't be the first time I heard that; probably won't be the last," countered Carter, still with a comical confidence.

As they headed home, there was a terrific exchange between the three inhabitants of the SUV. Carter never had the thought of being nervous around Kimmee. He was funny, kind, confident, and endearing to Kimmee and, more importantly, her mother. It was like the Carter of old never existed.

"Oh, dear, I need to stop and get gas. Would either of you like another drink or snack for later while we stop?" Diane pulled into a gas station, not realizing it was a little out of her comfort zone and maybe not as safe as she would prefer.

"Diane, let me get that for you. What octane do you prefer?"

As the tank was filling, Carter headed inside to buy drinks. As he did, he saw a man walking up from the street with everything he owned in a shopping cart. Carter noticed that his front wheel was wobbling loose, and the cart had to be much harder to push than need be.

As Carter exited the store with his drink order, the man was sitting beside his cart in the parking lot. Instead of taking the drinks to the girls, he headed toward the homeless man.

Kimmee and her mom had not experienced a lot of homelessness and were somewhat nervous that Carter went over to talk to the man. But they watched the exchange diligently from the safety of the SUV.

They saw Carter hand the man one of the drinks and then kneel down to look at the loose wheel. He then headed to the SUV to give Kimmee and Diane their drinks.

"Diane, are we in a rush to get anywhere? I'd like to help this man if I could. It shouldn't take that long. Would you mind?"

"Of course not; take all the time you need, dear."

Carter opened the back door, grabbed his backpack, and returned to the man. Kimmee was curious and followed him. Carter started to work on the wheel but needed some light and handed her his cell phone.

"Kimmee, will you hold this light for me?"

"Thank you, young sir." Said the homeless man as he eyed the two. "Well, you two sure make a handsome pair."

Kimmee and Carter exchanged an attractive glance, but neither opposed his observation.

"I was part of a handsome pair once, if you can believe that. But that was before, you know, life stuff started to happen — before I lost my leg," and the man lifted his pant leg. "See, what'd I tell you? I'm bionic!" He laughed out loud with a raspy threshold they could hear on Mars.

"The name's Maurice, at your service. How ya do? I caught a case of them frostbites back a spell — lost the sucker. I should have been living life right, but I was somehow living it on the left. Alcohol could have been involved — just sayin'. Anyway, looks to me like both of you still have all your body parts, so if you buy us some beer, we can celebrate all our body parts, both past and present. What do you say?"

"Nice try, Maurice. Maybe another time. But I'd gladly buy you some food or something else you need."

"I sure would enjoy that, young sir. I'm easy; a loaf of bread and a jar of peanut butter would do me just fine and last a good long while. Maybe a six-pack — of bottled water. Got you good, didn't I?"

"Maurice, let me get that for you while Carter finishes your wheel." Kimmee scampered into the store.

Maurice looked at Carter. "You did good, young sir. She's kind of pretty, a lot more pretty than you, I'd say." He laughed.

"Really? I hadn't noticed. She's not my type; she has crooked toes."

"Young sir, as long as she doesn't have a crooked head, she'll do just fine. Just keep a pair of socks on her."

The two men laughed together as Kimmee came out and delivered the food.

"So sorry to hear about your feet, young lady."

"Excuse me? What about my feet?"

"Carter said they have a mutiny going on; your toes are all rebelling against each other."

"Oh, he did, did he?" Kimmee hit Carter again.

"Okay, Maurice, that's enough. See how violent she is? Now get off your lazy butt and try pushing your cart."

Carter stayed with Maurice as Kimmee headed back to the SUV.

"Kimmee, I think your dad would approve of this one."

Armstrong barked his two cents worth of approval as well.

"I think so, too, Armstrong. He wants to come to church with us tomorrow after we go for a ride. I hope you're okay with that."

"Of course, I wouldn't want it any other way."

Carter made one last minor adjustment to Maurice's cart.

"Okay, what do you think?"

"I'll be darned, old Bessie feels like butter. They're gonna call me 'Greased Lightning' because of you. Thank you, young sir."

"Okay, Maurice, you take care of yourself." And he grabbed his backpack.

"Carter, I know I'm an old, broken-down fool, but that girl there, she's special."

"Yeah, maybe, but I'm just not sure I can get past those toes."

Maurice reached down and removed his leg and quickly started to beat Carter with it as he was laughing.

"What the heck are you doing?" Carter dodging the absurdity.

"I'm the fastest leg in the West, and I'm beating some sense into ya."

"Okay, okay! I'll give her a shot — if she's lucky."

Maurice started hopping after him and laughing as Carter ran to the SUV. Kimmee and her mom didn't know what to think but couldn't help laughing at the mere *Three Stooges* of it all.

"What was that about?" Kimmee asked as Carter removed his backpack and placed it in the seat with him.

"Well, if you must know, he tried telling me you were special. But I set him straight and told him I didn't know if I could get past those toes."

Kimmee started hitting him as well. "Oh, you'd get past them if you're lucky!" she said as he tried to protect himself.

"Don't you mean if you're lucky?" And they playfully scuffled. As they did, Carter's Bible with the cards from the homeless and his note from Darius fell out of his backpack.

Kimmee's curiosity kicked in as she quickly reached for them.

"What are these?"

"You have two eyes; take a look."

"Maybe I will?"

"Maybe you should."

Kimmee started reading them as Carter organized his tools back into his backpack. While she read, her mother had silent tears, wishing her husband was there to watch their daughter fall in love. Their love story unfolded before her eyes as she watched backward through her rear-view mirror. — A mother just knows things. *I wish you were here to see this, honey; I think you would like him. I miss you so much.*

Kimmee finished reading every comment, thanking him. "Wow, Carter, this is special! How nice! So why did all these people sign this for you?"

"Well, what happened was Dedacciai took me to a homeless camp to have dinner with three men. Truthfully, I was scared to death at first — but as I got to know them, it became awesome.

"Dedacciai decided to re-celebrate my 25th birthday with my new friends that night because my actual birthday was a disaster. Let's just say it ended with my dad's boot in the middle of my birthday cake. It was awful, but this was great. The Dedacciai even surprised me with a cake that night, and we had an amazing time. It was probably the best birthday I've ever had.

"The homeless men told these unbelievable stories about their lives. The things they've overcome and the love and camaraderie they had for each other inspired me to want to help them somehow.

"They had three bicycles at the camp that were in horrible condition and needed to be fixed. The Dedacciai and I decided to come back the following day, which was Thursday morning, and surprise the men by me fixing them. So, while fixing their bicycles, a lady named Jules asked if I could look at her bicycle. One bicycle led to another and another and another — and by day's end, I think we fixed around forty or fifty bikes."

"Carter, that's really sweet. How good of you." Diane commented.

"Thanks, Diane, but the story's not over. Here's where things take a turn for the weird."

"Again?" Kimmee retorted.

"Yes, again. If you haven't figured it out by now, anything that has to do with the Dedacciai is going to have 'weird' involved. So, Wednesday night after my birthday at the homeless camp, I heard the Dedacciai sneak out of his room at 3 a.m. — I didn't know where he was going, but I found him at the IHOP just down the street.

"As we sat and talked about my relationship with my dad, one thing led to another. Before I knew it, somehow, the Dedacciai convinced me to remove this stupid nose ring I wore and had a memorial service for it."

"A memorial service? Really?" Kimmee commented as both she and her mom sat, intrigued.

"Yes, Dedacciai doesn't do anything half weird; it's all or nothing with him. He even said a eulogy for the darn thing, which he named Naustris, before burying him in a Styrofoam container full of used coffee grounds."

"Oh, my God, he actually did that?" Diane exclaimed.

"He did, but the cool thing was, I found out that my nose ring was a symbol of hate, and I only wore it to hurt my dad because he hated it so much. Which was all true; I just never realized it till then. There were also some cooks and waitresses who attended the service. It was probably one of the best funerals ever. But the thing is, it truly helped me bury my hate for my dad. In fact, on our way back to Austin tomorrow, I'm going to see my dad and hopefully ask for his forgiveness. Because I could have made things easier for him, but I didn't. The thing is, I never realized that I should. I never once thought that. If he forgives me, I feel like it's the final step to forgiving him. You know — I'm just ready for this. I'm ready to overcome all the hate and have a great life with a new perspective!"

Kimmee and her mom fought back the tears for Carter, fascinated by the strange but wonderful events of Carter's time with the Dedacciai.

Kimmee continued and read the card with the poem from Jules.

"Oh, my God, 'when we transform life from "One Day to Day One"!' That's an amazing poem. I love that; I want that." She handed it to her mom to read.

"I know, right? Jules is a special lady. Her daughter had been taken away from her because of an abusive relationship. Chaplain, one of the homeless men I met at the camp, is this amazing man who counsels everyone in the homeless community. He told her she should write poetry to help deal with the loss of her daughter and to keep her mind occupied, but she didn't really take his advice.

"So, while I was fixing her bike, she was telling me about all this, and somehow, we had a conversation about how 'one day' we'll do this, and 'one day' we'll do that, which led to 'One Day I'll do this' and 'Day One I did that.' Later that night, she came to the hotel and surprised me with those cards."

"They're beautiful," Diane and Kimmee commented.

"I know; they mean everything to me. That day in the field, fixing everyone's bicycles, was the first God experience I ever had. My life has changed so much since I met the Dedacciai, and now, with this God experience, I think it will get even better. That's why I would like to attend church with you — if possible?"

"Why, absolutely, Carter; it's our privilege," Diane insisted.

"Okay, you two, I'm going to head home now. Carter, thank you so much for sharing everything with us tonight. It was wonderful to hear."

Diane started the SUV and drove away. As she drove, she felt compelled to give her daughter and Carter a sense of privacy. She raised her rear-view mirror just enough and turned on some soothing music just enough as well.

"Hey, Carter, here's one more. What's this one for?" Kimmee looked over the note.

"That's from Darius, the homeless man who helped me name the Dedacciai after his bike. You see, the night he found us, he insisted we stay at The Lancaster Landing. I knew I couldn't afford it when we got there, and I panicked. But Darius not only insisted that I stay at that hotel but that I ask for a specific room number as well and said it wouldn't be as much as I thought. He wouldn't take no for an answer; believe me, I tried.

"So, I unloaded the bicycles, took them in, and returned to get the Dedacciai. But when I did, Darius had disappeared and left that note with him sitting in his wheelchair. That's how I found out his name was Darius — from the note.

"I ended up telling the clerk behind the desk my story. I didn't know it then, but she was the owner. In the end, she told me I was a hero, and for saving his life and rescuing the bicycle of a total stranger, she gave me two rooms for two nights for $200. It was a miracle, and somehow, Darius was right about everything."

"Wow, that's amazing," Kimmee said as she reflected on the stories of the stranger that intrigued her and seemingly touched her heart. She was unaware that she could have feelings for someone this quickly. And she wasn't the only one, as she watched Armstrong lick Carter's hands and roll over on his back, insisting on a belly rub.

Kimmee read the note. Knowing its origin allowed her a deeper connection with the words and the deeper meaning behind them. She gasped and held it tightly to her chest as she finished reading. Kimmee was caught up in a perfect emotional storm from the past few days. And now, from the note, the cards, and the stories she had heard from Carter.

She enjoyed their banter and his kindness. She was impressed by his willingness to help the less fortunate, and thankful to have experienced it firsthand with Maurice. In a nutshell, she was twitterpated.

She paused and began thinking of her father. It was his wish she would fall in love with a man of substance, with a personality she wanted to spend her life with, regardless of how much money fit in his billfold.

She re-read the note again, slowly. As she finished, she turned to Carter. "Darius is right, you know — you do have a good heart."

Carter reread the letter, puzzled by her reference to Darius being right about his heart. This time, perspective changed everything.

Carter,

About your wish to rewrite your story— It is commendable of you to first recognize that your story needs to be rewritten. Like anything worth reading, the author you pick to help rewrite your story is most important. An author is the poet of your emotions, inspires what's already inside of you, and unveils the most buried parts of you. An author reveals the powerful capabilities that live within you and releases the unlimited possibilities of the human spirit. An author induces kindness and compassion by showing the same. You have a good heart; use it. Chapter One is sitting in this wheelchair. I hope your rewritten story turns out to be a beautiful and well-written novel.

~ Darius~

"You have a good heart; use it." Carter hadn't noticed those words before, but now that he did — everything changed. *I'll be damned; it is him. Just look at all that perspective.*

Kimmee gently placed her hand on Carter's heart. "That is one of the most beautiful notes I have ever read. I love this man's heart."

"That's nice because somehow, he's my heart, and he's the one who helped me create the Dedacciai — and I think, best of all, he's the one who led me to your heart."

Kimmee placed her head on Carter's chest and closed her eyes. She looked at him with her pupils wide and kissed him on the cheek — then with a reminiscent breath.

"I think my daddy would really love you — please don't let him down."

"I'll give everything I have to make sure that doesn't happen — And I'll give you everything that I am becoming to make sure you are proud of me as well. Kimmee, I promise you — I won't let you down —"

Carter's response was worthy of the moment as his words were the gravitational pull that unleashed the emotional tsunami whirling inside her. And Kimmee gave Carter a kiss for the ages. A kiss that showed that this was something special. A kiss that seemed open to the possibility of a love that was true, and a life that was built upon helping others together, and in their own separate ways."

Every great love story starts somewhere. Tonight, Kimmee and Carter's had just begun — and it was going to be epic.

Behind, a white, mid-sized cargo van with red tail-lights followed in the distance. Its mission to redeem the passenger's heart was now complete as it faded into the darkness, never to be seen again from human view — But then again?

Chapter Twenty-Eight

A Lot Can Happen In One Day ...

Or Is It Day One?

Kimmee and Carter had spent the previous twenty-four hours inseparable. Carter was now well-versed with the movie *Serendipity*, and Kimmee had experienced IHOP at 3 a.m. They stayed up all night, talking and laughing, and watched the first tentacles of light that started their day riding around White Rock Lake.

Carter experienced a community of believers while celebrating church with Kimmee and her mom. The music was engaging, majestic, emotional, and inspirational. Carter embraced being a part of the church community with Kimmee by his side.

She was all in on investing in Redemption Bicycle Consignment shop, and Diane decided to invest as well. Kimmee wanted to help find the perfect spot for the bicycle shop and would call upon her father's business associates to help. She wanted the best property for the best price and to fully understand the lease or purchase contract.

She was determined to help Carter get his driver's license because he needed to pick up and deliver donated bicycles in the future Redemption Bicycle Consignment van. Kimmee also convinced Carter to open the shop in Austin to be closer to her and the Dedacciai.

She was taken with the heart of the man who rewrote his life story under the Dedacciai's care and authorship. Maybe the plea Carter threw into the universe was why Darius showed up that fateful night — to set in motion a plan to restore what he knew was a good heart that struggled and suffered at the hands of hate. But whether it was some galactic plan or mere fate, his heart cleaned up well, as did Carter.

Kimmee took him shopping that Sunday afternoon before heading back to Austin. She made sure her man looked fine, with a new hairstyle and outfit. She enjoyed shopping for him, and he was happy to oblige.

The drive home was filled with lighthearted banter and engaging substance-driven conversations. It seemed like it took only minutes to arrive in Georgetown as Kimmee pulled into the Ducane residence, absent of external lighting and void of any car.

Carter stayed in the vehicle, silent and staring at the house that looked like it was dead, emotionless — while trying to suppress his anxiety by holding onto a confused confidence for Kimmee's sake.

"What are you thinking about?" she asked softly.

"Hmmm — I was reliving a conversation with Dedacciai."

"These are always interesting. What was this one about?"

"The Dagobah Cave."

"The dog went bah what? You two never disappoint, so what is that?"

"It's a scene from *Star Wars* where Luke Skywalker is training with Master Yoda. He must enter the Dagobah Cave, where he confronts Darth Vader, his father, although he didn't know it at the time. But before he enters, Luke asks Yoda what is in the cave, and Yoda answers, 'Only what you take with you.'

"So yesterday, Dedacciai, or in this case, Master Yodacciai, talked to me about confronting my dad using the Dagobah Cave metaphor. He tried to get me to take only positive emotions, like love, forgiveness, and God, into the cave. I thought I had this handled, but now that I'm outside the house, I'm not so sure."

"Well, how about taking something else into the cave — me?"

Carter was flooded with scenario after scenario of why this was not a good idea.

"I don't know about that. I have no control over how my dad will act, and I'm sure he's got to be halfway to passing out by now. I really like you — like really, really like you. I'm afraid of what you might think or if you might associate my dad as a future version of me. I'd rather you meet him after I handle things with him. I mean, nobody wants to see how the sausage is made."

Kimmee laughed. "My daddy said that all the time growing up, especially when negotiating a new car price for my mom."

"So, we agree; you'll let me go make the sausage first before you meet him," countered Carter, thinking he had won with sound logical reasoning.

But Kimmee was unwilling to give up just yet, as her curiosity about what was in the Ducane Dagobah Cave was hard to let go of, so she brought out the 'Hazel Mints.'

"Carter," she said, slower, sultrier while batting her eyelashes as if that were an Olympic sport. "Didn't you say something about obtaining your permanent breeder's license if you could forgive your daddy? Not that I'd let you use it, but I wouldn't want you not to have it."

There was a harrowing drop of Carter's Adam's apple and the thud of a gulp that was felt in Kansas — Kimmee was not playing fair.

"I wouldn't mix up the heart I know has changed with the one that hasn't. So, let me be very clear on the matter — I don't mind watching sausage being made if it will lead to a really great sausage later."

His testosterone level massacred every ounce of logical reasoning. Seconds later, they stood on the front porch.

It was 8:34 p.m. when the first knock grabbed the attention of the Ducane household. And Russell Ducane was heard questioning the air around him, "Who the hell is knocking on my goddamn door this time of night?" he grumbled.

It took some time for the front door to open as they listened to the rustling of the deadbolt and door handle before it flew open.

"Who the hell do you think you are, knocking at this time of—?"

In his inebriated state, Carter's dad had to process the transformation of the man who stood on his front porch before he started his asshole routine.

"What in the hell do you want!?"

"Dad, I'd like to talk — I want to make things better."

"Better? You're a dollar short and a biscuit too late for that. Besides, I thought you left in a blaze of glory, big man? Ain't no surprise you couldn't make it, though. I told Rose you'd be back. Where is that woman anyways? Rose, it's time for another beer — Rose! Get out here. I need more beer. Besides, you might want to see this. Someone came begging for his old room back!"

Rose rounded the corner and screamed as she threw her arms around Carter, crying with both pain and joy. She pulled Carter and Kimmee inside, where she could get a better look. Rose gasped for air at the transformation, then looked at Kimmee.

"Are you responsible for this? Pardon me; my name is Rose; what's yours?"

"Hi, Rose, I'm Kimmee Attwood, and I'm only partly responsible."

"Carter, let me look at you," as she continued her analysis of what all changed.

"It's gone; it's actually gone." Rose touched his face while her thumb stroked his nose, acknowledging the vacancy. "What happened to it?"

"It got buried in a Styrofoam container full of used coffee grounds, along with my hate. Which is why I'm here."

"Coffee grounds?"

"He's telling the truth; it really happened," Kimmee added.

"Carter, it's been so hard not to talk, but you made me promise not to contact you."

"My damn beer, Rose, where is it?"

Her face hard, Rose crossed her arms over her chest. But the Rose of old still chose to open a beer for her infantile husband.

"That's more like it, dear." He slapped her on the butt as she walked away.

His mom flinched.

"Sorry, can't do it!" Carter launched a verbal assault on his dad.

"You need to tell Mom you're sorry. She doesn't like that; it's disrespectful and embarrasses her. Why are you such a freaking idiot?"

"Well, Son, that didn't take long; already back to your old bag of tricks, and now you're trying to show off for your little friend over there. Is she one of those barflies where you work? How much you payin' her to be here anyway?"

"That's it; you're done." Carter grabbed his dad by the collar and threw him to the floor.

"Carter — NO! — Not again!" Rose yelled.

But it was too late. Russell managed to get off the floor, laughing.

"Is she blind or just deaf and dumb?"

Carter launched again, overpowering his dad, and pinned him against the wall; his fist cocked back, ready to end him.

As he held him against the wall, deciding his fate, Carter sensed the acid of hate coursing through his veins and felt disgusted for how easily he got to this point. He uncocked his fist, released his dad, and raised his hands, surrendering.

"I'm sorry — Dad. Do you hear me? I'm sorry." Carter turned to his mom and Kimmee. "I'm sorry. I'm so sorry you had to see that. This is the absolute opposite of what I came here to do." His eyes moved back toward Russell.

"Dad, I want you to know you're right — that your son is a failure."

"Tell me somethin' I don't know, idiot," Russell cocked back.

"Okay, I will. I came here tonight to forgive you, but I failed. I came here to tell you I loved you but failed at that, too. I came here to ask for forgiveness because I could've made things better but chose not to. I could've been a better son to you in so many ways. But I failed at all of it."

Shocked by what she heard; Rose grabbed Kimmee to brace herself from falling.

The scowl on Russell Ducane's face lifted slowly, and Carter studied it for the first time since he was born.

"Wow, they're greenish-brown," Carter remarked.

"What are you talking about? —" Russell asked, confused.

"Your eyes — they're greenish-brown. I didn't know what color they were, but a good son should know that about his dad. That's why I'm here, to learn about my dad, and that can only happen if I forgive you — and you forgive me. I want you to forgive me. If you ever want to have a discussion like that, man to man, let me know."

With that, Carter walked out the front door, disappointed, and his mom stopped him on the porch, latching onto his neck, crying.

"I love you, Son. Please don't give up on him. Please, please, please don't give up on him — Don't give up — for me."

"This isn't what I had in mind; I needed this to go better."

"Carter, honey, please give it some time. Just don't give up — I beg you."

"We'll see, Mom; it's up to him."

While Carter and his mom talked, Kimmee walked back in to grab her purse. Russell looked over at her, and they made eye contact.

"Sorry, I just needed to grab my purse."

He gave no response, but her inner voice made her take a chance.

"Mr. Ducane," Kimmee said politely.

"Suppose you need to get your two cents in about somethin', I said."

"Not really — I understand how you could misunderstand things."

Russell scoffed. "And what is it I supposedly misunderstood, little lady?"

"Well, for one, I have to pay Carter to be around me, not the other way around." She gave him a wry wink, which dismantled his asshole personality and left him unable to respond.

"I'm Kimmee. It's possible we might be around each other for a little while, that is, if your son will have me. He's a terrific man, sir, and could be a terrific son — that is if you let him. That's all I have to say. Goodnight, Mr. Ducane," and she started walking before stopping. She decided to take another chance and walked up and gave him a much-undeserved hug before getting her purse and walking out to the porch.

"Sorry, I just needed to get my purse."

"Kimmee, you're such a sweetheart. I'm sorry about what Russell said earlier." Kimmee placed her hand on Rose's arm. "Rose, please. Don't give it another thought."

"Okay, Mom, I love you. We'll talk soon."

Carter cracked open the front door to get one last look at his dad. He saw him glaring at a can of beer with a dazed look of confusion before Carter closed the door.

"I'm so happy that you're here, Son. I can't believe what I see. But more importantly, what I don't. Now, Kimmee, you take care of him for me."

"Trust me, Mom; she will — I love you."

Carter hugged his mom as she cried, hoping he wouldn't give up on what he had started.

Kimmee could tell Carter was upset as she started the engine.

"I'm sorry you had to see that," Carter said, covering his eyes briefly. "I had this whole Dagobah Cave scenario perfectly laid out in my mind, but I failed. And I definitely brought some hate and anger into the cave. I don't think Master Yodacciai would be very proud of me right now. I feel like I let him down."

"Carter, he would understand. You didn't let him down because he knew what you were up against. Just try to relax and calm your mind. I want to take you somewhere my daddy would take me when I was upset. Is that okay?" Kimmee searched Google before heading out.

Meanwhile, the Ducane Dagobah Cave wasn't entirely without a transformation, as Rose Ducane found an inner strength, she never knew she had.

"Russell, for twenty-five years now, I have let you run over me, degrade me, yell at me, and make me get your beers because you act like an infant that can't open his own damn beer. And I have done it for you, to be a good wife and keep the peace, but YOU are an asshole! Yes, I said asshole — you asshole!

"I don't care anymore what you do right now because I am furious. If you want to hurt me, then do it. But before you do, think about something other than your damn beers for once. Did you see our son tonight? Did you? He was amazing. He got rid of that nose ring and tried to have a conversation with you, to forgive you, and ask for forgiveness.

"But you said nothing — and you did nothing! Did you see Kimmee? She's wonderful! How could you call her a barfly and ask if he paid her to be here? And then ask if she was deaf, dumb, or blind because she cared for our son.

"I hate you right now; I can't believe how big of an asshole you are! Do you want to hit me? Go ahead — because right now, I'd rather live anywhere else than be here with you. What's it going to be, Russell? I'm tired of this; we have a son we can be proud of together if you give him a chance. — But if you don't, I'm out of here. I'm tired of this life. And for the first time in my life, I see hope. We have a real chance at having an element of normalcy. I want that; if you don't, then get the hell out of my life!" Rose ran down the hallway and slammed the door to her room, crying.

Russell Ducane had never been spoken to like that by Rose. But tonight, Carter changed the rules on him without warning, and now, Rose had followed suit. He had never had a problem looking Rose or Carter in the eyes while berating them, yet suddenly, his world was different. Russell was confused because if he wasn't speaking harshly to Rose or Carter, he didn't know what to say or how to act. It was like living a foreign language he didn't speak.

But as dysfunctional and intoxicated as he was, he somehow knew being an asshole to Rose right now was not a good idea. Russell stared down the pictureless hallway, envisioning what life would be without his family. He had a decision to make. A decision that lay behind the closed door at the end of the pictureless hallway.

— Meanwhile, less than a half-mile away —

"Whenever I was upset, my daddy would take me to Wendy's for a Frosty. It was usually late at night, kind of like you and Dedacciai at IHOP."

Kimmee looked behind her at the Dedacciai bicycle sitting in the back of the SUV.

"It's bizarre how I saw him riding that bicycle in the rain at midnight while in Wendy's drive-thru. But it gave me comfort thinking of my daddy that night, and it gives me comfort being here with you," Kimmee said softly.

"I'm happy being here with you too, honored that you'd include me in you and your daddy's Wendy's thing. But truthfully, I'm embarrassed at what happened back there. I didn't want you to see the sausage being made, but I thought I had this.

"But then, with all your darn sausage talk in the driveway, I really, *really* wanted to earn my breeder's license. Guess I let you down, didn't I?"

"Not that I'd let you use it, but I wouldn't want you not to have it." Kimmee again with her cryptic message.

"The pressure was just too much; now I'll never earn it."

"Oh, you'll earn it, alright, just like you'll earn your normal driver's license for your redemption shop. Just relax — somehow, it'll work out, I promise."

"I don't want you to associate who I am with who he is. It scares me that you might change your mind."

"Carter, please don't worry. You saw yourself as losing control tonight, embarrassed because of me, and feeling you let the Dedacciai and me down. But what I saw was you defending my honor. What I saw tonight was how you treated your mom. I also saw what you're up against with your dad."

Kimmee's phone rang.

"Sorry, I need to take this." She stepped out of the car.

As she got back in, she had a concerned look.

"That was a friend of mine; she was having trouble with her husband and wanted to know where I was because she needed to talk. I told her I'd talk to her more about it after a while."

"Hey, if you need to talk to her now, let's go. Or if you need to talk privately, drop me off somewhere; I'll be alright. It's funny, but I've learned what it means to be there for somebody. I didn't know how important that was until I met Dedacciai."

"You see, Carter, that's the heart of the man I truly care for because of who you show me you are. The talk's good, but the walk's better." Kimmee kissed him on the cheek and gave him a meaningful hug.

Time passed when suddenly, there was a hard knock at the back of the SUV, startling the two. Carter couldn't see who it was and reached for his brass knuckles.

"Stay here; let me take care of this."

Carter exited the car and saw his mom and Russell in the distance. On the ground in front of them were two cases of beer. Kimmee exited on the other side, already knowing who was there.

Russell started off by talking to Kimmee. "I'm sorry, Kimmee, for what I said earlier. It wasn't right. I haven't been right for a long while. I hope we can start over — if that's okay?"

"I'd very much appreciate that, sir."

"Son, is that offer still good — to talk when I'm ready? Your mom made me some coffee and knocked some sense into me. I'd like it if we could chat about it. There's a nice patch of grass under that tree over there; would that do for ya?"

Carter was stunned as he looked at Kimmee.

"This is my friend, the one I was telling you about, who called."

"You are really something, aren't you?"

"What can I say? I like how sausage is made."

They smirked at each other and then walked toward the designated U.N. peace patch.

Kimmee and Rose hugged as Kimmee whispered, "I'm glad we exchanged numbers; thanks for calling."

"Believe me; it was a godsend," Rose softly acknowledged, "the timing couldn't have been better." They released their hug and then witnessed the two men awkwardly begin their peace talk.

"Son, I'm not sure how to start this sort of talking thing."

"Dad, if it's okay, I'd like to start anyway because I have a lot to say. First, I haven't been a very good son, and I'm very sorry. I could have made things much better around here, but I blamed you for everything. I blamed you for my life not being better, although it wasn't your fault nor your responsibility; it was mine. I could've helped you and been your ally; instead, I was your enemy."

Rose grabbed Kimmee in anticipation.

"I like that I know what color your eyes are now, but there's so much I don't know about you. If you would allow it, I want to get to know you, not only as my dad — but as my friend."

The calm timbre of Carter's voice washed over Russell, and his face softened, leaving his skin tingling with warmth.

"You see, Dad, I have a new perspective on life. When I was young, you and Mom protected me from the severity of my heart condition. You downplayed my transplant as a minor operation, so much so I put it out of my mind. And because you did that, it never became a crutch for me to get sympathy from it, or become a victim of it.

"But instead, I thought riding a bicycle all my life made me a victim because I felt 'less than' for not having a car. In fact, it became my identity. I thought I hated you for it all this time. But it turns out I want to thank you, Dad, from the bottom of my heart because if it weren't for you, I would have never found the one thing that gives my life purpose — my bike."

"Uh, say what now? Are you thanking me? — for your life? Did you lose your mind out there along with your nose pierce thingy?" Russell asked with a less inebriated astonishment.

"Yes, Dad, I'm thanking you. I'm beyond thanking you. If I had gotten everything I thought you owed me, like a car, I would've stopped riding my bike. But not having a car was one of the biggest blessings of my life."

"If you say so — you're welcome. But I'm not totally sure I follow."

"You see, because I rode bikes all my life, I had to learn how to fix them. Because of that, I discovered that being a great bicycle mechanic means I have something to offer this world because I have a way to help people in need. It changed me. I realized that the very thing I hated most about my life was actually the most crucial thing in my life.

"But in high school, I allowed myself to be a victim because I had no car. I let the girls make fun of me and make me feel horrible. Truth be told, I wanted to kill myself over it so many times."

Rose gasped, hearing his darkness, and Kimmee held her.

"But the thing is, none of it was true, and they were wrong about me. I have an amazing heart, and I know my heart better than anyone — and in a way, most people would think unthinkable." He signaled his mom to come closer.

"Mom and Dad, I have learned so much since you last saw me. I've learned that I'm powerful when forced — caring when needed — and I seem to have a knack for wanting to help people. And I'm darn funny, which I never knew. But knowing who I am gives me confidence. And now, with my abilities, I want to open my own bicycle consignment shop that serves the community and helps people."

His mom clutched her heart with one hand as the other touched her mouth.

"Oh, honey, that's wonderful," his mom said passionately. "My son, the mechanic. I'm so proud of you, dear."

"I know, Mom. I'm very excited about it. But I want to finish by telling Dad I'm so sorry that, for years, I wore my nose ring to hurt him. Dad, I knew what I was doing. I knew I was hurting you, but I was defiant and used it as a weapon against you — although it hurt both of us.

"So, I'm here to tell you I love you, Dad. — I want to repeat that — I love you, Dad. And I'm here to ask you to forgive me, and I'm here because I can make things better. So please, Dad, will you forgive me?"

Russell Ducane had to sit down on his makeshift cases of beer, thinking, absorbing what he had heard. He had never been asked for forgiveness before. His head began to shake like a volcano before it erupted, and he placed his head in his hands to steady it.

As he sat contemplating how to respond, he twirled his hair, an endearing trait Rose used to love early in their relationship but had not seen for decades. As she watched, she experienced suppressed emotions not felt since they created Carter by accident twenty-five years ago.

Russell stopped twirling his hair and looked up at Carter.

"Son, I forgive you, but something feels wrong. I don't feel deserving of your forgiveness. But I'd really like to — I think I'd like to get some help. Somethin' inside me wants to earn your forgiveness by being a better man. I'd like to keep talking with ya and working on things between us. Would that be alright?"

"Are you kidding? There's nothing I'd like more."

Rose and Kimmee witnessed the extraordinary spectacle and were crying, proud of Carter and Russell.

"Well, it's settled then." Russell lifted himself from the beer cases, picked them up, and walked toward the road.

"Well, don't just stand there; follow me," he commanded as he placed his beers on the ground in a strategic spot and opened a case.

"This calls for a celebration." He grabbed a beer and turned around to a captive audience. As he looked them over, he opened his beer and lifted it as if to make a toast.

"In the rain, through the pain, while insane — now down the drain!" He turned toward the street and poured the beer down the storm drain before opening another.

"Well, what ya folks waiting on? Dang beers ain't gonna pour themselves out, are they?"

It was a strange occurrence for a strange man, but it was the Russell Ducane way. Rose and Carter joined in while Kimmee stood back and witnessed the outcome of the Dagobah Cave. However, Russell would have none of it and called Kimmee out.

"C'mon, Kimmee Lou, get in here. Anybody that can put up with Carter for more than an hour is family, as far as I'm concerned," and Kimmee joined in. "The name's Russell Ducane; it's nice to officially make your acquaintance." Russell was suddenly full of southern charm as he addressed Kimmee.

"Who is this guy? And what did you do to my husband?" Rose yelled. Then she leaned in and gently kissed him — the first in over a decade.

They laughed hard as they poured the remaining seventeen beers down the storm drain. On that night, on that strange stretch of road, the Ducane family experienced something they had never experienced before — joy, love, and laughter.

Carter took out his phone and captured the inaugural moment that united them as a family. That picture became the first family portrait that adorned the wall of their house — no — their home.

As they poured the last beer down the drain, Russell put his hand over his heart. "May them bastards rest in peace."

They sat down in their patch of grass, and Carter told his mom and dad all his ideas for the Redemption Bicycle Consignment shop. His ideas consumed them; it was the first time Russell Ducane was proud of his son. But even more importantly, it was the first time he was proud of himself.

During the evening's conversation, the forgiveness flu swept the Ducane family. Russell wanted to be a better man, and there was talk that he might join the halls of Alcoholics Anonymous while Rose and Carter joined Al-Anon in support.

Carter could hardly wait to tell the Dedacciai how well the Dagobah Cave scenario finally went. He texted him the family selfie with Kimmee and his family pouring the beers down the storm drain.

"Congratulations, young Carter! The Dagobah Cave went well, I see. What a fantastic photo! Proud of you I am, Young Carter! And I'm so happy for you and all of you!

"Your training is now complete. I will send your breeder's license in the mail post haste — That will be $24.95."

"What the 'F' Master Yodacciai? Crook, you are; why the $24.95?"

"The breeder license business ain't cheap, you know. There are state and local taxes, licensing fees, ice cream fees, shipping, and handling. This isn't a breeding charity I got going on here — The Dedacciai's got overhead!"

"YOU! – ARE! – SO - WEIRD!"
"NO! MAYBE YOU ARE NOT WEIRD ENOUGH!"
"I LOVE YOU, DEDACCIAI!"
"I LOVE YOU, TOO, CARTER."

"Today is our Day One. Let's seize it, my friend because our wish has already been written by Jules, and I quote:

> The lesson here is to remember this,
> the next time our life hands us a twist.
> It only takes that thing that needs to be done,
> to transform life from One Day to Day One.

A year from now, we'll hold it high,
or we'll see it in the mirror while passing by.
It will live in the pages we wrote or the art that we drew,
all because we followed Day One with Day Two.

Chapter Twenty-Nine

Even Bicycles Deserve A Second Chance

Epilogue

You couldn't miss the twenty-foot-tall, forty-foot-wide replica of the Dedacciai bicycle as it sat on top of the canopy, proudly displaying the name:

REDEMPTION BICYCLE CONSIGNMENT
Where Even Bicycles Deserve a Second Chance

And that was what Frank A. Beansley's vision had in mind when he custom-built the 'can't miss' proposition to the public, daring them not to look as they drove by.

"Go big or go giant!" Frank shouted from the roof while working on a special 26th birthday project for Carter.

"Going giant still isn't the same as going full Noah's Ark, is it?" Miami touted.

"Did God commission you in a dream to build Beansley's big-ass Bicycle to ride through some upcoming flood?" Alabama yelled.

"Frank, in Genesis 6:14-16, God told Noah that the ark was to be 300 cubits long, 50 cubits breadth, and 30 cubits high. How many cubits is that thing?" Chaplain asked.

"I don't know, what's a cubit? Guys, I'm sure this isn't anywhere close to the actual Noah's Ark; this is much smaller," Frank debunked.

"Are you sure?" Alabama questioned.

"Not really?" Frank conceded.

The Redemption Bicycle Consignment shop van pulled into the parking lot to unload bikes for consignment. Lance bolted out of the van to see his people scattered in the parking lot as everyone took turns petting the Redemption Bicycle mascot.

"Such a good boy you are — yes, sir, Lance is a good boy," he repeatedly heard as he made his people rounds, Miami playing with him last.

Carter exited the van and opened the rear cargo doors.

"Hey Miami, I dig the new RBC Gambucci Security shirt you designed."

"Thanks, Boss; did you see the warning on back?"

"No, turn around. — 'Don't Even Think About It! Gambucci Security.' Oh, that's great; I love it!"

"Well, happy 26th birthday, Mr. Carter. Hard to believe it's been a year since we had your campsite birthday."

"Thanks, Miami. I guess it's tradition to celebrate my birthday on a day other than my actual birthday. But I wanted Kimmee's mom to be able to come down and celebrate."

"Is everything set for tonight?" Miami asked.

"That's what I'm fixing to find out. Kimmee will be here in a few minutes to go over her lists."

"She's damn amazing, Carter. She's been working her ass off to locate everybody from all your wild-ass stories and get them here. She wants to make this special for you."

"I know she does. I can't believe this is my life. That damn Dedacciai!" he said sarcastically.

"Did Frank finish the lighting project I had him working on?"

"He's been up there all morning bangin' on shit and stringin' shit all up and down and sideways from one end of the sign to the other."

"Good, get Chaplain and Alabama, and let's get these new bicycles inside and tagged for consignment."

"You got it, Boss Man."

A small SUV pulled into the parking lot as Miami yelled for the two to help. A happy, six-year-old, auburn-haired sprite young lady named Megan popped out of the vehicle and ran and jumped into Miami's arms.

"Hi, Uncle Miami Gambucci Rowland Hawthorne." She gave him a big kiss and hopped down to find her other uncles, Carter, Chaplain, Alabama, and Frank.

"Come and get 'em, boys; we hit the motherlode," yelled the mother of the six-year-old as she opened the back of her SUV. Julie hugged everyone before directing them to three large boxes in the back compartment.

"Where did all these books come from?" Chaplain quizzed.

"From all my social media peeps following me now that I'm a published poet, thanks to Carter and Connie Sue Lancaster."

"Did someone say, Carter?" The energetic six-year-old daughter, who was reunited with her mother, Jules, ran and jumped into Uncle Carter's arms.

"I love you, Megan; it's so good to see you."

"I love you, too, Uncle Carter. Where's Aunt Kimmee?"

"Oh, she will be here any minute, and I bet she can hardly wait to get her hug."

She kissed Carter before wanting to play with Lance.

Jules ran over and gave Carter a huge hug. "I'm so proud of you. Just look at this place! Did you ever think in your wildest dreams you would own a successful bike shop and that I would be a published author — *and* have a bestselling poster — *and* get my daughter back? Thank God for you and Connie Sue. It's hard to believe how 'One Day' did indeed transform to 'Day One,' and now it's already been a year — or should I say Year One?"

"Are you kidding? Every day I see your 'One Day' poster proudly displayed where everyone can see it and, more importantly, buy it. And speaking of which, I probably need to order another 50 posters; they sell like hotcakes."

"You got it," she said as Frank appeared from the roof.

"Hi, Jules. That Megan is a firecracker of happiness, isn't she?"

"Thanks, Frank. I thank God every day that she is back in my life, and I never take one ounce of happiness for granted."

"Amen to that," Frank said as Jules returned to her SUV.

"Well, Boss, I think I spelled everything correctly, but as you know, I'm not highly Educamated, so it's a crapshoot. And I used all-male Christmas lights, so we should be good."

Carter laughed, "I think you meant Edumacated, or is it Edmucadated? I'll have to borrow Dedacciai's copy of 'The Idiot's Guide to Spelling for Weirdos.' Frank, besides, you're not as dumb as everyone thinks. I'm sure you spelled everything close enough. — I just hope the lights behave and do the trick."

"Me too! — Carter, I'm honestly honored to have invested in your Redemption; it's a big deal to me. Really, I mean, it's cool, it's unique, and it's great for the community."

Carter waited a few beats — — — "Is there a punchline?"

"Not yet. I can't be funny when I need to poop."

"There's the Frank I know and love, who is always full of crap. But seriously, thanks for saying that and for believing in me. I really do appreciate you. Now go poop because a world without funny is a world without Frank. The planet needs you, so hurry up and poop!"

Frank starts to unbuckle his belt.

"Not here"

"Why not? There are no signs posted." He chuckled. "By the way, I told *your* Kimmee I would help her set up and do whatever she needs. My man with the big-ass tailgate cooker will be here around 5:30, and I told him I would also help him get his rig set up to cook the hotdogs, starting at 6:30."

"You're an amazing guy, Mr. Frank and Beans. I marvel every day how you gutted out this huge lease space and did what you did."

"Just protecting my investment, my man. This is a special place. And speaking of which, I finished our special project inside and have sheets covering above the doors to the new rooms. Do you know what you want to say?"

"Yes, I rehearsed it with Kimmee last night."

"Dude, she's wonderful. You're one lucky man."

"Yeah, I know. These rooms were her idea; she's freaking amazing. I have you, Connie Sue, and Dedacciai to thank for all my relationship advice and breeder's license training. Seriously, Frank, your advice helped me a lot. I use something from what you said every day."

"I'm sure you do. I wish I had someone as amazing as me when I was a yearling."

"I'm not sure about that; you might have become normal and civilized, and that's not a good look on you."

"True, who wants to be normal? I spit on the ground of normalcy. I'm just glad me and Dedacciai found you when we did."

"Technically, I found the Dedacciai when I saved him before naming him — literally!"

Frank laughed. "No truer words have been spoken. Okay, I'll be inside at six when the Dedacciai and his family arrive. Then I'll do my part while you present your speech."

"It's going to be wonderful. I can hardly wait to see what you created."

"Yes, I would be, too. There really needs to be two of me in life. Like a chess game where I see the other me do all the cool things, like hop weirdly on horses, take castles, and capture pawns, bishops, queens, and kings. That sounds like the best of both *me* worlds."

"Not a good idea for the world. It can barely handle the craziness of Frank Andrewchow Beansley it is bequeathed with already."

"All true. Alrighty, then, I'll be ready when you are for your special birthday project later; just give me the old signal-a-roo when you're ready."

"Will do." And Carter gave a practice man-nod.

"Attention! Attention, everyone!" Miami yelled into his fifty-watt electronic megaphone. "Entering the realm of Redemption is our queen, Lady Diane Attwood, and her daughter, the Duchess of Austinopia, the lovely Lady Kimberly James Attwood."

A full-size SUV pulled into the parking lot, hosting Kimmee and Diane.

The two women got out, laughing as they made the rounds, hugging everyone before Kimmee commandeered the megaphone.

"Thank you, Overlord Gambucci, for that aspiring introduction. We must accomplish much before our honored guests arrive for Prince Carter's Birthday Extravaganza.

"I'm so happy I'm the one who gets to put on such a spectacle for my Prince Charming. So, let's get this party started." Kimmee ran over and gave her man a big kiss.

"Happy 26th birthday, honey. I love you, you know."

"Really? I couldn't tell." He kissed her again. "Okay, enough of this love stuff. I need to open the place for business while you and your mom work Frank ragged."

"Hi, Aunt Kimmee," as she felt a little finger repeatedly poking her. Kimmee scooped the little auburn-haired girl up to her waist.

"I can't believe how big you are getting, Princess Megan."

"I know I am; it's fun to get bigger." Megan kissed her as her mom walked up to Kimmee.

"Megan can't wait for you and Carter to babysit her again; it's all she talks about these days. You know, Carter is my knight in shining armor. I'll forever be in his debt for helping me get my daughter back."

"I know he is, and I'm so blessed to be pulled into his orbit of unique people who had such an impact on his life. And because of you and the Dedacciai, I found everyone he has ever talked about while they were together. I want him to have the best birthday ever!"

"It's going to be so fun for him to see everybody. I love how happy you two are. Thanks for letting me be his friend."

"Are you kidding? Thanks for letting us witness your rise to fame! He's so proud of you, and we couldn't love that little Megan anymore if we tried."

"Come on, everyone," Carter yelled, "Shop's going to open soon, and you know how things get around here on Saturdays. Some kids are coming in who want to earn their bikes. They can help Chaplain wipe off these books and put them on the shelves of the newly built library room."

Yes, indeed, the Redemption Bicycle Consignment Center was a special place for the community and was embraced by such, as donations were abundant. In the six months since the store had opened, it became a beacon of hope to the homeless and poor.

One of the two newly built rooms housed Chaplain's counseling center, doubling as living quarters for Alabama, Miami, and Chaplain. There was also a large kitchen area for the men, and a large walk-in shower, that doubled as a bicycle wash station, a new service available to paying customers. Frank had also engineered hidden pull-down beds in the walls so they would be out of sight while the counseling center was open.

The second room was a community library that the homeless and poor took pride in having. Chaplain ran the operation beautifully, along with Alabama and Miami.

Alabama managed the chores for kids who wanted to earn their bicycles. He had a well-organized table where up to six kids could address and label the large amount of RIDESTRONG AND REDEEM YOURSELF wrist bracelets. The income from the sale of the bracelets was used to fix the donated bicycles from the community. They also fulfilled online T-shirt and cycling jersey sales.

Frank built a unique display box into the side of Alabama's bed to house his most recent AA chip while he slept, which was currently his sixth-month chip. It was a gift to show his friend how proud he was of him for joining AA. Alabama had a special relationship with another AA member he met in the program, a man named Russell. The two men helped each other be accountable in the program.

Yes, indeed, it was a well-oiled, community-based bicycle shop, and they all took pride in doing their part. But today, the owner turned 26 years old, and they planned a party in his honor with a hotdog cookout in the parking lot.

The guest list was a perfectly reconstructed list of the lives Carter and the Dedacciai had touched during their time together. Kimmee monitored texts to ensure all would be present as she reviewed the list repeatedly.

With Jules' help, she located all the bicycle owners who had their bicycles fixed in the Field of Dreams and Despair that signed his card.

Also attending the celebration would be Tiny Dancer, along with the attendees of his nose-rings funeral, as well as Brandon, Charley, and Connie Sue Lancaster. There were also several of Frank and Beans' Friday Freeloader friends, most importantly of which was their hero, Officer Scott.

She located Emily Showalter and her daughter, whose van they had fixed, along with several grandmas working that day. They also found Drew and Kelly Simmons and their new Siberian husky, Skyler Two.

Best of all, Carter's parents, Rose and Russell Ducane, whose lives have been profoundly changed by a love for each other never thought possible. And of course, the Dedacciai, a.k.a. Jacob and Bellavia Garrard, would be there with their family, Jack, Jordyn, August, Evan, Amelia, and their five-month-old daughter, Camille Grace Garrard, or Cami Grace as her Grammy Bell and Papa Jobe called her.

Finally, Carter's medical team, who had been monitoring Carter's every heartbeat for the past year, wouldn't dare miss the party. The team comprised of the Clicker, Dr. Gary Stidham, Dr. Charles Johnson, and Dr. Kevin Slavin.

Kimmee wanted it to be a birthday to be remembered, and so far, every indication was that it would be. She had hired a DJ with his own portable stage, which would be helpful for announcements. In addition, Kimmee and her mom had rented tables and chairs and were meeting the rental companies as they delivered to let them know where to set up in order to leave room for the large tailgate trailer cooker to pull in when it arrived.

She also met with the catering people from The Lancaster Landing, who brought a specialty red velvet cheesecake blend birthday cake courtesy of Connie Sue Lancaster. Kimmee placed it in the refrigerator with a sign threatening the life and limb of anyone caught peeking.

After a day of Frank helping her string up solar lights, decorate windows, and place floral arrangements on the tables, she triple-checked her list of everything she wanted to accomplish and mentally signed off.

It was perfect timing, as it was a little before 4 p.m., and Kimmee and her mom wanted to freshen up and return in time for Carter to do the same. As they said their temporary goodbyes, Kimmee surprised Carter with a new birthday ensemble she had purchased for him.

At 5:30 p.m., the tailgate trailer pulled into its designated spot. The proprietor started the slow-burning charcoal under a rich hickory and applewood blend that would ignite the olfactory glands of humans near and far.

It was now 6 p.m. as the Dedacciai and his family arrived. They were led in by Frank as Kimmee had planned. Carter had cleaned up well and looked dapper in his new birthday garb as they welcomed the Garrard family.

Squeals and hugs of all sizes, shapes, and decibel levels permeated the shop as everyone ran to greet little Cami Grace Garrard. The Garrard family also became reacquainted with Kimmee's mom, Chaplain, Miami, and Alabama.

"She is so beautiful," Diane said, and Amelia handed her the baby for a closer look. "She's just precious; my husband would have loved to have a granddaughter as beautiful as her."

The infant started to cry.

"Well, maybe he still can. Carter does have his breeder's license," the Dedacciai touted as Kimmee made her response. "Dedacciai, he does; not that I'd let him use it, although I wouldn't want him not to have it."

Carter yelled at him, "See what you started. There she goes again with that sideways cryptic messaging system she has. My license is pretty much null and void."

"It is until you make an honest woman of me."

"Whoah!" Everyone laughed and yelled, egging her on for her zinger.

"She's darn right, Carter; what's the holdup?" Diane asserted as she and Carter exchanged a glance.

"I don't know — She has those darn crooked toes. Has anyone else seen them?"

"You'd be lucky to have them," Kimmee played.

"Would I? — Ouch!" Carter yelled as Kimmee punched him in the arm, followed by a kiss.

"Yes, you would." Kimmee moved the attention off them and presented Alabama to everyone á la a *Price is Right* model.

"Bama, you're looking good, my friend," the Dedacciai stated.

"It's just because Kimmee here got me all dolled up at her *salon*," denoted Alabama, using exaggerated air quotes.

"Regardless, you wear your six-month chip well," he added.

"He's not the only one," a voice sounded while entering the shop.

"Russell — my friend!" Alabama yelled as they hugged each other.

"Dad, let me get a picture of you two holding your six-month chips together."

"I'm so proud of you, Dad," as Carter hugged him. "How's the new car driving?"

"It's amazing, son. Thanks for helping me get back on the iron horse."

"Dad, it wasn't just me. Kimmee made a lot of calls to get all the legal stuff straightened out and help get you back on the road."

"Hi, Russell," Kimmee said as she hugged him and Rose. "I'm glad my dad's associates could help get your legal mess straightened out. Besides, everyone deserves a second chance in life. What's that saying again? 'REDEEM YOURSELF AND RIDE STRONG!' It seems like I've heard that somewhere before."

While everyone chuckled, Carter walked up in front and took command.

"Okay, everyone, follow me. I have something rather special to show you before we head outside to the party."

They walked over to the newly renovated rooms, where the doors were covered with sheets. Frank stood near the rooms as Carter began.

"Welcome, Dedacciai, his beloved Bellavia, and the Garrard family, along with my parents, Russell and Rose, Kimmee, and Diane, and my extended brotherhood, Frank, Miami, Alabama, and Chaplain. Thank you so much for coming; it's wonderful to have you here on my alternate birthday day.

"To the Garrard family, I would like to say that without your dad, I don't know where I'd be today. But I know it wouldn't be in the presence of this much love and a chance to serve my community through bicycles. This past year, I have gotten to know you, and you have gotten to know me and my story. A story of how this man, your father, my author, and my Dedacciai, rewrote my life into what it is today, for which I am forever grateful.

"But every story has individual chapters that make our book complete. And in my story, there is one chapter that has a profoundly powerful meaning. This chapter brings together a whole community connected by one exceptionally beautiful and beloved individual.

"So, with that in mind, Frank made something for my birthday, but it's really for all of us and our community, and I'd like to present it to you now." Frank removed the sheets, revealing his custom-made signage:

The Addison Hope Garrard Community Library

and

The Addison Hope Garrard Counseling Center
Where There Is Hope For All Who Enter

Custodian and Counselor: M.C. Chaplain

The gasps penetrated the room, and everyone clasped onto one another in grace and tears — But most of all, for Hope. There were no words powerful enough for what the gesture meant to all who stood facing the monumental words.

Chaplain instinctively stood before the families and broke the community of silence. "Please bow your heads — Dear Jesus, Lord, and Savior; it was a special angel who brought us together here, for each other, and for the community. May Addison Hope's love and light shine in us all, and may her wings grow bigger and stronger each and every day as she becomes the guardian angel of our souls.

"We love you, Addison Hope Garrard. We know you are watching over us and giving hope to this community, hope for those who seek knowledge from a book, and hope for anyone brave enough to seek counsel. And hope toward changing their lives in the form of redemption. And we look forward to the day when we meet in Heaven once again — and the people said —"

"AMEN," the group answered.

The audience stood mesmerized before Evan and Amelia were able to walk toward Carter, giving him a hug.

"That's truly magnificent, thoughtful beyond measure. Our angel will absolutely give hope to all who enter. What a wonderful gesture; thank you so much."

The rest of the crowd shared tears and accolades as well.

The Dedacciai felt compelled to say a few words as he stepped to the front.

"Community. I want to thank Chaplain, Miami, and Alabama for allowing Carter to experience what community truly means. That night in the camp was what I believe to be the pivotal moment when Carter genuinely learned what community was all about for him.

"Watching you three razz and love one another inspired him to want to repair your bicycles, and, of course, God took it from there. Carter, watching you grow as a compassionate human and helping you open this fantastic facility has been extraordinary.

"And now, memorializing Addison Hope the way you have — there are no words big enough to express our gratitude. Also, I want to thank Frank for the beautiful, handcrafted signs honoring our angel.

"But now, we have a party we need to transition to, and we can't go all weepy-eyed to greet your birthday guests. So, in the spirit of honoring

Addison's life, I brought you a birthday gift — duh! I kinda had to." He placed his hand on Carter's back and patted him.

"You see, I would read Addison a poem by Edgar A. Guest called 'It Couldn't Be Done' whenever she accomplished anything new. And it meant so much to me to share that poem with her.

"So, in that same spirit, as I watched you accomplish opening this community bicycle shop, I, too, believe you should have an Edgar A. Guest poem. And it should hang where all patrons entering this establishment can see. And I thought this was the perfect poem that also tied into Addison's spirit."

His son, August, handed Carter the gift. Carter opened it and read the heading. Then looked at the Dedacciai, giving him the man-nod for approval as he turned it around to the small crowd and showed the 2' x 3' custom-framed poster entitled:

IF I POSSESSED A SHOP OR STORE
By Edgar A. Guest

"If I possessed a shop or store,
I'd drive the grouches off my floor.
I'd never let some gloomy guy
offend the folks who come to buy.

I'd never keep a boy or clerk
with a mental toothache at his work,
Nor let a man who draws my pay
drive customers of mine away.

I'd treat the man who takes my time
and spends a nickel or a dime
with courtesy and make him feel,
that I was pleased to close the deal.

Because tomorrow, who can tell?
He may want stuff I have to sell.
And in that case, then glad he'll be
to spend his dollars all with me.

The reason people pass one door,
to patronize another store,

> is not because the busier place
> has better skills or gloves or lace,
> or cheaper prices, but it lies
> in pleasant words and smiling eyes.
>
> The only difference, I believe,
> is in the treatment folks receive!"

"Dedacciai, it's just outstanding, my friend; I love it! Thank you." Everyone had a look before Kimmee spoke.

"Okay, I don't see how Carter's birthday party could start any better, but we have food, presents, and people outside who want to share this day with you. So, I want all of us to go out first, and then Frank will announce for Carter and Dedacciai to come out. Okay, let's do this."

The crowd was boisterous with applause as the family and friend entourage walked out first. Carter and the Dedacciai listened to Frank for their cue, and, of course, Frank had to be Frank.

"I first smelt these two a year ago. Sorry, I first *met* these two a year ago while riding with The Friday Freeloaders on one of our 100-mile rides."

The Freeloaders made a loud commotion at the mention.

"That's when I first met Carter and saw the Dedacciai bicycle. To put this moment into perspective, it's the equivalent of when a young man sees his first pair of T-tops on a Trans Am. You never forget when, how old, and how many pubic hairs you had — Five, the answer's five if you're wondering. — That's going to be much funnier a few ounces from now when the beer kicks in. — Am I showing my age? A lot of the kids out here are looking at each other. 'Trans-Am, T-tops, what the heck is that?' Well, I'll tell you what that is. It's a big freaking deal, just like what's hiding behind door number one. So, let's make some noise for the headliners this evening. Give it up for my friends and yours, the Dedacciai, and the birthday boy himself, Carter Duuucc-caaaaaaaaaane!"

The partygoers went wild for Carter and the Dedacciai as they were ambushed by the faces that had changed the course of Carter's life.

Kimmee had organized an atmosphere of fun and excitement. Music played, beer flowed, and lives intermingled. Carter and Kimmee made the rounds and happened upon Cathy and Timothy Morton.

"Kimmee, these are two amazing people. This is Cathy and Timothy Morton. I met them in the Field of Dreams and Despair; they had two classic Schwinn bicycles now proudly displayed at Cycledelic Bikes."

"It's so nice to meet you both. Who's this little angel?" Kimmee asked while Carter remembered Cathy, pregnant in the field.

"This is Addison — Addison Marie Morton."

As she said the name of her angel, Carter recalled how emotional the Dedacciai was in the field when she told him the baby's name.

"Cathy and Tim, come inside for a second; I need to show you something."

They stood looking at the Addison Hope Garrard Community Library a minute later.

"Addison Hope was the Dedacciai's granddaughter. She passed away just before you met him in the field. None of us knew it at the time; he had kept everything bottled up inside."

"Oh, my God, that's why he collapsed when I told him my baby's name." Cathy began to cry. "He told me my little angel already had a voice."

"I wanted you to see this because it was a blessing for him when you told him her name. It would be nice to find him and let him meet your angel. I know he would appreciate it. Also, Brandon is out there somewhere if you want to reminisce about your bicycles."

They thanked Carter and left to find the Dedacciai.

"You're a good man, Carter Ducane. Just using that big heart of yours everywhere you go to heart-splain everything to everybody."

"Heart-splain? Is that all I am to you, a big heart that goes around heart-splainin' his way through life? I'd rather be looked at as a piece of meat with a breeder's license."

"Not that you can use it, although I wouldn't want you not to have it."

"I'm no grammar expert, but that sounds discombobulated to me, and cryptic, and weird — much like the Dedacciai's mental state."

"Hey, don't talk about my surrogate father like that!"

"Why? Cause you're a chip off the old block? Ouch!"

Kimmee followed through with her routine punch before kissing him.

"Let's go, Big Heart; you got more people to heart-splain what's happened the past year."

Time passed, beer flowed, and Carter and Kimmee found themselves in front of the crowd, garnering everyone's attention. Carter took over the DJ's station and grabbed the microphone.

"Thanks, everyone, for coming; I can't tell you what it means to have everyone here tonight. Each one of your faces represents a chapter of my life, a beautiful chapter authored by my friend and yours. Let's hear it for the Dedacciai!"

Everyone cheered wildly as the alcohol level had risen.

"But the fact of the matter is that none of us would be here tonight if it weren't for Kimmee James Attwood. That's right, everyone would be at home relaxing, cutting their toenails, reading the directions on their microwave dinners, and I'm not *even* going to speculate what Frank and Beans would be doing. But I'm pretty sure there would be flashing lights, loud sirens, and Officer Scott would be missing a pair of handcuffs. Am I right, Officer Scott?"

"Just a routine Saturday night for me," he pandered back.

"But I have some shocking news. Kimmee here isn't what she seems. Everyone thinks she's smart, pretty, and beautiful on the inside and perfect on the outside. And that she's an amazing daughter and friend, is compassionate, a hard worker, organized, that she takes charge of situations, blah, blah, blah, blah, blah. But she's not perfect. Oh, no! Far from it. A few minutes ago, while inside, she had the audacity to call me a name."

"That just enforces how smart she is!" the Dedacciai yelled.

"Thanks, Dedacciai; I thought you were on my side?"

"Nope! Think again — Team Attwood."

The crowd laughed, taunted, and played along.

"Well, think what you want, but Kimmee James Attwood is a name-caller. That's right, and she had the audacity to call me Big Heart. That's right; she called me Big Heart. Not so pretty now, is she?"

"Wrong, more beautiful than ever!" Gambucci yelled with his fifty-watt megaphone.

"Hey, this woman took it a step further and not only called me Big Heart but said that I needed to come out here and heart-splain to all my friends what has happened to me for the past year. Can you believe that?"

"Yes," Gambucci simply said in the megaphone as everyone hooted.

"So, I'm going to take her advice and try to heart-splain a thing or two. I want to start with Connie Sue Lancaster; would you please come to the stage?"

Connie Sue walked up, hugged her friend, and grabbed the microphone.

"I do declare; this man looked nothing like this the night we first met — Bless his heart. He cleans up really well, don't you think?"

Carter received catcalls from the audience.

"So, a huge shout out to Kimmee about that undertaking. Well done, girl." And the catcalls increased. "And to the Dedacciai for all he did to change Carter's heart. I just want to say that Kimmee calling you Big Heart is a perfect name for you. I knew you had a big heart, maybe not quite from the moment I met you, but a few minutes later, when you told me you had just rescued this total stranger and his bicycle. And from that point on, these two had the biggest ol' stories every night. So, I look forward to the movie version of *Big Heart*, starring Mel Gibson." She handed the microphone to Carter as the audience hooted and hollered.

But Frank had to be Frank and stole the microphone.

"Wow! Thanks, Connie Sue. I didn't know I'd have competition, and just to set the record straight, Mel Gibson would be playing Carter, the one with the Big Heart, not the Dedacciai, the one with the Big Farts — Correct?"

A cross-section of laughs and cringes were hurled at the stage as he continued.

"The other problem is, who could they cast as the Dedacciai? Because I've never met anyone quite like him. And if someone else is out there just like him, that should terrify all of us!"

As the laughter continued, Carter took back the microphone.

"Oh, boy, Frank and Beans, ladies and gentlemen. I think we can all agree there's a little bit of the pot calling the kettle black in that last segment. Because if there is someone else out there like Frank and Beans, that should triple terrify us all!"

More laughter.

"So, I wasn't finished heart-splaining to Connie Sue. What I want to say is you are a good friend who helped teach me about relationships. And I honestly believe without your guidance and without your Bible and direction toward God, it may not have been the right time to meet my Kimmee, and we wouldn't be here. So, I will forever be in your debt.

"But I also want to thank you for something else. Would Jules and her wonderful daughter, Megan, come up here? If anyone here has not read the poem 'One Day' by this woman, Jules Benton, you're truly missing out. And a shameless plug here — her poems are available inside for sale to support Jules and the shop — Just saying!

"Anyway, when I met Jules, her daughter had been taken away because of some horrible circumstances. But during our conversation, something sparked the need for her to ride home and write this amazing poem and bring it to me that night. And through a series of events, Connie Sue read it, loved it, and then heard that Megan was separated from her mother. Connie Sue Lancaster would not stand for it, and that's why this beautiful girl is here with us today." Carter lifted Megan to an enormous round of applause.

"Okay, I'd like Miami, Alabama, and Chaplain to come on stage and for everyone who had their bikes fixed to gather in front. A year ago, in a field far, far away. I followed Dedacciai to a homeless camp, where I was scared to death to go. But Dedacciai insisted, and I pushed through.

"That night was when I met these three men. Hearing their stories and watching them interact as we celebrated my impromptu birthday gave me a whole new perspective on life, which Dedacciai informed me was my birthday gift. Everything that happened to me that night inspired me to fix their bicycles and the bicycles of everyone standing in front of me. If that night hadn't happened, I don't think we'd be standing in front of The Redemption Bicycle Consignment Center. So, thank you all for allowing me to fix your bicycles because they changed the course of my life. Thank you."

A heartfelt round of applause permeated the air.

"Also, I'd like to thank Charley and Brandon from Cycledelic Bike Therapy. I met these two while fixing the Dedacciai bicycle after I saved it from being stolen the first time. Then, Officer Scott saved it from being stolen a second time. Shoutout to Officer Scott."

Everyone hooted and hollered.

"Anyway, Charley and Brandon heard what I wanted to do in the field that day and gave me a boatload of tires, tubes, patches, tools — you name it. They donated it to help everyone standing here. Brandon also came out to help fix bicycles, and because of that, I began working for them before I opened my shop.

"Today, they help me by taking in trades that we sell here at Redemption, which has turned out to be a win-win for both of us. So, thank you, Charley and Brandon."

The two men gave appreciative man-nods and smiled.

"This scares me a little, but could I have Crazy Frank and Beans back up here? Now, I know you've all heard Frank — but hearing him is different than knowing him. And it is my sincere honor to know him. And if you don't know, Frank is the one who completely remodeled the lease space for Redemption. And earlier, before the party, Frank made some beautiful signage that everyone must go inside and see before leaving.

"The signs pay tribute to an angel whose name is now on the Addison Hope Garrard Community Library and the Addison Hope Garrard Counseling Center that gives hope to our community. I'm so honored for that angel to be a huge part of my life and our community. And I'm incredibly honored to have the entire Garrard family here with us tonight, especially their newest angel, Camille Grace Garrard."

As a profound, heartfelt round of applause erupted, the sincerity rode the air.

"I'd also like to tell my parents, Rose and Russell Ducane, how much I love them and how proud I am of our family. We are a true miracle," Carter stated as the applause lingered.

"Okay, so let me get back to something that happened earlier. Kimmee's mom, Diane, asked me what's the holdup on making her daughter an honest woman."

Eyes grew, and hearts gasped at the possibility of where this might lead, and Kimmee's head turned and looked at Carter.

"Okay, men, help me out here. What does this mean? Earlier today, the Dedacciai reminded everyone that I now have my breeder's license. Kimmee retorted, and I quote, 'He does, not that he can use it, although I don't not want him not to have it,' or something like that. Tell me, how's a guy called 'Big Heart' (Carter using exaggerated air quotes) supposed to respond to this sideways cryptic messaging system she has? And then she has the monumental gall to tell me that my breeder's license, which I worked ridiculously hard for, mind you, is no good, and I quote, '… until you make an honest woman of me.'"

A communal "Whoa!" launched into the air, egging Carter on in anticipation.

"Diane, you asked what the holdup was of making an honest woman out of your daughter? I think it's obvious; it's her grammar. It's her cryptic, irregular, discombobulated grammar.

"But I'm a man with a 'Big Heart,' with a team of four doctors here tonight wanting to poke and prod on me every chance they get."

The doctors nudged each other in pride while the Clicker gave Carter his man-nod of approval.

"So, Kimmee James Attwood, let me try to heart-splain something to you in front of everyone here. My life is the most amazing life I could ever imagine or hope for. These people with us here tonight, many who have watched us grow together and many who have seen us for the first time, can tell what love is by simply watching us interact.

"But what I want you to know above all else is that as wonderful as it is to have all these people in my life — and it absolutely is, you amplify all of it and make my world better because I have someone to share my joys and triumphs with. If there's one movie quote to take from our love story, it would be that *you amplify m*e; you amplify my life, my heartbeat, my everything. And the most important thing that happened to me this year — is you."

Carter said it with such sincerity, kindness, passion, authority, and love that the crowd honored him with a beautiful silence.

"So, with my 'Big Heart and Frank's attitude of going big or going giant, would you please turn toward the building?" And against the darkness, the twenty-foot-high, forty-foot-wide display of male Christmas lights came on.

Carter Ducane
Will You Marry Me?

"What the —?" Carter turned and looked at Frank in embarrassment about why he put his name on the sign instead of hers. He turned to explain the mistake but found Kimmee James Attwood on one knee, holding an engagement ring.

The audience shrieked in excitement for Kimmee as The DJ handed her a microphone. But Carter countered by getting down on one knee and facing her with his own ring as Carter started.

"That was supposed to say, 'Kimmee, will you marry me? — You hijacked my proposal,"

"Sorry about that, but it only cost me a home-cooked meal to hijack your plan."

"Frank, I thought you were on Team Carter?"

"Nope, Team Attwood, dude!"

"I'm a modern woman, and I know what I want, and I couldn't take a chance that you wouldn't ask. Frank's been in my back pocket for months in case you got some big idea."

"I just love how that mind of yours works."

"I know; it's a really good mind," Kimmee countered.

"It has to be to offset those toes," and she punched Carter again.

"Well, I'm a modern man, and I know what I want, too, and that is for Megan to be our flower girl. Can you handle that?"

"Well, I'm just fine with that."

Megan squealed as she ran on stage and gave them both a hug and a kiss.

The Dedacciai yelled, "Does this mean Carter is going to breed?"

Kimmee yelped with authority — "Bet your ass he is, Dedacciai!" And the crowd went wild.

"Will someone actually ask the other to marry them?" Frank yelled.

Kimmee raised her hand as if to go first.

"Carter William Ducane, will you marry me?"

"Bet your ass I will!" Carter yelped back.

The two embraced in a passionate kiss. As they exchanged rings, a huge boom startled everyone as Frank surprised them with a fireworks display. A flying bride and groom flew down and hovered above Kimmee and Carter as the Clicker practiced his drone skills for the upcoming Halloween season of fright.

The parking lot was jubilant with love, laughter, hope, and grace from all the lives that had intersected because of an angel named Addison Hope Garrard. They were thrilled while standing under Kimmee's marriage proposal that could be seen in the forefront with a star-spangled sky of fireworks as the backdrop. It was EPIC!

Meanwhile, behind all the hoopla at the back of the crowd, a chocolate-brown 1985 Yugo had pulled into the parking lot. A man of Russian descent sat on the hood, admiring the fireworks while holding a tuxedo-colored bunny.

After the Clicker flew the bride and groom drones over the party guests, he noticed the man on the Yugo and walked toward him. As he got closer, it was undeniable that it was his rabbit, Bunny.

"Who the hell are you, and why do you have my rabbit?"

"I think I can answer that," said a tall, thin man wearing an old suit and sandals that seemingly appeared from nowhere.

"Nice bunny rabbit, Ivan."

The Clicker looked at the Russian and studied him, as he had never actually seen what Ivan looked like all these years.

"Well, that explains the hideous turd-brown Yugo. Now, dammit, Ivan, why are you here, and why do you have Bunny?"

"That's what Clicker want to ask, not why there is ghost man standing here?" as Ivan scooted further away with eyes glued on the ghost man.

"Ivan, don't be scared," Darius replied. "Ghost Man is not going to hurt you. Besides, you both know who I am and why I'm here."

"Yes, Ivan do. Yesterday was anniversary of Bronson death time. Sorry for you, Mr. Darius Montgomery — or do Ghost Man now prefer Darius Ducane?"

"Darius Ducane — I haven't been called that since my first foster family chose to watch me after our parents left Russell and me at the firehouse. After my foster family adopted me, they changed my name to Darius Montgomery, but you both already knew all that, didn't you?"

"Yes, new family keep you from knowing truth till you older." Ivan responded. "Sealed court documents for family. They had best intentions for you, best intentions. American family insecurity, they not want to lose you — you know — emotionally. Good people still."

"I know, they were great people. When they told me I had an older brother, I tried to find him for years, with no luck. When I became a lawyer, I had access to more resources and finally found an address. My wife and I even went by his house once after Bronson died to try and have some type of family connection. We thought it might somehow heal our relationship. Boy — were we wrong about that! It was so hard to hear Russell yelling at his family while standing outside on the porch. We felt terrible for them, but my wife and I were on the brink of divorce, and our relationship wasn't strong enough at the time to intervene and try to give relationship or family advice.

"However, in my research to find my brother, I learned that his wife Rose worked at the local library. On each anniversary of Bronson's death, I vowed to visit our old house every year at 3:28 p.m., the exact time he died and then go visit his grave. While visiting, I went by the library to try and get to know Rose. I just felt this need to somehow be connected to family.

"I introduced myself as Darius Montgomery, and told her I liked science fiction, and even wrote science fiction as a hobby. We bonded over books and writing, and I told her I came here every year to visit family. I could tell she was desperate for anyone to talk to her with a kind voice, and we became acquaintances who would see each other once a year.

"She told me about Carter's heart condition, and I asked how he was doing whenever I saw her. And then, one year, I went to the library, and she wasn't there. I was told that Carter was in the hospital and desperately needed a heart. They said he was nearly out of time, and saving his life would take a miracle. I rushed over to the hospital and sat in the parking lot, lonely, not able to talk with my only acquaintance in life. Even if it was on a yearly basis, she was the only piece of a family I had.

"The truth of my life back then was that I didn't want to be on this earth without my son. I just didn't know when I would end it. But when I learned about Carter, I knew this was my chance to end my suffering, as well as his, by giving him his life back.

"I spent the rest of the afternoon and evening contemplating if I had the heart to actually do what it would take to give Carter my heart."

Darius peered at the stage where Carter and Kimmee danced below their Christmas light proposal while fireworks solidified their love under a star-filled October sky.

"Just look at my heart; how happy am I right now? I knew giving Carter a more genetically matched heart would give him a real chance to have a long, healthy life. I'd say it worked — wouldn't you, Dr. Jezercak?"

"It works for now; I'll make sure it continues. You've given me what I needed to know. You have been a worthy and honorable adversary."

"Don't look Ivan right now. Don't need Clicker Man and Happy Ghost Man see Russian cry. Crying not Ivan best people feature."

"Ivan, why did you pick a turd-brown 1985 Yugo?" Clicker asked.

"Ivan love to drive Yugo. Make Ivan feel like home in Russia. — How bout Darius man? White van still putting along?"

"Of course, but I might need you to make me an up-to-date car tag."

"Ivan be happy to help Ghost Man van. Where do I mail to?"

"Therein lies the rub, my friend — therein lies the rub."

"Ghost Man, sir. Ivan is honor meeting you. Ivan feel your heart for why you do death night. You a good Ghost Man. Ivan not make poopy pants, or hide in bunker if Clicker Man calls about Ghost Man."

"Thanks, Ivan, I appreciate that — I think. However, I like your Renaissance rabbit portrait collection you have down there. It gives your bunker a nice vibe."

"Ghost man see that? — Ivan embarrassed. Ivan confess Ivan do much business with Etsy. Ivan favorite guilty pleasure place."

Darius chuckled before he turned his attention toward the Clicker.

"Dr. Jezercak, there is one last thing, and you're not going to like it — but I know about Amber Wood."

"If you tell anyone about her — I'll kill you!" he responded immediately.

"Kind of a moot point, don't you think?"

"Why does Clicker man want Ghost man to double die for? Ivan just now make friend with Ghost man, and now Clicking man want double death. Clicker need anger derangement course like Ivan suggest year ago. Clicker really need to learn to stop and smell the balls in life? If Clicker smell more balls, Ivan think Clicker man be in way more happy place."

"Ivan, I told you before, it's supposed to be 'stop and smell the flowers' — you idiot."

"Dr. Jezercak, he's not wrong about that," Darius interrupted, "besides, aren't you already smelling the flowers? Why not tell Ivan about your little flower arrangement with Amber?"

Bunny became upset, and Ivan handed Bunny to the Clicker as he took a calming breath.

"Darius, go ahead and tell him. But Ivan, if you tell anyone — I will find you and kill you."

"Amber Wood was a student that worked hard in his class but struggled. She would come to his office for help and would confide in him about her complicated family situation. Dr. Jezercak helped her realize the direction of her life and her dream of owning a flower shop someday. So, he helped her with her grades, and she became a botanist.

"Dr. Jezercak helped her get funding, and when she opened her shop, he became her first customer and wanted to help her get started. So he made an agreement to purchase an expensive flower arrangement each week if she would deliver it to the Medical Examiner's office. But there was a catch. He had her put a different name on the card each week to mess with the office staff at first. But later, as he met women outside work, he would tell them about the flower shop.

"Women started sending flowers to him because they thought it was sweet of him to help his student. Over the years, Amber would make sure that on the weeks when no one sent flowers, she would send one with the name Bunny on it. Years later, when he got his pet rabbit, he called her Bunny."

"Ghost man say Clicker man do nice flower scheme to make mess with office people, but same time do Amber flower sale business. Ivan confused, so very confused about Clicking man having heart feelings. Ivan check Hell, see if Hell do a Freeze-over."

"You're a good man, Dr. Jezercak. I think you can trust Ivan not to tell anyone."

"Amber was a good girl — she deserved a better life. It's the one thing I'm genuinely proud of that no one in my inner circle knew about — until now."

The Clicker then paused before changing subjects.

"Darius, speaking of white vans earlier, how is it you can drive a van, or appear to certain people without others seeing you. How do you do that?" The Clicker asked curiously.

"Well, if I told you, you wouldn't believe me." Darius acknowledged.

"I don't believe in any of this anyway, so humor me. I still need to know if I have a brain tumor causing these crazy hallucinations."

"Okay, if you insist. The day I killed myself, a guardian angel with special soul-catcher privileges rescued my soul and presented me to a special heavenly tribunal. You see, what earth refers to as Heaven doesn't like it when mortals kill themselves, and there is a possibility that someone could end up in what earth calls Hell. But in the case of suicide, an angel with soul-catcher privileges rushes in and rescues the soul before it ends up in Hell without a tribunal hearing the case.

"However, on the opposite side of the spectrum, people who sacrifice their life to save another are given the highest honor in Heaven. John 15:13

says, 'There is no greater love than this: to lay down one's life for one's friend.'

"Lucky for me, my guardian angel pleaded my case that I did indeed lay down my life for Carter's. So, I became an angel, then a guardian angel, and then from there is a hierarchy of privileges and clearance levels until you reach soul-catcher status — which I am currently.

"Now unlike Prime Being One, or God, as he's known on earth — God can see everyone's entire life. However, my ranking only allows me to see up to three Earth years ahead or behind. My ranking also lets me choose when, where, and who sees me. It also permits me to enter dreams, if necessary, or interact in the human space by driving a van, for example.

"So, being a soul-catcher is what I do as my heavenly job all year, but I always schedule time off to make it back here for October 4th. It's kind of a thing in the afterworld to visit on the day of your demise if you have the right clearances. Well, that's my story and I'm sticking to it."

He paused briefly while Ivan and the Clicker processed what they heard.

"Oh, who am I kidding," Darius interjects. "I told you earlier when I was talking to Rose, I loved science fiction and dabbled in writing when I was alive. That was my science fictional version of the Great Beyond. It was called The Soul-Catcher. I thought the premise might make for an interesting book. So maybe I'm just messing with you — I'll let you decide."

"Darius, I have to admit, that's pretty good writing because if there was an afterlife, a hierarchy of privileges is how I'd do it."

"Holy Balls, Ivan afterlife with Bunny screwed if Clicking man ever run Afterworld."

"Ivan, you'd be fine, I'm sure I'll need you to hack into a few galaxies far, far away," the Clicker assured Ivan before turning back toward Darius.

"So, am I to take from all your gobbledygook that you're not going to answer my questions on how you can do what you do?"

"Here's my answer, Dr. Jezercak. You, of all people, should know by now, there has always been a reason for me to visit you, and tonight is no different. Besides coming here to see my heart full of joy with Kimmee, there is a reason why I brought up Amber Wood. Would you like to know why?"

"I'd find a way to kill you if you didn't tell me." The Clicker responded.

"Okay, you asked for it — on September 24th of next year, she will experience a devastating event which will completely blindside her. Even if she is warned, it is going to happen. On that day, she will need you, so I suggest marking it on your calendar now to take the day off. And what happens on that day will answer whether my gobbledygook is just that — gobbledygook.

"So, next year on October 4th ought to be a big bowl of interesting because no one can see the future — that would be preposterous — right, Dr. Jezercak?"

"Ivan, until we meet again."

"Yes sir, yes sir — Same time next year, Ivan hope."

"And you better be here," the Clicker demanded. Darius responded with a certain look that prompted the Clicker's hair on the back of his neck to rise. Clicker took out his phone. "Reminder, Take off work on September 24th next year — Family Emergency."

Darius and Dr. Jezercak gave each other a man-nod out of mutual respect.

"Sounds like a good plan for now. Okay, boys, that's all I got. It's time for me to do my thing, so when you turn your head, I'll be gone. You know, Ghost Man School 101 stuff. One day, you'll see — I promise." Darius looked toward the unbridled revelry one last time as the Clicker and Ivan followed, and when they looked back, he was gone.

Ivan turned to the Clicker. "Ivan sorry Clicker man not know Ivan did a Bunny borrow — Ivan had government business to take care of. You know, topple this, topple that. Ivan take off-clock time for Carter party to see how Heart Boy is doing. Then Ivan would have Bunny back before my clicking American friend got home — promise. But Ivan had to play with Bunny while in America. Much better to do actual Bunny holding."

"I can see that." Clicker admitted. "I'm glad you were here to meet Darius."

The two men from opposite sides of the world fist bumped and turned their attention toward Kimmee and Carter. Ivan and the Clicker took pride in what they had accomplished behind the scenes with Darius to help Carter get to this point and would continue their mission to keep him healthy.

The party revelers went deep into the night. There was so much love, so much hope, so much community, so much alcohol, and way too much Frank and Beans — Because Frank had to be Frank.

Two and a half months later, the same revelers reunited on a cold winter's New Year's Eve in the Dallas church where Kimmee and Carter started their spiritual journey.

It was a beautiful ceremony. Megan set the stage by gracefully throwing rose petals and lining the path for Kimmee's surrogate father to walk her down the aisle and give her away. The Dedacciai then stood by Carter as his best man.

His Bellavia, Kimmee's surrogate mother, stood by her as her matron of honor.

Two hearts stood before a beautiful and diverse community of people. They took turns saying heartfelt vows to one another before they kissed as husband and wife to make it official.

During the reception, the Dedacciai stood honored and gave an emotionally charged wedding toast, reiterating how there was a spoke for everything in life. He then presented them each with a red anodized spoke to symbolize their love.

He explained his bicycle analogy of how they were now an intricate part of each other's metaphorical life wheels and their actual bicycle wheels, as Carter would add the red spokes to those later.

The reception proceeded and was a wonderful event with cake, dancing, drinking, music, and, of course, Frank and Beans — a lot of Frank and Beans. He, too, gave an honorable toast to the happy couple.

"Everyone, please raise your glass. — To my friend Carter, a man who I have come to know as a man of great honor. A man who has served his community with honor and a man who has become an honorable and great friend to all of us. A man who has become a wonderful son and a man who I know will be an honorable husband to Kimmee. So, with that in mind — I'd like to make a toast to honor — May he get on her and may he stay on her!" — Kimmee immediately howled out — "Bet your ass he will!"

The crowd erupted with laughter, but none more than the bride, Mrs. Kimmee Ducane. The DJ immediately amped up the music to match the joyous intensity, which continued to the end...

That night, after all the revelry, Carter William Ducane finally used his breeder's license.

Nine months later, three precious words would bless their lives.

— Darcy Hope Ducane —

And yes — there is definitely a spoke for that.

THE END

THE RIDE TO REDEMPTION

by Rick Swyden

I can't thank you enough for reading my novel.
I hope you enjoyed the emotional journey and would like to
support my work by leaving a review on Amazon.
It would, of course, mean the world to me.

Feel free to also send an email to rick@rickswyden.com
to let me know what you thought
and be kept up to date with future works as well.
There truly aren't words big enough to tell you how grateful I am
that you took a chance on a 200,000-word novel from a first-time author.

May the wind be always at your back in life so you too can enjoy the ride.

Sincerely, Rick Swyden

About the Author

Rick Swyden is a man of many passions. Top of the list is his wife Susan and five children, Christopher, Chase, Ryan, Alex, and Allison (Twins). He currently has five grandchildren, as of this writing, but suspects there will be more.

One of his earlier passions in life was playing the Bass Trombone and owning an 18-piece Big Band at the age of nineteen, making him the youngest orchestra leader in the country at that time. His big band once opened for The Buddy Rich Orchestra, and he has met many other Big Band leaders such as Woody Herman, Stan Kenton, Doc Severinson, Maynard Ferguson, and Count Basie.

At age fourteen, he was a Duncan Yo-Yo State Champion which led to him winning a Three Speed Bicycle, which in turn led to perhaps his longest lasting passion of all, cycling.

Some forty years later while riding his cherished Dedacciai bicycle. An idea for a novel came to him while riding around Lake Hefner in OKC and his life would never be the same, as writing 'got its hooks' in him — the result of which, perhaps you just read.

As this is his debut novel, he currently does not claim any literary awards. However, he was given a finger-painted award for best dad ever from his then five-year-old daughter and later from his kids as a coffee mug he uses for Hot Chocolate while watching Hallmark Christmas movies year-round. Somehow, he thinks this should count toward some type of off-off-off Broadway version of a Pulitzer Prize award.

Rick aspires to update this page one day with actual literary awards and looks forward to the possibilities in the years ahead.

Made in the USA
Coppell, TX
26 August 2024